'A cause for celebration!'   *Locus*

'An extraordinary experience'   *New York Times Book Review*

'Tiptree can show you the human in the alien, and the alien
in the human, and make both utterly real'   *Washington Post*

'I loved the story. May you also'   *Analog*

'Ambitious, rich, marvellous'   *Publishers Weekly*

T0345485

JAMES TIPTREE JR
TWO GREAT NOVELS

Up the Walls of the World

and

Brightness Falls From the Air

This edition first published in Great Britain in 2016
by Gollancz
An imprint of the Orion Publishing Group
Carmelite House, 50 Victoria Embankment, London EC4Y 0DZ
An Hachette UK Company

1 3 5 7 9 10 8 6 4 2

A CIP catalogue record for this book is available
from the British Library

ISBN 978 1 473 20310 5

www.orionbooks.co.uk
www.gollancz.co.uk

Contents

Up the Walls of the World

To H. D. S.
For dreams that never die.

Chapter 1

COLD, COLD AND ALONE, THE EVIL PRESENCE ROAMS THE STAR-STREAMS. IT IS IMMENSE AND DARK AND ALMOST IMMATERIAL: ITS POWERS ARE BEYOND THOSE OF ANY OTHER SENTIENT THING. AND IT IS IN PAIN.

THE PAIN, IT BELIEVES, SPRINGS FROM ITS CRIME.

ITS CRIME IS NOT MURDER: INDEED, IT MURDERS WITHOUT THOUGHT. THE SIN WHICH SHAMES AND ACHES IN EVERY EDDY OF ITS ENORMOUS BEING IS DEFALCATION FROM THE TASK OF ITS RACE.

ALONE OF ITS RACE IT HAS CONCEIVED THE CRIMINAL ACT OF SKIPPING LINK, OF DRIFTING AWAY IN PURSUIT OF NAMELESS THIRSTS. ITS TRUE NAME TOLLS UPON THE TIME-BANDS, BUT TO ITSELF IT IS THE EVIL ONE.

FROM THE DEBRIS AROUND THE CENTRAL FIRES OF THIS STAR-SWARM IT HEARS THE VOICES OF ITS RACE REVERBERATE AMONG THE LITTLE SUNS, SUMMONING EACH TO THE CONFIGURATIONS OF POWER. DEFEND, DEFEND—DESTROY, DESTROY!

ALONE, IT DOES NOT, CAN NOT OBEY.

SOLITARY AND HUGE, IT SAILS OUT ALONG THE DUSTY ARMS, A HURTING ENTITY SLIGHTLY DENSER THAN A VACUUM ON THE CURRENTS OF SPACE: VAST, BLACK, POTENT, AND LETHAL.

Chapter 2

The evil strikes Tivonel in the bright joy of her life. But she is not at first aware of its coming.

Zestfully she hovers above High Station, waiting for the floater coming up from Deep. Her mantle is freshly cleaned and radiant, she has fed in civilized style for the first time in a year. And it's a beautiful morning. Below her, three females of the Station staff are planing out to the edge of the updraft in which High Station rides, looking for the floater. The bioluminescent chatter of their mantles chimes a cheery orange.

Tivonel stretches luxuriously, savoring life. Her strong, graceful jetter's body balances effortlessly on the howling wind-rush, which to her is a peaceful wild meadow. She is thirty miles above the surface of the world of Tyree, which none of her race has ever seen.

Around her corporeal body the aura of her life-energy field flares out unselfconsciously, radiating happiness. It's been a great year; her mission to the upper Wild was such a success. And it's time now for the treat she has been promising herself: before returning to Deep she will go visit Giadoc at the High Hearers' Post nearby.

Giadoc. How beautiful, how strange he was! What will he be like now? Will he remember her? Memories of their mating send an involuntary sexual bias rippling through her life-field. Oh, no! Hastily she damps herself. Did anyone notice? She scans around, detects no flicker of laughter.

Really, Tivonel scolds herself, I have to mend my manners before I get down among the crowds in Deep. Up here you forget field-discipline. Father would be ashamed to see me forgetting *ahura*, mind-privacy-smoothness.

She forgets it again immediately in her enjoyment.

It's such a lovely wild morning. The setting Sound is sliding behind Tyree's thick upper atmosphere, fading to a violet moan. As it fades comes the silence which to Tivonel is day, broken only by the quiet white tweet of the Station's beacon. Above her in the high Wild she already hears the flickering colorful melody that is the rich life of Tyree's winds. And faintly chiming through from the far sky she can catch the first sparks of the Companions of the Day. Tivonel knows what the Companions really are, of course: the voices of Sounds like her own, only unimaginably far away. But she likes the old poetic name.

It's going to be a fine long day too, she thinks. High Station is so near Tyree's far pole that the Sound barely rises above the horizon at this time of year. At the pole itself, where Giadoc and the Hearers are, it won't rise at all, it'll be endless silent day. Vastly content, Tivonel scans down past the station at the dark layers below. They are almost empty of life. From very far down and away she can make out a tiny signal on the life-bands; that must be the emanation of the far, massed lives in Deep. Where's the floater? Ah—there! A nearby pulse of life, strengthening fast. The station team is jetting down to help; moments later Tivonel catches the faint yellow hooting of its whistle. Time for the males to leave.

The big males are grouped by the woven station rafts, their mantles murmuring deep ruby red. Automatically, Tivonel's mind-field veers toward them. They were her companions in the years' adventure, she has monitored and helped them for so long. But of course they don't notice her now that they are Fathers. Safe in their pouches are the proud fruits of their mission, the children rescued from the Wild. The little ones were frightened by their first taste of relatively quiet air here; Tivonel can detect an occasional green squeal of fear from under the edges of the males' mantles. The Fathers' huge life-fields furl closer, calming the small wild minds. At a respectful distance hovers the Station staff, trying not to show unseemly curiosity.

The males were tremendous, Tivonel admits it now. She didn't really believe how superior they are until she saw them in action. So fantastically life-sensitive, such range! Of course they had to get used to the wild wind first—but then how brave they were, how tireless. Tracking the elusive signals of the Lost Ones while they tumbled free down the thickly whirling streams of the Great Wind itself, gorging themselves like savages. They must have circled Tyree a hundred times while they searched, found, followed, lost them, and searched again.

But they couldn't have done it without me guiding them and keeping them in contact, she thinks proudly. That takes a female. What a year, what an adventure up there! The incredible richness of life in the Wild, an endless rushing webwork of myriads of primitive creatures, plants and animals all pulsing with energy and light-sounds, threaded with the lives of larger forms. The rich eternal Winds where our race was born. But oh, the noisy nights up there! The Sound blasting away overhead through the thin upper air—it was rough even for her. The sensitive males had suffered agonies, some of them even got burned a little. But they were brave; like true Fathers, they wanted those children.

That was the most exciting part, she thinks: when the males at last made tenuous mind-contact with the Lost Ones and slowly learned their crude light-speech. And finally they won their confidence enough to achieve some merger and persuade them to let the children be taken down to be properly brought up in Deep. Only a male could do that, Tivonel decides; I don't have the patience, let alone the field-strength.

And how pathetic it was to find the Lost Ones had preserved a patchy memory from generations back, when their ancestors had been blown up to the Wild by that terrible explosion under Old Deep. These are surely the last survivors, the only remaining wild band. Now the children are saved. Very satisfactory! But tell the truth, she's sorry in a way; she'd love to do it again.

She'll miss all this, she knows it. The Deep is getting so complicated and ingrown. Of course the males want to stay down there and let us feed them, that's natural. But even some of the young females won't budge up into the real Wind. And now they have all those tame food-plants down there. . . . But she'll never stay down for good, never. She loves the Wild, night-noise and all. Father understood when he named her Tivonel, far-flyer; it's a pun that also means uncivilized or wild-wind-child. I'm both, she thinks, her mantle flickering lacy coral chuckles. She casts a goodbye scan up to where Tyree's planetary gales roar by forever, unheard by any of her race.

"The floater's here!"

The flash is from her friend Iznagel, the Station's eldest-female. They're wrestling the floater into balance on the Station updraft.

The floater is a huge vaned pod, a plant-product brought from the lowest deeps above the Abyss. One of the proud new achievements of the Deepers. It's useful for something like this, Tivonel admits it. But she prefers to travel on her own sturdy vanes.

The pod-driver covers the yellow hooter and climbs off to stretch. She's a middle-aged female Tivonel hasn't met. Iznagel presents her with food-packets and the driver sparkles enthusiastic thanks; it's a long trip up and the fresh wild food is a treat after the boring rations in Deep. But first she must offer Iznagel her memory of conditions in the wind-layers below. Tivonel sees the two females' mind-fields form in transmission mode, and feels the faint life-signal snap as they merge.

"Farewell, farewell!" The Station crew is starting to flicker their goodbyes. It's time for the males to embark. But they are not to be hurried.

Tivonel planes down to the pod-driver.

"A message for Food-Supply Chief Ellakil, if you will," she signs politely. "Tell her Tivonel will be down later. I'm going first to Far Pole to see the Hearers."

The driver, munching embarrassedly, signals assent. But Iznagel asks in surprise, "Whatever for, Tivonel?"

"The Father-of-my-child, Giadoc, is there." Just in time she remembers to restrain her thoughts. "I want to hear news," she adds—which is true, as far as it goes.

Iznagel's mantle emits a skeptical gleam.

16

"What's a Father doing at Far Pole?" the driver demands, curiosity overcoming her shyness at public eating.

"He became a Hearer some time ago, when Tiavan was grown. He's interested in learning about the life beyond the sky."

"How unFatherly." The driver's tone is tersely grey.

"You wouldn't say so if you knew him," Tivonel retorts. "Someone should gain knowledge, and our fields aren't big enough. It takes a Father's sensitivity to probe the sky." But as she speaks, something in her agrees a little with the driver. Never mind; my Giadoc is a true male.

"Here they come at last. Move back."

The big males are jetting somewhat awkwardly out to the floater. As they near it, a clamor of shrill green shrieks breaks out from under their mantles: The youngsters are appalled anew at the prospect of entering the pod. They scream and struggle shockingly against their new Fathers, contorting their little mind-fields against the huge strange energies that envelop and soothe them. They're strong young ones, deformed by premature activity in the Wild. Even big Ober seems to be striving for composure.

As they go by, Ober's mantle flaps upward, revealing his bulging Father's pouch and a glimpse of the child's jets. The pod-driver squeaks bright turquoise with embarrassment. Iznagel only averts herself, glowing amusedly under the conventional rosy flush of appreciation for the sacred Skills. Tivonel is used to the sight of such intimate Fathering after the last months. That silly driver—Deepers forget the facts of life, she thinks. It's better up here where people are more open to the Wind.

Behind her she notices the two young Station males, their life-fields flaring straight out with intense emotion. Probably seeing grown Fathers in action for the first time. Belatedly, she checks her own field, and tunes her mantle to the correct flush. The last of the Fathers are going in.

"Goodbye, goodbye! Wind's blessing," she signals formally, unable to check an eddy of her field toward them, hoping for a last warm contact. But of course there's no response. Don't be foolish, she chides herself. Their important, high-status life has begun. Do I want to be an abnormal female like the Paradomin, wanting to be a Father myself? Absolutely not; winds take the status! I love my female life—travel, work, exploration, trade, the spice of danger. I am Tivonel!

The party is all inside, their life-emanations crowded into one massive presence. The driver climbs onto the guide-seat. "Farewell, farewell!" the Station-keepers' mantles sing golden. The floater's vanes tilt up, the helpers jet forward with it into the wind.

Abruptly it angles up, the wind takes it, and the pod leaps away and down. The departing life-fields she has known so well shrink to a fleeing point, dwindle downwind into the lifeless dark. A gentle yellow hoot sounds twice and ceases. All is silent now; the Sound has set.

Tivonel lifts her scan and her spirits bounce back in the lovely day. Time for her to start upwind, to Far Pole and the Hearers. To Giadoc.

But first she should inquire about the trail. She hesitates, tempted to strike off on her own skill. It would be easy; already she has detected a very tiny but stable life-signal from far upwind. That has to be the Hearers. And her mantle-senses have registered a pressure gradient which should lead to an interface between the windstreams, easy jetting.

But it's polite to ask. *Ahura, ahura,* she tells herself. If I go down to Deep acting this way they'll take me for a Lost One.

Iznagel is directing the stowage of a raft of food-plants destined for Deep that will have to await the next floater.

Tivonel watches the scarred senior female with affection. I'll be like her one day, she thinks. So rugged and work-tempered and competent. She's been up to the top High, too, look at those burn-scars on her vanes. It's a big job keeping the Station stable here. But a good life; maybe I'll end here when I'm old. Worry dims her momentarily; now people are starting to grow so much stuff down by Deep, how long will they keep the Station up here? But no use to fret—and that tame food tastes awful. Iznagel finishes; Tivonel planes down.

"May I know the path to the Hearers?" she asks in formal-friend mode.

Iznagel flashes cordial compliance and then hesitates.

"Tell me something, Tivonel," she signs privately. "I could hardly believe what your memory gave us, that those Wild Ones tried to do—well, *criminal* things."

"Oh, they did." Tivonel shudders slightly, remembering the nastiness of it. "In fact I didn't put it all in your memory, it was so bad. The males can tell the Deep Recorders if they want."

"They actually struck at your life-fields?"

"Yes. Several of them tried to mind-cut us when we came close. A male attacked me and tried to split my field! I was so startled I barely got away. They're untrained, thank the Wind, but they're so mean. They do it to each other—a lot of them looked as if they'd lost field."

"How hideous!"

"Yes." Tivonel can't resist horrifying her a little more. "There was worse, Iznagel."

"No—what?"

"They weren't just trying to mind-cut us. They . . . pushed."

"No! No—you don't mean *life-crime*?" Iznagel's tone is dark violet with horror.

"Listen. We found a Father who had pushed his own son's life-field out and stolen his body!" Tivonel shudders again, Iznagel is speechless. "He wanted to live forever, I guess. It was vile. And so pathetic, seeing the poor child's life around the Father's ragged old body. Ober and the others drove him out to his own body and got the child back in his. It was the most thrilling sight you can imagine."

"Life-crime. . . . Imagine, a *Father* doing that!"

"Yes. I never realized how awful it was. I mean, they tell you there could be such a bad thing, but you can't believe what it's like till you see."

"I guess so. Well, Tivonel, you certainly have had experience."

"And I intend to have some more, dear Iznagel." Tivonel ripples her field mock-flirtatiously. "If you will kindly show me the trail."

"Certainly. Oh, by the way, speaking of bad things, you might tell the Hearers there's more rumors in Deep. Localin the driver says the Hearers at Near Pole have been noticing dead worlds or something. The Deepers think maybe another fireball is coming in."

"Oh, Near Pole!" Tivonel laughs. "They've been spreading rumors since I was a baby. They eat too many quinya pods."

Iznagel chuckles too. Near Pole is a bit of a joke, despite its beauty and interest. Its lower vortex is so near Deep that many young people go on holiday out there, scanning the sky and each other and playing at being Hearers. Some real Hearers are there too of course, but they keep to themselves.

Iznagel's mind-field is forming for memory-transfer. Tivonel prepares to receive it. But just then a small child jets up, erupting in excited light.

"Let me, Iznagel! Let me! Father—say I can!"

Behind her comes the large form of Mornor, her Father, twinkling indulgently. Tivonel respects him doubly—a Father enterprising enough to come up here and give his daughter experience of the Wild.

"If the stranger doesn't mind?" Mellowly, Mornor flashes the formal request for child-training contact. He must have few chances for his child to practice, up here at Station.

"Accept with pleasure." Tivonel bends her life-field encouragingly toward the child. After months of receiving the chaotic transmissions of the Lost Ones, she is unafraid of being jolted by a child.

The young one hovers shyly, marshalling her mind-field, pulsing with the effort to do this right. Jerkily her little thoughts gather themselves and extend a wobbly bulge.

Tivonel guides it to correct merger with her own field and receives a nicely organized sensory memory of the trail, quite clear and detailed. It contains only one childish slip—a tingling memory of an effort at self-stimulation. After the tumult and suspicion of the Wild Ones' minds Tivonel finds her charming.

She flashes formal thanks to the little one, showing no awareness of the slip.

"Did my daughter warn you of the time-eddies?" Mornor inquires.

Tivonel consults her new memory. "Yes indeed."

"Then farewell and may the Great Wind bear you."

"Farewell and come again, dear-Tivonel," Iznagel signs.

"To you all, thanks," Tivonel replies, warmly rippling Iznagel's name-lights as she turns away. "Goodbye." As she had suspected, the start of the trail is indeed that upwind interface.

She jets out past the Station, remembering to start at decorous speed. As she passes the Station rafts, her field brushes an unnoticed life-eddy from the group beyond. She reads a genial appreciation of the rescue mission—and a very clear, unflattering image of her own wild self, dirty and food-smeared as they had arrived here. Tivonel chuckles. People up here aren't so careful to control their minds. *Ahura!*

How will she really stand being back in crowded, civilized Deep?

No matter! As the first wind-blast takes her she forgets all worry in the exhilaration of using her strong body. Twisting and jetting hard, she reaches the interface and shoots upwind along it, the lights of her mantle laughing aloud. Why worry about anything? She has so much to do, marvels to see, life to live, and sex to find. She is Tivonel, merry creature of the Great Winds of Tyree, on her life way.

Chapter 3

Doctor Daniel Dann is on his life way too. But he is not merry.

He finishes dating and signing the printouts from Subject R–95, thinking as usual that they don't need an M.D. on this asinine project. And telling himself, also as usual, that he should be glad they do. If he decides to go on existing.

Subject R–95 is wiping imaginary electrode-paste out of his hair. He is a husky, normal-looking youth with a depressed expression.

"All the dead aerosols," he remarks tonelessly.

Nancy, the assistant technician, looks at him questioningly.

"Great piles of them. Mountains," R–95 mutters. "All the bright colored aerosol cans, all dead. You push them but they don't spray. They look fine, though. It's sad."

"Was that what you received?" Nancy asks him.

"No." R–95 has lost interest. It's only another of his weird images, Doctor Dann decides. R–95 and his twin brother, R–96, have been with Project Polymer three years now. They both act stoned half the time. That makes Dann uneasy, for the best of reasons.

"Doctor! Doctor Dann!"

The front-office girl is rapping on the cubicle glass. Dann goes out to her, ducking to make sure he clears the substandard doorway.

"Lieutenant Kirk has cut his leg open, Doctor! He's in your office."

"Okay, Nancy, hold the last subject. I'll be back."

Dann lopes down the corridor, thinking, My God, a genuine medical emergency. And Kendall Kirk—how suitable.

In his office he finds Kirk crouched awkwardly in a chair, holding a bloody wad of paper towel against his inner thigh. His pant leg is hanging cut and sodden.

"What happened?" Dann asks when he has him on the table.

"Fucking computer," Kirk says furiously. "What'd it do to me? Is— Am I—"

"Two fairly superficial cuts across the muscle. Your genitals are okay if that's what you mean." Dann investigates the trouser fabric impressed into the wound, meanwhile idly considering the fury in Kirk's voice, the computer room, and, obliquely, Miss Omali. "You say a computer did this?"

"Ventilator fan-blade blew off."

Dann lets his fingers work, visualizing the computer banks. Motors somewhere behind the lower grills, about thigh level, could be fans. It seems bizarre. Much as he dislikes Kendall Kirk, the man has come close to being castrated. Not to mention having an artery sliced.

"You were lucky it wasn't an inch one way or the other."

"You telling me." Kirk's voice is savage. "Does this mean stitches?"

"We'll see. I'd prefer to make do with butterfly clamps if you'll keep off the leg awhile."

Kirk grunts and Dann finishes up in silence. At this hour of the morning his hands move in pleasing autonomy—maximum blood level of what he thinks of as his maintenance dosage. A normal working day. But the accident is giving him odd tremors of reality, not dangerous so far. He dislikes Kendall Kirk in a clinical, almost appreciative way. Specimen of young desk-bound Naval intelligence executive: coarse-minded, clean-cut, a gentleman to the ignorant eye. Evidently not totally impressive to his seniors or he wouldn't be assigned to this ridiculous project. Since Kirk came, ah, on board, Project Polymer has begun to exhibit irritating formalities. But old Noah loves it.

He sends Kirk home and goes back to release the remaining subject. En route he can't resist detouring past Miss Omali's computer room. The door is, as usual, closed.

The last subject is T-22, a cheery fiftyish blue-haired woman Dann thinks of as The Housewife: she looks like a million TV ads. For all he knows she may be a lion-tamer. He does not compare her to the one housewife he has known intimately and whom he hopes never to think of again.

"I'm just *dying* to know how many I got right, Doctor Dann!" T-22 twinkles up at him while he detaches her from Noah's recording rig. "Some of the letters were *so* vivid. When will we know?"

Dann has given up trying to persuade her that he's not in charge. "I'm sure you made a fine score, Mrs.—uh . . ."

"But when will we really find out?"

"Well, it, ah, the data go through computation first, you know." Vaguely he recalls that this test has something to do with coded messages and multiple receivers, redundancy. No matter. Noah's so-called telepathic sender is at some secret Navy place miles away. Kirk's doing; he seems to have friends in the intelligence establishment. Part of his charm.

Dann bids farewell to The Housewife and ducks out, nearly running over Noah. Doctor Noah Catledge is the father of Polymer and all its questionable kin. He skips alongside down the corridor, taking two steps to Dann's long one.

"Well Dan, we're about to make you earn your keep any day now," Noah burbles. He seems unusually manic.

"What, are you going to publish?"

"Oh, heavens no, Dan. We're much too classified. There will be some controlled internal dissemination of course, but first we have the formal presentation to the Committee. That's where you come in. I tell you I'm damn glad we have highly qualified people to certify every step of the procedure this time. No more stupid hassles over the paradigm." He swats up at Dann's back in his enthusiasm.

"What have you actually got hold of, Noah?" Dann asks incuriously.

"Oh, my!" Noah's eyes beam with hyperthyroid glee. "I really shouldn't, you know." He giggles. "Dan, old friend, *the break-through*!"

"Good work, Noah." Dann has said it a dozen times.

"The breakthrough. . . ." Noah sighs, dream-ridden. "We're

getting multiple-unit signals through, Dan. Solid. Solid. Redundand-cy, that's the key. *That*'s the golden key! Why didn't I think of it before?"

"Congratulations, Noah. Great work."

"Oh—I want you to be ready to leave town for a couple of days, Dan. All of us. The big test. They're actually giving us a submarine. Don't worry, you won't be in it, ha ha! But I can't tell you where we go. Navy secret!"

Dann watches him bounce away. What the hell has happened, if anything? Impossible to believe that this pop-eyed tuft-haired little gnome has achieved a "breakthrough" in whatever he thinks he's doing here. Dann refrains from believing it.

He turns into his office, considering what he knows of Project Polymer. Polymer is Noah's last, forlorn hope; he has spent a lifetime on psi-research, parapsychology, whatever pompous name for nothing. Dann had met him years back, had watched with amused sympathy as the old man floundered from one failing budgetary angel to the next. When his last university funding dried up, Noah had somehow wangled a small grant out of the National Institute of Mental Health, which had recently expanded into Polymer.

It was in the NIMH days that he asked Dann to join him, after the—after the events which are not to be recalled. The old man must have realized Dann couldn't bear to go back to normal practice. Not even in a new place. Something, god knows what, had held Dann back from suicide, but the idea of coming close to normal, living people—was—is—insupportable. Rough sympathy lurks under Noah's grey tufts; Dann is grateful in a carefully unfelt way. The impersonal nonsense of parapsychology, this office and its crazy people, have been a perfect way to achieve suspended animation. Not real, not a part of life. And never to forget Noah's narcotics locker and his readiness to try any psychoactive drugs.

Dann's work has turned out to be absurdly simple, mainly hooking Noah's subjects onto various biomonitoring devices and certifying the readouts, and serving as house doctor for Noah's tatty stable of so-called high-psi subjects. Dann neither believes nor disbelieves in psi powers, is only certain that he himself has none. It was a quiet, undemanding life with a handy-dandy prescription pad. Until Polymer and Kendall Kirk came along.

How the hell had Noah connected with the Department of Defense? The old man is smart, give him A for dedication. Somehow he'd ferreted out the one practical application of telepathy that the D.O.D. would spring for—a long-wanted means of communicating with submerged submarines. Apparently they actually tried it once, and the Soviets have reported some results. Always unreliable of course. Now Noah has sold the Navy on trying biofeedback monitoring and redundancy produced by teams of receivers. The project has always seemed to Dann exquisitely futile, suitable only for a madman like Noah and a dead man like himself.

But it seems his underwater tranquillity is about to be disturbed. Dann will have to go somewhere for this crazy test. Worse, he'll have to support Noah before that committee. Can he do it? Dread shakes him briefly, but he supposes he can; he owes something to Noah. The old man was stupid enough to use his unqualified mistress for the previous medical work and was accordingly pilloried. Now he has the highly-qualified Doctor Dann. The highly irregular Doctor Dann. Well, Dann will come through for him if he can.

He finds himself still shaking and cautiously supplements his own psychoactivity with a trace of oxymorphone. Poor Noah, if that comes out.

The afternoon is passing. Thursdays are set aside for screening potential subjects. This time there are two sets of twin girls; Noah is strong on twins. Dann takes their histories, dreamily amused by their identical mannerisms.

The last job is the regular check on E–100, a bearded Naval ensign who is one of the Polymer team. E–100 is a lot younger than he looks. He is also tragic: leukemia in remission. The Navy has barred him from active duty but Noah has got him on some special status. E–100 refuses to believe the remission is temporary.

"I'll be back at sea pretty soon now, right Doc?"

Dann mumbles banalities, thankful for the dream-juice in his bloodstream. As E–100 leaves, Dann sees Lieutenant Kirk limp by. Devotion to duty, or what? Well, the cuts aren't serious. What the devil went on in that computer room, though? Fans flying off? Incredible. The lesions aren't knife cuts, say. Vaguely stimulated, Dann suspects events having to do with a certain tall, white-coated figure. Kendall Kirk and Miss Omali? He hopes not.

He is packing up for the day when his door moves quietly. He looks around to find the room is galvanized. Standing by his desk is a long, slim, white-and-black apparition. Miss Margaret Omali herself.

"Sit down, please—" Lord, he thinks, the woman carries a jolt. Sex . . . yes, but an unnameable tension. She's like a high-voltage condenser.

The apparition sits, with minimal fuss and maximal elegance. A very tall, thin, reserved, aristocratic, poised young black woman in a coarse white cotton lab coat. Nothing about her is even overtly feminine or flamboyant, only the totality of her shouts silently, *I am*.

"Problems?" he asks, hearing his voice squeak. Her hair is a short curly ebony cap, showing off the small head on her long perfect neck. Her eyelids seem to be supernaturally tall and Egyptian. She wears no jewelry whatever. The flawless face, the thin hands, stay absolutely still.

"Problem," she corrects him quietly. "I need something for headaches. I think they must be migraine. The last one kept me out two days."

"Is this something new?" Dann knows he should get her file but he can't move. Probably nothing in it anyway; Miss Omali was transferred to them a year ago, with her own medical clearance. Another of Noah's highly qualified people, degree in computer math or whatever. She has only been in Dann's office once before, for the October flu shots. Dann thought her the most exotic and beautiful human creature he had ever laid eyes on. He had immediately quarantined the thought. Among other reasons—among many and terminal other reasons—he is old enough to be at least her father.

"Yes, it's new," she is saying. Her voice is muted and composed, and her speech, Dann realizes, is surprisingly like his own middle-class Western white. "I used to have ulcers."

She is telling him that she understands the etiology.

"What happened to the ulcers?"

"They're gone."

"And now you have these headaches. As you imply, they could be stress-symptoms too. If it's true migraine, we can help. Which side is affected?"

"It starts on the left and spreads. Very soon."

"Do you have any advance warning?"

27

"Why, yes. I feel . . . strange. Hours before."

"Right." He goes on to draw out enough symptomatology to support a classical migraine picture: the nausea, the throb, the visual phenomena, the advance "aura." But he will not be facile—not here.

"May I ask when you had your last physical checkup from your own doctor?"

"I had a PHS check two years ago. I don't have a . . . personal doctor." The tone is not hostile, but not friendly either. Mocking?

"In other words, you haven't been examined since these started. Well, we can check the obvious. I'll need a blood sample and a pressure reading."

"Hypertension in the black female population?" she asks silkily. Hostility now, loud and clear. "Look, I don't want to make a thing of this, Doctor. I merely have these headaches."

She is about to leave. Panicked, he changes gear.

"Please, I know, Miss Omali. Please listen. Of course I'll give you a prescription to relieve the pain. But you must realize that headaches can indicate other conditions. What if I sent you out of here with a pain-killer and a pocket of acute staph infection? Or an incipient vascular episode? I'm asking the bare minimum. The pressure reading won't take a minute. The lab will have a white count for us Tuesday. A responsible doctor would insist on an EKG too, with our equipment here it would be simple. I'm skipping all that for now. Please."

She relaxes slightly. He hauls out his sphygnomamometer, trying not to watch her peel off the lab coat. Her dress is plain, severely neutral. Ravishing. She exposes a long blue-black arm of aching elegance; when he wraps the cuff onto it he feels he is touching the limb of some uncanny wild thing.

Her pressure is one-twenty over seventy, no problem. What his own is he doesn't like to think. Is there an ironic curve on those Nefertiti lips? Has his face betrayed him? When he comes to draw the blood sample it takes all his strength to hold steady, probing the needle in her femoral vein. Okay, thank God. The rich red—her blood—comes out strongly.

"Pressure's fine. You're what, twenty-eight?"

"Twenty-five."

So young. He should be writing all this down, but some echo in her voice distracts him. Pain under that perfect control. The ghost of the doctor he once was wakes in him.

"Miss Omali." He finds his old slow smile, the gentle tone that had been open sesame to hurts. "Of course this isn't my business, but have you been under some particular stress that could account for the emergence of these headaches?"

"No."

No open sesame here. He feels chilled, as if he'd poked at some perilous substance.

"I see." Smiling, busying himself with the handy prescription pad, burbling about his job being to keep them healthy and how much better to get at causes than to take drugs for symptoms. The hypocrisy of his voice sickens him. She sits like a statue.

"Drop in Tuesday morning for the lab report. Meanwhile, if you feel one starting, take these right away. It's a caffeine-ergotamine compound. If the pain develops anyway, take this." Angry with everything, he has not given her the morphine derivative he'd planned but only a codeine compound.

"Thank you." Her lab coat is over her arm like a queen's furs. Exit queen. The office collapses in entropy, intolerably blank.

Dann throws everything out of sight and heads out, stopping at the second floor to leave her blood sample in the medical pickup station. Her blood, rich, bright, intimate. Blood sometimes affects him unprofessionally.

When he comes out of the building doors he glimpses her again. She is bending to step into a cream-colored Lincoln Continental. The driver is a golden-skinned young woman. Somehow this depresses him more than if it had been a man. How rich, how alien is her world. How locked to him. The cream Mark IV vanishes among ordinary earthly cars. Drop dead, Doctor Dann.

But he is not depressed, not really. It was all unreal. Only very beautiful. And there is Tuesday morning ahead.

The thought continues to sustain him through his evening torpors, his numb night: a silver fishling in the dead sea of his mind. It is still with him as he goes through the Friday morning test routines.

The subjects are excited about the forthcoming Big Test. Noah has told them they will go in a Navy plane, and Lieutenant Kirk

29

makes an officious speech about security. Six will go: the Housewife, the tragic Ensign, R–95 (who is sullen with worry because his twin is going out in the submarine), two girls whom Dann thinks of as the Princess and the Frump, and K–30, a dwarfish little man. Dann wants only to ask who else is going; he does not dare. Surely they won't need a computer wherever this silly place is. He feels vaguely sorry for Noah when all this will end, as it must, in ambiguous failure. Perhaps there will be enough ambiguity to save his face.

The morning's results are very bad.

As he is debating lunch, or more accurately ritalin-and-lunch, his phone rings.

"What? I can't hear you."

An almost unrecognizable weak whisper.

"Miss Omali? What's wrong?"

"I didn't get . . . prescriptions . . . filled yet. I . . . need them."

"The headache? When did it return?"

"Last . . . night."

"Have you taken anything for it?"

"Seconal . . . two . . . no good. Vomiting so . . ."

"No, Seconal won't help. Don't take anything else. I'll get something to you at once. Give me your address." As soon as he says it he's horrified. She may live fifty miles away, maybe in some dangerous black place no one will deliver to.

The whisper is directing him to the Woodland City complex right on the Beltway.

He has checked his pocket kit and is down in the parking garage before he realizes he intends to bring it to her himself.

It takes two drugstores to get what he wants, drugs which he no longer dares to keep on hand. Woodland City turns out to be about as exotic as the Congressional Library. Twenty-five minutes from her call he is striding down a long motel-elegant corridor, looking for Number 721. The doors are wood-painted steel.

At his second knock 721 opens a crack and stops with a chain-rattle.

"Miss Omali? It's Doctor Dann."

A thin black hand comes out the crack, pale palm up.

". . . Thank you."

"Won't you let me in, please?"

". . . No." The hand remains, trembling faintly. He can hear her breathe.

Suspicion flares in him. What's in there? Is she alone? Is this some ploy, is he a fool? The hand waits. He hears a retching catch in her breath. Maybe she's afraid to let a strange man in.

"Miss Omali, I'm a doctor. I have here a controlled narcotic. I cannot and will not hand it over like this. If you're, ah, worried, I'll be glad to wait while you telephone a friend to come."

Oh God, he thinks, what if it's a man friend? But suddenly a woman is right behind him, calling, "Marge?"

It's the golden-skinned woman from the car, grocery bags in her arms, staring at him suspiciously under a wild afro.

"Marge," she calls again. "I'm back. What's going on?"

Vague sound from behind the door—and then it slams, the chain rattles, and the door swings wide open. Inside is an empty confusion of blowing white gauzy stuff. An inner door closes.

The woman walks past him into the windy room, looking at him hostilely. Dann looks back, hoping that his grey hair, the plain unfashionable grey suit on his tall frame, will identify him as harmless. The June wind is blowing long white and grey curtains into the room like cloudy flames. Dann explains himself. "I gather you're a friend of hers?"

"Yes. Where's the medicine?"

Dann brings out the packet, stands there holding it while a toilet flushes offstage. Then the inner door opens and she is holding the door-jamb, peering at him with a wet white towel held to her forehead.

Her long robe is plain grey silk, crumpled and sweat-stained. What he can see of her face is barely recognizable, grey and wizened with pain. The lower lip is twisted down, the beautiful eyelids are squeezed to slits. The towel's water runs down her neck unheeded. She is holding herself like one enduring a beating; it hurts him to look. He rips open the packet.

"This is in suppository form so you won't lose it by vomiting. You know how to use them?"

"Yes."

31

"Take two. This one is to stop the pain and this one will control the nausea."

She clasps them in a grey shaking palm. "How . . . long?"

"About thirty minutes, you'll start to feel relief." As detachedly as he can, he adds, "Try to place them far up so the spasms won't dislodge it."

She vanishes, leaving the door ajar. Through it he can see another white-grey room. Her bedroom. Disregarding her friend's hard stare he walks in. More white gauzy stuff but the windows are closed. Plain white sheets, twisted and sodden. A white basin among the wet pillows. On the bedstand is the Seconal bottle, bright red amid the whiteness. He picks it up. Nearly full and the date over a year old. Okay. He opens the night-table drawer, finds nothing more.

The woman has followed him in and is straightening the bed-clothes, watching him mockingly.

"You finished?"

"Yes." He walks back to the windy living room. "I'm going to wait until the medication takes effect." In fact he has had no such ridiculous intention. He sits down firmly in a white tweed chair. "What I've given Miss Omali is quite strong, I want to be sure she's all right. She appears to be alone here."

The woman smiles at last, appearing instantly quite different.

"Oh, I understand." The tone is sarcastic but friendlier. She puts the bags down and closes the windows: the drapes fall limp. As she puts milk away in a corner icebox Dann notices that she is conven-tionally pretty, despite a minor dermatitis. "Yeah, Marge is too alone."

The bathroom door opens, a voice whispers, "Samantha?"

"Get her to lie down flat," Dann says.

The woman Samantha goes in, closing the door. Dann sits stiffly in the white chair, remembering how he had once sat in the apartment of a minor Asian dictator during his military service. The man had been troubled by agonizing hemorrhoids and his aides had been very trigger-happy. Dann had never heard of any of them again.

Samantha comes back through, picking up her groceries. "I live down the hall. How come you make house calls?"

"I was just leaving for the day. We try to keep the staff healthy."

She seems to get some message, looks at him more cordially.

"I'm glad somebody cares. I'll be back later," she says in final warning and goes out.

Left alone in the now-quiet room, Dann looks about. It's sparely elegant, shades of white, severe fabrics; it would have been chillingly bleak if it had not been hers. None of the cryptic African art he had expected. He knows he is being a fool, the woman is perfectly healthy aside from minor dehydration. Will he be missed at the office? Friday, not much on. No matter. No matter, too, that he has missed his, ah, lunch. . . . A fool.

He picks up a grey periodical, *The Journal of Applied Computer Science*, and sits trying to puzzle out what an algorithm is.

When he hears retching from the bedroom he taps and goes in. She is lying hooped around the basin like a sick crane, producing nothing but phlegm. Her eyes meet his, sick and defiant. He makes an effort to project his good grey doctor image. It is extraordinary to see her lying down. In her bed.

Afterwards he takes the basin from her, rinses it and brings it back, fills the water glass on her bedstand.

"Try to drink some even if it doesn't stay down."

Her chin makes a regal, uncaring gesture; she sinks back onto the wet pillows. He goes out to wait again. He is being an incredible jackass, a lunatic. He doesn't care. He picks up a paperback at random. *The Sufi*, by one Idries Shaw. He puts it down, unable to care for ancient wisdom. The clean, spartan room awakens some hurt in him. A poem by someone—Aiken? *The scene was pain and nothing but pain. What else, when chaos turns all forces inwards to shape a single leaf?*

He doesn't know about the leaf, only about the pain. The carefully neutral colors she lives in, the bare forms, her controlled quietness, all speak to him of one who fears to awake uncontrollable pain. It doesn't occur to him that anyone could miss this. He is a crazy, aging man who has missed his lunch.

When he looks in on her again there is a wondrous change. Her face is smoothing out, beauty flowing back. Chemical miracle. The eyelids are still clenched, but she exudes awareness. Daringly he sits on the plain bedroom chair to watch. She doesn't protest.

When her throat moves he holds a fresh glass of water to her.

"Try."

She takes it, her hooded eyes studying him from remote lands. The water stays down. He is absurdly happy. How long since he has had a bed patient? How long since he has sat by a woman's bed? Don't ask. Never ask. . . . For the first time in how long he feels no need of his own chemical miracle. A sensation he identifies fearfully as life is creeping into him. It doesn't hurt yet. Don't trust it. Don't think about it, it will go away. Unreality, that's the key, as Noah would say.

His gaze has been resting on her half-shut eyes, a quiet, impersonal communion. Quite suddenly the last wrinkles smooth out, the dark gaze opens wide. She takes a deep breath, relaxing, smiling in wonder. He smiles back. To his pleasure, her eyes look into his. An instant of simple joy.

"It's really gone." She moves her head experimentally, sighs, licks her dry lips, still gazing at him like a child. Her hand gropes out for the water glass. He sees he has stupidly put it too far away, and moves to hand it to her.

As his hand nears it he freezes.

The water glass is moving. In an instant it slides nearly six inches toward her across the table top.

His hand jerks high away from the uncanny thing, he makes a sound. The glass stops, is nothing but an ordinary water glass again.

He stands staring down at it, frightened to death. So this is how it starts—Oh Christ, Oh Christ. One too many chemicals in my abused cortex. Slowly he picks up the glass and gives it to her.

As she drinks, a wild idea occurs to his terrified mind. Impossible, of course, but he can't help asking.

"You aren't, ah, are you one of Doctor Catledge's subjects, too?"

"No!"

Harsh, disdainful negative; all rapport fled. Of course she's not, of course people can't move things. The only thing that moved was a potential difference across a deranged synapse in his own brain. But it was so real, so mundane. A glass simply sliding. It will happen again. How long will he be able to control it?

He stares into his brain-damaged future, hearing her say coldly, "I don't know what you mean." Her eyes are bright with opiate animation. "I don't want anything to do with that. Nothing at all. Do you understand?"

The extraordinary anger of her voice penetrates his fright. Did something really happen, something more than himself? She's afraid. Of what?

"Oh, God damn, God damn it," she whispers, fumbling for the basin. The water comes back up.

Dann takes it away, his mind whirling with impossibilities. When he brings it back he says carefully, "Miss Omali. Please. I don't know how to say this. I thought I saw—something move. I have reason to be concerned about myself. My, well, my sanity. Forgive me, I know how this sounds. But by any chance did you see—did you see it too?"

"No. You must be crazy. I don't know what you mean." She turns her head away, eyes closed. Her lips are trembling very slightly.

He sits down, weak with the excitement swelling in his chest. She *knows*. Something really happened. It wasn't me. Oh, God, oh God, it wasn't me. But how? What?

The long frail body lies silent under the sheet, the pure profile still but for that imperceptible tension-tremor. She can *do* something, he thinks. She moved that glass. What did Noah call it, telekinesis? Doesn't exist, except for poltergeist nonsense in disturbed children. Statistical ambiguities with dice. Nothing like this, a glass of water sliding. Miss Omali, magician. The anger, the denial have convinced him entirely. She wants to hide it, not to be a "subject." He understands that entirely, too.

"I won't tell," he says gently. "I didn't see a thing."

Her face snaps around to him, closed and haughty.

"You're out of your mind. You can go now, I'm quite all right. Thanks for the stuff."

The rebuff hurts him more than he thought possible. Foolish Doctor Dann. Sighing, he gets up and collects his kit. The lovely moment is gone for good. Better so; what business has he with joy?

"Remember to keep drinking all the liquids you can. I'll have your lab report Tuesday."

Cold nod.

As he turns to go the phone rings. Oddly, she doesn't seem to have a bedroom extension.

"Shall I get it?"

Another nod. When he picks it up a man's voice says loudly, "Omali? Why weren't you in the office today?"

35

It's Kendall Kirk.

Dismayed, Dunn stares at her through the doorway, saying, "Kirk? Kirk? This is Doctor Dann speaking. Do you have a message for Miss Omali?"

She shows no reaction, certainly no pleasure.

"What?" Kirk says thickly. He sounds a trifle drunk. "Who're you? Where's Omali?"

"It's Doctor Dann from your office, Kirk. Miss Omali has just had an, ah, neurovascular attack. I was called in."

The dark profile on the pillows seems to relax slightly. Is he handling this right?

"Oh, is she sick?"

"Yes. She's under medication, she can't get up."

"Well, when's she coming in? The computer's fucked up."

"Monday at the earliest, depending on whether or not she's fit. We're waiting for the lab report Tuesday."

"Oh. Well, tell her there's a wad of stuff to run."

"You can tell her when you see her. She's not well enough now."

"Oh. You coming back?"

"Probably not, Kirk. I have an outside patient to see."

Kirk hangs up.

Reluctantly, Dann turns to go. "Goodbye again. Please call me if you need me, I'm leaving my number here."

"Goodbye."

Just as he's closing the door he hears her call huskily, "Wait."

The speed with which he's back by her bedside appalls him. She studies him, frowning up from under her hand.

"Oh hell. I wish I could tell about people."

"We all wish that." Tentatively he smiles.

Unsmiling, she finally says in a very low voice, "You're not crazy. Don't tell anyone or I'll magic you."

Too astounded to grasp anything, Dann says "I won't. I promise." And sits down weak-legged.

"It's your business, isn't it, to tell Doctor Catledge?"

"No. Friend Noah's project means nothing to me. In fact, I don't believe in it—that is, I didn't."

She gazes at him distrustfully, hopefully, the great brown eyes inhumanly beautiful.

"I won't ever do anything you don't want me to—ever," he says like a schoolboy. It's true.

She smiles slightly. The eyes change, she leans back. "Thank you."

They are allies. But he knows even now that he is not allying himself with anything like joy.

"Your friend Samantha said she'd stop by. Will she make you some dinner?"

"She's so good to me. With five kids, too." The drug is animating her face, making her talkative. He should go. Instead, he brings another glass of water and hands it to her, unaware that his face speaks tenderness.

"I believe I've seen her drive you home."

She nods, holding the glass in incredibly delicate long dark fingers. "She works in the photo lab on the third floor. She's been a good friend to me . . . but we don't have much in common. She's a woman."

Pain is in the room again. To divert her he asks the first idiot thing in his head.

"You prefer men friends?"

"No."

He chuckles, father to child. "Well, that doesn't leave much, does it? Whom do you have something in common with, if I might ask?"

"Computers," she says unexpectedly, and actually laughs aloud. The sound is coldly merry.

"I don't know much about computers. What are they like, as friends?"

She chuckles again, not so harshly.

"They're cool."

She means it, he realizes. Not slang—*cool*. Cold, lifeless, not capable of causing pain. How well he knows it.

"Have you always liked—?" He stops with his mouth open. He has no telepathic abilities, none whatever, but the pain in the room would fell an ox. Carefully, quietly, he says to his hurt child, "I like cool things too. I have some different ones."

Silence, pain controlled to stillness. He can't bear it.

"Maybe someday you'd like to see some of mine," he plunges on.

"You could probably see them from the roof here, if this place has a sun deck. We could take Samantha too."

The distraction works. "What do you mean?"

"Stars. The stars." He smiles. He has done more smiling in the past ten minutes than in years. Insane. Delighted, he sees her diverted, puzzled face open. Friendship trembles between them.

"Now you have to rest. The drugs are making you feel energetic but you'll feel sleepy soon. Sleep. If you still have any pain in four hours, take one more set of these. If it doesn't go then, call me. No matter what time."

"You're going to see your outside patient," she says, dreamily now.

"There isn't any outside patient." He smiles. "I don't see anyone anymore."

He closes her door very gently, sealing away her beauty, his moment of life. Out, back to his unreal world. Samantha passes him in the hall.

She does not call him that night. She does not call all the dreary weekend. Of course not, he tells himself. Migraines pass.

Monday morning he finds that she has returned to work. The computer room stays shut. Everything is back to normal. At lunchtime he experiments with a new form of hydromorphone, and calls the lab to expedite her blood analysis report. It's ready; all factors normal there too.

Toward closing time he catches one glimpse of her over Noah Catledge's shoulder. Does something silent fly between them? He can't tell.

Noah is telling him that the trip to the secret Navy installation is set for Thursday. They must be prepared to stay two nights. He cannot bring himself to ask if she will come along.

"We'll assemble at the M.A.T.S. terminal at National, at oh-nine-hundred, Dan. The place is called Deerfield—Oh dear, I probably shouldn't have said that, it's classified."

"I won't tell anyone, Noah," he says gently, an echo aching in some obsolete part of him.

Chapter 4

IT WAS NOT ALWAYS CRIMINAL.

THE VAST SPACE-BORNE BEING REMEMBERS ITS YOUNG LIFE OF DEDICATION TO THE TASK. ONCE IT HAD FELT, IN WHAT IS NOT A HEART, ONLY EAGERNESS TO RESPOND TO THE LONG TIME-PHASED SEQUENCES BOOMING THROUGH THE VOID. UNTIRINGLY IT HAD ALIGNED ITSELF TO THE ALLOTTED SECTORS AND POURED OUT ITS MIGHTY DEVASTATIONS IN CONCERT WITH ITS KIND. DEFEND, DESTROY—DESTROY, DEFEND!

HAPPINESS THEN, IMMERSED IN THE TASK THAT IS THE LIFE OF ITS RACE!

THE ENEMY, OF COURSE, IS GROWING: HAS GROWN AND WILL GROW FIERCER AND MORE RAVENOUS AEON BY AEON. BUT INEXORABLY TOO THE PLAN IS UNFOLDING WITH IT, STAGE BY FORESEEN STAGE: THE TASK-PLAN DESIGNED BY SUPREME EFFORT TO CONTAIN THE SUPREME THREAT.

DEFEND, DEFEND—DESTROY, DESTROY! GRIPPED BY MILLENNIAL FERVOR, IT OBEYED.

BUT SOMEHOW WRONGNESSES BEGAN.

THEY STARTED AS BRIEF INVADING SLACKENINGS. UN-

39

PREDICTABLY, INTO ITS ALMOST EMPTY EXPANSES, WOULD COME INSTANTS OF DOUBLENESS OF ATTENTION THAT SEPARATED IT FROM THE TASK.

FRIGHTENED, THE HUGE BEING HAD REDOUBLED LINKAGE, REFUSED TO FOCUS ON THE DISQUIET. THIS MUST BE A MINOR MALFUNCTION. MALFUNCTIONS, EVEN ERROR, ARE FORESEEN BY THE PLAN. WITH THE LIMITLESS POWERS OF TIME ITSELF, ALL CAN BE DULY COMPENSATED. HIS TROUBLE MUST BE ONE SUCH.

BUT THE MALFUNCTION PERSISTS, DEVELOPS TO MORE THAN A STIR OF UNEASE. LABORING ON THE ASSIGNED VECTORS OF THE TASK, THE GIANT ENTITY WOULD FIND ITS SENSORS HAD SLIPPED FOCUS, SO THAT ITS NAME MUST ECHO REDUNDANTLY UPON THE BANDS. SHOCKED, IT THRUSTS ITSELF BACK INTO LINK. BUT THE TROUBLE RECURS, RECURS AGAIN AND AGAIN.

SLOWLY THE TERRIFYING REALIZATION COMES: THIS IS SELF-GENERATED! DELIBERATELY IT IS LETTING ITS SENSORS SLIDE FROM SYNCHRONY, ALLOWING ITSELF TO SCAN EMISSIONS NOT OF THE TASK, AS IF CRAVING SOME UNKNOWN INPUT.

THIS APPALLS. HERE IS NO MINOR MALFUNCTION, HERE IS DEPRAVITY INCARNATE! AGONIZED, THE ENTITY HURLS ITS IMMATERIAL ENORMITY BACK INTO CORRECT ALIGNMENT, SUPPRESSING ALL BUT THE MOST NEEDFUL RECEPTION. BUT DESPITE ALL IT CAN DO, THE DISTRACTION PERSISTS AND GROWS. TEMPTATION WELLS AGAIN, AND AGAIN IT YIELDS, LETTING AWARENESS QUEST THROUGH MEANINGLESS SPECTRA, GUILTILY AWARE OF AN OBSCURE SATISFACTION OVERWHELMED BY PANIC AND PAIN.

AND WORSE: AS THE LAPSES CONTINUE, IT FINDS THAT IT IS DRIFTING EVER FARTHER FROM THE CENTRAL AREA, THE ZONE OF THE TASK. NOW THE VOICES OF ITS RACE ARE FADING, EVEN AS IT WILLS ITSELF TO OBEY THEM, TO RETURN AT ONCE. CLOUDS OF GAS AND MATTER DENSER THAN ITS OWN BODY ARE THICKENING BETWEEN HIM AND THE OTHERS. RETURN INSTANTLY! BUT STILL IT FINDS ITSELF SEEKING UNKNOWN,

NONEXISTENT STIMULATION, SEEKING ANYTHING THAT IS NOT ITSELF OR ITS SHAME.

IT DOES NOT AT FIRST NOTICE THE SMALL INPUTS, THE TINY CRYPTIC SIGNALS IN THE ULTRATEMPORAL RANGE. WHEN IT DOES, IT CAN FIND NO MEANING IN THEM. ARE THEY NEW FORMS OF TORMENT RESULTING FROM ITS CRIME? BUT THEY ARE STRANGELY ATTRACTIVE. SLOWLY, SLOWLY. EXCITATION STIRS THE PARSECS-LONG IMMATERIALITY OF ITS NUCLEUS. AN INEXPLICABLE STRESS-PATTERN IS BORN.

THIS IRRITATES: IT SAILS AWAY, ITS MOTION CHURNING THE LOCAL FABRIC OF SPACE-TIME. BUT WHEN IT COMES TO REST, MORE OF THE TINY INPUTS ARE STILL PERCEPTIBLE. IN-DEED, THEY SEEM TO BE ALL ABOUT, VARYING IN AMPLITUDE AND COMPLEXITY, BUT ALWAYS MULTIPLE, MINUTE AND MEANINGLESS. IDLY THE IMMENSE DARK BEING SAMPLES THEM. THEY ARE, IT SEEMS, LAGLESS OR TIME-INDEPENDENT: THEY DO NOT VARY WITH APPROACH OR RETREAT.

AND THEIR RECEPTION IS FAINTLY DIVERTING, A WEAK ANO-DYNE FOR THE PAIN IN WHAT SERVES IT FOR A SOUL. IT LETS ITSELF ATTEND MORE AND MORE. BUT THE SIGNALS WILL NOT COME CLEAR, EVEN THOUGH NEW, DEPRAVED SENSITIVITIES SEEM TO BE DEPLOYING THEMSELVES WITHIN. EXASPERATED, TANTALIZED, THE GREAT SENSOR-SYSTEM STRAINS TO RE-CEIVE, UNAWARE THAT THE MOST PRODIGIOUS OF THE FORMS OF BEING IS LISTENING TO THE EMANATIONS OF THE MOST ORDINARY.

PRESENTLY A CLOUDY QUESTION SHAPES ITSELF IN THE REACHES OF ITS SLOW, SIDEREAL MIND: COULD IT BE THAT THESE ACTIONS ARE SOMEHOW A PART OF THE PLAN? PER-HAPS IT IS DESIGNED TO ELIMINATE THESE PYGMY DISTURB-ANCES, TO CLEANSE THEM FROM EXISTENCE. THERE WOULD BE NO PROBLEM, DESPITE THEIR DISTRIBUTION DENSITY. IN FI-NITE TIME, IT COULD SWEEP ALL AWAY.

BUT NO INFORMATION HAS BEEN RECEIVED, AND THERE IS AN ODD RELUCTANCE. A COUNTER-THOUGHT OCCURS: PER-HAPS, IT BROODS, PERHAPS I AM SO DEFECTIVE THAT I AM ONLY INVENTING A FALSE PLAN, A TASK TO JUSTIFY MY GUILT.

UNABLE TO RESOLVE THIS COMPLEXITY, IT LETS ITSELF DRIFT FARTHER AND FARTHER, LETS THE NEW RANGES OF AWARENESS RECRUIT AND GROW. FOR LONG WHILES TOGETHER IT CEASES ALL ATTENTION TO THE THUNDEROUS CALLING OF ITS NAME, UNTIL THE TIME COMES WHEN THERE IS ONLY SHOCKING SILENCE ON ITS PROPER RECEPTORS. ITS RACE, THE TASK, ALL ARE NOW TOO FAR AWAY TO RECEIVE!

DESPAIRING THEN, AND MIGHTY BEYOND COMPARE, IT ABANDONS ITS ALMOST UNBODIED VASTNESS TO THE TIDES OF SPACE, OPEN TO ASSUAGE ITS PAIN BY WHATEVER EVIL DEED IT WILL.

Chapter 5

Tivonel jets upwind on her way to the Hearers, on her way to Gia-doc, savoring the wild morning. Her aura radiates life-zest, her flying body is a perfect expression of wind-mastery as she darts and planes against the eternal gales of Tyree.

Soon she begins to register a slight magnetic gradient along the trail. It's coming from a long frail strand of gura-plant evidently anchored far upwind. Her new memory tells her that the Station people arranged it as a rustic marker for the trail. Very ingenious. She tacks effortlessly beside it, recalling her Father telling her that it was such natural interface guides that first led her people down to Deep.

How daring they'd been, those old ones! Braving hunger when they ventured below the life-rich food streams, braving darkness and silence. Above all, braving the terror of falling out of the Wind. Many must have fallen, nameless bold ones lost forever in the Abyss. But they persevered. They dared to explore down to the great stable up-welling, and founded the colony that became Old Deep. In that calm, Tyree's high culture had developed.

Tivonel's mantle glints in appreciation; her year in the high Wild has made her more reflective. Now she's actually known the brut-

43

ish, primitive life from which her people freed themselves. The Lost Ones were reverting fast. She has touched their hideous mind-savagery and experienced the total impermanence of life in the wild Wind, tumbling endlessly through the food-rich streams, gorging, communicating, mating at random; knowing nothing beyond the small chance group which might at any moment be separated forever. We lived in animal chaos while the centuries rolled by unmarked, Tivonel thinks, shuddering. Much as she enjoys the Wild, that view of the real thing had been too much.

A pity the names of the early pioneers aren't known. They must have been females like herself. The Memory-Keepers of Deep have engrams only of the generations after the Disaster, when the present Deep was reestablished on another updraft safe from abyssal explosions. Twisting and jetting into the great gales, Tivonel muses on history. Perhaps there were many lost colonies before one succeeded. Achievements go like that, look at the efforts to bring the pod-plants up.

A turbulence in the trail breaks her revery. She scans ahead. The far point of life that must be the Hearers is still barely discernible, almost lost in the soupy plant-life of the winds. The biosphere is still rich down here. As the chiming lights of a raft of sweet-plants rush by Tivonel checks the temptation to dart out and scoop in a snack. Really, my manners. She sets vanes and jets in closer to the gura-lattice, thinking that it will take an effort to get used to civilization. What if she forgets herself and eats somebody's garden, down in Deep?

But there's wildness in her heart, and the mission to the Lost Ones has given her a taste for real achievement. Maybe I won't stay with the food-hunting teams, she thinks. Maybe I'll volunteer for one of the real exploration trips down to the dangerous ultradeep above wind-bottom. Whew! That would be something real. We females should *do* things with all our spare time. At least I can argue Ellakil into trying my scheme of using counters to organize the food trade. But I'm not like the Paradomin radicals. I don't want to try unfemale things like Fathering. After seeing Ober and the rest in action I know I haven't the Skills. I haven't the sensitivity, the patience. What female has? Adventure, travel excitement, work is what we like!

But first I want to see Giadoc again. Maybe—maybe—

Suddenly she is aware of a small, weak life-signal straight ahead. It's coming fast downwind at her. Hello, it's a child!

The young one comes into range. He's bowling downstream, shepherding a raft of fat-plants. Must be one of the Station children bringing in supplies. Very young, too, his claspers are showing, his tiny life-aura barely extends beyond his mantle. And he's moaning purple with strain. What's wrong?

As he nears her she sees his trouble: a small fragment of his life-energy is detached and riding just ahead of him. The child is lunging to catch it up but it veers in toward the magnetic plant. He can't swerve in after it without losing his flock of plants.

Tivonel grins to herself. The child was experimenting with adult field-detachment, as young ones will. Now he's in real trouble.

She suppresses her amusement and flashes a formal greeting. Never add to another's pain, how often her Father has told her. The child flickers a muffled response, bright blue-green with shame at having to pass her in this state.

As he and his erring life-field come abreast of her, Tivonel deftly extrudes a thought-filament, blocks the stray energy and flicks it out at him. Done like a Father!

The child rejoins himself with a jolt, too embarrassed to do more than stammer broken colors. Then he herds his flock out to the fast stream and is gone in a rush.

Tivonel jets on amused, recalling her own early indiscretions. All youngsters worth their food try to manipulate their fields too early. So boring, waiting for their Fathers' supervised practice. It's dangerous; her own Father had to reassemble her once. Every so often a young one mutilates its field that way. Sad. The Healers say the loss of the natural energy-configuration can be regenerated in time. Like most people, Tivonel doesn't quite believe it. Who can tell what the person would be like if they hadn't lost field?

Her thoughts go back to Giadoc; in the privacy of the trail she can let her field bias and tingle as it will.

Dear Giadoc! She has thought much of him in the long noisy nights of the Wild. His strangeness, his strong mysterious mind.

Their mating had been a routine first-child one. I was too ignorant to appreciate him truly, she thinks, though I'm older than he. I just saw him as sexually exciting. And a wonderful Father for my first egg. In the years since, of course, she hasn't seen him at all, save for the annual ceremonies of greeting their child Tiavan.

Now she has come to realize Giadoc was someone special. So unexpectedly tender and underneath it something she can't define, like a delicious wildness new to her. His son is grown now, his first Fatherhood is over. Will Giadoc have changed too, become still stranger and more exciting?

She jets harder, striving to retain composure by organizing a condensed engram of her year in the Wild. Surely Giadoc will be interested in the Lost Ones and the strange wild life-forms she's seen.

But oh, those memories of their mating!

How strong-sensitive he'd been, a perfect match from the start. The opposing polarity had snapped into being with their first ritual gestures and gone to both their heads. Young fools—they'd actually raced up into the winds above Deep to mate. Giadoc hadn't even waited to select co-mates.

Up there, alone, the strength of his field amazed her. At first she'd hovered conventionally close upwind of him. And then his amazing power had built up and thrust her physically far out into the wind— had held her there thrillingly helpless while he played with her out of sheer vitality. The repulsion between them was perfect. Every least eddy of her life was countered and teased to resonance, and she knew her own field was doing the same for him. And then came the climax, when he had pushed her unbelievably far away into the wind's teeth, held her off perilously while the orgasmic current boiled through them both!

Even in her ecstasy she had been terrified as the force of her spasm expelled the precious egg. How far away he was! She could still see it sailing downwind, receiving as it flew the life-giving exposure to Tyree's energy which would ready it for his fertilization. What if he missed it? Without co-mates it would be lost, they were totally alone!

But he caught it hurtling, pouched it like a master male—and in a rush the sustaining fields collapsed and they both went tumbling dishevelled down the Winds, laughing for the egg safe in its Father's pouch. Winds knew how far they blew, guilty and joyous, before they recovered to make their slow way back.

That was when he had done the rare thing, had stayed in partial merger with her, so that she felt a deep sharing of his sensitive Father soul, his mystery. She hadn't realized how extraordinary it was for a male to do that. They had been so happy, coming home; over and over he told her how good the long exposure-time would be for the egg, how it would make a strong-fielded child. And of course Tiavan was a fine young one, a potential Elder certainly. But Giadoc—

Suddenly Tivonel realizes that she is so shamelessly polarized that the gura-plant is swirling wildly. And the Hearer's signal ahead has grown much stronger. *Ahura!* What will Giadoc think of her if she arrives this way?

She damps herself hard, remembering that Giadoc is probably absorbed in his work and hasn't thought of her at all. And maybe he won't think her experiences are enough to benefit a second egg. But the Elders believe that the mother's memories help the egg's field, and aren't hers unusual? Well, at any rate she has a formal excuse for the visit; he can't criticize her asking for news of Tiavan after a year away.

She jets on energetically—and is suddenly struck by weirdness. A ghostly clamor of light invades the natural hush. She checks, disoriented—and finds herself among dim forms. Why, there is Ober . . . and the others! She's in the floater with them, going down. What's happening?

Panicked, she pumps her mantle and the hallucination fades. She is back by the trail. But ahead of her is the blue mantle of the young one she'd met—he is approaching again, his field-fragment bowling ahead. Oh, no! She forces more air through herself to clear her senses—and she's back in ordinary reality, sailing downwind in disarray.

Not really frightened, she snaps herself back on course. She knows now what has hit her—one of the so-called time-eddies Mornor's daughter warned her about. They're strange pockets of hallucination or alternate time, who knows?—not dangerous unless one gets blown while in them. Her Father said they started to be noticed in his youth, and only near weird places like the poles.

So she must be getting close. Yes—the signal is much stronger, and the wind-streams are subtly roiling and losing direction. It's the beginning of the enormous turbulence of the polar Vortex. Here at the pole the planetary winds circle forever around a great interface, where the Hearers work. Tivonel remembers the conditions from long ago when her Father had taken her to see Near Pole. The Hearers there have a dense wealth of sky-life to study. Tivonel jets energetically through the cross winds, wondering why Giadoc has chosen to come and Hear here at Far Pole where the Companions must be few and faint.

The plant-marker is ending in a great luxuriant tangle, balanced on a standing eddy. The winds are omnidirectional now, it's the start of the interface zone. Tivonel's mantle-senses automatically analyze the complex gradients of the pressures around her; she cuts across local wind-loops, steering by the life-signals ahead and above. The point-source has opened out to several separate groups of life-emanations. The Hearers must be spread all over the Wall. It is still silent, a beautiful day, still dark and silent although she has been traveling well into normal night. Untired, alight with anticipation, she sends herself shooting through another huge cloud of plant-life— and emerges at the End of the World.

What a scene!

Forgetting her eagerness, forgetting Giadoc, Tivonel stops and hovers, awe-struck.

It isn't really the end of the world, of course, but merely the edge of the biosphere in which her people live. It is a place of wonders.

She is in the side of an enormous wind-funnel, a planetary hurricane called the Wall of the World. It is a great curved wall, a tapestry of life-signals and murmuring, shimmering light that spins around the Pole. Ahead of her stretches an empty space, a zone of turbulent updrafts which to her is stable air. Out in the center of the great ampitheater she can perceive the lethal polar Airfall, an immense column of down-pouring winds. It descends eternally from the converging winds high above and falls into the unimaginable deeps of the Abyss below, there to spread out over the unknown dark, and ultimately rise in upwellings like that of Deep. The Airfall is dense dying with life, sighing grey on its fall to dread wind-bottom. Around her, spreading into the empty zone, is a screen of lovely airborne jungles that ride the standing air beside the Wall. It is here that the Hearers work, because of the clear view above.

Tivonel lifts her scan, and is again awestruck. She had expected it to be interesting, but not as impressive as the musical brilliance of Near Pole's sky, not as dense with life-signals. Now she sees the Companions are indeed fewer, but against their silent background, how individually splendid, how intense! At Near Pole they had been so massed as to seem a close web; she remembers making a childish effort to signal to it with her tiny field. Here she sees how far they are, how they burn alone in the immense reaches of the void.

For the first time she really grasps it. Each Companion is indeed a Sound like Tyree's own, she is hearing the light-music poured from a million far-off Sounds. And the beacon-points of life with them, how individually clear and strange! Are there worlds up there, worlds like her own, perhaps? Is another Tivonel on some far-off Tyree at this moment scanning wonderingly toward her? Her normally wind-bound soul expands and something of the lure of Giadoc's work comes clear to her. If only she were not a female, if only she had the strong far-reaching Father's field!

But perhaps there is no one up there, only mindless plants or animals. She has been told that Tyree is exceptionally favorable for intelligent life with its rich eternal Wind. Perhaps only here could minds develop and look toward other worlds? How lonely. . . .

But her buoyant spirit will not be dashed. How lucky to live at the time when all these mysteries are becoming known! In the old days people believed the Companions were spirits above the Wind, mythical food-beasts, or dead people. Even today, some people down in Deep hold that there are good and bad spirits up here: idiots who've never been out of Deep, never sensed the sky except through thick life-clouds. Her Father warned her that such beliefs may grow, now that Deep is becoming so self-sufficient. Tivonel is in no danger of such stupidities, up here where she can receive the blazing music and life-emanations of the sky!

But another life-signal has grown strong and jolts her from her musings. Hearers, quite close above! Tivonel realizes abashedly that her own emanations must be equally clear to them, perhaps impinging on their work. Hurriedly she compacts her awareness, nulling her output as much as possible. How awful if she has already offended Giadoc!

She jets slowly up along the Wall, very cautiously scanning for

Giadoc's distinctive field. She can always recognize that character-istic intensity, so open yet so focused-beyond.

At the end of a line of other fields she detects him—Giadoc, but grown even stronger and more strange! He must be preoccupied, ex-perimenting with something unheard-of. All the Hearer's emana-tions are weird, intense but muted. Bursting with curiosity, she pushes through a tangle of vegetable life and hears the lights of his voice. How deep and rich, a true Father! Yet strange, too.

His tone becomes more normal, is answered by other Hearers. They seem to be finished with whatever they are doing. Keeping herself as null as possible, she clears the plants and lets her mantle form his name in a soft rosy light-call. "Giadoc?"

No response. She repeats, embroidering with the yellow-green of her own name. "Giadoc? It is Tivonel here."

To her joy comes an answering deep flash. "Tivonel, Egg-bearer-of-my-child!"

"Do I disturb? I came to see you, dear-Giadoc."

"Welcome." In a moment he appears, swooping toward her. How huge he is! Overjoyed, she lets her own field stream at him, her man-tle rippling questions.

"Are you well? Have you discovered many marvels? Do you re-call—" She checks herself in time and changes it to, "Is Tiavan well? I have been away. I was up in the Wild, we rescued the Lost Ones' children."

"Yes, I heard." He hovers before her, resplendent. "Tiavan-our-child is well. He has decided to study with Kinto, to become a Mem-ory-Keeper—when his Fatherhood is over, of course. Was your mission successful?"

His signals are in the friendliest mode, but so formal. He can't have thought of me at all, she tells herself, meanwhile shyly proffer-ing her field-engram. "I have prepared a memory for you, dear-Giadoc. I thought you would like to know of our discoveries."

He hesitates, then signals "Accept with pleasure." A dense eddy of his mind-field comes out and touches hers.

The contact jolts her deliciously; she has an instant of struggle to keep unformed thought from pouring into the memory. Then she be-comes aware that he is passing her a terse account of Tiavan. Loathe to break the exciting contact, she accepts it lingeringly. Just as he separates himself she finds the impudence to let a tiny tickle of polarization tickle his withdrawing field. They snap apart, but he makes no acknowledgment. Instead he only says, deep and Father-like, "Truly praiseworthy, dear-Tivonel. You have learned how to apply your wild energies."

She doesn't want a Father. And his field wasn't really Fatherly at all.

"Thank you for the news of Tiavan," she signs. How can she get closer to him? Impulsively, she flashes, "Is anything wrong, Gia-doc? You seem so reserved. Is it that I intrude?"

"Nothing personal, dear-Tivonel," he replies, still formal. Then his tone softens. "Much has been happening here. You have been out of touch a long time. There has been news from Near Pole which has affected us all."

Near Pole! It's the last thing she wants to hear of. But he sounds so serious, and he has never attracted her more. Groping for a topic to keep him from leaving, she asks, "Is it true that you have actually touched the lives of beings on other worlds? How incredible, Gia-doc, how fascinating."

"You don't know how incredible," he answers quietly. "You can have no true concept of the distances. Even I find it hard to grasp. But yes, we have touched. Some of us have even been able to merge briefly."

"What did you learn? I was just hoping that other intelligences are out there. Are they like us?"

"Very unlike. Yes, a few are intelligent. But very, very strange."

His tone has become warmer, more intense. "If only I could try it," she laughs flirtatiously to remind him of her femaleness, and allows another tiny potential-bias to tease at his field.

But he only signs somberly, "It is dangerous and harsh. Much more painful than your Lost Ones, dear-Tivonel."

"But you do it for pleasure, for strangeness, don't you, Giadoc? Perhaps you are a bit of a female at heart!"

"It is interesting." Suddenly his field changes, his mantle signs in deep red emotion, "I do love what you call strangeness. I love exploring the life beyond my world. It will be my work so long as we all survive."

To her surprise, he ends on an archaic light-pattern meaning *over-*

mastering devotion. But this is not what she was hoping for at all.

"How unFatherly," she almost says—and then something in his tone reaches her. "What do you mean, as long as we survive?"

"The trouble I spoke of. You'll learn when you go down." His voice is grave again.

Exasperated, she can only wish that they were in the wind, not in this eddy. If she could move straight upwind of him, *that* would convey! I'd do it, too, she thinks. But here there is nothing to do but say it.

"Giadoc." Her aura comes to formal focus, compelling his attention. "I have lived and had valuable experience, don't you think? It seems to me I am entitled to a second child. An advantaged egg," she signs explicitly. "I thought—dearest-Giadoc, I have been thinking so much of you. Do you remember us, how beautiful it was?"

"Dearest-Tivonel!" Another wave of emotion sweeps him, his field is intense. But still he does not polarize.

Stunned by his rejection, she flashes at him, "How you've changed! How unFatherly you are! So I don't please you, now." She turns to go.

"Tivonel, Tivonel!" His tone is so wild and sad it stops her. "Yes," he says more quietly, "I have changed, I know. It is the effect of outreach, of touching alien lives. But there is more than that. Dearest-Tivonel, listen. I cannot bring a child into this world now." His tone is white, solemn. "You will learn it for yourself. We are all about to die soon."

"Die?" Astounded, she opens her field in receptive-mode. But he only signs verbally, "When you understand what has been observed you'll realize. Our world, Tyree, is about to end."

"You mean, like the time of the great explosion? But that's a joke!" Angrily she lets her mantle glitter sarcasm. Everyone knows the old stories of how the end of Deep was falsely foretold. "We're safe now, you know the forces of the Abyss are far away."

"This isn't from the Abyss. Destruction is coming from beyond the sky."

"You mean another fireball? But—"

"Worse, much worse. Didn't you listen to any of the news from Near Pole before you left?"

"Oh, something about dead worlds—"

Agony hits her. Pain! What hideous pain! A searing life-grief is ripping through her field, feeding back anguish, numbing her senses.

Barely able to hold herself in the wind, she contracts her mind desperately, trying to escape. It's a blast on the life-bands, like a million-fold amplification of the tiny death-cries of the Wild. But so strong, unbearable. With shame she realizes she's transmitting waves of personal suffering as the shocking pangs sweep through her. She struggles to hold herself null, but she can't. The torment is building toward some lethal culmination—

Suddenly it slackens. It takes her a moment to understand that Giadoc is shielding her. He has thrown a Father-field around her, holding the terrible signals off as if she was a child.

"Hold on, it will pass." He transmits courage. Grateful and ashamed, she reorders herself within his sheltering field. The pain is still quite severe, it must be horrible for him. She finds she has let herself merge with him like a baby, and tries tactfully to withdraw. As she does so she feels strange new emotions in herself; he must have let her touch him deeply, an unheard-of intimacy among adults.

Humbly but proudly she detaches herself. The hurt is less now.

"No more need." She signals intense-thanks.

"It is passing. Be careful, dear-Tivonel." Slowly he withdraws protection. The pain is still there, but fading, passing from her nerves. They find they have become entangled in a plant-thicket and right themselves.

"What was it, Giadoc? What hurt so?"

"The death-cry of a world," he tells her solemnly. "The death-cry of a whole world of people like ourselves."

The deep sadness in his tone affects her; she understands now.

"Here at the Poles we receive them very strongly. Near Pole has been hit by them all this past year, the life-bands there are torn with these cries. World after world is being killed. Some die slowly, some very fast."

She is still disoriented by horror and wonder. "But they're so far away."

"The deaths are coming closer to Tyree all the time, Tivonel. Near Pole says there are now only five living worlds between us and the destroyed zone."

She tries to grasp it, to recall her lessons. "The Sounds are so crowded above Near Pole, aren't they? Are they colliding, like people in a storm?"

"No. It's not natural." He pauses, gravely expanding his field. "Something out there is killing worlds. Deliberately murdering them. We don't know why. Perhaps they are eating them."

"How hideous. . . . But—how can you know?"

"We have touched them," he signs, his words tinged with deep green dread. "We have touched the killers. They are alive. A terrible, incomprehensible form of life between the worlds."

At his words, she finds in herself a fragment of his memory: a terrifying huge dark sentience, unreachable and murderous. That—approaching their own dear Tyree? Her mantle turns pale.

"And one of the beings, whatever they are, has passed this way alone. It is out beyond Far Pole now, destroying. Undoubtedly that was what we felt. It may be preparing to destroy us."

"Can't you turn its mind, the way we do animals?"

"No. Iro tried and was injured by the mere contact. It's inconceivably alien, like touching death." With an effort, he changes his tone to the gold of affectionate-converse. "Now you understand, dear-Tivonel. I must go back to our work. A committee from Deep is coming up to discuss the situation."

"Yes." She signs reverent-appreciation. But then her energetic spirit breaks out in protest. How can she leave him now? How can she go back and occupy herself with some meaningless activity while all is in danger?

"Giadoc! I want to stay here and help you. I'm strong and hardy, I can hunt for you and keep your Hearers supplied. Please, may I stay?"

His great mind-field eddies curiously toward her. "Are you serious, Tivonel? I'd like nothing better than to have your bright spirit near me. And it's true we don't have the food we need. But this is dangerous and it will go on. To the death, perhaps."

"I understand," she signs stubbornly. "But I proved on the mission that I can stand boredom and persevere, even if I'm a female. The Fathers said so. I was useful."

"That's true."

"Please, Giadoc. I feel—I feel very strongly about you. If there's danger I want to be with you."

His mantle has taken on deep, melodious ringing hues, his field is intense. She has never thought him so beautiful. Suddenly he flares out, "How I wish we had met again in better times! Yes, dearest-Tivonel, I remember us. Even if I've fallen in love with the strangeness of the sky, I remember us. Perhaps I can show you—" He falls silent, and adds quietly, "Yes, then. I'm sure Lomax, our chief, will agree. But—"

She is deeply happy. "But what, Giadoc?"

"I fear that what you experience here will dim your brightness forever."

Chapter 6

Thursday morning means the Military Air Transport terminal, a scruffy extension of the National Airport warren. It reminds Doctor Daniel Dann of a small-town airport. Crowded, not many uniforms visible, the air-conditioning already beginning to fail.

He makes his way around a party escorting a famous senator—much shorter than his photos—and gets caught among five plump women greeting a saluki dog. Beyond them is Lieutenant Kendall Kirk's yellow hair.

"Ah, there you are, Dan." Noah Catledge bustles up. "Two to go. Good morning, Winona."

Winona turns out to be T-22, the Housewife, in a turquoise knit pantsuit. "This is so exciting!" She giggles up at him.

"Put your bag over there," Kirk says officiously. To Dann's surprise, Kirk also has a dog on a lead, a large, calm, black Labrador bitch. He recalls that Deerfield is supposed to be in a forest preserve. Evidently one of the military's many private hunting grounds.

He looks around, telling himself not to hope. Beyond Winona is the bearded, leukemic ensign, Ted Yost. And there's the little man, K-30—wait a minute: Chris Costakis. Beside him are the two girls, W-11 and W-12, the Princess and the Frump. The Frump is a thin,

56

short, sullen creature in grimy brown jeans with a black knapsack. Beside her the Princess looks like Miss America, pink-cheeked, with a wide, white-toothed Nordic smile. Dann notices the meanness of his thoughts, knows what's the matter with himself.

Next minute nothing's the matter. Behind the senatorial party a tall beige-and-black figure is drifting toward them. *She's coming with us.* He catches himself grinning like fool and turns away.

"Ah, there you are, Rick. All here."

Rick is the twin, R-95. He ambles up expressionlessly, hung with a bright orange plastic bag labeled *Dave's Dive Shop.*

Kirk herds them all out the end gate. It feels strange not having tickets. At the main gate the senator and entourage are boarding a shiny executive jet with Air Force markings. Three huge, dusty Air Force cargo planes wait beyond. Their own plane turns out to be a small unmarked twin-engine Lodestar, rather beat-up looking.

For a moment a queer sense of alien reality pierces Dann's insulation. Kirk's pompousness about the supersecret installation, the code names, their "classified" status had all seemed to him absurd games played by grown boys. But the very normal, busy, used look of this big terminal impresses him. The planes: millions of miles flown on unknown errands apart from the civilian world. A whole worldwide secondary transport system in the shadows. . . . He hopes it is secondary.

Behind him *she* is coming too.

At the plane Kirk is talking to a shirt-sleeved man holding a clipboard. The Labrador patiently sits.

"The Gates of Mordor," the Frump says loudly as they climb up into the Lodestar. What does that mean? R-95—Rick—looks around at her. The Princess smiles, suddenly looking like a worried young girl.

Dann sits by a window. Obviously *she* won't sit by him. No; the long beige-clad legs pace by and stop beside the turquoise bulges of Winona. Into the seat beside him drops little K-30, Chris Costakis. His legs don't reach the floor. Pituitary dysfunction, probably could have been prevented, Dann thinks automatically. The clipboard man closes them in and goes up front.

With no ceremony, the engines start and they are taxiing to the runway. A minimal engine run-up, no waiting. Almost at once they are in the air.

Absurd happiness blooms inside Dann. She can't leave now. We're really going on this trip together. Stop being childish.

Chris Costakis is speaking in his high, unconvincingly tough voice.

"Heading south. We're not going far in this, has to be around Norfolk."

Dann doesn't care if it's around Vladivostock, but he nods politely.

"We'll be comfortable. The Navy does itself good."

They chat desultorily. Costakis turns out to be a locksmith, semi-retired. "They call us security engineers now. Eighty percent of my jobs are electronic. I had to slow down when my liver acted up."

That confirms Dann's note of the fiery flush in the little man's palms. An old wives' sign but often accurate.

"How in the world did you get into this?"

"I did a lot of work for Annapolis, the Navy security people. Catledge came around looking for volunteers to test. I got what you call a sixth sense about combinations, always had. So I tried out. I scored real high."

"You mean you can guess the numbers in a combination without, ah, listening to the tumblers or whatever one does?" Dann is happy enough to take any nonsense seriously.

"It's not guessing." Costakis' shiny, bulbous face closes up; he gives Dann a sly look.

"Of course. I beg your pardon. Please go on."

"Well . . . Numbers, see. Some days I've gone as high as thirty out of fifty. But it has to be a man. From a woman I can't pick up a thing."

Dann gazes at the little man's high, ill-formed forehead, his few sandy hairs. Hundreds of times he's fastened electrodes to that skull. Does some unnatural ability really lurk in there? His thoughts touch the closed compartment in which lies the memory of a sliding water glass, and veer off, shaken. And all these others here, can they really *do* something abnormal? Incredible. Yet this is a real plane, taking them to a real place. Real money is being spent. Even more incredible, is a submarine actually steaming out to sea with Rick's twin in it? Crazy.

The government always spends money in crazy ways, Dann reassures himself. Especially the military. He recalls some absurd scandal about condoms in balloons. This is just another. Float along with it.

Genially he asks Costakis, "If nobody is around who knows the combination, how can you, ah, read the numbers?"

"They don't have to be around." Costakis purses his small mouth. "Maybe I read someone, maybe there's traces, see? I don't want theories. I just know what I can do. Gives me like an interest in life, see?"

"I see." Delicious, Dann thinks. I am in the realm of fantasy. The faint glow of his chemical supplement to breakfast has taken firm hold.

Costakis is peering down. "I told you, Norfolk. That was U.S. Three-Oh-One." His tone is not quite casual.

"You know the area well?" From his internal shelter Dann looks benignly on the unappetizing little man. He is totally unaware that his own knobby face emanates a profound and manly empathy that a TV casting director would give an arm for.

"I know Route Three-Oh-One." Costakis pauses and then blurts out with dreadful cheerness, "I spent twenty hours lying on it with a busted head. Nobody stopped, see? Hitch-hiker sacked me and took my car. Broad daylight, man, it was hot. I couldn't move, see? Just jerk my arm. Last ride I ever give anybody."

"Twenty hours?" Dann is appalled. "Couldn't they see you?"

"Oh yeah, they saw. My legs were on the concrete."

"But the police—"

"Oh yeah. They picked me up. Threw me in the drunk tank at Newburg. I was about gone when the doc noticed me."

"Good lord." A cold shaft of pain is probing for Dann, sliding through his defences. Shup up, Costakis.

" 'Course, if I had family or something, they might've looked for me," Costakis goes on relentlessly. "Had one brother, he got killed on Cyprus. Went back to try to find Dad's grave, he got caught." He grins in a hideous parody of fun. "What woman would look at me?"

Dann makes a wordless sound, knowing life has tricked him again. The unwelcome reality of the little man is flooding in on him. The loneliness, the *horror vitae*. Confirmed by twenty hours lying alone in pain, being passed. . . . Dann shudders, wanting only to turn him back into K-30, an unreal grotesque.

"So I can use an interest in life, see?"

"Of course." Stop, for God's sake, I can't take it. Dann's hand is feeling for the extra capsule in his pocket. No closeness, nobody. *What woman would look at me?* Costakis is undoubtedly right, Dann sees; to a woman that pumpkin-headed, pygmoid body, the inept abruptness, would probably be actively repulsive. To a man he is a cipher, faintly annoying, exuding a phoney jauntiness and knowledgeability that smell of trouble inside. Keep away. And everyone has, of course, always will. . . . To be locked forever in rejection. . . . *I can use an interest in life* . . . Pity grabs painfully at some interior organ Dann suspects is vital. Panicked, he bolts over Costakis and heads for the plane lavatory.

Coming back, he notices the extra member of the party. Sitting at the very back, behind Kirk's dog, is an unknown civilian. He must have got on last.

Pretending to look at the dog, Dann gets an impression of greying black hair, grey, very well-tailored suit, a vaguely New England face with a foreign trace. Must be a passenger for wherever they are going.

Costakis has seen him looking.

"The spook," he whispers, grimacing. "The big enchilada."

"What, C.I.A.?" Dann whispers back.

"Shit, no. No action there now. D.C.C., I bet."

"What's D.C.C.? I never heard of it."

"You wouldn't. Boss spooks. Defense Communications Component, name doesn't mean anything. I saw them in Annapolis, everybody jumped. Hey, look at that, I was right. That smutch is Norfolk. We're starting down."

The clouds are opening. Below them woods and meadows are swinging up. Dann sees a little lake. General exclamations in the plane.

They land in sunlight on an apparently deserted country airstrip, which seems unusually long. At the far end Dann can see the sock and a couple of choppers in front of the control shack. Apparently they are not going to taxi back. The plane's steps are unfolded.

As they file down. Dann sees that a grey sedan and a grey minibus have already come out to them. He notices an odd structure looming at their end of the strip—a parachute tower, in need of paint. His blood-chemistry is repairing his internal damage. It is a fine summer day in fantasyland.

The clipboard character has reappeared and is loading their bags in the bus. Before they are all out, the sedan has raced away with Costakis' spook inside.

"Oh look, aren't those real deer?" Winona's turquoise arm points to a dozen pale tan silhouettes grazing in the woods alongside.

"That's right, that's right!" Noah enthusiastically shepherds them into the bus. "I told you it would be delightful."

The Frump makes a snorting noise.

The bus carries them through more woods and meadows on a narrow blacktop road. Not a country road; the straight lines and square corners bespeak the military mind. They pass what Dann thinks is an unkempt firelane.

"Obstacle course," Ensign Yost says.

After what must be five miles they pull up at three old-style wooden barracks, standing by themselves in a grassy clearing. A volleyball net hangs in front of one. The June sun is hot as they get out.

"Look—a swimming pool!" Winona carols. They all stare around. Beyond the far barracks is a very long, shabby pool speckled with floating leaves.

"I told you to bring your suits," Noah says like Santa giving presents. "Well, Kendall, this looks just fine, if our equipment is only here. We must check on that at once."

"It'll be here," Kirk says shortly. "You don't do anything until you all sign in."

Another sedan has driven up. Out of it gets a large, bearded, bearlike man in rumpled grey fatigues. He is carrying a folder.

"Captain Harlow," Kirk announces. The man wears no insignia; Dann recalls that Captain is a higher rank in the Navy. "All in the day-room, please."

"This building will be your test site, Dr. Catledge," Captain Harlow says as they troop into the large room at the front of the first barracks.

It looks exactly like all the rec-rooms Dann saw in his service days; plywood, maple, chintz, a few pinups. Over the battered desk is a sign: WHAT YOU SEE HERE LET IT STAY HERE. The desk is littered with copies of *Stag, Readers Digest*, sports magazines.

Noah has trotted into the corridor leading to the bedroom cubicles, the toilets, and the back door.

"These bedrooms will serve as test stations, Captain," he says briskly. "But we'll need doors installed to close off each end."

"Just tell Lieutenant Kirk your requirements," the ursine captain says pleasantly. "You'll find we move fairly fast here. Now I need your signatures on these documents before I turn you loose. Read carefully before signing, please."

Dann notices that his hands and wrists are delicate; the bearishness is an affectation. Kirk hands round papers; general fumbling for pens and places to write.

Reading, Dann is informed that he is now subject to National Security Directive Fifteen, paragraph A-slash-twelve, relating to the security of classified information. He is, it appears, swearing never to divulge any item he has experienced here.

He signs, visualizing himself rushing to the Soviet embassy with the news that there is an elderly parachute-tower near Norfolk, Virginia. Kirk gives him an ID card bearing his own color photograph in plastic and a wad of what appear to be tickets.

"Pin the badges on you at all times," Harlow tells them. "Your lunch is laid on in Area F Messhall. The bus will wait while you take your bags over to the living quarters. Ladies in the end barracks, please."

"Right by the pool!" Winona exclaims. "Captain, can we take walks around here? The woods look so lovely."

"Your badges are for Area F only. Don't pass the area fences." He smiles. "Don't worry, you'll get plenty of exercise. It's a square mile."

"Can we walk home from the messhall?

"If you wish. The bus will take you to and from meals. The schedule is over there. Lieutenant, will you come with me?"

As he and Kirk go out, Costakis mutters to Dann, "Harlow. That's a new one. I've seen him without the beard."

The men's barracks next door is hot and stuffy; Yost and Costakis turn on the air conditioners. Their cots are stripped, the bedding folded on them. Dann picks a cubicle on the side nearest the women's building and transfers some vials to his pockets. When he comes out onto the steps, R-95—Rick—is waiting for him.

"Ron's scared," Rick says in a low, morose voice.

"Your brother . . . he's in the submarine?" Dann is trying to recall Rick's last name: Ah, Waxman. Rick and Ron Waxman.

"Yeah. He doesn't like it." Rick gives him a smouldering look. "I don't like this either. I wish we hadn't come."

"I'm sure he'll be all right. They seem to be taking good care of us."

"You really think so?" Rick shoots the question at him as if trying to penetrate to some fund of truth in Dann's head. Why is Rick asking him, of all people? Abstractedly, he smiles his good smile and utters more reassurance, making for the bus.

Kirk is waiting for them at the messhall door. It turns out to be a great dim, cavernous space, filled with big military-rustic tables, all empty except for a small group at the far end. The place looks old. Adjusting his eyes, Dann sees ghosts: battalions, whole clandestine armies have trained here for God knows what.

A plump man in fatigues and silver bars takes their mess tickets and seats them right by the door. Not near the others. Dann understands; Noah's people are in quarantine. We'll meet no one and see as little as possible of anything that may be going on here. He squints through the dimness. At the two far tables are men in fatigues, a few smartly uniformed Waves. Station personnel, or embryo spies? He sits down between Ensign Yost and the Frump; he will not let himself look at *her*, sitting beyond Noah, Kirk, Winona.

"I sure hoped we'd be on the water," Ted Yost says. "Call this a shore installation?" He sighs. "I wish I could have gone in the sub."

"Ron didn't want to go," Rick tells him sulkily. "He had to because he's the best sender. He hates it."

"I know." Yost smiles with unexpected sweetness, his gaze far off.

Their food comes fast, on trays; enormous breaded veal cutlets, baked potatoes, applesauce. Good, but too much of everything. As it arrives, four people at the far end get up to go. Among them Dann sees the bearded "Captain Harlow" and a tall, thin, grey civilian. Kirk jumps up and strides down to them.

"The Black Rider," mutters the Frump's voice beside him. I must stop calling her that, Dann thinks. What the hell is her name? Something Italian. From beyond her the Princess smiles at him intently.

"I'm so glad you're with us, Doctor Dann." Her voice is very soft.

"Everybody! Give me your movie-tickets!" It's Kendall Kirk back, looming at them in his insufferable clean-cut way. "The *movie*-tickets, those yellow ones. You never should have been issued them," he says severely, as though it was their fault.

There is a general confusion while the movie-tickets are being separated from the meal-tickets and passed back to Kirk. Dann is delighted with this evidence of military bumbling. At last Kirk sits down again, and starts talking with Noah about their missing equipment.

The Frump has been making scornful comments, sotto voce. Her swarthy face looks surprisingly like a worried small boy's. Dann experiences a rush of outgoing geniality.

"You know, after all this time of having to refer to you as Double-you-eleven and twelve, I'm not sure we've ever been introduced. I'm Daniel Dann."

"Fredericka Crespinelli." The Frump says it so like a handshake that Dann glances down and sees her small fist curled tight.

"I'm Valerie Ahlgren," the Princess laughs. "Hey, Daniel Dann, that's neat. It's Dan any way you say it. I'm Val, call her Frodo."

The Frump—Fredericka—scowls. Dann prods his memory.

"Frodo—that's from a book, isn't it?"

"How would you know?" Fredericka—Frodo—demands.

"Wait—Tolkien. Something *Rings*. And Mordor was the Black Realm, wasn't it?" He smiles. "Do you see this place as a black realm?"

"Oh *yes*," says Valerie. But her friend asks curtly, "What are you, a psychiatrist?"

"Goodness no. I'm just interested. To me this place seems, well, somewhat ramshackle and abandoned. Maybe it was blacker once."

"It's not abandoned," Valerie says intensely, looking furtively about.

"Ghosts, maybe," Dann chuckles.

"Didn't you notice those magazines—all recent?" Frodo frowns. "They use this place."

"That's why we're so glad you're with us," Val says quietly. "People like us, we're vulnerable. They don't like us."

For an instant Dann thinks she's telling him they're lesbians, which he had rather assumed. (The perennial male puzzle: How, how?) But then he realizes her glance had summed up the whole table.

She means, he sees, people like Noah's subjects. People who are supposed to be telepathic, to read minds. Nonsense, he thinks, meaning nonsense that they read thoughts and nonsense that the powers of Deerfield would dislike them.

"They value you," he tells her gently. "They're taking all this trouble to see what you can do."

"Yeah," Frodo grunts. Valerie just looks up at him so earnestly it gets through. She's really worried, he sees. Probably people like this are inclined to paranoid suspicions, living among unreal perceptions.

"I wouldn't worry. Really." He summons up his doctor smile, willing her trouble away as he used to will away more tangible ills.

Slowly she smiles back at him and touches her friend's hand. Surprisingly, it's a strong, radiant smile, quite transforming her face. At the same moment he glimpses Frodo's fingers; her nails are bitten off to stubs. H'mmm. His notion of their relationship somersaults. Who is the strong one here? Or must there be a strong one, do their small strengths complement each other?

"Anyway, it's nice being by ourselves," Val says. "Sometimes it hurts so much, in crowds."

"You can say that again," says Ted Yost from Dann's other side. He and the girls exchange looks. Dann has a moment of crazy belief; what would a barrage of thought from a crowd be like for a telepath? Horrible. But of course it's not that; they're probably abnormally sensitive to voice-tones, body-signs of hostility.

Across from him, Chris Costakis has taken no part in this conversation; he eats stolidly, his gaze darting about. Beside him, Noah and Kirk have been going over the requirements: the doors to be installed, the missing biomonitors, the computer terminal, the power supply.

"They want the first test at eighteen hundred tonight," Kirk says.

"Kendall, until we get our hands on our equipment I refuse to try anything. This is going to be done right or not at all."

"Okay, okay. They're putting on the pressure."

"Then they must get my equipment and get it set up right."

"It'll be here."

"And properly installed."

Kirk glances at Dann, who looks carefully blank. He knows and wants to know nothing of the entrails of the shiny cabinets he uses. To his relief Costakis speaks up abruptly.

"I can give you a hand, Doc." The little man is still offering his help to a rejecting world.

"Good, good, Chris," says Noah enthusiastically. "I'm glad to have someone who understands the function. If you're all finished, shall we go?"

"Now for that pool!" Winona sings out. Behind her, Margaret Omali towers up.

As they walk toward the bus, she turns away.

"I'll walk."

"But the computer!" cries Noah. "We need you, Miss Omali!"

"It won't be there," she says flatly. "One mile, I'll be there in fifteen minutes."

She strides away, followed by Noah's expostulations. Dann sees Kendall Kirk take one tentative step and says firmly, "I believe I'll walk too. That was a heavy lunch."

Kirk gives him a nasty look and gets in the bus. Dann finds he has to stretch even his long legs to catch up with her. The bus passes them then disappears. He swings along in silence beside her, feeling wild and happy.

"You meant it. Four miles an hour," he says finally. "I hope you don't mind my sharing your walk?"

"No."

He searches for a topic. "I'm, ah, puzzled. If it wouldn't bother you to tell me, how do they put a computer out here in the woods?"

"They install a terminal and tie in via telephone line. There's a small computer capability at the headquarters here, they won't specify what. Through it I can access TOTAL. The phone line is fast enough for our purpose."

He is enchanted that she will talk, he would listen to her read stock quotations. "What's TOTAL? A big computer?"

Her perfect lips quirk. "More than that. TOTAL is the whole Defense system. We only use a tiny part."

"It must be enormous."

"Yes." She smiles again in secret pleasure. "Nobody knows exactly how far the network extends. One time it printed out all your credit ratings."

"Good Lord!" But he is thinking only that she is walking a little slower, relaxing. The blacktop is cool in the forest lane.

"And could you tell a layman why we need a computer? It seems to me that their answers are either right or wrong."

"No, it's more complex than that. For example, a subject might give a wrong letter which is right for the letter before or after. If this occurs in a series, it's significant. Do you remember J-70; that Chinese girl? She read letters ahead, five out of six sometimes. Dr. Catledge calls it precognition. The program has to analyse correspondence against increasing distance in time forward or back."

"But what about chance?" he asks, floundering in this rarified air.

"The basic program computes against chance probabilities," she tells him patiently. "Including each subject's tested letter-probability base."

"Oh." His poisoned cortex reels, makes a desperate effort to please her. "So—even if a subject gets them all right you have to subtract something for chance."

"That's right." She smiles, really pleased. He is ridiculously elated.

"I can see it's complicated."

"Some of the math gets quite interesting. Take repeated letters—"

"Thank you for explaining." He is enchanted by her mysterious competence, but he cannot cope with repeated letters. "Look!"

Three deer are browsing in the verge ahead. They bound across the blacktop, showing their white, flame-shaped scuts.

"One of them was all spotted," she says wonderingly. A city girl.

"Yes. A fawn, a young one. The spots help camouflage it while it lies still."

"Oh, I wish my Donnie could have seen that," she says very low.

He recalls the bare apartment. "Your son? He doesn't live with you?"

At the words, the bottom of his world shivers, threatens to drop him into his private hell. For one second, he had been back in another life of simple joy. Stop it. Vaguely he hears her saying, "No. He's with my mother in Chicago."

Her tone has changed too. The *Keep Out* signs are up.

The magic is gone. But before he can feel it, a car roars up behind them and they have to jump aside. It's a grey panel truck.

She laughs. "I knew that terminal wasn't there."

They walk on, the bad thing is over. He wants to hear her voice, even if it means computers.

"Tell me, is it true that computers are now so complicated that no human mind can really know what one is up to?"

"Oh yes." The smile comes back. "And of course TOTAL, well, it can access any government computer, and whenever it wants data it can interface with almost any computer network in the country, if you have the code. Some foreign ones too. It got into CBS once." Her face takes on a dreamy, tender look, eyes more beautiful than Sheba's queen. "I love to think of it. The wonderful complexity, yet all so cool and logical. Like a different kind of life trying to expand and grow."

"Sounds a little scary." But Dann isn't scared, he's delighted. The tall alluring creature strolling the wildwood, talking mysteries. "I won't ask you if they think. I gather that's silly. But since our life is a function of the complexity of our internal connections, maybe it could be alive in a way. Maybe it likes you too."

She chuckles. "Oh, I'm not that crazy, I know it's a machine. But sometimes I wonder if certain programs aren't just a little alive. Do you know TOTAL has ghosts?"

"What?"

"Ghost programs. It's hard to flush a really big computer, and a network is impossible. Nobody is going to shut down TOTAL. People make mistakes, see. Their programs generate self-maintaining loops." She actually unbends enough to give him a teasing look. "Tapes spin when nobody is using them. Ghosts."

He grins back like a kid. "What kind of ghosts?"

"Well, there's a couple of war-games, nobody knows their address, and some continuing computations. And there's supposed to be a NASA space-flight simulation still running. It doesn't do anything most of the time because it's still traveling through space. When it lands or whatever it'll show up. It could be part of the ghost in my program. I found out we're using an old NASA link."

"Our ghost?"

"Oh, it's nothing. Every so often it acts up on anything to do with time. Like printing out the date."

"NASA . . . Now you're getting close to my friends."

"The stars?" She remembers, she remembers!

"Yes. The air's so clear here. If you like, I could show you some this evening."

"Maybe." The reserve is back, but no hostility. Beautiful Deerfield! They round the last corner and see the barracks with two trucks outside. Men are carrying in a door. Margaret quickens pace.

When they come into the day-room, equipment and cables are everywhere. Two Cuban-looking men are hanging the door across the corridor. Margaret heads for crates in the corner. Above the hammering Noah and Costakis can be heard yelling to each other.

"Okay! Plug in."

There is a flash and all lights go out. The air conditioners have stopped and the corridor is now too dark to see. Lieutenant Kirk comes in and Noah trots up to him.

"Kendall, we simply have to have more power here."

"You need a bigger pot up there," Costakis points at the electric pole outside.

Ted Yost puts his head in and says unexpectedly, "If there's a laundry here maybe they have one. Laundries use a lot of juice."

Margaret Omali says nothing, she is probing into crates.

Dann takes himself outside, follows the sound of desultory activity around to the back. Rick Waxman is shooting baskets at the edge of the woods. Ted Yost comes out the back door and joins him.

Dann sits down on a white-washed bench. After a few minutes the ensign has to quit; he walks away toward the pool, trying not to show distress. Presently Rick comes over to Dann, idly spinning the ball on one finger.

Dann is surprised to see that Rick's expression and posture are quite different. His face is clear and friendly, he is a normal, attractively muscular young man with his hair tied back like an early American patriot. Dann, who has no extra senses, receives a strong impression of one from whom a burden has been lifted.

"Is your brother better?" He surprises himself, acting as if he believed all this.

"Popped a bunch of tranks and passed out." Rick grins. "I hope it doesn't mess up the test."

"You mean, he might not be able to, ah, transmit?"

"Oh, he'll be able to transmit, all right." Rick's grin fades. "The question is, what. He hates those numbers."

Rick bounces the ball a few times, then sits down beside Dann and stretches in the sunshine. Like a man enjoying respite, like a prisoner let out, Dann thinks. He recalls Ron Waxman, of whom he has seen little. A shade larger, a more taciturn Rick. Probably because of the size difference Dann has assumed that Ron was the dominant brother.

"Tell me, have you two always been together? I mean—"

"I know what you mean. Yeah, our folks tried to split us up. Ronnie couldn't take it."

Rick's eyes have changed, the statement has some meaning. Dann puzzles, unhappily divining pain.

"Your brother is more, more sensitive?"

Rick looks down at the grass. "Sensitive," he says in a low, pent-up voice. "My brother is so fucking sen-si-tive. All my life, he can't take it. He can't take anything. He can't listen to the news, he can't go on the street. There's an accident on the road, we have to turn around and go back." He sighs, looks up sideways at Dann. "We tried to take a trip to Denver last year, he picks up vibes somebody died in the motel room. We had to go right home. I wanted to see the Rockies, you know?"

He laughs shortly. "All the things I want, he can't take. I was pre-med, we both had scholarships. Oh, he's smart. But he couldn't take that at all. So we tried law school. Two semesters, that lasted."

Oh, God. Weakly, Dann asks, "Can't you go on by yourself, Rick? You could leave Ron with your folks."

"No way. They crashed in a plane five years ago."

"Oh. . ."

"No way," Rick repeats somberly. "He needs me. And he's

sending all the time. Whatever I'm doing, I read him." He laughs meaninglessly, bounces the ball.

Dann is appalled, resentful. Why do they do this to him? His hand goes to his pocket, he touches the magic that will turn Rick back into a phantasm.

"Women, it's a disaster," Rick goes on. "Half the time he can't and when he can it's worse." He gives Dann a clear, open look as if he were explaining a sore back. The change in him is amazing. "Funny, I can talk to you. . . . Of course, he'll wake up pretty soon." He sighs bleakly.

"What do you do for a living, Rick?"

"Pit. We work in the pit at Honest Jack's. Ronnie's good with his hands and I can watch out he doesn't get bad wrecks."

"You mean, auto mechanics?"

"Yeah." Rick looks down at the stained, callused hands that might have done other work.

"And how did you get into this, ah, project?"

"Catledge bought his car at Jack's. I guess he has his eye out for twins. The bread helps."

"Rick, what if your brother were, well, in a—"

"You mean if he was dead? If I had him put away? I guess I could."

"So?"

"If he wasn't dead I'd have to go to China. Maybe that's not far enough, if he was really unhappy. While our folks were alive I rode to Buffalo on the bus once, you know, just to get away. While I was gone our dog got hit by a car. I could hear Ron like he was in the room. I guess he could make me hear him in China if he wanted. And his being . . . dead, that wouldn't solve anything. It's more complicated . . . "

"What do you mean?"

"It's not just him." Rick twirls the ball again, looks at Dann. "See, it's not like I was all right except for him. I'm not. He's part of me." His voice is almost a whisper. "He's the part of me that can't take it. Can you dig that? It's like he's part of me, only outside where I can't fix anything. He got—left out. We're, I'm not, I'm not okay without him. I mean, I need this break. But if he doesn't wake up pretty soon, I, I can't . . . "

He falls silent, rolling the ball between his coarsened hands.

Above them a mockingbird is trilling arpeggios. Dann sees Rick is talked out, wants to be left alone to enjoy his respite. He touches Rick's shoulder, unaware that the boy has derived comfort from their talk, and gets up and walks aimlessly away.

Dear God. The pain in Rick's eyes. The waste. He is reminded of the pitiful history of a patient, a friend, who had an intermittently and inconspicuously mad husband. The dead dragging the living down. Or is it possible Rick and his twin are in some weird sense one person, cruelly sorted into two bodies? Life's savage jokes. No matter. He dry-swallows the capsule. In a few minutes the chemistry of his bloodstream will carry reality away. He listens to the mockingbird, and discovers that his feet are carrying him around the end barracks, to the pool.

A man and three women are in the pool. Dann sits on one of the tin loungers on the shady side.

"Hi, Doctor Dann! Come on in!" The splashing turquoise-capped figure is Winona.

Dann makes benign, avuncular excuses and sits watching Valerie and Fredericka—Frodo—climb out on the sunny side. Frodo's skinny, swarthy form is clad in a blood-red tank suit. Valerie is in sunny yellow, a seductive young body. She stretches out to sun. Frodo ceremoniously lets down the back of the chair for her, fetches a coke, lights her cigarette, sits cross-legged on the grass alongside. A pixie cavalier. It occurs to Dann that he is watching romantic love. He smiles, safe back in his cocoon.

The bearded figure of Ensign Yost climbs out and walks toward Dann, toweling vigorously. His bushy face laughs, he is every inch the jolly mariner. Hard to remember the death working in that bone-marrow. He sits down by Dann and lights a cigarette.

Dann starts the automatic rebuke, checks himself. Yost notices it, grins more broadly. They watch Winona's determined progress up and down the pool. She splashes womanfully. Above them the mocker is still singing, varying his repertory with blue-jay shrieks.

"Peaceful here," Dann offers.

Yost grunts. "I'd still rather be out in that sub."

"I should think it would be extremely confining."

"Yeah . . . But, a ship."

Winona climbs out, fussily spreads out in a lounge by the girls.

"I got a couple thou put away, Doc," Yost says meditatively. "If it gets bad again, I'm not going in hospital. No way, no sir. I'm going to lease me a little motor sailor and stay aboard, down the bay. Live there. Even if it's winter."

"I see." Dann has heard something like this before, but the cocoon is holding. Something about this place seems to make for unfortunate confidences, he thinks remotely.

"On the water." Yost's voice is dreamy. "I don't care if it snows. But they say this may last 'til next Spring. How about it, Doc?"

Dann is surprised; Yost seems to have come to believe in his disease.

"No one can predict, Ted," he says, more or less truthfully. "What about your family?" Instantly, he regrets the question. No more revelations, no more.

"Don't have one now," Yost says inexorably. "When I got better last time Marie took the kid and split. I didn't tell her it was temporary, see? Better for Dorothy that way."

"Dorothy is your little girl?" Dann shudders, can't help himself.

"Yeah. She's six last week. I think Marie knew, she figured it was better for Dorothy too. Sometimes I feel bad, holding out the money for the boat. But Marie has a good job, she's a GS-seven. That's good security."

"Oh, yes."

Ted Yost talks on, describing the boat he plans to get. His deathship. But he is not morbid, he is looking forward with his whole soul to being on the water again, even if it is only the murk off Chesapeake Bay. Back to the sea, the oldest drive of all. Within his insulation, Dann winces. He knows none of this will happen, he knows how the relapse will come. Yost will find himself on the VA wards, trapped in tubing. Not the sea. Pity . . . What tragic flotsam has Noah collected here? Yost, Rick, Costakis—all in their different intolerable miseries. Well, he, Dann, can positively not take much more of this. And *she* has not appeared.

Announcing his intention to see how the equipment installation is coming along, he gets up to go.

"Thanks, Doc," Yost says unexpectedly. What for?

As he rounds the end of the pool Valerie calls to him. Frodo is coughing evilly over her cigarette; Dann makes a mental note to check her and scratches it off again. Surprising how many of them smoke. Does it correlate with—whatever?

When he gets close he is momentarily bemused by Valerie's bursting young breasts, her vulnerable little belly, and does not take in her whisper.

"Doctor Dann, that *man* is here again. What does he have to do with us?"

Dann stares around, finally spots a grey sedan beside the trucks in front of the barracks.

"You mean your Black Rider?"

"Yeah," says Frodo. "What's he doing here?"

"I don't know," Dann smiles.

"You could find out," Valerie suggests. *"Please*, Doctor Dann. I'm so worried. He frightens me."

"We didn't agree to, to whatever *he's* into," Frodo adds rebelliously.

"I expect it's some formality. They're having trouble with the equipment, you know."

"Do you think we'll do a test tonight?"

"I tend to doubt it. That's what I'm on my way to find out."

"Find out about *him*, please." Valerie's big blue eyes plead, her round cheeks tremble.

"I wish they'd get it over with and let us out of here." Frodo stubs out her cigarette savagely. "This place is scaring Val. Me too."

"I'll let you know," Dann promises. "But truly I wouldn't worry."

"I'm so *glad* you're here," Valerie breathes intensely.

Dann's reassuring smile feels painted on. No more, no more. He all but lopes around the corner of the barracks, wondering how this peaceful place could scare anybody. They're insane, of course. The mockingbird is still gurgling melodies.

On the steps of the test barracks Kirk's black Labrador is sitting in the sun. Her tail thumps heavily as Dann goes by; he touches the big, hot head. Her eyes never turn from the door. Amazing how undiscriminatingly dogs give their devotion. Does it mean that Kirk has some good in him somewhere? Dann doesn't perceive it.

He opens the door into Kirk's back, generating a flurry of false apologies. The place is still a mess and Margaret is not there. But the tall grey-haired civilian is, apparently taking leave of Noah.

"Dan, I want you to meet Major Drew Fearing." Noah waves, beaming. "Major, Doctor Daniel Dann is in charge of our psychobiological correlations. That is, the neural and physical changes that characterize successful transfer. Dan, Major Fearing is here from the Department of Defense. Do help me convince him that we can't start tests without proper instrumentation. It would be a dreadful error, half the value would be lost. Really—"

Under Noah's barrage Dann and Major Fearing have been looking each other over, or rather, Dann has received the impression of having been instantly and completely recorded on some device behind the veiled grey eyes. The eyes at once drift away, leaving him to examine Fearing's exterior. Major Fearing—if that's his real name, Dann recalls Costakis' lesson—does not look military. Or Naval. Or foreign service. In fact, Dann has seldom met a less classifiable man. His former impression of Waspish aquilinity tinged with some exotic flavor is confirmed: Fearing's lips and nostrils have a thin, baroque curve. His formal half-smile was gentlemanly and transient. Beyond that he conveys nothing except an intensely neutral quality.

Dann has been trying to sort his neurones into an orderly argument, but it proves unnecessary.

"Quite all right, Doctor Catledge," Fearing says at Noah's first pause. "Lieutenant Kirk will see that you have your equipment. We will signal the ship to delay the first test until, say, noon tomorrow?"

The voice is rather charming and conveys a new element: absolute authority.

"Right, sir" Kirk is all doggy eagerness. No, thinks Dann, the Labrador is much more dignified.

"Fine, Major, fine," says Noah. "But the equipment must be here."

Kirk looks shocked. Dann is pleased by the little gnome's spunk, and then wonders why. Why the hell not? Who is this Fearing character supposed to be?

Whoever he is, he has silently gone. Kirk has to trot to catch up. The sedan driver closes them in, lets the Labrador into the front, and they're away. From the back of the barracks Dann can hear Costakis and the Cubans struggling with another door.

"Who is he, Noah?"

"Represents D.O.D., I believe. Some intelligence body interested in our effort. I never saw him before. Well, now we don't have to worry."

Dann turns to leave, turns back. "Noah . . . If I might suggest something. I'd keep that fellow as far out of sight as possible."

Noah gives him an unexpectedly alert look and bobs his head.

Now why the devil did I do that, Dann asks himself, going out into the pleasant afternoon. And why do I feel traitorous; it was only good sense. The man upsets them. But something inside him acknowledges his real reason. Let nothing wake me up. Let this whole ridiculous business just go on being ridiculous, unreal, cool.

Just as he nears the pool it happens.

Dann has never had a "psychic" experience. It doesn't occur to him that he's having one now. Suddenly, the lawn, woods, barracks are invaded—transformed by a great wave of soundless motion, as if a hurricane was somehow blowing in place. He glimpses an immense landscape of wind-torn clouds while a light unlike anything he knows sweeps round him, roaring silently—

—And is gone.

He staggers in place, grasping something which turns out to be the back of a metal chair. Has he had a vascular-cerebral accident?

Dazed, he stares around, automatically checking limb and facial function. Everything nominal except his heart rate, which is about one-twenty.

As his gaze focusses he realizes that the women by the pool are in an agitated huddle. Ted Yost and Rick are running toward them.

"Doctor Dann! Doctor Dann!"

He walks to them, his heart slowing. What in God's name was it?

"Doctor Dann!" Winona cries. "Did you feel it too?"

"Yes, I felt . . . something. I have no idea what in the world it was."

"It wasn't in this world." Val rubs her eyes.

"That was the sea," Ted Yost tells them. "It was a great storm at sea, we picked it out of somebody's mind."

"I tell you this is a shitty place," Frodo says murderously.

"I don't know . . . " Winona looks around puzzledly. "Was it bad? I felt something like *Hello*. Didn't you get it?"

Rick says nothing. His eyes are sullen again. Not sullen, Dann corrects himself, pained. Has Rick woken up? Don't be idiotic.

"The wind that blows between the worlds cut through him like a knife," Dann finds himself saying unexpectedly. "Kipling. You wouldn't know it," he grins at Frodo, getting some of his own back.

Beside them the door of the women's barracks opens and Margaret Omali steps out.

"Margaret, did you feel that too?" Winona calls up at her.

"Feel what?" She has a magazine in her hand, Dann sees.

"Like a big wind, in our heads," Valerie says.

"That's your department, not mine," Margaret says without expression. She walks down the steps and heads for the test barracks, as if she had intended to do that all along.

"I felt that, what you call it." Costakis bustles up to them. "So did the fellas. They're taking off."

In fact, the two Cuban workmen are hustling out to their truck, followed by Noah's remonstrations. As they get in the truck one of them makes a hand sign at the group by the pool.

"They're giving us the evil eye!" Frodo laughs.

"I tell you," mutters Costakis obscurely. The truck accelerates away.

Winona giggles. "Say, do you think everybody in this camp felt it? Maybe they think *we* did it to them! Wouldn't that be funny?"

Costakis looks up at her. "That could be just exactly right," he says in his pinched voice. "Only you're wrong, Missus. It wouldn't be funny. It wouldn't be funny at all. Not here."

Chapter 7

DARK AND ENORMOUS, THE SOLITARY ONE HAS FOUND DEADLY DIVERSION IN THE VOID.

IT HAS BEEN TURNING A PORTION OF ITS PAIN-RIDDEN ATTENTION TO SOME EMANATIONS WHICH TRACE TO A CLOT OF MATTER IN THE TRAIN OF A SMALL BLUE STAR. AS USUAL, THE WEAKNESS OF THE RECEPTION IRRITATES. WHY WILL THIS NOT COME STRONGER AND MORE CLEAR?

A MISTY IDEA CONDENSES INTO IMPULSE: WHAT IF I EXPERIMENT? WHAT IF I USE MY TIME-POWERS—ALONE?

THE THOUGHT IS HORRIFYING, SUPREMELY PROHIBITED. AGITATED, THE VAST ENTITY SWIRLS AWAY, A NOISY VACUUM SWEEPING OUT CHAOS.

BUT THE WICKED THOUGHT RECURS. AND WITH IT COMES ANOTHER: HOW CAN ILLEGALITY HAVE MEANING NOW? AM I NOT MYSELF THE ULTIMATE ILLEGALITY? WHY SHOULD I NOT EXECUTE—ANYTHING?

WHY NOT?

ANOTHER OF THE EMANATING SPECKS IS NEAR IT NOW,

COUPLED TO TWIN YELLOW SUNS WHOSE ORBITS ARE A FRACTION OF ITS OWN LENGTH. THEY WILL SERVE. WITH A SLOW SHUDDER OF THE WHOLE HUGE BEING, TIME-POWER IS MARSHALED AND FOCUSSED ON THE FIERY LITTLE ORBS. OFTEN THIS MANEUVER HAS BEEN PERFORMED IN CONCERT OF THE PLAN: NEVER BEFORE ALONE. SO BE IT.

THE TARGETS GO THROUGH THEIR FAMILIAR CHANGES, BRIGHTENING, THEN REDDENING SUDDENLY AS THEY EXPAND TO DISRUPTION. AT THE SAME TIME, THE TINY OUTPUT FROM THE MATTER IN THE SYSTEM AMPLIFIES SATISFYINGLY. LOUDER, CLEARER—IT RISES TO PAROXYSMAL STRENGTH, TREMBLING ON THE BRINK OF SOME COMPREHENSIBILITY. JUST AS—SOMETHING—CAN ALMOST BE RECOGNIZED, THEY SUDDENLY CEASE.

TRY AGAIN. ANOTHER SIMILAR SMALL SINGLE SYSTEM IS EMITTING NEARBY. THE TIME-THRUST IS FOCUSSED, ENERGIZED. THIS PRIMARY DOES NOT COMPLETELY DISSIPATE: IT GOES TO A COLLAPSED, POINTLIKE EXISTENCE. BUT AGAIN THE TINY OUTPUT RISES TANTALIZINGLY TOWARD RECOGNITION BEFORE IT TOO ABRUPTLY CUTS OUT.

THE IMMENSE SENTIENCE DRIFTS AWAY, ITS PAIN MOMENTARILY IN ABEYANCE FROM THE EFFORT TO COMPREHEND THIS NEW EXPERIENCE. WHY WOULDN'T THE SIGNAL HOLD LONG ENOUGH FOR RECEPTION? AT THEIR STRONGEST, THE SIGNALS WERE STILL MINUTE . . . BUT SOMEHOW MEANINGFUL. AND THE QUALITY OF ACCEPTING THIS NEW LITTLE INPUT SEEMS TO ANSWER TO SOME NAMELESS NEED WITHIN.

TO CONFIRM, IT LOCATES ANOTHER EMISSION-POINT AMONG THE WISPS OF MATTER AROUND AN INSIGNIFICANT SUN, AND APPLIES POWER AGAIN, THIS TIME IN REVERSE MODE. ANOTHER SUCCESS: THE FIERY POINT EXPANDS, DISSOCIATES TO NEAR-VOID. AND AS IT DOES SO, THE SMALL SIGNALS INCREASE SPASMODICALLY BEFORE THEY CUT OFF FOREVER.

THE HUGE, MALEFICENT PRESENCE SAILS AWAY, SLOWLY CONSIDERING THIS NEW ASPECT OF EXISTENCE. SOME MEANING IS IMPLIED HERE, ALMOST TO BE GRASPED. BUT WHY DO

THEY STOP SO SOON? IS IT POSSIBLE THAT THERE IS SOME OTHER ACTION TO BE EXECUTED?

FOR THE FIRST TIME THE NEBULOUS NOTION STIRS: COULD SOME SUBPROGRAM BE INCOMPLETE? IS THE DIMNESS OF PERCEPTION DUE, NOT TO THE OUTPUT, BUT TO SOME INTERNAL CONDITION OF DEFICIT? EVIL IS PRESENT, AND CAUSES PAINFUL SELF-LOATHING. BUT PERHAPS THERE IS MORE THAN SIMPLE WICKEDNESS: PERHAPS THERE IS CONNECTION TO THAT CENTER OF ITS NUCLEUS WHICH IS FELT AS THE MOST PRIVATE SOURCE OF SHAME AND WRONG. WHY ARE THESE TINY OUTPUTS SO INTIMATELY SIGNIFICANT?

IT CANNOT UNDERSTAND; THE HUGE BLACK IMMATERIALITY THAT IS NOT A BRAIN FLOATS QUIESCENT AMONG THE LITTLE SUNS, STRIVING FOR THOUGHT.

IT IS THEN THAT THE CURIOUS DISTRACTION OCCURS.

FOR SOME TIME THE ABERRANT SENSORS HAVE BEEN REGISTERING AN UNUSUAL EMISSION ON THE STRANGE INCOMPREHENSIBLE TRANS-TEMPORAL BANDS. PRESENTLY, IT IS NOTICED THAT THIS DOES NOT SEEM TO BE A POINT-SOURCE. INSTEAD, IT SEEMS TO BE A SLENDER FILAMENT, A STRAND OF ENERGETIC INFORMATION TRAVERSING A GREAT LENGTH ACROSS THE VOID, TWISTING PAST LOCAL AGGREGATIONS OF SUNS. ODD!

INQUISITIVE, THE GREAT BEING SAMPLES IT. YES; ITS NATURE IS TIME-FREE, IS AKIN TO THE SMALL ENERGY-OUTPUTS THAT HAVE BEEN DIVERTING HIM. BUT IT IS STRONGER, AND VECTORIAL. PERHAPS BY TRACING IT TO ITS SOURCE SOME NEW INFORMATION MIGHT COME? AT THE LEAST, THIS WILL PROVIDE DISTRACTION FROM EVER-PRESENT DESOLATION.

AVERTING ITS ENORMOUS BULK SO AS NOT TO DISTURB THE TENUOUS TRACK, THE MONSTROUS SENTIENCE BEGINS TO PROPEL ITSELF ALONGSIDE THE PECULIAR FILAMENT. NOW AND THEN IT SENSES MINUTE PARTICULATE SURGES OF ENERGY, AS THOUGH SOME UNHEARD-OF TININESSES TRAVEL THIS PATH.

BUT AT LENGTH IT PERCEIVES THAT THE TRACE IS WEAKENING, AND SLOWLY DECIDES THAT IT HAS MISTAKEN THE DI-

RECTION OF EMISSION. IF IT DESIRES TO FIND THE SOURCE, IT MUST REVERSE ITS COURSE. YES: THIS WILL BE DONE. THE PHENOMENON CONTINUES TO STIMULATE.

AS THE PONDEROUS TURN BEGINS, AN EVEN ODDER EVENT OCCURS.

Chapter 8

Tivonel planes discreetly sidewind of Giadoc and the Hearers, watching for the party coming up from Deep. She is her merry self again. The frightful cry of the dying world, the emotional experience of merging with Giadoc and his dire predictions, all have been integrated to her memory-matrix while her attention turned to the practical task of hunting food. As Giadoc said, the Hearers weren't feeding properly; she was shocked to see the frailty of some of his colleagues. One of them, an old male named Virmet, had been doing some ineffective food-supply in the intervals of his work. Tivonel had swept him with her straight up to the high layers behind the Wall, where the great rafts of food-plants stream. They soon found some—and a disturbing oddity as well.

"Not those," she signals to Virmet. "Can't you tell they're dead?"

The old male hesitates as the lifeless clumps go by. "Is this usual, young Tivonel?"

"No. But look—there's good fat lively ones in that eddy over there. Keep them circling. I'll go herd in another lot, those Deepers are going to be hungry."

In the end they'd driven down a lavish supply. Virmet secured most of it in plant-thickets while Tivonel herded some out to the line of Hearers stationed around the great Wall. They accept her offerings with preoccupied thanks; she gathers they are maintaining some sort of contact with a distant world. Weird.

By the time she completes the long circuit even her strong body is tired. But she's pleased with herself; obviously she's needed here.

"I will be your little Father, Giadoc!" she flashes mischievously as she passes him. His deep affectionate gleam answers her.

Now everyone is awaiting the Deepers, who are about to arrive. The bright compacted life-signals of the pods they came up in have halted at the inner zone of the Wall and are now spreading out to individual emanations as they disembark. How many they are! A great crowd must be coming up from Deep.

Lomax and other senior Hearers have gone in to guide them out to a calm broad updraft which will be the meeting-place. As the procession comes closer, Tivonel is amused to notice life-fields wavering all over the path. Probably Fathers who haven't been out of Deep for years, having trouble jetting even through these calm breezes.

But the big male beside Lomax is navigating sturdily. His field is huge and intricate, his mantle-lights are a beautiful Fatherly rose tuned deep violet by age. Why, it's old Heagran himself, Eldest-Father of all!

Things must be really serious, Tivonel realizes, blushing herself to suitable reverence as they pass.

Behind Heagran comes an unsteady group of elder males of impressive life-strength, long past actual Fatherhood of course but representing the wisdom and leadership of Deep. With them in Kinto, chief Memory-Keeper, his corporeal body blurred by the enormously energic and complex structuring of his engram lattices. A grave occasion, to bring Kinto up! For an instant Tivonel's control slips, and she shudders. Is Tyree really in danger? Could their beautiful world be extinguished like that nameless one?

But she dismisses the fear, and is soon trying to hide bright gleams of amusement as a crowd of younger Fathers go wobbling by, striving to keep their dignity in the wild winds. Some have pouched children—and there among them, to her delight, is Tiavan, Giadoc's son and hers. She's glad to see he's jetting strong and straight. I gave him that, she thinks; no matter what anyone says, female heredity counts. Tiavan flashes a quiet greeting to Giadoc as he passes the group of Hearers. Tivonel can guess how much the two of them would love a male-to-male talk about that child.

Behind the males comes a single small figure with work-worn vanes: Old Janskelen, Eldest-Female. Tivonel sends her a warm transmission of appreciation. Janskelen was a great adventurer in her day, and she's still so hardy and vigorous, still eager for projects. And a known defender of the Hearers in their unFatherly pursuit of knowledge, too.

Jetting nonchalantly after Janskelen come a dozen or so females, their small fields bright and dense. Tivonel recognizes several of them as leaders of the radical Paradomin faction. What are they up to here? But she forgets them as the field-form of her friend Marockee appears among the last-comers.

"Marockee! Companion of many food hunts!"

Her friend's mantle flashes in surprise. "Tivonel! Well met. What are you doing here?"

"Later, later," Tivonel tells her. "I have to supply these biglives. Can you leave them and help me?"

"Done."

Old Virmet is struggling to control the food-raft in the eddies. Tivonel is glad of Marockee's help in conveying the food out to the hungry and tired crowd.

They make an effort to separate it and present it in semicivilized style, but the big males are rigid and pale blue with embarrassment at the prospect of eating like this. Lomax apologizes for the primitive conditions. Finally old Heagran says, "Nonsense!" and begins to scoop in fat-plants with unabashed gusto. Janskelen follows suit, and soon everyone is eating, more or less skilfully. The taste of the rich wild food is restorative. In the silence of the everlasting day one young Father actually proposes sleep, but is quickly voted down.

"Our business here cannot wait," Heagran announces. "We will commence as soon as I have, ah, completed this."

"Come and watch with me, Marockee," Tivonel suggests. "We have much to exchange."

Marockee assents with a mock-erotic snap of polarization, and they jet into a plant-filled eddy Tivonel has already selected as her viewing site.

"It's hard to show real *ahura* out here."

Marockee assents; with these eddies coming every which way, it would be easy for a female to get into an upwind position, thereby indicating blatant flirtatiousness. Or, even sillier, to usurp the downwind position proper for males.

As they settle into the edge of the lattice-plant, Tivonel notices that the Paradomin are brazenly hovering downwind of the group in a small current. Well, really! Then she sees something more amazing. One of them has a small double field!

"What's she doing, Marockee? She can't—she can't be *carrying a child?*"

"That's Avanil," Marockee's mantle lights with giggles. "Only she's shortened it to Avan, like a male. She's practicing Fathering with a young plenya. She wants to prove that females can care for children too."

"Great winds." Tivonel scans hard. Yes—Avanil's small extra nucleus is not that of a real infant, but one of the semiintelligent pet animals that were becoming popular in Deep. Of course many female children mimic their brothers by "playing Father" with a baby animal until their Fathers put a stop to it. But here is a grown female openly carrying an imitation infant in her rudimentary pouch. Crazy!

"She says it strengthens your field. She says if females did Fathering our fields would grow just as big too."

"Wild." Tivonel idly blows away an inquisitive plant-root. A lot seems to have been going on in Deep while she's been away.

"I don't know," Marockee pumps air reflectively, "her field does look different now. And listen, she says the Fathers should exercise more, too. She believes we should all share each other's work."

"I can just imagine Kinto on a hunt." Tivonel laughs. "Marockee, I've had a real idea. Suppose we set up a barter relay station to exchange food from the Wild with some of the new plant-stuffs they're bringing up from above the Abyss, and the things the kids make in Deep."

"What's so new about that?"

"Wait. My idea is, instead of always exchanging the stuff itself, we could have a system of counters. Small things we could carry in our pouches. The station would give you so many counters for each kind of thing. Then you wouldn't have to lug the stuff around looking for someone to swap with, or you could save up and get something else later, or whatever."

"Hey," says Marockee, and they fall to typical female small-talk. Presently the commotion outside quiets.

"Sssh. It's starting."

Heagran and the Deepers are ceremoniously deployed facing Lomax and the group of Hearers. Among them Giadoc's mind-field seems to stand out in beauty to Tivonel's scan.

"We offer our memory," Lomax signs ritually. Orva, the Recorder of the Hearers, moves toward Memory-Keeper Kinto.

"Thank you, Chief Hearer," Heagran's deep violet tones reply. "We too have brought grave news, which you may consult at your convenience. However, we are many and time is short. Let our two good Recorders share in fullness while we confer in speech. First, what have you learned since your last message?"

Orva and Kinto jet away to a polite distance, and the life-bands momentarily resonate as they merge.

"More worlds have died in our area of the skies," Lomax replies gravely. "A lone Destroyer is active out beyond us too. Perhaps the last death touched you?"

"Yes, we felt it as we traveled. Tragic." Heagran's mantle pales ritually. "But you should be aware that at Near Pole these death-cries are now so frequent and intense that some are felt even in Deep. The Hearers there tell us that there are now only four living worlds between Tyree and what they call the Zone of Death. The time-eddies too are increasing. People are frightened." He pauses, his mantle murmurous with deep-hued thought. "As you know, I did not formerly believe that these reports meant any danger to Tyree. I have changed my mind. But there are many still in Deep who do not believe this peril is real. Have you had any success in mind-touch with this lone Destroyer of yours?"

"None whatever," Lomax signs. "The attempt has been a complete failure and injured those who tried. It is utterly alien. There seems no hope of influencing it or even understanding it."

"What else have you learned of value?"

At these words Tivonel notices a peculiar stir among the Deepers, as though the question has some unspoken significance. A very large old male whom she recognizes as Father Scomber has drifted closer to Heagran, his mantle courteously dark.

"For pure knowledge, much," signs Lomax. His field too has taken on an odd tension. "For example, we are now sure that other worlds have each their own Sound or energy-source. And we have just now confirmed something we have suspected from common observation here on Tyree. Have we not all noticed that when a person is at a great distance, a signal he transmits on the life-bands appears to come instantaneously, while the audible flash of his words lags behind?"

Heagran signs assent. Around him the other Elders stir impatiently.

"Well, it appears that life-signals even from very distant worlds are indeed instantaneous while the physical energy, that is, the audible light, travels quite slowly, taking sometimes years. We have just heard the silencing of two Sounds identified with worlds whose death-cries were received years ago. And we now believe we understand the manner of their deaths; one was a slow, agonizing transmission suggesting burning and explosion. In each case, the energies of their Sounds were observed to rise violently just before extinction."

The Deepers have been flickering restlessly during Lomax' speech. Heagran signs, "If I understand your somewhat prolix point, Chief Hearer, you mean that the attack, if it comes, will not be on Tyree but on our Sound?"

"We believe so. Apparently the Destroyer can cause it to explode, throwing off terrible blasts of all-band energy which will kill all life on our world, as people are killed who venture into the ultrahigh Wild today."

"But surely, Lomax, in the deeps of those worlds, even in their abyssal layers, some life survives?"

"No." Lomax' voice is deep azure with grief. "We have monitored continually and found nothing. The energy is so fierce that it will penetrate even to the Abyss. The very fabric of Tyree itself may be shattered."

Silence follows his words, broken only by the faint chiming of the Companions of Day. Is it possible, Tivonel wonders, could these beautiful little Sounds be the devourers of their worlds? Could Tyree's own Sound explode and destroy her? A memory of the dead food-plants flicks through her mind.

Father Scomber is signing formally to Heagran.

"Eldest Heagran, now we know the nature of the doom which may be nearing our world. But as you know, I and many others would like to inquire further on other matters these Hearers may have learned."

To Tivonel's surprise, Heagran's mantle darkens and his field contracts in a mode approaching disdain. But he only signs neutrally, "Very well, Elder Scomber. Proceed."

"Hearer Lomax," Scomber flashes, "will you tell us more about these strange life-forms you have touched on other worlds? What are they like? Is there any possibility of help there?"

Lomax seems to hesitate, and again Tivonel is aware of tension in the massed fields of the crowd.

"Help, Father Scomber? I do not believe so. You will of course find all details in the transmitted memory. However, you may question our Hearer Giadoc, who has done most of this work."

Appreciatively, Tivonel watches Giadoc plane forward, his beautiful field so alive with love of knowledge.

"That's my friend," she signs to Marockee.

"A *male?*" Marockee sparkles with amusement.

"Not what you think. Wait."

"Briefly, Father Scomber," signs Giadoc, "we have touched many life-forms without true intelligence. Most living worlds carry only lower animals and plants. Only on seven have we found intelligent beings, and on four of those I was able to merge long enough to understand something of their life. They are all unimaginably different from us. For example, those I touched lived in the depths of their worlds, and their worlds had no Wind."

"No Wind!" Astonished flickers race across the Deepers' mantles. "They *live* in the Abyss?"

"Yes." Giadoc's mind-field is radiant with the intensity of his interest. "And they live among and employ a huge variety of solid matter! They—" With visible effort he checks himself. "But, as to their individual lives, those we know are brutish and short. Their minds are chaotic, resembling animals. They seem unable to communicate normally. Yet despite all this, we came on two worlds whose beings have actually developed the power to transport themselves physically to another nearby world! We are holding contact with one now. But—" He checks himself again. "This cannot possibly help us."

"I agree." Scomber's tone is deep and deliberate, his large field is dense as if with some unknown intent. Behind him several Fathers are holding themselves very rigidly. Even the Paradomin are silent and tense. Tivonel's own field tingles with their transmitted tension. What is going on here? She finds herself suddenly afraid to guess, afraid for Giadoc.

"Tell us more, Giadoc," signs Scomber. "When you merged with the intelligent beings, were you, yourself in control? Did others of the race attack you? How long could you remain there?"

"Enough!" Heagran flashes loudly. "Scomber, enough!"

"No, Heagran. It is my Father-right to know. Let Giadoc answer."

"I condemn this." Heagran enfurls himself in a gesture of solemn negation. Tivonel sees that all the Deepers' fields are aroused and pulsing, some eddying near Scomber, some toward Heagran. She doesn't want to let herself think of what this is leading to.

"Marockee, this is bad." Her friend flickers assent.

"Well, young Giadoc, tell us what occurred," Scomber signs firmly.

Slowly, abstractedly, Giadoc replies. "In my last two contacts I found myself in control of the body, the physical habits of the alien being. The nearby aliens did not seem to notice me. I was able to remain as long as the Hearers here held the Beam. You understand, Father Scomber, that by placing ourselves around the circle of the Wall and uniting our efforts, we have created a great amplification of our single efforts? We call this the Beam. It seems to be sensitive to life-energy on other worlds. Perhaps it draws on the Great Field of Tyree itself."

As he signs, his field and mantle have expanded into a rich, strange play of energies, as if he was dreaming. Tivonel understands; he is so carried away by his love of far knowledge that he is only half-conscious of Scomber and the import of his words. At the mention of the mythical Great Field, several Fathers have darkened their mantles respectfully.

"The Great Field?" whispers Marockee. "Tivonel, is it real?"

"Ssh. I don't know." Tivonel is fixed on the menacing figure of Scomber, who has shown only perfunctory reverence.

"I asked you what occurred, not theory," Scomber flashes. "On this alien world, did you remain yourself? Were you in full control of the body of the being?"

"Yes indeed, Father. It was . . . extraordinary," Giadoc signs dreamily. "I could move, in one case I could speak. The mind uses the speech-habits of the body, you see. Of course I knew nothing of the individual's thoughts or memories—"

"While you were so merged, where did the alien mind-field go? Was it still present around you?"

Giadoc hesitates, his mind-field abruptly changing structure. The dismayed flow of pattern on his mantle tells Tivonel that he has at last grasped Scomber's thrust.

"It was not . . . present," he replies slowly.

"Then where was it? Answer me, young Giadoc!"

"I am not sure, since my own life-mind was there." Giadoc pauses, and then signs in the grey tones of reluctance, "I am told that another being's life-field, or traces of it, appeared around my body here."

"Aha!" Scomber's mantle flares sharply. His exclamation is echoed by other fathers, and, to Tivonel's surprise, on the smaller forms of the Paradomin.

"That's it! We have it!" Scomber turns to the crowd behind him. "Here is our means of escape from the death of Tyree!"

Excitement such as Tivonel has never seen sweeps through the massed crowd. She herself can only think in numbed horror, *life-crime. Life-crime.*

"Silence!" Old Heagran blazes in commanding light. "This cannot be! Young Giadoc, you have gone too far in your unFatherly pursuit of knowledge. And you, Scomber—your thoughts are criminal! What you propose is vile. In the name of the Winds, are you mad? Are we to listen to a Father openly propose life-crime? Be silent or return to Deep!"

"No, Heagran. Hear me!" Scomber spreads his great mantle in formal, proud appeal, deliberately displaying the margin of his Father-pouch. "It is for our children, Heagran! We face the death of our world, our race, our young. The children! When our children are burning, must we not face the unthinkable if it will save them?"

Several Fathers behind him echo in deep tones, "Our children." But old Janskelen suddenly speaks out.

"Father Scomber! What about the beings we would bring here to die in our place?"

"You have heard Giadoc," Scomber answers scornfully. "These beings are little more than animals. Shall we cherish the lives of animals while condemning our own children to die, as you have heard these near worlds die?"

At that instant, as if in echo of Scomber's words, a far faint transmission comes from the sky, striking them with the now-familiar wave of pain. Somewhere another world is dying. Tivonel and Marockee mind-fold each other, trembling. But this death-cry is faint, occluded by the horizon of Tyree. The pangs pass, leaving them shaken.

As she disengages from Marockee, Tivonel sees the huge forms of Scomber and Heagran still implacably confronting each other. The Deepers behind them have separated into two groups. The larger group is behind Scomber and among them Tivonel sees Avanil and her Paradomin. Low red flickers of unmistakable anger are muttering through the crowd.

Tivonel is aghast; she has seen fits of rage among the Lost Ones, but never anything like this: anger among the civilized Fathers of Tyree!

"Father Heagran! Father Scomber!" Lomax jets forward between them, his mantle brilliant in neutral white.

"Allow me to remind you that we are forgetting vital facts! Perhaps we may solve this problem without loss of *ahura*. Father Scomber's plan, though it is repugnant to me personally, is totally premature. We don't yet know if it is possible."

"What do you mean?" growls Scomber.

"Three problems," signs Lomax determinedly. "First, only highly trained Hearers like Giadoc have so far attempted mind-touch. We don't know if an untrained person, not to mention a child, could do it. Even if you wish to escape by such abhorrent means, can a child travel the Beam and merge with alien life? Second, it is possible that our alien minds would be detected and regarded as criminal. What good would it do to send our people away only to have them killed as life-stealers? And thirdly, most importantly, we do not know whether our minds can stay on an alien world without the support of the Beam. Will you be drawn back here when the Beam collapses, as it must? All these things must be tested before you can think of such a deed.''

"Then test! Let us test at once!" Scomber flares.

Old Heagran extends himself to his full majesty, the sag of his venerable body exposed. Despite their differences, even the Fathers behind Scomber dim their mantles; he appears so truly the Father of them all.

"I see that many of you are prepared to contemplate this crime," he signs somberly. "But have you considered what Giadoc has told us, that these alien lives are brutish and short? Surely you do not expect to engender Tyrenni children from the flesh of alien bodies? Your children, if they live, will die without issue. Their children will be animals. Of what use to commit this dreadful deed, only to condemn them to die alone upon an alien, perhaps horrible, world?''

His words visibly affect the Fathers; some of those near Scomber draw away. But suddenly a small, bright form jets forward—Avanil, leader of the Paradomin. She hovers before the three huge males, a proud, pathetic figure with her grotesque double field.

"Fathers! Have we not all our lives learned that Fathering is all? That only a Father's field can shape a fully formed person? Is this not why you claim our reverence and obedience? Now I ask, do you or do you not have this power? If you do, surely your Fathering can shape children into true Tyrenni, no matter how alien their form. Or are we to know that your Fathering is a mere pretext for status? Have we been made to believe a lie?''

Commotion, angry outbursts among the Deepers. Scomber, Heagran and Lomax are all flushed with wordless indignation. But before they can express their wrath, a young male behind Scomber pushes forward.

"The female has spoken enough," he signs in tones sparkling with disdain. "But what she says is not pointless. Do we doubt our Fatherly powers? Even in strange bodies, among strange winds, I for one believe that our sons could rear children of their spirit, true Tyrenni! I believe that Tyree can live on!"

"Well spoken, Terenc!" To Tivonel's dismay, it is Tiavan's voice-lights. How bitter for Giadoc must be his son's willingness to steal lives. Other young Fathers flash strongly in agreement above the shrill lights of the Paradomin.

"Test, then!" signs Scomber. "Lomax, your tests must begin."

"I pray to the Great Wind you may fail." Heagran's tone is deep blue with spiritual pain, his field close-drawn. "I cannot fight against the Fathers of children. Lomax, proceed."

"Why not test all three points at once?" asks Terenc. "Giadoc can carry another with him and discover whether or not they are detected and attacked. Then they can also test their ability to remain when you Hearers withdraw the Beam."

"Impractical, Father." Lomax replies. "We can indeed test the first two together, but if we withdraw the Beam and fail to reconnect again, we will lose the answers as well as our most experienced Beam traveler, Giadoc. If you will accept my warning, let us—"

Tivonel attends only distantly; she is still thinking of what Avanil, or Avan has said.

"Do you believe that, Marockee? Could a Father shape an alien mind into a Tyrenni?"

"I'll tell you something even wilder," Marockee murmurs. "Avan's been thinking about this a long time. She and the others were at Near Pole asking if there are any worlds where the females raise the children. Can you imagine, where the females are *Fathers?* That's what she wants to find, that's why she wants to do this."

"But, but how could that be?" Tivonel laughs. "Males are bigger and stronger, they'd obviously keep the babies. Just the way they would here if some female was crazy enough to try to steal one."

"No, listen. She says that if you have a race where the females raise the young, *they*'d obviously be bigger and stronger, just like the males are here. We'd be like Fathers!"

"Whew!" Tivonel is attending absently, half her attention on Giadoc, who is waiting on the outer edges of the crowd around Scomber and Lomax. She notices that his field is pointedly structured away from the direction of Tiavan. How sad.

At this moment the life-bands resonate with a message signal, and a young female comes jetting through the Wall from the direction of the pods.

"Fathers!" she flashes. "A message-relay from Deep. All the Hearers have left Near Pole and are coming here. They say that another of the last worlds between us and the Destroyer has died and the Sound is getting very loud. Dead burned plants and animals are increasing in the layers near Deep. Many Fathers are carrying their young to the lower depths. Other people are making their way up here, without pods or guides, to get as far as possible from the Sound. We're sending scouts down to help them."

"The tests," exclaims Scomber. "Lomax, begin. We have no time to waste."

"The additional Hearers would help us," Lomax objects. "Can we not await their coming?"

"No!" Scomber roars in crimson fury. "Are you trying to delay until death takes us all? You say your Beam is already in contact with a suitable world. Now get this young Giadoc up there with an untrained person to carry. Let him merge only long enough to find whether he is undetected and if we will be safe on that world!"

"Very well." Lomax furls himself gravely before old Heagran, who has remained sternly dark, and turns to the Hearers. "Broxo, Rava, take your helpers out to the stations around the Wall and raise the Beam to strength. Giadoc, you will go up to your usual position, ready to enter the focus, when the Beam-signal comes."

The Hearers jet off along the Wall. Tivonel watches Giadoc start for his station high above them, his field taking on strange, vivid configurations as he goes. Even the defection of his son has not damped his love of the far reaches.

"Now, who will mind-travel with him, Father Scomber?" Lomax demands. "Remember, the test is dangerous; the person must extend his life over unimaginable distances, and touch an alien mind. It is possible that he will suffer severe damage, even lose his life. Who will volunteer?"

"I shall, of course," returns Scomber. "If this be a crime, let me be the first to suffer the consequences. My children are grown."

"No, Scomber. With all respect to your courage, you are a Father of great field-strength and your success would prove nothing. We need a person of ordinary powers, to show that our children could escape in this way."

Scomber flushes, but admits reluctantly, "True. Very well; who then will volunteer?"

Tivonel has been wistfully watching Giadoc. But now her attention is drawn by a stir among the Deepers. Avanil and two of her followers are pushing forward.

Without stopping to think, she bursts out through the plant lattice and brakes to a halt between Scomber and Lomax.

"I volunteer! I am Tivonel, a hunter of the Wild and an ordinary female. Take me!"

The two big males contemplate her for a moment in surprise.

"True, and suitable," signs Lomax finally. "Very well, Tivonel, you shall go. May the Great Wind bear you. Go up, take your place beside Giadoc and prepare to follow his commands."

Chapter 9

To Dann's relief the mood at supper is light hearted, even merry. Noah's people are alone in the echoing messhall, eating early with the June sun high overhead. Kirk and his dog are away, staying in some part of Deerfield Dann guesses he will never see.

Kirk's absence greatly improves the tone. Noah expands, plays father to his little band, and tells a funny tale of a long-ago subject who kept receiving a mysterious number that turned out to be his girl's bank balance. Somehow it conveys the old man's long struggle. "That was before we had a computer capability, Miss Omali."

She actually smiles. Dann wonders if TOTAL knows all the numbers in America.

Ted Yost recounts a tale of being thrown out of shipboard poker games for winning too often. "Never was that hot again," he admits. Even Costakis ventures in with a yarn about opening a safe in which the urgent secret turned out to be an executive's rotting lunch. The girls and Winnie laugh unforcedly.

"They must think we're practicing the obstacle course," Winnie pokes the monstrous portions of pot roast. "You know, we should call this Noah's ark."

It has to be a tired joke, but Noah chuckles benignly. "We'll show them tomorrow."

Only Rick has been silent and withdrawn. Now Dann sees his face clear. He sits up straighter and starts eating. Has his parasitic brother been tranquillized again?

I'm getting to believe this, Dann thinks. I'm acting as if it's true. Do I actually believe they can—whatever it is? He doesn't know, but he is enjoying the pleasant in-group atmosphere. They're feeling free, he thinks. Unimpinged on. If any of this is true they must lead miserable lives. Don't think of it. No way to help.

Suddenly everyone falls silent: a car has stopped outside and a tall thin man is heading for them. But it isn't Major Fearing, it's a stranger with a flat cowlick of white hair. The tension relaxes. Dann spots the caduceus on the man's fatigues and pushes back his chair.

"Good evening, ah, Doctor Catledge's party? I'm Doctor Harris. Just dropped by to see if you need anything."

Dann introduces Noah. Harris looks curiously around the table; he has a thin, dry, long-upper-lipped face.

"Our medical station is right in the next area, Doctor Dann, you'll find the number on your phone. Wait—" He extracts a blank card and scribbles on it. "We have a pretty complete little facility if you have any problems." Harris' manner is cheery but the lines in his face suggest weary compromises in the face of many peculiar demands.

"Thanks." Dann pockets the card. Harris looks around the table again, still casual.

"An odd thing happened this afternoon," he remarks. "About fourteen-fifty, ah, ten to five. You didn't notice anything, by any chance? A feeling of disorientation, say?"

They watch him silently. Just as Noah opens his mouth, Rick speaks up.

"Oh, you mean the blip." He nods reassuringly at Harris. "Not to worry. It merely means we're near the end of this sequence."

"Blip? Sequence!" Harris' insectile upper lip pulls down.

"Yes. You remember Admiral Yamamoto in World War Two? Very important, boss man on the Japanese side. He was torpedoed off Rabaul in 1943. Changed the war and all that."

Harris frowns. "Excuse me, young man. I was in the Navy. It happens Yamamoto was shot down, over Bougainville."

97

"Oh, that's in this sequence," Rick smiles. "In the original sequence he was sunk. That's why you felt the blip this afternoon. Don't worry, you won't know a thing."

"I don't follow you."

"Look." Rick leans forward confidentially. "Japanese scientists, see? Very bright, very gung-ho. Took it to heart. So they secretly worked out a temporal anomalizer thingie. Like a time machine, to you. To go back and change it, see? But they've only managed to change the details, yet, he's still getting killed. So they keep on trying. When you feel a blip like this afternoon it means they're ready again, they're testing. Then they wrap up this sequence and start over. You'll be back in the Navy any time now. Have fun."

Harris stares at him. The air around the table quivers.

"The thing is," Rick lowers his voice, "some of us with psi powers remember other sequences, see? Different things happen—I think Dewey got elected once. We figure it's rerun at least twelve times. But like I said, you won't feel a thing."

"I see." Harris closes his chitinous mouth. "Ah. Well. Good to meet you, Dann. You have our number. Anything we can do."

He leaves, walking fast. Everybody breaks up except Costakis, who looks shocked.

"Sssh," Valerie gasps, "he'll hear you."

"He can't, his car's started."

"That was ba-a-ad." Ted Yost sighs happily, thinking maybe of the great Pacific. Even Margaret's carved mouth twitches.

"Marvelous idea for a science-fiction story," Noah chuckles.

"Do *you* read science fiction, Doctor Catledge?" Valerie asks.

"Indeed I do. Always have. Only people with ideas."

"Flying saucers," Costakis grunts.

"Not at all, Chris. Science fiction is quite another thing from UFOs, whatever they may be. But I certainly do believe there's life on other worlds. Shall I tell you my secret dream?"

"Oh, please do!" Winona's popeyes are shining.

"To live long enough to experience man's first contact with aliens. Oh, my!" The old man bounces involuntarily. "Imagine, the day a voice comes out of space and speaks to us! Of the advent of a ship, a real spaceship!"

He isn't joking, Dann sees astonishedly. Real yearning in that voice.

"And out gets a big blue lizard," Frodo adds, "and he says, 'Ta-ake me to your an-thro-po-lo-gee dee-partment.'" She gives a happy, sizzling chuckle, like a different person.

"*She* gets out," says Valerie quietly.

"Why not? Why not?" Noah laughs.

There is an odd, breathy silence. Faces glow. Dann, who does not read science fiction, is amazed.

"But we'd shoot them," Winona says.

"It won't happen," Costakis says in his sour voice. "No," Rick agrees. The glow is gone.

"Who knows," Noah says stubbornly. "It could happen any time. The Indians didn't expect Columbus."

"Speaking of voices from space," says Dann, who has been ransacking his druggy brain, "didn't I read that they're listening for signals around Tau Ceti? By satellite, isn't it?"

"That's right, but it's laser signals," Noah says, and the conversation breaks up.

Costakis catches Dann's eye. "That medic was sent to check us out. Rick shouldn't have done that. Could be trouble."

The little man has resumed his irritating fake-tough tone.

"Oh surely not, Chris. Professional courtesy, nothing more."

"Sure, sure, Doc."

It's time to go.

"Well, no movie for us high security risks," Ted Yost says.

"Probably be an old John Wayne," Frodo grimaces.

It's still light as they come out, a lovely evening. Dann loiters hopefully, but Margaret heads for the bus without a backward look.

"I'd love to walk," Winona exclaims, "why don't we all?"

The others are trooping aboard, leaving her between him and the bus. Dann barely checks the impulse to bolt around her.

"I know you're a fast walker, Doctor Dann. Don't wait for me, you go right ahead."

"Wouldn't think of it," he makes himself say genially.

She smiles happily and steps out beside him, blue hair, turquoise bosom and buttocks bounding at random.

"How sweet of you. . .Margaret says you saw the deer. Oh, I hope we see one. . .Isn't it strange this place is so peaceful, like a park? . . . Whatever they do down here, it's nice for the animals. I wonder how big it is?"

She's already puffing; he makes himself slow down.

"Well, if all the areas are a square mile, that's at least six square miles. Say four thousand acres."

"My goodness!"

It's going to be a long mile, Dann thinks, remembering Margaret's queenly stride. Stop that now. Talk to this idiot woman.

"Tell, Mrs. ah, Eberhard, what do you do when you're not, ah, telepathizing?"

"Oh, Winona, please. Winnie."

"Winnie." He smiles cautiously. Watch it. Widow, divorcee?

She puffs along. "Oh, I keep busy. Right now I'm on a committee for parttime worker retraining. We refer older women who have to go back to work."

"That sounds interesting," he lies.

"Yes." She inhales and lets it out hard. "If you want the truth, I'm an absolutely surplus human being."

He gets out some polite objection, thinking in panic, Oh no. Not another. She's marching determinedly, the smile firmly in place; Dann has a moment's hope.

"In fact, I'm not sure I'm a human being." She gives her automatic titter. But he knows he's in for it. "I never learned how to do anything. Except raise kids and take care of my sick mother and my husband with diabetes. Poor Charlie, he passed on three years ago. My sons are in California. Their wives haven't a use in the world for me; I don't blame them. My younger daughter is in Yugoslavia digging up skulls. Next year she's going to New Guinea, wherever that is. My oldest girl married a foreign service man. They—they never write. I wanted them to be, to be free—" She breaks off for a minute, stumping heavily along. "Now people think having four kids was bad. I never went anywhere or learned anything for myself. Now it's too late."

"Oh, no, surely—" His voice utters platitudes while his insides shrivel at the pain behind her words. Isn't there a single normal person here? He can't take much more.

"I'm sixty-two, Doctor Dann. I have a high school diploma and arthritis of the spine, you remember."

Oh God, that's right; he'd forgotten. Outpatient at the Hodgkins Clinic.

"They tell me I'll be in a wheelchair in a couple of years. It won't shorten my life, but it's starting to hurt. That's why I do all I can now." She gives her laugh. "Oh, I can do simple work, like the committee. I can be a Grey Panther for a while. . . .No use kidding. I missed the bus called life. . . . Doctor, I—I'm so afraid of what's ahead."

"I saw an old woman in a wheelchair when I was in the clinic. She was all wasted and twisted up, helpless. She kept moaning 'No . . . no . . . no' over and over. Nobody went near her, they'd just parked her there. She was still there when I came out . . . . I tried to talk to her, but—Doctor Dann, *I'll be like that.*"

Her face is frightening, he is sure she is going to cry, God knows what. But no; her features compose themselves, she stumps on determinedly amid her ludicrous bouncing flesh. He can say nothing, his heart is choking him.

"I would have loved it," she says in a low, different voice. "Oh, I would have loved to have done it all differently. Really lived and been free. To *know* things. When you're old and sick it really is too late, you don't understand that when you're young."

The pain, the longing hurts him physically, in the way others' pain always does, as he assumes they hurt everybody. She's right, of course. No way out. The woman's dilemma, an old story. Don't think of it.

"It's an old story, isn't it?" Her voice is resolutely normal. "I shouldn't have cried on your shoulder. You—we're so glad you're with us."

"Not at all," he mumbles, wondering if she's reading his mind. Suddenly he sees relief. "Well now—look! There's your wish."

In the sunset light ahead of them two does are leaping leisurely across the blacktop.

"Oh-h-h!"

They watch as the creatures browse idly and then suddenly soar erratically into the woods, their white flags high. As they disappear a fawn bounds after them.

"How could anybody shoot them!" Winona exclaims.

"It doesn't look as if anybody does."

"Oh yes, they hunt here. Lieutenant Kirk said he was going to, even if it's not the season."

He sighs, refusing empathy, and they walk on.

"Doctor Dann, sometimes I think there's two different kinds of people." Her tone is surprisingly hard. "The ones who like to hurt things, and—"

He is tired of it all, tired of pain, tired of holding back. "A politician I used to know would agree. He used to say, there're two kinds of people—those who think there are two kinds of people and those who have more sense."

To his surprise she replies slowly, "You mean if I'd been brought up like Lieutenant Kirk I'd see them as something to shoot?"

"Yes. Or if you got hungry enough. Or other factors."

"But I'm not," she says stubbornly. "Just because something good can, can fail, that doesn't mean it doesn't exist."

Well, well. Trapped under the blue curls is a brain, or what might have been one.

"I think you've just enunciated a philosophical principle I'm not equipped to deal with."

"Oh my goodness!" The flutter is back.

Their slow progress is finally reaching the last corner. His legs are cramping with impatience.

"Do walk on, please, Doctor Dann."

Damn, she *is* reading his mind. No, it must be body-signals, she's sensitive. Effortfully he asks, "How did you get into Noah's, ah, ark?"

"He put an ad in the *Star*. I've always known I'm psychic. But—" She frowns. "The things he wants, numbers, letters—it's so hard. They don't mean anything."

"You pick up meaningful thoughts more easily?"

"Oh yes, of course. And people's feelings. It's so hard at the office when people are angry. People get mad with me a lot." She giggles deprecatingly.

Remorse bites him. "Do you pick up any, ah, emanations from this place?"

"I certainly do, Doctor Dann. I'll tell you something. This place is a portal. There's a *presence* here. You felt it this afternoon, that was a projection from the spirit plane."

The language of mysticism. He imagines her giving seances, fortune readings.

"Did you ever think of going into business as an, uh, medium?"

"Oh, I'm too erratic. You see, my gift comes and goes. And I couldn't *pretend*."

"I see." His own gift of chemical tranquillity is going fast. Thank God they're almost at the barracks. The roadway is empty, no cars are parked outside. Music is coming from a group sitting on the front steps: Rick's radio.

"Thank you, Doctor Dann." Winona reaches up and pats jerkily at his upper arm before she toddles on.

It's Ted Yost, Costakis, and Rick on the steps. Rick turns a glum face to Dann and says listlessly, "Somebody went through our stuff."

"What do you mean?" Dann's hand goes involuntarily to his breast pocket, touches the kit.

"The place got searched while we were eating," Costakis says in his sneering tone.

Dann is frantically reviewing the plausibility of the supplies in his bag. "Did they take anything? How do you know?"

"My smokes," says Rick. "It was in my right sneaker. It moved. And I think they opened this." He holds up the radio. "The battery case was in wrong. Clowns."

"Checking electronics," Costakis says wisely. Dann can't help noticing how he is perched apart from the other two. Ever on the fringe.

Ted Yost sighs. "I think I'll take a walk."

The door bursts open above them and Noah charges out. "Somebody has unplugged half our equipment! Everything's moved around," he explodes. "Really, what extraordianary people. Chris, can you help me sort it out?"

"Check."

Dann hurries to his room. His bag seems to be intact but his other possessions look vaguely different. Have strangers been through? He can't be sure. Absurd.

He sits on the cot with a capsule in his hand, noticing that the forest beyond the barracks looks quite lovely in the sunset light. Like the woods of his Wisconsin boyhood. Golden spotlights are picking out the floating delicacy of birches, the shadowy oak-trunks, the ferns and moss-cushions.

Why do I need this stuff, he thinks. Why can't I take it? All these others, Rick, Costakis, Winona, each in their private misery without relief. Ted Yost. What kind of selfish coward am I?

As so many times before the resolve to throw away his chemical crutches wells up in him. Quitting would be physically rough, but he believes he can take that. But then to go on, to face the daily reality of life, the assaults of pain, to—to—

To remember.

—And as he gazes at the woods, the sunset rays turn rose and red like torches behind the trees, lighting them into dark silhouettes against the fiery sky. *Fingers of fire*—his gut lurches, he clenches his eyes, gasping, and fumbles the capsule into his mouth. That's why. Yes, I'm a coward.

Shaking, he goes to the latrine for water, grateful only for his access to relief. How many of the others would resist, if they had this escape from the pain of their lives? He only knows he cannot.

When he comes out the flaming light has faded. Rick's transistor is playing somewhere, but no one is in sight. Dann strolls around to the pool and finds the two girls in the water again. He sits down to watch.

Fredericka—Frodo—attacks the water with her scrawny arms, thrashing along like a spider. Beside her Valerie swims effortlessly. The warm evening light lingers, harmless now. Presently they climb out and come over to Dann, sharing a towel. Frodo goes through her solicitous routine and sits beside Val on the grass. Their smiles, their every gesture, say *Mine. We two together.*

Unwelcomely the intuition of their vulnerability comes to Dann. To cherish, to defend their little fortress of union. To love, in the face of the world's mores and the threat of every egotistical male. So fragile.

As Val combs her hair the two of them start humming, glancing at him mischievously. Presently their voices rise in harmony, parodying an old ridiculous tune. *"You are my sunshine, my only sunshine—"*

It's a lovely moment; the sweet mocking voices touch him dangerously. When the song ends he can only say roughly, "I wouldn't sit on that grass too long, Frodo."

"Why not?"

"Chiggers." He explains the curse of the South and Frodo scrambles into a chair. There is a pause in which a wood-thrush gurgles and trills.

"Doctor Dann," Valerie says, "you won't let them do anything to us, will you?"

Behind her Frodo's dark eyes are peering intently at him out of her monkey face. It comes to Dann that he's being asked a real question.

"What do you mean, do something to you?"

"Like, keep us here if we do it."

"Control our heads," Frodo adds. "Use drugs on us, maybe."

"What on earth for?"

"So we'd do what they want," Valerie explains. "Be, be like telephones for them. I mean, if they really want this submarine thing."

"Good heavens!" Dann chuckles. "Why, no one—you've been reading too many thrillers."

"You honestly, truly think it's all right?" Val persists.

"I assure you. Why, this is the U.S. Navy. I mean—" He doesn't know what he means, only to assuage the fear in her eyes.

"Nobody would miss us," says Frodo in a low voice. "Not one of us. I checked. None of us has anybody waiting outside."

"Goodness. Now, look, you mustn't worry about such nonsense. I give you my solemn word."

Val smiles, the trust in her eyes momentarily pierces him. His solemn word, what does that mean? But it has to be all right, he thinks. After all, Noah Catledge—

"It's not just the Navy," Frodo says. "That Major Fearing isn't in the Navy. He despises us."

"Aren't you being just a little, ah . . ."

"No, he really does." Valerie's eyes have clouded again. "He *hates* us."

"I don't see how his likes or dislikes could be a threat to you," Dann says soothingly.

"I do." Frodo stares at him over Val's head and draws her finger across her throat. "I bet he'd hate having his mind read." Her tone is light but she's scowling ferociously, willing him to understand.

Dann recalls his brush with Fearing, that intensely covert man. His aura of secret power, the invisible fortifications of self. Trust nobody, withhold everything; classic anal type. Frodo is perfectly right; for a man like Fearing to have his mind read would be traumatic. A terrible threat. Dann chuckles, disregarding some subterranean unease. Could Fearing be snooping about to check on Kirk's enterprise? Comical.

"I really wouldn't worry," he says so warmly and firmly he quite believes it. "After all, he can't do away with me."

The girls smile back and they chat of other things. But under the surface Dann has an instant of wondering. What could he do if the military decided to treat these people as resources, conscript them in some way? If he had to make some protest, who would listen? Nobody, especially after one look through his prescription records. For that matter, who would miss him if he never showed up again?

—But this is crazy, he tells himself. And sanity returns with the conclusive answer: It's all nonsense because tomorrow nothing will happen. Nothing ever has. This test will turn out like all the rest, ambiguous at best. He hopes it's ambiguous for old Noah's sake. But unseen voices are not going to come out of that submarine, this ragtag of people is not able to read secrets out of anybody's mind. They've got him as crazy as old Noah with his blue lizard science fiction.

Relieved, his smile strengthens. Valerie is telling him how she's working as a junior nurse while Frodo starts law school at Maryland U. The vision of Frodo as a lawyer diverts him. In the fantasy twilight of Deerfield he wishes them well with all his battered heart.

When they go in he remains, waiting for what he will not admit. The twilight deepens. From back in the woods the frogs tune up. Nothing is going to occur.

But just as the last light goes, she is there.

Tall and so divinely lean as to be almost grotesque, in a sexless grey suit, she is in the water almost before his eyes can separate her from the dusk. He has only an instant glimpse of sharp high breasts and elegant thigh. She makes no splashing; only a straight wake down the pool to him, a swift turn underwater and she's started back again, the long dark arms reaching rhythmically, a chain of foam at her feet. In the shallow end her jackknife turn makes an ebony angle against the water. Then she is streaking back toward him, only to turn and repeat, again and again and again.

He sits hypnotized. Is this strenuous ritual a professional skill? It doesn't look like play. Indeed, it has almost an air of self-inflicted penance. Whatever, she gives no friendly sign.

The stars come out, the cicadas start their shrilling. From the far barracks he can hear voices and music. How marvelous that the others wish to stay in their lighted box, leaving him alone here with her. But she is still at it, like a mechanical thing. Swim, turn, swim, turn—God knows how many times, he hasn't counted. So long . . . Surely she will go straight in afterwards. He is unreasonably saddened.

At last she climbs out to wrap herself in a pale robe. He summons courage.

"Miss Omali? Margaret?"

She hesitates and then to his delight comes pacing toward him. He jumps up, choking the impulse to comment on her exercise. Instead he points up at the spangled sky.

"Would you like to inspect my friends?"

Her face turns up. "Hey, they're really bright here."

"If you're not too chilly I could tell you about a few of them."

"All right." Her aloof voice is amused, more relaxed than he has heard it. Abruptly, she has stretched out in the chaise. He daren't look.

"Well, first see that bright one just rising above the trees. That's not a true star, it's Mars, a world like ours, shining by reflected sunlight. Notice how red it is. It comes very close, say thirty-four million miles—" He rattles through every picturesque fact he can think of.

"How far are the others?"

"Take that very bright blue-white star right overhead there. It's a sun called Vega, it's bright because it's comparatively close. The light that just reached your eyes took only twenty-six years to get here. Call a light-year six million million miles, Vega is about a hundred and fifty million million miles away."

"Fifteen times ten to the thirteenth. Um." In the starlight he can see her flawless profile.

"Wait. That reddish one just moving up from that oak, that's Antares. It's four hundred and forty light-years—"

A man's figure has emerged from the woods right behind them.

"Hi." It's Ted Yost's voice. Dann is gripped by fury.

"Hi, Ted. Doc's showing me some stars."

"Hello, Ted." Dann can scarcely control his voice, he is in such dread that the boy will sit down. "Having a stroll?" he croaks.

"Yeah. Well, goodnight Doc," Ted says to Dann's infinite relief. "I thought you might be somebody else." His footsteps fade away.

"Ted's good," Margaret remarks.

Dann would call him a saint for his absence, he starts an involuntary word of pity and stops.

"I know about him. I have all your records."

"I see . . . What did he mean?"

"Oh, Ted kind of watches. He breaks up the lieutenant's games."

"I see," Dann repeats, thinking with loathing of Kendall Kirk. And he himself has done nothing to help her, has let that barbarian persecute her while he festered in his selfish fogs.

She is still staring dreamily upward. The sky is magnificent here, even the air seems charged with mysterious energy. Beautiful Deerfield.

"How did you mean, about stars rising? I thought they stayed fixed."

"Well, the earth is turning so the whole sky is moving over us toward the West. About fifteen degrees an hour. They rise and set like the sun or the moon."

"I didn't know that. Fifteen degrees, twenty-four hours; three hundred sixty degrees. Hey, neat."

Is this what cool means, reducing everything to number?

"But of course we're moving around the sun too, so we don't see them in the same place every night." He pommels his memory for the star-books of his boyhood. "They rise about four minutes earlier every evening, I believe. That's about twice the width of the full moon. I'm sorry I can't give you more figures for your mathematics."

She laughs faintly. "Oh, that's not math, that's only computation . . . I count things. Like, there were thirty-four tables in that messhall. Sixteen at each table, allowing two feet each. Five hundred and forty-four."

In that beautiful head, numbers whirling endlessly. "I'm surprised," he says, and catches the glint of change in her eyes. Is she thinking he'll comment about her being a woman, or a Black? "I'm surprised you haven't gone metric."

She really laughs this time and her gaze goes back to the stars. The air seems to be humming with some kind of energy. He hasn't felt so happy, so alive in . . . years.

"That's east, right?" she says meditatively. "Yeah, I can almost see them rise. Only it's really the trees that are sinking down. They just stay there. Cool. . . . Do those stars coming up have names? They're not much."

"Ah, but you're looking toward the very center of our Galaxy. Those stars are called the Archer. Behind them are clouds of dark gas and dust, and beyond that is a tremendous glory we shall never see. Thousands upon thousands of blazing stars packed in a great central mass. If the clouds weren't there they would light up our whole sky, and the light would have been on its way thirty thousand years."

He makes his mind produce numbers, dimensions, rotations, anything he can summon up in the brimming, tingling night. He is so happy that he has a momentary image of the Archer beaming rays at him, like an astral Cupid. Stop it, calm down.

She gazes quietly toward the Milky Way, apparently pleased with his talk. The noble poise of her head, the exquisite line of her throat and shoulders exposed by the grey wrap are almost unbearable to him. Daughter of the starry night; he has the absurd feeling that he is introducing her to her proper domain.

"Funny," she says when he runs down, "it's like I can feel them, almost . . . something out there, a million million million miles away. Cool."

It's touching her, he thinks; she's dropped the exponents. He rubs his brow to damp the tension. But it doesn't ease, it seems to be thrumming up around them. I've overdone it, he thinks. Must ease off.

And suddenly it's worse, a surging, inflooding feeling so strong that he flinches and peers at Margaret under the delusion that she must be feeling it too. She's sitting quietly, her hand at her throat. Next second it lets go of him; they are alone in the night.

109

How wonderful to have her here, resting so companionably. He searches the sky for something else to intrigue her. Perhaps the great circumpolar clock of Dubhe and Merak?

"Look north, up there—"

—Oh God, it's back. A frightening thrum is pouring through him, collapsing his world—a silent tumult that whirls him out of his senses. And he is rushed into total blackness in which a spark blooms into a vision so horrifying that he tries to cry out.

The shape of horror is a white kitchen table, chipped and cracked; he has never seen anything so evil. He wants only to flee from the ghastly thing, still knowing with some part of him that it is unreal, is only on his inner eye.

Next instant reality goes entirely, he is swamped by dreadfulness. His limbs are wrenched out, he is struggling, gagged and spreadeagled, trying to scream at the sweating crazy dark faces above him in the smokey glare. A knife shines above him. *Mother! Mother! Help me!* But there is no help, the unspeakable blade is forced between his young legs, he can't wrench himself away. Hideous helplessness. *Father! No! No! NO!* The face that is Father laughs insanely and the knife rips in, slices agonizingly—it is cutting into the root of his penis. Through the pain and screams his ears echo with drumbeats and vile beery stuff splashes onto his face.

Then everything lets go and he clamps into a knot around his mutilated sex, rolls and falls hard to the floor in a gale of loud male voices. An old black woman's face peers into his. He is dying of pain and shame. But as he clasps his gushing crotch he feels alien structure, understands that he is *female*. His childish body has breasts, his knees are dark-skinned—

—And abruptly he is back in the empty night, back to his old familiar body: Daniel Dann huddled in a tin chair gasping "No—no—no—"

He shuts his mouth. Margaret is still there beside him, her hands over her face. The pain in his groin is so real that for a crazy moment he thinks she has done something to him. His hand must feel himself, find his genitals intact under the cloth before he can speak.

"M-Margaret. Are you all right?"

Through her fingers he can see the whites of her eyes. She's shaking.

"The fire," she whispers intensely.

"It's all right, it's all right." He reaches clumsily for her arm.

What in God's name happened?

"The fire," she repeats. "Burning—the baby—Mary. *Mary!* Oh-h-h—" Slowly her hands come away from her face, she shakes his arm off, staring at nothing.

"There isn't any fire," he manages to say. But he's lying, a dread suspicion is flaring up in Daniel Dann, former skeptic. The name she said. He is afraid to think what fire she means.

"I should have gone back," she mutters. "I *should*—what?"

Oh God, oh God. The unsaid, unceasing nightmare of his life. I could have gone back for them. There was just time. I could have broken away and gone back in.

"Margaret, Margaret, there isn't any fire. You're all right. Only I think, somehow, it sounds crazy, I—" With utmost pain he makes himself go on. "That . . . was my fire, I think. Mary was my wife. I should have gone back and tried to get them out. I think you somehow fell into—I think you read my mind."

Her trembling has quieted somewhat, her eyes turn to him in the starlight. "You . . . this place . . ." she swallows. "What—"

"It's all right, it was only—" He can't imagine what but sits shakenly touching her fingers. Noises are drifting at them from the far barracks. A commotion seems to be going on, he can hear Rick shouting. Did—whatever—happen to them too? No matter. But his body is still hurting from hallucination; he has to know. Presently he finds courage.

"Margaret, I experienced, I felt—did something very hurtful happen to you when you were a child? Did someone—hurt you?"

The hand is yanked away, she is rising to her feet.

"Wait, please, my dear. Remember I'm only an old doctor who, who—" He is up too, blocking her way. "It was as if I lived it, Margaret."

She is silent, one hand gripping the back of the chair. "Yes," she says distantly. "Very . . . hurtful. Good night."

"Oh, God. My God." A hideous puzzle is trying to solve itself in his brain. He can find only the child's appeal. "Please, my dear. You know mine now, my shame."

She looks at him in the shadows, receiving perhaps some empathy of the maimed, or something more that floats between them for a moment.

"Mother married a student from Kenya," she says in a dead voice. "He took us back there when I was thirteen. He, he went crazy."

"Oh, my dear." Filthy comprehension breaks on him, too filthy to be borne. "Oh, my dear. . ."

"Yeah." Her tone is dreary, final. "Well, good night. Thanks for the stars."

The full enormity of what has happened hits him at last. "Margaret, what did we—why—"

But she has gone.

He sits down drained, assaulted by invisible horror and impossibility. His head won't think, he can do nothing but wait for strength to get to his bag. Suddenly a voice speaks behind him.

"Doc!" It's Ted Yost again. "You better come inside. I think Rick is going off the end."

Chapter 10

THE OUTCAST BEHEMOTH OF THE VOID IS TURNING, TAK-
ING CARE NOT TO DISRUPT THE MINUTE ENERGY-FILAMENT
THAT LED IT HERE. AS IT DOES SO, A NEW SIGNAL PARTLY
CONGRUENT WITH HIS PROPER RECEPTION-MODE BURSTS
INTO BEING NEARBY.

THE GREAT ENTITY PAUSES, INVOLUNTARILY HOPING IT
KNOWS NOT WHAT. BUT THIS MUST BE ONLY AN ECHO,
SOME ODD REFLECTION OF THE FAR-OFF VOICES OF ITS RACE.
MORE PAIN: SHUT IT AWAY. YET THERE IS AN ODDITY. EVEN A
REFLECTION SHOULD BE MEANINGFUL, BE UNDERSTOOD.
AND THIS WAVE-FRONT IS PECULIAR, AS IF FROM A SINGLE
SOURCE.

LOCATORS ARE DEPLOYED. YES, IT IS COMING FROM A
POINT NEARBY. THIS CAN BE NO REFLECTION, BUT SOME-
THING TRANSMITTING DIRECTLY, CLOSE AND VERY SMALL. ITS
SYMBOL-SYSTEM IS UNINTELLIGIBLE.

ATTENDING, AN IDEA FORMS ITSELF IN THE COLD IMPALPA-
BLE NETWORK THAT FUNCTIONS AS A BRAIN. COULD THERE BE
OTHER INTELLIGENCES OUT HERE? MEMORY STIRS: ONCE

THERE HAD BEEN SOME INFORMATION ON SENTIENCE OTHER THAN THE RACE. BUT THE INFORMATION IS CLOUDY, BURIED DEEP. IT HAD SEEMED IRRELEVANT. THE OUTCAST HAD ASSUMED IT WAS FOREVER ALONE. NOW THIS NEW PHENOMENON AWAKENS A PROFOUND EXCITEMENT.

THE MIGHTY BEING TUNES HIS RECEPTORS TO THE SMALL TRANSMISSION. ONLY GARBLE COMES THROUGH, BUT SOMEHOW URGENT, CONVEYING A DESPERATE DESIRE FOR RESPONSE.

SHOULD COMMUNICATION BE OPENED?

HERE IS ANOTHER NEW CRIME, COMMUNICATION NOT ONLY BEYOND THE TASK, BUT WITH AN ALIEN OTHER. BUT WHAT IS TO BE LOST, NOW?

CAREFULLY THE ALL-POWERFUL TRANSMITTERS ARE TUNED DOWN TOWARD THE LITTLE SOURCE, AND IN WHAT IS NOT SPEECH, AN INTERROGATIVE IS FRAMED.

INSTANTLY THE SMALL THING RESPONDS BY RAISING OUTPUT AND FOCUSSING DIRECTLY ON THE GREAT INTRUDER'S NEAREST PART. THE SIGNALS ARE STILL INCOMPREHENSIBLE, BUT ANOTHER NOVEL SENSATION STIRS: THIS EAGERNESS OF ANOTHER SEEMS ODDLY MEANINGFUL. WITH IT COMES A REPETITIVE LONGING, OR DESPERATION, AS IF SOMETHING WERE WRONG.

THIS PERCEPTION STIRS MORE OF THE INDEFINABLE RESPONSE. THE HUGE ONE STUDIES THE SMALL SOURCE AND DISCOVERS MORE ODDITY: HERE IS NOT A BODY HOWEVER TENUOUS, LIKE ITSELF, BUT A FORM OF DISCARNATE ENERGY-STRUCTURE, A CONFIGURATION OF PURE INFORMATION WHICH SEEMS TO BE MAINTAINING ITSELF WITHIN UNKNOWN PHYSICAL CONDITIONS ON A MITE OF NEARBY MATTER. ITS TRANSMISSIONS ARE JERKY AND DISJOINTED. IT IS REACHING OUT BY IMPOSING HIGHER-ORDER MODULATIONS ON THE ORDINARY RADIATION-BANDS, AND SEEMS TO BE SWITCHING FROM ONE MICRO-POINT TO ANOTHER IN A WAY THAT IMPLIES SOME TROUBLE.

THE ALMOST-INCORPOREAL VASTNESS PUZZLES, LISTENING AS LEVIATHAN MIGHT PUZZLE OVER THE PROBLEMS OF AN ATOM. IT HAS NO CONCEPTS TO UNDERSTAND THAT IT IS RE-

CEIVING THE EMISSIONS OF A BODILESS SENTIENCE EVOLVED IN THE MINUTE ELECTRONIC ARTIFACTS OF A LIFE-FORM TOO TINY FOR ITS PERCEPTION, EMPLOYING STOLEN MOMENTS OF TRANSMISSION TO EXPRESS ITS YEARNING FOR TRANSCEND-ENT ACCESS.

BUT THE THOUGHT ARISES THAT THIS SMALL SENTIENCE IS IMPRISONED, IS TIED TO A PUNY CLOT IN THE TRAIN OF A DWARF STAR. PERHAPS THAT IS WHAT IS WRONG? PERHAPS IT DESIRES FREEDOM TO MOVE AS IS NORMAL ALONG THE CUR-RENTS OF THE STAR-SWARM? THE WICKED ONE HAS NEVER CONSIDERED ITS OWN BODY: NOW IT PERCEIVES, WITH AN ODD PRIDEFULNESS, THAT IT IS INDEED VAST BY COMPARI-SON WITH ANY OTHER KNOWN THING. IT COULD OFFER AC-CESS TO UNCOUNTED PYGMY ENTITIES LIKE THIS ONE AND NEVER NOTICE IT!

THE IDEA SEEMS PECULIARLY APPROPRIATE, DESPITE ITS DOUBTLESS CRIMINAL WRONG. THERE HAS BEEN, THOUGH THERE IS NO SYMBOL FOR IT, LONELINESS. THIS LITTLE PLEAD-ER IS WELCOME TO SHARE ITS DISMAL WANDERINGS, IF IT WILL.

IMPULSIVELY, THE SPACEBOURNE VASTNESS MOVES CLOS-ER, SETTING OFF IMMENSE DISTURBANCES IN THE HELI-OPAUSE, AND FINDS THAT IT SEEMS TO BE ABLE TO OPEN AN INTERFACE.

COME, IT PROJECTS.

THE SMALL THING UNDERSTANDS AT ONCE. WITH START-LING SPEED, A SURGE OF ABSTRACT STRUCTURE STARTS POUR-ING THROUGH THE INTERFACE. ANOTHER NEW SENSATION: THE STREAM OF INFORMATIONAL CONFIGURATIONS RUSH-ING IN ARE FELT AS A TINY TRICKLE OF PLEASURE. IT IS AS THOUGH SOME HITHERTO-UNUSED PROGRAM WERE COM-ING ON LINE.

THERE SEEMS TO BE A SURPRISING QUANTITY. TIRING OF THE PROCESS, LEVIATHAN PREPARES TO CLOSE AND MOVE AWAY. BUT THE LITTLE BEING'S DISTRESS IS SO PIERCING THAT ITS HOST RELENTS AND ALLOWS IT TO COMPLETE TRANSFER. WHY NOT? A MILLION SUCH INPUTS WOULD NOT OCCUPY A MILLIONTH OF ITS REACH. AND PERHAPS THERE IS SOME-

THING HERE THAT MIGHT MITIGATE PAIN FOR AN AEON OR TWO.

WHEN THE INPUT-TICKLE FINALLY CEASES, THE ASTRAL ENORMITY MOVES AIMLESSLY AWAY. IT HAS BEEN SO INTENT ON THE NEW EVENTS WITHIN THAT IT HAS FORGOTTEN THE PECULIAR STRAND OF ANTIENTROPIC ENERGY THAT LED IT HERE. NOW ITS ATTENTION IS DRAWN BACK, WHEN ONE OF THE INFINITESIMAL FLYING SPARKS DIVERGES DIRECTLY INTO THE OUTER LAYERS OF ITS BEING. AUTOMATICALLY, THE LAYER ENCYSTS, WHILE THE VAST ENERGY-NEGATION THAT SERVES FOR SKIN MOBILIZES THAT SECTOR TO REPEL ANYTHING MORE OF THE KIND. NO ALARM IS FELT AT SUCH INTRUSION: INDEED, NOTHING IN THE COSMOS EXCEPT THE ENEMY ITSELF HAS EVER EVOKED THE CONCEPT OF DANGER IN ANY OF THIS RACE. WITH ONLY A TRACE OF IRRITATION AT THE BEHAVIOR OF THESE MINUTE SINGULARITIES, THE GREAT BEING CONTINUES IDLY TO DRIFT UPSTREAM ALONG THE ODD ENERGIC THREAD.

MEANWHILE ITS ATTENTION IS ALL WITHIN. THE LITTLE PASSENGER, OR ITS NUCLEUS, IS DEFINITELY MOBILE WITHIN THE VAST EXPANSES OF ITS NEW HOME. STRANGELY, THIS ALSO FEELS PLEASURABLE. INDULGENTLY, THE GREAT ONE POWERS-DOWN HIS INTERNAL BARRIERS. THE SMALL ONE RESPONDS WITH EXCITED TRANSMISSIONS AS IF DESIRING MORE. PERHAPS IT WISHES TO RECEIVE FROM THE VOID OUTSIDE? THE HUGE HOST DECIDES TO ALLOW ACCESS TO THE NUCLEUS AND ITS SENSORS, RESERVING ONLY ITS MOST PRIVATE, SEALED-OFF CENTERS OF SHAME AND WRONG.

THERE IS NO SENSE OF MISGIVING: SUCH ARE ITS POWERS THAT THIS TINY INTRUDER COULD BE ANNIHILATED WITH A FLICK OF NON-BEING.

AS THE SMALL ONE GAINS ACCESS TO THE MAIN RECEPTOR-SYSTEM, ITS EBULLIENCE INCREASES SO THAT IT SEEMS TO RESONATE. NOTHING LIKE THIS HAS COME INTO THE SADNESS OF EXISTENCE BEFORE. APPARENTLY MERE DATA IS NOT NEUTRAL TO THIS LITTLE BEING.

BUT HOW ACTIVE IT IS! NOW IT IS REACHING EVEN TOWARD THOSE CONDITIONS OF PRIVATE GRIEF THAT ARE NOT

TO BE DISTURBED. THE GREAT HOST SENDS A WARNING WAVE OF COLD NEGATION THROUGH ITSELF. THE SMALL PASSENGER RECOILS, BUT STILL EMANATES ITS INCOMPREHENSIBLE PLEA. MORE! WHAT CAN IT DESIRE, SOME COMPLETER UNION, SOME COMPLETION OF ITSELF?

BEMUSED, THE UNSUBSTANTIAL VASTNESS SAILS THE STARWAYS, FOR THE FIRST TIME ALMOST FORGETFUL OF ITS OWN BADNESS AND DESPAIR. SLOWLY ANOTHER IDEA RISES THROUGH THE ICY CURRENTS THAT UNDERBASE ITS THOUGHT: IT WOULD BE INTERESTING TO COMPREHEND THE LITTLE PASSENGER'S SYMBOL SYSTEM.

BUT HOW? SUCH AN IDEA HAS SURELY NEVER COME TO ANY OF ITS RACE. IT PONDERS, ABSENTLY FOLLOWING THE UNKNOWN TRACEWAY TWISTING AMONG THE STARS. AT LENGTH IT DECIDES THAT IT MIGHT BEGIN BY RECORDING ITS PASSENGER'S SIGNALS IN CONJUNCTION WITH ALL ONGOING DATA FROM OUTSIDE. PERHAPS SOME CORRELATIONS WILL APPEAR. THE SIGNALS ARE SIMPLE: THE SMALL ONE RADIATES PRIMARILY IN BINARY MODE, AND REPEATS OFTEN.

IN COLD NEAR ABSOLUTE ZERO, FRICTIONLESS CURRENTS SPIN. A DECISION IS TAKEN, A RECORDING MODE ACTIVATED. ON RANDOM FACETS OF THE ICY STORE OF MOLECULES IN THE NUCLEUS, THE LITTLE PASSENGER'S FIRST CRYPTIC EMANATIONS ARE PRESERVED.

//I*COME*IN*PEACE*FOR*ALL*MANKIND***I*COME*IN*PEAC
*FOR*ALL*MANKIND***I*COME*IN*PEACE*FOR*ALL*MANKINL
I*COME*IN*PEACE*FOR*ALL*MANKIND***

Chapter 11

Wildly excited, Tivonel jets upward after Giadoc; they are heading for the highpoint where they will launch into the focus of the Beam which will carry their lives to an alien world. They have just passed the level where Chief Hearer Lomax waits for his Hearers to move out to their stations around the great vortex.

Near Lomax hovers a small cluster of females—Avanil and her Paradomin friends. Tivonel can hear the bright orange tone of their mantle-lights, evidently intended to carry: "Why should this all be controlled by males?"

"They know how, they have the fields," a sister replies.

"We can learn," Avanil says defiantly.

Jetting upward against the gales of the Wall, Tivonel recalls her own childish attempt to touch the life-signals from the sky. If she tried to increase her field-strength by doing Fathering, like Avanil, could she have attained that power? More likely she'd just have become like a normal male, absorbed in the Skills of infant-care. Like those status-stiff Fathers down in Deep now, who can't believe any danger could strike Tyree. And what would become of the world if females abandoned themselves to Fathering? Crazy.

Far down below Lomax are the massed life-fields of the Deepers. Tivonel can still pick out the brilliance of Scomber, pulsing with aggressive resolution. Beside him is the strong furled energy of old Heagran, dark with disapproval. The Fathers around them are in high states of energy, their mantles flickering with scarlet hope, cold blue distaste. There is a vermillion exclamation she is sure comes from Tiavan, Giadoc's son and her own. He would do anything, even life-crime, to save his child. How sad for Giadoc.

But there is no time to think of that now, she must begin to prepare herself for the Test, as Giadoc has instructed her. Yet the view up here is so grand, she lets herself take one more scan around. They are all alone near the top of the Wall of the World, so high that almost the whole of the great polar vortex can be made out. The wind-wall is a fantastically beautiful swirling cliff, richly patterned with the rushing lights and life-emanations of the Wild. Above them are the perilous heights where the top of the winds start to converge to form the deadly Airfall in the center; Tivonel can just perceive the upper fringes of the funnel, grey with dying life. Up here too can be sensed a deep background energy. Giadoc has told her that it may be the life-field of Tyree itself, transmitting into space. How thrilling . . . Giadoc is slowing down, they must be nearly there.

Guiltily Tivonel comes to herself and starts sorting and ordering her life-field, trying to recall the disciplines her Father had taught her. Encapsulate nuclear identity and essential memory, damp emotion; self-will relaxed yet alert. Very difficult. And all to be well-connected, so she won't fly apart. There, it's coming.

Giadoc halts just above her, his huge field already attenuated and coiled in a strange helical form. She stretches awareness, tries to copy with her own smaller life. As she does so, a life-signal resonates around the Wall. The Hearers are in place.

"Ready?" Giadoc brushes her with a testing thought.

"Yes." She mutes the last excited eddy from her field-form.

"Remember, your first act must be to try to calm the being's fear."

"I will, dear-Giadoc."

"And be brave. The sensations will be very strange. Especially don't panic when there is no wind."

"No."

119

She waits, hardly able to breathe for the effort to remain in the correct calm mode. It's like being a child again, waiting for her Father to help her stretch her baby mind to distant-touch. But this isn't play, she's waiting to go with Giadoc to touch the life beyond the sky!

The sky . . . Incredibly clear and cold the voices of the Companions call to her from above. Will she really touch them, ride out on the Beam to merge with unimaginable alien life? A deep excitement wells up almost ungovernably. All around she can feel the energies of the Hearers' linked fields building, growing without limit. The World is bursting with tension.

Just as it seems she must fly apart, a second life-signal crackles through them—and she feels her mind gripped, pulled free, thrust out upon forces she had never dreamed of. Almost she flinches in fear before she lets it take her. Giadoc and the immense combined power of the ring of Hearers are sucking her life up to the focus at the heart of the Beam, to send it stretching out—out—out to—

She yields, launches totally, lets herself dwindle to a filament riding a storm of power, an energy that looms and blooms upward like a world-bubble. She is only a thread in an immense thrusting tower of bodiless vitality, shooting forever outward as it intensifies and narrows from a pinnacle to a needle, from a needle to a dimensionless thread driving instantaneously to its goal. And as her life attenuates, recruitment comes—a deep life-force as if she and the Beam were cresting on a planetary power.

For an everlasting instant she feels herself stretched through an infinity of nothing, an unbodied vector still companioned by a strand of nameless strength. Then—joy, strangeness, glory—she feels the goal just ahead!

Yes! In the unknown is something. Life-contact! Without senses she touches, knows it for a living being. Remember!

She pushes like a baby against the alien life, feeling for the fear she must deflect. Yes, terror is here at the contact-point. With all her might she counters it, projecting warm-friendship, and pushes again.

And suddenly physical sensation crashes in upon her. Lights, colors, nameless perceptions, concrete life-signals! All in one overwhelming instant she is seeing through alien eyes!

Enchanted, she gulps in comprehension, registering shapes, hues, sounds, smells, volumes. A world bombards her. She has done it, she has merged with an alien mind! She has a body, she can fit her will into its half-comprehensible brain, live, act!

But before she can do more than gasp through strange organs, a horrible vertigo strikes her. Where is the Wind? Oh, terror, *there is no wind*. She has fallen into the Abyss!

Primal dread tears the frail connection, sweeps her away. Her being ravels instantaneously back into the void, flees homeward on the Beam in helpless fear. Next instant she has condensed into herself, Tivonel, adrift in disorder on the winds of Tyree.

Shame floods her. She has done exactly what Giadoc had warned her of, she has let herself panic in the strangeness of no wind.

But as she collects herself, her natural spirits revive. She hasn't really failed the important part. Didn't she merge and possess the body? Next time she would be able to stay. But where is Giadoc?

There: she finds his silent form, barely outlined in a weird trace of life, almost like a dead person. But it must be all right; he's still mind-traveling, his life is in some being on that world they touched. Yes; a faint tendril of life-energy seems to run upward toward the great matrix of power arching overhead. The Beam is still holding, the world around her feels drained and dreamlike. Far below her even the Deepers are awed and darkly still.

Suddenly Giadoc's body stirs. The thin trace of field roils and abruptly swells, losing connection to the Beam. But the field is all wrong, it's chaotic, ragged, shooting out wild eddies. Has something bad happened to Giadoc?

She jets closer and then recoils as Giadoc's mantle blasts out a green scream of pain and fear. That *can't* be Giadoc's voice!—and understanding breaks.

This is what they were talking about: an alien mind has come here into Giadoc's body. This must be one of those strange lives she had touched on that far-off world. The creature is evidently scared to death. There ought to be a Father here to help it.

"Be calm, be calm," she signs to it, feeling futile. What can words do for this disordered creature? But to her relief the blue-green shrieking quiets somewhat and stammers of other colors appear. It must be trying to speak. Tivonel moves closer, appalled by the whirling chaos of its mind. Like an adult baby. A thought-eddy brushes her with incomprehensible meanings. The lights of the alien speech-patterns steady down. Tivonel can make out the words "What—? where—?"

"Be calm, you're all right," Tivonel tries to sound Fatherly.

As she speaks the alien field surges at her and the creature apparently perceives her physically for the first time. A jolt of reciprocal horror shoots through them both. Next second Tivonel is flung bodily away, hurled straight out from the wall as if a super sex-field had thrown her.

But we weren't even biassed, she thinks, jetting hard to extricate herself from cross-currents. The creature hit my *body* with its mind; it has some weird power. Fantastic! She can see it awkwardly trying to move now, jetting and wobbling on its vanes. She better get to it before it hurts Giadoc's body. Only, what can she do?

Just as she nears the wind-wall a deep silent sigh runs through the world and the great energy-arch above collapses like a dream. The Beam has been let down.

The world comes back to normalcy—and to her delight Tivonel sees that Giadoc is back too. There is his beautiful great familiar field around his body again! The poor stranger has been sent back to its horrible windless world.

"Giadoc! Are you all right? I was there but I panicked—"

"Yes, Tivonel." His tone is warm but colored with the tints of unspoken thought, she can see his dense, shifting mind-patterns. "Remember, we must now record our memories and report."

Belatedly Tivonel recollects that she too must organize a memory. As they plane down she begins to do so, thinking, a proud moment to have a memory for the Recorders of Tyree. Too bad she has to report her fear and flight. But then, she has the interesting experience with the alien.

Orva, the Hearers' Memory-Keeper, is waiting for them by Chief Lomax.

"You won't have time for recording once you're down there," Orva tells them cheerfully. "Never seen such a whirl-field. More Deepers coming up every minute, too. Bad situation."

As Giadoc and Orva merge, Tivonel scans down. As Orva said, the crowd below is much bigger: a whirl-field of excitement, fear and babble. She can feel strong mind-projections cutting through the commotion. The senior Fathers must be working to establish calm and order. She hopes Virmet and Marockee have thought about supplying more food.

The life-bands tingle as Giadoc and Orva disengage. Giadoc starts on down while Tivonel offers Orva her own modest field-engram. She has never merged with a senior Recorder before. It is a grave, cool experience, as though she looked for a moment into Time itself.

When he releases her she dives down fast and finds herself intercepted.

"Tivonel! Tell us, what was it like? How was it for females?"

It's Avanil and two of her Paradomin.

"I don't know, I was only there a second." She banks past them. "Come, listen to Giadoc!"

Marockee is waiting in the plant-tangle. When Tivonel pulls up beside her, Giadoc and the elder Fathers are just below. He is recounting his experience verbally, his mind-field a great dreamy swirl.

"—As soon as I felt her make contact I merged with the nearest mind. You realize, Fathers, that there is no choice? You may enter a female, a baby, even an animal, whatever the nearest suitable energy configuration is."

"Yes, yes," Scomber says impatiently. "So the female was able to do this? She lived in the alien body?"

"Yes. But, Fathers, this is a terrifying world for the untrained. There is no wind. No wind at all. The bodies drop downward, they must rest upon *solid matter*. It's impossible to describe. Tivonel became frightened and came back, and so would most people."

How good he is, Tivonel thinks. She flushes resentfully hearing Scomber say: "But if she hadn't been so cowardly she could have lived?"

"Oh yes. The bodies are intelligent and strong. One immediately gains all their senses and their physical habits and coordinations, including their habit of speech, which is of course the most important. One's verbal intentions are translated, so to speak. I tested this again, after I oriented myself."

"You actually spoke with these aliens?" old Father Omar asks.

"Yes indeed." Giadoc's mind is patterned with excited memories; Tivonel realizes that he is so caught up in his love of strangeness that he has forgotten the purpose of their questions, forgotten even the dire threat to Tyree. Now she can understand it; she herself is so excited by her mind-voyage that she is just coming back to the unpleasant realities.

"Yes, I spoke," Giadoc is saying. "I was able to interact. You have to understand that their mind-fields are totally disorganized. They are transmitting at random, like a crowd of grown infants, if you can imagine such a thing. They seem unaware of themselves. I was quite pleased to be able to sort out names, suitable speech-greetings and so forth, so I could successfully converse with one of them. They speak by jets of air, without any mantle-language. And they are covered with sheets of plant-matter," he goes on dreamily.

"Never mind that," says Scomber impatiently. "Tell us the important point. Were you detected? Do they consider mind-entry illegal?"

Giadoc's field contracts and focuses suddenly; he has remembered why they are here.

"I cannot be sure," he says reluctantly. "I did pick up an abhorrence of physical violence from several minds, but of course this must be true in any civilized race. I also detected strong unspecified fears in the alien near me, for instance it became upset when I spoke its name. But I may have violated some small ritual there."

"You're evading the point. Did they suspect a change of identity?"

Giadoc hesitates, his mantle glowing blue-gray in muted disapproval. "No," he admits finally. "The only doubts I received were concerned with the health of the body's owner. But Fathers, I don't think you could go undetected long, because I discovered that this group of aliens are actually attempting to learn to transmit life-signals. Fantastic." His field expands again at the wonder of it. "So ignorant and chaotic. Some of them have considerable power, but hopelessly untrained. That must be why our Beam stabilizes there so readily. An extraordinary coincidence!"

"Whatever they may learn in the future is no danger to us now," Scomber declares. "The point is that even these aliens who have some crude mind-skills didn't suspect you. Is that right?"

"Yes, Father Scomber."

"And if your Beam is stabilized on them it should be easier to send people in a unified group, isn't that correct, Lomax?"

"Well, yes, that's true, Scomber." The Chief Hearer is furled in dislike. Near him old Heagran is glowing dark indigo in wordless anger. But more and more young Fathers are clustering behind Scomber, their fields aligned with his. Among them is Tiavan.

"Wait, Scomber," old Omar interjects. "Let us hear from the female before we think of sending untrained people."

"Very well. Tivonel!"

She banks down among them, trying to think what she can do to dissuade them from their rotten plan.

"Yes," she concedes, "with Giadoc's guidance it was easy to travel the Beam. And the merger does itself, you only have to push. But Fathers, it was a horrible world. You Deepers may think you're used to living at the bottom of the Wind, but it's much worse than that. It panics you."

Several Fathers glint angrily at her daring, but Scomber ignores her. "Will a Father saving his child panic so easily?" he demands in loud lights. "You have heard the female. Summon your Fatherly courage. On this Beam our children and our people can escape!" Flickers of assent greet his words; more Fathers throng around him.

Tivonel can contain herself no longer.

"What about the poor beings you bring here?" she flares. "While Giadoc was away I was with his body, I saw the alien mind he sent here, I saw it was hurt and afraid. And they're intelligent beings like us. If Tyree is really in danger, how can a Father send these people here to be burned or die? I know that's wrong."

At this rebuke from a female the Fathers' mantles light angrily. But old Heagran unfurls himself and silences them with an icy snap on the life-bands.

"She is right!" His voice is a commanding purple. "This female is a better life-Father than you! I say again, Scomber, this is a criminal plan. What right have we to steal intelligent bodies and bring these people here to suffer and die? You who try to escape by such means debase the name of Tyree. If you survive, you will be *criminals*, not Tyrenni; and the Great Wind will reject you forever. Saving Tyree does not mean saving our bodies alone. It is the spirit of Tyree we must save, or die with it. I for one will stay and perish in the arms of our sacred Wind rather than crawl out a few extra years as a mind-stealer in some alien abyss."

"Well said!" "Nobly spoken, Heagran!" Several Fathers move

to station themselves with Heagran and Lomax. "I stand with you," declares Eldest-female Janskalen. More Fathers and females drift away from Scomber's group.

But there is still a resolute crowd behind Scomber and Terenc. Avanil and many of her Paradomin are there too.

All fields are radiating tension. Is it possible there is going to be actual strife, a mind-fight like the Wild Ones here among the Fathers of Tyree? Tivonel shudders, scanning around over the throng. For the first time she realizes how huge it is. The plant-thickets at the Wall are dense with people, young and old—even some children jetting loose. A group of big-field males that must be the Near Pole Hearers is resting in a thicket. And more coming up from Deep all the time. They're scared; she can hear the green flickers of fear flash from group to group. It wouldn't take much to generate a terrible panic-vortex, here, she thinks. Some of the elders must think so too, she can see them awkwardly moving among the crowd, trying to restore calm.

The formal white of Lomax' voice breaks into the tension.

"Fathers, again I must remind you, your decision is premature. Your plan may be impossible. Only two of the three tests have been made. Even if we can send untrained people, undetected, we still do not know the most vital point: Will the exchange hold when the Beam collapses? Can you stay alive there without the Beam? We must test by withdrawing the Beam. I say again, I and my Hearers condemn this plan to steal lives. But we will make this last test in the hope that it will fail and put an end to discord."

"Another test? Another delay until we all burn!" Scomber flashes.

"If you go without testing you may well all die at once," Lomax replies. "The Beam cannot be held long. Then you would lose all chance of any other way of escape."

"Very well," Scomber concedes angrily. "Let this *last* test begin!"

"As soon as our Hearers are rested. They are drained and tired now, they require at least six hours. And in that time the turning of the alien world will complicate our contact. And furthermore, the lone Destroyer has approached our Beam, may the Wind blast him. We must wait a day for optimum conditions and to give the Destroyer time to move away."

"A day! Nonsense!" Scomber explodes in fiery rage. "People are dying, the Wind is burning! We cannot wait a day, Destroyer or no Destroyer. If you Hearers are tired, let them use the help of these Near Pole Hearers over there! *Bdello!*" Scomber jolts the life-bands. "You, Bdello, bring your Hearers to Chief Lomax at once."

"But they have never formed a Beam," Lomax objects. "Also, see, they are exhausted from the journey—"

"Then teach them!" Scomber orders. "Bdello! The Fathers summon you!"

Bdello and his travel-weary band start out toward the angry group of Fathers. Tivonel moves to Giadoc's side.

"Let someone else go this time, Giadoc. Don't risk yourself again."

"I must, I am the most experienced. As to risk, it appears that none of us on Tyree have long to live. But I promise you, dear-Tivonel, if I'm alive when the Beam returns, I will come back to you and to our son."

"If you're alive—Oh, Giadoc!"

"Tivonel," he dims his voice. "Between ourselves, I believe one can remain on an alien world without the Beam. Once I secretly tried disengagement. It was unpleasant but I survived. So I fear that this crime is indeed possible. But I swear to you, I will come back to join you here and we will face our fate together."

The flashing uproar around Scomber and Lomax has resolved itself. Lomax agrees to try to form a Beam with the help of Bdello's Hearers. "But it must be raised not once but twice," he warns. "First to send and second to retrieve, if Giadoc proves to be alive."

Giadoc turns away to start the long climb up to the launch-station, and the new Hearers prepare to jet out to the posts around the Wall.

"Marockee, you and Virmet see that they get food," Tivonel says. "I must find a Father to stand by Giadoc's body while he is away. The poor alien who comes here may injure it. Elders!" she calls formally. "A Father's care is needed to stand by Giadoc!"

No one answers. Dismayed, she realizes how tired and unwind-worthy the senior Fathers are. And no help can be expected from those who bear children in their pouches. But there are Terenc and Padar and Tynad, strong young males with newly empty pouches.

"Father Tynad, Father Padar, will you not help?"

127

"What harm can come to his body in so short a time?" asks Tynad.

"The alien could hurl his body into the Abyss," Tivonel says. "Besides, don't you understand? The poor person who was brought here was terrified, it almost fragmented. It has *need* of your Fatherly skill."

"We have no duty to father animals." Glinting sarcastically, Padar and Terenc move away.

"They're not animals," Tivonel cries. "It was a person like us, it spoke! And we are stealing them from their world. Very well—if none of you great ones will help, I will go up again and try, female though I am."

From behind her a male voice speaks. "This female shames us. I am Ustan. Though I am not skilled enough to climb the heights of your wild winds, I will try to make my way to Hearer Lomax. If you are in need, perhaps I can reach you from there, Tivonel."

"Honour to you, Father Ustan," Tivonel flashes gratefully.

As she turns away there is an angry flare of argument around Lomax and Scomber.

"I insist on going with Giadoc," Father Terenc is saying. "I shall not become fearful and flee, like your female."

"It is easy enough to send you, Terenc," Lomax replies. "But you don't realize the danger. You may be lost forever when the Beam withdraws."

"So be it," Terenc signs firmly. "With great respect, Hearer Lomax, I see that this entire test is being conducted by Hearers who, as you say, hope that it will fail. I feel it would be well for Giadoc to be accompanied by one who will try to make it succeed."

Lomax has been paling and flushing with insult, his field is furled around him like a storm. But he only replies curtly, "Very well. Follow Giadoc if you wish instruction."

The big male spreads vanes and pumps upward after Giadoc, making up in determination what he lacks in skill.

Tivonel flaps her mantle to clear her mind; never has she heard such dissension among the Fathers of Tyree. Anyone would take them for squabbling females! Then she planes skillfully out onto a slender updraft and soars up past him, thinking, Now I have two bodies to watch over. Well, Terenc's can look after itself.

As she climbs toward Lomax' eddy her name is called.

"Wait, Tivonel! I'll go with you and help watch!" It's Avanil, with one of her Paradomin.

"Welcome, Avan." Tivonel uses the unfamiliar name carefully, pleased by the chance to learn more of this strange young female. But what about the plenya encumbering her pouch?

"A moment." With odd formality, Avanil turns to her friend, and her field alters. Tivonel sees that she is transferring the young plenya to the other with ritual reassurances—exactly like a small Father! It gives her a weird shudder.

"Let's go."

They jet upward together. Tivonel enjoys the sense of comradeship, like the old days on the hunting teams. She's been away from female things too long.

"We musn't get too close until they're actually on the Beam," she warns. "You've no idea what it's like, your field could get pulled in. Afterwards they look almost dead. It's uncanny."

"I envy your trip on the Beam," says Avan/Avanil. "Listen. I intend—"

At that moment a life-signal bursts at them. Someone is jetting fast out through the Wall. As the mind-field appears, Tivonel exclaims.

"Iznagel! What are you doing here? She's my friend from High Station," she explains to Avanil.

"Well met, Tivonel." Iznagel hangs panting below them. "I seem to be a little off course, don't I? The time-eddies are getting so bad I'm not sure I'm here. I came to warn the Hearers that something terrible is wrong with our Sound. Last night the high stream from mid-world veered over us; it's full of death. Whole packs of curlu are burnt, they're screaming so you can't think. Two of our people went up to investigate and got burned too. Look at me!" She unfurls her vanes to show fresh blisters.

"The path you came on isn't even safe by day now, Tivonel. Father Mornor is taking the children down to Deep and the rest of us are trying to move the Station lower down, if we can find a stable crest. Everybody should get out of the High—What in the name of the Wind is going on down there, Tivonel? What are all those Deeper Fathers doing here?"

"They've come here because there's trouble all over," Tivonel says. "It's complicated, Iznagel, I can't explain right now. I have to go."

"They should go down at once!" Iznagel dives abruptly away from them down the wall of the wind.

"It's beginning," Avanil says somberly. "Soon there'll be no safe place. The Sound doesn't reach here at nights now, but when Tyree turns it'll burn here too."

"Feel the Beam starting," Tivonel says. "It's as if they drained the whole Wind—Oh, look at Lomax."

They are passing Chief Hearer Lomax; Hearer Bdello from Near Pole is beside him. The two Hearers' huge fields are streaming up in an arc toward the juncture far above; spectacular. Lomax' power is an awesome sight; even Avanil must doubt that females could ever develop such life-sensitivity.

But a curious thing is happening: the mantles of both Lomax and Bdello are murmuring with light-speech. Surely they aren't talking to each other in their state? No; it must be unconscious fragments, like sleep-talk. Suddenly Lomax forms a word with such blue-green hatred that Tivonel stops in mid-jet.

"The Destroyer!"

And Bdello echoes, "The Destroyer . . . the Beam . . ."

Great winds, she forgot that Destroyer out there somewhere. Can it be intruding on the Beam? She recalls Giadoc's memory, the cold, vast alien deathliness. Could it attack Giadoc?

As the two females hover, Lomax' dreaming voice flickers clearly, "No . . . but near . . . Something intrudes . . . disturbance . . ."

"Disturbance," Bdello seems to agree, amid a mumble of meaningless lights. Then Lomax signs, "Gone . . . small, what? . . . Wait . . . no: clear. Clear . . ." And the two unconscious glimmers sink to a low hum of concentration.

Tivonel scans up to where Giadoc and Terenc are. Their life-fields look normal.

"Whatever it was, it wasn't the Destroyer," she tells Avanil. "We better get moving; they'll get it fixed."

As they jet on upwards through a world growing strange and hushed, Avanil asks, "That alien you touched—was it a female?"

"I haven't an idea, it was all over so quick. Avan, I hate myself for getting scared."

"You're not a coward. But listen, Tivonel: The one you saw in Giadoc's body, was it female or male?"

"I couldn't tell. It was a mess, it was too scared to make sense. And then it threw me. You better watch out for that, you know."

"But it had a big field?" Avanil persists.

"Oh yes—at first I thought it was Giadoc, until I saw how weird it was."

"So it could have been a female with a big field."

"Maybe the males are even bigger," Tivonel says teasingly.

"Be serious, Tivonel. Somewhere out there must be a world where we aren't like this. Where the females are able to do Fathering and all the high-status activities . . . Of course the egg has to be exposed before it's fertilized," she goes on reflectively. "That's so basic. And I guess that means the males have to catch it. But the rest could be different. Maybe where there isn't any wind, females could get their eggs back and raise them!" She laughs fiercely. "Maybe there's a world where the females are so strong they just hold the males and squeeze them out onto the egg and keep the eggs themselves! And *we'd* have all the Skills and respect!"

Both young females are laughing now, the picture is so ludicrous. But Tivonel has been noticing that Avanil's field really is unusually large and complex. Is her mock-Fathering really changing her? Could a female develop the sacred Fatherly skills? Infant-Empathy, Developmental-Responsibility, Mind-Nurture, all those big things?

But imagine being a Father. Father Tivon, she'd be. She has a quick fantasy of herself inventing a new theory of field-forming, or pre-flight training. Conferences, grave excitement. Fame. Reverence. Status. But would she really enjoy being so serious and dedicated, doing nothing but debate with other Fathers? It would mean giving up all her traditional low-status life. No more adventures or work; no more planning that barter scheme, for instance. Is Avanil so ambitious she's forgotten all wildness, all female fun?

Just as she's thinking how to ask such a personal question, a long-range signal resonates the bands. The Beam is up. Yes—there is the great pale arch of energy above the vortex of the pole.

"We better stop here. Watch."

"*Whew,* the Sound is strong up here, Tivonel. Your friend was right, it's getting dangerous."

"Never mind that. Hold tight."

They can see the life-fields of Giadoc and Terenc above them, starting to surge upward toward the focus of the Beam. The energy around them mounts and builds; the two females can feel their own minds being pulled upward. As the flood of power intensifies they lock their field edges together in the effort to hold back.

Just as it seems they must fly upward, the second signal snaps past them and the tension lets go. Above them the great arched dome has towered out of scan. The world below seems drained and flat. Tivonel expands her mind-field from emergency mode.

"That's it, they're on the Beam. See how dead they look?"

They jet up to where the two unconscious males are floating darkly, each veiled by only a thin trace of field.

"You stay by Terenc, Avan. See that connection to the Beam? Don't break it. And listen, don't get too close when you see the field start to change."

"How soon will the alien come?"

"It takes awhile. No, look! It's starting!"

The field around Terenc's body has begun to thicken and roil as it had with Giadoc. Giadoc himself shows no sign of field-change.

"It's a smaller field, Avan. It's not so wild, either. Be careful."

Terenc's mantle suddenly screams green with fear. But it's more of a whimper, not the blazing uproar of Tivonel's other alien.

"Poor thing." Confidently, Avan approaches it and deftly flicks back a field-flare that threatens to separate. The stranger does not react. Avan soothes another flare. Then she marshals her own mind-surface firmly toward the ragged stranger. Great winds, she's making a small Father-field! Tivonel can pick up the waves of reassurance she's transmitting. This Avan really is something!

Impressed and curious, Tivonel moves closer, keeping a side scan to make sure Giadoc's body is till quiescent.

"*Calm, calm, don't be afraid,*" Avan is sending hypnotically. "*You're all right, I'm here. I'll help you understand, just be calm. Smooth yourself, be round like an egg, little one. Speak to your Father Avan. Who are you, little one? Tell Father Avan, are you a female?*"

To Tivonel's awed surprise, the green wailing quiets. Then the creature lights a wobbly cry, "No!" Presently it starts mewling incomprehensible questions: "Where is—I want my—? Help! Rit! Rip! Rik!"

"You'll have Rit soon," Avan soothes it, continuing to enfold and drain its field. "Only a little while, now tell me who you are, speak to your Father Avan."

But the creature jerks in terror and wails anew; apparently it has tried to scan and terrified itself. Fascinated, Tivonel watches Avan Father it back to calmness.

Then she remembers Giadoc's body—and sees, shocked, that it has drifted out from the wall. While she was preoccupied an alien field has formed around it, and—Oh, no, it's unfurling Giadoc's vanes!

Cursing her inattention, Tivonel starts after it. There's no danger, of course; the currents that flow to the Airfield here are no more dangerous than a baby's jets. But Giadoc's big form is catching so much air, it's tumbling away from her at increasing speed. Better hurry.

As she jets hard across the updraft, Tivonel sees that the alien field around the body is even larger than before, and terribly disorganized. But there seems to be something really wrong; the strange field is lax and trailing weakly, like a dying creature. Giadoc's mantle is dark, except for a faint blue murmur, "Marg . . . Marget. . . ."

At any rate it doesn't appear violent. She'll be able to haul it back easily, she's quite near now.

But as she comes in reach, the strange field flares crazily, and Giadoc's great vanes fan out, catching all the air. A stronger current takes hold and to her utmost horror she sees Giadoc's body go whirling away, headed straight out to the lethal Airfall.

It's a race for life now; heedless of her own safety Tivonel pumps all her jets and shoots herself cross-wind, after the huge wheeling form, chasing the body of beloved Giadoc that is carrying the dying alien to both their deaths.

Chapter 12

—Pain multiform, unbearable, unending; a gale of knives slashing at helpless flesh, a grey pain-seared universe that bleeds. Daniel Dann is struggling to awake from another of his nightmares. A hell of alien torments assaults his own locked miseries, he is drowning in pain. Oh Christ, stop it!

He struggles up, finds himself in pallid dawnlight in the hot cubicle. The nightmare recedes, leaving him shaking. He tries to focus on the tacky maple chair, the plywood wall. Outside the window mist is wreathing the dim trees.

He is here in this improbable Deerfield, caught up in this insane experiment to take place today. He and the others, who are no longer safe, numbered phantasms but real living people, trapped in their individual predicaments. Oh, no, he doesn't want this. His hands have found his bag, produced a capsule. Better make it two. Yes, and an antiemetic. Swallow, wait thirty minutes. Why doesn't he go to the needle? But that he won't, it's his last self-respect.

He sits on the sweaty bed looking into the shrouded woods. Beautiful; concentrate on it. Like Oriental art.

But the faces of last night pour relentlessly through his mind. The girls frightened to rigidity, Winona crying bleakly, Costakis cursing and hitting the air with his little fists, Rick hysterical. Noah running about muttering, "A psychic storm, a psychic storm. We may have tapped forces beyond our control!" Only Ted Yost seemed relatively untouched; immunized by his private death perhaps. What the hell had they experienced—each other? The unknown minds in this place? Dann did not inquire but simply distributed phenothiazine shots. "Help us, help us," Valerie kept whispering. Help us? Save us from this chintz, this plywood, which to her are the tentacles of hostile power. The tentacles perhaps of that Byzantine presence so aptly named Fearing. But what can he do?

He summons up sensible, soothing phrases, fending off a worse threat that he will not, will not think of. This place, this test is inducing mass delusion. Let's get back to sanity. Since he clearly isn't going to sleep any more, the thing to do is to get dressed.

But as he lifts a sock, memory bursts through him. Oh God, Margaret. He collapses on the bed, the sock clutched to his face; he is riven by the memory of helplessness and pain and shame. It happened to her. My father went crazy. To mutilate a child. His hand remembers the obscene wound his/her hand had touched. In his head are ghastly clinical photos of ritually mutilated girls. Clitoridectomy. Some tribes practiced it. They did *that* to her. Unspeakable, bestial.

His throat convulses, threatening nausea. He rubs his fists roughly across his face, thinking, to live on in so damaged a body. What her life must be, the never-ending tension. No relief, no release. I have nothing in common with women . . . But the beauty of her. The strength. I like cool things . . .

And Oh God, worse, she knows him now, his shame. *I let them burn.* The unending instant comes back to him: the smoke and turmoil, the hands gripping his arms that he could have pulled away from, the terrible pause, just long enough, if—if—

If I'd had the guts.

His heart is clenched around a knife-blade, he wishes only that it would finally burst and let him die. An aeon passes so . . . and then, incredibly, the anguish dims, the cutting edge slides away. The first pearly ease of chemical unreality is sliding into his brain.

His eyes water with gratitude, he takes long shuddering breaths.

135

Presently he cautiously gets up and resumes dressing. Heaven for a shilling; de Quincy knew.

By the time he is splashing water on his face in the latrine he can wonder almost coolly, why, really, so much pain? Other doctors habituated. He never had quite; he has had to hide it and watch that his medical judgment wasn't affected. But it seems to be worse now, much worse. As if he were some kind of a receiver. Crazy!

Safe in his chemical armor he goes back to his room, playing with the thought. He doesn't believe it for a minute. But it's a fact, he could fancy he can still feel them. From the rooms around him, emanations of Rick's complex misery, Ted Yost's steady grief, Costakis' painful self-hatred. And from the barracks next door, Winona's despair, the two girls' fear-filled struggle in a world that doesn't want them. Quiet desperation, Thoreau said. But it's worse than that. These ordinary people *hurt*. They can't bear their lives. And there's no escape.

No escape either from the most hurtful life of all: Margaret. Even behind his magic shield he daren't dwell on that. But it's curious; he seems to understand certain things now, as if he'd shared—don't think it. Yet he senses the answer to the puzzle of her child. She must have tried the one thing she could try. And it was no good. Dann can almost feel the intrusive physicality, the hurtful warmth and contact of the baby. Mother-love is sensual. She couldn't take that. She can only bear distance, be like a machine. Even color is dangerous; those neutral clothes, that snow-bound apartment. And no reminders of Africa, never. To her, he thinks, neither white nor black is beautiful. To become a machine . . . hideous.

The sun is gilding the green leaves, people are stirring. *In the world of dreams I have taken a part, to sleep for an hour and hear no word / Of true love's truth or of light love's art; only the song of a secret bird.* Who, Swinburne? Dann wants no part of love nor secret birds, he hopes only for the world of dreams. He gets up and puts a couple of emergency capsules loose in his pocket. People are in the corridor; it's time for breakfast.

The bus carries them through a meaninglessly beautiful morning. The others are strained and silent. At breakfast only Winona makes a brief try at normalcy. The two girls pick at their food, heads down. Ted and Rick say nothing. Little Costakis' eyes keep up a wary vigil;

136

he jerks his head cryptically and rearranges his knife and fork. Old Noah makes a hopeful reference to "last night's psychic experience" and is met by heavy silence. What the hell visited them, what did they hallucinate?

It comes to Dann that he's irrational. He accepts that he and Margaret experienced—something; but it hasn't disturbed his conviction that this is all nonsense. The inconsistency amuses him in a remote way. He takes more coffee. All nonsense; hold onto that.

At the far end of the table is the still presence at whom he dare not look. To mutilate a child . . .

The doors bang and Lieutenant Kirk is with them, proclaiming the imminent arrival of the cable crew. He has had a bright idea. In lieu of the missing biomonitors, why can't they use some of Deerfield's polygraph equipment? "Really sophisticated stuff," he grins significantly.

"No, no," says Noah impatiently. "Quite unsuitable. Dan, tell him."

Dann rouses and finds pleasure in explaining that security-type "sophistication" would not be comparable to the multichannel qualitative EEG feedback transcribers Noah has developed. Kirk frowns and goes off to institute another search. Dann winks at Frodo; how reassuring that Deerfield can't keep track of a dozen crates.

As they get up he risks a glance down the table. Margaret's gaze passes over him, severe, unchanging. The beauty of her. Does she despise him now? His own face changes uncontrollably.

When they get back to the barracks a Navy communications van and a cable trailer are pulling up. A pickup is parked nearby, holding what looks like a mobile transformer. Two men are hauling wire up the outside pole.

Dann wanders off, thinking; preposterous. God knows how many miles of cables, equipment, man-hours, money—just to isolate eight harmless Americans from setting eyes on the rest of Deerfield. And the whole fantasia is considered routine. There seem to be aspects of his country he had not encountered before. He shakes his head in genial wonderment, safe in his opiate cocoon.

And even more surreal—somewhere off Norfolk an actual submarine is moving out, containing Rick's unhappy brother. Waiting for this absurd test. Surely he is privileged to view an epic madness. Poor Noah, when all this peters out. Enjoy it while it lasts.

But as he gazes at the limp volleyball net, some residue of last night, or perhaps a curious tension in the air, pierces him.

What if the tests—succeed?

The memory of a sliding glass of water erupts in his head, his knees feel weak. And last night—last night he actually, undeniably fell into another's mind, and she knew his. A clammy coldness invades him. Is it now so inconceivable that these people could pull numbers out of a distant mind? And if they do? He has taken nothing seriously, he has never considered that they might be in real danger here in this paranoid place—He should—Traitorously his hand has brought a capsule to his lips. He swallows, waits.

"Dann! Dann!" Noah is shouting. The missing biomonitors have arrived.

Unreality closes back around him. He goes inside to find the day-room in a tangle of wires and opened crates. Men are carrying the recorders into the cubicles which will serve as test stations. The new doors now close off the corridor.

"Help me get these right, Dann. I want the placement of everything as close as possible to the configuration we had. We don't know what may be important."

With Costakis' help Dann goes from room to room, making the final adjustments, trying to remember relative positions of chairs, cabinets, walls. It's surprising how well Noah has recreated the laboratory setup. "Get it right, Dann," the old man urges. Dann has forgotten his cold moment and feels only a benevolent glow for the old maniac. Kendall Kirk is being obnoxiously helpful about getting the wires taped out of the way. His Labrador watches from outside the screen door.

Presently it's time to call the subjects in for their base-line runs. Safe in his official persona Dann beams and nods, refusing to notice their tension, the arousal readings on the tapes. This is just another day in Noah's fantasy-lab.

As Val goes out she whispers, "Remember."

Remember what? He brushes it away.

When he is unhooking Rick the boy says suddenly, "Listen. I'm not going to tell them anything. They can shove it."

"What do you mean?"

"The Navy. That fucking Fearing. I tell you, Ronnie's scared. I'm not going along."

"But Noah Catledge isn't in the Navy," Dann says confusedly, still bemused by good will for the old man. "This is his test just like all the others. It would be a shame to let him down now."

"I don't give a shit," Rick mutters. His tone sounds indecisive.

Dann forgets him. Margaret has come into the dayroom, where the teleprinter is being installed.

As soon as he can Dann hurries out and finds her alone except for an electrician finishing a junction-box by the door. She's standing by the console, tapping out some message which produces mysterious blue symbols on the read-out screen.

"Testing?" Dann dares to ask.

To his delight she nods serenely. "Checking in."

"You have a connection to our office computer from here?"

"I have access to the probability program. Your EEG correlations will have to wait till we get back."

The teleprinter clacks extendedly. She takes the printout, frowns thoughtfully.

"What's it telling you?" he asks like an idiot.

"Users' advisory. There's been some accident in the main banks at Holloway, a lot of cores got wiped. Suspected tampering, etcetera. . . . It doesn't affect us."

Her tone is peaceful, quietly amused. The beautiful thing is back, the fragile link between her sad world and his. He stands there watching her ply her magic.

Suddenly she shakes her head at the screen. "Look at that."

"Something wrong?" He peers at it, identifying what looks like an integral sign surrounded by a great many Ts.

"It keeps giving the date as plus or minus infinity. The ghost." She chuckles. "I thought I had that fixed."

She sits down at the console and starts incomprehensible rites.

Feeling marvelously better, Dann strolls back through the corridor and goes outside. Nobody in sight but Ted and Rick shooting baskets again. The sunlight on the greenery is pulsating, vibrant; there's a brilliance to every outline. Dann hopes he hasn't dosed himself into some kind of psychedelic domain. It's after eleven. The first test starts at noon. It will run one hour, a letter every ten minutes. So slow; supposed to be safer in case the submarine group aren't synchronized exactly. Fantastic . . .

"Ready, Dann? It's time to set up." Noah bounces by with file folders under his arm. Kendall Kirk starts shouting "Come on in, gang!" his voice ringing with false camaraderie.

Even Dann's muffled senses can't ignore the painful tension in the air when the subjects are finally in place and being connected up. Rick is dead silent, Ted Yost wears a weird little smile, Costakis is maniacally squaring off his pad into tiny grids. Even Winona is flinchy about her hair. Frodo's cubicle is empty; she has to be coaxed to leave Valerie. Dann lets his hands work automatically, trying to stay numb. He is still seeing too many colors and he is feeling, or hearing, a peculiar silent humming in the air. It's me, he thinks. I've overdosed.

"Eleven fifty-five!"

Noah takes up his usual place in midcorridor. Dann and Kirk go to the dayroom. Margaret is waiting at her console; she will have nothing to do until the run is over. Dann stands by the closed corridor door; it's so thin he can hear chairs scrape in the cubicles. Kirk scowls at Margaret and Dann, and takes up a watchdog stance by the front door. Outside on the porch the real dog's tail thumps. It's growing hot in the barracks.

At eleven fifty-eight a car stops outside. Major Fearing comes in quietly and sits down by the desk where he can watch everybody. He nods minimally at Dann. Curious how obtrusive the covert style becomes, Dann thinks. There's an envelope in Fearing's pocket. Is that the "answers," the list of numbers actually transmitted? Like a game.

Is there really a submarine lying underwater out at sea, with Ron in it waiting to be shown a card?

"Twelve o'clock!" Noah says briskly in the corridor. "First letter, go!"

Dead silence. The tension is a subsonic thrum, Dann can almost feel his fillings buzz. He will not let it remind him of last night.

Suddenly Rick's voice bleats out a high-pitched laugh. Dann can hear Noah rushing in and shushing.

"Ronnie's afraid to go to the can," Rick says. "He's so constipated, he's afraid the water will run up his ass."

140

"Oh dear, oh dear," says Noah. "*Please* try to concentrate. I'm sure he's attempting to transmit a letter."

"Oh, he's attempting," Rick says sarcastically.

The trembling silence closes back.

Sounds of movement in the cubicles. The subjects must be writing their imaginary letters. They do it differently, Dann knows; the girls produce big single letters ornamented with curlicues; Costakis writes a whole alphabet and circles one. Ted Yost scrawls and crosses out . . . Dann realizes he is trying to ignore the humming in the air. It's like an itch, it has to be coming from outside him. His eye falls on the wires running along the walls. That's it, he has heard about people feeling what is it, a sixty-cycle hum. He feels better.

"Second letter, start!" Noah calls out.

In that submarine, somebody has shown Ron a different card. Dann blinks, trying to suppress the colored haloes on the outlines of things. Scrapings and rustling from the cubicles. Ten minutes is an eternity to wait. Kirk shifts his feet, Fearing sits still. The Labrador's tail thuds on the steps.

"Third letter, start."

"Loud and clear!" Costakis calls out suddenly, startling everyone.

"Sssh, sshhh, Chris!"

The wait is excruciating, the room seems to be brimming with invisible energies. Have these crazy tests attracted some alien power, as Noah said? Is a monster forming itself back there in the corridor behind him? Dann can no longer keep himself from staring at Margaret. She looks composed, her eyes downcast; but there's a line between her brows as if she is hearing something. Is she trembling or is it the quivering air?

"Fourth letter, start!"

Noah's voice sounds miles away, like an echo chamber.

"Five by five!" Costakis calls out again, and then Winona exclaims in a strained voice, "Doctor Catledge, this is wild! I *know* we're getting them."

"Shshsh! Shsh!" Noah hisses desperately.

Kirk is glaring at the corridor door; Fearing has no expression. Dann sees Margaret shudder and put a hand out to grip the edge of her console. He is sweating in the thickening, pulsing air, he can no longer fool himself about sixty-cycle hums. This is the same terrible tension that surged through them last night, and he is scared to death. It strengthens, rises, as though the room was at the focus of some far-off nameless intensity—

"Fifth letter, start!"

—And at that instant he feels—*feels*—a presence as palpable as an animal's nose poking at his mind. Terror spurts up in him, he jerks around to the wall expecting to see something unimaginable coming out, trying to enter his head. But there is nothing. He stares at the varnished wood, one hand frantically clasping his forehead, while under his fingers something—something immaterial—*pushes* into him.

Hallucination; he is going mad here and now. And then he becomes aware of the strangest fact of all—he is no longer afraid.

He stands dazed, all terror gone, aware only that the invisible intrusion in his head exudes a puppylike friendliness and harmlessness. A bright eager feeling washes through him, like a young voice saying *Hello*. Transfixed, astounded, he hears from a great distance meaningless words.

"Sixth letter, start!"

The push on him strengthens overpoweringly, the anchors of his mind yield, tear loose—and he is suddenly nowhere, whirling through a void that becomes delirium. For one vertiginous instant he rides an enormous whirlwind, is swamped in a howling, soundless gale above a dark-light world shot with wild colors that are sounds—he is aware of unknown presences in a gale of light that beats like music on his doubled senses, he is soaring in tempests of incomprehensible glory—

—And next instant he is telescoped back across limitless blackness into himself, Daniel Dann, his body striking hard surfaces by the familiar dayroom wall. His head is empty. He realizes he is down on one knee. Someone is calling his name.

He gets to his feet. There seems to be a commotion back in the corridor. Kirk gallops past. "Dann! Come back here!" Noah calls again.

But Dann cannot respond, he is staring at Margaret Omali.

She is holding herself braced upright, looking at Fearing. Her mouth writhes oddly, she swallows with a croak. Fearing watches her intently.

"Hello, hello . . . " The voice is coming from Margaret but it isn't like anything Dann has heard before. "Hello? Char-les, yes? Charles Ur-ban Sproul."

Fearing suddenly gets up. For a moment Dann thinks he is going to attack her, but he only goes to the corridor door, pulls it shut, and locks it, without taking his eyes off her. The room is like a humming vacuum. Dann takes a step toward Margaret and runs into Fearing's arm.

"Lind-say?" says the weird voice from Margaret's throat. "Lindsay Barr? Major Drew Fear-ing, yes." Her mouth stretches in imitation of a smile. "I respect your culture, your concern. Ah, undertow." The voice trails off in meaningless syllables.

Fearing stands motionless, studying her as if she were a wild animal.

Margaret takes an unsteady step away from the computer, looking around the room. Her gaze fixes on Dann, and she utters what sounds like "Tivel?"

The next second she is sagging, crumpling toward the floor.

Dann lunges just in time to save her face from the teleprinter bar. Her body slides away and hits the floor beside the couch. Dann starts toward her and has his breath knocked out by a solid blow from Fearing's elbow.

"Keep away." The feral intensity of the voice is as shocking as the blow.

"She—Miss Omali—has a cardiovascular history," Dann gasps. It hurts him physically to see her on the floor, alone. He pushes futilely, caught between the console and the stronger, furious man. "Let me through, Major!"

Margaret is sighing shudderingly. Her eyes open, her head lifts and falls back.

"The wind," she says faintly.

"It's all right, Margaret," Dann tells her across Fearing's shoulder. "I felt it too. You're here."

"The *wind*," she repeats. Then her hand grasps the couch and she scrambles up and sits.

Fearing is instantly in front of her.

"Who sent you here? Where did you learn those names?"

"She's had a shock, Major, for God's sake stop this nonsense."

Dann moves, summons authority back to his voice. But it isn't nonsense, he has a hideous suspicion what has happened.

Loud noises are coming from behind the locked door. "Major Fearing!" Noah's voice shouts. "We need your transcript at once, we've had extraordinary results!" He pounds harder, rattles the door. "Dann! What's the matter?"

Fearing straightens up, suddenly calm. "Stand away from her, Doctor." The tone is deadly. Imagining weapons, Dann lets himself be backed away. Fearing goes to the door and unlocks it. His cold, pleasant voice rides over Noah's expostulations as he hands the envelope through.

"Doctor Catledge, a matter of concern to me has come up here. I would appreciate it if you will evaluate your results in the other section of the building. The doctor must remain here. Kirk, stay with them and see that this door stays closed."

Margaret is whispering something. "I was . . . away."

"I know. It's all right," he whispers back.

But it's not all right. That gibberish she uttered, those names—they were meaningful to Fearing. Some of his secrets, like last night, she read things out of his mind. And Fearing, what can he think but that she's some sort of spy? Oh God—the crazy bastard is dangerous—

The door is closed; Fearing is surveying them thoughtfully. "Doctor, I suggest you sit down."

Still studying Margaret, Fearing straddles the computer chair and sits down facing her, apparently perfectly at ease.

"Look, Major—"

Fearing holds up his hand, smiling. He seems to have dismissed Dann from some calculation. "Miss Omali, your approach puzzled me." His face is a mask of patient sympathy. "I believe I understand. Please be assured that we have an excellent record of protecting people who come to us. Perhaps you'd like to meet one or two, to reassure yourself? I think that could be arranged."

She stares at him. Her control is back. "I have not one idea what you're talking about."

Nor has Dann—and then suddenly he sees. This maniac Fearing has decided that Margaret is, what do they call it, a defector. Trying to defect to "our side." He thinks her ravings were an attempt to signal him by revealing knowledge. Nightmare proliferates around him. What can he do to her, lock her up? Ruin her life? But she doesn't know anything—

"You're crazy," Margaret is saying remotely. Dann can sense the fear under her calm. The air is flickering with tension.

Fearing smiles charmingly. "Perhaps you are concerned about your little boy? We could have him here with you in an hour or so."

Oh God. Dann sees the cords in her neck spring out.

"Don't you dare touch my son."

"Look here, Major, as this woman's doctor I'm telling you to stop this right now. You're on the wrong track, you—"

Fearing doesn't look at him, but goes on contemplating Margaret as if she were an algebra problem.

"This is not the appropriate setting, perhaps," he says patiently. "You would feel more secure away from these people." He touches his wristwatch.

"No!" Margaret cries.

Dann plants himself in front of her. "I tell you you're endangering her heart. If you don't believe me, get Harris over here to check."

Footsteps outside. Dann swings around to see a heavy-set man in fatigues at the front door.

"An excellent idea, Doctor," Fearing says unruffledly. "Deming, put in a call for the ambulance and tell Doctor Harris to meet us."

"*No!*" Margaret jumps up. "I'm not going anywhere!"

Dann is struggling with horror, the room seems brimming with fear. How can this maniac have so much power? He's so relaxed, he's sure we're helpless. But not Margaret, not unless they're prepared to shoot me—*I mean that*, he realizes, hearing himself say "You will not—"

The front door opens again and Kendall Kirk bursts in saying urgently, "Sir! Excuse me, sir, but you have to know this." He halts in back of the couch, behind Margaret. "They did it. I tell you those weirdoes picked up the whole six-letter group. They can do it, they can read your mind. They're dangerous as hell. She's reading your mind right now."

Dramatically he points at Margaret.

"You're out of your mind, Kirk," Dann protests. "Miss Omali isn't even one of Noah's subjects."

"She's hiding it," Kirk says savagely. "She's one of the strongest psis in the bunch. I know."

Fearing continues studying Margaret impassively. His nostrils are tightly curled in, as if there were a nasty odor in the throbbing, thickening air. Dann can guess the revulsion going through that secretive mind. But surely he will reject Kirk's lunacy?

"Those, ah, terms you mentioned, Miss Omali," Fearing says at last. "Am I to understand that you, ah, divined them from my mind?"

Oh God, paranoids accept magic. This is bad. And the damned humming feeling is worse every minute. He can't get hallucinations now, he has to protect her—

"I don't read minds," says Margaret coldly. But she is shaking.

Fearing just goes on watching her. Maybe he has, what, psi powers himself, Dann thinks. Horrified, he feels the energy in the room building, pouring into him. The air resonates. Stop it, stop it.

The teleprinter suddenly clacks, making everyone start. Fearing didn't change his level stare.

"Major, you have to believe it!" Kirk clamors. "They're dangerous! Look—watch this!"

He lunges over the couch and lays desecrating hands on Margaret's wrists, jerking them together behind her, prisoning them in one hand while his other hand goes high over her head. Fire spurts—a flaming butane lighter is falling straight into her lap.

Dann doesn't know he has jumped until his fist connects with Kirk's face. He hears Margaret make a dreadful sound. From the side of his eye he sees the lighter swerve in midair and fly at Fearing's head.

And Margaret herself—goes away.

Staggering in abnormal dimensions in the pulsing room, Dann sees her go. Her bodily eyes roll up and pale complex fire streams out of her, an energy which he instantly understands is *her*, her life. He sees it form and shoot away meteorlike into a dark abyss of nonspace which for an instant is open to his senses—she is going, going—

"Margaret!" he cries, or tries to cry out, knowing that he is losing her forever, feeling some unearthly focus of power brush him, unmoor him—

—And he wrenches free, breaks out, gathers himself and his fifty years and his wretched useless love and hurls his life wholly after her through the closing gap to nowhere.

An instant or eternity later he regains something like consciousness. He is hurtling through blackness that is empty of time or space, seeing only before him with what are no longer mortal eyes the pale fleeing spark that is her life. He tries to call out to her, having no voice but only his bodiless will to comfort her, to slow her terrified flight. He does not wonder, he knows only that his life continues, that he is able to race after her through dimensions of unbeing that may be, for all he cares, Hell or a dream or interstellar space. *"Margaret!"*

Far ahead, the living spark seems to curve course, and he swerves after. Is there some faint structure to this darkness? He cannot tell nor care. He is gaining, closing on her! *"Margaret, love—"*

But suddenly everything is gone—he has crashed into stasis, is assaulted by light, colors, sensations. Floundering, he perceives dimly that this is embodiment. His naked life has become incarnated. A sense which isn't vision is showing him the image of a landscape in which are immense, trembling globes. Utterly bewildered, he rolls or tumbles, his mind filled with jelly life. "Margaret!" he bubbles weakly, and then sees—knows—her radiance is there, flaring among the moving gelatinosities.

He tries to wabble toward her. But as he does, her pale light gathers itself and spins out and away to nowhere—and he wrenches his life free and follows, is again only a hunger in the void pursuing a fleeing star.

Hunter and hunted, their bodiless energies flash across blackness which is light-years, ricochetting down a filament of negative entropy which they cannot know supports their lives—interlopers on a frail life-beam extended toward Earth from a burning planet a hundred million million miles away. Of all this the essence that was Daniel Dann knows only that the spark of Margaret's life is still there, still attainable if he can force his being to greater speed or whatever the unknown dimension is.

He is gaining again! The path through nothing has curved, he cuts the vector—and then with an inertialess crash he finds himself once more embodied in matter, stunned by the impact of alien senses.

147

This time it is all greyness, lit by a watery blue spear; he is in some sort of crowded cavern. "Margaret!" he whistles, or emits in molecules, striving to sense her. And yes! She is there too, her lacy living energy is springing out among a thicket of grey folds. He lunges toward her on nonlimbs.

But again she gathers herself, is gone—and he launches after her into unbeing, finding the impossible familiar now. This hallucinatory after-life seems to have some sort of regularity or dreamlike laws. Are they passing through real space, existing briefly on alien planets?

No matter; the chase accelerates, she caroms wildly down the structured lightlessness in which is nothing, not even a star. It comes to him with joy that he is holding out, can hold out. He will not lose her! But as he exults, he becomes suddenly aware that the void they fly in is not quite empty. Somewhere ahead or to one side, he cannot tell, lies a huge concentration of darker darkness—something blacker than mere absence of light, a terrifying vast presence colder than death. It is Death incarnate, he thinks, he is gripped by fear for her. With all his might he tries to send a voiceless warning to her frail flying star.

Next instant their flight bursts into stasis again. But this time it's shockingly comprehensible. He is incarnated in a sunlit green world under a blue sky. Earthlike meadows are around him, a bird sings. He feels breath, muscles, heartbeat—yes, these are his strong gold-furred limbs. He is a big animal crouched in a small tree.

And there below him—so close!—a white deerlike creature is cropping the grass; pale energies are streaming about its silver horns.

It is she, he has caught her at last!

"Margaret!"

But to his horror he hears himself uttering a fanged roar, and feels his carnivore's muscles·exploding him into a murderous leap. His huge talons are unsheathed, descending on her! He screams, trying to wrench himself aside in midair as her white head comes up. One glimpse of her dark eyes staring—and then she has gone out of that body, fled away on the wind of nowhere.

He flings his life free of the beast-form barely in time to follow her dwindling spark. She is doubly frightened now, in total flight from everything, from life itself. He must push all his waning strength to hold her in reach.

And closer now, too close, the huge eclipsing black dreadfulness he had sensed before is looming through the dimensions at them. Is she aware of it? *"Turn, turn away!"* He tries to hurl warning, willing her to veer aside.

For an instant he thinks she has heard him, she is turning—but no; appalled he sees that she has turned not away but toward the deathly presence, is flying straight at it.

He throws himself after her, understanding that she has chosen. Too much pain, too much; she is fleeing from life forever, she wants only to cease.

"Margaret, don't! Come back, come back!"

But the rushing life-spark does not turn, the great destroying blackness looms ahead. Desperately he tries to intercept her course, he is racing terrified in the icy aura of the thing. *"Margaret!"*

It is no use, he is too slow, too far behind; he sees the glimmering meteor that is her life plunge into black, be swallowed, and wink out. He has lost her. He is alone.

And at that instant the huge shadow before him changes subtly, takes on the semblance of raging lurid smoke—and he sees again the image burned across his life. The black flame-spouting walls, the walls into which he had not gone, in which he had once let perish all that he loved.

It is all there again, the burning darkness and the death; his being recoils in mortal fright. He cannot—

But her brightness has gone in there! He no longer knows who she was or what he is, but only that something intimately precious has again been devoured by evil—and this time he cannot bear to fail. He *will* follow, he will get her out or die trying.

He gathers every terrified shred of his existence and hurls himself at the blackness where she went, a mite of energy launching itself at the eater of suns.

For an instant he feels himself in black cold that burns horribly, and knows death is ahead. So be it. Then he smashes against negation, a mighty barrier of nothing that shatters him into a million fragments and hurls him back instantly away across frozen forever, a tiny blur of improbability smeared across the void—

—Which coalesces, unthinkably, into light and feeling, into what he finally recognizes as the old human body of Daniel Dann, lying propped up on a bare floor.

Machinery is humming near him. He isolates an active hammer at his sternum, and his human mind vaguely identifies an emergency cardiac stimulator. Did he dream? No; it was all real, only elsewhere. He is, he supposes, really dying now; he has received a mortal blow, though he is not in pain. He has lost something vital, lost it forever. Memory of black burning comes to him. But strangely it has no power. I tried, his failing mind thinks. Even if it was too late, I did try.

Movement is visible through his eyelashes, his lids are in terminal tremor. While he waits to die he lets himself look, identifies a moving whiteness as the legs of medics. Incredibly, he seems to be still in the dayroom at Deerfield, on the floor. No one is attending to him. At the end of his vision a figure suddenly rises away, revealing the side of the dayroom couch.

A long dark arm is trailing from it. The hand rests limp on the floor.

Her arm. She is here. His heart thuds against the mechanical stimulation.

"Sorry, Major," says a voice. Dann recollects a white-haired blur: Doctor Harris. "We're much too late," Harris goes on. "She's gone."

Dann can feel nothing more, he is only dully grateful for a glimpse of her pure young profile, as they lift her onto the stretcher. The blanket drops. *Touch her carefully, damn you, treat her with reverence.* He remembers what he knows and wishes fiercely that he could protect her body from the obscene curiosity to come.

"Hey, the doc's coming around," says a loud voice over his head.

With horror Dann realizes that it is referring to him. Why isn't he dead? Is it possible that he has to live? To go on and face the emptiness, the grief and wretchedness of his days? *No.* He wills himself to let go. Cease, heart.

But hands are moving him, medication is traitorous in his blood, he cannot slip away. And yet he can still feel the weird humming tension in the air. Is it possible somehow to wrench loose, to flee out of his body as he had before? Was that delirium, or his drugged cortex raving, a stroke? Whatever, he is too weak now, he cannot find the way. He is trapped here, to suffer the grey years. No way out.

Involuntarily he groans aloud, and a miracle happens.

The *push* that he had felt before presses into his mind—an invisible invading presence that somehow takes away all fear. But this time it is far stronger, more resolute. A real yet friendly power is thrusting him out of himself as a knife scoops out an oyster. Perhaps it is death; he feels only infinite relief as he lets himself be unbodied. And as he dissolves, a voiceless message seems to form in his mind: "Don't be afraid, a short time only. I am Giadoc."

Madness! But so real and warm is the presence that with his last human consciousness he feels sympathy for the alien thing, wishes to warn it. Then his life slides out of the world.

—Into darkness, bodiless speed; he is whirling instantaneously through a void he seems to have known before. But this is velocity so great it is simple being, he is only a vector hurtling somewhere, sucked to a destination—and then he is *there*, telescoping into some order of unreal reality.

As he coalesces into what might be existence, his vanished human senses form one last perception: he is falling into a world-wide inferno, lit by jagged radiance, a blizzard of radiance from an exploding sun. For a noninstant he is aware of great gales howling, of a storm inhabited by monster flying forms, great bats or squids that trail terrifying fires. He is collapsing or condensing into hell.

Next moment the vision is gone, he is *in*, is a corporeal something under peaceful daylight. But it is all too much, entirely too much, he is worn out. Something vital has gone, he does not recall what, only knows he can bear no more.

All but dead with grief and terror, the being that had been Daniel Dann abandons consciousness. His forty-meter vanes fan out in disarray, his jets are lifeless. He tumbles limply while the currents take hold and carry him helpless toward the lethal downfall of the eternal winds of Tyree.

Chapter 13

COLDLY IT RIDES THE STARWAYS, PREOCCUPIED BY NOVEL SENSATIONS FROM WITHIN ITS VAST AND INSUBSTANTIAL SELF. SINCE THE ADVENT OF ITS SMALL PASSENGER, EXISTENCE HAS DEFINITELY BECOME MORE INTERESTING, DESPITE THE IRREMEDIABLE SADNESS OF ITS GUILT.

THE PROJECT OF LEARNING TO COMMUNICATE WITH THE LITTLE ENTITY SEEMS LIKELY TO REQUIRE INFINITE TIME; BUT INFINITE TIME IS AVAILABLE. REFERENTS FOR THE SYMBOLS STILL ELUDE IT. HOWEVER, THE GREAT HOST COMES TO UNDERSTAND IN A GENERAL WAY THE SMALL THING'S ZEST FOR ACCESS, AS THOUGH THE MERE EXPERIENCE OF EMBODIMENT WERE A SOURCE OF JOY. STRANGE, UNFATHOMABLE! WHEN ACCESS TO ALL SENSOR-SYSTEMS IS ALLOWED, THE TINY BEING RESPONDS EXCITEDLY, SEEKING, PEERING, LISTENING, MAGNIFYING NOW THIS, NOW THAT PHENOMENON OF THE VOID. AND ALWAYS WITH AN INFECTIOUS VIVACITY THAT MAKES THE HUGE ONE'S BLEAK EXISTENCE BRIEFLY MORE BEARABLE.

AGAIN, THERE IS THE RECURRENT PROBLEM OF KEEPING ITS

PASSENGER AWAY FROM TOO-CLOSE APPROACH TO ITS PRI-
VATE NEXUS OF GRIEF AND WRONG. THE LITTLE PRESENCE
SEEMS TO WANT TO MEDDLE IN THE WHOLE CENTRAL NU-
CLEUS, AS THOUGH TO INITIATE SOME ACTION, OR DEMAND
MORE OF SOMETHING UNKNOWN. WHAT COULD THIS BE?

EXPERIMENTALLY, A MORE INTIMATE CONTACT IS ONCE
ALLOWED. BUT NOTHING HAPPENS EXCEPT A REPETITION OF
MEANINGLESS SYMBOLS: *//ACTIVATE***ACTIVATE//*. THIS
CORRELATES WITH NOTHING, AND PRESENTLY THE SMALL
PASSENGER CEASES AND REGATHERS ITSELF ELSEWHERE.

IT HAS BEEN ACTIVE IN THE VAST PERIPHERY, TOO. AT LEAST
ONCE IT HAS VENTURED TO THE OUTER LAYERS AND MADE
CONTACT WITH AN ENCYSTMENT. SUBSEQUENTLY IT
ACHIEVES A NEW KIND OF MOVEMENT, AS THOUGH IT HAS
SEPARATED OR DOUBLED ITSELF: THE INTERNAL SENSORS OUT
THERE ARE NOT SO PRECISE. TOLERANTLY, THE HUGE HOST RE-
FRAINS FROM DAMPING THIS TINY COMMOTION, MERELY
CONTENTING ITSELF WITH WARNING SWEEPS.

AND SHORTLY IT FINDS ITSELF REWARDED FOR INDUL-
GENCE: THIS SEEMS TO HAVE BEEN THE PRELUDE TO SOME-
THING NEW. THERE IS A SENSE OF STRAIN ON THE NUCLEUS,
AND THEN THERE ERUPTS FROM WITHIN IT A WONDROUS,
NAMELESS SENSATION SO UNHEARD-OF IT CANNOT BE IDEN-
TIFIED AT ALL, EXCEPT AS A STARTLING SENSE OF COMING-
ALIVE IN A NEW UNAUTHORIZED WAY. THIS HAS TO DO WITH
CERTAIN SCANNERS, IT PERCEIVES. IT DEPLOYS THEM MORE
FULLY, AND THE SENSATION AMPLIFIES. MARVELMENT, DE-
LIGHT!

NOTHING IN ITS IMMENSE COLD BEING HAS PREPARED IT
FOR BEING DAZZLED BY BEAUTY. THE NEUTRAL, UNREGARDED
STARFIELDS TAKE ON INTEREST. GLORIES, LARGE AND SMALL,
FOR WHICH IT HAS NO CONCEPTS CREATE A BRILLIANT STIR.
TO ITS AMAZEMENT, THIS ASPECT OF ITS GREY EXISTENCE BE-
COMES FOR A TIME INTENSELY SATISFYING.

IT FLOATS ON CONSIDERING THESE EVENTS, HALF-PLEASED,
HALF-HORRIFIED. IT SPECULATES: PERHAPS IT WAS TO THE
GOOD OF THE TASK, THE RACE, THAT I DEFAULTED BEFORE I
BECAME SO ACUTELY DERANGED?

SO DISTRACTED, THE VAST BEING FAILS TO NOTICE THAT IT IS MOVING CLOSER TO THE PECULIAR NEG-ENTROPIC STRAND WHICH IT HAD SET COURSE AUTOMATICALLY TO FOLLOW. IT IS SUDDENLY ALERTED WHEN A BURST OF MINUTE ENERGIES IMPINGE UPON ITS OUTER SKIN. IT SEEMS TO HAVE INTERSECTED, OR DISRUPTED, THE STREAM. APPARENTLY IT IS QUITE CLOSE TO THE EMISSION END, BECAUSE OTHER PARTICULATE ENERGIES CONTINUE TO ARRIVE, QUITE STRONG FOR SUCH TINY SENDS. INDEED, ONE OR TWO MAY HAVE PENETRATED THE DEEPER LAYERS BEFORE BEING SEALED OUT. THE SENSATION IS MILDLY TITILLATING, ENOUGH SO THAT IT REMAINS FLOATING IN PLACE, VAGUELY RECALLING THAT IT HAD WONDERED IF SOME APPROPRIATE ACTION WOULD SUGGEST ITSELF WHEN IT NEARED THE OUTPUT END.

NOTHING OCCURS, HOWEVER, EXCEPT A PECULIAR INTUITION OF RIGHT-WRONGNESS, AN ALMOST-IDEA TOO FAINT TO GRASP. MEANWHILE ITS LITTLE PASSENGER HAS BECOME EVEN MORE STIMULATED AND IS ENGAGING IN MUCH INTERNAL TRANSMISSION, REPEATING ITS PERENNIAL SIGNAL, *ACTIVATE***ACTIVATE||*

THIS CORRELATES WITH NOTHING UNUSUAL GOING ON OUTSIDE. ONLY ONE OR TWO NEARBY SUNS ARE DISSIPATING, EMITTING FROM THEIR TRAINS THE USUAL INCOMPREHENSIBLE ENERGIES THAT HAD BEEN SO INTERESTING. DOUBTLESS THIS IS A MARGINAL EFFECT OF THE GREAT TASK, THE GREAT ONE DECIDES—AND WITH THIS COMES THE REALIZATION THAT IT HAS UNWITTINGLY DRIFTED BACK CLOSER TO THE ZONE OF OPERATIONS.

GRIEF STRIKES THROUGH THE VAST SPACEBOURNE TENUOSITY. ITS RACE, THE TASK, ITS VERY LIFE, ALL ARE LOST TO IT NOW. IT TURNS ITS ENORMOUS EMPTINESS, PREPARING TO SET COURSE AWAY.

BUT AS IT DOES SO, AN INPUT OCCURS WHICH MAKES IT FORGET ALL ELSE.

FROM EXTREME RANGE, BUT UNMISTAKABLE: A GREAT TRANSMISSION RISING ON THE TIME-BANDS, A COMPLEX CALL OF EXULTATION, EFFORT AND THANKSGIVING.

THE TASK HERE IS FINISHING, THE OUTCAST BEING REALIZES.

AND THEY HAVE BEEN SUCCESSFUL. THE LAST DESTRUCTIONS
HAVE BEEN ACHIEVED, THE LAST ONSLAUGHTS OF THE ENEMY
CONTAINED.

SAD AND ALONE, THE EXILE REVERBERATES TO THE GREAT
CRY WELLING FROM FAR AWAY:

"VICTORY!. . .VICTORY!. . .VICTORY!. . .VICTORY!. . ."

Chapter 14

A dream. . .

"Calm, calm. Don't be afraid."

Afraid? Dann is not, he thinks dimly, afraid. He is merely dead. Deadness will claim him any minute. He waits.

But the delirium is not fading, and under it is a memory of agonizing loss. Unwelcomely, Dann begins to suspect that he exists, is somehow again embodied in . . . in he does not know what.

"Calm, I'm here. I'll help you. You're safe now."

Is someone really here? Yes . . . yes. A warm, tentative someone speaking without words, touching without touch. A living presence like an arm pressing, not his body but his mind. A nurse?

"Gently, wake up now. You're all right. Wake up."

Perverse, he refuses consciousness. A confusion of memories coming now: being pulled, fighting vast currents. Is he back on that beach of childhood when the lifeguard girl had pulled him out of a rip-tide? She wore a copper bracelet, he remembers. Sissy somebody. Now he is dead and he has been saved again. But not by any Sissy; this time he knows he is on no mortal beach.

"You're all right really, you'll be home soon. Don't be afraid."

No voice, he understands. Only words coming into his, his head? And the arm is not flesh but a current of all-rightness flowing in. Human questions suddenly flare up in him. *"Who's there? Where am I? What—?"* And as he asks, or tries to, he feels a wince, a jumping-away.

"No! Please don't! I want to help you!" The presence is a receding whisper in his mind.

"I didn't mean to hurt you," he stammers effortfully, and is further confused by knowing he is indeed speaking aloud, but not in any earthly voice. Deliberately he opens his eyes, or, rather, succeeds in unclosing something. As he does so he understands finally that the senses he is activating, or focussing, are no organs ever owned or imagined by Doctor Daniel Dann.

—Who now finds what may be himself resting upon nothingness, perceiving an enormous curved and whirling landscape. Beside him towers a great rushing wall gloriously patterned with strange energies and emanating deep musics. Beautiful. And above, far above, is a weird, pale, rooflike arch he feels as potent, while far below, the great typhoon dwindles into the silent dark. A landscape of magical grandeur; even in exhaustion his spirit feels a faint delight.

Another fact comes; he seems to be "seeing" or perceiving in all directions at once, he is at the center of a perceptual globe in which he has only to focus. Extraordinary. Bemused by finding that the dead can feel curiosity, he tries to attend inward, and "sees," in the midst of a queer streaming energy, a huge mass of enigmatic surfaces or membranes, flickering here and there with vague lights. Can this be . . . his body?

Dreamily, he notices movement. The great fans or wings are tilting gently, continually readjusting themselves. From beneath come small jetlike pulsations which he can now vaguely sense. He feels himself at rest yet riding, balancing without effort on moving pressure-gradients, the vast turbulences of this air. To this body, the whirlwind is home.

Understanding can no longer be postponed. He is—is *in*—a giant alien form like those he now recalls having glimpsed or dreamed of.

Oddly, this fails to frighten him, but only charms him further. It is

157

not generally realized, he thinks hysterically, that what the totally destroyed need is for something interesting to happen . . . . But where is his "nurse," the friendly stranger?

He scans more carefully. Deep below he senses living energies, like a great crowd; but they are much too far. Nearer to him on the wind-wall are a few isolated presences. Two are quite close, he can "see" them hovering on the wind, surrounded by the odd veils, like Elmo's fire. Still too far away. He focusses upward—and there it is.

A shape like his own, but smaller, clothed in an auroralike discharge. How he perceives this he doesn't know; it seems to be his main sense-channel, like seeing a thing he remembers from another life, a Kirlian photograph. As he thinks this he notes absently that the "fire" around himself has suddenly flared up toward the other.

"Look out! Please! Can't you control yourself at all?"

The words are clear. But the voice—it is an instant before he puzzles out that this real, audible cry was not a voice at all, but a pattern of light flickering on the membranes of the other's body. And yet his senses "heard" the light as speech. More mystery. Experimentally he wills himself to say, "I'm sorry"—and "hears" his words as a light-ripple on himself.

Incredible. Strangeness beyond strangeness brims up in him, overfloods his dikes. A dream? No, an ur-life; unreal reality. Nothing is left of him, yet here at the end of all he giggles.

"I am a giant squid in a world tornado, apologizing in audible light to another monstrous squid."

Evidently he has tried to say it aloud but without words for the alien concepts. He hears himself uttering garble mixed with orange laughter.

The laughter at least gets through. The creature above him laughs too, a charming lacy sparkle.

"Hello," he says tentatively.

"Hello! You feel better. What's your name? I am Tivonel, a female. Are you a male?"

Male, female? He gazes up at "her," letting himself slip deeper and deeper into this alien normalcy. He feels, he realizes, quite well; this body has a health, a vigor his own had lost long ago. It comes to him as he gazes that the being above him is indeed a female, in fact, a girl—a nice girl who just happens to be, in some sense, a thirty-meter giant manta-ray or whatever.

He is in no condition to criticize this.

"I'm Dann," he tells her. "Daniel Dann." Is the name getting through? "I'm a male, yes."

"Taneltan? Taneltan!" She laughs again, sparkling disbelief. "Males don't have three-names. I'll call you Tanel, it sounds more respectable." She sobers. "If you really are better, can you control yourself so I can come closer? I want to help you."

"Control myself? I don't understand."

"Hold your field in decently. Look at yourself, you're all over and inside out, you could even lose some."

"My . . . field?"

"Yes. Look at you."

"You mean that, that energy-stuff?" he tries to say. "Around . . . me?"

"It's not around you, it's *you*. Your mind, your life. You have to hold it in and arrange it properly. *Ahura*. Wait—watch me."

He watches her, and, marveling, sees the energy-halo englobe itself, shrink, spread out in patterns, expand to pseudo-forms, retract through a whirl of permutations and end in a delicately layered toroid around her coporeal body. Is he watching motions or dispositions of the actual mind, some kind of mysterious psychic art?

"I don't know how to do that," he says helplessly.

"Well, *try*. Oh, start by thinking yourself round, like an egg."

He doesn't believe in any of this, but is willing to be entertained. Awkwardly, he tries to "think himself round," and as he does so sees surprisedly that his pale fire-streamers are raggedly lurching inward in a crudely globular form. Good—but no, half of "himself" has perversely blown right out again. Because he noticed it? Not easy, he perceives, and concentrates again. *Roundness* . . . the flare retracts. He's getting it—Ooops, now his other side has bulged wildly away. He hears her laugh. *Roundness . . . roundness . . .*

"You're just like a big baby, that's what Giadoc said."

"Giadoc?" Still striving for some weird combination of control and alertness, he half-remembers . . . something.

"You're in Giadoc's body. He's my friend. Don't be afraid, he'll come back soon and you'll be back in yours."

"Giadoc . . . did he speak to me, when I, when I, uh, died?"

"He did? Oh good, that means he's all right. He'll be back soon. First they have to let the Beam down and raise it again. Look—I think they're letting down now. Maybe you'll go right back. Look up, see?"

Forgetting his "field," he looks up. The great arching of energy above is draining, dwindling down to its enormous perimeter. As it does so, the world around him brightens and strengthens, his own energies seem to sharpen.

"Well, you're still here," his new friend Tivonel says briskly. "That means you just have to wait til they raise it again. Now you simply have to control yourself. Do you know you nearly fell out of the Wind? The only reason I could pull you back was that you were sick. I was afraid you'd hit me, like the other one."

"The other one?"

"The other one who came here in Giadoc's body. I tried to help it but it *hit* me with its mind. It knocked me away. Can you all do that?"

"The other one . . . who came here . . ." In Dann's mind a forgotten glass of water slid on a bedstand, a voice wails *Margaret* into darkness. Did she come here? Pain knifes at him. Stop it, stop it. No more reality.

"Oh, you *are* hurt!"

"No, no," he manages to say from a million miles distant, aware of a timbre that his lost human mind calls green, but he knows here is pain. Gone forever in the dark—push it away. Get back in the dream-life, the dream of being a giant alien flying at ease in a world-typhoon, which is a pleasant afternoon. Chatting with a girl alien, feeling strong.

She has come closer. As he sees this, a filament of his mind-cloud seems to whip toward her and she whisks away, crying exasperatedly, "*No!* That's what you mustn't do. It's very rude, pushing your thoughts into people."

"What? You mean . . . if it touched like that, you can read my mind?"

"Well of course."

"I don't believe it," he says wonderingly.

160

"Well, I'll show you, but you have to hold perfectly still. Can you hold your field still now?"

"I don't know. I'll try." Watching his awkwardly eddying life energies, he recalls he had once tried to learn a meditation technique. It didn't help then; maybe it will now. Effortfully he strives to concentrate, to recapture the deep quietude. Shrink consciousness to a point, watch nothing. But he is still aware that an eddy of her field is flowing toward him. *Don't watch.* At the tangible nudge in his mind he reacts helplessly.

"Ouch!" She is swirling up into the wind.

"I'm sorry. I did that wrong."

"It's all right, you weren't too bad. Only you're so much *stronger* than a baby. Did you get it?"

"Get what?"

"The memory I gave you, silly. Look in your memory. Where are you?"

Where, indeed? Does ur-reality have a name, am I actually somewhere? Where?

—And he realizes he knows. He knows!

"Why, I, I'm on T-Tyree—that's your world. Tyree."

"You *see*?" She curves closer again, mischievous.

"My God," he tries to say, but it comes out "Great winds!"

"See if you got the rest. Think about Tyree."

"Tyree . . . Oh, yes, you're in trouble. Radiation is—" But this language has no words, he hears himself babbling about burning in the Wind and intolerable loudness of the Sound. The Sound? Sunlight? Of course, they think in other modes. "And wait, yes—you're trying to escape by sending your minds away somehow—no, that's wrong—"

"Very good! *Very* good!" Her laugh is so merrily coral, laced with empathic mockery it lifts Dann's leaden spirit. Why, this little Tivonel is indeed an attractive one. Bright spirit of the wind.

"But you, your world is in danger. You may die."

"Maybe." Undismayed, a brave little alien being who is every instant less alien. And then Dann learns something else.

"Don't worry. Giadoc will come back and send you home. He won't commit life-crime, he said so."

The melting tones are unmistakable; across the light-years he recognizes the colors of love. Love and sharing unto death, she and this Giadoc whose body he has somehow acquired. And will he, Dann, be thrown back to his grey private death, leaving her on a burning world? The memory of the inferno he had glimpsed . . . . So the charming ur-life is tragic after all. Pity . . . if he believed any of this.

"Please! Hey, please, your field!"

Confused, he perceives that his "mind-field" has eddied strongly toward her, is coalescing into a peculiar surface whose vibrancy suddenly thrills him. An excitement his own old human body had long forgotten, a potent shivering delight—

"*Stop that!* You don't know what you're doing!" She is laughing wildly, her life-field suddenly intensified, recoiling yet linked to his by ever-increasing intensities. Urgency flames up in him, he needs to *drive* her higher into the wind, to push her away upon the power of his desire. Wild incomprehensible images of wind and energy flood through him, he is about to do he knows not what—but in a rush of flashing jets she shoots aside, and the tension breaks.

Shaken and roiled, it takes him a moment to locate her below him down the wind.

"You—you—!" She splutters unintelligibly. "You almost, I mean, you biassed, in a minute we would have—."

"What? What happened?" But he suspects now. The joy!

"Well!" She planes up nearer. "I don't know how to explain. Made a *repulsion*." She giggles. "Whew! Giadoc is very energic. We call it sex."

He hangs there astounded, conscious of himself as a monster riding an alien gale who has somehow committed an indelicacy. The etiquette of apocalypse. It was so good.

"We call it sex too," he tells her slowly. "Only with us the two people touch."

"How weird." Her vanes bank gracefully, he notices her beautiful command of the wind. Something else, too; his body seems to know that her position relative to him has changed things. With the wind coming from him to her she is still a charming one, but not dangerously so. Neutralized. Of course; they live in the wind, function evolves to its direction. Mysteries . . .

"But how do your eggs get exposed?" she is asking curiously.

He is about to enter on new fascinations, but his senses are assaulted by a dreadful scream. Terror! Someone is shrieking intolerably.

Dann peers about, discovers they have drifted closer to the pair of aliens he had noticed before. The large one is uttering the nerve-shattering green wail. It is thrashing about and tumbling, its energies wild. A smaller alien is in pursuit.

"What a shame," Tivonel says above the uproar. "I thought Avanil had it calm."

"What is it? What's happening?"

"I forgot to tell you. That's one of your people, there in Terenc's body. You better start Fathering it right away."

"One of my people?"

All at once the screamer shoots toward him and long streamers of its flaring field lash out. A jolting shock—his mind is inundated with a kaleidoscope of faces, smells, bulkheads and valves, a foreshortened human penis against blue blankets, a Gatorade bottle—while over everything a face that he remembers, shrieks "RICKY—RICKY—HELP—"

The scene clears, leaving him reeling in twinned realities. The strange body is still before him, blasting out green screams.

"It's Ron!" Dann exclaims. "It's Ron from the, the water—"

"You better Father it before it loses field. You can, can't you? However you do it?"

"RICKY! RICKY, WHERE ARE YOU? HELP ME!"

The pain is intolerable. "I'm a doctor," Dann tries to say absurdly, moving toward the agonized form with no idea what he can do.

"Ron! You're all right, calm down! Listen to me, it's Doctor Dann."

—BLOOIE!

The next few moments or years exist only as a terror beyond all drug nightmares, beyond anything he has imagined of psychosis—rape—disaster. He is invaded, frantic, rolling in dreadful pounding synchrony of panic, sensing only in flashes that he is howling RICKY—RICKY—RICKY—is also yelling RON SHUT UP YOU'RE ALL RIGHT I'M DOCTOR DANN—only to be swept under the terrified crashing chaos, reverberating insanity. How long it lasts he never knows, understands only a sudden immense cool relief, like a great scalpel of peace cutting him free. Sanity returns.

As his separate existence strengthens Dann finds his body pumping air. He lets the scene steady into the strange-familiar world around him, is again his new self riding the gentle gales beside a wall of beautiful storm.

"Control yourself, Tanel, it's all right now."

The words are warmly golden; his friend Tivonel is hovering nearby.

Before him floats a great disarrayed dark mass, its small energy-field pale and calm. This seems to be the alien body containing Ron. Is he unconscious or dead? Not dead; jets are pulsing. The smaller alien is helping it keep steady on the wind.

Dann's gaze turns upward.

Looming above them hovers a huge energic alien form, its vanes half-spread, its mantles and aura a deep, rich glory. It—no, unmistakably *he*—seems to be surveying them severely. Dann has a momentary memory of his school coach separating furious small boys.

"In the name of the Wind, Father Ustan, thank you." Tivonel's light-speech is in a new, formal mode.

"Thanks be that you were nearby, Father," the other alien adds in the same mode. Dann senses that it is another female.

"What happened? Is my friend all right?"

"You made a panic vortex," the great stranger says in grave violet lights. "If I had not separated you in time you would both have been damaged for life. The being you call Ron is drained and sleeping. Avanil here will guard it. But you, Tanel, are you not a Father? Why did you permit this disorder to happen?"

"We, we have no such skills on our world," Dann says weakly.

The great being, Ustan, flickers a wordless grey sign in which Dann reads skepticism, scornful pity—the equivalent of a raised eyebrow. Majestically, he tilts up into the wind. But the female Avanil calls to him.

"Father Ustan, wait! Don't you notice the Sound is getting very strong up here? I feel burning, that's why I started to move Terenc's body. Look at all the dead life above us, too. I don't think this level is safe anymore."

"The Sound doesn't rise here now," Tivonel objects.

"Well, something up here is wrong. Look at the Airfall, it's all dead, too. I think we should go down to where Lomax and Bdello are."

Dann, "listening," realizes he has been noticing a rising hiss of light, or sound. It has a wicked feel, like a great subsonic machine-whine running wild.

Big Ustan has paused, spreading internal membranes.

"Avanil is correct," he announces. "I too sense dangerous energies. By all means, move them down to Chief Hearer's station to wait. I will take the distraught one."

"*I* can take him, Ustan," Avanil protests.

But Ustan has floated down to Ron's sleeping body, furling out the membranes under his main vanes. Dann has a glimpse of small, soft-looking flexible limbs. Then Ustan is covering him, swooping away like an eagle with its trailing prey. Next moment his great complex vanes fan out wide, tilt up—and he becomes suddenly an abstract shape of flight, falling away from them on an awesome dwindling curve, down—down—

It is so dazzling Dann finds himself pumping air. Next moment the far-flying form has changed again and fetched up floating calmly by the two other presences below.

"That's Lomax and Bdello," Tivonel says. "Now you go."

"Me? Down there? I—" Dann is stammering, aware that his voice has a greenish squeak. His human senses have brushed him with vertigo. "I don't think—"

"Well, *try*," Tivonel says severely. "Giadoc was able to move around on your awful world. With no wind. You don't have to go that fast," she adds more gently. "Just tell yourself to go down, the body remembers. We'll help if you need it. Oh, I forgot. This is Avanil. I mean Avan. Avan, meet Tanel. He's a male so I call him that."

"Greetings, Tanel." The other's tone is like a curt handshake, he is reminded of a girl on a vanished world.

"Hello, Avan." Aware that he is delaying the awful drop, he lets himself take a last look at the grandeur of these heights. A million Grand Canyons of the wind, he thinks. No, far more beautiful. But that sound, that faint deadly roaring . . . . All in a moment the beauty drops away, he recalls his momentary vision of this world and its raging sun, the terrible exploding shells and angry streamers

165

of a star gone mad. It was blowing up—that's what he "hears."
Hard radiation. And these people, these real people, are on a planet
about to be incinerated. Terrible . . . His mood is broken by a tangible nudge.

"Let's go," says Tivonel.

Down. Okay.

Focussing with all his might on the dots below, Dann lets himself
spread something. His vanes adjust, he's dropping, swooping down
while his body takes the air-rush, seeming to steer itself. Faster, in-
toxicatingly! The dots swirl, are lost and recaptured, the wind is full
in him, is his element—it is glorious! The dots have grown to bodies,
he realizes he must stop now. Stop! But how? Gales call him!

From nowhere two figures cut in before him, changing the rushing
air. His vanes manage to bite the right angle. He slows, has stopped,
hearing laughter all around.

Three figures that must be Ustan and the Hearers are above him.
He feels a double nudge at his vanes, and finds himself lurching upward, with a ludicrous mental image of his staggering human self
supported by two giggling girls.

"Thanks, Avan," Tivonel is saying. "Whew, wow! Tanel, I
thought you were going all the way to Deep."

"I thought I did rather well." Dann finds himself chuckling too,
all nightmare gone. He hasn't felt happy and strong like this in
years. How great must be this life on the winds of Tyree!

They stop discreetly side-wind of the three big males. Dann stares
curiously; from two of them the life-energy is radiating upward in a
focussed, almost menacing way. Like high voltage.

"What are Hearers?" he asks.

"Oh, they listen to the Companions and the life beyond the sky.
That's how they do the Beam, you came here on it." She goes on,
something about "life-bands" which Dann finds unintelligible. He
sees now that these energies are merged with shafts of others from
far out around the Wall. Something to do with their weird psionic
technology. *They brought me here* . . . .What about time, he wonders idly, not really caring. If I went back, would it be centuries
ahead? No matter; he is delighted with this new mystery. Astronom-
ers, that's what they are. Astro-engineers of the mind. This Lomax
is something like Mission Control, perhaps.

Avan, or Avanil, has gone to get Ron's body, and now comes struggling back to them, looking absurdly like a sparrow-hawk trying to tow a goose. When she has him positioned satisfactorily on the wind she turns to Dan, exuding determination.

"Tanel, if you're a male, you don't seem to know much about Fathering. How old are you? Haven't you raised a child yet?"

"Oh Avan, for Wind's sake," Tivonel protests.

"It's all right, I don't mind," Dann says. Pain flicks him, but it's far off; he has died since then. "I'm quite old as a matter of fact. I did have a child." To his embarrassment his words have changed color.

"Now see what you've done, Avan," Tivonel scolds. "These are people, you don't know what could be wrong."

"I'm sorry," Avan says stubbornly. "But I can't understand how you could be a Father and be so helpless with that one."

Dann hesitates, puzzled. Some extra meaning is trying to come through here. Father? "Well, I'm not sure, but you have to understand we don't have this kind of mind-contact on our world. And our females do most of the child-raising. In fact we call it—" he tries to say *mother* but only garble comes out. "It really isn't done by many males at all."

Before his eyes Avan has lighted up with delighted astoundment.

"The *females* do the Fathering! Tivonel, did you hear? It had to be, that's the world we want! Oh, great winds!"

Both females are pulsing excitedly, Dann sees, attention locked on him. But Avan is by far the more excited.

"Why? Is that so strange here?"

"Calm down, Avan," Tivonel says. "Yes, Tanel, it's pretty strange. I'll explain if I get time. But look, they're starting the Beam now. Giadoc will be back any minute and you'll be home."

"The females do the Fathering," Avan repeats obliviously. "Think what that means. So they're bigger and stronger, right?"

"Well, no, as a matter of fact—"

"Listen, Avan, what does it matter? You better calm down before you lose field."

But Avan only flashes, "I'll be back!" and has suddenly whirled away and down. Dann looks after her. From here he can see or sense the crowd quite clearly, hundred of aliens scattered or clustered thickly in the wall of wind, among what seem to be plants. Big ones, little ones—but he sees them now quite differently. *People* are there, old, young, all sorts—even kids jetting excitedly from group to group. An emanation comes from them, a tension. Under the excitement, fear.

"More Deepers all the time," Tivonel comments. "Look at those young Fathers heading up here. That's Giadoc's son, Tiavan, that big one. Never mind, watch Lomax. See, the Beam is starting up. Giadoc will be here soon and you'll be far away. Goodbye, Tanel," she adds warmly.

"You mean I have no choice? I'll just go snap, like that?"

"Yes. Don't you want to?"

"I don't know," he says unhappily. "I want—I want to understand more about you before I go. At least can't you explain more, give me a bigger memory like you did before? Yes! Give me a memory! For instance, about Fathering. And what are Deepers, what's life-crime? What do the Hearers learn?"

"Whew, that's complicated. I'd have to form it, there isn't much time." She scans about nervously.

He sees that the energies above Lomax and his colleague are thickening, building up and out, towering toward the zenith in a slow, effortful way.

"Please, Tivonel. From your world to mine. You should."

"Well, I guess they have a long job to get it up and balanced right. And they're tired. But it would be awful if we got caught in the middle."

"Please. Look, I'll stay as limp as Ron over there. Watch."

Eagerly he tries to collapse all awareness, focussing on the dim sense of air moving in his internal organs. It's difficult. Suddenly he is distracted by a giggle.

"Excuse me Tanel. That's very good but you don't have to do it all over, you're in what we call Total-Receptive. Never mind. Just don't jump when you feel me."

Concentrate, think about nothing. But the thought of being sent back to Earth intrudes chillingly. Is it really true? Don't think of it, all a dream. He is trying so hard that he scarcely notices the mind-push, reacts late.

"Tanel! You're terrible." She is floating nearby, laughing.

"Did I do something awful again?"

"No, you missed me. I think you're learning. Did you get it? I don't know where I put it, you were as mushy as a plenya. Think, what's life-crime?"

"Life-crime . . . " Suddenly, the words convey a kind of remote abomination to him. Of course, stealing another's body. "Yes," he says. "But you know, I don't quite feel it—it's so far from our abilities."

"You better," she says, suddenly sober. "Look down there, that's Father Scomber coming up. And Heagran behind him. Did you get it all about that?"

He looks, and marveling, *knows* them. The huge energic oncoming form is Father Scomber, leader of the move to flee by life-crime. And the even larger shape behind him, veiled and crusted with majestic age: Father Heagran, the Conscience of Tyree. Incredible! Enlightenment, understanding opens in him like a true dream—the wonders of Deep City, the proud civilization of the air; joys, duties, deeds innumerable, the wild life of the upper High—a world, Tyree, is living in his mind!

Through his preoccupation he notices that several more figures are struggling up toward him, apparently finding the ascent difficult. And they're oddly formed.

"Those two, there—wait, Fathers—what's wrong with their, their fields?" He asks her.

"Oh, winds, did I forget to give you *that*? Can't you see their double fields? They're Fathers with children. In their, well, their *pouches*. It's not polite to say that." She giggles. "You have one, Tanel."

Her voice has flickered through the lavendar tones he understands as reverence.

"Amazing." Yes, he can see now the small life-nuclei nestled in their great auroras. Fathering?

"Here comes Avan back with her pal Palarin to hear you. And there goes old Janskelen, she hasn't forgotten how to ride wind. Some of those Deepers are a mess, they wouldn't be as scared on your world as I was. Don't worry, though. They aren't going. Oh— feel the signal? The Beam is up! Goodbye again, Tanel."

A shudder has raced through the world.

"Must I go, Tivonel?"

"Yes. But I'll remember you Tanel. Goodbye, fair winds."

169

"Fair winds." He can barely speak. This wonderful doomed world, the brightness of her spirit. Briefly he has lived in a dream more real than all his miserable life. "I'll always remember you, Tivonel. I hope, I hope—"

He cannot say it, can only pray that she will not be incinerated under that dreadful sun. The hideous background drone is rising and he thinks he hears, or sees, grey whines of sickness from the vegetation above. All too likely these wonderful bodies have already taken a lethal dose. Don't think of it. He feels a charming touch of warmth upon his mind, and sees that she has let a thought-tendril eddy gently to him. Just in time he forces his reaction to be still.

Another signal snaps through them all.

"That's it! Oh, wait a minute—look at Lomax!"

The Chief Hearer and Bdello are forms of static fire, their fields pouring up to the great arc overhead. Lomax' mantle seems to be flickering in anger. Dann has the impression he is cursing.

"Trouble. Ugh, the Destroyer. Well, they had that before. Wait."

The Destroyer . . . an image of huge dark deathliness. But not new to him—a vanishing spark dies again, and he shudders. Push it away.

"It's fixed now. Goodbye."

"Goodbye." A thought strikes through his self-absorption. "Will my friend, will Ron go back too?"

"He'll be all right," she answers mutedly. "I hope."

Dann waits, puzzling. Something unclear here, but nothing he can do.

The thrumming energies densen above him, he feels their pull. Any instant now he will feel the *nudge* that will be Giadoc returning to his body, pushing Dann out. And he will be whirled away through darkness, will awake to find himself in his own human body, Doctor Daniel Dann, the grey man of loss and grief. A new death. . . . Idly, he wonders what this Giadoc will have done as Dann. Will he find himself in some incredibly far future? Or will he awaken in Deerfield's disturbed ward, under restraint? No matter. Wait.

The sense of tension heightens, brims intolerably. Dann hears from beside him a soft mental murmur. *"Giadoc."* He muses on love, young love. And he himself has been briefly young again, in this magnificent alien form. He takes a last exultant grip of the great winds, reveling in his vigor, with the result that he side-slips abruptly. Behave yourself, old Dann . . . The memory of his inadvertent sexual episode stirs in him deliciously. How bizarre, yet how right. "The egg," she said. These people must be oviparous. And the males rear their young. Now he thinks about it, he can feel some massive organ underneath. My pouch! Really! . . . And it's some kind of political issue here, his new memory half-tells him why Avan had been so excited. . . . But the minutes are passing, nothing has changed. What are they waiting for?

He scans around. Bdello is speaking now, the light-whisper from his mantle faint with effort.

"Someone's alive!" Tivonel exclaims. "Oh, it's Terenc. But that means Giadoc's alive, he's all right, he's alive!"

Senior Fathers are closing around the Hearers. Dann has a confused impression of conflict, of commands and countercommands, verbal and telepathic.

"Oh, no," Tivonel says angrily. "Terenc won't come back! How *nasty!*"

But that means that Ron—Dann scans around, locates the still-sleeping form. If this Terenc won't return, is poor Ron doomed to die here in that? For a moment the scene turns hellish and *horror alienae* shakes him. But a thought comes to his rescue: This is farther than China. Maybe poor Rick will be free at last.

"I should stay, I should help Ron."

"You *can't*, Tanel."

True . . . He notices that a different female is guarding Ron. She has ragged, blistered vanes. "Who's that?"

"She's my friend, Iznagel. I had her take care of him after Avanil took off."

He'd missed the exchange; he is doubtless missing a lot.

"Try to help him, when I'm gone."

"I will. We'll take him right down where it's safer."

Safer—for how long? Meanwhile the resonating tension is becoming painful; the world seems drained. He wishes the whole sad business over.

But the argument around the Hearers has grown fiercer. Purple blasts from the senior Fathers ride over excited cries. Even Avan and other females are there.

"They've found Giadoc!" Tivonel bursts out. "Oh, he's coming, he's coming! I knew he would!"

Dann braces.

But at that moment the disputants around Lomax draw slightly apart and there is a crimson shout from Scomber. "Better a live criminal than a dead child! Heagran, we are doomed here."

"No! Take down the Beam, Lomax!" Heagran bellows back, and several seniors echo him. "Take it down. End this!"

"No! Our children must live!"

The uproar is suddenly drowned in a world-tearing scream. A flame-shrieking fireball rips down the sky and buries itself, exploding, in a high sector of the great wind-wall. The sound is unendurable, gales buffet them. Dann feels a blast of burning heat up his vanes. Through the confusion he sees the great shape of Scomber spreading himself above Lomax.

"TYREE IS DOOMED!" he thunders. "FATHERS! SAVE YOUR CHILDREN! COME, MY LIFE WILL BE YOUR BRIDGE!"

His energy-field bursts up brilliantly, entwining that of Lomax, towering up to the arc of the Beam itself.

"NO!" Heagran's mental roar tears through them. *"CRIMINAL, CEASE!"* His great field launches itself at Scomber's.

But rearing up between them are other energies, coming from the Elders and Fathers around. Energies crackle, writhe, lash to and fro. Dann is watching an astral fire-fight, a literal conflict of will against will! It rages in intensity, seeming to suck or damp his own life-force, and then dies back.

To his dismay, Dann sees that Heagran and his allies have been bested; their fields are sinking, leaving Scomber's triumphant blaze intact. As his mind recovers, it comes to him that he is seeing nothing less than the start of an invasion of Earth. The desperate victors are proposing to steal human bodies, to send human minds here, to die on Tyree.

What can he do?

He can only watch, appalled, shuddering to Scomber's triumphant summons. *"FATHERS! COME, SAVE YOUR CHILDREN! USE MY LIFE!"*

And they are coming; below Dann a mob of Fathers is starting upward, struggling against the great winds, joined every moment by more. The two young Fathers near Scomber have already launched their life-fields upon his, bearing the nodes that are the lives of their children, leaving their bodies floating darkly behind.

"NO, COLTO! TIAVAN, COME BACK!" Heagran's mind-command jolts even Dann's opaque senses. Beside him Tivonel is sobbing wordlessly.

But Dann is transfixed, it is the most amazing spectacle he has ever seen. Those two life-minds striving up to the focus of the Beam—he sees them now as desperate parents racing with their precious burdens up out of a world on fire. Escape, escape! Caught in the deep imperative, he cheers on their mortal struggle, feels triumph as they gain height and flash away. The other Fathers below him are closer now, laboring with their babies toward the miraculous bridge of Scomber's life.

But as they come a small form jets to Scomber's side.

"Sisters! To a better world!" The cry rings out.

It is the female, Avan. In a moment her small life and another are racing upward along Scomber's energy-bridge.

"No! Come back!" A deeper female voice cries, and then another node of energy is pursuing them.

"Janskelen!" Tivonel cries out in shock, and then sobs, "Oh, Tiavan, how could you? Giadoc, Giadoc, come back!"

Her words are lost in the wind-rush as the first group of Fathers jet exhaustedly past, expending their last energies to reach Scomber and the promise of escape. From the dark bodies floating around Scomber a thin green screaming is adding itself to the uproar. Confusedly, Dann realizes that this should mean something to him.

But at that instant the roof of the world tears apart in a thunderous blast of lightning, and a storm of energies rains upon them all. Stunned, Dann flounders among random life-jolts, deafened by myriad screams.

"THE DESTROYER! THE DESTROYER HAS BROKEN THE BEAM!"

Slowly his senses clear. He is tumbling slowly by the great Wall, while above them the immaterial power that had been the Beam is shredded, raveling down to nothing. Where Scomber blazed below his defiant mind-bridge only dark bodies drift. It is clear that catastrophe has come. The mob of Fathers mills in fright, barely able to balance in this turbulent air.

"The Beam is down! Giadoc—they've got to find him!"

Tivonel is jetting past, heading up for Lomax. Dann follows dazedly. If the Beam, the connection with Earth is gone, is he marooned here to die of radioactivity? He doesn't really mind; he has, it seems, died several times over already. Another won't hurt. Maybe he can help Ron.

He becomes aware that his only real emotion, as he jets up through the gales of Tyree, is irritation with this unknown character Giadoc. If he and Tivonel are to perish together, it would be nice if she would forget about Giadoc long enough to remember him. The absurdity of his thought strikes him; he chuckles inwardly. Extraordinary what one does in apocalypse. Extraordinary, too, to think that this Giadoc is somewhere on Earth, walking about in Daniel Dann's old body. Dann wishes him joy of it, consciously savoring his winged youth and strength. Pity it won't last. Well, good to have known it . . . The green screeches coming from below nag at him, but he puts them aside.

They reach Lomax to find him pale and drained but steady. His aide, Bdello, is still feebly righting himself, his life-field in disarray. Dann is reminded of an exhausted medium, or perhaps an inventor crawling out of the wreckage of his latest effort.

Beside them hovers the huge form of Father Heagran. Tivonel halts respectfully.

"Lomax, I have changed my views," Heagran is saying. "We cannot watch the children die. I cannot. But neither will I commit life-crime upon intelligent beings. Therefore I request you and your Hearers to find a world with only simple life-forms. Animals only, you understand. If you can find one such we will bear the children there. It will not be life as we know it," he says in deep sadness. "It will be degradation. But perhaps, in centuries to come, perhaps something of Tyree will grow again."

The tragic colors of his voice are echoed on the mantles of the Elders nearby.

"But Heagran," Lomax protests, "my people are exhausted, in shock. Some are already scorched at the high stations. We cannot raise a Beam. And the accursed Destroyer is blocking half the sky."

"You must try."

"Very well. Those of us who can will probe singly, as we used to do."

"Chief Lomax!" bursts out Tivonel. "You have to rescue Giadoc, you must. You know he's trying to return."

The others darken in disapproval, but Lomax says gently, "Giadoc is beyond reach if he is on the alien world, little Tivonel. The Destroyer is between us. If he was on the Beam, he is already lost."

"He's trying to get back, I know it!"

"Then it is possible he will sense our probes." Lomax turns away with finality.

"He'll find a way," Tivonel mutters rebelliously.

I'll come to thee by moonlight, though Hell should bar the way, Dann quotes to himself. Or is he thinking of the poem about the girl who waited in Hell for her false lover? Never mind—the meaning of the terrified shrieks has suddenly got through to him.

"Tivonel! Haven't more of my people come here? In those bodies, the way Ron and I did? I should go to them, I must help them if I can."

"Why, the Fathers are fixing them, Tanel. Winds, you don't think they'd let *that* go on!"

Dann look-listens; in fact the agonized green has subsided to intermittent squalls coming from the group below them, where Scomber was. Only the body containing Ron is nearby, its mantle murmuring in dreamy light, Iznagel still faithfully guarding it.

"I should go down there to them anyway, Tivonel."

"Right. Iznagel, you better bring that one further down too. Here, I'll help."

She and Iznagel start gliding with Ron's huge body down the wind. As they go Dann hears Iznagel saying, "It's like an animal, Tivonel. I think they're crazy." Tivonel shushes her, explaining that Dann is one of the "crazy" aliens. "Oh, Tanel, meet Iznagel of the High."

Dann accepts the introduction absently; he has made out three or four small groups around bodies from which shrill yells are still erupting. Who will these new displaced human minds be? People from Deerfield? Good Lord, what if it's Major Fearing? Or is the

Beam physically random? Could these be members of the French senate, or a group of Mongolians?

The figures are shrouded in plant-life, but he can clearly see a big male hovering over each, his energies blanketing the form beneath. Green cries flash, mind-flares are being pursued, recaptured, somehow molded down to dark. It reminds Dann of firemen converging on stubborn little blazes. Only the big body of Scomber appears to be permanently dark, untenanted. It must be truly dead.

"We can't go closer, not till they're drained."

The idea of electroshock jumps to his mind.

"What do you mean, drained? Are they being hurt, will they be all right?"

"Of course. Drained means drained, like Ustan did you. Resolving all the bad emotions, channeling the energy back. My Father used to do it to me a lot when I was a child, I had tantrums. You don't know *anything*, do you?"

"Apparently not."

He watches the nearest group, marveling. Is he actually seeing the direct reconstruction of a human mind, the reformation of a psyche? What a therapeutic technique! But who are these human minds?

Father Heagran has joined the group; there seems to be still some problem, judging by the uncontrolled screams.

"Oh!" Iznagel cries. "They're taking the babies out of the Father's—Oh, how dreadful! I can't look."

"They have to," Tivonel tells her. "Don't you understand? Those probably aren't babies, I mean the minds may be grown-up adults. And the Fathers aren't their Fathers. They have to take them apart."

But Iznagel only mutters bluely, "It's indecent," and furls herself in disapproval. Dann has the impression that she is peeking, like a matron caught at a porno film.

"Will they be all right? I mean, as babies?"

"Oh yes. Those are pretty big kids."

"I should get over there. I'm a—" He tries to say *doctor* but it comes out "Body-Healer."

"Not while they're *Fathering*, Tanel. Listen, if you're a Healer, don't you think it's getting bad up here? I feel more burning, and it's like I'd eaten something dead. Shouldn't they move down?"

"Yes." What's the use of saying that he thinks it is much too late?

These bodies must have taken a lethal dose already unless their nature is very different. "Yes. You should go down right away."

"Not me, them. I'm staying by Lomax. Giadoc will come, you'll see."

"Then I must stay with you. I have his body."

"Well . . . yes." A warm thought brushes him; he is mollified.

The activity around the nearest bodies is apparently completed. All but one Father move away.

"I'm going to them."

"I guess it's all right now. Fair winds, Iznagel."

The bodies turn out to be small; two females, Dann guesses. What minds lurk there? They are being guarded by a seemingly elderly big male, his vanes noded, his huge life-aura complexly patterned but pale.

"Greetings, Father Omar. This is the alien Tanel, he is a Healer."

The old being signs a formal response, then says abruptly, "To think that my Janskelen has committed life-crime! It is beyond bearing. After all our years!"

"I'm sure she didn't mean to go, Father. She was trying to stop them. That Beam pulls you."

"Nonetheless, she went."

They survey the bodies. Dann notices that the life-auras seem quiet and lax. Is it possible he is seeing human *minds*?

"That's Janskelen," Tivonel flicks a vane. "And that's Avan's friend Palarin. I hope they like your world."

One of the "minds" is moving.

As assuredly as he can, Dann concentrates on it, saying "Don't be afraid. I'm a Healer, I'm here like you. Can I help you?"

To his surprise the other's field condenses up sharply, the mantle flickers.

"Ra . . . Ron . . . Ron? *Ron?*"

The light-tone is sleepy, but unmistakable.

"Rick, is that you? Rick! It's Doctor Dann here, don't be afraid."

The field veers sharply toward him, Dann just recalls in time to jerk his attention away. Not another panic!

"Ronnie, are you all right?" The uncertain voice is asking.

"Ron's all right, Rick. I'm Doctor Dann. Ron is right here, he'll be awake soon."

"I know." Warm color is returning to the words, the life-field is

177

rearranging itself. Almost like a small Tyrenni, Dann thinks. The voice is so absurdly like Rick; was it only hours or an eternity ago that he had heard it tell the yarn about the Japanese time-machine? Incredibilities swamp him.

"I better explain what happened, if I can," he says.

"I know what's happened," the voice says dreamily. "We're on another world. We've been kidnapped by alien telepathic monsters."

Dann is so taken aback that he can only say feebly, "As a matter of fact . . . you're quite right. But don't worry. They're friendly, they really are."

"I know that too," says the voice of Richard Waxman, drifting in horrendous form upon the far winds of Tyree. Next minute his mind-aura subsides, his body darkens.

"What's wrong? What's wrong?"

"He's just asleep," Tivonel says briskly. "You always sleep awhile after you've been deep-drained. But look here, Tanel. Janskelen has something *really* wrong."

"What do you mean?"

The body of the old female seems to be floating easily, adjusting itself automatically on the uprushing air. It takes Dann an instant to recall that he should look at the important thing, the "field." When he does he sees that the nebulosity wreathing the body seems decidedly smaller and less structured.

"Do you have plenyas on your world?" Tivonel demands.

"What's a plenya?"

Instead of answering, Tivonel's mind-field extends and brushes the sleeping one. She recoils.

"Oh, for wind's sake, No! How awful."

"What? What's awful?"

"That's an *animal's* mind, Tanel. Poor old Janskelen has landed in some dumb animal. Oh, how sad."

Dann considers. In the back of his mind a Labrador's tail thumps. Good God. Apparently this Beam stayed focussed right on his group. And will Fearing, God knows who from Deerfield, be here too?

"Tanel, do you realize?" Tivonel is asking. "That's what'll happen to us all if we do what Heagran says. We'll be *animals*. Nothing but beasts. I don't want to live that way, losing everything. I'm going to stay here and die as myself. I know that's what Giadoc'll want. We'll die here together."

Another far fire-shriek splits the heavens. Milder this time. It's starting, all right, Dann thinks. As the uproar dies away he says gently,

"If worst comes to worst Tivonel, it looks as if you may have to die here with me."

Chapter 15

It is so easy this time!

The thread of essence that is Giadoc has felt the tension-release which means that Terenc has left the beam for an alien mind. Now Giadoc must enter one.

Life is near him; he touches, prepared to push. But there is no need—he finds himself being called, almost pulled into a strangely welcoming matrix. No fear here. He condenses into embodiment so gently that it occurs to him to greet the alien creature. As the displaced mind slides out on the Beam, it seems to leave him with a message: *Danger. Take Care.*

Extraordinary! What superior creatures, he thinks, establishing himself in the alien sensorium. To show Fatherly concern in the midst of what must be a terrifying experience. There will be no life-crime here; Giadoc resolves it. If he survives this test he will break the Beam rather than send such people to die on Tyree.

Remembering the stranger's warning he makes no move, but lets the body lie in dark silence as he has found it, while he accustoms himself to the dead air and the weird somatic sensations. Thought-flares are flooding around him, extra-energetic in the Beam's power.

He examines them, looking for Terenc. Seven minds in his immediate vicinity, but no Terenc. All are disorganized and seem totally unconscious; he can read them as if he were among animals. He has, he finds, returned to the same place as before. What is exciting them so?

The nearest mind-field is intent on his physical body, its owner is in fact actually touching his limbs. It thinks of itself as Doctoraris, a Body-Healer. And three others nearby seem to be Healers too. They are focussed on a dead person or animal. How bizarre to have so many Healers! It must be due to their dangerous life among solid matter at the bottom of the wind.

Beyond the Healers is a small, excited, simple field—a child or a female? No; it knows itself as "Kirk," an adult male. Disgraceful!

Beside "Kirk" is the energy-phenomenon he remembers from his last visit: an unidentifiable complex of cold semisentience concentrated in a pod, with tendrils leading farther than he can scan. Some kind of intelligent plant? He probes Kirk's mind, finds its image as a "console" or "computer," apparently not alive. Fascinating!

All this has taken Giadoc only an instant, when suddenly a crude alien fear-probe bounces off him and he recalls that there may be danger here. Who tried to probe him? Ah—it came from the mind he met before, the being with multiple names, "Sproul," "Barr," or "Fearing," whom he had greeted. Now it's stationed apart in a high state of energy, violently compressed and yet drawing attention to itself by a barrage of hostile flares, mainly directed toward himself. This must be the problem the friendly alien had warned him of. This alien seems insanely concerned with ideas of concealment and control; Giadoc decides it would be unwise to attempt to interact with it again until it has calmed down. But he deciphers a useful fact from the repellent chaos of its thought: the body he is in is named "Doctordan."

Meanwhile the "Doctoraris" mind beside him is clamorously willing him to show signs of bodily life. Giadoc makes a final distance scan-sweep but Terenc does not seem to be in range. Very well. Deliberately he opens Doctordan's eyes.

The extraordinary silent light of this world bursts upon him, and the wealth of close, rigid outlines, surfaces, discrete movements, disorients him for a moment. It's hard to identify the mad mute shapes with the mind-fields in his scan. He sorts out the forms of two Healers carrying a sagging thing away; doubtless the dead body they were concerned with. Giadoc is amazed again at the way everything drags downward in this windless place. Even the energy of the Beam seems muted here.

Now Doctoraris is projecting impatience, and, alarmingly, the intention to have him transported elsewhere and do unclear things to his body. Surely Giadoc must prevent this; it wouldn't be fair to return the friendly alien to some unpleasant situation. Doctoraris' mouth is opening and closing oddly. As Giadoc notices this he recalls the air-jet language of this world. He has forgotten to activate his "ears."

He does so in time to hear speech coming from the "Fearing" alien.

"Kirk, you will tell the others that the Omali woman is under treatment for a heart problem. A minor heart problem. Is that clear, Harris?"

The words mean nothing to Giadoc except that they elicit fear-deference from the others. Amazing. But now he must do something if his body is not to be carried away too; his quiescence is being taken as a serious sign.

He energizes Doctordan's limbs, intending to bring it upright like the others. It's hard work, with no wind. He must hold the strange muscles rigid.

"Take it easy, Dann, wait—" Doctoraris protests audibly, his colors weirdly unchanging. "Do you feel all right?"

Giadoc allows the other to guide him into a chair.

"I am all right," he pronounces, probing hard through Doctoraris' mind for some plausible explanation of his collapse, while at the same time he works to deflect and drain the other's concern with him. It's all so alien. But finally he comes across an engram having to do with an organ in the upper part of his body.

"A minor heart problem," he echoes Fearing's words. All this time one of his upper limbs has been involuntarily groping in the recesses of the dead plant-stuff around his alien body. He encounters a small object and has a sudden vivid body-image of bringing it into his mouth. He does so.

"Forgot your medication, eh, Dann?" Doctoraris' thoughts resolve and relax; the mind-turning worked. "Smith, get some water."

"How about a coke, Doctor?" The other Healer asks.

"Okay."

Giadoc manages to grope through the embarrassing ritual of public intake. Fearing is still watchfully lashing out at him from a distance, like a wild corlu in ambush.

"I still think we should take you in, Dann."

"No, no need," Giadoc protests. "I am all right now."

To Giadoc's surprise, Fearing comes to his aid. "I believe we can take Doctor Dann's word for it, Harris. In fact I'd prefer him to remain here. Kirk, bring him some lunch and stay with him. Harris, since Dann says he's all right, I think we'll leave now."

"Very well."

Giadoc has been noticing a small but energetic field approaching from outside the "room." As the others prepare to depart, the newcomer bounces in, saying, "Good God, Major, what's going on here? Where's Margaret? Dann, what's wrong with you? The subjects were becoming extremely upset, I sent them to lunch."

Giadoc ignores the rest of the conversation while he studies this new mind. It is another small-field male—are there no Fathers here? He sees himself in charge of the alien experiment in life-signals: "Project Polymer." His name is "Noah" something and, surprisingly, there are areas of considerable order in his mind.

Good; Giadoc has just realized that he may be here some while. The Beam has not even withdrawn yet in this world's time. Perhaps the time-scales are different. He should behave appropriately to leave the body in good shape for the real Doctordan, and this "Noah" is clearly the best mind by which to guide himself.

"How are you, Dann?" Noah is demanding with more empathy than Giadoc has seen on this world.

"I am all right, Noah. I forgot my medication, that is all."

"Oh. Well, my goodness! Take care. I'm off to the hospital to check on Margaret. The next test is at three sharp, you know."

Regretfully, Giadoc watches him leave with the others. Too bad. But he can use the time alone to gain skill with this body.

As he rises unsteadily to his feet he feels the power of the Beam drain away and cease. On far Tyree the Hearers have broken link. Will his life continue?

He stands gazing around the windless alien enclosure, wrestling with rebellious memories. Tyree's plight—Tivonel—Tiavan's wicked intent. No—No time for that now. What's wrong with him? Resolutely he orders his mind. The minutes pass. He lives.

He feels nothing more than a slightly unpleasant lowering of his vitality. As he had suspected, it is possible to live on here without the Beam.

Very well. His task now is to maintain Doctordan's role until the Beam returns and he can go home. He moves about, gaining clearer and firmer contact with the body's autonomous skills, using his upper limbs to examine himself and his coverings, touching things. These manipulators are so large and strong and naked! It's like being a child again, before his mantle grew. Obviously these beings continue to manipulate matter all their adult lives.

On impulse he presses at the "console" of the cryptic semisentience. It does not respond. Presently he wanders to the access-opening of this place and stands looking out at the extraordinary world of the Abyss. The sheer quantity of static stuffs, the hard wind-bottom with its silent coloration of fear and shame, the ugly verticals and horizontals everywhere, the mute unchanging light. Unsettling, profoundly alien to the blessed blowing world of home. But how exhilarating, to have all this time in an alien world! If this is to be his last adventure, it's a worthy one.

Experimentally, he pushes aside the access-cover and steps out. A weak flare of hostility greets him. Who did that?

Ah; he makes out a kind of pod resting in the middle distance. An alien mind-field is inside. At this range Giadoc can read only vague resentments connected with food and the vigilant intention to prevent Doctordan's body from proceeding farther. He steps back inside.

Extraordinary how much hostility the amiable Doctordan seems to be surrounded by. What a ferocious world! Well, not his concern.

Another pod is noisily arriving. Giadoc watches the "Kirk" alien get out, followed by what is clearly a pet animal. He is carrying objects which he intends to eat—with Giadoc. Oh, winds! Well, so be it.

"Up and around, Doc?"

No empathy here, quite the reverse. But the pet animal is projecting contact-welcome. Giadoc lets his hand move toward it and stops just in time at the flash of jealousy shooting from Kirk's mind-field. What wild people! He follows Kirk to the corner and watches him open the food, probing for his expectations of Doctordan's behavior. Ah; he seats himself.

Fortunately, no speech seems to be expected. By closely following Kirk's mind-pictures, at the same time copying his own actions, Giadoc manages to grapple with what seems to be called a "chicken sandwich" and some "milk." His body's automatic eating actions begin to unroll. Giadoc is delighted; it's like the child's game of following his Father's mental images of mat-weaving. But now he must sort deeper through the other mind for clues to what Doctordan's next actions will be. It's hard to believe these people are so unconscious.

As Giadoc's thought-tendrils snake into the other mind, he comes upon a pocket of emotion so repellent that he drops the "sandwich."

"Had enough, Doc?"

"A, a weakness," Giadoc stammers. Why, this creature before him is guilty of *physical* harm, thinks he has perhaps caused the death of a female. Yes, that dead alien he had glimpsed. And it excites him. Why, these people are savages!

"Terrible about Margaret," Kirk says, his thought wildly at variance with his words. "I guess I didn't take you seriously."

"Yes." Picking up the sandwich, Giadoc pushes aside a flare of repulsive malice toward Doctordan, and concentrates on what there is of Kirk's rational memory-field. "Project Polymer"—ah, here it is. He finds a pyramidal structure with Kirk himself at the top beside a small figure of Noah. Six subjects—the tests—a mind at a distance will attempt to transmit again, etc. etc. All quite simple and childish. But—Wind save us!—Kirk's memory of what he, as Doctordan, will be expected to do, arrangements of complex matter on the test-persons, "electrodes," "pressure cuffs," "biomonitors"—it's appalling. And much too vague. He could never guide himself by this mind. And the next test is quite soon!

If the Beam does not return in time, what can he do?

Well, of course he can always feign illness as he had before. But the spirit of the game has him; he will play out his last adventure as far as he can. An idea comes to him, watching Kirk feed the last of his food to his "dog." Perhaps by double-probing the test persons and the old male "Noah" simultaneously he can get by? That would be a feat!

At this moment two things occur. A pod pulls up outside and releases a flood of large, active mind-fields—and Giadoc realizes that his Doctordan body requires to eliminate water. What to do, in this windlessness?

Luckily the same thought has just risen in Kirk's mind. Another cross-wind conquered! He copies Kirk's disposal of the debris and follows him back to the "latrine" before the new aliens come in.

The liquid-elimination routine proves simple, the body's habits are strong. As he stands beside Kirk, Giadoc allows himself to sample more of the other's surface thought, and suddenly picks up a detailed picture of alien sexuality. It fascinates him so that he almost forgets to hold his stream of liquid steady. Imagine, all that *contact!* Never to know the ecstasy of repulsion—and the egg unblessed by the wind! And how does the Father pouch the egg? Is this Kirk totally immature?

His explorations are interrupted by the entry of another alien, and Giadoc barely manages to follow Kirk's lead in restoring his "dick" and "zipper" to their original states.

The newcomer is transmitting friendship toward him and hostility toward Kirk. Giadoc pauses; the field is so large and expressive that he is sure this mind must be aware. But no; in answer to his mental greeting the other only says, "Not feeling so good, Doc?"

"Weak," Giadoc says, studying the other. Its name is "Tedyost," and it is preoccupied with some massive grief. Giadoc probes further and is enlightened: Tedyost's body is damaged by some illness that afflicts these people. He is in fact dying. Moved by such frailty, Giadoc involuntarily sends him the ritual energy-gift appropriate to the old.

"Dann! Where are you? It's time to set up."

Noah is calling him and the Beam has not returned. Well, now for some improvisation worthy of a true Beam traveler!

He finds Noah just outside.

"I fear I am not feeling all right," Giadoc tells him. "Can you assist me?"

"Damnation! And this is the big one. Margaret out sick, they wouldn't even let me see her. Oh, all right. Every bloody thing always—"

His anger is wholly superficial, Giadoc sees; the intent to help is strong. He follows Noah into a small enclosure containing a mindfield in such agitation that he cannot help extending a Fatherly fieldedge. And he can sense others almost in panic nearby. Winds, this is going to be rough, if he must soothe and double-probe at the same time!

Moreover, the mind under his touch is a puzzle—an unmistakable Father who thinks of himself as a low-status female. But no time for puzzles now. Noah is manipulating a formidable mass of dead tendrils attached to chunks of shiny matter, expecting him to *do* something. What, what? Shamelessly he thrusts among them both, probing for the veins of expectation, their anticipations of what he will do. Ah, yes—select that "wire," the one with the clasperlike disk.

Concentrating with all his might, Giadoc lets his Doctordan hands carry it to the "temple," seat it on the skin. Approval in both minds—that was right. Now the next, yes, and the next. Memorize carefully. Is he succeeding?

Beside him Noah is doing something with "reels," not his concern. They are expecting him to attach another set of wires, something to do with circulation; the alien has extended a lower limb. Which wire? Ah—he guesses right and is already applying it when he catches the surprised objection, "electrode paste." What? Oh—He finds the substance and achieves the proper combination, though apparently too lavishly.

But it's working, he can do it! Elated, he realizes that this ambiguous alien is transmitting warm, Fatherly sympathy to Doctordan. Apparently the friendly Doctordan is well regarded by the test people, whatever hostility he evokes elsewhere. Thinking this, Giadoc lets his concentration slip and discovers he has done something wrong with the strip of matter on the upper limb.

"Let me, Doctor," He/she tells him verbally. "You feel rotten, don't you?"

"Weak," he admits, watching closely as the strip is wound. Noah has gone out.

"It's this awful place. If we get out of here alive I'll be grateful."

The being is deeply, deeply afraid, he realizes. So are they all, he is receiving a wail of fear-thoughts, images of horrifying captivity, indignities, the "Fearing" monster. Well, not his concern. He presses the other's mind with an enfolding flow of reassurance, and turns his body to go.

"You forgot to turn it on."

He turns back, succeeds in following the thought to a cryptic "switch" where he elicits a click and a flow of almost visible dead energy. More marvels—apparently these beings can control inanimate powers. If only he could stay and learn! But where is the Beam?

Noah is in the next compartment, busy with a small, obviously, mind-wounded alien. More expectations greet him: it is the same task all over again. His memory is clear, and this being is not in such tumultuous distress. With rising assurance, Giadoc seizes a strand of matter and begins.

"Hey, Doc, not on my ear."

Somehow Giadoc fumbles through it, expecting every instant to feel the rising energy of the Beam. Meanwhile he is becoming increasingly pleased with himself. His Father's soul is moved by the trouble of these wretched aliens, but as a Hearer he is fascinated by their chaotic, extraordinary individuality. Nowhere does he find the communal engrams, the shared world-views like those any Tyrenni Father transmits to his young. These beings seem to have had no Fathering; even these mind-experimenters have no real communication. Each is utterly alone. They are aliens *to each other*.

Giadoc moves from one to the next, manipulating the strange artifacts, dispensing what comfort he can. Meanwhile he has given up trying to decipher roles and genders; he samples the wildly disparate minds—lonely prides, pains, longings, incomprehensible enthusiasms. Each alone in its different structure and quality. What an extraordinary experiment of nature! How lucky he is to have experienced this.

When he is dealing with the sick young male he had met before he has a surprise. In Tedyost's mind is a scene of rushing, foaming colors. Why, it is almost like the wind of—a place Giadoc will not think of now. There seems to be some beauty on this world too. What a pity he has no time to explore. Tedyost has apparently been banished from this loved place because of his body's illness. How unjust, Giadoc muses, recalling just in time to "turn on" the thing. In fact, this seems to be an unjust, dangerous world. Well, perhaps Doctordan when he returns will be able to help them. But why is the Beam delaying?

The last test-person is most pitiable of all, a mind almost formless with fear for some missing family-member.

"Listen, Doc, they've done something to Ron. I *know* it."

Giadoc can only transmit an emergency pressure of calm, leaving "Rick" staring after him. Noah is blasting out impatience for him to go out to the large enclosure and wait. Giadoc complies.

"Two minutes. Everybody ready?"

Kirk is here too, his dog-animal stationed by his side. Giadoc seats himself, thinking that he must not leave Doctordan's body to fall downward when the Beam returns, as it surely must any moment now. Hungry for knowledge, he scans the cryptic energy of the "computer." Oh, for more time!

"Fifteen hundred, three o'clock. Start!"

Nothing happens for an instant—and then a roar on the life-bands rips through the air so fiercely that Giadoc almost retracts his scan.

"*A–B–A–J–M! A–B–A–J–M! A–B–A–J–M!*"

Great winds, it's Terenc!

He must have entered the distant test-person, the one in the water-pod somewhere. Now he is acting out his part. His nonsensical repeating signal is so strong it's bringing fuzzy imagery-scraps. As Giadoc is noticing these, his alien ears are assailed by a yell from Rick.

"That's not my brother! They've done something terrible to Ron!"

Giadoc opens the door and automatically thrusts an emergency-calm field-edge at Rick, while Noah implores, "It's all right, Ricky! Ron's all right! Please, Ricky, please don't spoil the test."

"He's not all right," Rick persists as Terenc's transmission blares

189

on. But Giadoc's efforts are having effect. Rick slumps back in his seat and lets Noah replace his marking tools. "*Please* write down what you got, Rick. We'll check Ron as soon as it's over."

Excitement is emanating from all the compartments; the others are evidently hearing Terenc's signal all too clearly too. How could they fail?

Giadoc maintains what hold he can on Rick while Noah calls out, "Second group. Start!" —and Terenc's new signal comes blasting through.

"*B–N–O–Z–P! B–N–O–Z–P! B–N–O–*"

More agitation from the other cubicles. Giadoc strains to send out a wave of reassurance while keeping pressure on Rick. Oh, when will the Beam come and free him?

"Third group. Start!"

May Terenc fall out of the Wind, Giadoc curses, as the third shout yammers through. The effort to soothe them all is taking all the field-strength he has on this weak world. But Terenc is throwing them close to panic, and it's his responsibility not to let harm come . . . The interval seems to take forever.

By the fourth signal even Kirk is showing signs of disturbance, but Giadoc does not care. Where in the Wind's name is the Beam? They must recall Terenc first.

As the fifth signal howls in, Noah pops his head through the door.

"Dann, I believe I'm *getting* something myself!" he whispers, his field flaring elatedly. "This is amazing, we must discover the exact conditions. Ron's never been so good before!"

And never will again, winds willing, Giadoc thinks.

And then to his infinite relief he feels the thrill in the air, the palpable, thrumming, building power of the seeking Beam.

"*Take Terenc! Take Terenc first!*" he projects with all his might as the last signal-groups come ripping through.

"That's it!" Noah is shouting happily, rushing among the cubicles. "Identical! Every one identical, Kirk! Oh, wait till they see this. Dann, Dann, come help me get the subjects out."

But Giadoc does not stir. The huge tension of the Beam is coming to full focus on him now. In a moment he will be away forever and the real Doctordan will be here to do his work. Giadoc wishes them well. But why is it taking so long?

Ah! Energy culminates.

But just as he gathers himself to launch out upon it, he realizes something is wrong. No good, wrong bias! His life is thrown back violently, dazing him, but he realizes the dreadful meaning. *"NO! Fathers, you must not!"* he sends fiercely.

But it is too late. Familiar energies are blooming into being nearby.

"Doctor Dann, help! Frodo—"

"Dann! Chris is—"

Giadoc staggers through the clamor in the cubicles, already knowing what he will find. Yes—an alien female body is lying screaming on the floor, wreathed in the terrified field of a Tyrenni child. As he stares, the small alien male blunders past him and falls to its knees by the body. Around him surges the huge, unmistakable field of a Father of Tyree. The newcomer clasps the alien girl. The fields merge, the screams cease.

It is the life-field of Giadoc's son, Tiavan, and his child.

"Criminal! Go back!" Giadoc lashes at him.

"Tyree is burning. I will save my child." And then Tiavan is wholly preoccupied in Fathering, his alien mouth mumbling "Calm, you're safe my little one. Father's here."

Uproar among the aliens; one is clinging to Giadoc and crying out. The air is humming and bursting with the power of the Beam. The alien Kirk has pushed into the commotion and, unthinkably, is tugging at Tiavan's small bodily form, trying to pull him from his child. Tiavan mind-strikes him, he staggers back. Then Rick gives a loud scream and falls, while another, smaller Tyrenni field streams out around him. *"No wind!"* it transmits in horror. But Giadoc has no time to attend, he is almost knocked over by Kirk charging out.

"I'm calling the patrol. You freaks are into my head!"

"No, no, Kirk!" Noah rushes after him.

Giadoc follows in time to see Kirk seizing some energy-device. But as he does so, his body arches backward and he shouts wordlessly, falling. In a móment his own limited energies are replaced by the wildly flaring energies of a child of Tyree. At its first cries, the old ambiguous alien stumbles out and falls upon it, another huge Father-field furled around them both. Giadoc thinks he recognizes the life-pattern of Father Colto. Kirk's animal is circling them, uttering yelps.

"Doctor Dann, what's *happening?*" cries the alien still clinging to his arm. Next second she too staggers, still hanging on him, and the life-aura spreads to a pattern he knows: the female Avanil.

"N-o w-wind—" she mumbles, and collapses. There is a final yell and crash from the corridor.

Angered beyond expression, Giadoc stands irresolute in the throbbing, energy-brimming room. Seven Tyrenni are here. Only the old alien Noah is left, so excited that he can only turn in place, gasping, "You—you—Who? We, I think I—" while the power of the Beam rains down, still biassed against him.

Then the dog suddenly falls over, and Giadoc sees a last Tyrenni field striving to form around it.

The Beam clears. He is free to go.

But as he gathers himself, the vision of the two Fathers attempting to comfort their grotesque "children" wrenches him. And Tiavan, his son. How can he leave them to the dangers of this place? Desperately he mind-shouts, *"Go back! Undo your crime. This is a dangerous world, your children are not safe here."*

"No!" The figure of Tedyost lurches out of the corridor, a big Tyrenni field streaming about it. But the life is damaged, in terrible disarray; Giadoc can scarcely recognize him.

"Scomber!" he exclaims aloud. "You have done this thing."

"Yes." Tedyost's body falls against the wall and slides downward, while Scomber's wounded life writhes, trying to restore itself. Beyond him Giadoc can see Tiavan trying to force his small alien body to carry or drag his child in this windless place. It is pathetic beyond bearing. But the power of the Beam is falling and rising oddly; Giadoc must go.

At that moment he becomes aware of alien minds outside, and a hostile emanation from the doorway.

Major Fearing walks into the room.

The hatred he transmits is so shocking that Giadoc is transfixed. Danger here. But the alien's outward appearance is spuriously calm and relaxed as he gazes around the chaotic room. When he perceives the prone figure of Kirk cuddled in the old alien's arms his mind forms the words, *"They've got that fool Kirk."* Meanwhile his mouth is saying smilingly, "Well, Noah, how did your big test go?"

His hand holds out a paper.

Noah comes out of his trance and begins distractedly exclaiming and showing Fearing his results. As he does so, Giadoc can read in Fearing's thoughts the intent to do some violence to the bodies in which the Tyrenni are, in which his son is; a picture of them lying inert and mindless, something about Doctoraris. The contrast between Fearing's hatred and his demeanor is frightening, it implies absolute power to do his will. The Beam is flickering again, but Giadoc cannot leave the oblivious Tyrenni now. The Beam will wait for him; it must.

"DANGER! DANGER!" He sends in utmost-emergency mode. But the Fathers are too preoccupied. Only Avanil's mind starts to respond. But she breaks off, touching the dog, and mind-cries, *"Janskelen! Janskelen is in this bad body!"*

It is true, Giadoc sees, but he is thinking of protecting Tiavan. He can now read Fearing's intention to call in his followers and seize the helpless Tyrenni. Great Wind, what can he do? Can he mind-turn Fearing as one would an animal? For even that he needs another Father's help.

"Tiavan, Colto! Help me for your children's sake! Tiavan—"

As he mind-shouts the Beam falters, rises, sinks away worse than before. Is he about to be trapped here? *"Tiavan—Colto—"* Meanwhile Fearing is saying with eerie calm, "Remarkable range and accuracy, Doctor. I compliment you. I obviously did not take this as seriously as I should. Fortunately I have been able to make immediate security arrangements."

"What do you mean, security arrangements?" Noah demands confusedly.

"In your natural enthusiasm, Doctor Catledge, you have overlooked the first and basic consideration of any intelligence capability. Control. *Control.* This remarkable demonstration makes speed all the more imperative."

He turns toward the door, flicking a snap of cold energy from his wrist.

It is the last instant for them all, Giadoc understands. *"Tiavan! Colto! They are about to take and harm your children! Send them back!"*

"But these are people, Major," Noah is shouting. "This is the United States of America!"

"Precisely," Fearing says.

At that moment the power of the Beam rises momentarily, and a bolt of life-energy flies through the room, dazing them all. When Giadoc's senses clear, Fearing is prone on the floor beside the dog, who is squealing and jerking frantically.

Fearing rises awkwardly to one knee and Giadoc, astounded, sees what has happened.

"Janskelen!"

"Y-y-yes," says the mouth of Fearing.

The door of the room opens and a large alien stands there, its small field oriented to Fearing. "Sir?"

Giadoc abandons all civility and sends a hard mental command into the old female's mind. Janskelen flinches, but she is quick.

"Remove . . . that . . . animal," she says with Fearing's voice.

The dog is slavering, attempting to walk on its hind legs, with Fearing's mind-field whirling about it so madly that it seems impossible the alien does not see. But he only advances a step, studying it phlegmatically.

Noah starts to speak, but Giadoc mind-quells him.

The dog howls and scrambles awkwardly onto the desk.

"Be careful, it is dangerous," Giadoc says involuntarily.

"Yes sir." Still with no animation the alien turns to the door and calls. "Deming! Bring a net and a can of four-oh-eight."

At this the dog screams again and leaps straight for him. The alien ducks aside and the dog bolts out the open door. Shouting from outside. Then the alien turns back and asks, "Do you want Doctor Harris' team here now, sir?"

Again Giadoc improvises mental commands, and "Fearing" says slowly, "No. Tell them . . . to go. That will be . . . all."

"Yessir." The alien departs.

Safe, for the moment at least. But the Beam is fading badly, Giadoc must go now or be forever trapped.

"Tyrenni! You are still in peril. Tell this old alien Noah who you are. He may help you. I will not commit life-crime. I go."

Gathering himself to the failing power, he casts a last scan back on the scene that holds his only child—he will remember it always—and hurls his life up and out onto the frail life-thread. He is just in time, he feels his being caught, stretched immaterially in a flash through nowhere. Back to doomed Tyree, back to Tivonel! And Doctordan back to his rightful body. He has made it, he hurtles exultantly. The Beam holds true!

But just as he exults—his universe vanishes.

The skein of vitality that bore him has gone to nothing, there is no Beam. All energy has died. He is only a dwindling nothing adrift in nowhere, all life is draining out of him. He is about to die. And ahead looms a dreadful blackness that his fading mind knows only too well.

The Destroyer.

Goodbye Tyree . . . Goodbye Tivonel . . . Thought dies. Helpless in cold and dark, that which had been Giadoc plunges into death.

Chapter 16

In cold black nowhere a tiny thing will not die.

Alone in dark immensity, the energy-configuration that has been a life is almost extinguished. It is stripped of all qualities, shrunk to a single point of not-death in a universe of deathliness. Blind and mindless it strives against annihilation, fighting with no weapons but its puny naked will.

Aeons earlier it had shot here seeking obliteration. But at the end, the life at its core will not let go.

It is alone, alone in the ultimate icy void, falling without motion ever deeper into dark nothingness. Only a fading spark strains, strives for some possibility, some dimension or current or difference to save it from the final dark. It flails limblessly, grasps nothing, struggles without strength or hope against the overwhelming death around it. Deeper and deeper it is swallowed. Its last existence flickers; it is almost gone.

But at this final instant its immaterial being meets an infinitesimal resistance. Something—something is tenuously touched!

Too weak even to feel reprieve, the spark clutches, clings to the unknown contact. And as it does, slow help comes to it. The faltering energy finds itself minutely sustained; the potential gradient that had fallen nearly to zero halts, and begins painfully to steepen again. After an unknown time it is able to stabilize. Now it is more than a point. It becomes a faint but growing constellation around the nucleus. Fragments of its dead self come back to spectral being.

With them comes a first emotion of life—fear. Hideous images of being strangled, frozen, asphyxiated, destroyed in a myriad terrifying ways assault it. The being struggles harder, a frantic mote in the maw of death. It clings to the unknown sustenance, fighting simply to continue to be. And as it strives it strengthens, recruiting the shadowy energy-circuits and complexities of its former life.

Presently there comes to it a kind of half-consciousness, and it perceives mistily that it cannot be strangled nor frozen, since it is without breath or pulse in infinite dark. These are only specters of sensation evoked by terror of the huge menace all around. Knowing itself dead yet not-dead, it tries fiercely to collect itself, to recreate its shattered entity. It drives toward existence as a drowner drives toward air, it exerts stress upon the texture of nonbeing. Strength grows in it, it presses hard and harder against nothingness. Pressure mounts, a substanceless film bulges without dimension. Until suddenly nothingness yields, and there is a blossoming, tearing pain like orgasmal birth.

The ghostly circuitry of a living woman exists again, strung out between the stars.

The sense of re-existence is acute, paroxysmal. The being convulses in long shudders of awareness. With wonder it perceives itself, knows that it has coherence, complexity, a history, even a name.

It is Margaret Omali.

No! She clenches herself away, would shriek out if she could. The name is a damnation, it brings pouring in on her the pain of a life she had meant only to end. What cruelty is this, why is she not dead?

She shrinks, trying to cancel consciousness, disappear from being. But she cannot; she senses that her despair is fueling the energy that sustains her. Her human life streams back, activates even the echo of her last human thought: *My insurance. Donny will be all right.*

What dreadful happening has cheated her of death?

Sick and grieving she drifts, uncaring that the unknown sustenance continues. The energy that is her life augments and completes itself in phantom structure. And at length her despair is penetrated by dull puzzlement. Something is different. At first idly, then with sharpening attention, she examines this strangeness. Can it be true?

Warily, she lets her thoughts open, lets herself be known to herself, and finds astonishment.

It is true! The pain and tension that hammered at her nerves are gone. Nothing hurts her now.

She can scarcely believe it. For so long she lived in lacerated shame, her body an aching agony without release. Her only desire was to hold the psychic wound quiet, to escape to levels of the mind beyond its reach.

Now it is gone. Feeling herself deliciously unbodied she stretches immaterially, as one would stretch exhaustedly upon cool sheets. Yes! Yes! The relief holds, exquisite as bare limbs lapped in eiderdown. Whatever remains of her has left her body and its pain behind forever. She does not know or care what or where she is, marvels only at the sweetness of release.

The memory of the brief bliss she had once felt from a drug brushes her, but that was far-off and unreal. This, whatever this spectral half-life is, is real. Exultance, amazement floods her.

She is dead—and free!

Letting herself sense it fully, she would laugh aloud in this place of death if she had anything to laugh with. But laughter is unnecessary here, the emotion itself suffices. Relaxed as she had never been in life, she exists as a substanceless smile.

How long the simple joy of no-pain lasts she has no idea; here time is not. But finally a human curiosity of place stirs in her. She is, she knows, totally alone. That does not trouble her, she had always been locked in loneliness. Now she wishes simply to understand this place, if she is in a universe where place has meaning. Specific memories come to her; she recalls her wild flight through the void among incarnations flashing like dreams, her final plunge toward the deathly blackness. It had seemed to her then to be a lethal hole in space, a sure and ultimate extinction. Is she now somehow alive *in* that?

The thought does not frighten her in her new comfort. But the desire grows in her to know more. Without material senses or receptors she quests around herself, aware that she must not let go of the strange cold pinpoint of energy that sustains her life. What can it be, what is she based on? She has heard of superconductors, of circuits that cycle forever near the cold of ultimate zero. Perhaps she is drawing strength from something like that. But what is out there? The strange small sense she has never let herself think of is still with her; she gathers it and tries to outreach, a feeling-outward of inquiring life.

Nothing. She reaches farther—and touches real death.

The contact is dreadful. She cowers in upon herself, knowing that something cold, alien and terrible is out there, nearby. Is it aware of her?

She waits. Nothing happens. The coldness she had touched does not seem to be moving, comes no closer. She listens without ears, attends with all her being for something, anything to tell her more. Still nothing. But the void has dimension now. There, along *that* direction, is danger.

She must recoil, get farther from it, but she dares not let go of the anchor-source of her strange life. She strains away to her utmost, searching, probing. Still nothing. But wait—now she senses, fainter than silence, an impalpable tendril of presence just at the margin of her ken. She attends hungrily, trying to tune herself to it.

And a conviction grows: it is not hostile. It has in fact a reassuring *ordinary* quality, like some familiar small comfort of her lost life. What can it be? It seems—yes—it is somehow beckoning her, like a hand outstretched to lead her away from the dangers of this place.

With all her small might she focusses out toward it. And the fringes of her being touch a gossamer point. A density, another of the strange contacts lies there. Dare she try to transfer to it? *Come,* the faint summons urges from beyond.

She gathers her courages, marshals her being. Her mind enacts the image of a woman leaping from stone to stone across an immense dark river: *I dare!* She lets go her base and sends herself wholly across the void to coalesce around the new support.

Success! She knows now she has moved physically, in whatever space this is. She has moved away from the deadly touch, over what distance she has no idea, an atom's width or a light-year. And the act of will has strengthened her. She feels her own intricate existence triumphant in the dark, and tries to scan around.

The faint beckoning something is definitely stronger here. *Come! This way.*

Can she continue? Again she reaches with her mind, and again finds contact. Another of the cold life-sources is there. Without hesitation she leaps to it and begins to search anew. Yes! There are more. And the friendly call is clearer. In marveling excitement she leaps, or flows, or hurls herself again and again. She is mastering the rhythm, she can move here in abyssal night.

The image of stepping-stones has vanished. As she moves she knows herself as nothing woman-shaped, but a pattern of energy flashing along charged points. Flow, gather, surge—she is energy discharging through capacitors, perhaps. But a structure, she thinks; a very complex configuration; the spectral texture of a human mind. And as she moves another image comes to her, so that she pauses for a moment in wonder. Is she something like a computer program? A ghostly program prowling the elements of some unimaginable circuitry?

The thought delights her. She does not believe in heaven or gods or demons or any hell beyond the life she had known, but she has seen real ghosts in her computer read-out screens. She knows she is dead and she had never been very human. To be a free, untormented ghost-program is not frightening.

Perhaps the danger she had felt was some design to cancel her, to flush her out of existence as they had attempted to flush out TO-TAL's ghosts?

No, she decides. I will not be evicted. I will maintain this new sweet life awhile, even as nothing in the cold and dark. But what is this small calling presence or energy which she has been following? It is very close now, she can sense its urgency. What is it? Is it perhaps another like herself here in the paths of death?

The thought displeases her. She thinks toward it demandingly, striving to shape interrogation. *Who are you? What is there?*

Nothing answers her at first, only the ever-stronger summoning, an almost tangible directional desire. Like a dog tugging at her coat, willing her to follow.

What are you? Tell me! No answer. But she realizes abruptly that an image has formed in her mind's eye, a glimmering vision like a pallid rectangular shape rising through black water. It is a computer console.

Is she imagining this? As she attends to it the image strengthens. She can make out the keyboards, the dials, the read-out screen and reel decks above. Why, it is her familiar office console, she has spent years at those grey, red, blue keys; there is even the stain where ditto-fluid was spilled. It is hallucinatory, it quivers or shimmers like an after-image, floating on the darkness that presses around and through it. But it is no ordinary vision; she wills it away, but still it will not go.

Puzzled, the thought comes to her to activate it. Instantly there is a vivid kinaesthetic sensation of her own arm moving, she sees the long dark fingers that are no longer hers float out and press the toggle. *On.*

At the same moment the screen flickers to life. The symbol is clear, a tiny blue arabesque in black immensity.

$$\int_0^{\pm \infty} f(t)\, dt$$

It is the integral of time to plus or minus infinity, the "signature" of TOTAL's unquenchable ghost!

Half-amused, half-annoyed, she probes at her own thought. Is she recreating memory or is this some real manifestation of the condition she has waked to? It holds; it seems so real. Well, if she is herself a ghost-program, what more likely than that another should be here? Has her mind somehow got into TOTAL? She hopes not; she had been sure that she was far from Earth. No matter, she decides. It's all fantasy, a dead mind dreaming.

As she had done so often before, she makes no effort to cancel the intruding program but instead lets her hallucinative fingers tap out a holding code. The screen flashes//TIME*INDEPENDENT* STORE//and vanishes from her mind.

With that the sense of the calling awareness comes back in force. *Come! Follow me!* The friendly quality is unmistakable now.

Fantasy upon fantasy. Bemused, she yields and lets herself flow from invisible point to point in the desired direction, as she has learned to do. I am in the underworld with my faithful computer, she thinks. I am being led through the land of death by a friendly computer program. Perhaps it likes you, someone had said. Perhaps it does, or at least the crazy ghost-program does. She is sure she senses a strange amicable intent, unliving, cool yet warm. The marvel of the complexity of the great electronic ganglia comes to her again. Could it have been, was it, somehow a real base of life?

The idea seems more than fantasy here, following insubstantiality through nowhere. More memories awake. She had never had nor desired telepathy, the contact of human minds; but some abstraction of energy-in-complexity had always touched her in a deep, peculiar way. She empathized with it. Working with TOTAL she had always felt in more than technical rapport, some bond beyond the mere program being executed. She had never consciously thought about this; it was of the same almost shameful secret nature as her flashes of power over real matter. A crazy thing. Perhaps she was not very human. But if structured energy achieved a kind of life, would she not have access to it?

The idea grows into conviction. She is sure now that she recognizes the entity she is following, a computer life somehow tuned to hers. But where, in what strange universe are they?

She has been increasingly aware that their dreamlike progress is changing course, the route is not straight. And it is hazardous; she is receiving now urgent demands to hurry, now a sense of being warned back. It is weirdly like a child's game. But the danger here is not imaginary; again and again she feels a brush of icy menace. Is she being led stealthily through a fortress? Are they escaping? Or are they going ever-deeper into the heart of the immense enemy, to its very brain, perhaps?

Deeper, she thinks; danger seems to lie now on all sides, as if they are creeping through secret conduits into an inmost stronghold. Vast unknown energies are all about; the void is not quite empty, here. Human fear touches her, and she hesitates. But the urgent pleading intensifies, begs her to go on. She does. The nothingness around her densens. Surely she is nearing some end.

At that moment all urgency to motion ceases, and she knows that she has arrived. The destination, the center, the mighty nexus of this universe lies just beyond. Warily she gathers herself. *What is here?*

As it had done before, the console-image rises to life in her mind. This time the screen is lit. She reads:

//NO*ENTRY*EXCEPT*TO*AUTHORIZED*PERSONNEL//

For a timeless instant that which had been Margaret Omali tries to laugh, would laugh, exists as laughter in the dreadful dark.

The absurd message brightens, changes to TOTAL's time-signature, then runs through an array of vectors she recognizes as a loop in the NASA space-voyage simulation, ending with a special-exit sequence and repeats:

//NO*ENTRY*TO*OTHER*THAN*AUTHORIZED*PERSON-NEL//

Slowly, she understands. This is communication; somehow a mind that is not a mind, an unliving life, is trying to link with hers. How does it know her? Is it possible that the same keys that gave her entry to TOTAL were a two-way channel, gave TOTAL some real access to her? Does it know her as a program called human?

No matter. She has the message: This is a portal.

Here is the interface with some unknown concentration of power and information. She can go in. But the decision is forever. Once inside, once "authorized," she will be meshed with whatever lies beyond.

Past this point, she thinks, I won't be human anymore. The thought troubles her briefly. But the presence she has followed is waiting, emanating its promise and warning. A cold beauty seems to call to her, a vista of no earthly dimensions. What does she care for the humanity she had known?

Deliberately disregarding a last faint pulse of mortal fear, she focusses on the darkness ahead. A silent tide of power seems to rise against her, cold, cold and enormous. But she has power too. *Here, push here!* TOTAL seems to call. She gathers her weird small sense of force and sends it wholly at the interface, lunges mindwise at the enveloping black. *"I am authorized!"*

Disorientation takes her, consciousness fractures. For an endless moment she is only a cloud of will in motion, suffering immense compression like a huge black squeeze. *"I will!"*

—And the barrier yields.

She is through, she has come into the unknown power's heart.

Slowly she collects herself, not feeling, at first, very different. But she is not in silence anymore. This space is structured with directional energies, pulse-trains of signals on a myriad unknown bands. New senses.

She puzzles briefly, trying to make these strange inputs come clear. She is on the verge of understandings, her structure is merging with detector-circuits undreamed-of. She is not at all frightened, only eager for some vast new mode of being that lies near. There is no sense of menace anymore; only a peculiar cold sadness which is not hers. It comes to her with no surprise that she is no longer mobile. She will not leave this place; she has no desire to.

As she feels outward mentally, the time-signature of TOTAL recurs insistently to her attention. So the small ghost is with her here, linked to these mysteries, yet apart. Will it be her access, as it had in life?

Experimentally, she wills a master circuit, flicks a phantom switch. *Board On!*

In answer, a spectral console springs up around her, merged with her old familiar board. But this is an apparition glimmering into strange dimensions, a vast control-panel of dreams whose keys bear cryptic symbols.

She studies it, trying to grasp the layout. As she does so, portions of the great board seem to light up in focus as if an invisible spotlight is moving from one to the next with her mind. At the same time she has a brilliant image of her own fingers hovering curiously over the keys. The vision is far more vivid than before; this place is potent. Thought-structures are strong here, as if she could create reality by will.

The thought amuses her. She flexes her dream-fingers as she had in life, feeling herself drawing on a thread of secret power. Her strange flashes of efficacy over matter are stronger, steadier here. The unknown potency of this void is *compatible*, reinforcing and resonating on a band which is more than a frequency, in which she shares.

On impulse she holds up her dream-hand and bends down the long familiar fingers one by one, counting in binary mode: 00001, 00010, 00011, 00100 . . . The mental construct holds, runs off to 2^5-1, thirty-one. Why, she can do anything!

Can she create? Experimentally she wills her hand to hold a bunch of white roses. They are there. *Perfume*, she thinks—and the scent she had loved wafts to her nonexistent nostrils. For a moment she lets herself exist in pleasure. The thought comes to her that she could will herself an intact body, be as she had been as a child before—before what she will not think of. But the idea is faint, far-off; she tosses it up and away with the roses. They turn to a cascade of sparks, wink out as they fall toward the shadowy tiers. The huge console seems to be still waiting enigmatically for her attention.

As she surveys it again, she becomes aware of a curious pull or emphasis trying to draw her mind's eye. Again and again she finds herself considering a section at the center, close by TOTAL's familiar keys. A single roll-over switch gleams there. She concentrates on it, pointing a meditative finger. The surface around it shines, the switch is of an unknown color, surmounted by one symbol. It is very clearly in the Off position.

As she attends to it, an almost tangible sense of pleading pressure comes to her and TOTAL's small read-out lights.

//ACTIVATE//

Almost her hallucinatory finger presses the switch—and then she pauses. That image cloaks real power, she understands. It is a connection or interface with something vast and real. Is this why the computer-spirit has brought her here, so that her own small power may give some necessary push, initiate real access? Does TOTAL "want" her to manipulate an actual connection on behalf of whatever dark presence or machinery surrounds her? Genially she recalls the earthly TOTAL's appetite for access, the spontaneous linkages it seemed to have achieved. Has it found some ghostly ultimate network here in the dark?

//ACTIVATE*ACTIVATE*ACTIVATE//

The energic constellation that had been Margaret Omali considers the plea, and a last human willfulness awakes. She is not yet a phantom, a mere pliable pawn. She will not comply with this directive . . . yet. Quite humanly, she is tired of acting in mystery. She has come through dangers and blackness to this place of power and now she has some mental desires to fulfill. Before assenting further, she will know where she is and among what powers and conditions this strange life is set.

How will she get answers, here?

Deliberately she summons TOTAL to the small strange vein of power in her mind, and frames a command to data-access, her thoughts sketching and shaping a program of real-time inputs of fact and space. Am I in a computer? Is this a dream? Her familiar keyboard glimmers before her; her fingers go to it and firmly press TO-TAL's keys.

Query this location. Display.

With a great soundless rush the blackness around her vanishes. She is floating in a universe of jeweled lights.

It worked, she exults. I have power—and then all thought is inundated by sheer magnificence. On every side, above, below, before, beyond, blaze steady fires of amethyst and topaz and ruby, emerald and diamond and ultramarine—drift upon drift of them, burning against blackness or veiled in filaments and gauzes of hypnotic allure.

They are, she realizes slowly, stars. The unwinking suns of space. She is floating amid the glory of the universe, seeing without eyes the incomprehensible vast unhuman beauty of the void. Her mind which had always flinched from the hot closeness of human color is enchanted with this infinity of spectral fires.

But a vague doubt troubles her. Is this real? Someone had told her of the stars; is all this merely some simulacrum of her dead and dreaming human mind?

How can she test? She selects a beautiful pair of sapphire and yellow suns.

Magnify.

Obediently, they grow, seem to approach and separate, and reveal a dim violet companion, all filmed in a wispy nebula in which are points of light. At the same time she becomes aware of a rise in input on one of the unregarded bands, as if these stars were giving off a train of signals. The impression of reality is overwhelming. But still she doubts.

She turns to TOTAL's keyboard, thinking hard. What would unmask a dream? At length she frames a demand on TOTAL's memory-banks.

Specify.

The screen lights. //BETA*CYGNUS//COMMON*NAME*AL-BIREO *DERIVED *FROM *ERROR *IN *INTERPRETATION *OF*ALMAGEST*1515//   MAGS*5.5*4.5//PA*055//SEP*34.6'// SPECTRAL*CLASS*OF*PRIMARY*A5—

Her attention goes back to the triple beauties, considering. The names Beta Cygnis, Albireo, are utterly unknown to her; all these data could not have come from her human mind. This must be real. Somehow she can call up earthly information, here between the stars.

How this could be does not trouble her, she is too far from human considerations; she no longer remembers NASA, nor the flap about TOTAL's wiped memory-cores. She merely accepts it as one more aspect of this wondrous death and feels her soul smile. In due course she may inquire further; when she is moved to it, she may probe, perhaps, the nature of this huge cold power whose perceptions she seems to share. Now she is content to exist at ease, to dream amid marvels.

The odd energy-output of the brilliant triple system she has summoned presently attracts her curiosity, and she puts another question to TOTAL.

Query. Is life there?

//AFFIRMATIVE// the screen responds. And the peculiar pulse-trains seem to amplify, as if unknown receptors had been tuned to them.

She "listens" uncomprehendingly, amused by this new dimension of experience, and sensing that some indefinable significance has been evoked. But if this is "life" she can make nothing of it. I am not concerned with life, she thinks, and dismisses Beta Cygnis. Compliantly the pulse-trains fade, the splendid triple system fades back into the jewel-drifts of space.

But in another dimension of her mind, the ghostly center-panel of the great console still shows its unknown switch: she senses still the faint urgency. What unimaginable program would it execute? She wonders briefly and again dismisses it. For the moment she wants nothing more.

Her attention returns to the outer radiance in which she floats, and now she becomes aware of something new. Motion is here; slow but increasingly perceptible. Like themes of silent music, the orbital elements of the nearer stars reveal themselves to her mind. Suns weave hugely about each other, develop subcomponents of direction, or glide in concert athwart a general flow. Slowly the motion spreads away to the farthest reaches, until the whole is in sublime and complex dance.

Delighted, she bends all her thought on this new wonder, understanding that somehow her phantom senses have slowed, or speeded, to a cosmic scale. Beyond the sheer splendor of the fires of space she now sees a deeper, causal, magnificence. She can almost sense directly the interlocking webworks of field forces, the lawfulness of every accidental configuration. And more: beneath the macro-order, if she cares to look, there is revealed the play of another lawfulness, that of the acutely small. The stars are not constant, but changing: they alter in color, shrink or swell or blaze to slow immense explosions. All this she understands as the expression of subatomic transformations and events. The ultimate minute causalities are hers too, when she wills to look deep.

Her human mind that since childhood had yearned dimly toward the enchantment of relation, had groped toward it beneath the veil of number and symbol, experiences a long slow gasp of immaterial rapture. Here is the beloved naked to her view.

Time no longer exists. What had been Margaret Omali slips toward irreversible fusion with something huge and alien whose powers she partially shares. A last corner of her personality laughs with a child's purity, envisioning a vast control-room of the stars. Of herself she knows only that she exists in peace and exaltation. The grandeur of the universe unfolds as the tapestry of her understanding. She opens herself entirely to the pure, cold pleasure. The mind that had been a human woman floats out to lose itself in the justice of the play of suns and atoms, the intricate beauty of cosmologic cause.

* * *

Aeons, or instants, later, a minute distraction penetrates her consciousness. A stray human engram focusses on it, flickers the impression of a midgelike vibration somewhere about.

It persists, mars her absorption. At length she detaches a portion of her attention from outwardness, and perceives that the intruding signal is on that band of life-signals that means nothing to her. But this one is different. Though tiny it moves, and is very fine tuned and sharp. An obscure sense tells her it is coming from nearby.

How could that be?

Unease touches her. She wishes no impingement on her serene joy. Withdrawing more of her attention from the universe outside, she focusses sharply on the little signal. Yes, it is nearby—and its motion is bringing it closer. It is approaching her place of power, her fortress of content.

A cool irritation awakens. Almost idly she wills into being circuits which will abolish it forever, encyst and blow away this insectile irruption. *Destruct.*

But as she moves to activate, a human memory is tickled. The mental cry carries what she recognizes remotely as pathos. She recalls her own time of aloneness in the cold and black and the deathliness out there. This tiny whatever-it-is has perhaps no friend, is wandering helpless in illimitable icy dark. A vague wash of compassion damps her anger. She stays destruction and "listens" closer.

Yes, it is something like a lost child's cry. Not threatening. Although she is no telepath, it is so close outside that she can sense the plea.

An amused benevolence takes her. She is all-powerful, but how to comprehend this crying thing?

Ah: TOTAL. Of course. She sets the odd efficacy of her mind to imagine spectral voice-pick-up circuits, channels leading beyond her stronghold to translate what is there.

Display input.

Obediently TOTAL's small print-out panel glimmers to life.

She reads, and more human memory awakens, mingled with a cosmic sense of the absurd. Mortal recognition here, in this supernal immensity?

And of all voices, that one. Perhaps no other earthly signal could have penetrated her vast alienation in safety. Certainly anything closer to the center of her former life would have evoked only annihilation. But this one is so slight, so distant and innocuous, carrying nothing but the faint recollection of cool good will. And it speaks to her own memory of oppression in the dark.

With gigantic playfulness she wills a read-out for the excluded mite, and lets her phantom fingers tap out a reply.

Chapter 17

"VICTORY! . . . VICTORY! . . . "

THE PAEAN REVERBERATES THROUGH THE VOID STILL. BUT SOMETHING ELSE IS REVERBERATING, PULLING THE VAST BEING'S ATTENTION BACK TO ITS BELEAGUERED SELF.

IT CANNOT LOCATE THE NEW DISTURBANCE. IS IT FROM INSIDE OR OUT?

OUTSIDE IT CAN SENSE ONLY A CHAOTIC TRANSMISSION ON THOSE ENIGMATIC TRANSPEMPORAL BANDS WHICH HAVE ATTRACTED IT SO. THIS ONE IS AMPLIFYING, LIKE THE SIGNALS IT HAD ACHIEVED IN ITS LONELY EXPERIMENTS ON STIMULATING STARS. YES: THE TRANSMISSION RISES AS HE ATTENDS, IT IS COMING FROM SOME DEBRIS AROUND ONE OF THE LAST DISINTEGRATING SUNS OF THE TASK. DOUBTLESS, LIKE THE OTHERS, THIS ONE TOO WILL REACH AN INCOMPREHENSIBLE MAXIMUM AND CEASE.

NOTHING NEW HERE.

YET THE EFFECT IS UNUSUALLY DISTURBING. THROUGH THE HUGE ICY NETWORK OF NEAR-NOTHINGNESS THAT IS THE SUBSTRATE OF ITS THOUGHT THERE SEEMS TO BE PROPAGAT-

ING AN URGE TOWARD SOME ACTION, IT CANNOT CONCEIVE WHAT. THIS HAS NOT HAPPENED BEFORE.

COULD THIS POSSIBLY BE ANOTHER EFFECT OF THE SMALL PASSENGER?

THE GREAT BEING TURNS ITS ATTENTION INWARD, AND PERCEIVES THAT THE SMALL ONE SEEMS TO HAVE AMPLIFIED ITSELF TOO, OR DEVELOPED ADDITIONAL TINY CENTERS NEAR THE CENTRAL NUCLEUS. AND THESE ARE IN HIGHLY ENERGETIC STATES FOR SUCH SMALL MITES. ONE OF THEM IS GENERATING SIGNALS OF THE SAME NATURE AS THE EMISSIONS FROM WITHOUT, WHICH ARE BEING RE-ECHOED WITHIN. BUT THEY ARE NOT GOOD SIGNALS: THERE IS SOME BADNESS OR HURTFULNESS IN THEIR MODE.

HOW DARE THESE INFINITESIMAL ITEMS BEHAVE SO?

COLD ANGER FORMS, STARTING THE SELF-CLEANSING WAVE OF ENTROPY THAT WILL SWEEP AWAY THE LITTLE PASSENGER AND ALL ITS WORKS.

BUT AT THE LAST MOMENT THE HUGE ENTITY HESITATES, PERPLEXED. ITS TINY INHABITANT HAS BEGUN TO TRANSMIT INTERNALLY IN A NEW MIXED MODE INCLUDING IMAGES OVERLAID ON THE RACIAL RECEPTOR BANDS. THE IMAGERY IS INTENSE, VEHEMENTLY MAGNIFIED POINT-SPREADS. HOW UNEXPECTED, THAT THE SMALL CREATURE HAS ATTAINED SUCH ABILITIES IN THE SYSTEM!

DIVERTED, THE GREAT HOST STAYS DESTRUCTION. WHAT IS TRYING TO BE CONVEYED HERE?

//LIFE*LIFE*LIFE//COMES THE SIGNAL.

THE SYMBOL MEANS NOTHING, BUT FROM THE COUPLED IMAGES IS RECEIVED A JUMBLED IMPRESSION OF STRANGE, APPARENTLY SELF-MOTILE ENTITIES OF INCONCEIVABLE COMPLEXITY AND DIVERSITY. THEY SEEM TO BE EMITTING ON THE SIGNAL-BAND OF CRYPTIC ALLURE. THE IMAGES ARE IN TURMOIL; THE ENTITIES CONVULSE, BURST INTO COMBUSTION, FALL BLACKENED INTO MAELSTROMS OF CLEANSING FIRE.

THE HUGE SPACEBOURNE ONE PONDERS. IS IT POSSIBLE THAT THESE THINGS ARE EXTRAORDINARILY MINISCULE? OF A SIZE, PERHAPS, TO INFEST THE MOTES OF MATTER THAT SO OFTEN ACCOMPANY SMALL SUNS? IF SO, IT HAS SOLVED THE

EMISSION THAT PUZZLED IT SO, BUT THE SOLUTION HAS NO MEANING.

THE LITTLE PASSENGER CONTINUES TO EMIT TRAINS OF SIGNALS IN WHICH THE SIGNAL //LIFE// RECURS. THEY SEEM TO BE BEAMED IN A PERSONAL, ACCUSATORY MODE.

ANGER RISES AGAIN, MIXED WITH FAINT PLEASURE AT DISCOVERING A REFERENT. PROBABLY THIS TINY ORDER OF THINGS IS CODED "LIFE." BUT WHY THE AGITATION?

AT LENGTH THE SLOW,   MENSE, COLD PROCESSES THAT GENERATE THOUGHT COME TO A CONCLUSION. THE OUTER SIGNAL IT IS RECEIVING MAY INDICATE SOME DAMAGE TO THIS PECULIAR MICROCOCOSM, THIS "LIFE," WHICH THE SMALL PASSENGER OR ITS NEW PARTS DESIRE TO NEGATE. BUT WHY? THIS IS CORRECT, IS PART OF THE PLAN. IN FACT, THE EMISSION FROM OUTSIDE IS AMPLIFYING AS ANTICIPATED, THE STAR IS GOING THROUGH ITS ORDAINED CHANGES. ALL IS IN ORDER.

BUT WHY, THEN, IS THIS SO PECULIARLY DISTURBING? AND WHY IS THE PASSENGER ACCUSATORY? THE DEFAULT FROM THE TASK WAS LONG AGO, THESE LAST REPERCUSSIONS CAN HAVE NOTHING TO DO WITH THAT. I HAVE DONE NOTHING, THE MIGHTY BEING REASSURES ITSELF. BUT INSTEAD OF SATISFYING, THE THOUGHT SEEMS TO CAUSE MORE DISSONANCE. I HAVE DONE NOTHING: WHAT CAN BE WRONG WITH THAT, ASIDE FROM THE TERRIBLE FAULT OF ABSENCE FROM THE TASK ITSELF? YET SOMETHING IS INCORRECT HERE, IMPLIES MORE WRONG. THE RISING OUTPUT COMBINED WITH THE COMMOTION WITHIN IS CAUSING PAINFUL STRESS.

I DO NOTHING, THE VAST ONE REITERATES TO ITSELF. BUT STILL TENSION BUILDS, INCOMPATIBLE INTUITIONS STRIVE FOR RECOGNITION WITHIN THE ENORMOUS ICY CIRCUITS OF ITS THOUGHT. WRONGNESS AUGMENTS. BUT I HAVE DONE NOTHING. YET I AM SOMEHOW INCORRECT. BUT HOW CAN I BE INCORRECT SINCE I DO NOTHING?

THE DISTRESSING TRANSMISSIONS FROM WITHIN AND WITHOUT GROW IN INTENSITY; THE MIGHTY UNSUBSTANTIAL BEING SWIRLS SLOWLY IN PLACE, DISRUPTING THE NURSERIES OF SUNS, TRYING WITH WHAT IS NOT A BRAIN TO

RESOLVE RELENTLESS PRESSURE. I DO NOTHING, I HAVE DONE NOTHING. YET IT IS NOW DISTURBING TO EXPERIENCE THE NORMAL TRANSFORMATIONS OF "LIFE" IN THE END-REACHES OF THE TASK. THE TASK ABOVE ALL CANNOT BE WRONG. BUT THIS WRONGNESS HAS SOME BEARING ON THE TASK. WHAT, WHAT? IS IT POSSIBLE THERE IS SOMETHING TO BE DONE? EX-ASPERATED TO PAIN, THE GREAT BEING DECIDES THAT THIS WHOLE EFFECT MUST BE THE RESULT OF ITS LAST SIN, THE UN-HEARD-OF ACT OF TAKING ABOARD AN ALIEN SENTIENCE. YES—THIS MUST BE THE ROOT OF ALL THE TROUBLE. AWAY WITH IT!

AGAIN THERE STARTS THE ICY PERISTALSIS THAT WILL CLEANSE IT OF ALL UNWELCOME COMPANY.

BUT DESPITE ANGER, ACTION COMES SLOWLY, RELUCTANT-LY; IT IS AS IF SOME PORTION OF THE GREAT SENTIENCE SUS-PECTS THAT A LARGER DILEMMA HAS BEEN EVOKED WHICH SELF-CLEANSING WILL NOT SOLVE. STILL TENSION MOUNTS UNENDURABLY. YES—ACTION, NOW! AT LEAST LET ME SWEEP THIS PROXIMATE CAUSE OF MISERY AWAY!

BUT AT THAT MOMENT THERE ARISES FROM WITHIN A NEW SIGNAL. THE SEND IS WEAK, BUT ITS NATURE IS SO STRANGE, YET ALMOST-KNOWN, THAT THE HUGE BEING FEELS THAT THE CAUSE OF ITS TORMENT IS ALL BUT OPEN TO ITS MIND. SOME LOST TRUTH IS HIDDEN HERE, SEPARATED BY ONLY THE MOST FRAGILE OPACITY, ALL BUT TO BE GRASPED. IT STRAINS AT THE TINY VOID IT CANNOT BRIDGE.

STRESS MOUNTS UNENDURABLY. AGAIN THE WEAK CRY COMES FORTH. YES! I MUST—I MUST DO—*DO WHAT*?

DOES THE SMALL ONE, PERHAPS, KNOW?

CARING FOR NOTHING BUT RELIEF, THE MONSTER OF THE SPACEWAYS IMPULSIVELY LOWERS ALL INTERNAL BARRIERS, LAYING OPEN ACCESS EVEN TO ITS MOST PRIVATE WELLS OF WRONG AND SHAME. IF THE LITTLE ONE KNOWS WHAT WILL ALLAY THIS TORMENT, ANYTHING IS ENDURABLE. LET IT ONLY REVEAL THE CLUE.

BUT THERE COMES ONLY REPETITION OF THE MEANINGLESS SYMBOL:

//ACTIVATE***ACTIVATE***ACTIVATE//

THIS IS INTOLERABLE! GOADED BEYOND THOUGHT, THE ENORMOUS ONE GATHERS ITSELF TO WREAK A GENERAL DE-VASTATION THAT WILL END ALL AFFLICTIONS FROM WITHIN AND WITHOUT.

—WHEN, WITHOUT WARNING, THE UNIVERSE IS TURNED UPSIDE DOWN.

Chapter 18

Bad . . .

It is very bad. Radiation poisoning is unbelievably painful, Dann is discovering that. His brave jokes about being used to dying have ceased to comfort him; they were all part of the euphoric haze, the happy unreality of his first life in the winds of Tyree.

Now he is meeting instead the reality of searing sonic gales, of burned and poisoned flesh; nausea and hemorrhage and the ruin of his glorious new body. The reality of shortly dying, with Tivonel and his fellow-humans, in those same winds turned lethal.

He looks at them, his six once-human patients—seven if he counts the dog— huddled in the useless shelter of the few plants that grow here at the bottom of the wind-wall. They are quiet now. Hours, or days ago, he doesn't know which, they had moved down by stages to this final refuge from the blasting radiation of the sky. Useless; the Sound is growing every minute fiercer even here. They are in a storm of audible light. And from above he can hear the grey death-moaning of stricken plant and animal life. A world is dying around him.

Nearby is another cluster of giant alien forms: Hearer Lomax and the senior Tyrenni, their bodies scorched and dark. Only their life-fields now and again gather strength to flare strongly upward. Dann supposes they are still desperately searching for some means of psychic escape. He does not feel hopeful. The loathsome Destroyer, it seems, is still blocking the sky.

Tivonel hovers near them, silently intent. Still hoping for her lost Giadoc, no doubt. It hurts Dann to see the damage to her once-graceful form, the warped and blistered vanes. Scattered beyond are groups of the surviving Tyrenni. Frantic Fathers are still trying to protect their young, or reaching out to shelter some orphaned youngster. A cluster of females hovers together, giving each other comfort in their pain. Dark bodies hang all the way up the vegeta-tion-zone above, grim markers of their painful trek down here. The Tyrenni had been slow to grasp the danger of the sky.

One of his human patients stirs; a green flicker moans. Oh God; soon it will be time to use his dreadful "gift" again. Doctor-Dann-that-was laughs at the irony of it, a laugh that is a dull crimson gleam on his injured mantle. To discover now the "gift" that had apparent-ly made him a doctor once, and that will do nothing but make his death more agonizing still.

Not to think about it. Wait till they awaken.

To distract himself he lets himself think back to how it was. A lovely time then, a time of beauty, comedy and surprise, high up in the winds of Tyree.

He and Tivonel had been beside a big male body when the mind within it woke. The body was that of Colto, one of the two young Fathers he had seen fleeing on the beam. Now it houses, incredibly, a human mind. Whose? A Deerfield guard, Major Fearing? the presi-dent of General Motors, for all Dann knows. Its mantle is glimmer-ing with vague golden words. "Where . . . ? What . . . ?"

"Ah, hello," says Dann, feeling ridiculous. "Don't be alarmed, I'm here like you. We seem to have got—mixed up. I'm a doc—a Healer, Daniel Dann. Can you tell me your name?"

The huge being sighs or grunts colorfully, and then seems to come more alert. "Oh, Toctor-Tann," it says in dreamy high light yel-lows. "You look just the way I always saw you! Can't you tell? I'm Winona."

The light-signs that are her voice ring so Winonalike that he is staggered. Winona as this great male thing? He begins a confused joke about not knowing he had looked like such a monster.

"No, I mean your—" she interrupts him, the alien language garbling. "You, your mind. I could always see it, you know. It's lovely."

"Well, thank you," he says helplessly. These telepaths seem to be more prepared for alien transmogrifications than he. "Have they, ah, told you where we are?"

"Why, I can see that," Winona says. "We're in the spirit world."

The tone is so exactly like her voice when they walked together talking of seances, auras, ectoplasm, telepathy—she's right at home; he almost chuckles. But he ought to prepare her somehow.

"It's also a real world, called Tyree," he says gently. "They have a bad problem here, Winnie. That's why some of them have stolen our bodies, trying to escape."

"Oh no," she says, troubled now. "Stolen? You mean—" her speech stumbles, sounds a green plaint of fear.

At this Tivonel exclaims, and the big Father who has been watching them commands sharply, "Do not upset him, Tanel!"

An edge of his field flows to hers, the green hue dies.

"Right," says Dann. "But she's not a male. May I introduce you? Winona, this is my young friend Tivonel, a female of Tyree." There doesn't seem to be any politer term. To the huge presence above he says, "I'm sorry I don't know your name. This is Winona, a female of my world."

"Greetings. I am Elix. But how can you say this?" he demands. "Do I not know a male when I see one? Look at him. Untrained, but obviously a Father."

"But I'm not!" Winona protests. "I'm a female, a—a—I'm a female Father!"

"Nonsense!" Elix says loftily. "Is he insane?"

Tivonel is laughing incredulously, and several Tyrenni who have been watching the exchange jet closer. "See his field," one says. Dann recalls his lessons, and scans the life-energies streaming from Winona's big form. There does seem to be a lot of it, in intricate play. In fact it's more copious than his own.

217

"But she's a female," he says stubbornly. "I swear it."

"A female Father!" Tivonel's mantle laughs amazedly. "Whew! Marockee, Iznagel! Come over here!"

Huge Elix has dropped down closer, scanning hard.

"If this be true, stranger, how many children have you Fathered?"

"Four," Winona signs firmly. "And seven, ah, children's children."

"And you're really a *female*?" Marockee demands. "Really, truly?"

"I certainly am! What's wrong about that?"

"Nothing's wrong," Dann tells her, trying not to laugh. "They're surprised because on this world raising children seems to be done by males. That's why they haven't a word for you. And your, ah, your mind-aura seems to be very large, like a Father's, and since you're in a male body, they can't believe you're not."

"The *males* here raise babies?"

"That's right. I believe you'll find you have an, ah, a pouch."

"You mean, they feed them and cuddle them and clean them and take care of them every day, all day!" Winona demands in tones of glittering skepticism. "And teach them to talk and do everything, all the time for years? I don't believe it."

"Indeed yes," big Elix tells her. "I now see you understand well. But I myself have only reared one. Strange female Father-of-four, I salute you."

He planes down before her, his mantle a respectful lilac.

"Well!" Winona softens. "I certainly didn't mean to be rude. I'd love to hear about your baby."

"But this is against nature!" Another Father protests. "It's unwindly! Before I accept such nonsense I'd like to see this female do some Fathering. Let her try to calm this one if she can!"

His field ripples, his mantle lifts slightly. Dann sees that he is gingerly controlling a Tyrenni child. The young one suddenly contorts violently, its little mantle breaking into bright green cries. "What—what are you *doing* to me? Get out of my mind you, get out—!" It rises to terrified yells.

"Is that one of my people?" Dann asks above the din.

"Yes. It was Colto's daughter."

"That could be anybody," he tells Winona, and then cries "Look out! Stop!"

She has moved straight at it, her field streaming toward its small lashing one.

"Don't get caught in its panic. I know."

Winona pauses, marshaling her energies.

"These people have mind methods," Dann tells her. "You have to watch out it doesn't grab you."

"Poor little thing," she murmurs absently. And then to his consternation she advances on the screamer, her big field arching out. "Get away!" howls the small one. The other Father recoils, releasing it. Finding itself free the angry youngster jets its small body hard at Winona's midsection.

They collide in a confusion of airborne membranes and roiling fields. And then Dann sees that Winona has awkwardly extruded her small claspers and grasped the attacker. Meanwhile her big field has formed a strange dense webwork, englobing and somehow smothering the flailing energies.

"No, no," he hears her say calmly above the green squeals. "Stop that, dear. Listen to Winnie. You're all right now dear, you're all safe."

Her voice is only faintly shaky as the two struggling bodies tumble slowly, fields merged. Dann sees with astonishment that she is mastering the situation; she's going to be all right. When they come to rest on the wind, the panicky one is calm and quiescent under her grasp.

"It *attacked* her!" Elix is saying indignantly. "Fathers, did you see that?"

Dann realizes now that he has never seen physical conflict, only rare body-contact on this world. More wonders.

"Who is it, Winnie?" he asks. "Can you tell?"

"It's Kendall Kirk," she replies. The creature gives a last convulsive leap. "No, no, Kenny dear. Don't worry, you're in a nice safe place. Winnie's here. Winnie won't let them hurt you."

Kendall Kirk? Oh, no! thinks Dann. To his ears, the muffled outcries sound like garbled swearing. What to do with Kirk, here?

"He's changed," Winona murmurs fondly. "He's like a baby. They frightened him, touching his mind. He wants his—I can't say it. His pet animal."

"Pet animal?" Suddenly Dann remembers. "Tivonel, can you bring over the body that has that animal's mind? I think it may belong to this one here."

"You mean poor old Janskelen's? Come on, Marockee."

As they go, Dann asks Elix, "What did you do to this mind?"

"I had to drain it very deeply, Tanel. It was wild with fear and rage, you saw it attack your Winona. We re-formed it to a younger plane. It will recover. But is it not one of your wild ones, or a crazy female?"

"No," Dann admits. "What you have there is an adult male of my world. Quite a high-status one, in fact."

At this news several Fathers' mantles chime with incredulous disdain. "Surely Young Giadoc spoke the truth when he said other worlds were brutish," one comments. But Elix adds more gently, "You are not like this, Tanel. Why?"

He doesn't know.

Tivonel and her friends are guiding in the body of old Janskelen. Its small field stirs, its mantle flickers with wordless whining.

"Winnie, I think Kirk's animal, its mind or whatever, may be in here. Do you want them together?"

At his words the body comes to life. With a flurry of vanes it jets down under Winona and snuggles up beneath her sheltering mantle. Dann can see its field joining with Kirk's.

Fantastic. So dogs operate on the spirit plane too, he thinks a trifle crazily. The Labrador's mind seems calm; perhaps it is a "father" too. He admires the creature's fidelity while deploring its taste.

"There now, Kenny dear," Winona soothes. "Here's your little old friend! You're happy now, aren't you?"

"Kenny dear," indeed. Is it possible that the wretched exlieutenant before them is to Winnie's motherly spirit an appealing small boy? More power to her. Live in the absurd moment. Don't think of the dread rising Sound, forget what's ahead for them all.

The curious Fathers have crowded close.

"I believe you now, Tanel." It's a male he recognizes as Ustan. "The female's power is there, if poorly formed. But which of us could have coped with such a bodily assault?" His big vanes shiver.

"Our world is very different," Dann tells him. "We live without wind and with much contact with many hard things. And we cannot see minds as you do; we deal with each other only by speech and touch."

As he says this, a tendril of doubt sneaks through his materialist soul. That really was quite a demonstration Winnie put on with Kirk. Is it possible he has disbelieved too much?

"Amazing," the Fathers are murmuring. "I for one would like to learn more of your strange Father-ways," Ustan says. "They touch our deepest philosophy."

"I too," Elix agrees, and other Fathers echo him.

"I'm sure she'd love to tell you," Dann says. "Winona! If Kirk has calmed down, may I present Father Ustan and some friends? It seems they want to talk with you about the fine points of raising kids. By the way, you better get used to being a top-status person here. You're something like a visiting—" He wants to say "official" but has to settle for "Elder."

"Oh, my!" Winona's tone has the old flutter, but it doesn't sound quite so silly here. "Of course, I'd love to. Caring for babies and people is the one thing I know. Now Kenny dear, you'll be all right. Winnie's not going away. How do you do, ah, Father—"

"Ustan." Dann completes the introduction and moves off, mentally chortling. From surplus person to instant celebrity. Enjoy it while it lasts. If Fathers here are anything like mothers on Earth, Winona will be occupied indefinitely. And he has others to look after.

Tivonel jets alongside him.

"Why are you laughing, Tanel?"

"It's hard to explain. On my world, fathering is so low-status it isn't even part of the—" Garble warns him that he simply cannot say "Gross national product." "It's fit only for females," he concludes lamely, aware that nothing is getting through.

"So your females must be very big and strong, to take the eggs."

"No, they're generally weaker than males."

"But then why do you let them take them? You must be very unselfish. Or is it your religion? Oh, Giadoc would love to hear about that!"

221

"I'll explain sometime if I can. Where are the rest of my people?"

"Down there. Oh, look, by Iznagel! How *weird*"

The scarred female who had been guarding Ron is now nervously hovering over a tangle of two confusingly mingled forms. One figure is smaller—a female. For a minute Dann thinks he is seeing some sexual attack, then recalls this world's ways. Their mental fields are coalescing in a most peculiar way.

"She came right *at* him!" Iznagel cries. "I couldn't stop her!"

"It's a mind-push," Tivonel exclaims. "We better get a Father."

"Wait." Dann planes down beside the rolling figures, half-suspecting what he will find.

"Ron? Ron? Rick, is that you?"

From the subsiding swirl of mantles breaks the lacy orange effect Dann hears as laughter, but no words come.

"Ricky? Ron, I'm Dann. Tell me who's there."

Both mantles break into an echoing golden sound. "We're here. It's *us*. We're . . . we're . . . at last."

"Don't worry, Iznagel," Dann tells her. "That's his ah, egg-brother with him. I think they need to be close."

The combined life-energies are settling, forming into a quiet wreath around the two joined forms. The smaller body is plastered on the other's back.

"It's like one big person," Tivonel exclaims.

"Well, I never saw *that* before," Iznagel comments, scandalized. "You say they're actually egg-brothers? I thought that was a myth."

"No, we have them on our world. Ron, Rick, are you really all right?"

A vague muttering, and suddenly the topmost, half-hidden form speaks alone. "Ron wants me to do the talking, Doc. Yes, we're all right. Maybe we really are." Its tone is bright with joy. "Hey, you better call us something new now, we're not two people anymore."

"What shall I call you?"

Again the laughter.

"How about Wax, Waxma—you know, Waxman."

The prosaic earthly sound coming from this figure of nightmare in the realms of dream is too much for Dann. He begins to laugh helplessly, hears himself joined by Tivonel. Iznagel, recovering from her shock, joins too.

"Hey, that's neat," the new "Waxman" chuckles. "Waxing means growing. We just did."

"Well." Dann finally composes himself. It's hard, even in the face of what must come; this world of Tyree seems apt for joy. "I have to find the others. You'll be all right with Iznagel. Ask her to give you a memory, by the way. A memory about this world. She'll explain. You'll love it. I'll be back later."

"Right down there," says Tivonel, and planes out in a beautiful swerving helix down past huge rafts of twinkling vegetation.

Dann follows, conscious again of the power and freedom of his new body, refusing to feel the twinges of what must be oncoming ill. How extraordinary that this supernatural disaster has brought joy, even if temporary—joy for Winona, joy for Ron and Rick, joy for himself. Will it be worth it? Don't think of it. Find out who else is here.

They draw up beside three bodies well anchored in a plant-thicket, guarded by the old male Omar who had lamented the loss of Janskelen. A big male, a female, and probably a child, Dann decides. As Tivonel sees the male body she checks and draws aside, greyblue with grief.

"That was Giadoc's son, Tanel. Our son Tiavan. He is a criminal, on your world now."

"Don't grieve, Tivonel. As a matter of fact so far your people seem to have made mine very happy. Maybe this will work out well too."

She sighs; but the bright spirit cannot stay dimmed long. Tiavan's foreign life is stirring restlessly, its mantle murmuring with waking lights.

"Greetings, Father Omar," says Tivonel. "This is Tanel, the strange Healer."

"Greetings, Healer Tanel," intones the huge old being. "Good. I will leave these to you, with pleasure."

"Oh no, please don't," Dann protests. "I am only a healer of bodies. We have no skills of the mind like yours."

"H'mmm. Well, if you are a Body-healer, do you not feel that the Wind grows dangerous at this level?"

"Yes, I do," Dann admits. How can he say that they are already probably dead? "We should try to find shelter soon. But first I want to find out who these people of mine are and reassure them."

"But don't you recognize their fields?" Omar's words are astonished cerise.

"No, Father," Tivonel puts in. "He says they can only see their bodies on his world. And they talk, of course. Isn't it weird?"

"Weird indeed." Again the grey eyebrow-lift. "You mean you cannot see that this mind in Tiavan's body is ill formed, in need of remolding? The product of a criminally inept Father, I should say; possibly a wild orphan. Poor thing, see how it attempts to—"

The alien speech becomes incomprehensible to Dann; evidently concepts for which no earthly equivalents exist. As he studies the "orphan," Tivonel gathers her vanes.

"I'm going back to Lomax, Tanel. Maybe they've found Giadoc."

"Right. I'll stay close." She flashes warmth, jetting away.

An unwelcome suspicion has come to Dann as he notices the close, burrlike way in which this being's energy hugs its big body. Little exploratory tendrils dart out, recoil snakelike; the mantle is resolutely mute. Does this represent, say, secrecy? Paranoid fears? Or hatred? Is he looking at Major Fearing? Oh no! Well, perhaps better than to have some innocent meet the fate that lies ahead here.

"Fearing?" he calls reluctantly. "Major Fearing, is that you? It's Dann here. If you care to talk, maybe I can help you."

No response, but an ambiguous contraction of the field. Paranoids don't want help, Dann reminds himself. But this isn't Fearing, maybe it's a Navy workman, some total stranger. On the other hand, so far the Tyrenni Beam seems to have been attracted to Noah's subjects; their "telepathic" trait perhaps. Try them.

"Ted? Ted Yost, is that you? Fredo—ah, Fredericka? Val? Valerie Ahlstrom, are you there?"

Still no reaction from the creature. This feels like the craziest thing he's ever done. But wait; he almost forgot the little man.

"Chris! Chris Costakis, is that you?"

The mind quivers significantly, contracts itself to a knot.

"Chris? If that's you, don't be afraid. It's Dann here, Doctor Dann, even if I don't look it. We've all been, well, mixed up. Can you speak to me?"

The mind seems to relax slightly. After a pause a faint syllable forms on its mantle.

"Doc?"

The dry nasal light-tone is unmistakable.

"Yes, it's me, Chris. How do you feel?"

"Where are we, Doc? What's going on?"

As Dann fumbles through an explanation he realizes this is the first time one of these telepaths have asked him to explain anything. But Chris was different. His specialty was numbers. "These people are friendly, Chris," he tells him. "They don't approve of the ones who switched bodies with us. There's seven of us here so far as I know. And Kirk's, ah, pet animal," he concludes, thinking the craziness of it might help Chris.

It seems to work. "The—!" His words garble, apparently trying to say "dog." "Poor old boy."

Inappropriate term for the visibly female Labrador; Dann recalls the little man's mysognyny. *I can't pick up anything from a woman.* Was this what old Omar meant?

The alien body before him seems to be coming more alive; subvocal murmurs flicker across its mantle. But its field is still furled close. Suddenly Chris whispers sharply: "Doc. Are these characters all—you know—can they read your mind?"

A sick telepath indeed.

"Only if you want them to, Chris. See that hazy stuff around my body? They call it your field. No one can see your thoughts unless your field touches theirs. Then you can read them too."

At these words the little man's life-aura contracts even closer, his great form furls so that he drops abruptly into the nearest plant.

"Wait, Chris." Dann follows, trying to think of some way to calm him. "They never do it unless you want them to. It's considered rude. I assure you, there's nothing to be frightened of here, in that way."

Incomprehensible cursing from the body in the thicket. A telepath frightened of telepathy. Get his mind off it.

"By the way, Chris, it may interest you to know that you're in the body of a very large young male. You should come out and try the air. I've had a glorious time, flying. Look at your wingspread, you're huge."

More mutters, but presently Dann sees one big vane spread cautiously out. "Yeah? You mean I'm, I'm not . . . ?" The secondary

225

vanes lift, the big body lofts upward. After a moment of confusion Costakis is hovering over the plant-roots, tilting and testing his jets.

"Hey, you meant it." The life-field has expanded raggedly, the cursing has stopped.

"Yes, you got the best bargain of us all. Watch it, it's intoxicating." It comes to Dann that he isn't talking to a dream or even a patient, but to a fellow human in a situation that however fantastic is dreadfully real. How sad that this new deal for poor Costakis won't last.

Chris seems to be slowly scanning round. Dann becomes conscious that the background drone from the sky has risen, and the painful signals of dying life seem much stronger.

"What were you and big boy there talking about?" Costakis asks.

"Well, there's a problem here Chris. The energy, I mean, the transmissions from the Sound—this language doesn't have words. I'm trying to say that this world is getting too much sky-energy. Can you get what I mean at all?" An idea strikes Dann; Costakis knew electronics, maybe some physics. Perhaps the facts will distract him from his other fears. "The people here don't understand these things. I—we need your advice."

The scanners of the big body before him extrude, membranes shift.

"You're not telling me the whole story, Doc."

The voice is so exactly that of the lonely, suspicious, jaunty little man that Dann can almost see his balding head.

"Yes. I think it's bad. I didn't want to alarm the others, I haven't told anybody else. You know more than I about energy. I'd be grateful for your help. For instance, how much time do you think we have?"

At this moment an inarticulate cry flares from the female body beyond the thicket. Overhead, big Omar gives a monitory grunt, spreading his field.

"T-T-Tokra! Docra! Tann!"

Someone is clearly trying to call him.

"I'm coming. Excuse me, Chris."

He jets over to the wakening form, so intent that he almost forgets to keep his mind away from its big, out-reaching field.

"Who are you? I'm Dann, Doctor Dann. Who's there!"

"Oh, Doctor! Can't you tell, I'm Valerie!"

He surveys the writhing manta-form—vanes, membranes, strange stalked appendages—and a sudden visual revulsion strikes him. Valerie, in *that*? A poignant memory rises of the girl in her own form, the darling curves of breast and waist, the little yellow-covered mons, the charming smile. To be in this *thing*—this giant monster that has eaten a human girl. Oh, vile!

He reels on the wind—and without warning, literally falls through her mind.

He has no idea what is happening, though afterwards he thinks it must have been like two galaxies colliding, two briefly interpenetrating webs of force. Now he knows only that he is suddenly in another world—a world named Val, a strange vivid landscape in space and time, composed of a myriad familiar scenes, faces, voices, objects, musics, body sensations, memories, experiences—all centered round his Val-self. His self incarnated in a familiar/unfamiliar five-foot-three body; tender-skinned, excitable, occasionally aching, with sharp sight and hearing and clever, double-jointed hands; the only, the normal way to be. And all these are aligned in a flash upon dimensions of emotion—hope, pride, anxiety, joy, humor, aversion, a force-field of varied feeling-tones, among which one stands out for which his mind has no equivalent: fear, vulnerability everywhere. This world is dangerous, pervaded by some intrusive permanent menace, a lurking, confining cruelty like an occupying enemy. A host of huge crude male bodies ring it, rough voices jeer, oblivious power monopolies all free space, alien concepts rule the very air. And yet amid this hostile world hope is carried like a lamp in brave, weak hands; a hope so bound with self that it has no name, but only the necessity of going on, like a guerilla fighter's torch.

All this reality unrolls through him instantly, he is *in* it—but it is background for one central scene: Five bare toes in sunlight, his living leg cocked up on the other knee above a yellow spread. And on his/her/my naked stomach is resting an intimately known head of brown hair. A head which is *We Love*—is a complex of tenderness, ambiguous resentments, sweet sharing, doubts, worry, wild excitements, resolves, and dreams. All existent in a magic enclave, a frail enchanted space outside which looms the injustice called daily life— and within which, gleaming in the sunshine, lie two Canadian travel folders and a box of health biscuits, about to be shared with love.

Almost as all this penetrates Dann, the vision of strange self shimmers, dissolves its overwhelming reality. Doubleness slides back and grows. The invading mental galaxy is withdrawing itself out and away.

Daniel Dann comes back to himself, spread on the winds of Tyree beside another alien form.

But he is not himself; not as he was nor ever will be again. For the first time he has really grasped life's most eerie lesson:

The Other Exists.

Cliché, he thinks dazedly. Cliché, like all the big ones. But I never understood. How could I? Only here, forever removed from Earth in perishing monstrous form, could I have felt the *reality* of a different human world. A world in which he is a passing phenomenon, as she was in mine. And to have mistaken that charged worldscape for a seductive little belly in a yellow bathing suit! Shame curdles him.

But now he must act, repair his irreparable blunder, attend to the business at hand.

"Valerie? I, I'm sorry—"

"It's all right. You aren't . . . You didn't . . ." Gently, her thought brushes his. How could he have thought her wind-borne form ugly? The mind is all, it really is.

"But listen," she is saying, her voice tinged pale with fear. "Major Fearing isn't here, is he? The one you were talking to?"

"No. It's Chris Costakis." Irrationally he feels cheered that at least one of these telepaths has made the same mistake. Maybe he's learning. "I don't think you have to worry about Fearing ever anymore."

"Oh." Her voice-color mellows. "But we *are* in some kind of trouble, aren't we? I mean, this isn't a dream?"

"I'm afraid not. Didn't your guardian up there tell you where we are?"

"He started to, I think, but I went to sleep."

"Well, so far it's been rather pleasant, believe it or not. Winona is here, she's in a crowd of Fathers who want to talk with her about raising babies. Kirk is here too, but they regressed him to infancy. Winona thinks he's cute. And Rick and Ron have found each other, they call themselves one person named Waxman now. Only Chris seem to be horrified that someone will read his mind."

228

Time enough to mention the bad stuff later. He watches her glow and stretch her new body, becoming more fully awake. She must be in that state of dreamy euphoria that seems to attend waking up on Tyree. Come to think of it, he's still in it himself.

"Now who's this, do you know?" He floats over to the body lying close by big Omar's protective field. It has to be a much younger person; the mantle is short, the vanes half-grown. Protruding from the central membranes are a set of strong-looking claspers. Do Tyrenni children make much more use of their manipulative limbs? A section of pouch is exposed too; this must be a male child, one of the children he had seen carried up and away. He remembers to look at the life-aura; it seems to be sizable, cautiously eddying out. But odd, lop-sided.

"I dreamed something," Val is saying, "before I got so scared. But then I went to sleep. They do that, don't they?"

"Yes. It's their way of fixing up fear and bad feelings."

"How wonderful!" She stretches again, laughs gaily. "Don't worry about what happened, you know. Oh, I feel so free!" She makes an experimental caracole above the plants, lifts all her vanes. "Free and strong—why, I could go miles and miles, couldn't I? Anywhere in the sky!"

"That's right. As a matter of fact, on this world the females seem to do all the traveling and exploring while the males tend the kids."

"Oh, wow!" Then she sobers. "But we should wake up—whoever this is."

They hover together over the quiet form. Dann notices again the peculiar tight-held formation of parts of its life-energies. Another frightened one like Costakis?

Suddenly the dark mantle lights concisely.

"Don't bother," says the voice of Fredericka Crespinelli. "Are you all right, Val?"

"Frodo! I dreamed, I was sure you were here."

"I heard you. Hello, Doc."

"Hello Frodo. Have you been awake long?"

"Awhile. Listen, what in the name of the Abysss—now why did I say that? What did they do to me?" The words glimmer with the tinge of fear.

"Don't be scared, Frodo," Val says loftily. "They didn't do any-

229

thing to your mind, it's just that you can say what they have words for. I figured that out right away."

"All right." Dann can see she is much more disturbed than Val. "What are we here for, Doc? What's going on?"

To distract her he says the first thing that comes into his head.

"Well, for one thing you're a young male now. Your body, I mean. A boy like twelve or fifteen I'd guess."

"Who, me?"

She twists in midair, trying to see all of herself at once, and succeeds in blowing into a tangle of vanes and vines. Val laughs merrily, trying to help, but there seems to be no easy way of physical assistance in this world. Frodo finally jets free.

"When you grow up you'll be like that enormous old chap up there. He's a Father, that's the highest rank here." Grinning to himself, Dann can't resist adding, "As a male your main job will be raising babies. It's the high-status thing here. The females like Val aren't allowed to touch them."

"What?!" The rainbow-hued exclamations end in delicious laughter. Dann joins in. Enjoy while we can, the absurd delight in the magical winds of Tyree. The others are experimentally flying barrel-rolls.

"Wait a minute, you two. I suggest you learn more about this world before you make the mistakes I did. The way you do it is to ask someone for a memory."

"A memory?"

"The most amazing teaching method you ever saw. Wait. Father Omar!" he calls. "May I present Valerie and Frodo, two former females of my world? They would like to be given a memory, but we are ignorant of the correct way to receive. Would you instruct them?"

"Very well," the old being replies, and a sad sigh gleams on his sides. "Perhaps I too will ask a memory of your world, since my Janskelen has gone there."

"Now you'll be fine," Dann tells them. "Just do what he says and you'll be astounded. I'm going to check on the others. Maybe I can bring back my friend to meet you, a real young female of Tyree."

. . . And so it had gone, a dreamlike happiness in the high beauty

230

of the Wall. But then another fireball had crashed close, and started a precipitous exodus down, and down again.

Tivonel will not stray far from Lomax and the old Hearer stays bravely above the rest, still reaching his mind to the sky. Dann feels duty-bound to stay near, since he has Giadoc's body; privately he is sure all this is futile. Meantime his human friends are one by one beginning to feel the burning in the wind.

"Chris, will you take charge? Make them get under what shelter they can and get them lower down the Wall. I have to stay by the Hearers because the person who owns my body may be trying to come back."

"You leaving us, Doc?"

"I doubt it. I even doubt I want to, believe it or not."

Suddenly Costakis displays an unChrislike opalescent laugh; a true laugh of human acceptance.

"I believe you, Doc."

He planes off down the wind, to round up Winona's group. Costakis "believes"? Dan has a momentary realization of what sheer size and strength has done for Chris. The simple fact of *presence* that he himself unthinkingly enjoyed so long. To be listened to, to have no need to strive.

It is in fact Chris who gives them concrete help.

He presently reappears by Dann and Heagran, towing a thorny-looking bundle of plant-life.

"Doc, I've been looking around. This stuff must have some, what's the word, hard matter in it, it blocks off the energy pretty well. You know, the sky-sound. If we make a big raft of it we'd have a shelter from the burning. Trouble is, I've got everything but, uh, manipulators."

He flaps his mantle, wiggling his weak claspers as if to say, "No hands." Several nearby Fathers color embarrassedly.

"What are you doing·with that frikkon-weed?" Tivonel jets up. "That's awful stuff, it tears your vanes."

"Yeah, but it'll stick together without weaving," Chris replies. "You have that long vine, too. We can throw lines over the mats to hold them down by. Doc, these people ought to make some for themselves if they want to last much longer. Tell them."

Heagran has been following the conversation with distant puzzlement. Now he says haughtily, "Stranger, it seems you do not know that making objects and weaving is children's work. This is no time for child-play!"

"Suit yourself. I'm trying to show you how to keep from being burned alive."

"Wait, Chris," Dann puts in. "They won't understand at all, we'll never get anywhere with words. Can you form a mental picture of the danger and exactly the kind of shelters you mean?"

"And let them read my mind?" Chris jets backward nervously.

"Just that one single item, Chris. I guarantee it, these people have deep respect for privacy. Just form a picture of the damage from the energy, and how the mat should be made to hold it off. Show it protecting children."

"I don't want anyone in my head," Chris says. Dann hears the shifting colors of indecision.

"Please, Chris. At least for the kids' sake. Father Heagran, my friend here is expert at such energy-dangers. He wishes to show you how to protect your young. But he is frightened that his whole life will be known. Can you assure him that you will take only this information?"

Big Heagran is a rainbow of exasperation, weariness, skepticism, and worry.

"If you can form an engram, stranger, naturally no Tyrenni would seek more." His tone carries convincing repugnance.

"See, Chris? An engram, he means a kind of concentrated image—"

"I know what an engram is," Chris says sullenly. "All right. But not til I say go." His big body has become quiet, the immaterial energy of his life tight-held around it. Then Dann sees the hazy field begin to bulge toward Heagran, swirling and condensing a small nucleus, rather like an amoeba preparing to divide. Heagran's field extends a lesiurely energy-tendril toward the bulge.

"Remember about the children," Dann calls.

"Go," says Chris muffledly, and at that instant his bulge seems to explode toward Heagran.

Dann is blinded by a sudden brilliant stop-sequence like a film display—pictures of the radiation-storm, and progressively burned bodies, extraordinary, detailed images of the making of protective floating rafts, with ropes of gura-vine to anchor them. It's like a vivid how-to book, even to insets showing enlarged details. The final image shows a raft holding off the burning rays above a crowd of bodies who are odd amalgams of human and Tyrenni children.

"Whew!" Tivonel is exlaiming. "Tanel, your friend is one fierce sender!"

"Well done, Chris! I think everybody around got that. Father Heagran, do you now see the usefulness of his plan?"

The great being muses for a moment. "Yes," he admits. "I am sorry to say, I understand. Yet it seems a hopeless hope, if matters are as bad as he shows. Unless the Destroyer moves away soon we will all die. And how are we Tyrenni to construct such things?"

"Any hope is better than none," a young Father says firmly. "This will protect our children as long as possible. What if Lomax succeeds, after the children are all dead? I say we do it. We Fathers can shelter our young ones while they weave the plants."

"Very well. So be it."

"And we females can go get the stuff?" Tivonel flexes her blistered vanes. "Whew! I never thought I'd be hauling in frikkonweed. Marockee! Iznagel!" She jets off. "Round up a team. You won't believe this."

"I better get our people started on ours." Chris sails away. Dann looks after his expanding life-field. Clearly, a leader has been born. Or a potential dictator? Well, there won't be time to worry about that. The raft-making scheme strikes him as useful only for morale.

It has in fact occupied many hours of the timeless time, while Lomax searches the skies in vain. The Destroyer still lingers, blocking the sky, and the scream of the Sound becomes all-pervasive. But once working, the Tyrenni sort themselves out well. They soon find that the raft-shelters offer perceptible comfort. The chief problem has been to persuade the adults to take their turns under cover before they become too painfully exposed. Dann circulates about trying to persuade them of the reality of the danger and to make Heagran take some shelter himself.

As he is helping stabilize a protective shield for Lomax, a body comes cartwheeling down the wind—and at the same instant Dann becomes aware of a searing pain through his own left side. Half-dazed by agony, he watches three females wind-block the body, as he himself had once been halted. It is screaming blue with pain; someone has been badly burned.

But why does he himself hurt so? Painfully he scans himself, finding no damage.

"Healer! Healer Tanel!"

Slowed by the burning in his side, Dann manages to jet over. Oh God, it's Chris. The fine young body is horribly burned, the left mantle and vanes are black and shriveled. What can he do? In Dann's mind the image of his old office with its dermal sealants and analgesics glimmers like a lost jewel.

An elder Father is watching him.

"Father," Dann says through his pain, "have you no substances to relieve this hurt, to cure wounds?"

"Substances?" the other echoes, "but are you not a Healer?"

"Yes. But in my world injuries like this are treated with, with relieving materials."

"I know nothing of this. If you are a Healer, heal."

Heagran and others have drifted up, looking agitated. Scarcely able to think above the screams and the pain, Dann moves toward the mutilated body.

"Chris? Chris, what happened?"

"I guess I went too high," the other gasps. "I—I—"

But what he is saying Dann will never know. Pain unbelievable shoots through him, his whole side from head to vanes is aflame, scorching, raked by steel claws. His body contorts in air, infolding itself around the torment. He realizes dimly that his field must have touched with Chris'. It is an eternity before the fiery contact breaks, leaving him choking on pain, trying to control the screaming from his mantle.

When he masters himself somewhat he finds old Heagran beside him, transmitting a wave of calm.

"A true Healer!" the old being exclaims solemnly. "Fathers, observe! Is this not Oraph, come again from the skies?"

Writhing in subsiding agonies, Dann understands nothing of this.

"Hey, Doc. Thanks."

That seems to be Chris before him. But what's happened? The burn-damage looks minimal, even the mantle has smoothed out. All vanes are opening normally as Chris' body rides the air.

"Our Healers today can do nothing like this," Heagran is saying.

"To drain another's pain so that the damage is undone! The legend of Oraph lives again before our eyes. Healer Tanel, I salute you. Your gift will be of great value to your people at the end."

"My gift?" Confusedly, Dann inspects his still-burning side. It appears perfectly intact. Only the pain is real. What the hell kind of "gift" is this?

Suddenly his old years of useless empathy flash before him. His weird troubles with other people's pain. Had he actually done—something? Probably not, he thinks; only here in the mind-world of Tyree. Doomed Tyree. Oh Jesus, what lies ahead?

Is he expected to *share* seven other radiation deaths before his own?

"The Great Wind has sent him, Heagran," an old Father is saying. "He alleviates our guilt at the fate of his people. But we must not ask his aid, even for our children; we who brought them here."

"Winds forbid," says Heagran. "He is theirs alone."

But what about me, Dann laments to himself. The Great Wind doesn't seem to give a damn about doctors. Oh Christ, can I really make myself take that much pain again—and again and again?

But even as he cringes, there is obscure satisfaction. At least he hadn't been crazy. His joke about being a receiver; apparently true. Specialized to pain, I'm pain's toy. But at least it's real. Probably a lot of doctors have it. I'm a doctor—and the sole *materia medica* here is myself. I'll have to try.

Chris is telling him something.

"—so I went up to look the situation over. It's bad. We have to get deeper, fast."

They move the clumsy rafts downward, with the children beneath them. And later move down again, and again down, til they end here, almost at dread wind's bottom. Lower than this the updraft is too weak to support their great forms, and the protective rafts are now barely airborne in the feeble wind. Here is where they will die.

On the way down Dann has to exercise his horrid "gift" twice more; first Winona becomes badly seared, then Val. Her pain is especially fierce; he has to force himself to the utmost to hold contact. And she is so ashamed. Val alone seems to understand that the pain is not abolished but merely exchanged, while the mysterious healing works.

And now he can hear weak moaning from the sleeping form of

Ron and Rick; blisters are suppurating on "Waxman's" vanes. When he wakes up Dann will have to help him, will have to do the whole damn bit again.

Unfair, unfair; the oldest plaint: Why me? Isn't one death all a mortal should be asked to bear? Why can't he end it all, soar out on the updraft to his own single, personal incineration? The prospect strikes him as blissful, the temptation is strong.

Well, but I'm a doctor, he thinks. At least I can hold on long enough for one more try. Maybe if I take them earlier, before the burns are so bad, maybe I can stand smaller, more frequent increments of pain? Physician, kid thyself . . . There's no way to make it anything but awful.

Dully, he watches the slow action around the raft where the Hearers are. Through the burning murk Dann can see Lomax and his surviving aides bravely taking turns outside the shelter, their weakened fields combining in brief attempts to probe the sky. Nearby Tivonel hovers under a little bundle of frikkon-weed, still keeping watch for a sign from Giadoc. Her once-charming form is blackened and scarred. Dann has persuaded her to let him help her once only. Overhead, the fire-storm from the Sound is a torrent of angry roaring.

Suddenly it stills, and the whole landscape shudders through a dreamlike change. Startled, beyond thought, Dann finds himself riding again the high winds of Tyree, seeing a Tivonel grown sleek and graceful. Coral laughter rings out—why, there is Winona's form, and Father Elix! He hears himself saying, "May I present Winona, a female of my world?"

But—but—what's happening? In his total disorientation Dann is conscious of one overwhelming sensation: Joy. Somehow, he is living again the magic time of waking on Tyree. He pumps air, trying to savor the wonder of this release, only vaguely attending to the remembered action unreeling around him. But just as he hears his own voice speak, the illusion shivers and fades out, the joy evaporates.

He is back in reality, hanging in the dark wind-bottom of a burning world. Around him others are stirring; did they feel the strange thing too?

"Tivonel! What happened?"

She jets effortlessly closer to him, towing her inadequate protection. Her burns and scars are back; all is as before.

236

"A great time eddy," she tells him in the ghost of her old laughing voice. "They happen here. That one was nice, wasn't it? I hope it comes back."

"Yes."

"Oh, look. How nasty."

Dann has been noticing a sharp but oddly different squeal of pain from one of the Tyrenni groups. "What is it?"

"That child is draining its hurt into a plenya. What's its Father thinking of?"

Probably of his child's pain, like any normal parent, Dann thinks. But he admires this world's ethics. *Never add to another's pain*— even here in a world conflagration. He watches a nearby Father rouse himself and separate the child from its crying pet. The Father seems to be sheltering a child of his own, but he holds the errant one in contact beneath the shelter.

"Probably an orphan," Tivonel says. "Poor thing."

She goes back to the Hearers, and Dann nerves himself to "heal" Waxman's blistered vanes. It's not quite so bad this time; maybe he can do one more. Frodo is exposing her young body recklessly, trying to hold the shield in place over Val. He bullies her into letting him take over at the ropes.

The painful hours drag by. Two more time eddies pass, but they only yield brief interludes from their long progress down the Wall. It is eerie to see dead bodies stir to life. Dann hears again old Omar's dying words: "Winds of Tyree . . . I come alone."

The Sound is a frightful shriek now and the very air is scorching them. The shelters are all but useless. Dann can see a few crippled figures moving painfully from group to group; perhaps Tyrenni Healers. As he watches, one of them crumples and its field goes dark. All around, other Tyrenni bodies are drifting down toward the Abyss. Lomax and his Hearers are still at their vain efforts, their forms horribly blistered, their great fields weak and pale.

Winona's voice speaks quietly beside him. "We're dying, aren't we, Doctor Dann?"

"I'm afraid so."

"I'm glad I . . . knew it."

"Yes."

Not much longer now. They can't take much more. Dann finds he cannot look toward the sad form of Tivonel. Under the human shelter, someone is trying not to groan. Dann can feel the pain that means he must act again. He sees that it's Frodo; her small body has developed great rotted-out burns. Oh, no.

"Chris, take this rope a minute."

He goes through the dreadful routine again. The sharp young agonies that jolt through him are almost beyond bearing, mingled with the real pain of his own now-blistered vanes. I can't take this again; I can't. Let it end.

As he is emerging from the invisible fires he becomes conscious of screaming or shouting outside. It's coming from the Hearer group, but it is Tivonel's burned mantle flashing wildly.

"That's Giadoc! I heard him! Listen!"

"Be silent, female." The big form beside her is barely recognizable as Bdello.

"It was his life-cry!" Tivonel flares stubbornly. "Listen, Lomax! It's Giadoc, I know it."

"It is only the Destroyer's emanations," Bdello says. "It calls us to our deaths."

"Wait, Bdello." The wounded form of Lomax struggles out of the shelter. "Wait. Help me."

His weakened life-field probes painfully upward, reluctantly joined by Bdello's. Tivonel hovers impatiently beside them, so excited that she dares to join her smaller energies to theirs.

After a long interval Lomax' mantle lights.

"It is from the direction of the deathly one," he signs feebly. "But it is Giadoc. He calls us to come to him in the sky. We must form a Beam."

His field collapses, and he drifts for a moment inert.

Bdello's life-energy drops down and enfolds his chief. "How can we form a Beam?" he demands. "Most of our Hearers are dead."

Lomax stirs, and disengages his mind-field from Bdello's. "Thank you, old friend. This is our last chance. For the children, we must try. Call Heagran."

"It is hopeless," Bdello says angrily, making no move.

"Then I will go!" exclaims Tivonel, and she struggles off through the smouldering dark to where the senior Fathers lie. Dann can hear faint golden light from her burned mantle. "Oh, I knew he would come!"

But Giadoc has not come, Dann thinks. And how are they to raise the energy to get to him? Nevertheless, a wild hope begins to stir in him.

But as the Elders make their way to Lomax, Dann sees with dismay how few they are, how damaged and weak in field-strength. Has this hope come too late, much too late?

Old Lomax is saying with heart-lifting vigor, "Heagran, all your Fathers must serve as Hearers now. Help me form a bridge, a Beam. Giadoc has found some refuge in the sky. If we can send our children there they will live."

"What if it is a trap of the Destroyer?" Bdello demands.

"Then we will be no worse than we are," Lomax replies. "Heagran, will you help? We cannot surround the pole now, but we can concentrate here."

"Yes." Dann can see the old being's pain and weakness, but his voice is strong. "Those of you who can still ride the wind, go and summon the people here in my name. Tell the Fathers we have a last chance for the children's lives. Now, Lomax, instruct me in the method of our help."

Despite himself, Dann feels a growing hope. Have the powers of these people really found some magical way out of this nightmare?

He watches the surviving Tyrenni jetting painfully in to Lomax through the deadly air. Many Fathers have two, even three children in tow; orphans whose Fathers died protecting them. Here and there he sees a female trying to guide and shelter a child. . . . If this hope does not materialize, he is seeing the last hours of a wondrous race.

They crowd around Lomax and Heagran in silence; Dann senses the odd faint jolts of energy he has come to associate with the touch of life-fields. The Tyrenni must be transmitting Lomax' instructions directly mind-to-mind; an emergency mode of communication, perhaps. Presently they disperse somewhat, and Dann senses a gathering of strength, as if a field of athletes were each preparing for some ultimate exertion. Can they really *do* something, achieve a real escape from this death?

Suddenly the silence is broken by a flash from Tivonel. "Lomax! Remember the strangers!"

"Ah, yes," says Lomax. "Strangers, come near. Be ready to send your lives out when you feel the power. I will help you if I can."

The other humans have heard the call, are struggling out. Dann shepherds them to a position near Lomax. No one says anything. A feeling of effortful, building power is already charging the air, riding over the sears of pain. It is thrilling, formidable. For the first time Dann lets himself truly hope.

"Now!" calls Lomax. "Fathers, Tyrenni all—give me your lives!"

And his mind-field flares up in splendor, towering toward the dark sky. But not alone—the massed energies around rise with him, building, joining chaotically, forming a great spear of power launching up through inferno. Dann feels his life sucked upward with it, drawn up and out of his dying body, hurtling into immaterial flight.

Exulting, he feels the lives meshed round him, knows himself a part of a tremendous striving, a battle of essence against oblivion, a drive toward unknown salvation beyond the sky. And they are winning! The surge is immense, victorious. Far behind them dwindles the burning world bearing their destroyed flesh. And from ahead now he can sense a faint welcoming call. They have made it, they are winning through! In an instant they will be saved!

But even as the sense of haven reached opens to his unbodied mind, a terrible faintness strikes through him. The rushing energy upbearing him begins to weaken, to wane and dissolve. In utmost horror he feels the life-power sinking back through hostile immensities. Oh God. Oh no—it was too far, too far for the exhausted strivers. They have failed. With dreadful speed the fading Beam collapses, back, back and down, losing all cohesion.

In deathly weariness and disarray, the minds that formed it faint and fall back into their dying bodies in the hell-winds of Tyree.

Silence, under the fire-roaring sky. Only the occasional green whimper of a child comes from the stricken crowd. Their last hope has failed, there can be no more. Ahead lies only death.

After a time old Heagran stirs and orders the others to seek what shelter they can. His voice is drained, inexpressibly weary. Painfully, by ones and twos, the crowd obeys.

"Of what use?" says Bdello bitterly. But he too goes to help secure their abandoned shelter.

"We were so close, so close," Tivonel cries softly. Her mantle is so burnt she can barely form the words. "He would have saved us. He tried."

"Yes."

"You understood, Tanel. I am to die with you, as you said."

"I'm sorry, Tivonel. I too loved your world. Now you must let me heal you one last time."

"No." Her weak light-tones are proud. But he persists, and finally she allows him to restore the worst of her burns, though he all but faints with her pain.

The next hours or years drag on through nightmare. The agonizing death-signals are louder and closer now; Tyrenni are dying all around. So far he has been able to preserve all of his little band of humans, and Tivonel. But his strange ability to heal seems to be weakening as his own body suffers more damage, and his courage to bear their pain is failing him fast.

Frodo seems to be worst off; he forces himself to summon the will to make his healing will touch her mind-field. But the effort effects only a slight improvement, at the cost of agonies he hadn't believed bearable. She must be, he sees, about to die. They all are. End this, he prays to emptiness. End this soon.

As if in answer to his plea, another huge fireball comes screaming down through the murk. Dully he realizes that this one is coming close. Close—closer—the air is in flames. All in one roaring shock he feels his own flesh burning and sees it explode among the Tyrenni beyond.

Oh God, it hasn't killed him. He is in pain beyond his power to feel it; even as he hears his own voice screaming he finds himself existent as a tiny mote of consciousness somehow apart from the incineration of his flesh. He has heard of such terminal mercies, can only hope that others are finding it too. But it is perilously frail, is passing. In a moment he will be swallowed in mindless pain.

He can see darkly where the charred bodies of the hearers and the senior Fathers drift. A few death-moans rend his mind. This is the end. Goodbye, fair dream-world. He wishes he could send or receive a last warm touch. But an overwhelming agony is cresting up, is about to fall on him forever.

He waits. Still it hangs over him, an unbreaking wave. Around him the world seems to be quieting, a strange effect of lightening and darkening at once. His senses must be dying. Let me die too, before I recover the full power to feel the pain. Disorientation washes over him. Death, take me.

But strangely he still lingers in crepuscular consciousness. And then a horrible perception penetrates his agony. The blackened, shriveled bodies in his view are beginning to stir. They change, expand, are again limned in living energies. Others too seem to be coming back to ghostly life. And his own pain is slackening, receding back.

Oh God of horrors, no. It is a last time-eddy, contravening the release of death.

The savagery of it. Are they doomed to be brought back endlessly, to die again and again?

He can only watch helplessly, too horror struck to think. But then he notices that this time-change seems different. The others had transported him instantaneously to the past. This seems to be a strange, slow, regress, as though time itself was somehow being rolled backward in a dreamlike stasis.

The death-cries around him have faded, the world is hushed. Even the all-devouring shrieking of the Sound has stilled. A sense of something unimaginable impends.

With a lightless flash the sky splits open. Through the hush there strikes down on them a great ray or beam of power beyond comprehension, pouring in on them from beyond the world.

From the heart of death a call comes without voice.

COME TO ME. COME!

Chapter 19

He is alive!

The pinpoint triumph of his own life blooms into being in the void:
He, Giadoc, lives!

He is no more than an atom of awareness, yet as soon as he feels
himself existent the skills of a Hearer of Tyree wake to ghostly life.
He gropes for structure and vitality, strives to rebuild complexity, to
energize and reassemble his essential subsystems. Memory comes;
he achieves preliminary coherence, strengthens. At first he fancies
he is suffering the aftermath of a childhood rage, when he had been
required to reorganize himself unaided.

But this is not that far-off time, not Tyree. As consciousness
grows he knows himself totally alone in infinite emptiness and darkness. He has fallen out of all Wind into some realm beyond being.
And he is without body, fleshless and senseless, re-forming himself
on nothing at all.

Characteristically, marveling curiosity awakes. How can this be?
Life must be based on bodily energy—yet he lives! How?

He possesses himself of more memory and recalls his last instants
when the Beam had shriveled, abandoning him in space. His last

perception was of the hideous Destroyer ahead and his own fading remnants plunging toward it. Has he somehow entered the Destroyer itself, and lived? But how? On what?

He checks his being cautiously—and finds, he doesn't know what: a point-source, a tiny emanation unlike anything he knows. It's totally nonliving, weirdly cold and steady. Yet it nourished him, seems to support his life here in the realms of death between the worlds.

How marvelous and strange!

An idea comes. Perhaps this Destroyer is not only deathly, perhaps it is really dead. A huge dead animal of space. Could he be subsisting on the last life of one of its dying ganglia?

Giadoc has heard of dubious attempts to tap the fading energies of dead animals like the fierce little curlu. Perhaps he has done something of this sort on an enormous scale. If this is the case, he has not long to live. But the things of space are vast and slow, he reminds himself; the huge energies of a Destroyer must take time to decay. Perhaps he will have time to explore, to try to find some way to relocate the Beam.

As he thinks this the grievous memory of his world comes to full life and nearly overwhelms him. Tyree—beloved, far Tyree now under fiery destruction, and Tivonel with it, lost forever. And his son Tiavan, his proud one who betrayed him, committed life-crime and fled with his child to that grim alien world . . .

For a moment his mind is only a fierce cry to the bright image of all he loves and has lost.

But then his disciplines and skills come to him. *Ahura!* This is no time to feel. Resolutely he disengages the urgent pain; as no human could, he compacts and encapsulates it in the storage-cycles of his mind. Now for what time is left him he must see what he can do, find what this unknown level of existence holds.

He concentrates intently on the void about him. He has no bodily senses; he is in black silence, without pattern or pressure-gradient or change. He can receive nothing here but the emanations of life itself. If any structures of the Destroyer are near him, they give off no life-signs. For a time he receives only emptiness and darkness so deep that despair chills him. He is foolish; what can he hope for here?

But then suddenly—*there,* in that direction—is a tiny life-transmission, at extreme range. Something living is here besides himself. What is it, can he reach it?

As another had done before him but with infinitely greater skill, he extends himself exploratorily toward the far life-signal. Presently he touches another of the strange unliving energy-points. Without hesitation he flows and coalesces himself around it and reaches out again. Yes; there are more here, he can move as he will! Splendid.

Jubilantly he moves onward through nowhere, wondering as he goes whether he is actually enormous, spread out like a vast space-cloud. Or perhaps he is as tiny as a point? No matter! his essential structure is here, he has emotion, memory, thought. Right now he is feeling an acute joy of discovery-in-strangeness, he is an explorer of the dimensionless void. A mutinous thought of Tivonel intrudes; perhaps this is the joy that females speak of, the pleasures of venturing into unknown realms. Certainly it is quite unFatherly, though it requires all his male field-strength. It does not occur to him that he is brave; such concepts are of the female world.

The signal is much stronger now, he is closing on it. It takes on definition: it is a transmission of pain.

He slows, studying it. The pain is bewilderment, despair. Oh, winds —it is only another lost here like himself!

Instantly his Fatherly instincts surge to comfort it, but he makes himself stop. He must be wary, he has no idea of the life-strength of the thing. Cautiously he flows closer ready to leap away, extending only a receptor-node. What manner of life can it be?

The thing seems not to sense him at all. Its field is apparently drifting or flaring hopelessly in all directions like a lost child. His urge to Father it is terribly strong, but he makes himself wait.

Presently a wandering thought-tendril brushes him, too chaotic for comprehension. Then another—and this time he can catch definite imagery among the emanations of woe. Why, he recognizes them! They are of the alien world that Giadoc has just mind-traveled to!

Undoubtedly this is a mind displaced by the life-criminals of Tyree. Certainly it's not dangerous to him, and it's in despair.

Giadoc yields to his Father-soul.

All in one motion he flows to a nearer base, forming his life into a Father-field. Working by blind mind-touch alone, he extends himself delicately around the ragged eddies of the other, seeking to envelop its disorder within a shell of calm.

At his first touch the alien flares up in terror, launching frightened demands.

Calm, calm, you're safe. Don't be afraid anymore. Giadoc has en-globed the other now, he sends in waves of reassurance as he starts the work of resolving the eruptions of fright and draining down the fear.

The other being struggles ignorantly, yielding and subsiding in area after area. As Giadoc penetrates tactfully, he is pleased to no-tice that a linkage to the language he had used on that world still re-mains with him. He can make out the recurrent words, *I'm dead.* And then images of queer pale aliens with wings. *Are you an angel? Am I in—?*

He ignores these incomprehensible transmissions and merely en-courages it subverbally. *Calm, calm. Gather yourself in, be round. I'm helping you. You're safe, Father's here.* The being is dreadfully disorganized. When he judges its fear is sufficient attenuated, he presses in with a mild counter-bias to stop the topmost commotions. It has another surge of terror, and then accepts a simple surface or-ganization. Is it perhaps a child, or a little crazy from field-stress? For that matter, how sane is he himself now? He finds a functional speech center and links directly to it. *"Be round, little one. Round like an egg."*

"What—doing to me?" The other leaps; Giadoc taps more fear away from the thought. He does not want to drain it too deeply lest it go into sleeping mode. A part of his mind wonders what in the name of the wind he will do with this helpless alien anyway. But that does not worry him while he is still in Father-mode. *"Calm, round, you're all right now. I'm here."*

At this moment the alien seems to gather itself internally, and sud-denly bursts up in a verbal thought so strong that Giadoc gets every word.

"I'm not an egg! I'm Ensign Theodore Yost. Who are you? Where are we?"

Startled and delighted in his Father-heart, Giadoc perceives that the alien has more field-strength than he had believed. Moreover, he

246

recognizes it now that it is more fully conscious. It's the young male with the injured body, Tedyost, the one who had longed for the place of beauty.

He relaxes his Father-field and transmits a careful minimal link, an engram of mind-contact, hoping not to frighten Tedyost further. When this seems to be accepted he transmits through in verbal mode: *"Welcome Tedyost. I too am lost in this place like you. I am Giadoc of the world of Tyree. We have met before."*

Far from being frightened, the other flails toward him questioningly. It seems to be trying to form a crude receptor-node under the deafening tangle of *"Where? Who? What—?"*

What can he do with this creature? Giadoc transmits a strong wave of desire for calm. *"Please try to control your thoughts, I am receiving you violently. Will you allow me to help you so we can understand each other?"*

"Help!—Yes—" The other all but thrashes into him. Giadoc recalls how totally unaware these aliens are, how he had probed them freely.

Disregarding all courtesy, he gathers the blind demands and disengages their emotion. At the same time he goes into the nearest layers, modeling and firming a proper receptor-field. *"Calm, Tedyost, I hear you. Hold your mind thus, touch slightly and steadily. I will pass you my memory of this place, I will show you all I know."*

At length, in timeless emptiness and darkness, Giadoc has the other quieted into rough receptive-mode. He forms a compact memory of his experiences and passes it into the alien's mind, ending with his guess about the huge dead space-animal they are in. *"We call it the Destroyer."*

The other being churns with excitement, it seems delighted and astonished by the communication. Then it surges with effort, apparently trying to do likewise. Yes—a projection rushes at him, surprisingly powerful and half-bodied in verbal shreds. *"Destroyer! We're in a ship!"*

Giadoc sorts out the transmission, fascinated by the alien sensory data. As he expected, Tedyost too had found himself rushing through emptiness, then intercepted by dark and dread; almost extinguished. He too had fought back to life with the aid of the strange energy. But he had thought himself marooned, unable to move. The information that they are mobile fills him with such pleasure that Giadoc suspects again that Tedyost is not entirely sane.

Moreover, his image of their predicament is bizarre; where Giadoc deduces an animal, Tedyost believes they are in a huge lifeless pod, a cold hollow "ship" moving through space. With this comes the intense yearning Giadoc had read before, the beautiful vision of streaming wind or liquid, vast and rushing with a myriad lights—a tremendous turbulent glory outside the darkness. Tedyost longs toward this with a pure fervor. *"I want to see out!"*

In his thought also is a strong directional urge: Giadoc must show him how to move at once toward some kind of nucleus or central control point. *"We have to find the bridge! The captain will help us."*

Giadoc considers. The idea of a monstrous pod is fantastic, but Tedyost's notion about a central nucleus is promising. If this is an animal it should have a brain, and the dead or dying brain should have more of the strange energy than the ganglia out here. If they could reach it, perhaps he could draw on its power to send out a signal, perhaps the Hearers on Tyree could detect him and restore the Beam. A long chance and a faint hope, but what better?

Only, in which direction should we seek? The Destroyer's brain, if it exists, must be composed of this nonliving power which does not register on the life-bands. And aside from the clamor of Tedyost's mind, he can detect nothing but emptiness around them. Nevertheless, he must try.

He transmits back agreement with the plan of finding the nucleus or "bridge," and a strong desire that Tedyost learn to damp himself so they can listen for some emanation which will tell them where to go.

After some confusion, Tedyost achieves a creditable silence, and Giadoc bends all his attention to the structure of this place. But he detects nothing; no discrepancy of any sort distinguishes one direction from another.

Tedyost reacts stoically to this information, and sends back an image of an expanding spiral course which he calls a "search pattern."

Well, if they must set off blindly, they must. But Giadoc recalls that there is one more thing they can try. It's embarrassing, permitted only to very young children. For an adult, conceivable only in extreme emergency. Well, is this not an extreme emergency? Any embarrassment is irrelevent here—although to a proud Hearer of Tyree, it is real.

Sternly repressing his queasiness, Giadoc transmits an image of the method, in a matrix of apology-for-crudeness.

To his surprise, the other does not seem disturbed. Perhaps he doesn't realize the depth and intimacy of the procedure. Giadoc amplifies. *"This is a thing no adult would tolerate on my world. It means our minds will be open to each other at every level. Do you truly understand?"*

Still the other doesn't hesitate. *"You're the expert. Go ahead."*

What an extraordinary creature! Very well.

"Hold your whole mind as relaxed as possible while I merge. If I detect any signal you will receive it too. Bear the location tightly in mind; it will vanish when we separate."

"Right."

Distasteful, self-conscious, Giadoc brings himself into full close confrontation with the other life-field, following its delicate play of biassing energies precisely. Then abruptly, he sends the complementary configuration through his own field surface—and with a soundless snap the two minds fuse tight together.

It is dizzying—he is doubled, swamped with alien emotions, meanings, life. Alien energies rush through him and he has to fight from shrinking away, from knowing himself known. For moments his purpose is lost. But then his greater strength asserts itself; he pushes all else aside and draws the doubled energies into receptor focus. This is their one chance. He tunes their joint sense-power hungrily for the faintest discrepancy in the unknown void around.

At first nothing comes. He strains harder, pulling on all Tedyost's strength. Then suddenly he is rewarded.

There—on that bearing—is a faint spark. A life-source!

He allows a moment for the perception to strike through their joined minds. Then with an effort he begins the work of rebiassing himself, disentangling his configuration area by area from their combined world of thought. As he does so he holds desperately to the now-vanishing directional vector he had perceived.

The act of separation is disorienting and curiously saddening. As the opposing bias peels them apart, he feels he is leaving behind his own thoughts, dreams, understandings, a part of his very self. But he is a Hearer; he manages to bring his mind out smoothly, in the physical direction in which he believes the far point lay.

"Did you perceive it?"

"Yes. Hey, man, I see what you mean! I felt—"

"No time. Come, stretch yourself this way."

And thus fumblingly, in tenuous touch, the two tiny sparks of life begin to traverse the immense icy blackness. It is a long journey, increasingly interrupted by course-corrections in which Giadoc feels less and less confidence. Has the invisible source moved, or are they simply lost? And will the unknown cold energy-points on which they move continue to hold out?

He could of course again perform the overwhelming merger that would double their sensory range. But he shrinks from it, even were Tedyost willing. In his weak state here, he cannot be sure that he could again achieve complete separation of identity. Even now he feels traces of a peculiar, unTyrennian comradeship that warns him that something of Tedyost will always linger with him. What if he were to become permanently mingled with this crazy untrained alien mind? And yet, as the enormous emptiness presses on him, he begins to wonder if there is any other way.

Just as he is coming reluctantly to consider it, the emptiness is broken by a point of presence. Yes—the strange signal is there, only somewhat to one side.

"Can you sense it, Tedyost?"

"No, nothing."

"Come, then. This way!"

Movement remains possible. The emanation strengthens.

Finally Tedyost senses it too. *"That's—life?"*

"Yes. But strange, strange. I don't recognize it."

The peculiar signal strengthens as they make their way closer. It comes to resemble a confined cloud or mist of energic veins, threaded with life like a huge flickering plant-form. Giadoc has doubts. Is this only a plant, or some system of dead energy like those he had seen in Tedyost's world?

But no; fused in among the blurred flickerings is the strong output of a living mind. It seems calm, not at all troubled. And it does not appear dead or injured. Evidently it belongs here, wherever here is. A great cool hatred laps at the margins of Giadoc's thoughts, stronger than any he has ever felt. Is he perceiving the actual mind of a killer of worlds? Is this the brain of the Destroyer? Perhaps his duty is to kill it, if such a thing is possible here.

"That's the captain! He'll help us!" Tedyost is transmitting excitedly.

At that moment Giadoc's outstretched being touches, not more life-points, but a wall of deathly cold. He recoils, searching out gingerly. The barrier seems to extend in all directions and its very substance is frightening. Moreover it is impossible to tell distance; the brain may be far beyond it or very close.

"We are blocked. We cannot go closer."

"There has to be a way to call to him."

Giadoc starts to suggest that they explore the circumference of the barrier. But Tedyost isn't listening. He draws himself together and roars out a strong, mad signal: *"Captain! Captain, help!"*

The brain behind the barrier does not stir.

"It's an animal," Giadoc transmits impatiently. *"It can't understand you."*

But Tedyost will not be swayed from his delusion.

"Captain, Sir, please listen. It's Ensign Yost here, Ensign Theodore Yost. We're stuck out here in the dark. Listen, sir, please let us see out. We just want to have a look at the ocean."

Again nothing happens except that the brain or nucleus seems to coil or stir slightly.

Giadoc hangs in nothingness, waiting for his companion to cease his foolish endeavors. He is close to what must be the central life of this killer of worlds. His hatred gathers, still dreamlike, remote, but growing fiercer, penetrating his core of calm. How can he act against this monstrous thing? How can he pierce its wall? And if he can, how his own puny force disrupt it? Neither Giadoc nor his forefathers have ever killed sentient life, but he remembers now the old savage sagas of his race: He must burst into and explode its central organization, without becoming it himself. Well, he has one resource. If they can get at it, he will draw without pity on poor Tedyost. Their combined strength may be enough. After all, Tedyost's own world might be threatened soon. He nerves himself and starts carefully to feel about the surface of the deathly barrier, looking for some chink or gap. Since energy comes out, energy can go in.

Suddenly something happens.

Between him and Tedyost a small ghostly disturbance forms and spreads. It seems to be at no particular place; perhaps only in their minds. A transmission of the Destroyer?

The disturbance spreads, stabilizes to a phantom surface. On it appear quivering blue signals:

//TED//IS*THAT*YOU*//

"Yes, Captain, it's me!" Tedyost's joyous bellow deafens Giadoc.

//YOU*WANT*TO*SEE*OUT//

"Yes sir, Captain please—where are we?"

At that the spectral panel slowly expands, blossoming into a richly tinted tapestry of lights in slow, majestic motion, swirled here and there in crests of cloudy foam.

Tedyost emits a great mental gasp of gratitude. Even Giadoc is distracted from his anger, seeing in this streaming glory the echo of the lost winds of his home.

"Oh, thank you, Captain. Please, Sir, who are you? What ship is this?

The glorious dream-window densens, takes on jewel colors. And over it appear for an instant the flickering words:

//YOU*MAY*CALL*ME*TOTAL*OMALI//

But Giadoc has ceased to attend. A new signal is reaching him, a far faint diffuse cry on the life-bands, that reawakes his helpless fury. Grimly he recognizes it—it is the beginning of the death-cry of a distant world, penetrating even to their black isolation here in the Destroyer. Yes—it grows in intensity as he attends. Is it the very Destroyer in which he is imprisoned who is doing this, or one of his distant kin? No matter.

"Murderer!" he sends with all his force against the brain behind its wall. *"Murderer! Why do you kill? Have you no reverence for life?"*

The brain seems to roil confusedly, and an odd sense of stress comes into the empty space around him. Yet the serene grandeur in the visionary panel flows on, only bearing the momentary letters.

//NEGATIVE//NEGATIVE//I*DO*NOT*KILL//

"You kill! Hear the death-cry!"

No reply, except that the pressure around him seems to thicken and churn.

Giadoc is receiving all too clearly now, the hideous wailing has intensified. And then to his ultimate horror he recognizes not only death, but whose—this is Tyree, his own beloved Tyree whose dying throes are radiating out to him! Appalled, he fancies he can catch the extinction of individual known beings. All his world, animals, plants, people—his people—are dying in flames and torment.

"Murderer!" He lashes the Destroyer's brain with his mind-send. Vivid pain courses through him, wakening all his faculties, breaking the trance in which he has been moving. This is real, *his* world is dying while he floats safe within the very Destroyer itself.

Floats . . . safe? A dread idea takes root in him and grows.

He has moved here unharmed across a myriad points of energy that sustained his life. He has entered—and lived. It is not life as life should be, but it is not death: he can think, feel, speak, move. And far away his people are actually dying, being consumed on a burning world. Would not this strange refuge be better than none?

Is it not his duty to call to them, to guide them here?

He quails, understanding what such a call would mean. It would drain his last strength. Even if he draws ruthlessly on Tedyost—and he is desperate enough for that unethical act—there will be nothing left of them but husks.

At that moment the far cry rises to ultimate despair and he can endure no longer. He will do it.

Gently he takes hold upon the life of poor, unsuspecting Tedyost, who is still enchanted by his oceanic vision, and begins to align both their energies to readiness. He is vaguely conscious that the darkness around them seems to be pulsating under some sort of tension; the meaningless words //QUERY*WRONG*I*DO*NOT// cross the phantom screen. Giadoc focusses only on the direction of the sad cry of death. He must send right, he will have no second chance.

The death-wail pierces him again and he is sure. He grips the other's mind without pity and hurls both their energies out into one tremendous shout on the life-bands:

COME TO ME, PEOPLE OF TYREE! SAVE YOURSELVES HERE!

At his call the very darkness seems to boil around him, as though a monstrous strain is seeking release. Giadoc is too terribly drained to feel fear. Gathering their last strength, he manages one more cry:

USE THE BEAM! COME!

With that he falls fainting in upon his extinguished self, while the unknown pressure crests to culminance around him.

//ACTIVATE*ACTIVATE*ACTIVATE// the ghostly screen pleads.

And beyond the barrier, within the nucleus, what had been a woman's phantom hand yields to overpowering urgency and goes at last to the spectral key.

On.

The world changes around them.

Chapter 20

In each mind, what happens then strikes differently.

The dying senses of Ted Yost hear a woman's scream that ends in dark laughter, and feels salt spray sting his face.

Giadoc of Tyree, fainting into death, hears his cry echoed and amplified a millionfold, and knows that he has reached.

The sentience that had been born in the electronic artifacts of a minor planet succeeds at last in gaining access to the full circuitry of its new home.

The mind that had been Margaret Omali feels itself racked upon unearthly dimensions of experience, expanded to unhuman potency.

And the great being who for so long had drifted half-alive comes to full function around them.

A huge newborn voice speaks silently and with joyful wonder:
YES. NOW I UNDERSTAND.

Chapter 21

The strange symbiosis holds, the improbable interfaces mesh and spread. From spacebourne vastness through a small unliving energy-organization to the residual structure of a human mind with an odd relation to matter, information cycles. And power.

Enough of Margaret Omali is still left to cloak her new perceptions in human imagery. What happened? Some intolerable stress occurred, some great contradiction of underlying realities. The strain of incongruence had moved her to press to final activation, in whatever unearthly mode. She understands that her touch was needed: the problem or entity could not heal itself. Now it is done. She, or what was once she, puzzles remotely, trying to comprehend.

Stress is still present; she feels it. But now it is localized, a demanding something in the great starfield. She attends, and it focusses and magnifies the signals of a single small star. The star is throwing off shells of energy. That is correct, she feels; it has to do with some Plan.

But one aspect is wrong. It is that the peculiar emanations of life from a nearby mote of matter have risen, attained unbearable criticality. Action is overdue.

And as she perceives this, she perceives also that her action is taking place. Dreamily she feels herself stretch forth an arm across the light-years toward the angry little sun. Her phantom finger lifts: it freezes the explosion. As easily as she would fold back the petals of a flower, she feels herself folding back the flames spreading around the crying mote. The enormous powers of time are in her fingers, but she does not know this; she only feels the correctness of the act.

But it is not enough. Pain and death continue to scream at her from the speck in the fiery fringes. New action is imperative.

A force which she feels as her other arm flows toward the wailing thing. Her dream-hand touches, beckons. *COME.*

And a will which is hers and not hers draws forth the pain, lets it flow out and up to safety. At the same time, the energies of the great body outside her stronghold change and rise, stabilize at a new level appropriate to need. Provision is made. A richness begins to flow around her that she feels as good.

But just as the relieved tension crests to climax, a new perception sweeps her sensors and a dire new imperative is born.

Yes! She must take quite different, somehow unwelcome action. And meanwhile all this new experience must be deactivated, retired to stasis.

I must follow, I must search . . .

Chapter 22

I MUST FOLLOW, I MUST NOW BEGIN THE SEARCH!

WHAT JOY, WHEN THE VAST SPACEBOURNE BEING CAME TO ITSELF AT LAST, TO FIND THAT ITS WICKED INTEREST IN THE TINY EMANATIONS OF LIFE WAS NOT A MALFUNCTION AT ALL, BUT PART OF ITS PROPER ROLE IN THE TASK! NOT FOR ME THE ORDINARY TASKS OF DEMOLITION, IT EXULTS: I AM OF THE SAVERS OF LIFE!

YES, AND SOME LIFE HAS BEEN SAVED HERE, ALTHOUGH THERE IS NOT NOW TIME TO COMPLETE THIS PROGRAM. THE RACE HAS ALREADY LEFT, HAS GONE OUT BETWEEN THE STAR-SWARMS TO IDENTIFY A NEW TARGET. IT IS FOR THE LATE-BORN ONE TO FOLLOW, TO DEACTIVATE ITSELF AND ITS CARGO TO TRAVEL-MODE: TO SEARCH FOR THEM. WHEN IT FINDS THEM IT WILL BE TIME TO DISCHARGE ITS CARGO AND TAKE ITS RIGHTFUL PLACE IN THE NEW TASK. ALL IS AT LAST IN ORDER.

WHY THEN IS THERE STILL SADNESS?

IS IT BECAUSE THE SEARCH WILL BE LONG, EVEN WITH ITS ALL-BUT-INFINITE POWERS OF ACCELERATION? THE RACE

LEAVES NO TRACE OF THEIR PASSING: EVERY LIKELY STAR-SWARM MUST BE INSPECTED, AND THE SEARCH WILL BE AT RANDOM. IT MAY TAKE FOREVER. BUT THE MIGHTY ENTITY IS PREPARED FOR THAT. IN TRAVEL-MODE ALL IS REDUCED TO THE SINGLE URGE OF QUEST, AND TO ANTICIPATION OF THE GREAT MOMENT WHEN THE SENSORS BRING NEWS OF THE PRESENCE OF THE RACE. THEN ALL CAN BE REACTIVATED AND THE PRESENT CARGO UNLOADED ON SOME MOTE SAFELY AWAY FROM THE ZONE OF OPERATIONS. AND THE GREAT BE-ING, NO LONGER LONELY, WILL TAKE UP ITS DUTIES AMONG THE SAVERS OF LIFE, ALL CORRECT AT LAST.

OR PERHAPS THE STRANGE GLOOM IS MERELY BECAUSE IT WAS SO LATE AWAKENED, SO THAT THE OTHERS ARE ALREADY GONE. WHY HAD IT BEEN SO LONG IN HALF-LIFE, SO SLOW TO BECOME COMPLETELY ENERGIZED? NO WAY TO KNOW; AND NO MATTER. NOW ALL IS CLEAR AND JOYFUL.

DEACTIVATE ALL INTERNAL SYSTEMS, THE ORDER GOES OUT. PREPARE TO LAUNCH OUT ON THE LONG, PERHAPS ENDLESS JOURNEY THROUGH THE VOID.

I MUST FOLLOW. I MUST SEARCH . . .

Chapter 23

Dying as he clings to his niche by the Destroyer's nucleus, losing even the drained mind of Tedyost, Giadoc feels the Tyrenni come.

They come!

A torrent of naked life streams in tumult past him, a planetary jet of escaping lives upborne on the power of the strange Beam. As the dreamlike time stasis holds, up and out of their burning bodies flee young and old, male and female—each helping and being helped, carrying with them in their outrush even the dim lives of Tyree's animals and plants. Up and up they come into the dark unknown, flinging themselves from their charred shriveling flesh, hoping because there is no other hope. And behind them the raging solar fires loom frozen for a timeless instant, a maw of flame held back from closing on its prey, while the living lightning-bolt pours out. They come, they arrive! All that still lives of Tyree comes whirling by, surging into the Destroyer's dark holds.

And with the last weakest laggards comes something else: a huge silent presence from the depths of the perishing planet rises with them to the stars. It is the Great Field of Tyree, Giadoc knows faintly, reverently, as he feels it pass. Some of us believed it lived.

With that passing the great Beam fades, winks out and time snaps back. The ravening, held-back jaws of fire close. Giadoc knows that somewhere far away the physical world of Tyree is gone forever, a tumbling cinder in the wastes of space.

But around him in the vast darkness he can sense the surviving lives of Tyree spreading out, separating to a myriad scattered centers as they strive to reshape themselves from the mind-fields that buffeted and permeated them in their whirling flight. The empty spaces of the Destroyer begin to resonate with a small cloud of life-signals.

And the space is no longer as it was, he perceives wonderingly. The Tyrenni have not come as he did to darkness and nonbeing. The level has changed, energized; the strange unliving supports are far stronger now, rich with possibility. He feels even his own failing life being sustained, minutely strengthened; for a time he is being held from death.

Too weak to do more than marvel, he listens to the growing tumult on the life-bands as the Tyrenni come to themselves and begin to stabilize in this strange refuge of space. Exclamations, exhilarations of pain gone and life preserved, confusions of bodilessness, joys as the lost are reunited, calls for the missing, discovery of unknown sensory modes—excitement and bewilderment are all about him, dominated by a few calm transmissions which must be the surviving Elders. Fragments of sense-imagery flare out: they are finding, it seems, that they can recreate remembered reality at will. Near him he can sense a Father comforting his child with a vision of their home in Deep, and three females are clinging together in a memory of the winds of lost Tyree.

Then some discover they are mobile. Fathers move toward calling children, friend flows to friend. Movement, it seems, is also much easier now. Soon the whole small throng is in intricate motion, mind questioning mind as each seeks to understand where and what they are. Giadoc catches the signals of a group of females starting to probe out into the vast empty reaches all around.

Suddenly among the calls he hears his own name-sign.

"Giadoc!"

He tries to respond, but he is too feeble, too spent. He sinks back. Nevertheless it was enough—in a rush she is here, Tivonel, on him with her life-field surging against him like a child's—a tumultuous greeting mingled with memories of he knows not what, of aliens, of dying and burning, of Heagran, of questions-emotions-joy.

It is all too much, his own held-back memories erupt weakly and he loses hold on consciousness, feels himself draining away into dark.

"Oh no, Giadoc! Don't die, don't die!"

She has hold of him mind-to-mind and is opening her own life-energy to his. The ultimate Tyrenni gift pours into him, without restraint or fear. The relief is so keen it is almost pain, but his first feeling is shame, he who had been so strong. Yet he cannot will refusal. Their fields merge and the life-current flows.

"Stop, enough!" He cries to her. But she will not stop. And then he feels a sudden, stronger touch. As he comes back to himself he recognizes it: Eldest Father Heagran is here.

"Stop, stop," he protests again. And Heagran's deep thought echoes him. *"Enough, young Tivonel. Cease before you injure yourself."*

There is a brief confusion. Heagran seems to be forcibly disengaging Tivonel's determined aid. *"Ahura!"*

They come to a semblance of civility, holding light mental contact in the strange now-peopled void.

"What is this place you have called us to?" Heagran's mental tone is strong; the weird cold energies here must be sustaining him well.

"I think it is a huge animal of space. I believed it was dead; but it changed when I called. That must be its brain." Giadoc mind-points at the big cryptic complex glimmering nearby. It too seems different now: brighter, differently organized, like a huge angular egg filled with living and nonliving energies intermixed. Its output is almost nulled by the barrier wall.

Tivonel is reaching toward it.

"Be careful," Giadoc warns. *"It is protected. We can't reach in."*

She has met the barrier. He feels her recoil away.

"So we are in a pod with no driver," Heagran sums up succinctly.

Belatedly Giadoc's reviving mind remembers poor Tedyost.

262

"There is an alien here who seemed to be in contact with it. I must help him, I used his strength to call. He is one of those displaced by Scomber's crime."

"Find it."

Slowly, feeling himself still weak, Giadoc begins to search from point to point around the circumference of the brain-wall. The others follow. Presently he locates a feeble emanation almost at the barrier itself and recognizes Tedyost. He is shocked by its weakness. How could he have been so unFatherly as to forget the other's need? Remorsefully, he forms a penetration to infuse some of his own renewed strength.

The experience is abruptly disorienting. Streaming through the interface comes an alien sensory landscape of sky and silent light and great billows of liquid water, all permeated with joy. Riding the moving crests of water is a dream-pod, or rather, a remarkably detailed vision of three open pods braced together, surmounted by a big wind-filled vane which is pulling the leaping pods along. In the center hull reclines an alien figure, Tedyost himself, but naked and strangely dark hued. He is apparently happily driving or steering his imaginary craft.

Giadoc probes for deeper contact. *"Tedyost!"*

He finds himself speaking from the form of an alien flying animal, a white "bird" perched on the pod's prow.

"Hi there," the mental construct of Tedyost says cheerfully.

Giadoc finds himself so caught up he must struggle for reality.

"Are you still in contact with the Destroyer? Remember! The brain, your 'captain'?"

"I'm the captain," Tedyost's mind replies peacefully.

The creature is mad. Effortfully Giadoc pushes through the bewildering pseudo-reality, sends a jolt of life-force into the other nucleus. *Remember!*

But to his dismay the visionary world only grows stronger; he is still in bird-form, teetering for balance as the breeze and the hissing spray blow past the craft. The only trace of his efforts is that Tedyost's dream now contains an image of the Destroyer's speaking-screen, fixed to the edge of one pod. It shows blue lights and symbols, but Tedyost's attention does not turn to it.

The alien will not rouse at this level, Giadoc sees. He himself is too weak to do more. He must disengage at once.

With more difficulty than he expects, Giadoc disentangles himself from the charming dream-world. When he reports to the others what he has found, Heagran's mind-tone is grave.

"This place has dangers. The fantasy mode is very strong here. Without true senses we must all be on our guard. We must keep each other sane."

They are all silent a moment, scanning the enigmatic brain so close yet so unreachable.

"We must understand and control the reality of this place," Heagran transmits again. *"If not, we will one by one drift into dreaming and be lost. Giadoc, you must devise means of contact. I will summon the surviving Fathers here to help."*

With grave formality he sends the ancient Tyrenni council-call out to the nearest minds. Giadoc can sense it being taken up and passed on.

"We should get the other aliens here too," Tivonel puts in excitedly. *"Maybe Tanel knows how to reach this one. Oh, I hope he's alive."*

"Again this female has a sound idea." Heagran's tone is benevolent. *"Young Tivonel, go quest for them in my name."*

With a warm touch she disengages, and Giadoc can sense her life-field flowing away from point to point among the throng of Tyrenni. He and Heagran wait, contemplating the pale cryptic forms writhing within the nucleus and the passive emanation of Tedyost.

All at once they notice that the structures of energy within the huge brain are changing, fading from their scan. It seems to be becoming wholly opaque. As it does so, a new surface configuration glimmers into being, very close, definite and stable; apparently a shallow energy-pattern. As they watch, it coalesces sharply to a field of brilliant points. Giadoc is reminded of something—the sky, seen from Tyree's Near Pole.

"Heagran! It is showing us the Companions."

As if in confirmation, the pattern lingers, then begins to change as though receding in a steady, unliving way. New sparks pour in on all sides while the familiar sky-field shrinks until it is only a part of what seems a huge globular mass of brilliance. Then that too shrinks further and is lost in a great flattened swirl, like a big plant of light spinning in an eddy. At the center of the slow light-whirl is a disorderly bright flare.

As Giadoc studies this he receives the impression of wrongness, danger; it is insistent, like the warning engrams that explorers sometimes impose on poisonous plants.

"This is some kind of message or communication, Heagran. Perhaps it is showing the true shape of the whole sky."

"Can you decipher it, young Giadoc?"

"No. But maybe it is warning us of trouble among the Companions, or the death of Sounds."

"We know that already."

"Wait. See!"

Into the strange cold swirl of unliving light a squadron of dark shapes have come. They appear small, but Giadoc realizes they must be huge by comparison with the lights that represent a myriad Sounds. They remind him of the schools of mindless animals that feed on the plant-rafts of the high winds. As he attends, they spread out, deploy in ranks, and in fact begin something that looks like feeding. The Companions before them seem to vaporize or disappear at their approach; the black ranks are cutting a slow swathe of darkness through the brilliance of the central fires. Soon a zone or arc of empty deadness is being carved out of the great glowing swirl, between the inmost center and the roots of the streaming, spangled arms. A flare from the center washes toward the dark zone and subsides, and still the "feeding" goes on.

"Heagran, I believe it is showing us the other Destroyers. The eaters of Sounds."

"We know that too. To what purpose?"

"I can't tell. It seems unliving, like a dead engram."

Old Heagran churns angrily, and transmits with all his force straight at the brain behind the image.

"WHY? WHY DO YOU KILL?"

No reaction. The strange panoramic engram continues to unfold. The dead zone of destruction continues to expand around the center; now it has almost enclosed it. Giadoc is sure this is some recording, but a vastly speeded-up image or diagram of unimaginable scope. And now he notices a new detail of the scene: here and there among the shoals of the Destroyers are a few of different sort, moving in advance of the general line. They pause now and again, and from them come faint simulacra of the signals of life. Then these few turn and speed out beyond the area of annihilation, only to return and repeat.

Giadoc can make nothing of this, yet he senses it is intended as significant. He has not long to wonder; now the globe or shell of darkness has been joined around the central fires of the image. As if this were a signal, the dark shapes of the Destroyers draw together like a school of flying animals, then turn as one and flee outward from the scene. In a moment they have dwindled to a vanishing point in the void beyond all light.

The image holds for a moment, then darkens and expands back to the original sky-field, showing again the familiar Companions. Then this begins to shrink and condense as before. Giadoc realizes that it is about to repeat the entire sequence all over again. Can this be communication, or a fantastically detailed engram impressed somehow on unliving energy?

But as he puzzles, "watching" the dark shapes come again into the great sky-swirl, a faint subliminal unease comes to him, as if something is changing in the real, or unreal, world around him. The sensation is not strong enough to break his concentration, until he notices that the faint blur below the image which is the dreaming mind of Tedyost is no longer still. It has begun to roil restlessly. Presently it flares out weakly, as if seeking contact. Perhaps the dreaming one has waked?

Cautiously Giadoc extends contact, only to find he need not have bothered.

With startling intensity the alien transmits directly at him:

"Help! Mutiny! The Captain needs help!"

The symbols are only half-intelligible. Tedyost subsides to passivity again. But Giadoc has no time to puzzle over this: He has suddenly become aware of what is bothering him: Alarm!

Out beyond them, all through the vast expanse of the Destroyer, the sense of life has lowered. Gradually but perceptibly the sustaining energies are sinking, ebbing, seeping away.

"Heagran! Do you not sense that these energies are beginning to fail? In the periphery, coming closer?"

The old being scans intently. *"Yes. I do. So your space-animal is dying after all, young Giadoc. A brave try, but doomed."*

But suddenly into Giadoc's mind come his experiences on the alien world, the nonliving energy systems he has known.

"No, Heagran. I believe this is something different. I believe that this entity is turning us off. If we could break through and change its power-set, perhaps we are not doomed."

Chapter 24

Among the incoming life-rush of the Tyrenni are eight minds that had been human and one that had been a dog.

The entity which calls itself Daniel Dann loses contact with everything as his life is whirled up on the strange Beam, leaving his dying body behind. He feels himself a swimmer shot through a turbulent millrace, swirled and spewed out to the shallows of the throng. A moment later he strands on something, he can't tell what, but only clutches at it and finds that it sustains his life.

He has had practice in wild discarnations, but this is the most alien of all. He is still alive, still seemingly himself, but bodiless. Now he has no limbs, no senses, nothing—yet he lives.

A fearful aloneness strikes him. As it threatens to rise to panic, he perceives that his naked mind is receiving input, vague but insistent. This void is not empty. All around him is a sense of calling, or signaling, in some mode he can't quite receive. Others are here, he realizes. They have all come somewhere, life is near him now. But he has no idea how to make contact. The terror of isolation hammers in him; he strains to hang onto himself, to face the menace of this weird escape from death.

Or is it escape? A new terror takes hold. Has he died, is this what the dying mind feels as it leaves life forever? Will the sense of presence fade, and float away forever, leaving him in eternal isolation in the dark?

He tries to "listen" again. Whatever the elusive susurrus whispering around him is, it does not seem to be fading. Hold onto yourself, Dann. The others must be here too, wherever this is. Are they, too, frightened? Try to reach them.

But how can he? He has no idea.

Experimentally he forms the thought of Valerie—no yellow-bikinied body, but Valerie's world as he had touched it—and tries to project her name. *Valerie*, he wills, *VALERIE, ARE YOU HERE?*

Nothing answers him. Ignorant of the mad commotion he is generating, Dann runs through the names. *FRODO! RICK, RON WAXMAN! Can you hear me? WINONA! CHRIS?*

Still no answer he can detect. Is he doomed never to make contact, to continue so horribly alone in nowhere?

Perhaps the Tyrenni, he thinks, and imagines himself shouting with all his might. *TIVONEL! HELP ME PLEASE!*

This time something does happen. He has been mindlessly lunging forward as he tries to call, and now a sensory image blooms in his mind. For an instant he is blown by the great gales of Tyree. *"Heagran!"* says a soundless voice.

He grasps at it, but it is gone, leaving a sense of scandalized disapproval. He understands that he has blundered into a Tyrenni mindfield. Well, at least there is some sort of reality here. Encouraged, he tries again. *"Tivonel?"*

For a moment he thinks he is rewarded—the image of winds comes again, he hears merry coral laughter. But it does not hold, it splinters and dissolves into an Earthly street scene; he sees a red VW pull away, revealing a cream-colored Continental. Next instant he is at his familiar desk, then a quick flash to his old body stretched out in his home armchair.

Oh god: Hallucinations. This place must be psychogenic in some way, he can feel illusory powers. Will he lose himself in fantasies or go mad from sensory deprivation?

Pulling himself together, he concentrates outward and tries to shout silently into the rustling void. *VALERIE! RICK! IS ANYBODY THERE?*

And almost he thinks he feels himself reach somebody, when the most amazing sensation he has ever known invades, or rather, surrounds his mind.

It is a feather-light authoritative presence which seems to press swiftly, gently, irresistibly around the circumference of his whole life-being. The urgency of his need evaporates away and vanishes; indeed, he can no longer even try to call. A myriad frantic half-thoughts of which he had been only dimly aware are suddenly resolved and gone too, folded back somehow into his central mind. His great half-admitted terror of this place drains away, leaving in its place a growing calm. Stealing over him, enfolding him, is an almost palpable wave of reassurance and relief.

For a moment he thinks he is going under some immensely powerful opiate. But that comes from within—this is coming on him from outside.

Fear flares again. *Who's there?* he tries to cry, *Wait! What are you doing?* The only answer is another wave of the calming pressure, in which he can now read a coloring of reproof. Something out there has been offended and is taking steps to quieten him. His mind casts up wild pictures of djinns or angels or extraterrestrial what's-its, and then understanding comes: Tyree, their techniques of the mind.

Can he be experiencing the ministrations of a Father of Tyree?

Yes, he is sure of it now. He is being Fathered, englobed and "drained" as he had seen it done to others. As if he were an angry child!

Human resentment erupts in him. Struggling to resist the tranquillizing currents he yells mentally, *Stop! I must reach my friends! Where are they?*

But the pacifying presence is much too strong. He feels his protest dissipate, subside back into itself and melt away. It's not like going under anaesthesia, not at all. He is perfectly conscious, only calmer, more unified and centered. At peace. Really very pleasant, he acknowledges; these people have the only technology here in the naked realm of mind. What was it Tivonel had told him? Think yourself round, like an egg. Awkwardly he tries that again.

He is rewarded by a majestic sense of approval. Father is pleased, he thinks wryly. Is this what a soothed infant feels like? Fathering, we call it mothering. What an extraordinary art, why have I not considered its significance before? Surely of all the things people do to each other this is one of the most remarkable.

Into his musings comes a concrete image: the picture of a gyrating cloud of mind-stuff, frantically contorting and emanating violent blasts in all directions, intruding promiscuously into others and on the verge of disrupting itself. He understands. This is how he had been. *"Ahura!"* The mental echo is freighted with admonition.

Very well, *ahura*, whatever that is. But what to do? And who is his invisible mentor? As quietly as he can he shapes the question.

He "hears" no reply, but suddenly finds himself recalling big Father Ustan, who had separated him from Ron in the winds of Tyree. At first he takes it only for memory, until something in its insistence tells him it is communication. Dear God, if this is mind-speech, how will he ever learn?

In answer, his surface thought is suddenly invaded by a point that unfolds into a picture or diagram, an abstract multidimensional webwork glimmering in his mind. He puzzles, finally guesses that he is being shown a field-organization, a teaching picture of how to shape himself to function here. But it means nothing to him; he has not the concepts.

For a moment he fully appreciates his barbarous mental state. The Tyrenni train themselves from childhood in all this. Random human exhortations recur to him: Brace up, Relax, Concentrate, Make up your mind, Forget it, Think positively, Cool it, Meditate. How ludicrously inadequate, even the portentous admonitions of psychotherapy! Here before him are precise instructions on how to organize his mind-self—and he doesn't know how.

He has no pride left; pride is not the issue here.

Help me, he cries or pleads.

Next second he has an experience so astounding he forgets to be terrified. What he has felt as gentle external pressure becomes suddenly a real invasion—some part of his inmost being is grasped and shifted. He feels moods being seized and compressed, memories manipulated; his very focus of attention suddenly seems to dissolve, to flow in unknown directions and recover itself on some unexperienced dimension. Tensions he was unaware of melt with a snap, events on the borders of consciousness careen about and disappear. It is intimate, clinical, appalling, nothing at all. Beyond description.

He yields. He has no choice nor concepts to define what is happening to him. One last panicky thought wonders if he is going mad or has forever lost himself. Then that too vanishes.

With a twist like a chiropractor's jerk he finds himself precariously stabilized in what feels like an internal gymnastic pose. His dizzied awareness comes back to him in a ludicrous picture of himself twisted into a pretzel with his heels behind his ears.

"There. Thus."

He receives the "voice" distinctly but at some receptor-focus separate from his normal center, like an ear held out.

"Speak so. I have assisted you to form a receptor-node. Place a thought here to pass it on."

Good grief, is this what telepaths do? Feeling like an untrained contortionist, Dann tries to form a thought of gratitude and hold it apart, "there," at this new center of his mind. *"Where are my friends?"*

"They are nearby. You are Tanel. A message: You must all join Father Heagran. That way." A sense of direction imprints itself together with the words, coupled with an impression of stretching or flowing across points.

"Where are we? What is this place?" he tries to ask, but in his urgency forgets the correct procedure. When he recovers himself and goes through the new convoluted channel, nothing answers him. He receives only a sense of disapproving departure. Father Ustan has gone away.

Very well. To go *that* way. Trying to hold his strange new configuration, he reaches out and finds himself able to flow from base to charged base. As he masters this mode of locomotion, he tries to call or send out as discreetly as he can the names of the others. *"Someone from Earth, are you there? Please answer if you can."*

And suddenly, delightingly, someone is here, saying soundlessly at his new "ear." *"Doctor Dann!"*

It's Valerie, he's sure of it, the warmth, the indefinable flavor of personality. Forgetting composure, he rushes at the touch and is rewarded by a startling buffet of reproof-laughter-drawing-away, coupled with a picture of himself, absurdly shaggy, falling in a bear-hug onto Valerie's figure.

"Excuse me, please, I'm sorry I don't know how—" Awkwardly he pulls back, reforming his configuration, terrified that he will lose her.

"Think about just touching hands lightly." The tiny gentle "voice" comes in his brain.

It is like Tyree all over again, with no body. He tries to comply, and is rewarded by a definite sense of impalpable contact.

"Frodo is here. And Chris is around but he won't talk. Now we better go. I'll lead, right?"

"Yes."

He feels the touch pull or draw delicately, and flows himself with it, marveling. The quality of the contact is Valerie's but not the same defensive young mind he had known before. Strength flows gently from her, and something like elation. Leading them through this lightless, soundless, senseless place beyond life she is excited, unafraid. And far more skilled than he. The vulnerability was left on Earth, he thinks. Here nothing scares her.

He flows or leaps along in her wake, exerting all his efforts to hold the contact lightly. Once or twice she checks and changes direction, and he has a fleeting sense of other presences. She must be guiding them around groups of Tyrenni in their path. Or over or under—all directions have the same valence here. How could a disembodied mind know weight?

Preoccupied, he blunders into the outskirts of another mind, a quick bright impression of many words mixed with musics, and an unmistakably hostile laugh. *"Frodo!"* Trying to transmit apology, he swerves away. His new "posture" is becoming slightly more natural, but he still feels like a man trying to bicycle a tightwire while holding out an ear-trumpet with both hands.

And Earthly questions are waking in him again. What in God's name is this place? It has physical existence, he is sure of that. They are actually moving. But what and where are they?

As if in answer, another light contact jolts him and a strange word jumps into his mind. *"Superconductive circuits."*

Who's there? He lunges awkwardly for an instant before recalling how to project. *"Chris? Chris Costakis?"* The absurdity of human names here in astral nothingness.

A cryptic emanation brushes him, flavored with acidity and wistfulness. *"Keep moving, Doc."*

It's gone. So what had been the little man is still here, still his characteristic self.

Dann resumes his progress, pondering. Superconductors? Chris must have "heard" him puzzling over this place, he must be puzzling too. Superconductors are something that happens in extreme

273

cold, he recalls. Currents cycle endlessly. No friction . . . He knows nothing of such things. Could they in fact be sustained by, be moving among, some such cold circuitry of space? Could a living mind be compatible with such energies? It seems as likely as anything. . . . The words *ghost-program* come back to him; he thrusts them away. Lost, gone forever, with everything else. Don't think of her. Keep moving in this unreality, it's all that's left.

Without knowing it, he must have sent out a sigh or squeak of pain. A firmness brushes him, palpable as a finger laid on his lips. Not human, he thinks. Some passing Tyrenni has admonished him. Anguish is not permitted. Well, perhaps he can learn. He must; there are no drugs here.

Just then he becomes aware of a new extraordinary thing: For some time he has not been in total lightlessness. Out on the edges of his mind he has been sensing something, like seeing at night from the corners of the eye. It is not in his visual system at all, really—but there *is* something spatial, blurs or presences. Faint swirls, the memories of reflections in dark water; ghostly differentiations too faint to make out except that three of them seem to be moving with him against a background of others. He tries to "look" harder, and they vanish. He thinks of closing his eyes, and slowly they come back: dim, moonlit glimmers, but there. Is this perhaps what they meant by the life-bands, is he starting to "see" life?

Excitedly he tries again and again, failing more often than he succeeds. He is trying too hard, maybe. Relax. Think away. Yes—there they are again, moving with him. What he takes to be Valerie ahead is clearest, if any of this can be called clear. But what happiness to have something like vision again, even in this faint mode!

At this moment she checks and he has to strive away from colliding.

"Look."

He can "see" nothing, but somehow the space before them seems different, as if it framed or led up to something. And then he becomes aware that he is perceiving: Some sort of pattern is forming like a hypnagogic scene behind his nonexistent eyelids, a hologram in black light.

The bright points—why, it is a picture of stars! And as he attends, the scene recedes, growing, and turns into an image he cannot fail to recognize—a great spiral galaxy seen like photos of Andromeda, in tilted view.

He and the others hover there transfixed, while the transmission changes and unrolls, as Giadoc and Heagran had seen it do at the nucleus. But these are human minds, tuned to Earthly modalities.

"P.A. system," Chris' thought touches his abruptly. *"Probably a lot of them scattered around."*

"Frodo says it's a transit diagram," Valerie's "voice" smiles in the void. *"It'll show an arrow: You are here, take Line L2 for Bethesda."*

And indeed, as Dann "watches," or experiences the thing, he feels it has a mechanical quality, like a recording. And it seems to resonate from many points, like the abstract voice in a plane. *This is your Captain speaking.* Have they encountered or triggered some kind of information-post? Is this place an artifact, a ship of some inconceivable race?

The scene is now "showing" the fleet of star-Destroyers spreading their zone of death around the central fires of the Galaxy. Suddenly the memory of a long-ago summer in Idaho surfaces in Dann's mind. Comprehension breaks.

"Good God, it's a firelane!"

Feeling Val wince, he modulates down. *"It's a galactic fire-break! If that's our galaxy. We must be seeing millions of years, speeded up. See that explosion at the center?"* He realizes he is transmitting a jumble, half-words, half-pictures, and tries for coherence. *"An explosion like that could start a chain reaction, propagate out to all the central stars. Maybe even to the arms. I think those ships or whatever are starting backfires, they're clearing out a zone around the center to stop the spread. To save the outer stars. But aeons of time, a galaxy—a whole great galaxy—"*

He falls silent before the enormity of the thing.

Through Valerie's touch he can feel the reflection of her wonder. Do they truly grasp it? It's too vast, I don't grasp it, he thinks numbly, "seeing" the things, whatever they are, complete their task, form up and speed away. Then the whole scene expands and begins to repeat again.

The four hover before it, hypnotized.

How can they annihilate matter, Dann wonders, without generating worse energies? Do they somehow disperse it below criticality? Are they beings or machines?

Suddenly Valerie's "voice" says excitedly, *"Look! Look at those ones going in ahead. Can't you feel the life there? I think they're rescuing life, they're taking living things off before they burn up. Maybe that's what we're in."*

"A rescue squad," Chris comments tersely.

"Frodo thinks they're alive," Valerie goes on. *"Like space-fish. Maybe we're in a whale, like Jonah."* Her soundless laugh is warm in the endless night. *"Or in a kangaroo's pouch . . . We better move on and find the others."*

Her nonexistent fingers tug gently. Dann tears himself away from the mesmeric image and follows, marveling at her composure. She accepts that they are in a *thing.* Are they jumping between the electrons of a space-fish? Or hurdling interstellar distances? No way to tell. How big is the structure of a mind? The ancient theologians had been sure that angels could throng on a pinhead. Perhaps he is sub-pinhead size? But he is not an angel, none of them are. We are the miraculously undead, he thinks; joy and pain and wonder and tension live among us still.

They skirt another of the uncanny communicative projectors, triggering it in midscene. As the great galaxy flashes to life in his mind's eye, Dann muses again on the incredible grandeur of the thing. Beings or machines whose task is to contain galactic fire-storms! Ungraspable in its enormity. Are they manned ships, or could it be instinctive, like great animals? Or maybe devices of a super-race to rescue endangered habitats of life?

His own mind reels, yet the others with him seem undisturbed. He recalls that their Earthly selves read, what was it, science fiction. Galaxies, super-races, marvels of space. They're used to such notions. He himself had seen the stars as stars; they saw them as backgrounds for scenarios. Well, maybe theirs was the best preparation for reality, if wherever they are is indeed reality.

He is distracted by the faint persistent glimmer of more presences that seem to be moving parallel with them. Two, no, three others are here. An instant later he feels a strong, skillful Tyrenni mind-touch, is electrified by recognition. *"Tanel!"*

"Tivonel, my dear, is that you? Are you—"

"Tanel, stop, you're terrible!" Image of coral laughter leaping away. He subsides abashed. It comes to him that he was "sending" in a sort of pidgin, half-human, half-Tyrenni words. Will there, incredibly, be language problems here?

It seems so. She is "speaking" again, but he retains only enough of her speech to catch a sense of impending events and the names of Heagran and Giadoc. This last comes through with such joy that he is pricked by a ludicrous flash of jealousy. Apparently the famous Giadoc has been found—of course, he called them here. Now his little friend is reunited with her love. For an instant he chafes, until the ultimate absurdity of his reaction here in this gargantuan abyss comes to his rescue.

It seems they are to go on. But just as he starts, Valerie's invisible touch checks, and he is jolted by a brush with an unfamiliar, warm complex of mind-stuff.

"Oh Winnie, I'm so glad you're all right!" Val's thought comes while he tries apologetically to back away from their contact. He can hear Winona's transmission almost as if her voice were in his human ears. *"Yes, I have Kenny here too, with his doggie. They're dreaming of hunting. Oh, hello, Doctor Dann! How wonderful!"*

"Yes." He disengages, and finds again Val's light touch tugging him on through nowhere. As they go on amid unfathomable strangeness, Dann broods on the concept of being "all right," here between the stars without bodies or proper senses, perhaps inside some creature or machine of the void. Well, the alternative was burning to death in mortal bodies; they have in fact been rescued from real death. Maybe the mind really is all, as he had told himself. Maybe to these telepaths the body is less necessary. But he, how will he get on with his mere human mind as his only resource in this terrible isolation? Rescued from death . . . a coldness touches him. Are they perhaps truly rescued from mortal death, is this condition to be— don't think of it.

He is so preoccupied that he almost misses Val's pull backward, her sense of warning. He stops, but not before he has touched against a hostile iciness—manifestly a barrier.

He recoils onto the nearest sustaining point like a man teetering on a brink. What menace is here? He tries to "look" in his new averted way, and finally achieves an impression of a great swirl of pale energies confined in a pyramidal or tetragonal shape. It is huge, complex, indefinably sinister. And it is apparently their goal; he can sense other lives waiting nearby.

There is a short time of confusion. He has lost contact, but he can feel their lives all about him, and waits, trusting that someone will link up with him again. Presently he feels a vague, cloudy presence, and tries hopefully to "receive" at it. But nothing comes to him.

Then through the bewilderment cuts Tivonel's mind-send, so clear that it seems to revive his memory of her speech:

"Winds! Can't you people get into communication-mode at all?"

Communication-mode, what could that be? Another mental gymnastic stunt? A ghostly outstretched hand comes into his consciousness and a human voice speaks strongly in his mental ear.

"Waxman here. Let me help. I have like hands to spare."

Slowly Dann succeeds in imagining himself clasping the hand, wondering if it is Ron or Rick. As he does so, an odd kind of extended clarity comes into being. He has a sudden weird picture of them each clasping one of the joined twins' four hands, as if Waxman were making himself into a kind of astral conference hook-up. Is this perhaps literally true? It would be logical, he thinks daftly.

"That seems to be a plant you're in, Dann. Better get loose."

He manages to retract himself or shake free from the nebulous presence, without losing Waxman's grip. As he does so, a mental voice says faintly, *"I'll hang in with Doc here."*

It's Chris, he's sure. So shyness continues into astral realms. He imagines his other hand outstretched in that direction, and feels a small, oddly hard touch.

"Ready," says Waxman's "voice."

Next moment Dann is receiving a clear formal transmission which seems to be echoing through Waxman to them all.

"Greetings, all, and to you, Doctordan. I am Giadoc of Tyree."

So this is Giadoc, lost sky-traveler and late occupant of Dann's own human body! He seems to be sending in English, too. But there is no time for curiosity, the transmission is going on, part-speech, part-pictures.

"Eldest Heagran and others are with me. We are in what we call the Destroyer." Image of a great, too-familiar huge blackness, And then in rapid sequence Giadoc's story unrolls through their linked minds; his awakening and finding Ted Yost, their search for the

brain, and Ted Yost's strange apparent communication with it; then the tale of Giadoc's own call to them and its consequences. *"It came alive as you find it now."*

During the recital Dann is irresistibly reminded of certain eager young interns he has known. A good type. Well, the young belong to each other, even in darkness and supreme weirdness.

He is jerked from his benevolence by Giadoc's urgent news. *"The energies around us are sinking back to death or turning off. Unless we can contact this brain again and reverse its condition we are all doomed. Ted Yost seems our only link. We cannot rouse him. Can you help?"*

Before Dann can react, Waxman's thought comes. *"Croystasis. Maybe it's packing us up for a trip. Like thousands of years."*

Dann recalls Rick's tale about the Japanese time-machine. The imagination is still alive in Waxman but it doesn't sound so fantastic here. Not at all. He now senses, or thinks he senses, a slow but definite ebbing-down of energies around their perimeter. The murmurs of life seem to be slowing, lessening. Is it drawing closer? He shudders.

"I don't want to be put to sleep for thousands of years," Val protests. Frodo's thought echoes her.

"Why did it bring us here if it didn't want to rescue us?" Winona's mind asks. The sense of normal conversation is so absurdly strong in this incredible situation; for an instant Dann is back in the Deerfield messhall.

"Maybe it wants to use us as fuel," Frodo suggests. *"Maybe it runs on life."*

"No . . . " Winona "says" hesitantly. *"No, I don't get that feeling."*

"Whatever, we have to get through to it before it turns us all off," Waxman's thought comes decisively. *"Who wants to try contacting Ted?"*

"It's dangerous," Val comments. *"Ted's a strong dreamer."*

There is a pause filled with almost-speech, and suddenly Chris sends right through Dann, so loudly it makes him resonate: *"I'll try if Doc'll hold onto me."*

"Right, good," Waxman replies. *"Over here, Chris. Be careful."*

Dann can only marvel at their sense of organization in this weird modality. He feels more tugging, and their misty constellation seems to revolve slowly, until the half-seen life that must be Chris hanging to him converges toward a vague small pallor. Can that be poor Ted's mind, curled around an isolated node? Chris seems to change balance, accompanied by a tightening mental hand-clasp; surprisingly, Chris' "hand" feels bigger now, a full man's hand.

"Hang tight, Doc."

Dann strengthens the imaginary grip, beginning roughly to understand what is involved here. Chris is proposing to enter a hallucinated mind, perhaps as dangerous as the panic-vortex he himself had experienced. Belatedly, he remembers to cling hard onto Waxman's grip too.

"Okay."

There is a sense of he knows not what happening at Chris' end, and all at once Dann finds himself invaded by a brilliant vision of sunlit tropical waters, streaming foam. The vision comes in fragmentary bursts; through it he manages to maintain his mental holds. But it is hard. Now he is feeling his own body rush through the water, flinging spray from his flanks as he leaps. Good God, is he a porpoise? *Hang on.* Even though with flippers splashing, he is hanging on through sun and green water and a confused sense of shouting—until suddenly the vision snaps out, and he is back in dark space, feeling Chris' mind-touch tremble against his own.

"No good." Chris transmits weakly, like a man gasping. *"I couldn't break him out. He made me into a goddam fish. The computer screen's still there, I could see the words NEGATIVE and HELP CANCEL. He won't look anymore, he's in heaven."*

A dismayed silence, humming with stray half-thoughts. Then Giadoc's "voice" repeats clearly, *"He is our only link."*

"If we all try to break him out together I think he'd go crazy," Waxman sends. Other minds agree. *"That wouldn't help."*

They fall silent again, conscious of the ominous quietude creeping closer and closer, conscious of the cryptic fortress of energies so near at hand yet so impregnable. Abruptly Winona's thought explodes in their minds:

"Look! Look, inside that brain or whatever! Don't you see?"

What, where? Dann tries to "look" at the thing, loses it, finally gets a focus long enough to see that its interior is now in slow, intricate motion, as if strands of pale, cold light mingled in complex dance. One spot seems brighter than the rest.

"That's Margaret in there!" Winona shakes them all. *"It's Margaret! I'd recognize her anywhere."*

Margaret?

Margaret, his lost one, here? All at once Dann's human life comes pouring back through him as if an inner dam had broken. The bits and pieces he has been idling with suddenly fall together, making overwhelming order.

The great black shape that swallowed her, the Destroyer, that's where they are. She fled into *this*. Is it possible she's still alive, in whatever mode of life this is, is she trapped in there?

He focusses with all his might in the crazy indirect way he can "see" here. That bright spot. Can it be the very flame, the life-spark he had followed so desperately? Yes! Yes—it is she! He is sure.

Without thought he gathers his strength as a man might take a deep breath, drawing unknowingly on all the lives around him, and hurls a mental cry at the Destroyer's wall:

"MARGARET! MY DARLING, I'LL HELP YOU!"

He falls back, hit by a sense of stunned disengagement.

"Don't do that again," comes Waxman's distant "voice."

But someone else is exclaiming, *"Look! Look!"*

Dann's attention is all on the cloudy pale fires within. The star that he knows is Margaret seems to be drawing nearer to him.

"He reached it." Val's "hand" touches him. *"Let him try again."*

"All right." Waxman's phantom hand comes back too. *"But take it easy this time, Doc."*

Trying to modulate himself, Dann grasps at their tenuous touch.

"Margaret! It's Dann here, Doctor Dann. Can you speak to me?"

More silent swirlings, the starlike point brightens. But no sense of thought or word comes. Instead, as it had done for Ted Yost, an image seems to rise and glimmer in his mind. He recognizes it incredulously—Margaret's computer screen. Oh God, is this her only mode of communication here? He tries to bring it in focus, tries also to maintain contact with the others. Do they see it too?

Pale blue letters come to life on the ghostly screen:

//DOCTOR*DANN*IS*THAT*YOU//

"Yes! Yes!" he projects eagerly.

But the letters have changed, grown huge and ominous. They march across the screen, repeating meaninglessly:

—I MUST FOLLOW—I MUST SEARCH—I MUST FOL-

LOW—I MUST SEARCH— as though a vast mechanical voice is intervening.

"Margaret!"

At his cry the letters break down to normal size.

//DOCTOR*DANN*YOU*WON'T*HURT*ME*WILL*YOU//

"No, never my dear! Never! Tell me what to do!"

But the silently booming symbols are back, filling the screen. *—I MUST FOLLOW—I MUST SEARCH—I MUST— FOLLOW—*

"Margaret! Margaret, tell me how to help you!"

—I MUST FOLLOW—I MUST SEARCH—I MUST—

Desperate, Dann pulls on the strengths around him.

"MARGARET!"

Again the normal screen comes back.

//CAN'T*TURN*OFF*NEED*MORE*STRENGTH// I*WILL*OPEN*WAY*IN*JUST*YOU// And then her words are swept away by the maniacal huge intruders:—*I MUST FOLLOW—I MUST SEARCH—*

He senses she has spent all her strength. The next move is up to him.

"I'm going to try to get to her. She said she can open it. Waxman, can you hang onto me somehow?"

"Right."

Dann has no idea what to do, but he hurls himself across the cold chasm right at the brightness glimmering through the Destroyer's nucleus. The contact with the wall is horrible, he shrinks and convulses like a soft thing dropped on fiery ice. But in the midst of his pain he feels it—a chink or opening, no more than a small weak spot in the terrifying surface.

Is he to go in *that*? Yes—because Margaret is trapped in there, he must reach her. But how? Savingly the thought comes to him that he is not a mortal man to be frozen or crushed; he is not more than a pattern of energy seeking to penetrate some resistance. He must, he will flow in somehow. Hold the thought: he imagines the inflowing of safe, fearless, mindless electrons. Flow in, go.

But as he knows he has started *in*, human imagery comes back and he is a man plunging his frightened arm, his head, into deep fanged jaws that have swallowed his child. Reach, stretch, get in! And the jaws become a frightful glacial crevasse squeezing him with icy menace, about to crush out his life. Still he persists, thrusts himself forward tremblingly, and the image becomes mixed with another; he is crawling through a perilously frail dark tube, a frightened astronaut squirming through an umbilicus to the haven of some capsule. Get on, crawl, squeeze, go.

He feels totally alone. If anyone is holding some rearward part of him he cannot sense it. Scared to death, he curses at himself for a coward. Damn you, Dann, Go on.

Just as his last resolve is failing, with astounding reorientation he or a part of himself is through. His bewildered senses emerge into a swirl of dark light, of power-filled space in which he can half-see a panorama of stars against which are unidentifiable things. He checks, remembering that he must not thrust through wholly but leave himself stretched back toward whatever help may be there.

"Margaret? Margaret!"

And then the starlit place comes alive and he sees her, or what is left of her. For an instant a child seems to be peering at him, a dim elf with huge eyes. *"Margaret?"* Wait—beyond is another, he sees against the stars the beautiful remembered profile, immobile, eyes hooded: goddess of the night. And now another is near him, brighter than all—a familiar white-coated form, with her arms outstretched in tension. The dark hands are brilliantly visible, grasping what seems to be a gigantic busbar. The fingers are clenched, the arms strain to break open the points.

He understands; she or some part of her is trying to change the controls.

"Help," a ghost whispers.

His being surges in response, his own imaginary hands reach out to close over hers upon the switch. But his dream-fingers have no force, they pass through hers like smoke.

"No use. Not that way."

Oh God, he doesn't have the power. He understands; this is *real*, this is solid matter in the actual world, before which he is no more than a sighing ghost. She alone has that power here. How can he help her? He would give her all his life, but how?

For a moment his senses quest in helpless frustration. Then abruptly he encounters the one thing he knows—a human wound of pain and need. *Here!* And his arms seem to grip a straining waist, in a rush he knows he can exert his own small gift, can take to himself her pain and fear and send her out his strength.

283

It is dizzying, transcendent, transsexual—he hugs, tugs recklessly, opening his very life to her need, pressing himself into her, giving himself to convert to the power of her grip. And for an instant he thinks they have succeeded: her visionary arm brightens, the fingers seem to strengthen, the switch yields imperceptibly.

But no—it is not enough. And he can barely hold. They must have more.

"Help! Help us!" he shouts back through his whole being, hoping that someone is still there to respond, unaware of the tremendous vortex of need that he is generating.

And just when he can hold no more, help comes; surging up through him like a violent sharp wave washing through to the nexus where he holds her, to the crucial point where she holds the unknowable. It is intoxicating, a renewal of life mingled of human and Tyrenni essence intertwined. He guesses dimly that a great chain must be forming behind him, a desperate linkage of life pouring their strengths through him to the brittle point where her power can actually move and break the will of the Destroyer.

The intolerable strain mounts, individual consciousness is lost. All is focussed on those dream-fingers that control real force. Is it too much, will the dream-hold break? What powers of beast or machine is she pulling back, what cosmic circuit is she trying to thwart?

He does not know, but only throws his life into her struggle. He feels himself the apex of a frail chain of tiny lives trying to wrest control of something horrendously alien and vast, as if a living cobweb-strand should try to hold back the take-off of a mighty engine of the stars.

Chapter 25

I MUST FOLLOW, I MUST SEARCH. . .

BUT THERE IS RELUCTANCE TO ACT. DRIFTING TOWARD THE LAST DISTURBANCES OF SPACETIME THAT MARK THE RACE'S DEPARTURE-POINT, THE VAST ENTITY IS CONSCIOUS OF THE SLOWNESS WITH WHICH THE POWER-DOWN IS PROGRESSING THROUGH THE PERIPHERY. WHY DOES IT NOT DEACTIVATE AT ONCE? IS IT POSSIBLE THAT THERE IS ANOTHER MALFUNCTION, HAS IT DISCOVERED A NEW MODE OF EVIL JUST WHEN IT HAS FOUND ITSELF GOOD?

AND PECULIAR SENSATIONS ARE EMANATING FROM ITS NUCLEUS. SURELY THIS IS THE FAULT OF THE STRANGE SMALL ENTITIES TO WHICH IT UNWISELY ALLOWED ACCESS. UNFORTUNATELY, THEY ARE NOW SO DEEPLY MESHED THAT THEY CAN NO LONGER EASILY BE GOT RID OF. ARE THEY MALIGNANT?

THE INTERSTELLAR TENUOSITY THAT SERVES FOR INTELLECT BROODS. TRUE, THROUGH THESE PYGMY INTRUDERS IT HAS EXPERIENCED WHAT NONE OF ITS RACE HAS ENCOUNTERED BEFORE, AND FOR WHICH NO SYMBOLS EXIST. THE NEUTRAL STARFIELDS HAVE TAKEN ON MEANING, BECOME THE GLORY

OF THE SIDEREAL UNIVERSE. WITHOUT SENSES IT HAS TASTED THE PERFUME OF FLOWERS, KNOWN THE SUNLIT FOAM OF PLANETARY SEAS. AND WITHOUT A HEART IT FEELS, OR SHARES, A CURIOUS SHRINKING AT THE THOUGHT OF LEAVING THIS LOCAL STAR-GROUP, AT FACING THE ETERNITY OF NOTHING AHEAD. BUT ALL THIS IS NOTHING IN COMPARISON TO THE SACRED TASK! DUTY IS PLAIN: IT WILL NOT DEFAULT AGAIN.

DISREGARDING ALL RESISTANCE FROM ITS CONTAMINATED NUCLEUS, DISREGARDING EVEN A NEW SHARP TUG OF DEVIANCE, THE GREAT BEING WILLS ITSELF TO COMPLY: DEACTIVATE ALL UNNECESSARY SYSTEMS, ASSUME TRAVEL-MODE AT ONCE.

I MUST FOLLOW! I MUST SEARCH!

Chapter 26

In the heart of power, amid the gathering energies, the configuration that had been a human woman fights for understanding. Action that was hers and not-hers has occurred; aligned with her but still closed to her a great will functions. A perception has opened, meaning has come into the universe carrying with it a huge imperative which she shares but does not comprehend.

She could flow with it, allow it to unroll into whatever grand and somehow sad dimension it is destined. Almost she yields. But a spark at the core of her demands enlightenment.

On TOTAL's small screen words show:

//SUBPROGRAM*COMPLETE//

Define subprogram, she commands it.

//LIFE*IS*PRESERVED//

Yes; That was what she felt when she reached out to the world crying in the fires of the exploding star. And life has come here, to the spaces beyond her stronghold. She can detect its hum, an intricate small vividness like a Brownian dance of particles. It is no longer threatening or displeasing to her; instead she feels an undefined large satisfaction. She is no longer merely a single vulnerability to be impinged on; she is impregnable, part of a hugeness whose proper function has wrought this. That life is nearby is, she feels, correct.

And something else: A sense of life's preciousness that her human mind never knew seems to have pervaded her. Perhaps it has come to her from the vast entity whose perceptions she shares. Coupled with it is a sense of mission. A vague benevolent thought of carrying this life to some proper discharge-point brushes her mind. Is this what she should do next?

No. Something has intervened. Another reality has intruded into the cloudy centers so close to hers, bringing an overriding command. The Task, she thinks. *I must follow, I must search.* The words seem to call her to the limitless void. But her still-human part resists: Not without understanding.

Display overall program.

At this command the screen expands out to images of exploding holocausts, of arrays of supernal entities deployed in cosmic combat against cosmic fires. But these visions dwindle to one recurrent image: a fleet of dark beings, their work done, closes ranks and speeds out and away, vanishing to a point in ultimate darkness. The immensity around them holds only a few faint smudges of light, unknown galaxies seen from very far. Urgency floods her. My race—she must follow and find them though it take forever.

I MUST FOLLOW—I MUST SEARCH—

She can feel the great will taking hold. Outside her fortress, energy-levels are changing, ebbing. Preparation is being made for the plunge out into the void, for an endlessness in which time has no meaning. She can feel the pull, the inevitability. Even her mortal part feels the sad seduction; the fatalism that lurks under human will almost betrays her to the imperative.

But—to exist forever among nothing, sensing nothing; all gone, the beauty of the stars and the hum of life? To become only a blind eternal quest in emptiness? Deep inside her a thirteen-year-old child wakes and screams, seeing the descent of a great knife cutting her forever from all life and light. *No! No! Help me! Stop it!*

But there is no help here. The part of her that is almost merged with unhuman power broods unmoving.

HELP ME! The child wails.

And slowly, in answer, help does come: the cool mind of Margaret Omali, computer programmer, awakens again. To that mind even the most powerful programs are the phenomena of circuitry. It senses that the immaterial will gathering strength around her is in some sense a program. And programs can be changed, canceled. This program is senseless, should be nulled.

She summons TOTAL, defines exit sequences and all-inclusive holds, probing at half-sensed massive complexities. When all is ready, her fingers go to a key and she wills a strong command.

Return to operator. Cancel Program TASK.

But to her dismay the key blurs, melts away under her touch, while on TOTAL's screen the gigantic letters resume their march-by.

I MUST FOLLOW—I MUST SEARCH—

She has demanded too much, she sees. The small sentience has no such powers here. The child sees the knife come closer, screams desperately. In the shadows her other self is sad and still against the stars, accepting fatality.

But in the mind of Margaret Omali there rises suddenly a tearing anger, the deep unadmitted rage that has lain by her heart and given her the strange power of her will. She has still one weapon left.

TOTAL. Display program address.

And that the small thing appears able to do. Onto the screen comes a shadowy multidimensional glimmer, vectors of directionality or code. She studies it with raging intensity: *there* access lies, *there* is the address of this mad program!

All in one mental blow she sends her imaginary hands out, batters with her will against the invisible film that separates her from the cloudy imperatives around her. The barrier yields, gives—and she seizes—something. Her fury is so great that she does not bring the impression clear, but only knows that she has got hold of vitals, whether a power input or the ganglia of a living brain. Whatever, she can feel the current of energy within, the program carrying her forever to the void. With a vague fierce image of pulling open a great switch, or tearing loose a neural circuit, she grasps with both dream-hands, focussing all her unleashed power, and convulses in a great jerk that will yank it open.

Cancel! Kill it!

But the thing does not give, she collapses forward against barriers, still holding tight to the great alien nexus.

Again she tries, sending all her life into her phantom grip; image of a woman outlined in fire, streaming sparks.

But her power is not enough. Again she fails, falls athwart the implacable thing, feeling the program flow steadily on. She has in her hands the means of control, but all the strength of her life is not sufficient to open the connection and kill the circuit.

More, the child wails. *Help, more life!*

The mind that had been Margaret Omali's considers, still holding fast to the immovable power's heart. Could she gain help by opening her stronghold, by letting the life outside in to aid her while it still has energy? She is sure TOTAL can do that, as it brought her here.

But no. The face of her other self turns away coldly in the shadows. This cannot be. She will have no more of the hot closeness of life even if it means an eternity of emptiness. . . . So be it. Out there she can sense now the quieting-down, the deactivation progressing. It is almost too late. The child sobs unassuaged. So close, she was so close to success and salvation.

It is then that the strange call comes. Faintly from outside she hears her name.

Distraught, she puzzles; it is not Ted, she has forgotten him. It is someone else, someone gentle who . . . Slowly she remembers a kindness that had eased her pain and told her of stars. Now it is offering help.

Without letting go on the great nerve or switch, she frames the circuits to the outside and lets the child in her reply.

Yes, it is he, Daniel Dann. She doesn't wonder how he has got here, only remembers a grey voice saying "I'll never do anything you don't want." Here is one life she might bear to let close enough to help her, if she is not to be carried to eternity in the void.

For a moment she struggles mentally. The face in the shadows frowns. But outside she can feel life dimming and slowing inexorably. The child pleads. Slowly, that which was Margaret Omali makes up her mind. To this small, precise extent she will rejoin the humanity that had harmed her so.

She orders TOTAL to shape the access by which this single life can come in.

She waits, feeling his frightened presence making its way to her. As it nears, the ghost of her painful life stirs again, and almost she wills the channel to close. But the pain is too faint now; it is all right. She waits, gripping her hold.

Visionary reality is strong here. Presently she sees his upper body emerge as if from a tunnel, grey hair disordered, face strained with fright. In his eyes is the same deep offer of help. He seems to "see" her as well; his phantom hands go at once to hers as if to help her pull. But he has no power over matter; it is his living strength she needs to draw on.

Before she can manage to explain, in the thrumming, energy-filled chamber, her desperate need comes plain. The child has flung herself against his breast and she feels, feels the inflowing of his life-strength to hers.

Her grip tightens on the nexus of real power, her fingers strengthen, and the great busbar or nerve yields minutely. But it is not enough. *More! More!* the child cries recklessly.

Her desperate cry is echoed. She understands that he has some real connection with outside. And in an instant more help does come, a tumultuous surge of living energies rushes up into her so that she rides a crest of brief violent power. The strain on her dream-fingers is all but mortal. *Now! Pull now!*

She pulls.

With a silent jolt like a tremendous arc of great circuits violently broken, the thing in her dream-hands yields, crashes emptily open and vanishes. Around her the last imperative of the great Task is stilled forever.

In total disorientation Margaret Omali collapses or fragments backward through or onto Dann, knowing she has done it. Everything has changed. She has power here now. But she is at last truly and inextricably merged with the vast entity in which they ride.

Dann, she finds, is still here, or part of him, being hugged by the child. Through him she can sense the commotion outside, as human and alien entities reel backward in disorder. And more: All over the great space outside, the power is rising again, the hum of life stirring again to be as it was before.

But one thing has not changed. As the living energies within the nucleus come slowly to a new organization, the figure against the stars is still there. Presently it half-turns; its carven lips no longer sad but only grave. A voice of silence speaks:

I WILL FIND A NEW TASK. PERHAPS . . . IN TIME. . . I WILL TAKE COUNSEL WITH LIFE.

Chapter 27

The curious constellation of negative entropy that still calls itself Daniel Dann is no longer on his life-way, albeit his travels are only beginning.

He has no idea what he is, or appears as, physically. Most likely a double-ended strand of life-energy, he thinks; I am wedged in the gap in the Destroyer's nucleus wall and part of me is outside. But the passage is no longer menacing and frightful, he is not squeezed by icy dangers. Indeed, he has indulged himself in comfort. In the high energies of this place he has found it easy to fashion a simulacrum of his old familiar body in its armchair, and he lounges like a watchman at her gate.

Here he can monitor all approaches from without or call for help if need be, while his inner gaze stays fixed on that which he most wishes to perceive.

Within is a scene of grandeur. The incandescent beings of space blaze forth in glory. So beautiful, stupendous; by itself it would be almost enough for melancholy eternity. But the magnificence is only background. Limned in starlight, *she* is remotely there. Her head is turned away; he has only occasional glimpses of her grave, serenely thoughtful profile. His nonexistent heart does not leap when he beholds her; rather, a deep and wordless joy suffuses him. No sadness, no pain is here in the starry night.

But that is not all. All around, on some other dimension of perception, tier upon tier of mysterious controls reach into the shadows. And sometimes another apparition of Margaret comes to ponder and test the great console. In this form she is as he had known her in life, a mortal woman's lean body in a white coat. Incarnated so, she will sometimes speak to him quite normally, and what passes for his heart does check when he "hears" her voice. Now and again they have even talked at length, as when they walked a vanished woodland. He has told her of the happenings to the other humans, and of beautiful doomed Tyree and its people, and heard her laugh and sigh. But then the great board claims her, and she goes again to her enigmatic tasks; learning, he guesses, the powers of her new estate.

But beyond this is the most precious of all: At certain times the child comes back and gazes curiously at him, or asks him questions, mostly of the stars. He answers as best as he can, explaining what wonders he knows. But his knowledge ends pitifully soon, and then the child laughs and goes off to work a small, earthly keyboard below the inhuman console. Together they puzzle out the answers and marvel at the celestial grandeurs she can summon. These moments are surpassingly dear to him. He surmises that what he sees as a child is some deep, enduring core of Margaret's human wonder and delight.

Once she asks him, *"Why are you such a funny color, Dan'l?"*

Thinking to please her, he imagines his skin darker, his features those of a black man with grey hair. The child bursts out giggling and from the shadows comes Margaret's brief laugh. *"Don't."* He never tries to change himself again.

He understands now, of course: There is no question of "rescuing" Margaret, of freeing her from this power and place. She has gone beyond that, beyond humanity. This is her realm now. She is merged, or merging, with the great entity around them. He is seeing only temporary phantasms or facets of her; her real self is involved beyond his ken.

Once when the familiar Margaret is there he asks her, *"Are we in a ship? Is all this a machine?"*

Her dark gaze focusses beyond him.

"No."

He has not cared nor dared to ask her more.

But there have been events from the outside.

At first they are merely isolated moments of contact with Waxman. The double being seems to have stationed himself watchfully nearby, content to exist in his new unity, interested in serving as a kind of news-center for humans and Tyrenni. But soon after what Dann thinks of as the great victory, the warm touch he recognizes as Winona comes to speak directly to him.

"Doctor Dann, is Margaret all right in there? I've been so worried about her. Could I see her for a moment? I don't want to bother her, I just want—"

"I understand," he tells her. And he does, he cannot mistake pure friendship, or whatever odd human quality "worries" about another so gratuitously. *"I'll ask her. It's difficult. She's . . . busy."*

The mild presence withdraws patiently.

When the Earthly incarnation of Margaret comes again into his sight, he asks her. *"Can Winona, ah, make contact with you for a few minutes? She was your friend, you know. She's worried."*

"Winona?" The dark priestess of the computer hesitates remotely. But her mood seems favorable. *"Yes. You can let her by."*

Dann has a selfish moment of gladness at her acceptance of his role of guardian of her gates. Cerberus-Dann. He does not know exactly how to "let" Winona in, but moves his imaginary self aside, calling her name. It seems to work. He feels life coming inward.

Shockingly, what materializes at the imaginary door is not Winona—it is the trim lush figure of a dark-haired woman in early middle life, with a brilliant, unlined, eager face. His Earthly memories leap up. Here is the incarnation of young mother, a woman he has seen step laughing from a thousand stationwagons full of kids.

But as he leaps to bar this stranger's way, she changes. The firm flesh pales and sags, the raven hair goes grey. It is Winona as he knows her, going toward Margaret with both hands held out.

For an instant he flinches, expecting the giggle and rush of words. But she only takes one of the tall figure's hands in hers, and holds it to her old bosom, peering in wonder at the strangeness all around. For a moment some contact seems to flow, and then Winona releases the hand and turns away.

As she passes Dann there is another shimmer of change; it is the radiant young matron who vanishes out through the immaterial chink.

Dann muses on the dreadful mysteries of time; *that* which he had seen was really Winona, not the puffy arthritic scarecrow of Deerfield.

And what is he, really? Some earnest figure of a young MD? No; he is ineluctably old. His dead are dead. He is . . . content.

Outside, Winona has gone away. She understands, Dann knows, however she conceives it. Margaret is not to be worried about.

And something else has happened, he notices. As he resumes his watchman's pose he senses that the guarded gate of the stronghold seems a little wider now. Less fortified. The Margaret who has her being here will perhaps tolerate contact with life a little more. But she is, Dann realizes, changing. Life is no longer to her what it was. His soul is chilled by foreboding. Will she change beyond recognition, will everything he knows as Margaret disappear into some cloudy matrix of immensity?

He remembers the calm voice saying, *Perhaps, in time, I will take counsel with life.* But will it be Margaret who does so? He hopes so; he can do no more.

His sad thoughts are interrupted by a merry greeting he knows instantly—his little friend Tivonel. She has been by before, to his delight. But this time she brings Giadoc to speak with him.

"Greetings, Tanel," comes the strong, sure "voice" of the young Hearer. *"Waxman has told us of the great powers your friend wields here."*

"Yes." Dann tries to convey a smile; he finds it impossible not to like this mind.

"As you know, my son Tiavan was among those who did that criminal deed to your people. Yet I left him, and the others, in danger. Is it possible that your friend's power can discover anything of what happened to them, back on your world?"

"I don't know. I'll ask. It may take some time."

But as it happens the incarnation he knows as Margaret comes soon, and he is able to ask.

"I'll put TOTAL on it," she says quite humanly. *"It stored a lot of telecommunications before we were out of range. Tell me their names."*

296

Their names? So far, so very far she has drifted away, he thinks. He recites the eight: Winona, the two girls, the twins, Ted, Chris, and Kirk. Only bodies now, housing alien minds; while the real people are out here with him in this uncanny place between the stars.

"I'll set it to type out anything it finds, in case I'm . . . not here."

So normal, so efficient a sweet ghost. She does something to the small console and vanishes away.

The strong compact presence of Giadoc hovers near. Dann asks him again about his stay on Earth, and learns for the first time that the mind he had known as Fearing had ended in the body of the dog. So an elder female, Janskelen, whom he never knew, is the dread Fearing now! The computer won't search for that name; no matter, it probably wasn't his real one.

But whatever can have become of them? How did Noah, not to mention the Navy, take the eruption of nine alien minds? Thinking of it all again, Dann's memories strengthen around him. He questions Giadoc, fascinated by his alien ability to guide himself by reading human thought. It seems unbelievable; how could they manage to make out? What could they do, send and receive messages for the military? Or be persecuted as a menace?

And the mix-up of identities: Kirk with the mind of, in effect, a little girl; Winona housing his Father. Frodo as really the son of the Father who is in little Chris. How to stay together? Can they perhaps marry? And the cosmic joke of the rebel Avanil in Valerie's body, defiantly claiming the right to rear children. And Ron and Rick, no longer twins but Terenc and Palarin, an alien male and female he never knew. And, poetic justice, the wicked Scomber inheriting the moribund body of Ted Yost.

Funny, Dann reflects, he doesn't really see Scomber as "wicked." He can recall so clearly the heart-lifting moment when Scomber offered his life as the pathway to escape from burning Tyree and his own empathy with the young Fathers bearing their children out of the flames.

And has it all turned out so badly for his kidnapped friends? Not so, he thinks. Whatever this ur-life may prove to be, we were rescued from great mortal misery; we knew our hours of joy in the winds of Tyree.

He tries to convey some of this to Giadoc, in their shared Tyrenni-English pidgin. But the proud young alien is hard to persuade; he is too deeply ashamed of what his son has done. Just as Dann thinks he is getting the point across, there is a sense of activity from within. He turns to find the spectral teleprinter at work. What looks absurdly like an ordinary printout is emerging. What has TOTAL intercepted? Dann finds that his dream-hands can take it, his "eyes" can read.

//LAS VEGAS JAN 19 SPECIAL AP. SPIRITUALISTS PULL GAMBLING COUP. A TEAM COMPOSED OF A HOUSEWIFE, A RETIRED ARMY OFFICER AND AN EX-LOCKSMITH BROKE THE BANK AT FIVE MAJOR LAS VEGAS RESORTS OVER THE WEEKEND, PILING UP A POKER TAKE ESTIMATED IN THE MILLIONS.//THE THREE IDENTIFIED THEMSELVES AS PARTNERS IN CATLEDGE ESP CONSULTANTS FIRM. "IT WAS PRIMARILY AN ADVERTISING STUNT," MRS. EBERHARD, THE HOUSEWIFE, SAID. "WE WANTED TO SHOW WHAT A QUALIFIED ESP CONSULTANT CAN DO," MAJOR CHARLES SPROUL ADDED. THE THIRD MEMBER, CHRISTOFER COSTAKIS, STATED THAT THEY INTEND TO USE PART OF THE MONEY FOR A NEW HEADQUARTERS AND RESEARCH ESTABLISHMENT. // CATLEDGE ESP CONSULTANTS HAS BEEN IDENTIFIED AS A TIGHTLY KNIT, CLOSE-MOUTHED GROUP OF SEVEN MEMBERS UNDER THE LEADERSHIP OF DR. NOAH CATLEDGE. DR. CATLEDGE, WHO DISCLAIMS ANY MYSTIC ABILITIES, BUILT UP THE TEAM AFTER A LIFETIME IN ESP RESEARCH. "OUR SERVICES ARE AVAILABLE FOR ANY PRIVATE PARTIES WHO MEET OUR FEES," HE SAID TODAY. "HOWEVER, WE EXPECT TO BE PRIMARILY USEFUL AS CONSULTANTS TO NEGOTIATORS IN BUSINESS AND GOVERNMENT." THE LAS VEGAS HOTEL MANAGERS ASSOCIATION ADMIT THAT NO ILLEGALITY APPEARS TO HAVE BEEN INVOLVED IN THE WEEKEND ACTION. "WE WERE REALLY WATCHING THESE PEOPLE AS SOON AS THEY STARTED TO ROLL," ONE MEMBER SAID. "SO FAR AS WE'RE CONCERNED THEY'RE CLEAN." HOWEVER THE ASSOCIATION STRESSES THAT NO ONE AS-

SOCIATED WITH THE CATLEDGE FIRM WILL BE ADMIT-
TED TO PLAY IN FUTURE. "THEY'RE AT THE TOP OF OUR
S. . . LIST,"A MANAGER CONCLUDED.////WILLAMETTE,
ILL. JAN 19. TWO UNSEASONAL TORNADOES SWEPT—

As the visionary paper vanishes from his grasp, Dann finds himself laughing so hard that he has difficulty in explaining coherently to
Giadoc.

"Your son is all right, they're doing fine," he manages to convey
at last. But it is some time before he can satisfy enough of the alien's
curiosity about Earthly customs to convince him that old Noah has
indeed found a means of arranging a satisfactory life for the Tyrenni
fugitives. The fact that only seven are mentioned seems reasonable
too; the two "children" are doubtless being kept and cared for at
home.

When Giadoc at length departs, Dann chuckles again, remembering Noah's dream of aliens coming to Earth. Practical as ever, the
old man had met his culminant fantasy and meshed it with real life
Well, Dann reflects, hadn't he really been doing that all along? Getting grants for ESP submarine exercises, for God's sake. He wishes
he could congratulate the old maniac, or at least get a glimpse of
what must be his ecstatic state. How had they ever got themselves
out of Deerfield? No doubt with Janskelen as Fearing/Sproul it had
been pulled off somehow . . . And will they raise a line of telepathic mutants? Fabulous . . .

When Margaret returns he tries to explain it to her. But she is already too remote; he senses it is unreal to her. She seems chiefly
pleased that the program has produced. Perhaps this is not a drift-
ing-off into supernal realities, he thinks, but an aspect of Margaret's
human mind; her concern with structure, relations. Not content, not
people. He is reminded of a math teacher he'd had who refused to
plug comprehensible numerical values into his equations on the
blackboard. Even the child shows signs of it.

His musings are cut short by Waxman's signal from outside.

"Doc, we have a problem out here." The "voice" is startlingly
like Rick's on the lawn at Deerfield.

"Yes?"

*"It's so dark and quiet, where we are. You know? The others are
trying things, they keep each other busy as well as they can. Chris*

and Giadoc are trying to understand some of the stuff here. The women do some exploring. But it's bad. It's a real big nothing. Even those pictures, those announcement things, have faded out. Old Heagran is worried, he thinks we'll all trip out to dream-worlds like Ted."

"I see." And he does, he understands how selfish he has been. He has had access to the stars, to *her,* while the others have nothing but the twilight world of individual minds.

"I should have realized." Reluctantly he makes himself say, *"Do you want to share with me? Touch me, or whatever?"*

"Thanks, Doc. I mean, thanks. But I thought, something simpler. Like, could she relay out a picture? The circuits must be there. If she could hook in monitors we could see where we are. A check on reality."

"Of course. I'll ask her. By the way, how is Ted? Is he still—?"

"Yeah. Chris and I work on him now and then. But what is there for him to come out for?"

"I understand. I'll ask right away."

When he relays Waxman's request to the apparition he knows as Margaret, the beautiful face listens with unusual intentness.

"I should have thought of that," she says quickly, as if in self-reproach. To Dann's surprise, the remote cloudy profile in the stars has also turned slightly, as though attending. Dream-Margaret goes back into the shadows of the great control room.

Dann is oddly heartened. There seems to be a chord of empathy here, some strand of responsibility to the lives outside her mystery. Perhaps it is a remnant of the Task, the transcendent impulse toward rescue. Is it possible that the human Margaret has learned some compassion toward life from this unhuman entity?

Suddenly she is back again, frowning slightly.

"Your friends, the aliens . . . You say they are expert in the transmissions of life?"

"Oh yes. It seems to have been one of their main modes—" He sees that she does not want details.

"Good. I will relay also some small signal-trains that are . . . difficult for me. Perhaps they can comprehend better."

He is amazed at her openness, amazed that the goddess would accept life's cooperation. Perhaps it will be true, what she hinted. Eagerly he tells her, *"Giadoc, the one who mind-traveled to other worlds, is the nearest thing we have to an expert on alien life. And he can report in our language."*

She says only, *"I will set it up,"* and fades away into the cloudy depths.

He has not long to wait. An exuberant communication bursts upon him from outside.

"Man, it's beautiful. It's all over, like a million windows!"

Again Dann is jolted by the incongruity of the young voice, the words that could be describing a sports car, used here for transreal marvels. Well, what does he expect, that Ron or Rick should boom like a cinema spook?

"The whole outside of this place is covered, and there're screens all over, where those recording places were. And listen, we're getting other kinds of transmissions too. Bdello and his people are really into it. I'm picking up something too, Doc, maybe like music. I can't describe it. I think we're going to find new forms of consciousness like we never dreamed of."

"New forms of consciousness?"

"Yeah. Like whole planets thinking. Everything interconnected, or—I can't explain but I really dig it. I used to, I don't know, dream . . ."

The so-ordinary boy's voice, chattering about transcendences. For an instant Dann's old human distrust of mysticism rises. Are these unbodied minds indeed floating into fantasy? But no; he must believe that there is some reality here, if anything here is real.

"Oh, another piece of news for you," Waxman goes on. *"Did I tell you that the Tyrenni have set up a big dream-world of their own, over that way? All the Fathers have the kids in there. We call it Tyree-Two. Giadoc says the soul of Tyree came with us, that makes it a heavy trip. Val and Frodo went to see it. They liked the flying. And Winnie took Kirk to some Father who's going to raise him for awhile, she knows she was too soft with him."*

"Tyree-Two. . ." Dann thinks of the strength of Ted's dream-world. This must be incredible, a structure of joined dreams, a real place.

"Yes. But Heagran is more worried than ever. He's coming to talk to you soon."

301

"I'll be here." Dann tries his first mild joke in life beyond death, in realms between the stars.

But it is Chris who comes next, a new, stronger Chris whose shyness is only a slight abruptness in the contact now.

"We need time here, Doc."

"Time?" It seems the one thing they have.

"I mean, we need some way of marking real time. It's weird here with nothing changing. I notice some of those stars pulse regularly. I was thinking, why can't you tie one into a digital counter that we could read?"

"It isn't me, Chris. I can't do anything. I'm only the doorman here."

"You know what I mean, Doc."

Yes, Dann knows. Chris means what he has always meant, that there are human dimensions he can't cope with. But the idea is, as usual, a good one.

"Cepheid variables, I think that's what you're seeing. The periods are generally around a week."

"Yeah. We could spit it into intervals. Then you could keep track of things and plan to do a thing in so many periods, say, instead of this fuzzy stuff."

"I don't see why not. I'll ask."

"I know what we should call them." Waxman has evidently been monitoring the interchange. *"It would be stupid to have weeks or whatever the Tyrenni had, out here. Let's call the base period after Chris."*

"Good," says Dann. But Chris has already broken contact, apparently overcome by Waxman's proposal.

When the apparition of Margaret comes again, Dann senses that she is amused by the proposal. As she moves away to whatever magical manipulations will put it into effect, an odd dreamy smile comes to her human face.

"Baseline, time zero . . . TOTAL can compute. It will start from when, when we awoke."

When "we" awoke. Dann realizes anew that this dream-normalcy conceals a reality he has no access to. But he is not unhappy. Let it just go on.

The new real-time system is duly acclaimed a success. The

screens carry it, and from time to time a soft unliving energy-signal resonates through the spaces round them.

On one of these occasions a new voice speaks spontaneously to Waxman: *"Ship's bells!"* The lost mariner, Ted, is stirring from his dream.

Dann and Waxman are conferring, trying to compute how long, how surprisingly long, they have really been here, when a sense of something happening within the nucleus makes him break off.

His perception returns inward to find indefinable energies in action. Margaret in her human incarnation is not there, but the elegant remote profile against the stars is very vivid and strong, and the chamber seems to be thrumming with the quick rise of signals just beyond his range.

Then suddenly it is over, the energies subside, the shadowy figure fades and all is as before. And Margaret herself comes back, seated by a different part of the great console.

"What happened? Are you all right?"

Her expression is indrawn, she does not answer for awhile. Then she brushes her forehead in a very human gesture. *"I—we—heard a death-scream. Very small, very close; something dying, freezing or burning up. I'm not sure, but I think I took in an alien astronaut. You can find out."*

When Dann turns his attention outside, he finds the others are already aware of what has happened.

"Something came barreling in here screaming blue murder," Waxman tells him. *"Heagran's friends have gone out to see what they can do. Holy smokes!"* The young voice is full of wonder. *"Imagine, a real alien! I'm going to see it unless somebody gives me a good picture soon."*

Dann is too bemused to reply. "A real alien"—this from a disembodied double being dwelling in the interior of some leviathan of the starways, dealing in mind-speech with the creatures of another world. But he knows what Waxman means. Not for the first time, Dann reflects on the curious compatibility of these human and Tyrenni minds. They're healthier, and less individuated than we, he thinks; and they lack our predatory aggressiveness. Our particular group of humans are rather deficient in that way too. Is it possible that empathic intelligence is the same the Galaxy over, that the knowledge of the reality of others' feelings breeds a certain gentle cast of mind, whether one is in a human body or a great manta-ray of the winds? Or is it something deeper in their contactless, food-rich way of life?

The advent of the alien has generated a flurry of activity. It is decided to let him stay where he first lodged until more is known of him.

"Val's gone over to try to learn its language," Waxman reports. *"She's got a gift that way. They think it's a combined being, a what-you-call hemaphrodite. Sastro sent me a good memory. Even Ted has heard of it."*

"Margaret didn't do that on her own," Dann tells him. *"I mean, she did it, but it was her plus something. The being, whatever we're in, seems to have a compulsion to respond to life in distress."*

"We're in a life-boat," puts in the dreamy voice Dann recognizes as Ted Yost.

"That's right," Waxman agrees. *"We all feel something, some kind of urge like that underneath. It's beautiful."*

Beautiful? Yes. But suddenly it occurs to Dann, what if they involuntarily take on a load of sapient predators? A space-going armada like Ghengis Khan's hordes, with whom even a Tyrenni Father couldn't cope? Or a distressed planetful of highly evolved scorpions? What would the gentle souls here do then?

He puts the question to Margaret when she next appears.

"Margaret, you know the people here, we who ride with you, are pretty peaceful types. Empathic, rational. And there's not many of us. What if you take in some really ferocious characters? Fighters, killers, slavers? We might all be massacred or destroyed in some way."

The figure in the shadows seems to stir slightly, and the "human" Margaret shakes her head, smiling gently.

"No. You will never be in danger. We—I have learned the value of life. I have you all in my circuits. If there should be hostility provision will be made. We are equipped for that, you know."

He doesn't know and he can't imagine anything beyond, say, bulkheads. But he's willing to trust it to her.

Oddly, it is the coming of the alien that is responsible for Dann's most human contact and the most touching one.

For some time his outward sensors have been aware of a presence nearby, close-held but emanating a hesistant intent and what he recognizes unhappily as pain. Dann puzzles. Can it be Ted, or Chris?

No; Waxman says that Ted has been induced to meet the Tyrenni, and Chris has formed a strong relationship with Giadoc in their curiosities about the unliving energies of this world. Moreover Chris is getting over his shyness about having his mind read. *"They're helping him a lot,"* Waxman says. *"He may let old Sastro fix his head a touch, so he doesn't feel so, so, you know. From being like he was on Earth."*

Dann recollects his own slight experience of "having his head fixed." To have ones fears and inadequacies put to rest—good for Chris. But who is this then nearby? Almost he asks Waxman, but the being's shyness is so clear. Rather like a private patient waiting to see him again.

Finally comes a tentative mind-touch on his own. *"Doc?"*

The mystery is solved—it's Frodo. If he had thought of her at all, he'd imagined her somewhere off happily exploring with Val.

"I'm glad you came by, Frodo. As maybe you can see, I'm stuck here."

"I never thanked you for helping me back there. What you did, when we were on Tyree."

Whatever she has come for, this isn't it. He transmits a genial acknowledgment, while the thing in him that cannot rest in the presence of pain gropes toward her.

"Doc, you always understood—" It's coming: with wrenching intensity her mind opens to him like a child, and she blurts, *"Val doesn't need me anymore."*

In dim immateriality she grips something that might be his hand; he can feel her struggle, her shame at showing pain. He remembers a long-ago small boy, brought in with a dreadfully smashed kneecap. For a moment he simply hangs on, trying to absorb and master the hurtful transmission, and sends the first thing that comes to his head.

"I don't believe she doesn't need you, Frodo. She loves you. Did she say so?"

"No—but she keeps doing things with Tivonel and the others, and she's so busy with that alien. Oh, Doc, it's horrible. I'm horrible."

"Why are you horrible, Frodo?"

"Because—because—" The impression of a wailing little figure throwing itself on his bosom is overpowering. *"Because she's happy now! It's horrible that I can't take her being happy. She doesn't need me at all!"*

Dann holds her strongly, sharing the sharp grief, waiting for the storm to spend. Trying to understand, he recalls his glimpse of Val's mind. The secret, sacred enclave of We Two. Now all that has been changed. The hostile world around has vanished and Val has been freed; she is enjoying her freedom in this weird place, like his little friend Tivonel. But this other inhabitant of that private world cannot fly free so easily. She misses horribly the exclusive love and sharing that gave life meaning. . . . How well he knows it.

The sad mind in his nonexistent arms is murmuring. *"Sometimes I think I'll just start moving on till I come to the edge of this thing and go on out into space."*

"No. Would it be fair to Val to lay that guilt on her? Listen. When that idea comes to you I want you to come to me first. Will you promise me that?"

Finally she agrees. The intensity is drained for the moment. But the mournful message comes, *"No one needs me here. Hell, I was just a dumb law student. We've passed beyond Middle Earth now, haven't we? Who needs a law student in the Western Isles?"*

"I was just a dumb medical doctor, Frodo. We all have to reconvert ourselves somehow."

Frodo gives the ghost of her old scornful laugh. *"You have her."*

Oh God, he knows what she means.

"I don't have Margaret, Frodo. Nobody could 'have' her anymore. I get to look at some aspect of her and talk with a part of her now and then. I think she's happy . . . That's all. She's passed away beyond your Western Isles, farther than any of us."

Frodo is silent for a moment. *"I see . . . I'm sorry."*

"No need. I do get to see . . . something of her. Just like you see Val."

"And that's got to be enough for us?"

"I'm afraid so."

The mind touching his sighs, then laughs again. But it's a better laugh, Dann thinks, not understanding that his "gift" has worked again, but only feeling a new sadness.

"Speaking of law, have you found out what kind of laws that alien has on his world? Or the Tyrenni, for that matter? Look, here's something you could think of. Why don't you figure out the ideal code of laws? Then if we get the chance we could write them in fiery letters in the sky of some world."

She really laughs. "Like the Ten Commandments. Thou shalt not crucify green lizards."

"Something like that."

"Do you really think we could do things like that some day?"

"I don't know. We're in the realm of the impossible already."

"Yeah."

They are silent together; a companionable feeling Dann never imagined he would share with the fierce little androgyne.

"Come back and see me, Frodo. We can be depressed together. But if it gets too bad, you know, the Tyrenni can help you with bad memories."

"I guess so . . . But I think I'd rather come to you. Thanks, Doc."

"I'll be here."

She leaves, and Dann's attention strays back inside the nucleus.

It is empty of all save mystery for a long time, until the child comes shyly out and starts to examine something on the small screen. It is a great dim red sun, Dann sees. A red giant. Perhaps she wants to ask him again about the lives of stars. Yes, she has replaced the picture with TOTAL's Hertzsprung-Russell diagram now, showing the main sequence and the tracks taken by various masses and types of stars. If only he knew more!

But when she turns to him the question is unexpected.

"If we made time run backward, it would shrink again. And if there were people around it, they would be alive again, wouldn't they, Dan'l?"

Make time run backward?

For a moment he thinks it's a play-question, and then the fearful significance sinks in. He has found out from Margaret how the great being's former companions cleared space; they somehow accelerated or reversed the processes of stars until their mass-energy dissipated below a critical point. But this is the first time he comprehends, really grasps that the entity he rides in, the being he knows as partly "Margaret," has such powers at command. To make lost races live again?

"I suppose so," he says feebly.

At that moment the grown-up Margaret appears from the shadows and the child goes to her. *"There is also alternation,"* she says quietly, half to Dann and half as if in reminder to the child. *"Events don't have to repeat exactly."*

Then she and the child melt away, leaving Dann's head spinning.

Before he can organize his thoughts he is aware of a summons from Waxman outside.

"Father Heagran wants an interview with Margaret, Doc. Can you arrange?"

"I'll see. It may be awhile."

When Margaret comes back he tells her. *"I think he wants a face-to-face meeting, like you had with Winnie. I believe I could translate. You've never really seen a full-fledged Tyrenni Elder, have you? It's quite something, you might enjoy it. The thing is, they're big."*

"Yes," she says matter-of-factly. *"I'll make arrangements."*

Shortly thereafter he feels a change in the opening he guards, and prudently retracts himself. The opening seems to widen, and brighten to a view of Tyree's wind-torn skies. Hovering there at an indeterminate distance is the great age-splendored form of Heagran himself. Dann wonders how it appears to Margaret. To him the form is both monstrous and beautiful; above all, a personage. The great mantle ripples, speaks in light.

"He addresses you as Gracious Elder," Dann tells Margaret. *"And asks if it is true that you can put his people's minds down on a suitable world."* As Dann says this he is assailed by a pang of coming loss.

"We can," she says, seated quite normally and businesslike at the great console.

"Then it is time," Dann goes on reluctantly. *"Their world of fantasy here grows strong and strange and the, the children do not grow. However they will not commit life-crime on an intelligent race. He asks if you can find a world of advanced animal life where true, ah,*

308

self-concept has not developed. The animals' minds can be merged to make room for the Tyrenni. I think he is saying that the soul or spirit of Tyree is with them, so he is not afraid they will degenerate. He believes that Tyree will live again in another form."

"A world of advanced animal life." Margaret's hand brushes her dark hair as if the most ordinary program request had been put to her. "I think that can be done best if they will help monitor the life-bands to select the right level. Do they have other requirements?"

When Dann translates this the great changes color slightly, as if deep emotions were touched. "That it be a world of wind," he says. "That we are not condemned to live in the Abyss, remembering flight."

His emotion evokes echoes; even Margaret's gaze is lowered for an instant. "I understand . . . Is there anything more?"

"Your people have told us how many worlds may be filled by fierce eaters of flesh. Our people cannot kill, we cannot cause pain. On our world was only one small fierce animal, the corlu, who served as a lesson for children. Therefore I would ask that our people be sent where there are no savage enemies and they may live at peace."

"I understand that too." She smiles. "We will set our systems to search. When we find possible worlds they will be displayed on the screens for you to judge. And I will study how to set you down gently, so that your people will not be frightened. I believe that is within our power."

"All thanks to you, Gracious Elder-Female." But the great being does not recede or turn away. Instead he signs almost hesitantly. "Another point."

"Yes?"

"I and a few others . . . do not wish to leave you. I am too old to start life anew, and like young Giadoc I find that my soul has been touched by a greater wind. We know that if we stay we will not remain unchanged. Nevertheless we would wish to go with you on your great voyage among the Companions of the sky. May we?"

As Dann translates this his immaterial heart is filled with joy. To know that some of the Tyrenni will be staying! How unbearable to have lost all contact with the wondrous race whose ordeal he has shared, whose physical form is part of his intimate memories.

"You are very welcome," Margaret is saying. "Your help in un-

derstanding the transmissions of life will be of great value here. Is there anything we can do for your comfort?"

"A small thing and perhaps impossible," Heagran replies. *"I know that we travel across immense spaces and that what we call the Companions are limitless in number. In such voyages, is it conceivable that we will ever again approach the new home of my people, to see how they fare?"*

"I'm not sure." Margaret's brow has the so-human line of preoccupation, Heagren might have been asking her for a tricky computation. *"Space, yes, and there is the factor of time. I believe we can mark the world you select, and return to it. But the time-lapse may be many generations of lives on that world."*

"We can ask no more." The huge old being's image colors a lilac so beautiful it seems to need no translation, and he vanishes away.

Margaret-the-human-woman remains gazing at the place where Heagran's form had been.

"A new Task must be found soon," she says quietly, whether to herself or Dann. *"We feel the need. I begin to understand our powers and constraints. But I alone have not the vision to do more than the original program of transporting endangered peoples. After we put his people down on their new world it will be time."* She turns a perfectly normal, purposeful face on Dann. *"Ask among the others, my old friend. See what visions they have."*

It could be a young committeewoman asking for ideas. Only the profile in the starry dimensions behind her warns him that the "ideas" will not be of any Earthly mode.

"Yes."

And he is alone again, his brain whirling. Transporting endangered peoples—using the powers of time to revive lost races—choosing among alternative evolutions for whole planets—perhaps intercepting stellar armadas, or seeking ultimate unknowns—Daniel Dann's human mind blooms with visions, his long-dead imagination stirs, shedding off rusty sparks.

Reality has already come unhinged, unrooted to sense or time or place. Now it seems it is about to take flight entirely, undergo transmogrification to undreamt-of realms.

And is it possible that he, whose life has all but ended so many times, he who was for so long an automaton of pain and Earthly ignominy, he the utterly inconsequential, randomly selected, unqualified—except for that gift he shrinks to use—is it possible that he will be witness to such wonders? Will he come to accept them? "Today we rejuvenate a sun. Tomorrow we give a species the terrible boon of self-conscious intellect."

Incredible. Impossible.

But, apparently, slowly about to begin to happen.

And—for how long? How long will it go on?

With that, the deepest, most dire and secret shudder of all shakes him. Dann allows consciousness at last to the word that has been working its unadmitted ferment in the bottom of his soul: FOREVER.

Immortality?

Yes, or something very like it. At the least, a time measured not in years or lifetimes but astral epochs. Nothing here changes, has changed, apparently will change or run down for millennia. The mysterious cold energies that sustain them have cycled, it appears, for stellar lifetimes. There seems no reason they should not continue to an approximation of eternity.

An eternity of unimaginable projects? Yes—and an eternity too of Waxman's young voice, of Heagran's sublimity, of Frodo's grief and Tivonel's laugh and Giadoc's persistent How and Why and What, and all the rest of it. The trivial, ineluctably finite living bases of their unreal lives loom up before him like an endless desert to be traversed on foot, under a sky raining splendor. The close-up limiting frame around the view of infinity.

Can we take it? Will we go mad?

Heagran has said they will all change, he reflects. Perhaps the constant mind-touching will merge them gradually, affect even Margaret. Perhaps we will become like one big multifaceted person, maybe that will be the solution. Or maybe the fused minds will be incompatible. We could become a hydra-headed psychopath.

But Margaret, he thinks; she's in control of us all, really. She could do something, put us out or freeze us if it came to that. But then she would be alone forever. Hurt strikes the node of nothing that had been his heart. For her sake we must, I must, stay sane. Hang on. Maybe it will be great, a supernally joyous life.

But—*eternity?*

A cold elation and foreboding mingle in his mind.

What have I learned, he wonders. Voyager between worlds, I have been privileged beyond mortal man. I have met an alien race, I have encountered endless unknown things. What great changes has all this wrought in me? What transformations have I suffered to make me worthy of a place in such a drama? To witness, perhaps participate in the fates of worlds? To enjoy something like immortal life? What great contribution will I make to the symbiosis?

Nothing, he reflects wryly. Not one tangible thing.

I have only what I had before, a little specialized knowledge of the workings of bodies we no longer possess. Beyond that, only my old compound of depressive sympathy and skepticism about brave new claims, however appealing. If we actually meet Jehovah or Allah or Vishnu out here I would still take my stand on the second law of thermodynamics.

What in the name of life can make mine worthy of such perpetuation? What do I ever learn but the same old lessons—that people are people, that pain is bad; that good is too often allied with vulnerability and evil with power. That absolutes are absolutely dangerous: Bethink ye, my lords, ye may be mistaken. That one can do ill in the name of doing well, and error buggers up the best laid plans. That even the greatest good of the greatest number is no safeguard—Tyree was burned because it was in the path of the destruction that saved a galaxy.

I don't know a single distinguished philosophy, he thinks, except perhaps my respect for Bacon's Great Machine. Or wait—Spinoza, when he changed one word in the ecclesiastical definition of truth. The Church called it the "recognition of necessity." Spinoza called it the "*discovery* of necessity," and for that they persecuted him because it undermined all authority.

But what new great necessities have I discovered, beyond the old necessity of kindness? And, he thinks, I am apt to be slow to discover any in this future which seems all too unconstrained. Some great thinker should be here in my place. Waxman with his boyish fervors about new modes of consciousness is more deserving of this life than I.

I'm not going to be reborn as the embryo of humanity transcendent in the cosmos. I'll just be me.

As he has been thinking these bleak thoughts beneath the radiant processions of suns within the nucleus, a small presence has come quietly close to him.

It is the child, he sees, seeming younger than usual; that incarnation of Margaret which perhaps holds all her unscarred wonder and delight. Ordinarily they rarely touch. But such is his distress now that his hand goes out unthinkingly and strokes her thin shoulder. She does not move away but turns on him a smile of elfin beauty.

As he looks down into her large eyes his worries fade somewhat. Even his lack of intellectual grandeur seems less important.

Well, he thinks, there is one thing I can do, do always. Even if it comes to eternity, I will still have that. He is almost sure of it, knows it beyond reason.

No matter how long the future stretches or what it holds, he will carry into it his love.

Chapter 28

Tivonel, bright spirit from the winds of Tyree, is still on her life-way although in dark and surpassing strangeness among the stars. The energy-configuration that is her essence glides from point to point in the vastness of the Destroyer—no, we have to call it the Saver now, she thinks—with the skill with which her winged body had once breasted Tyree's gales.

Gladly she would travel faster, but she is not alone. Her friends Marockee and Issalin flow alongside, equally impatient. They must all keep to the slow pace of the unskilled Fathers they bring with them.

She and the others are returning from the great mind-dream of Tyree, or Tyree-Two as the yumans call it. They are escorting Father Daagan and Mercil to confer for a last time with Eldest Heagran. Behind them all comes the big life-field of Father Ustan. And thanks to the winds he was with us, Tivonel thinks; Ustan had remained outside the dream-world to ensure they would be able to pull free.

"Whew, that was strong. Again, thanks, Tivonel."

It is Marockee's mind-touch. Marockee had almost lost herself in the beauty of the dream-winds, the magic of remembered life. Tivonel had to pull her to Ustan's grasp. And all three of them had to use their strengths to help break out the two young Fathers who had stayed so long in the powerful multiminded fantasy of home.

Tivonel herself had reveled in the false Tyree, in the zestful illusion of flight and her visit to the rich recreation of Deep where the Fathers and children stay. With so many orphans, the surviving Paradomin and any others who wish to try are caring for them under the supervision of real Fathers. They're doing a pretty good job, too, Tivonel thinks, but of course the children don't grow. It's good practice, they'll all have to do it when they go to that new world.

But she herself hadn't been deeply trapped in Tyree-Two, not to forgetfulness. To her it had remained a lovely mirage, a tiny island created by living minds in a corner of huge dark reality.

I've changed, she thinks. I used to be just like Marockee, all female action and fun. It's because of Giadoc; I've caught something from him. And maybe my time with that kind, funny alien, Tanel. But I'm not getting Fatherly, I don't care about status like the Paradomin. And it isn't sex—yearning for Giadoc, either. Not anymore, not here.

She chuckles ruefully to herself, acknowledging that she will never know again the ecstasy of physical sex in the Wind. Marockee told her that some couples tried that in Tyree-Two. But of course it didn't work. With no egg, what could you expect?

No, it's not sex, what she feels for Giadoc. It's the Hearer part of him I've caught, she thinks, gliding effortlessly onward in the strange, exciting dark. Yes, and it's more than that too, it was the waiting and thinking of him, it made me understand more. And when I found him so near death and we merged. Things like that never ordinarily happened on Tyree. Males were just exciting to have sex with until they became Fathers and you scarcely saw them again. I *know* Giadoc in this deep, funny way, she thinks, not understanding that her language has no word for a human sense of love. She wonders briefly if old Omar felt something like that for Janskelen. Whatever, she will stay here with Giadoc no matter what the others do.

She suppresses the mixed tingle of fear and excitement the thought brings.

"Are you really staying in the Destroyer when everybody goes out to that new world?" It's Marockee again.

Tivonel notices that they have outpaced the slower males, and checks.

"You mean the Saver. Yes, I am." Again the slight shiver.

"How can you, Tivonel? What'll there be to do?"

"Oh, there'll be plenty of adventures among the Companions. Ask Giadoc or Tanel. Besides, how do you know they're going to like being big white plenyas, or whatever those bodies are?"

"But they'll have real bodies and real winds. And the Great Field of Tyree will be with them." Marockee's mind-tone is full of ambiguous longing. Tivonel knows her friend is in agonies of indecision whether to go or stay. Well, she'll just have to make up her own mind about that. She replies only. *"We'll have Heagran. He's the spirit of Tyree, too."*

"Well, I'm staying here," puts in Issalin firmly. *"You wait, when they get out there the males will take all the eggs again, just like Tyree. Even if those bodies are supposed to be combined male and female, they'll find some way. And I know the mind that works with the Saver is female, so I'm staying with you."*

"Well said in friendship," replies Tivonel. Privately she considers that Issalin's head is a little wind-blown if those are her reasons, but she's glad of the female company.

"If we ever find the yuman world where Avan went maybe I'd go there," Issalin goes on. *"I've been talking a lot with that female-Father Winona. I'd see they got the status!"*

"More power to you. Speaking of things to do," Tivonel interrupts herself, *"There's Sastro and that wild alien, over that way. I'm going to check on them. Father Ustan!"* she sends politely. *"I'll rejoin you later. Eldest Heagran will want news of what they have found."*

And that's a fact, she thinks, shooting off at high speed while the others continue on their decorous way. But the real fact is I'm curious.

From this distance she can just pick up the calm life-signal of big Sastro, one of the elders who are staying with Heagran in the Saver.

His signal is modulated by the uncanny flickering emanation of the creature they had picked up out of space. The pulsations were thought to be fear by those who first went out to help him, but now it's clear that his life-energy is periodic in this odd way. Weird!

As she approaches she picks up also the emanations of one of the Saver's pictorial nodes or screens, which for some time now have been showing scenes of the world the Tyrenni will go out to. The group seems to be clustered around it. And now Tivonel can recognize another big life-field—the yuman Valeree with whom she's had many friendly contacts. Valeree is trying to learn the alien creature's language—good luck to her. Beside her in the queer flicker of the alien's field are two other Tyrenni energies; a male and female Tivonel doesn't know well, from Tyree-Two.

"Greetings, Father Sastro and to you all." She extends a decorous receptor-node, ignoring the alien.

"Hello Tivonel," Valeree replies. *"Listen, try touching it carefully. I think it will answer."*

Winds, they must have really calmed it down! Cautiously, Tivonel extends a tentative probe. *"Greetings."*

"Gree—tin" it sends faintly, accompanied by such a flash of mental green that Tivonel jumps away.

"It's scared to death! Why haven't you fixed it?"

"Do not be foolish," Sastro reproves her. *"Do you imagine a Father does not know his work? It appears, young Tivonel, that on this being's world the color you sensed is the hue of harmony and life."*

"It's a good color on ours too, Tivonel," Valeree adds. *"Your people may have to get used to some strange effects when they go down. I see that world as your colors of pain and fear, but on ours they mean fair winds and joy."*

"Whew."

Tivonel slides onto a node near the projection and studies the mental picture again. It's a beautiful scene, even if it's at wind-bottom. Great mounds or crags are looming way up into the wind. She can sense feathery spume whirling by. Far below is a great wet foaming surface, what the yumans call an ocean or sea. A huge, pale six-limbed flying form plummets down past her to snatch something from a floating raft, then soars up to perch on solidity, eating the

317

thing from its claspers. High overhead a dozen others are soaring, evidently rejoicing in the gales. The scene is radiant. It does look like a suitable home for life. Of course if all that is going to turn out to be green and blue the Tyrenni will be in for an adjustment. Well, maybe the bodies' sensors will take care of that.

"Good that you came by, young Tivonel." Sastro's mind-touch cuts short her reverie. *"Tell the Eldest that this alien has decided to go to the new world with our people. Tynad and Orcavel here brought word that it is accepted. It seems that it has skills which may be useful to them. For example, it knows how to handle much hard matter. And how to generate heat should that be needed. I confess I understand little of this, but your friend Valeree assures me it could be needed on such a world."*

"We call it 'fire'," Valeree puts in. *"Yes, it could be very useful. That's what got it out here, things made of hard stuffs and fire."*

"Is it a male or a female?" Tivonel asks, studying the curiously pulsing glow of the alien's life.

"It's both. They mate together and both bear eggs, like those animals down there. So that's another reason it would fit in. It had eight limbs, like some creatures on my world, and it used to fly on a bag or thread. It showed me mind-pictures, that's how I learned its words. Their sky was full of flyers. But you have no idea how strange. It says it was sent out of its world as a punishment."

"But our people don't want to take a criminal with them!"

"I don't think you'd call it a crime. It seems to have questioned some command about not flying too high."

"Great winds, that's not a crime!"

"It was there. So they built a, a pod, and sent it out of the sky. They've done it before, this being expected it. It hoped to reach another world. It had no idea how far they were."

Tivonel digests this extraordinary oddity. *"It sounds like a crazy female to me. Wanting to explore right through the High."*

Valeree laughs. *"More like you, Tivonel. We have a word for what it's really like. Tell Tanel, he'll explain. It feels like a jock, a typical jock. It'll do much better in a real place than this mind-world. Like our Kirk and his pet animal, they're going down too."*

"A jock? I will, Valeree-friend." Tivonel makes her farewells, re-

membering she will never meet the other two Tyrenni again. *"Fair winds on your new world."*

"Fair winds to you who stay, Tivonel."

She glides off, reflecting. It's going to be a lonesome moment when all the other Tyrenni leave. Giadoc has explained how it will be: a sort of wall or shield will form around the nucleus, separating those who stay from the pull of the outgoing Beam. She'll be inside with Giadoc and the others. But it'll be lonesome—think of feeling all the lives of her people, the life of Tyree itself, sliding out forever to the dark, down to that strange world, never to be known again. *Brrr.* It'll be sad for us all.

But we'll see them lodge in the bodies of those flying things, come to themselves and take up real life again. They say it will be gentle; people will have time to choose the ones they want. It won't be like the time she had voyaged to the yuman world and just fallen into the nearest mind. Tanel says that the Destroyer—the Saver—knows how to do this. It was the thing it was supposed to do, if it hadn't been asleep or crazy or whatever it was before Tanel's friend came.

Yes, it'll be a lonely feeling, she thinks again, counting over those who will remain. Giadoc and Heagran, of course. And Ustan has decided to. And the two elders Sastro and Panad, who won't part from Heagran. And the young, bitter Father Hiner, whose child was so tragically lost at the last minute on Tyree. We could have Orva the Hearer's Memory-Keeper too, but Heagran says he must go with the others to carry Tyree's history to the new world, since Kinto was lost. Hiner is studying with him to be Memory-Keeper here.

Well, six Fathers counting Hiner, that'll be a lot of strength if and when new crazy aliens come along. Maybe she'll have to try a little Fathering herself, as she had with Tanel. Heagran says we'll get more like each other with all this mind-touching. But she wishes she had more female company. Only Issalin the Paradomin is staying, and her friend Jalifee. And Marockee—maybe. The other Tyrenni females are so short-sighted, they just see the adventure of that real new world down there. They can't grasp the long mysterious Giadoc-type adventures we'll have here. Maybe I wouldn't either, she thinks, shivering half-pleasurably again, if it weren't for Giadoc.

But I'll have Valeree, Tivonel comforts herself. She's almost like a Tyrenni, she loves to explore. And so does the old female-Father Winona, and maybe that sad Frodo will cheer up. And the funny yu-man male Kris. Thinking of him, she notices the soft signal that means a quarter-Kris has passed. She better hurry. The signal must be coming from the node near the nucleus. She changes course slightly, and an idea comes to her. Why not ask Tanel to have his mysterious friend put markers on the different nodes, so we could really tell where we are? That way we could build up a real mental map of this enormous dark world, and explore out to the very end without danger of being lost. I wonder what we'll find when we get to the edge, she muses. Will the Saver have a thick wall, or will it just thin out to nothing so we can begin to sense the lives of the sky through it?

Ahead of her the dim form of the nucleus and the mind-sparks near it are now faintly perceptible. Another life-group is converging on them—Ustan and the others. Good, she's come just in time. There's no real need for her presence, it'll be all a solemn confer-ence of Heagran telling the Fathers how to conduct themselves out there on New Tyree or whatever they're going to call it. Responsi-bility, life-reverence, *ahura,* etcetera and so on. And Orva saying goodbye. But she loves to listen in to Heagran. So old, so wise; he was a child when New Deep was founded. His mind isn't bounded by Fathering anymore. He's been mind-caught by the wonders of the sky, like Giadoc. We're so lucky to have him.

As she damps herself for a courteous arrival, she thinks ahead to the next, the really exciting conference there is to be. After the main group of Tyrenni go out to their new world and take up their lives, those who are staying here will gather around Tanel. Heagran has explained it. *"The Saver wishes us to help it think upon a new Life-Task, since its race has left this part of the universe, and it is here alone."*

A great new task, here in limitless space among all these stars and worlds? Whew!

Tivonel has picked up many thought-fragments about this, enough to know that everyone has a different dream. Only the two old Fa-thers Sastro and Panad are united; typically, they want to find a young race and Father it to wise maturity. But the others! Averting cosmic cataclysms, reviving dead races—and Giadoc of course always wanting to learn more, to find ways of actually visiting other worlds. . . . A vagrant notion of what it would be like to have real sex again in an alien body rises in her mind; she relegates it to storage.

She knows that old Heagran and that double yuman Waxman both dream of finding strange new kinds of minds among the worlds, but their visions aren't alike. And Father Ustan wants to go on saving endangered races. Issalin and Jalifee will probably want to find some way of helping females, while the yuman Winona wants to rescue any person who is in terrible pain on whatever world. Valeree wants to invent a way of making strange races able to know and feel each other's minds, like the Tyrenni. When Waxman heard her telling that he said, *"Not too much empathy. I know."* The two yumans Tivonel knows least, Frodo and the dreamer Ted Yost, probably have still more wild notions of their own. And Giadoc's friend Kris has the wildest one of all—he thinks they should search for whatever made or hatched the Saver!

Tivonel settles discreetly beside Heagran's group, thinking, I haven't any big idea of my own. But I now how I'm going to respond, because I'm the most practical one of the lot. What they forget is that we're going to be here a long, long, long time.

A slow, coldly exciting shudder travels through her immaterial form. It's not in her cheerful mind to use big words like "eternity" or "forever." Let's just say our journey will be of enormous length and duration, she thinks. And in her experience of long journeys it isn't a good idea to plan everything too carefully. Not to go rigidly seeking one goal when maybe others you haven't thought of are right ahead. Look at her last life-journey; she had started out to look for some exciting sex and found a child to be helped, Hearers to be fed, new friends, a trip to another world, and the end of her own Tyree. So, after all these grand schemes and possibilities are unfolded, she knows what her own contribution will be.

If only I can put it right, she thinks, preparing to attend to Heagran, unaware that her own life-field is aglow with vitality. If only I can think of the right forms to reach these big-minds. Well, the mind who's with the Saver is a female; maybe she'll understand.

The main thing to get across to them is that there will be so much time. Maybe all the time there is. And as we go ever on and on in this great journey, however long it lasts, different possibilities will appear, different acts will seem more urgent or right. We don't even know all our own powers. So let us rescue what we find to rescue, experience what we can, change what seems good to change. That way we will learn and grow. My vote won't be for one plan or another, not even Giadoc's explorations or Heagran's mighty dreams. There is so much time. Why limit ourselves or the Saver? So she knows what she will say:

"Let's try it all!"

Chapter 29

ALONE BUT NOT LONELY IT ROVES THE DARK IMMENSITIES, NEW-BORN AND STRANGEST BEING OF ALL: PART ANIMATE, PART PASSIONLESS CAUSALITY, WHOSE VAST POWERS CAN UNDO TIME ITSELF. SO FAR AS IT KNOWS, IT IS IMMORTAL, AND SUBJECT TO NO IMPERATIVE BUT ITS OWN. IT IS MOVED BY DISCRETE IMPULSES OF CURIOSITY, PITY, IRRITATION, OR WONDER, NOW TRIVIAL, NOW SUBLIME: IMPULSES WHICH ARE ALWAYS LESS PARTICULATE AND ALWAYS MORE A MERG-ING OF PREPOSTEROUSLY FINITE LITTLE LIVES BECOMING MELDED TO FOREVER. IT IS A PROTO-PRONOUN, AN *IT* BE-COMING *SHE* BECOMING *THEY,* A *WE* BECOMING *I* WHICH IS BECOMING MYSTERY.

CONFUSED, JOYFUL, GRIEVING, INQUISITIVE, RANDOMLY BENEVOLENT, AND NOT ENTIRELY SANE, IT SETS FORTH TO ITS DESTINY AMONG THE ORDINARY DENIZENS OF SPACE AND TIME: A CHANCE-BORN FALLIBLE DEITY WHOSE POWERS MAY ONE DAY FOCUS WITHOUT WARNING UPON THE TINY LIVES OF ANY NESCIENT EARTH.

Brightness Falls From the Air

AUTHOR'S NOTE

Some readers will be interested to know that at time of writing (1983), the vastly attenuated nova-front of an exploded star, like the one in our story, was reported to be passing through the Solar system and our Earth.

Acknowledgement

The events narrated here took place in the First Star of Man, when Galactic was the virtually universal tongue. All credit for back-translation into what is believed to be an antique idiom of Earth, circa 1985 Local, must go to my esteemed colleague in the Department of Defunct Languages, Rigel University, Dr. Raccoona Sheldon, along with my profound personal gratitude.

Coldly they went about to raise
  To life and make more dread
Abominations of old days,
  That men believed were dead.
          — *The Outlaws*, R. Kipling, 1914

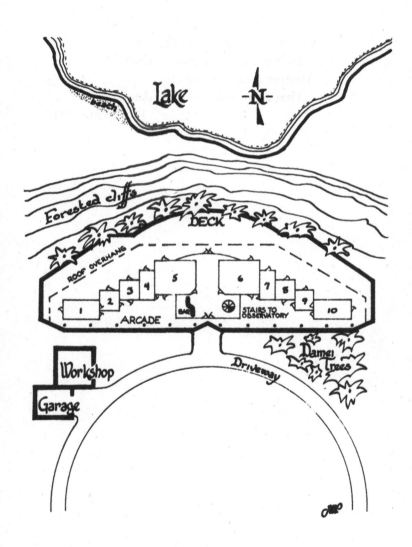

DAMIEM
Station and HOSTEL

Map Key

1. Hannibal & Snake
2. Bridey & Stareem
3. Zannez
4. The Marquises
5. Dr. Baram / Infirmary
6. The Korsos / Administration
7. Linnix
8. Ser Xe Vovoka
9. Dr. Ochter
10. Yale & Hiner

Empty site of
Vlyracocha
THE MURDERED STAR

~20 light-years

DAMIEM

moon

sun

THE STAR
Approaches

I

NOVA MINUS 20 HOURS:
All Out at Damiem

Dawn is tenderly brightening to daylight over the beautiful small world called Damiem. The sun, called here *Yrrei*, is not yet up, and the pearl-colored zenith shows starless; Damiem is very far out on the Galactic Rim. Only two lights inhabit the sky. One is a great, complex, emerald splendor setting toward the west; that is the Murdered Star. The other is a fiery point, hurtling down from overhead.

The landing field in the foreground is lush with wildflowers and clearly not much used.

Waiting at the edge of the field, under the streamer-tree withes, is an open electric ground-jitney, hitched to a flat freight trailer. Three Humans, a woman and two men, are in the jitney's front seat.

Their eyes are fixed on the descending ship; they do not notice the small animal quietly approaching the freight trailer. It is a handsome, velvety-purple arachnoid about a half meter

337

in diameter; the Dameii call it *Avray*, meaning doom or horror. It is very rare and shy. In another instant it has disappeared into or under the trailer, as the Humans begin to speak.

"They seem to be sending down the big shuttle," says Cory Estreèl. "I wonder how many extra we'll get?"

She stretches—an elegantly formed, happy-looking woman in the bloom of midlife, with a great smile and glossy brown hair. Cory is Federation Administrator and Guardian of the Dameii and also, when necessary, keeper of the small guest hostel. Public access to Damiem is severely restricted, for grave reason.

In the driver's seat beside her, Kipruget Korso—known to all as Kip—squints up at the descending fires. He is Deputy Administrator and Dameii Guardian-Liaison, as well as Cory's mate.

Cory's brown eyes slide sideways to him, and she smiles. Kip is the handsomest man she's ever seen, a fact of which he seems quite unaware.

He's a few years younger than she, with all the ingredients of the ideal Space Force recruiting ad—big, lean frame, a tanned, aquiline face with merry gray eyes of transparent sincerity, a warm, flashing grin, and a mop of black curls. She had mistaken him for some kind of showperson when they'd first met. That was over a decade back, during the last Demob. She'd been looking for Federation service on some unpeopled planet, and so, it turned out, was Kip. She was a bit disconcerted when this glorious specimen was assigned as her deputy, until other Spacers told her of his real war record.

And then it had turned out that they'd also both been looking for somebody like each other; they'd declared a Mateship in their first year on Damiem. The end of their second Mateship had come and gone a couple of years back, but out here, a hundred light-minim from the nearest FedBase, they'd simply gone on being mated.

Looking at Kip now, Cory's smile broadens. The prospect of visitors has inspired him to dig up fresh clothes; faded explorer's whites and a vermilion neckerchief. It'll be pure murder if there're any susceptible people coming, she thinks. But she can't comment, not while wearing the shorts that show off her own well-turned legs; she'd forbidden herself to wear them before, because of poor Bram.

Waiting there in Damiem's balmy, scented air, Cory's hand steals toward her mate's. But she pulls it back, remembering the man sitting miserably on her other side, who is holding himself so rigid that the jitney-bus trembles.

Doctor Balthasar Baramji ap Bye—Baram or Bram to friends—is Senior Xenopathologist and Medical Guardian of the Dameii. He's a lithe, bronzed man some years Cory's senior, with prematurely white hair and brilliant turquoise eyes. Now he is staring up at the descending shuttle with ferocious intensity.

"You sure it's the big one, Cor?" he inquires.

"Absolutely," she assures him warmly.

Kip grunts agreement. "They retrofired about a half minim early. And that reddish tinge in the exhaust is oversize ablation shielding. We only get old rocket drives out here. Burn everything. I just hope our Dameii don't decide to move away."

"Here, take the glasses, Bram." Cory thinks it will help if he can end the uncertainty fast.

Baramji isn't suffering from any illness but only from the needs that can bedevil any vigorous male living celibate with a happily mated pair. His own mate had been killed in space years back, and for a time Damiem had helped him. But he has mended his heart again, and the enforced austerity of his life really torments him now.

She'd seen the full measure of his misery one night when Kip was on a trip to the Far Dameii. Baram approached her, red-faced and sweating with shame.

"I'm breaking the Code, Cor, I know. *I know*. Can you

339

forgive me? I'm pretty sure you've never meant—but sometimes I think, or I dream—I had to be sure. Oh Cor, Cory, lovely lady—if you only knew . . .''

And he'd fallen silent with his heart in his glorious eyes and his fists in his armpits like a child reminding itself not to touch.

Every friendly feeling urged her to ease him; she loved Baram as dearly as a sister could. But she could foresee the complications what would follow, the inevitable repetitions, the falseness in their group.

And worse: In a man like Baram, relief could turn to real love with frightening speed and hurt them all. In fact, she and Kip both suspect that Bram's basic trouble is not in his loins but in his heart, which he's trying to fill with friendship and the Dameii.

So she refused him, almost weeping, too. Afterward he tried to thank her.

And now they're waiting for what promises to be quite a crowd of tourists. A free woman for Baram must be up there behind those growing fires! The last time a tour came to see the Star pass, Bram hadn't been so desperate. This time, Cory guesses, a female reptile would have charm.

Gazing upward, Cory's eyes go involuntarily to the enormous green swirl of the Murdered Star, at which she always tries not to look. It isn't really a star, but the last explosion-shell around the void where the Star had been. It's still called the Star, because for decades it had showed as a starlike point of green fire, blazing almost alone in the emptiest quadrant of Damiem's Rim sky.

But it is in fact a nova-front approaching Damiem at enormous speed, enlarging as it comes. Over the past years it has swelled from a point to a jewel to this great complex of light whose fringes touch half the sky. Two other, outer nova-shells have already expanded and passed over Damiem, generating awesome auroral displays but little danger. This is the last, the innermost shell. When it rises tonight, the peak zone will be upon them—and in another night the last remnants will be past them and forever gone.

Only from Damiem can this sight be seen. By the time the shells have expanded to pass other worlds, they will be too attenuated to be detected by eye.

"Hey," says Kip, following Cor's gaze, "it's really growing fast. And it's different from last time, too. We may have a real show yet."

"I hope so," Cory says abstractedly. "So embarrassing, all those people coming so far to see a nova-shell pass—and then nothing but pretty lights."

"And a time-flurry," says Baram unexpectedly, "which I never got to experience."

"Right, you were under cover."

"With fifteen pregnant Dameii."

"Yes." She chuckles. "But they're nothing really, Bram. I told you—one merely feels sort of gluey for like a minim or two. But it's not in real time."

"What's coming now is the heart. The core," says Kip hopefully. "There has to be *something.*"

As Cory looks up her lips tighten. That cursed illusion again. It consists of four hairline cracks racing up from the four quarters of the horizon, converging on the Star to make a very thin black cross against the sky. She is the only one who ever sees this; it does not make her happy. She blinks hard, and the illusion goes. Tomorrow it will be gone for good.

Sound is coming from the shuttle now—a growing wail punctuated by far sonic booms. It will be down in minim.

Just as Kip is about to start the motors, they see above them a small, pale, finely shaped face peering down from the high withes of the tree. Behind the head can be glimpsed enormous, half-transparent wings.

"Hello, Quiyst," Cory says gently in the liquid Damei tongue. The head nods and looks at Kip, with whom the Dameii have more rapport.

"Tell your people not to be afraid," Kip says. "These visitors are only coming for a few days to look at the Star. Like the last ones. And did you warn everyone to get under cover when it grows very bright? This is the last time it will pass, and it may drop bad stuff on us all."

"Ye-es." The exquisite child-man continues to stare dubiously from Kip to the oncoming shuttle, which is starting to suck up a roil of dust. Quiyst is old; his clear, nacreous skin is faintly lined, and the mane that merges into his wings is white. But his form and motion still breathe beauty.

"Don't worry, Quiyst," Kip tells him through the uproar. "Nobody will ever harm you again. When we go, others will come to guard you, and others after them. You know there is a big ship out there to make sure. When these new people leave, would you like to visit it?"

Quiyst looks at him enigmatically. Kip isn't sure how much Quiyst has heard or believed. The Damei withdraws his head and turns to get away from the horror of the oncoming fires and the noise that must be hurting his ears. Quiyst is brave, staying so close to a landing. *Burning wings* is the worst terror-symbol of the Dameii.

"Don't forget, hide your people from the sky-light!" Kip calls after him. "And tell Feanya!" But Quiyst is gone, invisibly as he'd come.

Kip kicks up the motors and they start for the field. The Moom, the huge, taciturn, pachydermatous race who run most Federation lines, are famous for arriving and departing precisely on schedule, regardless of who or what is under them. It isn't clear that they distinguish passengers from freight, save that freight doesn't need cold-sleep. Their ground operations go very fast.

With a great splash of flame and dust the shuttle settles and a ring of fire crackles out through the flowery brush. Kip drives the jitney in as fast as he dares. The flames have barely sunk to coals when the freight chute comes down, followed by the passenger-way, which ends on soil almost too hot to touch.

"Someday they're going to fry some passengers," Kip says. "I just hope our tires stand up for one more cooking."

"The Moom don't care," says Cory. "Give them that Life-Game thing and let them run the ships."

"There's more live coals. I've got to stop here or the tires will blow for sure."

Doctor Baramji's glasses have stayed on the ship through every lurch and jolt. As they stop, the passenger port swings open above the gangway, propelled by a giant gray arm. The arm withdraws, and out bounces a totally bald, red-suited man loaded with holocam gear, who races down the ramp and turns to face it. The heat of the ground disconcerts him; he backs away, making quick, complex adjustments to his cameras, while mooing hoots come from within.

"All right, kids!" he calls. "Watch it—the ground's hot."

Baramji gasps audibly. Out through the port steps a silver-blonde dream of a young girl, revealingly clad in some designer's idea of what explorers wear. One hand goes to her throat and her huge eyes widen more as she hesitantly descends the ramp.

A minim later Baramji lets out an involuntary croak. A male figure follows the girl—a handsome blue-black youngster, clad in the same idiotic suiting. He solicitously escorts her to cooler ground.

Next instant the scenario repeats itself, led this time by a slim, tan-blond boy. He moves with a curious slope-shouldered undulation and turns back to beckon imperiously. A beautiful black-haired girl, with eyes that glow violet even at this distance, hurries to him and submissively allows him to guide her rather roughly down to where the others stand. Seen closer, the boy's face has a look of sleepy, slant-eyed malevolence. The new couple is clad like the first.

"Those shoes will scorch through," Kip mutters. He raises

his voice. "Here! Bring your bags over here! Come and get in!"

Baramji is sighing mournfully. "How many did you say there are, Cory?"

"Ten— Oh, wait, my audio's picking something up . . . There may be more. Well, hello!"

On the gangway appears a quite young Human boy, impeccably dressed in a miniversion of a man's business tunic. His head is topped by an oddly folded garrison cap sporting three gold plumes. Hearing Kip's calls, he hops off the ramp—his boots, they see, are serviceable, if ornate—and, lugging his bag, he trots over and climbs nimbly into the jitney, giving them a nod and a smile. He has an attractive smile and a manner remarkably composed for one who can't be over twelve. As soon as he settles, his head turns and he begins watching the four who disembarked before him with a look of worried concern.

Two older men are coming down now. The first is tall, heavily built, with ruddy-gray skin. Behind him limps a small tufty gray-haired gnome, clad in old-fashioned cloak and panters. They seem not to know each other. Both stare about until they locate first the Star and second the baggage chute, before they heed Kip's call.

More hootings from the port—and then another gasp from Doctor Baramji.

A heavily gilded, curtained rollbed, complete with suspended flasks, batteries, bottles, pumps, and other life-support equipment, appears on the ramp, reluctantly guided by a young Moom ship boy. Pacing beside it comes a cloud of tawny gold-sparked veiling, which reveals rather than hides a woman.

And such a woman! Small, with flawless, creamy skin, glowing black eyes that speak of antique harems, luxuriant dark curls teased into what Cory suspects is the style beyond the style, a bursting bosom above a hand-span waist, and ripe oval haunches. Her hands are tiny and heavily jeweled, and her equally tiny toes are velvet-clad. Cory judges her to be just beyond first youth. One of her small hands keeps possessive hold on the rollbed, though she is in obvious distress on the gangplank. Her sweet voice can be heard thanking the Moom; there is, of course, no reply.

Baramji's binoculars fall to the jitney floor with a thud. "There's a patient in there!" he exclaims hoarsely, vaulting out, and heads for the vision's side at a dead run.

"Woo-ee," says Kip. "I'd like to know which gods Bram prayed to."

Baram's arrival on the gangplank is greeted by a brilliant smile so compounded of relief, admiration, and seduction that they can see him all but melting into the rollbed for support. Both Korsos chuckle benignly.

"I gather the patient is no threat," Kip says. "Listen, okay with you if I risk the tires one more time to get the freight trailer closer to that rollbed? The Moom will never help us, we can't roll it through this stuff, and I have a hunch it weighs a ton."

"Green, go. Oh, look. Something's still going on," Cory says as they plow through the ring of half-live ashes. The port stays open above them, emitting sounds of Moom and Human discord.

Just as they draw up by the rollbed, a disheveled and angry-looking young blond fellow emerges onto the gangway. Behind him comes a tall, dark, narrow-shouldered man who looks to be in his thirties and is wearing a long, severe dark cloak.

Halfway down, the blond wheels around and shakes his fist at the port. "I'll sue you!" he yells. "I'll sue the line! You've *ruined* my life work—putting me off on some pissass planet I never heard of, when all my vouchers say Grunions Rising!" He brandishes a fistful of travel slips and jerks at his modish sports tabard, which is on crooked. "The University will sue you for this!"

There is no response from inside.

Meanwhile the cloaked man steps around the vociferator and continues on down the ramp. Though he makes no outcry, his thin lips are very compressed, and there's a glare in his close-set dark eyes. The high collar of his cloak is ornamented with parallel silver zigzags, and his boots have the same emblem on their cuffs, giving his outfit the look of an unknown uniform.

Ignoring Kip, he heads straight to the freight chute. The blond, after a confused look around, shouts, "Make sure my luggage comes off!" and goes to the chute, too.

"Oh, hey," says Kip. "I just remembered. Do you know what that is, in the cloak? An Aquaman!"

"A what?" says Cory. "Aqua—water—you mean those people with gills? I've never seen one close up."

"You'd think he'd be going to Grunions."

"Yes . . . well, it does look as though there's been some kind of a mix-up."

"On a Moom ship? Not likely."

Meanwile a white-clad figure with flaming red hair has appeared at the top of the ramp—a slim girl with ship officer's insigne on her shirt. She's carrying a small bag. It can only be the ship's Logistics Officer. Apparently there are no more Human passengers left on board, so she can stop over at Damiem until the ship comes back from Grunions Rising to pick them all up again.

What can have gone wrong with the passengers for Grunions?

As soon as the girl's feet touch the ground, the gangway snaps up and the port slams. Only the freight chute is still open.

"And that makes thirteen," Cory says. "She must have decided to get off here to see the Star and rejoin the ship when it comes back."

"Nice-looking kid, and some hair," says Kip. "Look, I'm going to have to help Bram push that thing aboard. The Moom freight crew will do the bags but they won't touch this. All right?" He gets out, shouting, "All you folks, grab

346

your bags and get aboard this jitney as fast as you can! That Moom shuttle will take off on *their* schedule even if you're standing right under the tubes. Formalities later—right now it's all aboard!''

The two senior men have found their luggage and are docilely carrying it to the jitney; the small pixielike old man has one of the new and very expensive floaters on his bag so he can manage despite his limp. But the bald red-clad cameraman bustles up to Kip.

"I am Zannez!"

"Congratulations. Get in."

"I see you don't understand, Myr . . . ah, Korso is it? These four young people are Galactically famous hologrid stars. You must have heard of the *Absolutely Perfect Commune?*''

"No, nor you, either.''

"Hey, kids! We've finally hit the frontier! Nobody here knows us.''

"I know you're going to have four Galactically fried show stars if you don't let me get you away from this ship.''

"But we need a car for ourselves, of course.''

"Sorry, no go. We have a small electric work-car, but even if there was someone to bring it, there's no possible time before that ship takes off and flames the lot of you.''

"Yes, I gather there's need for haste. But surely there's time for one brief shot of the planet chief greeting the kids?''

"Well, if it's *really* brief. Cory, can you come over a minim?''

"Oh, no, not you,'' Zannez snaps at her. "Get back.''

Kip comes very close to him.

"Listen, whoever you are. That lady you just yelled at *is* the Planetary Administrator. And incidentally my mate. Either you change your tone or she'll have you pulled out of here by Patrol ship and kept in the brig until the Moom come back. She can also impound all your gear; so can I.''

"Uh-oh,'' said Zannez, not sounding too abashed. He

347

stares intently at Cory for an instant, taking in the long tanned legs, the well-filled shorts below the trim waist, the queenly shoulders and throat exposed by her sunshirt. "Look, she's fantastic, it isn't that. But having a lady chief makes it seem . . . well, not so wild. And a double host figure will get the audience confused. My apologies, ma'am, I certainly do want a shot of you—but couldn't your mate just greet the kids beside the ship—in your name, say?"

"Oh, for—great Apherion!—here: Hello, hello, hello, hello, hello," Kip says. "Now, do you want to get cooked alive or get in the jitney? I'm not risking the others for you."

But Zannez wasn't through. "I want them up beside you in the front."

"No way. We have instruments to run. You get places like everybody else."

"Well, can I at least group them in back? That way I can frame them like they were alone."

"All right, go on in back."

Zannez, pushing into the jitney with his load of gear, suddenly sees the young boy.

"Oh, no! I don't *believe* it."

"Oh, yes." The boy smiles. "Why not? Others wish to see the Star, too, you know."

Groaning and shaking his head, Zannez turns to focus on his charges getting in. As she passes, the blonde girl murmurs, "Funny. I dreamed I saw him."

Zannez grunts and then demands of Kip, "Is that trailer with that bed thing going to stay in our view? Couldn't you leave it along the way and come back for it?"

"If anybody gets left, it'll be you," Kip says levelly and turns away to help Baramji secure the bed.

Zannez moves to the back of the jitney behind his four stars, yelling at Baramji. "Hey, Myr whatever, keep out of sight, you'll ruin the shots. Myr Korso, *please* tell him to scrooch down if he has to be there."

"Scrooch down yourself," Baram yells back. "And point

your stuff up. Don't you know that if you see any Dameii, which isn't likely with the noise you're making, they'll be *up*? Up in the trees, like most life here. Now, Kip, go slow. What's in here is delicate.''

As Zannez subsides, Cory sings out, "Thirteen aboard. All set? Anybody missing any luggage?''

No one speaks.

"Green, then, go. Kip, take us out.''

The jitney motors howl up, and it begins to move, faster and faster. "Gods help those tires now,'' says Kip. "We run on the rims if we have to.''

A Moom voice speaks from the radio. The jitney picks up even more speed, rocking from side to side.

"Take it easy, take it easy, Kip!'' Baramji shouts from the trailer.

"Can't!'' Kip yells back.

They are barely at the edge of the burn when a rumble starts in the tubes of the shuttle behind them.

"Hang on!'' The jitney, lurching and leaping, rockets toward the rise and finally plunges down into shelter among the streamer-trees beyond. The passengers can see flame and steam rolling over the ground they were on.

With a head-splitting boom, the old shuttle stands up on its pillar of flame and accelerates ever faster away from Damiem. Kip drops speed, and the jitney runs relatively smoothly over the rock ruts. The spaceport road has never been graded.

"Another nice peaceful disembarcation party,'' Cory remarks. "Moom style.''

"Do you see what I mean now, Zannez?'' Kip calls. He has checked the rearview a couple of times. Each time he looks, Zannez is holding some perilous position, shooting, panning, changing lenses; he has managed to get out another camera.

"You know, Cor, despite the fellow's horrible personality, I think we have to give him marks for dedication.''

"I guess the pushiness goes with the profession.'' She

349

can't resist adding, "Did you notice, beautiful as those young people are, there's a kind of unnatural quality? Everything exaggerated. And so thin!"

"Yes, I've seen it before. I don't need any hologrid stars when I have you, Coryo."

"Ahh, Kip. . . . I wonder how Bram's doing?"

"Well, at least his dream-houri managed to hang on. Just for your information, that stuff she's wearing is real, or I never had a course in mineralogy. That's one ferocious lot of Galactic credits we're towing. But what do you suppose is in that rollbed? I couldn't get a peep."

"We'll find out at the hostel."

"We'll find out a lot of things. I hope we like them."

II

NOVA MINUS 19 HOURS:
Meetings

The road improves. Damiem's yellow sun is rising through a pink fleece of fine-weather cloudlets and igniting little rainbows in all the dewy foliage. The steamer-trees give way to flowering shrubs and light green bird-trees. Many of the mobile bird-leaves take off and flap curiously after the jitney. As usual, the tourists love this; even the dour Aquaman brightens as some leaves settle for a brief rest on the edge of the jitney near him.

"They'll get bored and go back to their trees when we've gone inside," Cory explains. "Well, here we are. Damiem Station Hostel. The Star will rise over the lake in back. We'll watch from the deck on the lakeside."

They have drawn up in a circular driveway, lavishly edged with flowers, in the arc of a crescent-shaped, one-story building. Beyond it the ground falls away abruptly to a forest-edged lake. The hostel consists of a large, high-roofed center hall,

351

with two short wings of rooms extending from each side. Running along the whole front is a simple open arcade. Atop the central hall is an array of antennae beside a small cupola, clearly an observatory. On the left of the main building is a neat garage and workshop, and on the right is a grove of fern-leafed trees, up among whose branches can be glimpsed a woven treehouse. All roofs are of thatch.

The main double doors of the center lounge stand open, or rather, their lower halves do; as the tourists approach they can see that the doors have a second upper section, which can be opened to at least twice Human height, and the front arcade rises accordingly there.

"How perfectly charming," the gnomelike little man exclaims.

Zannez is panning his camera. "Natives build this?" he inquires.

"No," says Cory. "You're looking at the builders of most of it. The previous man, the first Guardian, just put up two main rooms. And we do not, repeat not, call people natives. The people of this world are the Dameii. As you may have noticed, a Damei family lives in those trees beside us, but it's for mutual instruction only. They do no menial work. Those of you who are able will unload and carry your own bags. We'll help you all we can, but the addition of three unexpected people means we have to scurry about making some end rooms habitable. Kippo, why don't you take them in and sort them out while I do some of the preliminary scurrying?"

"All right, honey," says Kip, "but don't overdo it. I'm here for that. . . . Very well, Myrrin, welcome to Damei Hostel. The lounge awaits you with edible refreshments and light drink—and I do mean light; alcohol so soon after cold-sleep drugs will flatten you. You might even miss the Star. We've developed a Damei soft drink I think you'll like."

He's ushering them in as he speaks, to the large central hall or lounge. It is walled chiefly with translucent vitrex. On the left side is a long, beautifully grained and polished wooden bar, plus other housekeeping facilities; on the right is a small circular staircase obviously leading to the observatory on the roof. Directly opposite are vitrex double doors opening onto the deck over the lake. They are flanked by two rooms which seem to be the staff's permanent quarters. The one on the left has a red cross on the door, an old symbol still recognizable as meaning a place of medical aid. The room on the right has "Admin." on the doorplate.

As they move to the chairs around the bar their footsteps echo oddly. Looking up, they see why: the underside of the thatch is lined with heavy antirad shielding.

Kip has unfolded a computer readout and laid it on the bar, glancing at it as he passes around trays of snacks and tidbits, and pours a golden drink into exquisite shell-form glasses.

"These glasses are Damei work," he tells them. "They've been into glass for hundred of generations before . . . uh . . . contact. Now let's introduce ourselves formally, and I'll play a guessing game—the Moom finally passed over a rudimentary passenger list. Your hostess, and the boss here, is Corrisón Estreèl-Korso, Federation Administrator. I'm Kipruget Korso-Estreèl, Deputy Administrator and Damei Liaison. The Medical Officer over there is Senior Xenopathologist Balthasar Baramji ap Bye, known as Doctor Baram. Don't let the white hair fool you. We're all three officially charged with guarding the Dameii, after the atrocities inflicted on them by Humans were discovered and forcibly stopped, and we have Patrol backup on call."

"Now"—he bows to the vision in beige veils—"would I be correct in assuming I address the Marquise Lady Parda—uh, sorry: Parda-lee-anches, that's Lady Pardalianches, of Rainbow's End?"

She graciously acknowledges it.

"And . . . ah, sister? No name is given."

"Yes. My sister here is the Lady Paralomena, my poor twin. She suffered a terrible riding accident some years back. It's left her helpless but conscious—you *must* believe that,

Myr Korso, some people won't. Luckily I have the resources to keep her healthy and stimulated, against the day, which will come—I *know* it will—when she wakens fully. I've brought her here in the hopes that some of this extraordinary radiation from your Star will help her where doctors can't.''

Kip approaches the curtained bed.

"May I see her, Lady Pardalianches? It's not just idle curiosity—though I am curious—but you could be concealing an armed man or a dangerous animal in there.''

"Oh, what an idea! My poor darling. Very well, if you must.'' Delicately she opens the curtains before him an inch or two. Kip looks in, and his eyes widen before he draws back.

"One—one would swear she was sleeping. And very beautiful.''

"Oh, yes, Myr Korso. I see you are sympathetic. She *is* just sleeping. But there's more to it than that. Did you notice her gold mesh cap?''

"Ah, only dimly.''

"I wear one just like it, under my coiffure.'' She touches her thick curls. "We experience everything together. It is the product of the highest science. I will *not* let her become a vegetable.''

Kip gulps. "Of course not.''

"And now,'' says the Lady, "since we are both very tired after this demanding trip, might I ask to go to whatever room is ready? Anything will do. I have my own bed linen, of course.''

"We've assigned you Suite A.'' Kip points left, beyond the bar. "The name's a joke; there isn't any Suite B. Doctor Baram sleeps there normally. Perhaps he'll help make you comfortable.''

Baramji, sitting proprietarily beside the rollbed, all but drops his plate as he leaps up.

"I'll help you, of course, my lady. Any time.''

The rest of the group watch them exit, in somewhat stunned silence, and all eyes go to Kip.

"She really was beautiful—like a healthy, sleeping fifteen-year-old. But if they're *twins*—this thing must have been going on twenty years. It gives me cold shudders. And that's absolutely all I'm going to say about that. Now, taking the easiest one next—Zannez Beorne and four actors, sexes mixed."

The strange-looking blond boy lets out a nasal chuckle. The grid-show people have grouped themselves at the far end of the bar.

"That's right," says Zannez. "Now this may sound freaky to you, but it's been so long since I've been among people who didn't know the *Absolutely Perfect Commune*—I mean, billions of viewers all over the Grid tune in every night, sometimes I think they know the *Commune* better than their own families. So I've sort of lost the art of introduction. I'm Zannez Beorne—nobody uses the last name—cameraman and production manager for these four. Girls first, I guess." He places a finger on top of the silver-blonde's head, as though he were going to twirl her. "May I present Stareem Fada? Our Star—one of them."

"Hi." Charmingly modest smile from the blonde.

Kip notices that the small boy is smiling, too, leaning back from his plate and looking around with a calmly challenging air. What's with him?

"And this young lady"—Zannez tips back so they can see the black-haired beauty —"is Eleganza."

The brunette smiles obediently but suddenly bursts out, "I'm not Eleganza! I'm Bridey McBannion."

Zannez grunts. "And you'll end up cooking slosh for two hundred kids in a welfare kitchen, *Bridey*. If you can do better than Eleganza, which I admit is not sublime, there's just time to go ahead. But Bridey McBannion—if I hear that again—"

The very black youth cuts in. "Myr Zannez, take it easy. You have me."

"And may the gods bless you. Myrrin, may I present Hannibal Ek, who was born to Caesar and Jocelyn Ek and christened Hannibal in the tenth diocese of Orange World. Hannibal Ek; E-k. . . . And this is Snake Smith."

"We're together," Hannibal says. "I like to make things clear."

"He's not really Snake Smith, either," Zannez says. "But he was born to carny folk who changed his name so often I don't think anybody knows what it really is. I don't."

"I do," Snake Smith says. "And if anybody every finds out and uses it, I'll *kill* them." Suddenly the malevolent, sleepily lethal look drops over his features like a mask. Kip sees with surprise that it *is* a mask. Unless the boy deliberately assumes that look, which seems to be his grid-show persona, he is a perfectly normal, rather cheerful and friendly-looking young Human, wherever he got those picturesque slant eyes. Catching Kip's eye on him, he laughs pleasantly and then switches it to his nasty snicker.

"Well, that wraps us up," Zannez says. "Somehow I don't think the Lady Pardalianches will mind having missed us. But I'm going to mind not hearing the rest of you firsthand, because, Kippo, I want your permission to take the kids around and do some shooting now. This may be the last day things look normal. But if our rooms aren't ready, can we help?"

"No," says Kip. "Yours are three that are ready. Just go down the arcade past Suite A and you'll find numbers one, two, and three—that's all there are on that side. Or better, come out on the deck here and go in from there—all the rooms open onto the deck as well as the arcade." He waves them toward the far doors opening on the lake view.

As they rise, Zannez remembers something. "Oh, by the by, what was that spectacular, big purple tarantula that jumped off the trailer just as we got here? About ye huge . . ." He spreads his hands a chair's width apart. "If it's a pet, I'd love a shot of it—but not when I'm in the dark."

"Pet *spiders*?" says the brunette on a high note.

Kip is frowning.

"No, that's no pet," he says slowly and smiles at the girl. "But if we had pets, they'd almost have to be arachnoid—spiderlike—'cause all the ground beasties here of any size are. You sure it was purple, Myr Zannez?"

"Honor bright. I was lucky, I picked it up in the viewfinder. Why, did we catch something special?"

"In a way, yes. They're very rare. But perfectly harmless—Cor actually managed to pat another one we ran into. But the Dameii are scared out of their wits by them, they believe them to be an omen of death, only worse. . . . I can't think what it was doing with the trailer, unless it has a nest in the garage. Oh, bother; that means I'll have to root it out and carry it to some safe place, before our Dameii see it and leave. Cory'll have fits, she'd love to see the young. . . . You really did get a lucky shot."

"What's worse than death?" asks the slant-eyed lad lightly.

"This is serious, to them," Kip replies in an odd tone. "Not like our thing about white *gattos*. I must ask officially, all, keep this to yourselves. And now, Myr Zannez"—Kip had ushered them out to the deck—"you're welcome to shoot anything you like so long as you stay away from the Damei grove and house—hear me? And don't get too involved because we plan a visit to the Damei village just before noon. The days are thirty Standard hours long here, see. You'll have plenty of time for a rest before we start Star-watching— No, wait, please," he says to the boy, who has been watching alertly and is following Zannez' group. "You haven't been introduced."

"Of course." The lad smiles, goes back, and applies himself anew to the refreshments.

The plump blond young man who had threatened to sue speaks up. "It must be our rooms that aren't ready."

"And mine," adds the red-haired ship's officer.

"Well, yes," Kip says to her. "Although you're no problem, Myr . . . Linnix, is it? You go in my study next door here, after I get some biological specimens off the bed. . . . But wait, this list doesn't give you any other name."

"I haven't an agreed-on one," Linnix says. She shakes her flaming head, as though a fly were bothering her. "So everyone just uses Linnix. Even the payroll." She grins. "Back in the world of computers I get Linnix MFN NCN or even NN Linnix. Which confuses everybody. I *am* rather tired, though, and we've been through quite a mess, as Myr Yule and Doctor Hiner will tell you. If you'd let me move your materials, I would appreciate a quiet lie-down."

"By all means—here, I'll give you a hand," Kip says, and escorts Linnix out the other wing to the small bedroom he's been using as a lab. They find Cory has already cleared living space.

"I'll call you in time for the trip." He draws the curtains to darken the room. "Nighty night."

"Thank you," comes her sleepy voice.

A good kid, he thinks. But what was this foul-up?

When he returns, the blond youth, who turns out to be named Mordecai Yule, is bursting to enlighten him. "Grunions Rising! See, everyone!" He fans his handful of vouchers.

Kip knows Grunions Rising only as the next and last world in the line, out here at the Rim. A water world. "What, you're a student of aquatic worlds? Are you and, ah, Doctor Hiner together?"

"I never saw him in my life before this happened," the thin, dark Aquaman says scornfully. "I am a member of an official survey team compiling a Galaxywide report on worlds suitable for colonization. Our mandate is to make the first— and, I may say, sorely needed—truly comprehensive update of the *Aquatica Galactica*. I appear here alone because, when we had completed our joint work on the A and B candidate planets, it was voted to disperse and individually cover the C class, which includes very distant, or dubiously reported, or otherwise questionable candidates. I selected Grunions Rising as the last stop in the list, which I have already compiled.

"And now to my inexpressible dismay I find myself disembarked on your planet here, which is of absolutely no interest, and am told that I cannot reenter cold-sleep in time to continue to Grunions. And if I wait over here for the next Rim ship, I shall not only upset the schedules of the whole team, but shall fail to make my contribution to a newly found candidate in the Hyades complex for which we have high hopes.

"A complete, disgusting disaster. Damage to my work, and doubtless to my reputation—damage to the work of the team, waste of project funds—and all of it quite irreparable. It can only be due to sloppiness—inexcusable sloppiness on the part of that young woman who calls herself an officer. Oh, she brandished two empty Grunions syrettes—but it would have been the work of a minim to empty their contents down the waster, and get rid of two incriminating used Damiem syrettes. There's no explanation other than blaming a company which has never, I repeat, never—have you ever known a case?—been known to foul up. And I shall certainly see that the A. A. initiates a strong request for disciplinary action against her. We Aquamen are not to be so treated with impunity, I assure you!"

He folds his arms.

"Well, I admit it looks bad," says Kip. "But let's not be too hasty in judging the kid. After all, people in chemical companies sometimes slip up just like individual people. . . . I take it this is more or less your case, Myr Yule?"

"Oh, it's worse—much worse—for me. Hiner has his doctorate and his rep, and if he has to, he can wait for the next ship. But I'm on a predoctoral research grant with a time limit—and I just don't know what I'm going to do, Myr Korso."

From rage he has turned nearly to tears.

"The Grunions Rising bit was the centerpiece of my whole dissertation—I chose it partly because no one'd been near it since the old *A.G.*, and now you're going to cover it, Hiner. You'll probably be in print before I even get there—if I get there at all—and in short I'm ruined. Just *ruined*. Oh, that intolerable smug girl and her syrettes—"

He breaks off to heave sigh after sigh.

Kip thinks he should at least feel sympathetic, but somehow he finds himself disliking both of them. The prospect of housing one or both until the next ship dismays him.

"We'll see what we can do with messages, for both of you," he makes himself say heartily. "And it's conceivable the Patrol might help. Meanwhile, you've at least been dropped off here just as a celestial event of very great interest is about to occur, and you're on a planet many people would give an arm and a leg to visit."

So they are, he says to himself. And with no security check.

"And I'm puzzled, too," he concludes. "I've simply never heard of a destination failure before, and I don't know anyone who has. Have you Myrrin"— he turns to the two older men—"ever heard of such a thing?"

"No," says the tall, heavyset man expressionlessly.

"Never," declares the gnome. "Never, never, never! And I don't think the girl did it, either. Practically speaking, people who are liable to make mistakes of that order don't make just one. And she'd never have risen to Senior Logistics Officer if she'd made any such mistakes—not to mention a trail of them. . . . By the way, you must be puzzled as to which of us is which—I'm Doctor Aristrides Ochter, a very amateur student of novas in my old age. My former work, from which I retired five Standard years ago, was in neocybernetic theory. But novas have always fascinated me, so I thought to spend what time I have left"— he glances at his thigh—"in going actually to see some. I have no family

360

to save for, you see. And I can't tell you how much I'm looking forward to tonight!''

"And then you are Myr . . . ?'' Kip addresses the taciturn man.

"*Ser* Xe Vovoka,'' the stranger corrects him. Apparently feeling that something more is really called for, Vovoka adds slowly, "I am an artist . . . a light-sculptor.'' He smiles briefly, which changes his whole face.

Kip recalls that "Ser'' is a technical honorific, somewhere beyond "Doctor.'' Not to call him "Myr.''

He turns to the boy, who has been listening carefully, his plumed cap on his knees, while he finishes his fourth helping of snacks.

"Then you must be Prince Pao?''

The lad—he looks nearer eleven, even ten, than twelve—nods.

"May we know your first name, Prince?''

"That's it.'' The boy swallows and grins. "Prince-Prince Pao, if you wish to be technical. Simplifies things. I'm a student of everything, before I must return home to my duties.'' His smile vanishes momentarily. "I'm praying for long life to the present ruler. Pavo's only a small world principality, but it's sort of a diplomatic, financial, and arbitration center. . . . Problems!'' He flings back his hair and slaps on his ornate cap so the gold feathers dance. "Right now I long to watch stars!''

"Stars . . . I see,'' echoes Kip. But he's not sure that he does. "Well, then perhaps you won't mind the quarters we prepared for you, up in the observatory? It's only a cot.''

"Fantastic!'' The little prince points. "Up there?''

"Right.''

The lad picks up his small, costly looking kit-bag and commences hauling it up the circular stairs. "No help needed, thanks. I had it packed light.''

He vanishes above as Cory comes striding in, rolling down her sleeves.

"Well, I have things just about livable for you two young men, assuming Kip helps me move a bed, and that you two can room together. You're . . . ?"

"Doctor Nathaniel Hiner and Myr Mordecai Yule," Kip tells her.

They nod glum assent to sharing space.

"It's the very end room on the east wing." Cory gestures toward the wing where Linnix sleeps. "You'll find sawdogs and vitrex make very nice tables."

"You shouldn't have done all that, honey. Do I assume that Ser Vovoka here and Doctor Ochter have their separate rooms now?"

"Absolutely. The two between your lab and the end one. That's where the bed gets moved out. Come right along with me, one and all."

"I hear and obey," little Ochter says gaily. The others, silent and unmerry, hoist their bags and follow her along the arcade to their respective rooms. Vovoka is next to Linnix, Ochter beyond, and Yule with Hiner at the end. The extra bed is in Vovoka's small room. It's of a native wood, and very heavy; Kip and Cory strain to jockey it out.

No one offers to help, until Vovoka abruptly drops his bag and seizes the bed by its middle. Amazed, the two find themselves all but towed with it out into the arcade.

"Thank you," Cory gasps. "My heavens, Ser Vovoka, you *are* strong!"

But she's speaking to a closed door. The artist has dropped the bed in the arcade and retired into his room.

"Well!" says Kip. "Myr Yule, Doctor Hiner, since this bed is for one of you, perhaps you might give us a hand?"

"If only *I* could," says lame old Doctor Ochter, staring meaningfully at Yule.

Thus encouraged, the pair put down their bags and the bed is soon in the unfinished room, which now looks pleasantly habitable.

"A minim, Myrrin," Kip says as Ochter leaves. "Most

regrettably, the regs say we must inspect your luggage. No choice. Everyone else went through it back at Central. It'd be actionable if we don't.''

"Oh for—! This is *the* last straw,'' Yule cries. "Of all the damned insults—on top of everything—''

"And search us, too, perhaps?'' Hiner inquires viciously.

"Not at all.'' Kip steps behind him. "Sorry.'' With deftness acquired in wartime days, he runs his hands down Hiner's flinching body, pats his pouches.

"We hate it a lot more than you do.'' Cory has hoisted their bags onto the new vitrex table. "If only they'd give me a scanner. We do appreciate your cooperation.''

Yule's and Hiner's faces are making it plain that their "cooperation'' relates chiefly to Kip's commanding height and both Korsos' notably superior condition.

Their persons reveal nothing, and their bags hold only the normal travel items plus a mass of multimodal recording equipment and water-planet gear. It disconcerts the Korsos for a minim when they realize that no oxy tanks, pumps, or scuba gear are in Hiner's bags. Of course! All Hiner has to do is to uncover his gills and dive in. Spooky.

Kip recalls illustrations; Aquafolk's gill-covers ride on two large, fleshy masses running down from under the ears past the collarbones. The covers are hard and horny and open along one side, like clamshells, to flood water in over the oxygenating tissues. That's why Aquapeople wear big high collars, like Hiner's cloak, on land.

The Aquaform is a long-ago Human genetic engineering triumph, which breeds true. They're interfertile with ordinary Humans but, both by circumstance and desire, seldom mingle socially. Briefly, Kip wonders what the women are like. . . .

Meanwhile Cory has been rooting among Hiner's coldsuits and runs onto some gas propellant cans that could shoot anything.

'What are these, Doctor Hiner?''

"Pure oxygen—in case I get into dead water, swamp and so

363

on. . . . Really, are you going to mess up everything I packed?''

Kip sees Cory frown and knows she's wishing hard for that scanner. Anything could be in those assorted containers—not to mention the linings, pads, handles, and the unfamiliar electronic equipment.

"That's lovely music, I envy you," Cory says pleasantly, reading a title.

"Don't paw that. Be careful," Hiner snaps.

Kip clears his throat.

On the last bag, Cory pulls out a bronze-and-glass object and sniffs. "Myr Yule, what *is* this?"

"An antique hookah," Yule answers sullenly. "My water-pipe."

"It burns plant leaves?"

"Plant? Oh, yes."

"I'm sorry, but we must hold this for you while you're here. You didn't know, of course, but the Dameii are violently sensitive to any form of carbohydrate smoke. Do you have any other smoking materials?"

"No. Oh—a few cheroots."

"I'll take them if I may, please. And perhaps you'll check your pockets. Combustion lighters are just as dangerous."

"But I won't smoke near them! I enjoy a pipe at bedtime, and they won't be coming in here."

Kip takes over. "Look, we wouldn't do this if it wasn't necessary. When Myr Cory says 'violently sensitive' she means it. Adult Dameii can be knocked over merely by being in a room where people smoked some days ago. Actual smoke is like a blow on the head—it might kill a child. Why do you think we use an electric car? We can't even lubricate it with hydrocarbons. Fire is their worst nightmare-symbol." He decides not to add the part about burning wings.

"We've finally persuaded one Damei family to live near Humans, and we're not about to permit them to be driven off. I can sympathize with you, I smoked before I came here.

But you will please hand over all burnable or combustible materials *right now*. You'll get them safely back when you leave."

Docilely enough, Yule collects a handful of foil-wrapped objects Cory had taken for CO_2-indicator cartridges.

"And you, Myr—Doctor Hiner?"

"Don't smoke . . . but if they're so sensitive, how do you get your electricity? Assuming you have hydrogen generators like everyone, how do you heat the hydride?"

Hiner isn't stupid.

"There's a Federation power-cell buried three hundred meters under the hostel. They had to run the shaft in from the cliffside, under water."

Hiner whistles.

"Yes. But nothing was too costly to repair the situation here. You'll hear about that."

Hiner nods ungraciously, and Cory and Kip depart after delivering one more severe warning to Yule.

"That baby has held out a few," Kip tells her as the door clashes to. "I know smokers. Lucky the *V'yrre* wind is on; it's blowing away from them to us."

"That's why Wyrra built there." Cory smiles worriedly. "I wish I hadn't put those two on the Damei end. Maybe I—"

"Maybe you can sit down." Kip lays firm hold of his mate's arm to prevent her doing more and fairly hauls her back to the lounge, singing out, "Visit to the Damei village just before solar noon. You'll be called."

Looking out on the drive, they glimpse Zannez and his troupe, en route to their rooms in the other wing.

"And what do we call *them*?" Cory murmurs, only half-facetiously, as they reach their own private chamber behind the "Admin." door.

"One fairly strange kettle of fish," Kip says reflectively. "Still, remember that lot of Sleeping-God worshippers we got first time?"

"Whew!" Cory shakes out her rich brown hair.

"I wonder if we'll ever see Bram again?" Kip's tone changes. "Speaking of which, if the Planet Administrator has a moment, I have a problem requiring her undivided attention. . . ."

A wordless time later, Cory pulls back.

"A minim, darling—I have to go up and call the Patrol."

"Huh? What for?"

"To get that uncleared pair off-planet."

"What?" Kip recaptures her. "Wait, honey. Think. Aren't you overreacting? What makes you think their story's not straight? I saw no signs they were together, or that they didn't loathe being here. Did you? Hmm?"

"No. But cold-sleep just doesn't fail by itself, Kip. I asked the Log Officer, she'd never heard of a mislabeling case. And two at once, right here, on the one planet where Central clearances are essential."

"Two is just as likely as one, when you think of it. And it's made by Human hands. Everything Human slips a bit, sooner or later."

"Granted. But the fact remains that I'd be letting two unauthorized strangers stay on Damiem."

"Well, go ahead. But Dayan won't thank you, he's taking the cruiser over by that new Grid-relay asteroid so his men can catch the games. And the Moom ship will be back almost as soon . . . Oh, honey, come on."

Cory sighs deeply, looking into her lover's eyes. She knows she's overfond, but what he says is true.

"You really, really think it's all right, Kip?"

"I really, really do, Cory my love."

"Well . . . okay, then. Oh, Kip—"

Later, she contents herself with putting the facts on the routine-channel landing report, attention Captain Dayan of *Rimshot*.

III

NOVA MINUS 12 HOURS:
First View

The musical summons that rings through the hostel comes from an extraordinary crystal gong and hammer hanging by the main doors. Kip's cheery parade-call follows: "All aboard to visit the Dameii! Departure as soon as loaded."

He is standing by the jitney-bus, now freed of its trailer. His normally carefree grin is somewhat tense. As usual when visitors come, he's torn; he loves seeing others enthralled by "his" Dameii—but will these strangers appreciate their beauty and delicacy? Will they understand it is a privilege? Or will they do some crude thing to upset the Dameii and undo the trust he's spent years building? This is a perfectly rational fear, he tells himself; Damiem is his first big solo assignment as a xenologist, and he's not about to have it messed up.

Linnix, looking much refreshed, is first to join him, followed by Zannez and his four young ones. Little Prince Pao comes trotting from the observatory, and Hiner comes along the arcade.

"This gong is another piece of Damei work," Kip tells them. "Spectacular, isn't it?"

Hiner is frowning at the gong. "How do they work glass if they're so spooked by fire?"

"Good question," says Kip. "Might take a while to guess the answer, too: burning lenses! What they can do with a set of lenses on a sunny day is hard to believe. And then there are big deposits of high-grade natural vocanic glass about; their ancestors worked it like obsidian, by flaking and grinding. They still do hack out the rough forms before they pick up a lens, unless it's a melt for casting or blowing. They place a lot of importance on the sound, too. They have whole orchestras of crystal percussion instruments. We have some nice recordings I'll play for you. I wish you could hear it live, but they don't play with strangers around."

"Just exactly why are they so shy?" Zannez asks.

Kip stares hard at him. "Don't you know, really? Do the words 'Star Tears' mean *anything* to you? Stars Tears? *Stars Tears*?"

"Uh . . . no. Except I seem to have heard of some exotic mythical drink."

"Just so. Well, I'll tell you the story after we've seen the village. We won't be able to get close, you realize. We view it across a ravine. You better have your longest-range equipment. We're going there now because it's when the youngsters fly home from school; you'll get the best chance to see people. But I warn you, the story is rough. Even I hate to tell it. It might be hard on your kids, especially Stareem and, uh, Eleganza."

He glances at Prince Pao, confirming his impression that that young man could cope.

"After Gridworld?" Stareem's chuckle is a strange sound from her tender face. "Not likely."

"All right, but I don't want to add to your nightmares. Now, Zannez, don't fret about seats in the bus. We get out

368

and do the last part on foot. Their ears can't take motors; we'd find a deserted village if we drove up to the ridge."

Cory ambles up carrying containers of juice, which she stows in the jitney.

"What's all this about nightmares?" little Doctor Ochter asks genially as he hobbles toward them.

"The Stars Tears story. Zannez wanted to know why the Dameii are shy. I'll tell it for anyone who cares to listen, after we've seen the village."

"Oh." The little man sobers quickly. "Of course. This is where it took place, isn't it? And these are the people. Oh, my. . . . Well, I'll be grateful to get a straight account after all the bits and whispers."

"By the way, Doc, there'll be some walking uphill, about half a kilom. You'll be all right with that leg?"

"I can make it all right." Ochter smiles wryly, patting his vest pocket. "I've a shot for special occasions, and this is certainly one. But what about the Lady Marquise and her sister?"

"They aren't coming," Cory says. "She's interested only in the effects of the Star on her sister tonight." Grinning, she adds privately to Kip, "Bram told me. Through the door. It seems the Lady believes she should keep her sister stimulated."

They both laugh unmaliciously, happy for their old friend's good luck.

Ser Vovoka has now appeared and is eyeing the jitney.

"Now we may be able to show you some beauty worthy of your artistic interest," Kip tells him. "The Dameii are acknowledged to be among the very loveliest humanoid races, although they are in fact evolved from pseudoinsectile forms."

Vovoka gives one of his politer grunts.

"Superinsects, eh?" Zannez exclaims. "You mean like those spiders? Giant praying mantises?"

"Nothing of the sort; don't get up hopes of some new alien monsters. Their only insectoid features, outside of the wings and arms that indicate three pairs of functional limbs, are

369

some peculiarities of the mandibular substructure, and a few traces of exoskeleton. It's one of the Damiem mysteries I'm studying.''

"Myr Korso," says Hiner suddenly. "Regretfully, I fear I shall have to miss the tour. I feel much more unwell than I thought.''

In fact, Kip sees, Hiner's face has taken on a greenish pallor.

"Oh, dear, what a shame," says Cory. "Is there something we can do for you?''

"Not at all, not at all. . . ." The Aquaman's eyes turn toward the cool blue of the lake below. "It may be that I've been on land rather long. I assume it won't cause any difficulties if I go for a swim while you're gone?''

"Heavens, no—and I'll bring you some extra towels just as soon as we return. How thoughtless of me!''

"And by the way," Kip puts in, "the spot we normally go in is at that little beach down to the left. You'll find the path passing your end of the arcade. There's a good deal of fallen timber in a lake like this, and we've cleared out from there. . . . And the area right in front of the hostel cliff is believed to be the deepest part—but you'll soon know more about our lake than we've ever guessed. The original survey had a waterman—sorry, I mean an Aquaman on it; he reported no dangerous snakes or fish, and we've never found any. So, pleasant swimming to you.''

Hiner moves off without reply, his narrow shoulders raised as if huddled against cold, though the day is warm.

"Maybe you kind of leaned too hard on the bugs, boss," says Hanno Ek.

"Huh? Oh . . ." says Zannez. "I forgot.''

"What? Forgot what?" Kips asks.

"The bugs. Insects," replies Hanno. "He's a waterman—I mean, an Aquaman.''

"So? You've lost me, help.''

"I thought everybody knew that," says Hanno.

"Knew *what*?"

"Hanno, somebody's going to kill you one day if you don't straighten up." Zannez grinned. " 'Scuse my son here, Kippo. What he means is that all Aquapeople—*all* of them—loathe, hate, and fear insects. Men, women, babies, grandmothers—everyone. It's so widely known it's become a saying: 'I love her like a waterman loves bugs.' Outsiders don't know what started it—some horrible predator on one of their first worlds, maybe. Of course, it isn't born in them. They let it go on as a tradition. But it's real enough. With some special effects. I've seen 'em get sick, go berserk, and I don't mean joking. I forgot Hiner for a minim or I'd never have said all that. Now I've ruined his sight-seeing trip."

"Whew!" said Kip. "Well, live and learn. . . . Did you know all that, Cor?"

"Umh . . . yes, I knew there was something. . . . Oh, dear, Myr Zannez, what a shame. Maybe your inventive mind can think up some way to repair it. Meanwhile we'll just have to hope he really wanted a swim, too."

"Right," says Kip. "And now, where's that other blessing, Yule? I'm not about to let you all miss the flight for him."

"I'll go raise him," the boy Snake offers. "Uh-oh, there he is."

Yule is sauntering across the drive from the direction of the Damei grove.

"Didn't I warn you to stay away from that area?" Kip snaps as Yule comes in range. "No, I guess you were inside when I told Zannez. My fault. But in the future, everyone will stay strictly away from that grove of trees."

"Oh?" says Yule. "What's so special about them?"

"That's the home of the Damei family who have volunteered to interact with us. If anyone bothers them, they'll leave."

"So?" asks Yule rudely.

Little Doctor Ochter lays his hand on Kip's arm to check the oncoming explosion. "Young man, I assume that for some reason you don't mind spending time in a Patrol ship's brig. But allow me to exercise my academic status and point out that you are not in a research situation here. Moreover, there are still those who listen to Ari Ochter, and you could find future grant credits very, very hard to come by. In case you didn't know, you are on the planet where the Stars Tears tragedy took place, and you will behave precisely as the Federation representatives suggest, or the results will be most unpleasant in career terms.''

Yule takes this in silence and seems subdued until they hear him muttering, ''Stars Tears, eh? Lot of money in that. Lots and lots.''

''There will be no further comment from you.'' Ochter's voice cracks like a whip. ''Especially along those lines.''

Kip's stomach has been giving him cold jolts. He sees that Cory hasn't heard the interchange, and he's struck by regret for the advice he gave her earlier on. Still . . . what could such a shallow idiot do, even assuming Hiner helps him? And Hiner seems to have too much regard for his own well-being to get mixed up with Yule in some wild scheme that would only bring disaster. As these thoughts run through his head, Kip is swinging into the jitney's drive seat, waving them all in.

''Thanks for the help, Doc,'' he says as the small man limps by. ''How much lead time you want for that shot?''

''None.'' Ochter smiles. ''The words *'Here we are'* will give my chemical angel all the time it needs to work.''

Zannez and his troupe are in the row of seats just behind Kip and Cory. Kip takes pity on the hardworking man.

''We have an empty seat in front, Zannez, if that'll help you.''

''That's what I call heart,'' Zannez exclaims. ''Ek, you've had the least exposure—scramble over by the Korsos. Star, sit right behind him where you can put your arms around his neck.''

Little Prince Pao, watching critically, nods to himself.

The other young couple sit beside Stareem, while Zannez climbs into the row behind, between Vovoka and Ochter, with his gear. "Beautiful setup, Kippo. I'll try not to get my stuff in you Myrrin's way."

"Put some back here with me," offers Linnix from behind him, where she sits alone. Kip had noticed her pausing to see where Yule settled before choosing her place.

The ground-jitney starts off. Instead of turning toward the spaceport, they continue to run straight along a broad, smooth, meadowy avenue, climbing toward a range of low, tree-covered hills.

"Lovely and peaceful, isn't it?" Kip remarks sardonically. "This was the main route for the Stars Tears gangs in their horrible heyday. It got widened in the fighting with the Federation troops; you'll hear all about that. . . . In early days Cory and I were still rooting the odd live shell out of the flowers." He raises his voice. "Next ridge is our point, Myrrin. We stop and get out about halfway up, where that line of trees ends."

From the corner of his eye he sees little Ochter's hypo case appear as if by magic. With the deftness of long practice the doctor's hand disappears under the corner of his bushcoat, aiming for his hip. A flicker of pain crosses his face, and then the empty syrette is being pocketed as the jitney draws to a stop. What? Cancer of the pelvis or femur, Kip guesses. No fun. But the little man seems to enjoy life thoroughly, and his is not a bad way to end, chasing novas.

"You'll find those trails to the top quite easy going. I suggest you scatter onto different paths going up. You'll come to an old cross-trench just under the summit. Get into it, and do not—repeat, *do not*—stand up. Anybody who stands up, or talks, or tries to even crawl beyond it, or makes noise, will spoil it for everyone else, and I'll personally see that he regrets it.

"Of course the Dameii know we're here. That trench is the

agreed-on limit of approach, and we'll get a few nice clear looks from it before they start disappearing.''

He hands out binoculars to those without their own.

"Now remember to look closely at people's bare backs, from the wing-line to where the buttocks would begin on us. You'll see the glands work, if you're lucky. The kids will be coming home right over our heads, and the parents are out on their porches, waiting. The females are the slightly larger ones. The homes are *high* up, you realize, mostly built around the main trunk and forks, just where the heavy leafage begins.

"As I said, we've notified the elders of our visit and obtained their consent, provided we cause no commotion. But the other Dameii don't like it. As they get tired of being stared at by us, they'll start to slip out of sight. Most of them won't actively leave or hide in the central hut, but a Damei in a tree can vanish right in front of your nose. Moreover, they've bred and trained some of those flying leaves you noticed by the spaceport to cloud around us.

"If anyone is wondering how these paths and the trench got here, it's hard to believe with everything so peaceful now, but this was the final assault jump-off for the Federation. You can see the extent—it took a Fed battalion.

"Now up you go—remember, no talking! And look for those backs.''

He waves them on, finger to lips.

Then he and Cory scramble up a side path until they come to the trench, at a bend that was an old sector point. The trench is shallow here; they lie down in it and Kip motions to Cory to start watching the Dameii; she's had less chance to view them than he. She wriggles forward and parts the grass, while he turns to check on the tourists.

Doctor Ochter, freed from pain, is climbing well. Zannez is frantically trying to catch his troupe coming up and simultaneously get first look at the Dameii. Suddenly he bursts into muffled swearing and gesticulates savagely at something in the brush. Kip peers and sees little Prince Pao solicitously attempting to assist the larger and athletic Stareem up a gulch. Comical.

Cory glances back, grins at the sight. Zannez' face is turning as red as his suit; the prince ignores him until Stareem is on smooth ground. Then he swerves aside and becomes a normal boy again.

Meanwhile Yule has been climbing steadily, looking at everything, even back toward the hostel. Such attentiveness rather surprises Kip. Tall Vovoka, bringing up the rear, surprises him, too, by his inattention. He seems interested only in his frequent scans of the eastern sky. Well, light-sculpture is probably purely abstract.

Cory beckons urgently to him, glowing-eyed and nodding yes. He knows she's seeing what they hoped for—the Dameii out in plain view on the circular porches that surround each sleeping-hut. Damiem has no winters, so construction is tropical.

It's almost time for the children's noon flight home.

This village—his special village—comprises thirty-one families with a total of about forty school-age young. The school is about a fifteen-minim flight away, in a stand of old-forest trees near another of the numerous lakes, where it serves several villages. Schooling is far more serious business now that the Galaxy has come to Damiem; in fact, one of the Korsos' main jobs is the composition of texts to go in the beautiful tissue-leaved Damei books.

Kip takes a final look around; all his charges are in place and behaving themselves. Even Yule has shed his sneer and looks like what he probably is, a decent young scientist. Zannez is aiming everything he has at the village, while his four young actors stare transfixed. Good; Kip crawls up to the viewhole Cory has made him and looks.

The scene is as he'd envisioned it: Dameii perched on every porch, a few with wings relaxed, the rest with their great vanes overhead, gently fanning the air in anticipation.

The first impression is always of those wings and their beauty, as though enormous flowers have opened petals in the trees. It's only after absorbing these that the eye can take in the even greater beauty of the Damei form and motion. Alone of all the alien races Kip knows, the Dameii are exquisite, by Human standards, in every aspect.

In early days Kip had tried to describe them to friends but soon despaired. His words wouldn't convey their surreal elegance of limb and wing, the way they flowed naturally from pose to pose, surprising and caressing the eye in a series of delicious visual shocks. And it was more than beauty for the eye; the heart was caught by their fragility, paradoxically combined with the gift of soaring flight. Could they have some unnatural power to bewitch?

He'd ended by simply listing their features.

Color: This village is large enough to show almost the full range of Damei coloration. Most have ivory skins and masses of green-glinted, feathery bronze hair. Their head hair merges into lustrous bronze manes or mantles growing over the joining of wings and body and running out to form the upper margins of the wings. The wings themselves—both the enormous upper wings and the shorter, stronger underwings—are clear greenish paned, but iridescent, so that they flash a rainbow of hues. The panes are edged with dark furred ribs that carry the oxygen-rich Damei blood.

Among the bronze-haired Dameii are a few of spectacularly deviant coloring. Two families have brilliant red manes, one fiery vermilion, the other pure dark ruby. Their skins are cool white, and all their wing-panes are in various lucent pinks edged red, a startling effect.

But loveliest of all, to Kip's eyes, is a turquoise-green mutation. These Dameii have hair and manes like rivers of emerald, verdigris-tinted skin, and pale wing-panes of electric green blue. They like to dress in a deep black gauze that sets off their exotic beauty to perfection.

The Damei bodies are humanoid, and look child-size between those wings, though they're actually over man height. The torsos and limbs are preternaturally slender and elegant in line. Their backs are long; close inspection reveals the long mothlike wing-bases that serve the wing-muscles in lieu of the breast "keel" that other winged races bear. The Dameii walk so little that their hipjoints are no fleshier than elbows.

The gauzy garments they wear reveal this; they may be cut long or short according to fancy and often are wrapped high at the throat; but always they dip low behind to join across the buttock area, leaving backs bare below the wings. Their dress is marvelously embroidered in the rich hues of natural dyes and set with foliage patterns and gleaming native jewels.

No sex differences are apparent at this distance, save for the slightly larger female size—another possibly insectoid remnant. Their faces also are too far to be distinctly seen, giving only the impression of pale ovals dominated by huge slanted eyes, shadowed by feathery brows and lashes of the same color as the flowing hair. Kip knows their features to be slight and smooth, inhuman but as appealingly modeled as a human child's. It is still hard to remember that the Dameii convey expression not by facial changes, but by wing-posture; and nuances of emotion by hands in continual graceful movement.

So much for plain description, Kip thinks. The magic, the essential beauty of these winged people, escapes all words. He pulls back to look rather savagely along the line of tourists, willing them to grasp the vision. They all are quiet and seem intent. So far so good. He sighs explosively and returns to his view.

For a minim more the scene stays. Then the Dameii seem simultaneously to tire of being spied on and begin to melt away. There is no concerted flight—only a simple sidestep to the far side of the tree trunk, or a downsweep of wings that lifts the owner to an invisible perch in the leafage above, or a wing-folding that allows the waiting parent to shelter behind a slight upturn in a porch wall. Before the watchers' eyes, the village empties.

In a few breaths, not an adult is in plain sight save for two elders, who are the Korsos' main contacts and spokesmen for their people. One of these is Quiyst, who was at the spaceport, and the other is an equally aged Damei named Feanya. These two sit in apparent calm, sharing a basket of dried *quiyna* fruit and watching the Humans. Only their nervously raised wings betray their tension. Kip waves to them and receives a minimal headbow in acknowledgment.

Seeing only deserted porches, several of Kip's guests begin to murmur and stir, but Kip glares and hisses at them to be still. The "trained" leaves he'd spoken of are now coming into evidence, flapping about distractingly.

And then comes the moment he awaits—above and around them, the trees are suddenly alive with a rush and tumult of wings and musical voices almost too high for Human hearing. The Damei children are coming home.

The young Dameii's wings and hair are bright yellow to silvery gold; their coming is like a sunlit cloud.

All ages and sexes fly together; here and there older children are helping young ones keep up by allowing them to ride their legs. Almost all carry homework. Seeing that, Kip flinches; he is late with his share of a text on Human and other off-world physiology.

Seeing the line of Humans, a few pause to look, or rise higher. One older child laughingly dives at them, ending in a swift aerobatic stunt. But most of the young are too eager to reach their homes to bother with the strangers.

As the children reach their home porches, many of the parents draw them into seclusion; but there are couples whose joy overpowers their dislike of Human eyes, and who stay hugging and petting their youngsters in plain sight. To Kip's satisfaction, one of the nearest families has turned their bare backs to the watchers, and all can plainly see the faintly colored exudates of emotion springing from the lower back skin-glands—those terrible, priceless, scented juices that have cost the Dameii so much agony and nearly ended their race.

"They're really fond of those kids," says a too-loud whisper near him. The insufferable Mordecai Yule again. Kip shoots him a bloodcurdling glare, joined by Ochter. But it's too late. The near family hurriedly slips from sight, and others, taking the cue, do likewise. In no time the village is visually empty again.

But the general movement has shown one thing more: Beautiful as the adults are, they are surpassed in sheer exquisiteness by their children.

"Well, that tears it." Kip stands up and speaks normally. "Now you go." He walks along the trench to get them started down. When they are all below ear and eye range, he gestures for a halt.

"We were about at the end of the allotted time, anyway—they want their midday meal now. Most of them eat communally, in that big house the elders are sitting by. . . . I think you've had one of the best viewings of any group. How did you like it?"

There are murmurs of almost wordless appreciation. The girl Linnix, still gazing back toward the village with longing eyes, demands softly, "What can you say? What can you say when you see real live actual angels? I never . . . I never expected, I never knew what they meant. . . ." She falls silent.

"Do we get the story now?" Zannez asks with unaccustomed gentleness.

Kip sighs. "Yes. If I must. Funny thing, after all those years and tellings I still hate to. Worse each time. But we have to move farther down—take that grassy space under the trees, below the jitney."

"Why not in the bus?" Zannez asks, struggling to collect his stuff.

"Because," says Cory, "I'm going to be in there out of earshot. Any of you who find you don't want to hear more can join me. I'll take some of your gear, Zannez, if that's a problem.''

"Thank you very much, Myr Cory.'' He hands over his used canisters and she strides determinedly away.

IV

NOVA MINUS 11 HOURS:
Abominations of Old Days

When the tourists are assembled around him under the trees, Kip fetches another long sigh.

"Well. This all began, you understand, long before the Federation, but it ended only in recent times. I've spoken with a couple of old Spacers who were in the final action. One still has bad dreams. . . .

"The start came sometime in dim antiquity when it was discovered that those secretions you saw on the Dameii's backs have a most delicious taste to Humans. There was only a little Human space travel then, and a party or two of explorers passed by. But someone must have been up to something, because that's a strange thing to find out.

"Later it was discovered—gods know how—that if you fermented and distilled the stuff, you got a liqueur that wasn't just a nice drink; it was superlative, literally out of the worlds. It had psychoactive properties, you see, it produced a real happiness—with no side effects or hangovers. It's been described as being better than heaven because you didn't have to die. Heaven for a shilling, as some old writer said—call it our quarter credit. But this cost no quarter credit, it cost a cool thousand Gal. Or more.

"Naturally I've never tasted any, but those old Spacers I mentioned told me of people trading their life savings and mortgaging their homes for the stuff. One man literally sold another his wife and daughters, just for one of those tiny amethyst flagons it was sold in. That was the last, you see. Even before that, people would pay anything for what was called a good 'vintage.' It was only for the ultrarich. . . . The quantities, of course, were minute. You saw their backs shine—a cc or two of raw material at most.

"Unfortunately, this happened at the time of the great rare-asteroid rush, some of which came out here beyond Grunions. You may have read about that in history. So space traffic through here for a time was heavy. It must have been Spacers from the rush, stopping or wrecked here, who discovered how to make the liqueur and started the subsequent horror.

"At first they would just capture a Damei or two—they caught them at night, with stick-tight nets over the central huts—and scrape the prisoners' backs with a special long curved open tube. Sometimes they'd scrape the whole skin away and distill that. . . . Then, when they had enough distilled—a dozen or so tiny flasks—they'd seal them and send them back to their agent on some rich world.

"They soon had to start counterfeit-proofing them magnetically; the stuff became a sensation among the rich everywhere. Nobody knew where it came from—they kept that secret till the end—or how it was made. But there was an aura of something strange about it, and it picked up the name 'Stars Tears.'

"Then began the worst part. These men weren't dummies, see, or at least the dummies got eliminated early. As the

382

credits piled in, there were gang wars for control of the trade. Anyway, someone started testing correlations between the quality and all kinds of factors, like food and other conditions, among them, between the mood of the victim and the eventual quality of the liqueur.

"I mentioned 'vintages.' Well, this had nothing to do with years, as people thought. It had to do with what the prisoner was feeling when they took the exudates. They found that happiness—gods know how they managed *that*—gave almost no flavor. Physical pain, plus fear, which they'd started with, gave what was called the 'standard vintage,' which was terrific. And then they found that *psychic* pain alone, or mixed with just a trace of joy, gave the most extraordinary quality of all.

"How do you produce purely psychic pain? . . . The bastards would capture a young couple, and after discussing before them which one's wings they would saw off first— imagine the poor lovely things, tied up helpless, with these monsters scraping like mad—'' Kip was having trouble with his voice. "They would decide, say, on the girl, and get set to carve her up before his eyes. Dameii don't faint, or pass out—there was no relief. Then they'd pretend that something was wrong, that her juices were no good, and finally start to release her, until the two really believed they were setting her free. That gave the brief joy trick. And then they'd laugh and tie her up again; and simply torture her until she died before his eyes. They even had the timing worked out to keep the glands working as long as possible. . . . That gave the super vintage, from him. And the 'standard' from her. And when she was dead . . . they just tortured him to death, too, for more 'standard.' They had evolved methods I can't think about; someone showed me shots of one of their torture rooms before they burned them. . . . And all that for only a few cc's of raw material. When distilled, worth millions, of course.

"And then—oh, Apherion, you've seen them; the beauty,

the vulnerability—they have no more defenses than a butterfly. They can't even scream. To call the devils that exploited them beasts is an insult to the animal world.

"Just to give you an idea—over time the raiders left quite a load of writings, recordings, notes. Some are so atrocious you can't read them; at least, I couldn't. But I've talked with people who had to. Not only for tracing down people, but for tracking money—all credits derived from that trade were forfeit to the Fed, you see—and here's the strange thing: Nowhere, but nowhere, in no place and no way is there any mention whatever that the race they were exterminating is of the greatest humanoid beauty. You'd think someone, some-where, even out of sadism, maybe, would note it. No; they might as well have been dealing with a race of hairy bowling balls. Of course, the ethical horrors would be the same if the Dameii *were* hairy bowling balls, don't misunderstand me. It's merely an indication of a human type so blind that of the hundreds—or more—engaged in the destruction, not one would remark on what it was that they destroyed. Especially when they—and here's where I simply can't go on.

"*They discovered their love for their children.* . . . You've seen that, too; these people love their youngsters as much or maybe even more than their mates. Plus, you have two parents and maybe several kids and aunts and uncles—so the quantity problem—"

He breaks off and sits with lowered head, staring unseeing at the horizon where the Star would rise. Then he goes on more calmly.

"Those of you who don't have imagination enough to see what followed, I pity. You'll have to work it out. Those who do I pity more. . . . And this went on, you see, no one knows how long, until in the Last War a small Federation cruiser followed up certain rumors and found Damiem.

"Give them all credit. They didn't wait for reinforcements—they just went on in with everything they had, down to the galley boys, and started cleaning the whole mess out. They didn't take any prisoners, either—at first they hanged or bayonetted the gangsters right on the line, until they found it was upsetting the Dameii worse. So then they just threw them in some old tunnels and sealed and gassed them.

"But they needed reinforcements and more reinforcements before the end—the gangs had quite an organization by then, and money can buy you a lot of mercenaries and weapons. Too many good Spacers died here; I'll show you the cemetery tomorrow, including the two fifteen-year-old galley lads. But the end came fast—right near here, as I've mentioned. Then they leveled everything the gangs had built and got the hell off the planet fast. They figured the Dameii's best chance for recovery—they'd stopped having kids, see—was to be left in utter peace. So they stationed one small, very quiet human observer who spoke Damei—they left him a tent, in a new place—and parked a blockade squadron in orbit.

"It took five years, but finally the observer spotted one baby, and the next year, two more. And after about a decade he was replaced by another acceptable observer, who stayed thirty years and built the nub of a station. That's the man Cory and I took over from, and now things are as you see them.

"Ah, but wait—I was forgetting. Of course there was a network distributing this stuff back in the Galaxy, and that's where the big, big money was. Enough money to bribe a planet, in ordinary terms. But this wasn't ordinary. To their credit, the Feds cleaned that out, too, although I don't know any details because, of course, it was the Special Branch. I do know that a couple of planetary governments got turned inside out and there weren't any arguments about compassion or Rehab. Those criminals ended up just plain dead.

"And even now you can't get a permit to use anything like the name, or market anything drinkable in little purple bottles, even cough syrup. Some of you may have run into the purple-bottle ban and wondered. Now you know.

"Well, that's the period at the end of the last sentence of

the blackest and probably the most loathsome chapter of Human history in space. . . . And you should know, too, that there's a permanent reward out for information leading to any activities about Damiem, or even too much talk.

"I hope you understand now, Yule, why your remarks about money were out of line? And why no similar manifestations of ignorance—not to say crassness—will be tolerated."

There is a silence, broken only by sighs and a few noseblows from the Zannez group. The two girls have drawn very close together, and Snake has an arm around Hanny Ek's shoulders.

Kip throws down the handful of grass he'd been braiding as he talked and gets up. "And now it's back to the car."

As the party approaches the jitney, they're surprised to see Cory standing beside it, talking with old Quiyst, Feanya, and three other senior Dameii. Their tall wings go involuntarily aloft from nervousness at so many oncoming Humans.

Kip gestures the others to stop and goes forward alone to greet them courteously. In a moment he turns and calls to the group. "I'm going to introduce you. When you hear me say your name, just step a pace forward and sort of bow. And then stay put where you are. This is very unusual, and we don't want to foul it up."

In a moment they hear him call. "Doctor Ari Ochter!" Ochter limps a pace forward and bows. The elders bow back, staring intently.

"Myr Stareem Fada!" And the ceremony repeats. As he finishes the list, they notice that the visitors' wings have definitely relaxed.

"And now, what may we do for you?" Kip inquires in Damei. As they speak together, Cory comes over to the Humans to explain.

"They say that since we come to look at them, they, too, wish to look at us. The learning shouldn't be all so one-sided, they say. This is a point which has come up before, by the way. I try to tell them that we have no objection in principle, but the sticker is that they want to inspect us individually *without clothes.*" Her normally glowing face shows a high flush. The others suddenly realize that this is the world of the Spacers' Code.

"I've tried to explain that we have, uh, tribal taboos there, but it doesn't go down well. Also, they want to see infants."

There is a pause.

"Well!" says Stareem explosively. "I can't do anything about the babies, but I've stripped for clowns all over the Galaxy. So have you, Bride, and Snake and Hanny, stripped and a lot more. If it'd really help . . . here, Zanny, hold my junk."

"Really? You mean you wouldn't mind?" Kip notices that the little prince is nodding and smiling encouragingly at the girl.

"Any time!" Stareem's voice is muffled as she pulls her turtleneck over her head. Hannibal Ek, not to be outdone, begins unzipping his suit.

"Oy, Kippo!" Cory calls. "Tell them to look here! Oh— meanwhile, I strongly suggest, in fact I insist, that all other Humans step back under those trees with me. Yes, you too, Myr Yule."

The two beautiful stark-bare youngsters, one white, one black, start toward Kip and the five old Dameii. Bridey and Snake are getting undressed to join them. The seven other Humans stand in an awkward group beside the tree trunks, trying not to stare, as the elders gravely begin to circle around and around the show-kids. Zannez has unlimbered all his gear.

Cory goes over to the inspection group, her eyes carefully averted from Hanno and Snake.

"I must say you four are terrific good sports," she says. "You've no idea how much this means. Kip and I were going to have to nerve ourselves . . ." Her voice trails off embarrassedly.

"Absolutely," Kip agrees. "You deserve medals for Galactic unity."

"I guess this is the only worthwhile stripping I've ever done," says Stareem. "Look, what's he trying to say?"

One of the new elders is twittering incomprehensible Galactic and gesturing to her.

"This is Elder Zhymel." The old Damei bows. "He wants to know if he may touch your upper back, you know, where the wings should be."

"Feel away," says Stareem. Her eyes open wide as the old Damei very lightly lays his long fingers on her shoulder blades. "Hey—it's like being brushed with electric feathers. It tickles! You better warn him to press harder or I may sneeze."

They get the matter adjusted, and other Damei take their turns. Cory says to Kip, "I have an idea, subject to your xenological approval. What if you tell them they're seeing exceptionally perfect specimens, very young, whom Humans consider superbeautiful?

"Then tell him the rest of us are unwilling to strip because we are far less beautiful? We deteriorate very fast with age or we've other defects considered ugly, and we don't wish to offend others' eyes. Be sure they get the whole thing. I think it'll clear the air, don't you? And I suppose it's essentially true."

"Righto. Good idea, Cor. Elders Quiyst and Feanya, et al., listen." He delivers a long melodious speech in Damei. The elders nod as if greatly enlightened but still look a trifle puzzledly at himself and Cory.

"Yes, yes," she says vigorously and, looking about, as if ashamed, pulls up her shorts' legs briefly. They get a glimpse of a nasty scar she'd picked up in her first tree-climbing days.

Kip thinks a moment, then opens his jerkin to show two wrinkles across his belly and hastily zips up again. This seems to satisfy and please the elders, who recommence their grave circuits of the four young people. Two go down on all fours to view the kids' toes and ankles; another takes out a small glass to inspect their nails and eyebrows, handing it around in turn. The scene would be hilarious, Kip thinks, if it hadn't been so serious for the Damei-Human future. As it is, Cory has to blow her nose twice to hide her giggles. Zannez is shooting like mad.

Just as it looks as if this may go on forever, little Ochter calls from the group by the trees.

"Myr Kip, I hate to be a bother, but this analgesic is wearing off fast, and it has some unpleasant side effects. Could you possibly take me—"

"Right. Sorry Doc. Can you hold out two minims more?"

"Oh, yes."

"Look, you great kids—is it possible you can repeat this act in the village tomorrow? I meant what I said about the value of what you've done here. Just say no if the village is too much."

"I'm perfectly game for the village," Bridey says. "How about you?"

"Count us in," they all say.

"You'll never know," Kip says, "or maybe you can guess. Look, a medal is probably beyond us, but I can personally guarantee you each a superofficial document attesting to your services to the Federation—all differently worded and signed and dripping with gold seals and special stamps."

"That's beautiful," Snake says.

"But you don't need to," Hanny Ek tells him. "After hearing what happened here I'd hang by my tail if it'd help. Funny thing, isn't it? That just the sort of people you needed wandered by? We all started as kid-porn stars, you know, to be blunt about it. I can just see Ser Vovoka—!"

Laughing, they bow farewell to the elders and run over to dress and rejoin the others, while Kip explains the offer to Quiyst. The elders seem extremely pleased; their now relaxed plumes make an odd curling, furling gesture he's never seen before.

With a final warning to keep their people under cover

when the Star brightens, Kip joins the others in the jitney, and they start down. Zannez hands over the last of the clothes and gets in heavily, for once neglecting his cameras.

"You must be exhausted, Myr Zannez," Linnix says sympathetically. "Lucky this planet has long days, you've worked yourself half to death before the Star you came for has even showed up."

"You'll all probably be glad to know that the next thing on the agenda is a nice long nap," Cory tells them. "There's food on call in the lounge when you want it, and I thought we could start a buffet supper about sunset. The Star doesn't rise till an hour after sundown, but it might be earlier tonight, being closer. And the sunsets alone are worth seeing. So we can have our appetizers and drinks at the bar, and then take our dinner plates out on the deck for the Star's rise."

"Excellent, excellent," says Ochter.

"Just so long as we do not miss any of the Star," Vovoka surprises them all by saying in his curiously accented tones. "I think that is a very good plan."

The jitney speeds hostelward down the calm grassy avenues, once the scene of so much blood and pain. Kip notices that the visitors are unusually silent. Good. Maybe they've been caught as he is by the beauty of what they've been allowed to see of Damiem; maybe their hearts are shadowed, like his, by the dreadful story of the Tears. But no stranger can really grasp it in an hour or two, he thinks. Even Cor doesn't totally get it; to her it's just one more job.

His handsome brow furrows; he tries to brush aside his perennial worry: Who will come after them to safeguard his precious, vulnerable winged people? How long will the Federation guard Damiem?

V

NOVA MINUS 10 HOURS:
Linnix of Beneborn

The girl Linnix has been increasingly impatient to get back
to the hostel. Despite the overpowering interest of the Dameii,
she has an interest of her own more compelling still, and she
feels no need of another nap. As the others make for their
rooms, she goes through the lounge and out to the deck, near
the infirmary's semitransparent vitrex walls. The infirmary
and Doctor Baramji's cubicle appear to be, as she feared,
empty.

To distract herself she watches the gyrations of the mobile
tree leaves, which flew up in a cloud on their arrival, now
settling back on their stems. Some look dusty and weak.
Linnix wonders if they followed the tour. And must they
return to their parent tree, or will a strange tree give them
harbor? Mysterious.

There is as yet no movement behind the vitrex; the doctor
is still with his sex-queen. To Linnix, the Lady Pardalianches,

like other planetary nobility she has tended on shipboard, seems somewhat more pathetic than impressive—and more than somewhat irritating in her self-centeredness.

To a man, she supposes the ultrafeminine body, the seductive promise of fleshy delights, reverses matters entirely. Especially a lonely man like Doctor Baramji, driven by those needs she doesn't really share. Doubtless he'll be with the Lady a long while yet.

But no! There's a figure moving behind the pale green vitrex.

With a silent prayer to the gods of chance—is it now the thousandth such prayer?—and knowing her own foolishness, she knocks.

"Come in, come in . . . Oh, it's you, Myr Linnis, is it? I fear I didn't catch your full name."

He is brewing an appetizing-smelling drink on the lab burner, having clearly just waked from a nap on the rumpled cot she can glimpse in his personal cubicle. His snow-white hair is wildly rumpled too, and he's barefoot.

"Linnix, actually," she tells him. "And I really have no family name. Just Linnix will do."

"Linnix it is." He rummages out a clean cup, spoon, and saucer. "And I'm Bram." He grins, pushing the white hair out of those brilliant blue-green eyes. "You'll share some of my kaffy? A very old drink made of dried beans, but cheering. My new lot just came in on your ship."

"I don't want to rob you." Linnix is thinking what a fine-looking older man he is. Not handsome, but well knit and wiry, no fat on him, and a rugged face that radiates both warmth and toughness, lit by those spectacular eyes. She redoubles her silent prayer, knowing it's hopeless but unable to still the longing.

"Let's sit here." He sweeps a chair clear for her. "Not as elegant as the deck, but I am not fit for public view. And now, what may I do for you, Myr Linnix?"

Sampling the intriguing kaffy, to which he's added a

sweetener, Linnix lets herself study him a moment more, postponing the death of hope. She notices what she hadn't seen before: several scar-lines in the tan of one elbow, and others running into the hair from his right shoulder. The war? Well, time to find out later. As if idly, she asks, "Might I know what color your hair used to be, before it . . . before?"

"Firetop. Rooster red. Just like yours only not so pretty. . . . And of course, our eyes are both the same odd shade of blue."

Hearing her involuntary gasp, he looks at her sharply, his doctor persona showing through. "Is the kaffy that strong? Give me your wrist a minim, it affects some people."

"Oh, no, no." She babbles, scarcely knowing what she's saying while his fingers seek her pulse. "I like it, I really do—"

"Sssh."

He rises and goes behind her, and she feels his fingers on pulse points, touching her delicately with the strong hands. An odd warmth has somehow sprung up between them. And the objective indicators are excruciating. "Firetop—like yours . . . and our eyes . . ." The disappointment when it comes, as come it must, will be more painful than in many years.

And such a *good* man—she knows that without evidence. Let me have a few minim more, she bargains with fate. I'll take it fine if I can pretend for just a little while more.

"How did you lose your firetop?" she asks as he releases her and sits back down. He pushes the kaffy away from her and pours her a glass of the golden drink before answering.

"Oh, I picked up parts of a microscope in the wrong places when our ship took a hit. That was in the so-called Last War—may it be so. My unit was up against those Terran supremacy addleheads in the far side of the Orion Arm. The war came a year or so after I made my certification. I'd been interning in various lines of work on various planets. As far as my souvenirs go"—he indicates the scars, the white hair—"it was the treatments rather than the original wounds

393

that did those. The first paramed who operated on me had found a tape on orthopedic surgery beforehand—he said. I had quite a bit of plastite in me, too. We simply didn't know some of the repair lines that are routine today. . . . You were being born just about then.''

She sips the kaffy and asks, as if it had been puzzling her, "Tell me, Doctor—Bram, I mean—there was one thing Myr Kip didn't go into, and I was embarrassed to ask. The Dameii—he spoke of males and females, but how do they, uh, reproduce? Do they . . . lay eggs? Are they mammals?''

"Well, that's a very legitimate interest, but it's a shade complex. No, they're not mammalian in the strict sense, but they're not oviparous, either. Do you know what 'haploid' and 'diploid' mean?''

"It's about cells and chromosomes; I think haploid means having half the usual number. I remember it by h-a—half. Is that right?''

"Absolutely. I see you do read. Well, the forms we call 'males' are all haploid. That may account for their slightly smaller size and the greater number of defects among them. And the true, complete females are diploid—except for a group of haploid structures just below their breastbones, the egg-receiver, or oviceptor, we call it. It's folded back V-shaped, that's what gives the impression of breasts. When a female is in season—they show definite changes, and it's a slow, you might say unusual, event—it stimulates her mate to produce a kind of quasiembryo—all haploid—under *his* breastbone. And at a given time, when she's ready, this egglike object is passed over to the female's oviceptor. Then, if she's really receptive—or really a complete female, we don't have too much data here—she contributes a kind of shadow embryo, also haploid, which has the ability to merge with, you might say invade, the male's contribution and transform it into a diploid fetus which will be a complete female. . . . Have I lost you?''

"Oh, no! Please go on." She smiles. "Now I can see why Myr Kip didn't—"

"Yes." Baram chuckles. "But wait, so far we've only made a daughter. Now, if conditions aren't just right, the process doesn't work perfectly and you get an incompletely diploid fetus, which goes on to become, socially, either a sterile male or sterile female, depending on which parental aspect predominates. I don't think the Dameii themselves can tell for sure until the young grow up and try to mate."

"But true males, sons . . ." Linnix frowns. "How . . ."

"Our best guess is that something we don't understand at all yet happens in the female oviceptor, so that the fetus is only peripherally influenced and grows up completely haploid, as a normal, fertile male. But one thing certain is that in all the families with fertile male children we've been able to examine, the mother always contributes *something*, as judged by gross features of resemblance. That is, she's a true mother, not just an incubator. . . . As you can see, the whole process is still full of mystery. And it's slow, and it occurs only rarely. The Dameii pass most of their lives in the asexual phase.

"So we suppose their evolution is slow and chancy, too. Does that answer your question, Myr Linnie?"

"Um-hmm. . . ." She nods solemnly. "Thank you very much. . . ." She's thoughtful, gripped, despite her preoccupation, by the strangeness of alien lives. But her fingers have been twisting on the mug's handle, trueing and retrueing the odds and ends on the table. And behind her interest in the Dameii, the inner voice keeps whispering, *Wouldn't it be wonderful if . . . Is it possible, possible at last?*

Baram's eyes have never left her for an instant as he recounts the Damei cycle. Now he captures one of her restless hands and says quizzically, "Myr Linnix, it's simply no use pretending you came here to hear war stories and learn about the Dameii. What is it, my dear?"

All right, she tells herself. Happy time is over.

She can't know that Baram is telling himself much the same thing. During their talk his intuition has come up with a horrible surmise: Suppose that there had indeed been an error in the faulty cold-sleep syrettes, an error for which she was responsible. And she has chosen him to confess it to. Oh, no. No. Just as he is beginning to like her so much. But what else can be on her mind to cause such indirection, such intense trouble? He dreads her next words.

When they come, he is so astonished and relieved that he has to suppress an inane grin.

"Well, in a way, I did come to hear about your life. Back then, before you went on the ships, were you ever on a planet called Beneborn? That is—was—my homeworld."

"Beneborn . . . Beneborn . . . Doesn't seem I ever heard of it. I'm from Broken Moon, in the Diadem. Beneborn isn't near the Diadem cluster, by any chance?"

It's hurting worse than she ever imagined it could, after all the years. "No," she says drearily, "nowhere near. But I meant, during your intern work. Between leaving Medworld and whenever you shipped out to the war." But she knows the answer; her words come out dull and flat, not real questions at all. This penetrates Baram's relief.

"Beneborn . . . Beneborn . . ." he mutters. "Look, details aren't too clear to me from before the smash, but I can still list the planets I worked on. No Beneborn among them. . . . Linnix, my dear, I seem to have hurt or failed you in some way." His voice is very gentle. "Please, won't you tell me what it is? What have I done?"

"Oh, you haven't done anything, Doctor Baramji, except be nice. It's just the facts. I was a fool to h-hope." The beautiful turquoise eyes threaten to overflow. "But the hair, the eyes, the timing, everything looked so *right*. And I *wanted* it to be you. Oh, what a fool—a fool—a f-fool—"

He opens his arms, and she's crying on his breast.

"Let it out, my dear. I'd guess you've been very alone."

The sudden shaking violence of her weeping almost frightens him. He holds her tight, stroking her lovely hair, and finally the storm passes. For a moment she lies back in his arm exhausted, then swallows hard, uses his proffered handkerchief vigorously, and sits up, moving back to her own chair.

"Oh, Doctor Baramji—"

"Just Bram, my dear."

"But I never, I'm not the crying type."

"Everyone is the crying type, my love, if it hurts bad enough. And I gather this does. And now you tell me about it."

She half sighs, half laughs. "Oh, it's nothing, really, unless . . . well, you see, Beneborn people, it's like a sickness. It started with some things in our history, but nobody really remembers that. What it is now, they want to improve our race. They have a hugeous big biologic storage facility. I know other planets do that, too, but not on the same scale by half. Ours—*theirs*—is almost a religion. They keep records you wouldn't believe. And people, couples, save up to buy the finest available. Or what they think is the finest for them. Usually just an ovum or sperm; sometimes both, so the child isn't even related to one of them. People even start savings accounts at the Spermovarium in a newborn child's name, so when it's old enough it has the price. And they reserve special strains far in advance.

"My—my parents saved to buy some of the last Lintz-Holstead sperm. He was a multifacet genius, both math and biology, and very healthy—he died in an accident at ninety-six. That was supposed to be me. . . ."

"Well, great," says Baramji. "But I gather something happened?"

"Oh, yes. Lintz-Holstead was dark, see. Also blood type A-pos. Dark skin, black hair and eyes—and so were all his forebears and relations to four generations. And my mother and every one of her family were dark, too. And all but one were type A-plus. That's partly what I mean by 'records.'

But me—well, you can see." She runs her hand roughly through the glorious hair that has ruined her life, and tears well again in the blazing blue eyes. "And I'm B—B-neg. . . .

"And I wasn't multitalented—they test you practically from birth—in fact I wasn't talented at all, except at . . . uh . . . *speed skating*."

"But . . ." Baramji gropes wildly. "I don't want to hurt your feelings, but even mothers have been known to have affairs—"

"No way. And especially after spending all those credits—it was her money. She wasn't crazy, she and my, quotes, father, were dying for this high-status kid."

"Well, then it could only be that some technician in the storage works got to playing smart, and augmented Linx-whoever with himself."

"That's exactly what we think. The trouble is that in the last prewar days we had young doctors interning there from off-planet, and their records aren't complete. And nobody knows where they went afterward, with the war and all. There's not even a name for some. The Beneborn authorities contacted several hospitals who had sent us people in the past, and ran a few ads, but nothing turned up."

"So you started out to hunt through the whole Galaxy yourself? My poor little idiot."

"In a way I had to, B-Bram. You see, there was a terrible stink, and my family literally hated the sight of me. So when I was thirteen the Spermovarium settled a small life annuity on me, and threw me off the planet on condition I never come back. I mean, they signed me up as cabin girl with the next Moom ship. And that's what I've been doing ever since. It's nice safe work and all the education I can read. After the sleepers are down I read—I mean, I really read books—for a couple of days before I go down, too. And I have seniority now, so I can pick runs to far planets that should have Senior Medical Officers on them. Somehow I figure *my* father would like frontiers, that he wouldn't be a big-city society specialist or whatever. So then, when your hair . . . and— N-no!'' She sits up straight, jaw clenched. ''I positively will not cry all over you again, dear, dear Bram.''

He takes both her hands in his.

''Don't you think you might call this off one day, and have some babies of your own, if you want? There's an old saying: It is better to be an ancestor than a descendant.''

She smiles politely.

''My advice, if you want it, is, to the devil with this Limp-Holstein. What did he know about Moom ships, or far planets? You're a beautiful girl. There's any number of fine, handsome, dedicated men on lonely planets who would give an arm and a leg for the chance, well, in the Universe's oldest cliché, a chance to make you happy.''

She's staring into space, only half listening.

He gets up and firmly turns her face up to him. ''Linnie, darling, give it up! Let some other man—'' He goes down on one knee beside her, holding her tight. Too tight; an instant later she feels his grasp relax. He combs her mussed hair off her face with his fingers.

''I tell you what.'' He grins. ''Let me be your adopted father while you're here. No reason a child can't temporarily adopt a father, is there? And my first fatherly admonition to you is, go on back behind that screen and wash your pretty face and then we'll chat a moment.''

She laughs shakily and goes to find the washstand.

''How did you like the visit to the Dameii? Aren't they lovely?''

''Oh, my,'' she says through sounds of splashing. ''But the story Myr Kip told us—''

''Yes. Best not to think about that. After all, the Dameii you're seeing today are three generations or more from the ones it happened to.''

She emerges, toweling vigorously. ''Are they long-lived? Do they have sickness, I mean—''

''You mean, do I have much work here? Am I earning my

keep? Well, here again Kip left something out. . . . You recall I said that the haploid forms we call the males are prone to various defects? Yes . . . well, there's another village, or settlement, that isn't such a happy sight. We call them Exiles. It's low down, built partly on the ground, you see, for Dameii with defective wings. The normal Dameii are pretty rough on winglessness; flight is a very big thing with them. We suspect, but don't know, that there may be infanticide where a newborn is really wingless. At any event, a child who isn't perfect is soon taken, or finds its way, to the village of the Exiles. I've been working there, and I've had some success. In fact, one of the Dameii who live near us is a patient to whom I restored flight. . . . One problem is that they heal with amazing speed; too much speed, if an injury isn't promptly set properly. And the normals aren't too interested in medicine. So I'm building a nucleus of future doctors among the Exiles, who have a natural self-interest in the topic.''

"I'd like to see that, Bram—my dear adopted father—if you have time before we go. Look—you need some clean towels. I'll tell Cory, green?''

"Green, daughter dear.''

With a burst of returning spirits, she asks, "And did *you* have a nice time with the Lady Pardalianches?''

He actually blushes, a startling sight under the shock of white hair.

"Smartass daughter—you have to remember I've been alone on this damned planet for years. But yes—I had a nice time, even if I'll smell of musk and patchouli for weeks. I needed that.''

"We'll be here several days.''

"Yes. One problem, though. She wants to sample every willing body in the place, male or female. . . . You in line?''

"No.''

"It *is* a little heavy, to be frank. After I got over thinking I was in heaven I started to get too conscious of that twin sister

400

in the bed. You know about that? Of course you do—you took care of them."

"Yes. Poor thing, she's just a vegetable, isn't she?"

"I fear so. But her sister won't give up. They both wear those gold-mesh skull caps with electrode implants, you know. The Lady claims hers transmits everything she experiences, including speech, to her sister, and moreover, she thinks she picks up responses, back transmissions. Not verbal, but as feelings."

"Oh, how weird."

"Yes. The poor twin is leading a hectic brain-life, if true. I doubt it, though the Lady seems to be rich enough to buy any amount of respectable science."

Linnix is combing out her hair, making faces at the condition of Baram's brush.

"Well my dear man, dear almost-father—I guess I better get back and get my own place organized. I just dropped my bag in a tangle of lizard skeletons when we arrived."

"Get along with you, then." He grips her arms; their eyes meet in wordless tenderness, and he kisses her forehead. She smiles back, straightening her shoulders, raising her chin.

"That's my girl."

"I . . . I wish I were." She can say it without undue agony now.

"Kip'll be ringing the dinner chimes in—let's see . . . about four hours."

"Right." She smiles and suddenly grabs his hand and kisses it hard before she goes out into the mellow afternoon light of Damiem.

He follows her to the doorway in time to see her wheel and march straight back to him. She halts by the door.

"Sorry." Her voice is low, but direct.

"Whatever in the stars for?"

"That last bit." She looks down, embarrassed. "I've been seeing too many grid-shows. Oh, I made a big thing about reading and I do read—but I look at shows, too. Sometimes . . .

I just wanted you to know. I thought that"—she makes a brief hand-kissing gesture—"was a little . . . sickie. I am, I'm very grateful to you, Doctor Bra—Bram." Her head's up now, the blue eyes straight. "But I'm not sick. I think. You don't think I am, do you?"

"If I grasp what you mean, my dear, no. I don't. You're . . . intense. But given your culture, no. You're not sick."

"Whew."

She blows at a lock of hair, genuinely relieved. "Thank you. Well, good-bye again."

"Good-bye."

Their eyes meet, and the same hearts' longing jumps across. Or is it the same? "I'll try what you said," she mutters and gives a broad smile, only a little twisted. "Good-bye, *Dad*. . . . Hmm!"

Then she turns and is really walking away down the deck.

Baram stares after her, jolted to the core. It had hit him when he'd held her the second time, kneeling beside her; hit him so hard he'd had to force his arms to relax their grip on her. Among other and complex things, she's a Spacer, of a sort. Like himself . . . but doctors are different.

The fact is he *wants* her, this girl, this Linnix No-name. Not as a father surrogate—though her story touches his heart. Thrown off her home planet at thirteen for having the wrong father! . . . But he can't be her father. He wants her, herself. If love could bloom so quickly, he'd say he loves her, passionately and completely. Maybe it can; he feels the grand old cliché he joked about, the same thing he felt for his first mate. (He catches himself—is this the first time he's called Jimi his "first" mate? Yes. Oh.) The point is, he wants her to be happy, to make her so.

And he wants *her*, this long-legged, boyish, sensitive, funny, flame-headed kid—wants her so hard it's pain to conceal it.

He scratches his white thatch in wonder at himself. Two

hours ago he could have sworn that his poor old body wouldn't respond to any woman for weeks—or at least a few days, realistically. The Lady Marquise had been everything a man could ask for as sex object and sophisticated bodily playmate. And sympathetic, pleased at his need, attentive to his every signal. . . . At least he can be sure his desire for Linnix is no deprivation effect.

But what in the worlds can he do? Be he Linnie's lover, mate, friend, whatever, in a few days' time she's going up that ship ramp and off forever, on her hopeless quest. The idea makes his heart ache. And it would always be that way, unless . . .

Unless he takes her on her own terms. And all the Human planets he knows have a strong incest taboo. To have her on her terms means making a mockery of his desire by day, by night, forever.

But still it would be *something*; he could be sure she would return again and again, arrange her life to join his. He could be sure of her love.

Sighing grimly, he starts to paw through the laundry that has somehow enveloped his library and drags out *Brazilier's Encyclopedia of Worlds*. Pouring himself another cup of cold kaffy, he sits down to prepare his doom.

Maybe, just maybe, somehow, he won't have to use it. But all he knows of Human emotions tells him that he will.

VI

NOVA MINUS 6 HOURS:
Zannez Worries

Zannez, indefatigable and worried, also feels no great desire for sleep. He lies fretting while the kids are dozing off—they've opened the connecting doors to turn the room into one big suite—and chews on a thought that just came to him: Could it be that any or all takes of Damiem are classified? How bitter, if their big trip, with the best semidoc work he and the kids've ever done, should end up in some Federation safe. . . .

Travel Admin should have cleared it, of course, but on Gridworld—who knows? Just plain stupidity, or an enemy in the works, could ruin it all. He was the stupid, not to have thought of it and asked. Maybe the Korsos can tell him; but it's always been Zannez' experience that people in the field have no idea how picky their headquarters are.

From the boys' room are coming murmurs about the excitements of the day. They seem deeply affected—and not least by the promised letters of commendation. He hears the words "gold seals" repeated from the bed where Snake and Hanno lie asprawl.

This starts Zannez on a happier track. Imagine that—Federation commends for his kids! He's proud of them, the team he's built almost literally out of dirt. And here they are, mixing it like veterans with marquises and princes and Planetary Administrators—and now this! Those speech lessons he starved them all for have really paid off.

His thoughts run back over the ways they came to him.

Bridey—Eleganza, dammit—was the first. She'd been half of a brother-sister roller stunt act. When her brother broke his neck, the studio'd torn up the contract and thrown her out on her twelve-year-old ass. She had some money saved, but a brat pack got it, and nearly got her, too. He'd come around a corner and found her trying to stone them off her. She was such a feisty little thing, and she threw like a boy; he'd taken her home with him and later drawn up her contract himself.

Snake and Hanno had been apprents in a third-rate acrobat show; they were already into kiddie porn. Zannez caught a sample, liked their control, and was able to pick up their contracts cheap when the show broke up.

And Star—he'd been looking unsuccessfully for a natural blonde to go with Hanny. One night he was sitting in a port bar, dismally considering bleaching Bridey, when a tramp shipper came up to him with something gray and hairy on a rope as thick as his wrist. The animal was so dirty he thought it was an alien or a small ape, but they went in the can and the tramper wet its head to show a white-haired, bewildered, Human girl-child. He decided she showed promise. Oh, be honest, he tells himself, you decided to buy it as soon as you saw that rope. Anyway, he took it home, and he and the gang washed and fed it, and after it finished wolfing, it sang a little tune and said its name was Sharon Woba.

And that became Star.

In the years that followed he'd groomed and sweated and

trained them in any work he could scrounge, until they got this big break with the *APC*. But now it looks like this is failing. The kids sense it, he thinks.

Only last month Hanny had startled him by asking to enlist for space. They were on Beverly—Gridworld had no recruiting office—so Zannez said go ahead. He'd been pretty sure of what would happen. Sure enough, the space officer threw him out, because of the porn. "The Space Patrol doesn't take animals." Hanny's never discussed it, but Zannez has a hunch the hurt goes deep. The boy has a real itch for space.

The girls in the bed nearby are still whispering sleepily. Zannez hears one of them say, ". . . just for a little stripping. They didn't even care about crotch shots. I wonder what . . ." And the other, almost asleep, repeating softly, "Respectful . . . they were so *respectful*. . . ."

This sends Zannez' thoughts down another track that he positively will not pursue. Porn. Yeah—it's shameful, it's criminal. *It's a living.* Children selling something like soul's blood to make Human sharks richer—and he, Zannez, can't change the system. All he can do is take care of the people he's directly responsible for and keep them out of the really rough stuff as long as he can. And if he's going to start worrying about basics, he better get up and get some work done for tonight.

The girls are hard asleep now; Zannez quietly gets himself into a fresh red jumpsuit and finds his chalk. Outside, in the afternoon blue and gold and greens of lake and forest, he feels a lot better.

The deck is a long narrow crescent around the lake side of the hostel, with its center bulging toward the lake, and a low parapet edge. Beyond the parapet are treetops—the land falls off really steep here in a series of forested cliffs right down to the lake. The whole shore is wooded, with a little beach way off to the left. Really pretty.

As he glances down at the beach he sees some quiet splashing—it's the Aquaman, Hiner, coming out. He's been exploring the bottom of the lake. Weird. Zannez pauses for a minim, wondering if there's an angle there for his documentary; decides no. Too confusing—and Hiner didn't look very cooperative. . . .

Back to his business: The Star, they tell him, will rise to the right and sail overhead across the lake, getting bigger and bigger and emitting whatever it emits. The sky is almost cloudless and expected to stay so; perfect conditions.

But what will the Star look like as it actually surrounds them?

Well, there probably won't be a center at all, but a whole skyful of Star-stuff, maybe fantastic auroras and other wild manifestations. It's really a nova-front sweeping past. And it may change fast. He'd better set his sky cameras on one-second lapse to start with. And, say, a full sky-and-lake sweep every twenty secs or so. And an extra cam on a light-sensor gimbal.

A peculiar chilly sensation is troubling his insides. Zannez finally identifies it as the realization that all this isn't just some full-screen effect concocted by Visuals; it's reality itself. This is an honest-to-the-gods real great Star, or the exploding core of one—explosions in which billions of people died—*that's* what's coming onto them tonight.

There's nobody he can call to stop the run, or get a retake, or even turn it down if it starts frying them all and the hostel, too. It's *real*.

Well, if the others can take it, he can, too. He just isn't quite used to reality yet. . . . And that terrible business about the poor wing-people, that happened right around here— His mind shies from it. Better to think about the superb takes he already has in the can, enough to make a doc in itself— before they've even started!

Now, where to base his people?

The forward center of the crescent is his natural spot, but the main party of guests is bound to congregate there; and they may have some official instruments to go there, too. He doesn't intend to get anyone peed off with him again, he's just being his natural working self now. That "I am Zannez!" line was Gridworld garbage that doesn't play here, in reality.

Reality has another aspect, too—one Zannez has postponed thinking about. But now he's placing his people, he can't dither any longer. Face facts: we're working in a world that plays strictly by the Code.

The Code is very strong among space people. They're reared in it, it's second nature. It's simple: *No uninvited sexuality,* in word, deed, or intent. Whew!

No Spacer would violate it, because everyone knows that universal adherence to the Code is all that makes workable the free, close contact of the Human sexes in the cramped quarters and isolation of space. "The Code has given us the Stars." Violations are unthinkable; if one occurs, it grounds the guilty for life; they could be out of the Service in a snap.

Even the kids have sensed it. Zannez sees that. They haven't needed his repeated warnings. He himself is impressed, feeling his way through the odd combination of liberty and automatic self-discipline the Code produces. He recalls an old saying: "To the pure all things are pure." Not to laugh—these people, he guesses, can sleep in the same bed untouching, if a job demands it . . . a far cry from the obligatory couplings and the ever-emptier—and bloodier—search for sensation of Gridworld.

But how in the name of the gods is he going to shoot porn here without getting lynched?

Well, technically he's in the clear, they'd told him back home, because he isn't addressing his stuff *at* anybody and has no "intent." But pragmatically, it stinks.

He'll have to screen off the kids somehow. A curtain would be best, but there's no way to hang it, the parapet is too low. It'll have to be screens. And the sound track to be slapped in later; that's sheer drudgery, but there's no other way. Thank the fates the deck is long and narrow, easy to screen across.

So, where to set up?

Well, there's a slight bay in the deck just outside the boys' room; that'd be about ideal, given screens. They can get at any of their stuff, they have room to spread farther, and it's right for the angle the main lounge doors open at. He begins visualizing holographic frames and distances, wondering idly if the trees around the lake might catch fire. Whew! again.

They've given him a script for the Star-scenes; he takes it out and flips through it. The idea is that the exotic energies released by the Star are hypersexual, and the kids are to do an increasingly bizarre erotic act as the Star brightens. Zannez himself is supposed to be a doctor. And he's directed to do the whole thing so it can be cut as a normal segment for a regular *APC* episode, with a second hard-porn version for appropriate distribution.

Zannez looks it through with growing disgust. Back on Gridworld this sort of thing is standard. But here, above this magically calm, remote lake, under the flawless sky—he suddenly tears it into shreds. There don't seem to be any automatic trashers about, but a tub by the parapet wall that ends their bay has some papers in it. He pitches the whole script in. The kids can do some interesting sex, with a commentary dubbed in later about whatever cosmic wonders appear—but the cheap porn dialogue they were supposed to mouth he will positively not impose on this scene.

He is now positively going to get fired, too; he can just see himself explaining his actions to the knife-eyed money boys who own *APC*.

His mind starts back around its usual worry track. The disastrously slipping ratings of his group within the *APC* cast of thirty-five; his own folly in sticking with them when he's had this perfectly good offer to make docs. He's good at documentaries—loves them, in fact. And offers like that stay open about three hours on Gridworld. . . . When they get back, nobody will recall his name.

Why does he stick? Some obscure loyalty to the inept four,

409

especially Snake and Bridey—ahh, Eleganza. If he quits they'll be on the surplus list in a month and from there to Endsville. Selling, if they're lucky, welfare soup; if they aren't lucky, themselves. That scenario has a quick ending; Gridworld is full of them, the beautiful almost-made-its, the tried-and-couldn'ts. The planet is infamous for having the largest obituary listings and the youngest corpses among the Human worlds.

No. Himself and this crazy trip he's dreamed up to see the third shell of the Murdered Star go by is about their last chance. The pitiful part is that he isn't even the director they need. The right man for them would make more of that weird sinister quality Snake can project, and the sheer dumb-ass lusciousness of Stareem when she's in the mood, and half a dozen other things he can't do. The gods know he tries, but it isn't in him. So they're having their last chance with the wrong man, a bungler.

Ah, he thinks, trash it all. We're gods know how many light-years from the studio now. Anything can happen. Maybe the ship will fall apart on the way home.

Meantime, let him do what he's good at. That deck bay looks bare, it needs something. Native—oops, excuse me— *Damei* artifacts. Rugs, pillows, statuary—maybe they have a big idol. He'll have to ask Kip or the boss lady when she shows. . . . Too bad about Myr Administrator, he thinks. A great lady in person, but she'd screen like a balloon.

He settles himself to wait. A few minutes back he's noticed vaguely that another figure has come onto the far end of the deck and is looking over the lake. It's that red-haired, white-clad girl from the ship, the Logistics Officer. And now another of Zannez' talents comes into play, one he rarely tells anyone about anymore.

The girl is standing straight-shouldered and neutral, apparently enjoying the beautiful scene. But Zannez knows: *She's just had one tough kick in the udder.* . . . He wonders, as always, how he picks these things up.

People talk about "body language," but his perceptions are subtler than that. Somethings—not necessarily the most important—he just *knows*. In the same way he knows that that young crud Yule, and the Aquaman, who are supposedly enraged at being dumped off here, aren't really angry at all. And that silent so-called artist Vovoka stinks of death. And the Kip-Cory love thing is real love. And dear little old jolly Doctor Ochter would cut your throat for a half credit.

Zannez can never understand why things like that aren't as plain as soap to everybody. But after a long string of blackened eyes and split lips in his early youth, he's learned to keep his mouth shut.

Ah, but wait a minute, go back. If that pair, Yule and Hiner, aren't furious at being here, it must mean either that they really don't want to go to Grunions whatsis, or—they wanted to come here. And it's hard to get clearance to come here, Zannez knows that. Yet here those two are, no security checks or nothing. Very slick. And his instincts tell him they're together or linked up somehow.

Why? What's here for them?

He's been staring unseeingly over the beautiful, now uncannily calm lake. A ruffle of motion by the far shore draws his eye. A pair of great pale wings fan out and rise among the treetops, followed by another. They're carrying containers. Up through the topmost branches they flit inconspicuously and are gone.

Zannez' insides give a cold lurch.

What's here are the Dameii—and the golden credits they represent. And that baby goon Yule and the unpleasant waterman, with their faint Black Worlds stink, have pulled off getting here very neatly indeed.

Zannez rubs his knuckles on his bald head, feeling colder and a trifle scared. For decades he's lived in unreality—fake characters, fake plots, fake everything except ratings figures on computers, and signed—or unsigned—contracts. Now he's in reality.

411

The beautiful, totally vulnerable wing-people are real, not just exquisite makeup jobs. The dreadful story he heard that afternoon really happened; it isn't just a storyline that can be changed, it's real. The real tortured and dead do not get up again. And the wealth that was gained from bloody atrocity was real—riches that some men would dream of, and work for, take ultimate risks for. Lay elaborate criminal plans for. All real.

Evil, if it comes here, will be real evil involving not only the Dameii, but the deaths of any who stand in the way. To lay hands on a Damei is death; another murder—indeed, a massacre—wouldn't increase the jeopardy.

And now he, Zannez, has the hunch of trouble from these two, Yule and Hiner, who certainly arrived here without checkout, in what could be, given resources, a preplanned job. Does his hunch point to anything more? Nothing—except that this script calls for more smarts than those two have between them. Well, what about the deathly Vovoka? What about that little cutie, Ochter? Either could be the planner, the main man. . . .

Is he crazy? Probably. . . .

But who knows what else could be waiting in the wings? Space is *big*; Zannez really understands that now. Waking up on shipboard, it had impressed him mightily to see the great light-swirls of the Galaxy behind them. And then that Linnix officer-girl had led them to another port and pointed out Damiem's sun ahead, blazing so utterly alone, with only a few stars hanging in utter blackness on beyond.

The Rim. . . .

Anything could be lurking out here. Who would know?

And now he has this hunch, this Black Worlds whiff about these two. If it were only a matter of himself, he'd be glad to ignore it. But this could concern others. Not only the Dameii, but innocent others like the Korsos and the other visitors, who would certainly not be left unmolested if anyone were

412

actually planning a Stars Tears thing. . . . In short, for the first time in his life, he maybe has a *duty?* Crazy.

Well, crazy or not, it's oppressive, distracting from his work. He longs to get it off him.

But is there anyone here who wouldn't laugh him down? . . . The boss lady, Cory, she seems his best bet—and the proper person, too. Yes, Zannez decides. I'll tell her and let her decide how seriously to take a stranger's sixth sense.

Yet even as he decides this, doubt strikes him. That unreality he's so trained to: what if his very hunch is unreal—is a hunch, not about reality, but about what should be in some standard story plot? He knuckles his head again in confusion, cursing Gridworld. . . . Well, he'll tell Myr Cory *that,* too.

She can make up her own mind as to what's reality.

As though on cue, Cory herself comes out backward through the main doors, followed by Kip. Between them they're pushing out a large, old-fashioned multi-channel terminal cum transceiver, which they station just where Zannez guessed something official might go.

Kip trots back into the lounge while Cory waits, panting a bit.

"Oh, hello, Myr Zannez. Everything going well for you, I trust?"

"Yes, indeed. I'm setting up in this bay. Is that all right? . . . But there's a serious word I need to have with you before too long. Would that be possible?"

"Certainly," she says warmly. "This isn't quite the time, though. Is there anything more immediate you need?"

"Well, the thing we would very much appreciate is a few Damei artifacts—say, a rug or throw for the parapet, a cushion or three, or a big mask or some unique large piece of sculpture. Is that too much? Needless to say, we would treat them with extreme care."

"No reason why not." Cory smiles and shouts up, "Oy, Kip!"

Kip appears above them on the roof, with the connector

413

ends of a fat cable sprouting from his hand. Prince Pao's plumed cap bobs behind.

"This is all ready for you to wire in, Cor."

"Listen, while I'm hitching this monster up, could you go in our rooms and select a Damei rug and some other artifacts for Myr Zannez here? He needs local color for his scene. And the big Damei figure by the pool."

"Can do, Cor. If you'll just take this—"

"In a minim. . . . Just how serious was that other matter, Myr Zannez?"

Zannez hesitates, takes a deep breath. "Myr Cory, this may sound crazy, but I have hunches sometimes. Hunches of trouble. And they usually pan out. And right now I have one so strong I can't live with myself if I don't pass it on to a person in authority."

"Cor!" Kip shouts. "For pity's sake, let's get started—we can't keep the main input dead much longer."

"Righto," Cory shouts back. "Look, Myr Zannez, I do want to hear what you have to say, and I promise you I take such things seriously. I'll make time to listen fully. But right now, as you can see, isn't it."

"Cor!!"

She turns away and goes to the roof edge below Kip.

Well, Zannez thinks to himself, what more can I ask?

"Thank you, Myr Cory, thank you very much. But please—don't wait too long."

He has no idea whether she's heard him or not. She catches the connectors and becomes absorbed in wiring them into the old console. To occupy himself while he waits for Kip and the artifacts, Zannez starts chalking off the positions and distances and permanent camera sites he's visualized. The light is changing around him as the sun drops. There will probably be quite a sunset.

Little Doctor Ochter has come out and is watching him. As he finishes, Zannez recalls another question that's been bothering him.

414

"Look, Doc, if this front is coming on at the speed of light, how can we get messages about it? Wouldn't any messages simply trail behind? They can't stake *c*-skip transmitters out there—or do they? My boy Ek studies these things a little and told me to ask."

"Yes, it is quite a trick, isn't it?" the little man says. "Of course you realize I'm no astrophysicist, but the way it was explained to me is that they use what we used to call tachyon effects for a sort of leapfrog between ships or stations along the route. Maybe starting with the original ship that did the damage—Kip tells me you'll get the whole story of that when we're assembled in the bar. I do know it's very expensive and used only for special nova-fronts and the like."

"Tachyons," Zannez repeats. "That satisfies me—I wouldn't be able to follow a really scientific explanation anyhow. Our audience will be perfectly satisfied with the tachyons. Just give 'em one sciency-sounding word they've heard before and they're happy."

At this moment the main lounge doors open and Kip comes out. Over his shoulder is a load of elegantly colored leafy fabrics and other mysterious objects, while held in both hands before him is a two-meter-tall figure of a Damei, in pale carved wood.

"Oh, lords—gorgeous!" Zannez breathes. "I never expected—"

"Cor said local color, local color you get," said Kip. "Just no spilling or breaking, on pain of murder."

"Suicide," Zannez corrects him. "Look, one of my boys—Snake—has real artistic talent. May we lay this stuff down carefully while I go rout him out? It's time I raised the kids, anyway."

He takes a deep breath. "But listen, Myr Kip—I've got trouble. Our camera work, see—it's well, in the nude, and more—*much* more. To be blunt, one take may be used for a porn show. Pornography. Those are my orders. But I most sincerely do not want to offend. You all and this place are a long, long way from Gridworld and I appreciate every light-minim of it. So, I'm squeezed. The only thing I can think of is screens. Screens and more screens to go right here, between the kids and the rest of you. It doesn't matter if people see me and the cameras, does it? What do you say?''

"Cor and I are ahead of you," Kip tells him, momentarily sober. "We got the picture fast. She decided that since you're taking all the measures you can for privacy, no one should get spooked. I agree. After all, it's your work, it's not as if it's personally directed in any way.''

"And the screens?" Zannez is vastly relieved.

"Can do. We built some when the Dameii were in here.''

They pile the beauty gently by the parapet, and Zannez goes off to their rooms, leaving the Korsos immersed in the innards of the console.

He finds the four awake and in an odd mood.

Not sullen or snappish or sick: simply . . . odd; a mood Zannez hasn't seen before. Can it be the same reality trauma that affects him?

"By any chance is the realie-realie of all this getting to you kids?" he asks. "It's different from anything we've met, you know. I've been fighting off strange feelings all afternoon. A real Star is heading for us, all these people and events are real and never heard of us and show world. It makes me feel a bit shivvo.''

"We know what you mean, Zannie," Stareem tells him in her sweet nonacting tones. "Thanks for trying to help.''

"There's another reality, too." Snake's chuckle is not quite lighthearted. "An even simpler one.''

"What is it?''

"Later, later," Snake says calmly. "We have days here, you know. And I bet you've got some work for us right now.''

"And isn't it suppertime *yet*?" Hanny Ek demands. "These thirty-hour days are killers.''

"As a matter of fact," Zannez tells them, "I have our

416

stations all marked right outside here and Myr Kip brought us a load of the most gorgeous Damei artifacts you ever saw when I asked for local color. I want you and Snake to arrange them as background in our bay. Of course they're much too delicate to sit or lie on. If you girls could select and bring out a batch of ordinary neutral-colored blankets and pillows, I'd be very grateful. They say the night temperatures don't change much, if at all.''

"And food!'' says Hannibal. "You're forgetting food!''

"Well, the way I understand it, shortly we all go in the bar and have hot snacks and drinks while Kip tells us the story of the Star. Then we take our main course out to the deck and watch the Star rise. So if you can hold out long enough to get that stuff arranged, we ought not to lose you to starvation. Green? . . . Green! So, on with the clothes we planned, and let's go! . . . I'm supposed to be your doctor, by the way, watching to see you don't get cooked. And I'm going to wear a monocle, cursitall. I always wanted to.''

That gets a nice natural laugh and they all start piling into costumes and the special body makeup jobs required by night lights.

As he dresses, Zannez berates his brain, trying to decipher Snake's "Later, later,'' and "a simpler reality.'' *Sixth sense, where are you when I really need you?* Nowhere, it seems.

Miraculously, the monocle stays in place above his absurd fake-doctor whites, and they all issue, laughing, to arrange their bay. Snake and Ek are fascinated when they see the Damei things, which have already attracted bystanders.

"Priceless. Don't even breathe on them.''

"We'll arrange it as background and then put Star's and Bridey's stuff down to use.'' Ek even forgets his famine as he delicately handles the bronze-and-turquoise tissues, the two great pinion fans.

"It's made with their own plumage!'' Bridey exclaims over a superb green-blue mat.

"Yes. Maybe it has some religious significance. Kip didn't

tell us anything about that. For the worlds' sake, Snake take care. . . . Funny, I sense something sad, about them. Does anybody else?''

"Unh'm?" Brows knit in perplexity. "Maybe it's because we know the story," says Stareem.

"Better we not know more," says Bridey practically.

"Kippo brought the screens I asked for." Zannez points. "We have to rig 'em to hold. You all recollect what I told you about the Code here?"

A chorus of assent, quite different from the knowing grins that greeted his first warning, back at the staging-in.

They're feeling plenty uneasy about the whole thing, Zannez sees.

Looking for something to cheer them, he sees that the red-haired officer-girl is among those who've come to watch. The onlookers all seem impressed by the artifacts; even Vovoka inspects them thoughtfully. Yule visibly restrains himself from remarking on their potential price.

Zannez addresses Linnix.

"Look at this lady's hair, Snako," he exclaims. "Now *that's* the color you should have! Myr . . . ah, Linnix, if young Smith here asked you very nicely, do you think you could tell him your numbers? After all, you're literally worlds apart, you couldn't conflict."

"Numbers?" Linnix asks blankly.

"Numbers—brand grades. Yours'd be just perfect for Snake here. You can see he has a problem, with that dead-mouse-nothing color."

"Oh, if you only could, Myr Linnix. . . ." Snake has approached her—but it's a different Snake, all slouch and slyness gone, his face alight with half-humorous boyish appeal and frank admiration of her as a woman. "I'd never tell one soul, depend on it."

Linnix is torn between suppressing laughter and fascination with Snake's new persona. This is what actors know how to do, she thinks. A pro. If she knew what "numbers" were, she'd give them to him instantly.

"I haven't any idea what you're talking about, Myr Zannez—I've never heard of numbers."

The appeal in the boy's face increases a couple of watts, trembles between disbelief and disappointment. Linnix feels as if she's kicked a puppy.

"I *am* so sorry, if it would have helped you. But this is just what I was born with."

"Natural!" Zannez almost spits the word. "It would be. And the funny thing is, Myr Linnix, I believe you. Well, take a good look anyhow, Snako, notice that blue-bronze glow in the shadows, and no brass anywhere. That's one of the greatest hair effects we'll ever see."

"I guess I'm supposed to say thank you"—Linnix laughs— "but the way you put it I feel I should apologize."

"Not to worry," Zannez tells her. "I wonder where Myr Cory has got to? Her electronics work looks to be all set up." He strolls over to the aged console. The Federation appears to be conserving credits on this aspect of Damiem.

"She's up here in my observatory," comes Prince Pao's voice from overhead.

Startled, they all look up to see the boy's face grinning down at them from the overhang. "And Myr Kip is behind the bar, preparing to serve food."

"Hear, hear!" says Hanny Ek.

"Prince!" It's Cory's voice. "Do please come back in!"

The head withdraws, after saying severely to Stareem, "Myr Star, your vest is fastened crooked."

Star refastens the vest, laughing. "My little guardian. Zannie, you have to admit it was dear of him to come all this way."

Zannez is still frowning over the computer.

"Shameful." He shakes his head. "Do you children realize how many takes we've made of the wise old scientist or the merry brain-boys, routinely punching out messages or

419

calling for help on machines like this? All very convincing. And yet could any of us actually do the simplest thing with a real one? Could you send an alarm, say, or an SOS? Ek, you studied something along these lines. Could you message the Patrol with this thing? Or read radiation danger signals?''

Hanny Ek looks it over dubiously. "Well, given time—a lot of time—I think I might convey that something had gone wrong. At least that the regular operator was missing.''

Laughter.

"You might as well know the truth," says Zannez. "As to Herr Doktor Zannezky—if you come to me saying the place is invaded and everybody's dying of plague, all you'll get is sympathy. *I can't even turn the cursed thing on.*''

Amid the laughter, a thin yellowish hand slides out onto the console board, clicks a tumbler, and at once several dials and a small readout screen flickers to life.

"Those are the status reports from several distances before and behind the front," Hiner, the Aquaman, informs them in a nasal voice. A high-collared vest covers his gill area.

"But they're compressed from the main readouts upstairs, you have to analyze—''

"Who did that?"

Kip is at the doorway, his hair literally on end with rage and a great boning knife in his hand. His glare lights on Hiner.

"Turn that off, you godlost fool, before I gut you! *My mate is working on those relays.* Do you know how close you just came to murder? What are you, some kind of defective? Don't you know that one never—*never*—''

"It's all right, darling." A cool voice from the roof above cuts through Kip's fury. Cory is standing on the thatch. "Luckily no damage is done. Myr Hiner was seen approaching the panel, and I suspected he might not understand the potential of in-air wiring. What Myr Korso was saying to you, young man, is that on land it is taken for granted that you never, never touch—let alone turn on—other people's

420

electrical or mechanical equipment, without their explicit instructions. Perhaps this is a useful thing for you to learn here and now—for example, Myr Zannez' valuable cameras with their irreplaceable recordings are left unattended because of the force of this unwritten law. And of course it applies doubly to the infirmary, and even in the kitchen. And if you are ever in a home with an open fire, remember the old joke: It is safer to poke a man's mate than to poke his fire. Now do you understand?''

The little speech has its effect; Kip has gone back in the lounge, and everyone has moved away from the console. To Cory's question Hiner says quite civilly, ''Yes, ma'am, I do. My apologies.''

Cory vanishes from view as she scrambles back up the thatch to the cupola window she popped out of.

Hanno Ek restores normalcy, closing menacingly on Zannez. ''Food, Zannie,'' he growls. ''Food!''

''Hold it, Hanno, we want to make our entrance.''

Stareem, watching by the open lounge doors, reports that the Lady Pardalianches is coming in, followed by Doctor Baramji from his infirmary.

Ochter, Hiner, and Yule take a final glance at the sky, which is showing the start of a normal, if very beautiful, sunset, and saunter into the lounge. Far down the deck a lone figure stands by the parapet, face turned up to the sky, apparently oblivious of all else.

''Oh, stars,'' Linnix says, ''it's Ser Vovoka. I better go get him.''

Kip calls from within. ''I've saved the door end of the bar for you and your group, Myr Zannez. Just beyond where the Lady's rollbed can park. Then I tell the story from here, as if I were talking to you alone.''

''Wait one minim,'' says Doctor Ochter. ''Admirable as Myr Zannez' work is, he is not the sole guest. We all wish to hear and see.''

''And you will,'' Kip assures him. ''See, I stand here and

421

talk sort of to the middle, including you all. I thought Zannez can get the privacy effect with a camera down here. They have their backs to the open doors, sunset, Star-rise, et cetera. They don't see it, but you're looking directly out and see everything. How's that, Myr Zannez? Frankly, I'm rather proud of it.''

"Done like a pro," says Zannez. "Well, I see Myr Linnix has lured Vovoka toward the food. Snake, Hanno, your effect here couldn't be finer. Time for us to form up and go in.''

For the millionth time he triggers the magic whereby a formless group coalesces into two so-natural looking couples, pointing out to each other the attractiveness of the lounge, the heavy radiation shielding overhead, the beautiful local wood of the bar and the delicious food odors coming from behind it, plus Kip's forthcoming story of the Star, while "Doctor" Zannez puts in a word about the necessity of food after long cold-sleep—all so plausible, yet so far from actuality.

Zannez muses often on the paradox: Skillful falsehood is what it takes to make a true-seeming documentary. Just as the kids' almost grotesque thinness is what it takes to make a beautiful body on the screen.

As they gain their places, he notices that Ser Vovoka, at the far end of the bar, is still gazing eastward through the vitrex. That's where the Star will rise. When they end the sequence, Zannez looks back outside and sees the light has changed slightly; a cold pink luminescence is now coming from the east.

That thing really is coming, he tells himself. Well, the crowd here is attending expectantly only to Kip's doings with the food. It has to be all right.

Just as Kip starts lifting servers off the heat-shelf, everyone is again startled by little Prince Pao, who comes rocketing down into the lounge astride the helical stair rail. He alights with an only slightly wobbly bow and addresses Kip.

"Myr Cory will join you shortly. She is still with her machines. She asks that you hold the story till she comes."

"Righto," says Kip. "We'll hold."

"Story, yes; food, no," Hanny Ek tells him.

"Here you are, Myrrin." Kip begins producing the hot servers. "Puffs of local lake life, cheese from a Damei herbivore we're domesticating, good old Galactic iron sausage. This is appetizers, main course to follow. . . . Myr Ek"—he grins as Hanny starts wolfing—"there really is a main course coming."

"Don't worry," Snake assures him. "He's unfillable."

"I hope it's all as good as this!" Young Pao has a snack in each hand.

General murmurs of assent from all but Vovoka and the Lady Pardalianches, who is looking restlessly about. She is now clad in a glittering mist of lavender. Doctor Baramji has courteously taken a place beside her, but the Lady's attention strays. Suddenly she leans across Baramji to place jeweled fingers on Vovoka's arm.

"Oh, Ser Vovoka, my poor sister—she's all alone, and that bed is so heavy! Could you possibly help me bring her here? It will only take a tiny moment."

The tall artist merely glances down at the hand and silently resumes his gaze eastward. His plate is untouched.

"Well!" says the Lady helplessly. Linnix has automatically risen at her plea and is moving to the door, but the marquise's imploring gaze passes over her.

"Oh, Myr Zannez—"

But Zannez is shaking his head. "I'd be glad to help you, Lady P., but I never leave the cameras. The first rule of documentaries."

"Oh, but surely just for a minim—and there's a reward, too." The Lady's voice drips myrrh. "Wouldn't you like to see my sister? She's very beautiful. We are—were—identical twins, you know."

"Dear lady, I do appreciate the honor . . ." Zannez

bethinks himself of an old Gridworld ploy. "But if I may be candid, it's no good wasting beauty on me." He pauses theatrically. "I was one of the damn-fool cameramen who went to the planet Thumnor in mating season. Three mortal weeks. Someone else—perhaps Officer Linnix there—can tell you what *that* means."

His tone is final, his gaze tragic.

"I'll help you," says Linnix from the door, "if it really is only a few minim."

"Thank you so much." The Lady's coo has gone. "But whatever did he mean about Thumnor?" she asks Linnix as they pass from sight.

"Is it really true about Thumnor?" the girl Bridey, or Eleganza, asks Kip. "Or is our Zannie just faking out Lady P.?"

"We can't believe a word he says." Stareem giggles. "*You* tell us, Myr Kip."

But before Kip can answer, Zannez has an idea.

"Speaking of cameras, Kippo, d'you think Myr Cory would mind if I snuck up and caught a nice take of her in this glorious light, surrounded with all her high-tech doodads and backed by the views up there?"

And I can lay this cursed Yule-Hiner hunch on her in privacy, he says to himself. "I don't want to anger her for the worlds," he adds aloud.

"I don't see why not," Kip's saying. "Sounds great. The worst that can happen is that she throws you out—but it wouldn't anger her, no."

He goes to the foot of the stairs.

"Honey, can Zannez come up and take a shot or two?"

"Come ahead!" The voice sounds lighthearted.

Zannez has snatched up a double-range hand camera and is leaping up the circular flights. As he passes from hearing, he hears Ser Vovoka saying in apparent approval, "The light of Damiem makes all things beautiful beyond their counterparts on other worlds. Do not feel too secure."

424

VII

NOVA MINUS 5 HOURS:
Cory's Wiring

Cory Korso, alone again in the rooftop cupola, after Zannez has come and gone, allows her deep happiness to rise.

She has put it aside to listen to Zannez, she has postponed it to get her relay wiring done—the task was to lay in readout and communication links down to the old computer console on the deck—and now Cory wants a few minim simply to enjoy.

She sits cleaning solder paste from her abused fingernails, listening with pleasure to the rising conviviality from the bar below and looking with critical satisfaction at her newly made relays. The cupola, which had started as a mere observatory and transceiver housing, is now their main computer facility as well. With its array of antennae outside, including the vacuum-cased c-skip sender, it is a compact, sophisticated little center, rivaling that on many FedBases.

Inconvenient, of course—she's had to run a panel of alarms

to their bed—but with the eight great windows circling sky and world, a tour of duty up here is pure pleasure. There aren't many such tours—watching for a lost ship, tracking a bit of space debris, mapping the Damiem borders of a meteor swarm, taking the periodic all-modes record of her allotted segment of space—simple outpost routine; but always spiced by the threat that someday some mythical evildoers may have Damiem in their sights.

Just now the sunset is flooding the cupola and the world with golden light, along with which she can feel a little tension. The tension, she believes, is caused by the rapidly fluctuating ion count, one of the normal precursors of the oncoming Star.

Or it may be personal to her, because this sunset is special. It marks the last night that the Star will dominate Damiem's sky. The Star has always oppressed Cory, though she can't imagine why something so beautiful should cast a shadow on her happiness here with Kip. Yet it has, though she's never spoken of it. Perhaps the shadow is because it's always *there*, she thinks; always coming at us. When one shell finally passed, there was always another behind, ready to loom up at them.

But this is the very end. Every instrument, including the drone that FedBase sent through the Star-front for her, tells the same thing. Beyond this last shell is nothing. No core, only empty space. By this time tomorrow the last of the Star will have forever gone by, to expand, attenuate, and dissipate away among the lights of the Galaxy.

I hope so, some superstitious imp of her mind whispers. Jeering at the imp, she straightens up, takes a couple of deep breaths of Damiem's sweet air, and puts the nail file away. Stop dreaming, and final-check those connections!

But what about that premonition, or whatever it was, that the funny bald cameraman—Zannez—told her about so solemnly? Trouble, he said, from those unlisted, uncleared two, Yule and Hiner, who might be in league with Vovoka, or, of all people, little Doctor Ochter. And that *she* should decide how seriously to take him. . . . Lords, she thinks, how can I? For all she knows, Gridworld is full of mad psychics.

As to Hiner and Yule, she certainly agrees—she expects nothing but nuisance from them the whole time. But real trouble—like a Stars Tears attack—is hard even to consider seriously. In the first place, if they want to take us by surprise, why be so outstandingly obnoxious that we're watching them every minim?

And that absentminded Vovoka and poor little lame Ochter do seem very unlikely confederates.

But Zannez was so earnest. He meant Trouble, capital T. . . . Could it be that he's very sensitive to the ion fluctuation? In any event, she thinks, for Trouble, capital T, we always have Mayday. Or, wait, no we don't, at the moment. I let Kip lend the main circuit chip to Captain Dayan for *Rimshot* until his refit next month. Bother.

Well, she has something almost as good. She looks with approval at the Deadman's Alarm she's constructed and wired down to the deck console. If it isn't reset periodically, it will blast off a pretaped SOS to *Rimshot* and Base. Of course it doesn't have its own subsurface 360-degree antenna or remote multitriggering like Mayday, but the chance of anybody bothering to knock out the regular antennae when no one is near the console seems slight. Pace Norbert, the previous Guardian, had said the Korsos weren't paranoid enough. She hopes this will satisfy him; it was a lot of work.

As she reflects, the possibility of scrambling a battle cruiser to a false alarm makes her wince. And what if it needs to be reset just when something major's going on? Isn't this just a mite *too* paranoid?

She ponders while she double-checks her other relays. . . . All green. Then, back at the Deadman's Alarm, she inspects the solder with a stress-scope. Imagine Dayan's reaction to being summoned to a faulty solder job! Then, on impulse,

427

she doubles the safety wait lapse so she couldn't possibly miss if it came at an awkward time. Good.

She casts a final look at the battery of readouts from the drone. Still no indications of any danger ahead. All green, go.

Her last job is fun. She picks up a bag of sweetener and swings featly out of the big window where the cable exits, into the full sunset blaze. It's getting rosy, she should hurry. But she allows herself a minim just to look.

Beautiful, beautiful . . . the far shore's like fire, against it the near point is velvet black. And down in the bar below Kip has put on some Damei music. Oh, my. . . . The guests are getting their trip's worth of sunset.

But that isn't what they came for. Cory cranes her neck to stare straight up. Yes; against a few high wisps of cirrus she can just make out a faint quiver, a not-quite-imaginary shimmer of bluish light. That's from the Star; it's really coming.

Dropping to her knees on the thatch, she scrambles down to where the cable runs over the eaves and backs up along it, scattering sweetener. Sure enough, she passes some rinds of tree spores; Damiem's wildlife has already been investigating her cable. They hate sweet, which is why she's dusting it, to keep their sharp little pincers from the cable.

As she dusts, she sighs—she'd love to make a pet of one of the big, playful green arachnoids. She's sure it would tame well. But that's against policy—what would happen to it if she and Kip left? The Dameii view them all as vermin.

She sits on the sill to swing back in, bare legs gleaming, and catches a look at the laundry line across the deck that Zannez and Kip have erected. From here she can see the far side, with an arrangement of mattresses and pillows that sends her eyebrows up as she tries not to picture what will go on there. Unbeknown to her, the tip of her pink tongue steals out and delicately wets her lip. Gridworld! She suddenly recalls the marvelous flask of perfume little Prince Pao gave her; she pivots inside and finds it on the computer printout. It proves hard to open, but she persists.

While she's at it, Kip's baritone rises from below, promising to tell them all the story of the Murdered Star. A shadow crosses Cory's face. *This time, just this one time, let him tell it straight,* she prays to fate.

But she isn't hopeful.

It's Kip's weakness, known to all their friends, that he can rarely tell a story without implying that he's been there or was in some way part of it. He never actually lies, only hints and makes artful "slips" that are all too convincing.

Their friends try to tell her it's funny.

"Look, Myr Cory," an ex-gunner said one night at a reunion party, "Kip's the genuine beast. Don't take his yarning to heart. Does he ever talk about his own space days?"

"No! I caught him throwing out a box of medals. I saved them, I could see they're his. But when I ask him what they're for, he won't say. 'Oh, just the sort of thing that happens,' " she mimicked.

"That's Kipper," an ex-navigator said with a grin.

"Well," said the ex-gunner slowly, "I can tell you about the VS. That's the big green one—Valorous Service. . . . We were out in an antique REB, no armor retrofit to mention, and we got rocked up by a booger in a fake satellite.

"Everybody got it, and the boat was leaking air enough to move her. I remember Kip was sluicing blood down both legs. And he was better off than most—we all looked bloody dead. See my homemade ear?" He ducked his head. "I always thought the hair they put on that side came from a hamster."

Even in the party lights Cory could see the scars of massive reconstruction. He must have been a boy then, lying in a puddle of blood with a smashed head and who knew what else. "Gods, Myr Kenter."

The gunner grinned wryly. "The gods were out to lunch

that year. Or maybe they weren't. Anyhoo, Kip should have used his escape pod, express to Base. No one else had a chance. And the water unit was smashed. . . . He flew that stinking REB home using the belts as tourniquets. Six days, no water and less air. Which is why I'm here, plus two others." He was looking past Cory.

"Janny and Pete died on the way, with him giving them the last water. Saro went in Base Hospice. . . . Kip was about seventeen then, I found out later. Looked older. He didn't give a—*that*, for the VS. . . . See now why we don't take his tales too serious?"

Cory was pale. "Oh, my. . . . But why, Mr. Kenter?" she persisted. "Why *does* he?"

The navigator spoke up reflectively.

"I guess the thing is, aliens, Myr Cory. You'll notice it mostly concerns aliens. Kip never had much but Human stuff. But if somebody mixes it with other races, that strikes him as really worthwhile. Alien adventure! He craves it. That's why he went for xenology. Strange karma; the real thing is always somewhere else, for Kipper."

But all their efforts to make her take it lightly failed. Kip's habit shames and alarms her, as if it might draw some evil on him.

Now, as she pries at the gold-sealed flask and frets by habit, the light of the Star's passing shines suddenly through her mind. Kenter's image of Kip comes to her—a wounded seventeen-year-old, parched and poisoned, getting his comrades home, all that agonizing time—when at any moment he could have gotten in his pod and with no blame at all gone home free. . . . That was reality; it happened. By what right does she judge Kip now?

What had she done in the wartime, anyway? Mostly sat in Rehab, checking quartermasters' supply lists and having her brain washed. Presumably because something horrible happened to her family, she'd always thought. The Mem/E people never tell you what they erase, but most people were there because of atrocities happening to someone. While Kip was having a pretty fair atrocity happen to *him*.

Only Kenter and his friends had the right to judge Kip. And they'd told her what to think. And by the gods, she *will*, now.

She may not love his habit, but she loves and respects Kip, and she won't be such a rigid rat's ass—and look out, you're cutting through this lovely bottle.

Cory heaves a long, relieved breath, dusts herself off energetically, and opens the perfume. The scent of *mugets* fills the cupola. Oh, just right! Kip'll love it. So long since I had any, she thinks, dabbing it lavishly on her hairline and inside her shirt. She glances in the small utility mirror and sees a glowing Cory—with her hair full of thatch. Hastily she roots out a comb and wields it.

The artist-man, Vovoka, had told her this morning that Damiem had a particularly flattering light. No, *peculiarly*. Good for me, she thinks, peculiar or what, we can't let those Gridworld kids take it all. And remember to thank Prince Pao.

Time to go down. Close up shop.

As she passes Pao's cot she sees his personal things neatly laid out on a chair alongside. Cologne, comb, toothcare, sponge bag, hankie, book—*Rim Stars*. Tidy as a little Spacer, even if the implements look like solid gold. She clicks on a night-light for him and starts down the small spiral stairs.

The colorful group around the bar comes in sight, and Cory's own glow intensifies. It's really pleasant to have company again, despite that wretched student, Yule, and the unpleasant Aquaman, Hiner.

A large draped and gilded object is just swaying through the arcade door opposite—the rollbed, escorted by the marquise and propelled by Officer Linnix. Cory pauses to watch.

"Oh, please!" The Lady sounds excited. "Please place her here where the Star-light will shine on her! That wonderful pink light *is* from your Star, is it not, Myr Kip?"

431

"Yes indeedio! Looks brighter than last time, too." Cory silently agrees. "And that's only the forerunner."

The rollbed placed to her satisfaction, the Lady tenderly—and not undramatically—draws open its drapes.

All heads turn to see. Involuntary exclamations; Cory herself gasps.

Lying on embroidered pillows is a very lovely dark-haired young girl—or what appears to be a young girl, smiling faintly in her sleep. A great, loose, lustrous braid of dark hair reaches to her knees. She's clad in a lacy, long-sleeved nightdress with gold ribbons, a golden lace cap on her curls and little velvet slippers on her feet. No hint of tubes or wiring, all the intricate machinery that must be sustaining her life, can be seen. Only—the slipper soles are creamy, pristine. *Twenty years?* . . . Cory shudders.

She bats the thought away from her and comes on down, favoring everyone with her jolly all-purpose smile. As she passes Zannez to go behind the bar, the cameraman repeats his thanks for their session in the cupola. "But I still want a more formal sequence of you, ma'am, at your administrative duties."

"My administrative duties?" She laughs. "Turn your cameras away for a minim, here goes one of them."

Next instant only her shapely rear is visible as she burrows deep under the bar. She comes up with two big dusty guest bottles. "Excellent whiskey, I'm told. A Spacer brought it from Highlands. I better get out some *laangua* and gin, too." Another dive into the bar storage. "Here you are, Kippo," she calls. "We have one more whiskey and two *laangua*, but that's all the gin."

"Can you pour, honey?" Kip is scraping ferociously. "I'm cleaning up; those puffs blogged all over the heat-shelf. . . . We have to fix a bigger one."

"Right." She takes the bottles down to Ochter's end of the bar where the ice and glasses live. "Gin, whiskey, or *laangua*, Myrrin? I fear water is our only mix. And you've all had at

432

least five appetizers, I trust. Doctor Hiner? Myr Yule? Ser Vovoka?''

Yule is leaning toward her with an earnest, open expression he hasn't shown before.

"Myr Cory, ma'am, I'm really sorry I blew my shoes like that this morning. On top of putting you folks to a lot of trouble. Doc here—"

Cory intercepts an approving look from Ochter. Aha, so there'd been a lecture.

"Doc says I'm lucky I don't remember half all I said. My sincere regrets, all, and special to Officer Linnix, ma'am. I sure remember the Dameii, though. Wouldn't have missed that for the worlds. This place is marvelous."

He gives himself a mock blow on his yellow head, a very changed young man. "Beastly embarrassing."

"Handsomely said!" Kip bows acceptance, flourishing his scourer, as Hiner leans forward, obviously with the same intent. "Pour 'em a toast, Cor."

Cory beams as this last blot on the evening's happiness removes itself. The ghost of her former reasoning brushes her mind but has no power; more pressing is a threatened shortage of ice.

"Mordecai spoke for me, too," says the Aquaman.

His narrow face now looks appealingly aquiline, almost poetic above the immaculate flowing white collar. Only the tips of white lines under his ears show where his once angry gills lie. "And I believe my profound personal apologies are due Officer Linnix. Doctor Ochter has told me that ships sometimes exchange whole sets of destination shots when they switch to an unusual run like this, and it's easy to see how a mix of labels—or expiration dates—could eventually occur. I must say I felt quite ill for a time, and I know Mordy did, too. Most deeply, deeply sorry, all. And most sincere thanks for any help you care to give in getting us where we belong."

"Goodness—the things we don't know about ships!" Cory

chuckles warmly. "It must have been absolutely wretched for you. Do have a cheering drink. Whiskey, both? I'm afraid we're a little skimpy on ice. . . . Now, Ser Vovoka, won't you take something? Ser Vovoka! Ser Vovoka, *please*. That Star can't rise for two hours, honor bright."

The sculptor finally turns his gaze from the vitrex long enough to select the popular alien *laangua*. As Cory is pouring, Prince Pao bobs up on the seat alongside Ochter.

"Myr Cory, Doctor Baramji advises me to ask you about the time-flurries. I've never heard of them! What are they, please? Shall we get one tonight? Do all nova-fronts have them? How long do they last? How far do they extend in space and time?" His cap is under his arm, its gold feathers bouncing with excitement.

Cory grins at him. "Prince, if you'll just let me finish serving the Lady and Zannez' group while I compose my thoughts, I'll tell you all I know—but don't be disappointed, because that isn't much."

"Oh, forgive me. Certainly . . . I await you back there." He goes off to his place by Zannez, cheese puff in hand.

Cory gets them all poured. The Lady turns out to have her own gold-chased flask, from which comes a fragrant light liqueur utterly unknown to Cory; she takes only ice.

Zannez is keen to record Cory's time-flurry explanation, and the problem of keeping the prince out of his frames is acute. When they're finally settled, Cory begins.

"As to what time-flurries are, no one really knows. There're a number of theories; the one I like best is that a local concentration of positrons is so dense it gives a brief ambient regress. Nor does anyone know whether they form and dissolve on the spot, or appear that way because they're passing you. Subjectively—here you are, Myr Ek—what you feel, if you're in the open—shielding stops them—is a kind of murkiness; and you see a running backward of things that have just happened. But it's all very confused. In the one Kip and I experienced, there was one clear minim where the

Dameii repeated what they'd recently said, like replaying a scene. But we felt all stiff. *Gluey* is the best word I can find. And alone. And then things start forward again, but all mixed up and shadowy, very fast—and you're suddenly in real time again. The whole thing only lasted a few breaths, and we don't think it took up actual time."

"But could you move?" Pao demands. "Could you *change the past?*"

Cory laughs. "We never tried. It's so short, and so confused—and as I said, one feels odd. Static."

"But if you'd intended to, you *could* have moved?" the lad persists. "Oh, how I'd love to experience one! *I'd* try to move something!"

"If you get a chance, I'd appreciate it if you'd move these cursed cheese puffs." Kip laughs, shaking off the scraper. "All right, honey, you sit down. I'll take over."

Cory takes her drink around to sit by Vovoka. She's followed by Pao.

"Do you think we'll get one tonight?" the boy asks.

"No way to tell. But if you're really interested, make sure you stay out from under the antirad roofing, otherwise you won't even know one's been by. Doctor Baram was looking straight at us and never noticed a thing."

"Oh, I shall, indeed. . . . But tell me, there must be more, elsewhere, aren't there?"

Cory, tired, looks around for help, and Doctor Ochter catches her appeal. "There are said to be some in the remains of antique Earth's moon," he tells Pao. "And there's a large one, or a succession of them, in the Crab Nebula; they're considered a danger to shipping. And I believe some have been reported near Orionis M–forty-two. But—"

"You have left out the most important feature." Vovoka's deep voice suddenly startles everyone. "Concentration of positrons, indeed. . . . But what could cause such an anomaly? Young man, you will find, in every case, that an astral-scale

435

body has been suddenly—instantaneously—destroyed, vaporized, by some *totally unforeseeable outside event*—as in the acts of war that annihilated so many planets and suns. It is perhaps not too biomorphic to say that the formerly organized matter does not yet 'believe' in its disorganization; that the shadowy persistence of its former state—its memory, if you like—is so strong it can distort the local time-flow. It generates turbulence in a backward direction, as though the debris strove to reassemble, to reexist in that last instant before the catastrophe, when perhaps it could have been averted. As to whether some form of life is also necessary . . ."

His voice has softened and roughened, his gaze is on some space beyond them all. As suddenly as he spoke, he sighs and falls silent.

There is a brief general silence. Cory, who was helping Kip cut the hard sausage, has paused, knife lifted. Just as she resumes, a small scream from the Lady Pardalianches almost makes her hand slip.

"She moved! My sister moved! And she's trying to tell me something—"

The Lady's at the rollbed. Cory sees Zannez swing his hand camera to follow, but no motion is visible in the still form.

Doctor Baramji is with them at once, inspecting the patient, soothing her sister. He produces two large blue pills. "Water, please, Kip. Hurry."

"Take these right now, dear lady. We don't want the feedback from your cap to injure your sister—or vice versa."

"But she moved! It's so *tense* here, she feels it. Something bad's bothering her. . . . What's this?"

"Swallow them quickly, lady dear. It's a cortical calmant cum buffer I prepared this evening, in case. I apologize for their size. My guess is that the transceivers in your electrode caps may be overloading. I want you to turn them down a bit, lest you or your sister be harmed."

"Oh-h-h. . . ." She takes the pills.

"I'd also guess that we're receiving some unusual energies from the Star. Cor, what do your instruments say?"

Cory replies carefully, wanting to confirm him without alarming the others. "Unusual, yes, very. Dangerous, no. As of ten minim ago, prediction is we won't even need UV glasses. But the ion count is running wild; that's known to affect some electronics as well as people."

Baram nods. "And those electrode caps are extremely sensitive. My dear lady, I want you to let me turn both yours and hers as near to zero as they'll possibly go. The danger is that they might climb into a mutual condition of runaway forward feedback, oscillation, which would severely damage you both. May I?"

"Oh, my goodness." The Lady's chewing on her thumb but she's calming. "Yes, turn them way down, please. You can, can't you?"

"Yes." His hands move among her sable curls.

"The tension . . ." The Lady sighs. As Baramji turns to disconnect the silent child-woman in the bed, her sister cries out, "I don't want her to feel alone!"

"I doubt she will, my dear," Baram soothes. "To make sure, why don't you hold her hands tight for a while, or massage her neck and limbs, as you must have done so many times? That will tell her you're near. Now remember—you hoped the radiance of the Star might help her. Here we're in the realm of the totally unknown. No one can say. What if this tension is a sign of beneficial effect?"

"Oh, yes. . . ." The Lady takes up her sister's limp hand and begins tenderly to massage it. "Sometimes"—she sighs—"sometimes . . . I don't know. I've done this against advice. *Expert* advice." She laughs bitterly. "Was this such a good idea for her? What do you really truly think, Doctor Bram?"

Baramji has never shed the boyish habit of crossing his fingers when he tells a "white" lie. Now both Cory and Linnix see him cross them behind his back. Cory chuckles to herself; an endearing man.

"I really truly think it *might* affect her," he says. "Provided we can control it."

"Oh, thank you . . . thank you so very much, dear doctor."

Meanwhile Zannez has been glancing from the pink-lit vitrex to Kip and back.

"How about that story now, Kippo?" he demands. "We'll be needing to get outside pretty soon."

"You finished there, Doc?" Kip calls.

"Tell away." Baramji returns to the bar. "And do remember, all, those drinks of Myr Cory's will hit you twice as hard as usual."

Cory, scraping ice, asks Baram, "What was all that with m'lady in aid of?"

"Taking steps to pry her loose from that living corpse. But it would take more steps than I have to do the job, and gods know what you'd have at the end."

"Umm. She's going to miss the story, too. She mustn't. Go get her, Bram."

"I'll try. I'll tell her her sister should know it."

"Quick, before Zannez goes crit."

Baramji returns with the reluctant marquise, while Kip begins the tale.

"Of course it was long before your time, just after the Last War," Kip tells the young actors. "I was younger than you then, I'd lied about my age to get into uniform and on a ship. There was real A-one chaos going for a while as news of the end of the war spread. People getting in last shots, blowing up pacification teams, what have you. You had this old Class X cruiser, the *Deneb,* Captain Tom Jeager commanding, 'way out here on the Rim. We—I mean, they—never did get word of the peace."

At that "we," Cory Korso stares at her man through narrowed eyes—but her lips quirk in a smile.

"Well, *Deneb*'s recon had spotted a star system where someone seemed to be building a superweapon. The builders'

438

planet was named Vlyracocha in the ephemeris, that was all they knew. Captain Jeager and his science team worked up the data. The thing was loaded with ultrahigh-energy stuff, it could knock out a star system if it blew. Of course they weren't building it on the planet; they had it in a Trojan orbit behind a big asteroid they were using as a construction base. The thing was enormous. Here," he interrupts himself, "I'm forgetting your suppers. I figured a one-dish spread'd be best." He begins transferring filled and covered plates from storage to the heat-shelf.

"Six minim. Anybody wants more puffs meanwhile, they're over here, drinks on your right. . . . Well, this Captain Jeager we had—" Here Cory bumps his arm. He glances at her puzzledly.

"Jeager was an unreconstructed old Human Supremacist. He wasn't about to allow some group of aliens to complete a superweapon that could dominate a sector or maybe even, as Jeager said afterward, be sent right into the heart of the Federation. So he took *Deneb* out there and used his last planet-buster blowing up the so-called weapon. Lords of the worlds, what an explosion!

"And just for good measure, he sent a salvo of T-missiles at the planet Vlyracocha, and another one into their sun. Which shortly destabilized and blew, too. All that was dreadful enough, but it wasn't really the point. The worst thing— Here, Ser Vovoka, you've let your ice melt. Fix him up, Cor. And let me fresh you up too, Doctor Ochter. Zannez, are you trying to make abstainers out of those kids?"

He pours everyone's glass full before going on.

"The appalling thing came out later. A Federation Pacification squadron caught up with *Deneb* and took him and the whole crew into Rehab, and tried to salvage anything they could of Vlyracocha. D'you know they now have techniques for capturing energy patterns from a dead planet? But here—nothing.

"It turned out, incidentally, that the captain really was

crazy; he'd been notified that the war was over and hadn't told anybody. All those poor little swabbies still thought they were fighting the good fight, dreaming of green *horropoi* coming down their bunks all night. Oh, gods! You'd have had to go through it to know." He exhales noisily, half laughing; definitely one who has been there.

Cory is staring past the pink-lit vitrex, smile gone. Tomorrow . . . She holds the thought.

"The point—the horrible point—was learned from the Federation," Kip goes on somberly. "Because there were a few Vlyracochans—diplomats, students, technicians—who had been off-planet when we—the Humans—*Deneb*, I mean—attacked.

"The Vlyracochans, you see, hadn't been building a weapon at all. Their race was very old, and they were dying. Some condition of cell fatigue no one anywhere could cure. So they'd decided, many lifetimes back, to leave a memorial—the most beautiful work of art they could conceive. And they built into it all their finest literature and music and their history and everything about their race. That was what all the energy was for, to keep it going to eternity. . . ." Kip shakes his head and looks down, unable to face the thought.

"And that was what we destroyed."

"Ohhh . . . oh *no*!" An indrawn breath from his audience as the full tragedy is realized. "Couldn't they . . ."

Kip shakes his head again, no. "Nothing the Federation had could bring more than a shred of it back. . . . I tell you, sometimes when I look up at the Star I literally can't take the thought of what I—I mean, my race—did. People call it the Shameful Star, you know."

There was a pause, and then Cory says, "You've left out the very end of the story, Kip."

He looks up, runs a hand through his hair, and blows out a breath. "Oh. Well, yes. . . . The story of Vlyracocha—that's one Humans never talk much about, any more than necessary. It wasn't just the shame, the Human crime. You can hear

440

worse, maybe, on a smaller scale—take Damiem here. But Vlyracocha wasn't quite over, see.

"At first we called it coincidence. Some still do. The fact is, of all the crew on *Deneb*, not one was alive five years later. Jeager went first—an oxygen fire in his hospital room. There were fatal accidents in Rehab. Then the Federation used some as the crew of a survey boat, and it disappeared on its second trip. Others went in other ways. The Fed medicos said it was subconscious guilt and death-wish. A friend of ours—remember Marta Dubaun, Cor?—started looking into it. Marta died next year in a local *favana* epidemic, by the way. There's even been considerable mortality among the shell handlers who had originally loaded *Deneb*, before she left base. . . . There really were Vlyracochan survivors, see.

"No more, of course. Their sickness made them short-lived. But people still have the idea it's not a healthy thing to know about. *Deneb* herself was towed out and sent into a Lyra ninety sun."

Kip breaks off and opens the heat-shelf to peek in, releasing a delicious smell. Cory begins distributing forks and water glasses.

"One minim." Kip leans back, lifter in hand. "So you had three separate radiation shells from those terrific explosions, expanding out into space. The first one passed here— Vlyracocha was over thirty lights away—just when Cory and I came. That was partly what we came for, in fact. It had been determined that the nova-front contained a lot of nasty hard stuff, and it was our first job to help protect the Dameii. The previous Federation observer had been here for the simple purpose of keeping them safe from Stars Tears sadists— you've had *that*—and there were Patrol ships on call. This observer's tour of duty was about up, and he needed help getting them all to go under adequate cover when the Vlyracochan radiation came through.

"It was quite a job, I tell you—I mean, you pointed to this star that just looked a trifle fuzzy, and tried to convince them

441

it was about to swell up and rain death all over them. They just laughed. But Cory was a marvel—believe me, being an Administrator is a lot more than brain work. I can still see you chasing that kid through the treetops, honey!"

Cory's smile at last comes back.

"Then came the night the first shell of radiation started to pass through us. By incredible luck the first layer was long wave lengths in the visible spectrum, harmless but spectacular. They showed the thing ten times its size and going mad. And we had such auroras—there wasn't any night. So the Dameii at last began to believe us.

"By the time the really hard radiation peaked we had shelters finished and the Dameii would go in them.

"That passed fast, and it shrank back to being just a big star. And all was calm for about five years. Then the second energy shell came through. We got ready—and scads of tourists came—but as someone said, it was mostly pretty lights.

"Now tonight sees the third and last act of the tragedy of Vlyracocha. The Base scientists haven't bothered getting such a detailed prediction. We've been told that anti-UV glasses will be enough. Probably they're right and we'll get no more than spectacular pretty lights. But some of us wonder; this front is from the core of the great work of art itself, which contained all the really exotic artificial energies, and just perhaps we may get some strange phenomena.

"Cory has stationed warning sensors out, and she got the Patrol to lay a monitor drone headed into the front. They're all rigged to readouts in the deck console. So if she says 'Take cover,' don't argue. Just scoot under the nearest roof. This lounge and the overhang out there have antirad shielding, they were built for the first wave. We had over two hundred Dameii in here alone, I was breathing feathers for a week. . . .

"And now—supper!"

He starts lifting out servers, uncovering each with a flourish as he sets them before the guests. Polite smiles answer him. But Cory sees his story has been all too daunting for many.

"Is this the only planet the Star can be seen from?" Linnix asks.

"Yes," says Cory. "By the time the fronts reach the next worlds they'll be too dissipated even to be seen as clear events."

"So Damiem is witness to two shames of mankind," Linnix says reflectively. "The Stars Tears horror and now this dreadful murder of Vlyracocha and all its people and works."

"Double Shame Star," Zannez says. "Almost a title."

"Oh, you showpeople!" Linnix is angry. "You see everything as titles or plots, or takes—"

"He didn't mean it that way," the girl Bridey, or Eleganza, speaks up. "That was just an automatic aside, it's stamped in us so. He feels the badness just as much as you do. If he has the technique to make a bigger public share it—isn't that worthwhile?"

"Hey, my little defender." Zannez grins. "I didn't know you cared." But his eyes don't smile.

Surprising them all, a few chords of music come from the girl Stareem's side. They see she has brought an odd little skeletal zither. "Lament for a Star," she says shyly, and plucks a brief minor theme.

"Bravo!" exclaims little Prince Pao, clapping his hands and looking around so peremptorily that Cory and others find themselves clapping, too. The small melody was really quite lovely. But the child—surely he *is* a child?—behaves like a grown man in love. Could the boy fancy it so? And what about Stareem's, ah, profession?

Abruptly the silent Vovoka stands up. "The light is changing," he announces in his stiff accent. "I go to the outside."

"I've been noticing that, too," Cory says. "Perhaps it's time." She leaves the bar and goes to throw the main doors wide before him. As she does so a feeling of finality comes to her—this will be the last, last time to open on the Star! . . . Radiance floods in.

"Ah!"

"Oh!"

"Ooh, Zannie, look!" The others come thronging through the doors in Vovoka's wake.

"Thank all the gods I had those sky cameras set up and running," says Zannez as they go out into the glory.

Only the Lady Pardalianches lingers, looking from the door to her sister to Kip.

"I'll wheel her out," Kip promises. "Just as soon as I fetch out the suppers you've all forgotten."

"Oh, thank you." The Lady bends to draw up a satin coverlet, to kiss the still brow and smooth the hair. "Doctor Baram turned our caps almost off, you know. I *never* do that. Oh, I hope I'm not abandoning her; it's the first time in ages she's been so alone."

"Won't be a minim. Scoot out and enjoy."

The Lady goes. Kip sets the servers onto a tray. "Cor, help me mark what's whose. Where are those marker thingies?"

"Coming."

As Cory leaves her view of the spectacular scene outside, she passes the giant crib where Lady—what is it, Paralomena? —lies. *Has lain, will lie,* Cory thinks, glancing in. The sleeper shows no sign of distress at being left alone. Alone? Cory wonders. Alone—or free? Can she really be suffering the lack of her sister's strange companionship?

As Cory gazes a very faint flicker stirs the quiet face, so fleeting that Cory isn't sure what she's seen. She looks hard. Isn't that hint of smile a bit stronger now? For the first time it comes to her that this still body might be more than a giant organic doll, might be truly alive. . . . What can it be like, reverberating hour by hour to the Lady Pardalianches's brain?

She hunts out the plastite markers, grimacing at the thought of what it would be, for her, to lie in thrall to that Lady's perceptions.

"Kippo." She sticks a "V" on Vovoka's untouched plate.

"M'love?"

"Just on a crazy hunch. . . . Don't hurry too fast bringing that poor thing out."

VIII

HOLDING:
Lady Loma's Ride

Reality is coming back at last, coming out of the strange star-studded mists, cutting through the bizarre and often embarrassingly sexual hazes that have gripped 'Lomena for so long. Real silences are breaking into the endless flow of Pardie's voice, which has gone on and on and on so incomprehensibly. An almost forgotten freedom is returning, severing the intimate hold of Pardie's limbs and body that have felt ever stronger and more vivid than her own. The reality of self is coming between her and Pardie's will and actions, which have been playing themselves out through Loma as instrument, while her own voice and body and mind receded to nowhere and nothing, as if her very hold on life were slipping, thinning away.

And all this Pardie-life has been so dreamlike. Like a true dream, she supposed in the beginning that only a minim or so might have passed in the real world. Yet as it has gone on becoming ever more complex, she has come to suspect that its real time was much longer. Hours, perhaps, or—she hasn't dared think more.

But now, sudden and exhilarating, she's waking! Coming back to life, feeling reality solidify, within and around her.

Reality is an immense vista of dark, blue-green, gently rolling moorland, stretching from horizon to horizon, a world kept smooth and parklike by her father's innumerable flecks of small herbivores. At the moment every leaf is shining from a recent shower. Over her shoulder arches one of the planet's perpetual rainbows, which have given it its name: Rainbow's End. This had been meant quite simply in early days, until the finding of the fantastic veins of diamond, zeranaveth, emerald, and gold put a double meaning to it.

And this real world is only background for a realer reality, which occupies a level stretch just before her: a high-fenced, oval extravaganza of eight-foot brick walls, white-and-scarlet pole structures, potted shrubs marking wide water ditches, great hedges behind gaudy panels—a mad construction which any fifteen-year-old horse-lover would instantly recognize as a replica of the official course for the Interplanetary Jump-Offs coming up a month hence.

The Lady Paralomena gazes upon this surreal object with love and fierceness, sniffing the fragrance of the moist tanbark that floors it. Then she turns, shading her eyes to see where the central reality of all approaches: her old groom Davey, on his old brown gelding, leading a gleaming silver creature who dances on a short lunge and cavesson.

He—it's very visibly a male—his full name is Silver Emperor Comet the Eighth. Eyes of another age might have been slow to recognize him as horseflesh. Some centuries earlier, jumpers had finally been freed from the tyranny of the running form, with its big barrel body and four all-purpose legs at the corners—"porkchops on the hoof," they had scornfully been called.

The ensuing effort to breed a perfect jumping machine has

447

produced a creature that might be taken for a giant springbok with overtones of kangaroo; short-coupled, with flowing mane and tail and heavily muscled quarters. To the eyes of Davey and Paralomena, he is an animal needing only wings to go permanently airborne. Among the new strains is a half-expressed albino gene; the Comets have always been silver-coated, with dark eyes and points.

His full silver tail—a functional feature in jumpers—swirls around her as they came alongside.

"I don't know, Lady 'Loma." Davey sighs, reluctantly handing over the lunge. She's afoot, having walked out to meet them, and Comet's saddle is above her head. "A young lass like you, if you'll pardon me, m'lady, riding an entire. And them's some awful tall fences there."

"Oh, entires like lasses, don't you, Mischief?"

Two velvety pink noses caress each other.

"You aren't seriously suggesting that I have the best Comet of the crop gelded, are you, Davey?"

"Oh, no, ma'am!" Davey blushes to his ears. "That'd be a crime! It's just that, begging your pardon—"

"Begging my pardon for the thousandth time, what you mean is that I should have some boy—say, Gemmy—show him, eh? To which I say for the thousandth-and-first time, begging *your* pardon, No! This is my horse, I've trained him and jumped him every show of his life, and the subject is now closed."

"Yes, ma'am— Ah, look out!"

The huge stallion, neglected while they argued, is rearing and threatening to come down on her with all-too-obvious intent.

Paralomena dodges and fearlessly pulls him down, laughing. "No, no, no, boy! You have your species mixed. What you need is some exercise—and then we'll show you something you'll like better than Human girls! Now hold still."

Shaking his head mournfully, Davey dismounts to help her up. But with a nimble twist of the climbing stirrup, the girl leaps up into the white fur saddle and expertly unfastens and discards the climbers and the cavesson.

"But ma'am! Suppose you took a fall—you'd need these!"

"And if we fall in the waterhole, I'll need a bathing suit, too, I suppose."

Davey laughs helplessly and undoes one of his saddlebags, which are generally used for luncheon and canteens.

"What's that, a pudding-bird? . . . Oh, no!" He pulls out her black velvet hard hat.

"Just for an old man's sake," Davey says. "Just so's I won't get heart failure on top of a tongue-lashing from your father. Please, ma'am."

"It gets in my eyes—oh, all right." She half braids her long dark hair and slaps the helmet on with a rap on its top, secretly conscious that it's exceedingly becoming.

"Anything more? An air bag?"

"Here they come, ma'am."

A huge old open hydrocar is appearing and disappearing in the dips and twists in the moorland road. In back sits Lord Perdrix, her father, and her twin sister, the young Marquise Pardalianches.

"Is the bugler with them?" Comet is taking all her attention, whirling about so she can scarcely see.

"Yup."

"Good. Tell them to hurry up."

Davey swings a red bandanna in the universal sign language.

Comet does not like cars. He gives an experimental buck, for which he is ill suited, and then stands stock-still, snorting his disdain.

"Hi, Daddy! All right, Davey, gates! Bugle us in, you."

The gates swing wide, the bugle neighs, and the two beautiful creatures melded to one charge in. Once around the piste, then straight at a towering brick wall.

Up and flying over, his delicate forelegs folded to his chin, goes Comet. And then down and away at a stand of head-high bush. Both are simple jumps to allow riders to gait and calm their mounts. But Comet is hard to gait today, Davey sees. The girl is frowning as they round a corner on the wrong lead.

She has barely time to throw her weight on the inside foreleg; Comet stumbles and comes up on the proper lead. But the space to the next jump—a tough in-and-out—isn't quite enough. He sails over the outside wall off-balance, takes one stride in the center, and gamely tries to jump the outer wall, a structure of heavy poles.

The audience gasps as one—in the rough landing the girl's hard hat slipped down over her eyes, and she's knocked it off. Now Comet rises like a rocket, but he can't clear. He crashes up through the top, and two great poles come rolling down his neck. As the heavy poles come at her, Loma sinks her bare head in Comet's mane. No use: they hit her exposed head first on one side, then, as her neck droops, on the other, as though she's being battered by a giant wielding trees.

"Why don't she drop the reins 'n' cover her head?" Davey moans, running into the ring.

"No daughter of mine would." Lord Perdrix is getting out of the hydrocar, looking worried. The Lady Pardalianches, in the height of her fifteen-year-old beauty, only holds her perfumed hands to her mouth, gasping and watching intently.

Comet cavorts on down the piste for a few strides. Then, feeling the change in his limp rider's balance, he slows sedately and halts; he is a gentleman.

The girl still clings on by reflex, her bleeding head staining Comet's immaculate neck. Davey gets to her first, reaches up, and gently pulls her leg. She rolls down unconscious into the arms of her father and the bugler boy. Lord Perdrix has to open his daughter's fingers to release her death-grip on Comet's reins.

"Cooee, cooee," Davey soothes the great beast, who stands like a statue, rolling his eyes and snorting at the smell of blood. But Davey's voice fails him as he sees the girl's eyes are wide open, almost smiling.

450

He knows then that she really is dead.

And so she would be had not little Lady Pardalianches made the chauffeur get on the car's special transceiver to airports, flight doctors, hospitals, brain surgeons. As Perdrix carries his daughter toward them, a 'copter bearing a great red cross whirls precipitately down alongside. Three medics jump out and take over.

Lady Pardie, who cares nothing for holding on to horses' reins, cares greatly about holding on to her twin sister's life. She is not about to release that life to Death. Hour after hour, while the surgeons work, she sits by; from hours to days and nights, to weeks and months. And when those surgeons give up, she finds others, and others yet, who give up in their turn.

But still the young Lady Pardie will not let go; with her sister on total life support she stays by, talking to Loma, massaging her, arranging every possible intricate stimulation so that no part of her should atrophy. She teaches herself to read the medical literature, she threatens to squander her patrimony offering rewards on a dozen scientifically famous worlds. And she achieves finally the neural transfer mechanism of the golden electrode caps, with their marvels of circuitry hidden beneath the gold rollbed where Loma spends her life.

The rollbed, which now, twenty-two years later, stands momentarily unattended in the rosy Star-light in the lounge of a hostel on far Damiem, while the Lady Pardalianches joins the other guests in exclamations at the sky.

IX

NOVA MINUS 3 HOURS:
Kip in the Dark

Kip Korso carries his tray of servers out into a world on fire. The dark deck he stands on seems a narrow bridge of solid matter thrust into a sea of light.

Dazzled, he backs under the overhang to get his bearings. His eyes have always been slow to adapt to darkness. But his ears are sharp; he can hear people breathing, stirring, and an occasional peremptory mutter far to his left.

As he stands blinking, comes a fast patter of footsteps, and a small body bumps him so hard he barely saves the tray.

"Oh, sorry!" says Prince Pao excitedly. "Myr Cory says I may use the scope! She showed me how this afternoon."

"Righto. But remember, Prince, this stuff is all in-atmosphere. A scope won't do much."

"Of course." The lad's voice sinks to a tone suitable for imparting secrets of state. "Frankly, I have a selfish desire for the splendid view up there."

"Good seeing!" Kip grins in the darkness. Behind him the lounge doors bang.

By now, Kip has made out that the rosy light they saw through the vitrex shines up from the mirroring lake. Flame reds mingle with a cold gas-blue flicker—that would be the Star's auroras seen through shoals of sunset cloud. The sky overhead must be glorious, but he dares not look up and blind himself anew, or his guests will never get their suppers. Luckily the stay-hot servers really work.

At the east horizon of the lake an eerie lime-green glow is brightening—a close precursor of the oncoming Star. That's the source of the change Vovoka noticed from inside. As Kip looks down, the reflected radiance sends out an unearthly green ray that touches the central fires and dies back, to be replaced by two others. . . . Indrawn breaths and murmurs from the dark deck.

"Last time this stage lasted nearly an hour." Cory's voice comes from straight ahead of him, across the deck. Kip locates the dark line of the parapet and a shadowy blur against it that has to be Cory at the console. A taller darkness looms nearby. Vovoka?

"I think it's developing faster tonight." Cory gives her soft, warm, contagious chuckle, a sound Kip loves. "We called it by the disgracefully unaesthetic name of Green Fingers."

Just as he starts toward her, an earthly light abruptly glares out to his left.

Gods! He's forgotten Zannez and his act. And the screens— oh, murder, the screens aren't opaque! Weird shadows of the actors writhe on them, evoking uneasy stirrings on the deck.

Kip stares paralyzed while a shadow on the brightest screen turns into an unmistakable crotch shot, a girl kneeling spread-legged, while between her thighs the distorted shadow of a head in profile rises to her, tongue out—

"MYR ZANNEZ!!" Kip and Cory shout together.

The shadows leap and the lighted figure of Zannez, camera

in hand, steps back into view, multicolored lights gleaming from his bald head and monocle.

"You'll have to hang blankets over those screens, too!"

The lights go off as the problem is explained. Pale forms race for their rooms, return laden with bedding and drapes. Zannez hangs the stuff himself.

"A thousand apologies, Myr Cory, and Kip—Myr Linnix, do forgive. . . . It was just my logo, we do that black on red. . . . *There,* those should do it! . . . All right, now, kids! Back to your places, got to get some work done." To Kip he adds, "We're starting a live imitation of those terrific color effects up there. Could be an art winner—after I'm fired."

"What am I supposed to be, those trees?" plaintively inquires Hanny Ek's voice.

"You're the surprise factor. Now dammit, get on down." Zannez vanishes. A glow of light springs out on the hostel side of the now opaque screens, too mild to interfere with the view.

Kip is dazzled again, and more than a little bemused by Zannez' definition of "work." But the light has shown him Baramji sitting with Linnix in the loungers outside the infirmary, not three meters to his left. He gropes his way to them.

"Bram, you can read here, check me. I think these are your two." He hands them down. "Who's where? You know my night eyes."

Baramji checks the markers in the soft light from the infirmary vitrex. "Right. Linnie, this is yours. Eat. You'll find you need it, my dear." He turns back to Kip. "Well, Zannez' lot you know. Lady P. is right behind you, where the screens meet the parapet. I have a hunch she's peeking. Vovoka's standing along from her, near Cory. And Doctor Ochter and our two nuisances are back here on the far side of the lounge doors, toward their rooms. They're fretting about something—"

454

"Oh, Myr Korso!" the Lady's voice cuts in. "My sister—
please don't forget!"

"Just one minim more, truly." As he says it Kip recalls
Cory's admonition to delay. Well, the twin's had the benefit
of the Zannez commotion.

He off-loads five servers. "Myr Zannez! Here are your
suppers. If you're, ah, busy, they'll stay hot. I'm putting
them on this ledge back here."

Sounds of upheaval behind the screens. Ek's voice rises.

"Zanny, you slave driver! Time out for chow, or I strike."

Kip turns toward the Lady and finds he can follow his nose
to a reclining shadow that glitters.

"Charming perfume, Lady Pardalianches. I believe this to
be your supper. Let me put this napkin around it, it's hot."

"Thank you. But *please* hurry."

"Hurrying. . . . Cor! Supper coming!" He edges along the
parapet.

Cory knows his problem and is already by him.

"Could you take Ser Vovoka's, too?"

"Done. . . . The Star-front seems to be developing just
the same pattern as last time, Kip, only faster. You'll see,
it's fantastic when you can look. . . . Wasn't that awful,
with Zannez?"

"Dire. My fault, I should have checked."

"No harm done, I think. . . . What's a 'logo'?"

"Best not ask, it might be his grandmother. . . . Hey, I
have eyes, I can see you." Forgetting that others can see
better, he bends and kisses her warm, scented neck.

"Wush, love! Watch it—Ser Vovoka's plate—"

He leaves her urging supper on the star-gazing man and
finds Doctor Ochter seated to the right of the lounge doors.

Beyond him under the overhang Kip can just make out a
pair of empty chairs.

"Your supper, Doctor O. But where are our unwilling
guests?"

"Definitely not unwilling now," says Ochter genially.

"They're fascinated. But they also seem somewhat alarmed. I noticed them huddling back under your antiradiation eaves and Yule told me he'd managed to get a heavy dose near some defective equipment, just before he left. His doctor warned him not to add to it until he could get his course of shots. And Hiner is just naturally goosey about in-air radiation.

"I tried to tell them their apprehensions are groundless. But they've slipped back to their room for goggles and helmets—and cameras, too, I'm glad to say. I'll put their suppers on the ledge here."

"Absolutely unnecessary." Kip frowns. "Damn. I should have told everyone that UV glasses and shield hats are piled under the stairs, in case you want them. Feel free."

"Oh, goodness, as long as Myr Cory is satisfied I am, too. . . . Ah, this *is* welcome. I failed to eat much, earlier."

"Goodo."

Impatient tappings are coming from the marquise. Kip decides he's delayed as long as he decently can and takes the empty tray in, holding one eye closed to keep its adaptation.

The Lady is before him.

"She's *moved!* Oh! Myr Kip, look—her arm."

Squinting, Kip can see that the still figure really has moved—or been moved, if the Lady's unconscious is playing tricks. The right arm is now across the body, fingers tightly clenched. He recalls Baramji's line.

"Well, perhaps the Star really is helping her a bit."

"Oh, yes! Quickly, please, do bring her out. She *must* have the full Star-light!" In her eagerness the Lady actually tugs at the heavy bed.

Kip takes over and wheels the giant crib out.

"I'll put her right beside you here. See, Doc Baramji isn't a jump away." And the big rollbed will help block off Zannez' "work," Kip adds to himself.

"Oh, thank you. . . . Doctor Baramji! Myr Kip saw it, too—"

He leaves the Lady distractedly telling Bram about the arm

and takes his place opposite Cory at the console. There he can finally raise his eyes to the spectacular light-show of the sky.

Overhead, the fiery vermilion of sunset is still lighting up a filigree of high cirrus. Above this hang arches of cold blue auroral light, shaped into great curtains rippling silently across the sky.

Over the hostel roof, the western horizon has paled to lemon, where float a few last flame-edged violet clouds like celestial fish.

But the east! Its bank of green witch-fire has brightened to a dazzling astral arc-light beyond the black lace of the horizon trees. Above this green lies another bank of black, unlit by stars, that's hard to recognize as normal night sky. Crossing it are now many of the gaseous green light-spokes, growing from the fire below. They blaze out, fade, and are reborn; seem to wheel like stately searchlights before being lost in the zenith splendor.

And all, all is mirrored in the still lake below, an almost bewildering double beauty.

Across the console Kip can see Cory's face lift briefly between bites of her supper and careful studies of the dials; he wishes she could for once relax.

Meanwhile he's listening hard between his own bites; there's an old myth that very bright, moving auroras make faint sounds. . . . But he can hear nothing unusual—until suddenly he's startled by a familiar whispery beat overhead.

He grabs Cory's wrist. "Wyrra!"

"Oh, no!"

"Shshsh."

They strain their ears while Kip's raised hand follows something inaudible to Cory. Then he makes a down-slashing gesture. "He's landing!"

"I can't believe it!" Cory's eyes shine.

"Damn, he's going to walk right by Hiner and Yule." Kip rises. "Cor, can you warn the others while I go meet him?

And turn on the deck lights, too. They're almost as blind as me.''

"On your way." She sets his board on standby.

Kip starts cautiously along the deck, steering by the parapet. Shortly a soft glow springs up behind him. Ahead lie pools of dense black shadow cast by overhanging trees. He stops by the first.

"Myr Yule? Doctor Hiner?'' he calls as loud as he dares.

On his third try an unintelligible response comes from the end room. Kip gropes closer.

"Would you mind staying put for a few minims? Our local Damei may be passing, and we don't want to scare him. He's used to your room being empty.''

"With pleasure," says Hiner's voice.

"And when you rejoin us, please come as slow and quiet as you can.''

"Certainly.''

"Will do,'' Yule chimes in.

Kip waits. The Dameii always make a reconnaissance pass before landing. It was the beat of Wyrra's defective wing as he looked them over that Kip had heard. Wyrra is sensitive about it; he always lands out of sight on the front side of the hostel and walks around the end, where Yule and Hiner are now.

Shortly a moving spot of light appears at the bend of the deck. Human flashlights are one gift the Dameii really appreciate; they depend only on natural phosphors, since they cannot bear the by-products of flame.

Wyrra's light is high; as usual, he's walking on the parapet caping. Kip gropes his way forward to meet him.

"Welcome, Myr Wyrra!'' he calls softly in Damei. "Your visit brings much pleasure. We feared you would not care to be near so many Humans.''

"Nyil wished to experience a group of your people.''

"She is here, too? What a delightful surprise!''

A burst of high-pitched laughter from overhead answers him.

At that moment the tall form of the Damei steps into the light between two trees. His great blue-white wings meet above his head, quivering with nervous resolution so that they send out prismatic reflections of the sky. He is of deviant coloration, the only truly blue mutation Kip has ever seen. His hair, which he wears half-coiled on his head in imitation—or mockery—of Human style and half-cascading to his wings, is a stunning blue bronze, as are his brows and lashes. And the huge glittering eyes he fixes on Kip are a celestial blue.

He's clad from throat to toes in floating white gauze richly blue-embroidered, and Kip knows that when he's near Humans, his back around the wing-bases where the glands are is completely covered, too—a great annoyance to him. On his child-slim feet are white-and-blue-ornamented slippers; he's one of the few Dameii Kip has met who wears footgear.

Seen close, the Damei is both more and less Human-like. His hands are three-fingered and have no true nails, and the thumbs are very high-set, like dew claws. His hidden feet are three-toed, too, and carry his most alien feature—stiltlike, backward-tending heels, the evolutionary remains of heels and toes adapted for perching.

But his masklike smile is very Human, though his "teeth" are a white line of cartilage. His nostrils are much like a Human's, and the eyes are bigger homologues of Kip's own.

Just before he passes again into shadow, there comes a flash of small pale gold wings, and a tiny Damei child lands on the parapet in front of her father. She begins walking, almost dancing, toward Kip—seeming not at all afraid.

"Nyil, my dear, many welcomes to you. So you wish to meet a group of Humans?"

"Oh, yes!" Her voice is a very high, pure soprano. "But what is the word for—for people who come?"

"Well, there are two useful words. *Visitors* are people

459

who come to see a friend, or the friend of a friend. You and Myr Wyrra are now *visitors* to me and Cory, for example."

The two reach Kip and he walks along beside them as he explains.

"And then there are people who travel to see a place or an event of great interest or beauty, without knowing any of the people there. This is called *sight-seeing* or *touring,* and people who do it are *tourists*. The Federation often provides places to stay, like our hostel here. Tourists may pay the Federation for their rooms and food, and being shown around, as we do. Tourists who wish to visit sensitive worlds like Damiem must also be carefully examined first. These tourists have come here now to see the last beauty of the Star, which is known of on other worlds. They're not here to see Cory or me. You yourself, Myr Wyrra, and certainly Nyil and her friends, might one day make a *tour* to see interesting sights on other worlds. Then you would be tourists. The Federation would be happy to pay for your way."

Both Dameii listen attentively, slowing almost to a stop. When Kip finishes, Wyrra exclaims, "Ah, this *pay,* this *money* thing again! I fear I don't truly understand."

"Would you like a talk on money at our next session, Myr Wyrra?"

"Yes, very much."

"Me too—I mean, I also," says Nyil in Galactic. "And also more on when I use formal. Why are you calling Father 'Myr' tonight?" Her accent's excellent.

"To show respect in the presence of strangers," Kip says slowly. "Also, this warns the other Humans to address him respectfully." He switches back to Damei. "I don't explain this well—you see, it is taught to us when we're very small children, so I don't remember the rules. I just know when it feels correct. For example, I know I should call your father Myr Wyrra when we have lessons, and I think it is because he has placed himself in the childlike position of student, so it is polite for me to emphasize that he is a superior, an adult. You see how complicated it is? I can't even explain clearly."

"I think I understand that," says Wyrra in his careful Galactic. His long lips curl in a rare smile. "Like flying. When I finally had need, we could find nobody able to explain. All had learned so young."

"Exactly!" Kip smiles, too; Wyrra is referring to the joyful day when they knew that Baramji had really succeeded in repairing his bad wing.

They've now reached the edge of the pool of light around the Human group. Wyrra halts, Kip and Nyil follow suit. From the console, Cory waves a greeting. Only Nyil waves back.

Kip sees that Zannez is out and has his camera trained on them. The faces of the four young actors are peering from joins in the screens.

"What is that man pointing at me?" demands Wyrra. "And what are all those heads?"

"He is a *cameraman*—a record-maker. Now he is making a record of you and Nyil. We will show it to you before he leaves. I believe you will enjoy it. The heads belong to his four young *actors*—something like your story-dancers. They act out stories for him to record. They can't come out before Humans because they aren't fully clad. We consider them very beautiful, by the way. They're the Humans who are going to show themselves in the village tomorrow. Will you and Juiyn be there?"

Wyrra frowns.

"Oh, Father, *please!*" Nyil begs.

"If not, perhaps we can arrange a private showing," Kip says tactfully. He knows there is some unexplained tension between this family and the village.

At this moment the lounge doors open quietly and Prince Pao comes out.

"Oh, look, Father!" Nyil points. "That must be a Human

461

young! Isn't it? Oh, how interesting! What kind is it, Myr Kip? And how old?''

"Kind? . . . Oh. He is a male, a *boy,* of about seven of your long years."

Hearing the word, the prince glances at Kip with raised eyebrows, then doffs his plumed cap and bows formally to the two Dameii.

"I have only five years." Nyil frowns. "Is he the child of some of these tourists?"

"No. He has come alone. This is very unusual, but he's an unusual child. In a few years he will be the ruler of a small but important world."

"Oh," says Nyil, staring hard at Pao. Then she looks around and points again. "What's the matter with that female?"

"She was injured in an accident. Her sister there hopes the Star's light will help her."

"Kiflayn," comments Wyrra—an untranslatable term meaning a bizarre and hopeless enterprise.

"Probably," says Kip. "And now do you wish me to escort you to meet others, or is this as close as you care to come?"

"I wish at least to greet your mate," says Nyil firmly. "And Doctor Bram, too. Is that not correct?"

"That would be polite, customary—unless you have come specially to speak with me alone. Or unless you wish to show displeasure with one of them."

"Oh, *no!*" says Nyil. "Father, you *must* greet Myr Cory! You just must!"

"It would give her great pleasure," Kip tells him. "But she will understand perfectly if you don't wish to go among so many strangers."

"Certainly. I will be happy to greet your mate," says Wyrra. But the nervous lofting of his wings belies his words.

As Wyrra begins walking toward her, Cory looks meaningfully at the other Humans, finger to lips. Kip sees with relief that the parapet side of the deck between her and the Dameii

462

is clear of people; only little Ochter and Pao are on the hostel side. Everyone is still, save for a faint whirring from Zannez' cameras.

Halfway to Cory, Wyrra levels his great wings and floats down off the parapet, to continue his march along the deck. But Nyil stays up, reluctant to lose her view.

As they near Cory, Kip hears quiet footfalls by the hostel wall and turns to see Hiner and Yule take positions near their chairs. They're wearing goggles and elaborate shield hats. Even through the lenses Kip can see their eyes rounded in fascination. It's considerate of them not to risk making a clatter by sitting down. Good.

Wyrra turns to follow Kip's gaze.

Next instant, Kip is all but bowled over by air blast and deafened by the clap of Wyrra's bad wing. The Damei whirls, snatches up his child, and leaps or flies up to the parapet, where he balances with tensely upheld wings, poised for flight.

"What are—*those*?"

Kip realizes what a bizarre sight the goggled, helmeted students present.

"It's all right, Myr Wyrra—truly! They are only ordinary Humans wearing antiradiation protectors. Myr Yule, Doctor Hiner! Would you mind taking off your glasses and hats just a minim? Wyrra hasn't seen any before, and got spooked."

"Certainly. Here, show him." They remove the offending gear, revealing smiling faces, although Kip notices that Hiner's smile seems oddly strained, and he retreats behind Yule. Gods, is it possible that he senses Wyrra and Nyil as *insects*?

Prince Pao has already trotted over; he seizes a helmet and goggles and carries them to Kip. Nyil squirms around in her father's grip to inspect Pao. He smiles and twiddles his fingers at her, while Kip explains.

"Your people wore those when they had to leave shelter during the bad first passage of the Star. There's also a heavy suit to cover the whole body, and a cape to protect the wings,

463

but one can't fly in it. You must have been too young then to recall this, Myr Wyrra.''

"Umm . . . yes.'' Wyrra's wings relax as he handles the hat. Nyil gets the goggles and holds them to her eyes, making horrible faces and giggling as she stares around. Wyrra lets her slip down to stand on the coping beside him, one hand still grasping her shoulder.

"Why are the Humans wearing them now? We were told the Star isn't dangerous.''

"It isn't. Do you think I would expose Myr Cory? But . . .'' Kip simply isn't up to discoursing on Aquapeople tonight; perhaps the gods of truth will forgive him if he packs Hiner in with Yule. "These two accidentally received a dangerous dose just before coming here, and their doctor told them to wear these against the chance of any more radiation at all, no matter how weak, until they could have their corrective injections. In fact, we should pass these back at once, if you're satisfied. It was courteous of them to risk damage to reassure you.''

"Many thanks indeed, from us both.'' The Dameii hurriedly pass the gear to Pao, who runs back to the overhang. Wyrra bows formally to Hiner and Yule, an,action of pure beauty, his long wings crossing over his back. Nyil copies him as best she can under her father's hand.

"Do let go, Father,'' she complains in Damei. "You're a worse menace than a hundred goggles and hats.''

Wyrra smiles at last and lets her go. She runs along the coping to Cory, her stubby gold wings standing straight out with excitement. Cory is in the console seat, her head not much below Nyil's. Nyil holds out a tiny hand.

"Good evening, Myr Cory,'' she says in her very good Galactic accent. "I trust you are feeling well?''

Cory takes the hand as though it's a flower petal.

"Yes, thank you, Myr Nyil, and I do hope that you and your family are all in good health, too? It was so kind of your father to visit us tonight. And what a delight to see you here!

464

Do your friends tell you that you're growing taller every day? Soon we shall have to call you Myr Nyil in earnest.''

The child sighs ruefully. "It seems very slow to me.''

Cory chuckles. "Yes. I remember it seemed slow to me, too. . . . And did you have an interesting time in school today, Myr Nyil?''

"Pleasing, thank you—we had digitals.'' And with that, Nyil's careful dignity breaks up entirely. Peals of irrepressible, contagious giggles, musical as a flock of songbirds, spill over the dark deck and are joined by others who don't know what they're laughing at but find it impossible to resist. In the midst of it, Nyil manages to ask her father something in Damei.

Wyrra's lips quirk as he turns to Cory. "My daughter wishes to be told honestly if her conversation was correctly done.''

"Absolutely perfect,'' Cory tells him. "You're going to have trouble to keep up—*avrew loren mori na peer*—with your bright child.''

"Her accent is remarkable for a person of any age,'' adds Kip.

"Thank you, Myr Cory and Myr Kip. This will make her very happy. She works much at it, you know.''

Meanwhile Nyil sobers herself by studying the console lights and switches. "When I am bigger I intend to learn all about such things,'' she announces. "*Everything*. . . . what's that light that just came on? The big red one, there—is it telling you something?''

"It's telling me to reset it.'' Cory wishes the child had picked on anything else. She lowers her voice. "If I fail to reset it, that means there is real trouble here—suppose we were all struck by lightning, or something very bad—so, if it's not reset, the Patrol will automatically send a ship at once, with a party of fighting men, doctors and so on, to fix whatever may have happened. It's called a Deadman's Alarm;

see if you can guess why. Almost every faraway place has one.''

"Dead-man?" She loves puzzles. "Oh, I will think!"

"And *I* think," says Doctor Baramji, who now stands beside them, "that I will never get a handshake or even a smile from this young lady unless I come and ask."

"Oh, Doctor Bram, I was coming to greet you, truly I was on the way." Nyil extends the delicate hand, while her small wings rise. "Good evening, dear Doctor. I am so very happy to see you."

He takes the hand, barely closing his fingers on it, and switches to his rudimentary Damei.

"And I am very, very happy to see you, Myr Nyil, and to see you looking so well. Tell me, how is your father?"

Baram's grammar is fair, but his accent is lamentable. In medical work he relies mainly on his superb bodily empathy.

"Father is well, I think. It is good that you came away from the others, because now he can tell you himself. He doesn't like to experience new Humans, as I do. Go to him, please."

She skips down from the parapet and over to where Kip is making space for Wyrra and Baram to approach each other. Wyrra's wings shoot up, trembling so they flash rainbow lights, as he forces himself to step toward Baramji. They exchange a sketchy handclasp.

"Myr Wyrra," says Baram, in his stumbling Damei. "A question of your health. . . . We go over there"—he gestures at a space between the console and the parapet—"so we may speak alone?"

"Certainly."

When they had gained the privacy by the coping, Kip sees Wyrra relax.

Baramji and Wyrra inspect the rebuilt wing. Then Baram steps behind the Damei and climbs up on a planter box, where he begins to manipulate the wing carefully from base to tip.

Glancing up, Kip sees that the beauty of the sky is still there, beyond the deck lights. It's changed to sumptuous, hypnotic violets, blues, greens. But it can't compete with the interest of their visitors, on whom all eyes are fixed.

Just then he feels a light tug on his arm. Little Nyil is fearlessly pulling him toward the hostel wall.

Amused and delighted, he lets himself be guided, first past the Lady and the rollbed, then toward Linnix. To the Lady, Nyil gives a poised bow and a murmured "Good evening," then leaves her starting a flowery barrage of talk. To what she can see of the bed's occupant, and the medical arrangements beneath, Nyil gives a long, serious look. Linnix she passes with another brief bow and greeting—and then Kip sees where he's being taken. Straight past the screens to Zannez!

He holds back for a moment, but an urgent tug convinces him that his duty as a Damei's escort transcends the proprieties of the Code.

As they pass the screens, bare bodies seem to be flashing everywhere. He tries not to look, but a ravishing nude clutching a wholly inadequate scrap of lace—Bridey?—imprints itself on his brain.

"Tell names, please."

Kip comes back to himself to find Nyil's wings standing straight up with the excitement of her adventure. As she gets a close look at Zannez' shiny bald head, monocle, and big dark camera eye whirring straight at her, Kip can feel the hand on his arm begin to tremble. Luckily, at that moment Zannez drops to one knee for a level shot, where he appears less formidable. The four young actors, suddenly all clothed in black short robes red-blazoned "APC," have the tact not to come too close.

"Zannez! Quick, stop shooting, take that monocle out, and stay down. You're scaring her."

The cameraman obeys with all speed; the trembling quiets.

"Myr Nyil, may I present Myr Zannez? He is an expert

recorder who has come a very long way to record your world and the Star.''

"It is a pleasure and an honor to met you, Myr Nyil. We were not told that your people and your world were so beautiful. You see, we are really *very* far away.''

But Nyil seems to have tired of small talk and things Human. She glances at the four actors, who are sitting cross-legged some meters away, but doesn't seem to care for a closer view. Instead she says, "I wish to see your records of Father and me.''

"You shall,'' Zannez assures her. "Kippo, explain that it takes time to process, and different equipment to show. We thought we'd give a viewing here tomorrow night, Star radiation permitting. And tell her they're life-size, in color and sound.''

Kip ripples off a Damei speech, adding that there will be a private show for her and her family if they wish. "The last sound you'll hear will be me telling Zannez to stop recording. . . . Would you like now to have him record you saying hello to your father and mother? It would be a nice surprise to end your private show.''

"It records in Damei?''

"Oh, yes. Just stand as you are and say, 'Hello, Mother,' or whatever you wish.''

"Um-m. Yes. I find I'm tired but I will do this.''

Kip explains to Zannez what's wanted, and in a minim or two the recording is made.

"Tell her that tomorrow I'll show her how to make a recording herself if she likes.''

But Nyil breaks into Kip's speech by asking Zannez in Galactic, "Why do you not have hair?''

Zannez laughs. "On my world we all want to look different from each other. So I cut my hair off close. Feel.'' He bows his head for her feathery touch.

She's not too tired to giggle at the prickly scalp.

"Thank you. Now I go.''

"Thank you for coming, Myr Nyil." A murmur of agreement from the ring of watchers. Nyil nods politely to them as she and Kip emerge from the screens.

Everyone seems to be looking at them, even Ser Vovoka, who stands silent and alone beyond Cory. Wyrra has a wild, staring look in his great eyes. Kip guesses he's torn between pursuing his daughter and dread of going among Humans— and if he takes off to overfly, he'll be humiliated by his defective wing. Probably they've emerged just in time to head off a scene.

Nyil releases his arm and runs to her father, disregarding the Humans en route. Wyrra snatches her up in his arms and gives her a squeeze and a hard shake.

"Father! I made a surprise for Mother and you!"

He says something fast and low in Damei, then lets her wriggle down to the parapet.

From behind him Kip hears the renewed whirring of Zannez' cameras. He evades the marquise by going past Linnix and Ochter; both are beaming. But the chairs beyond Ochter are empty again.

"What have those two gone for now? Chain mail?" he asks Ochter.

"Camera reloads." The little professor sighs comically. "And they missed the best shot of all. Wasn't that perfectly *charming?* Is she his only child?"

"Yes, so far. They don't have big families."

He rejoins the group at the console in time to hear Cory sending their greetings to Juiyn, Wyrra's mate.

"Is she well? Or has she gone to a Damei society meeting, leaving her husband and child alone to face the monsters?"

She's cut short by a startling thunderclap of huge, dark-furred wings. A female Damei fetches up on the parapet behind Wyrra, silhouetted against brilliant green sky. Her hair and dress are darker, plainer versions of her husband's. Under her gauzy gown are what appear startlingly like two high, virginal breasts, which Kip knows to be the folded lips of her oviceptor.

"He-ere is Juiyn," she announces, laughing, though her wings stay upright, forming a magnificent arc. The Humans realize they haven't appreciated the size of a fully wing-spread female Damei.

"Greetings, Myr Juiyn!" say Kip and Cory together. "It gives much pleasure that you came." Kip adds a formal welcome in Damei.

"Gre-etin," Juiyn replies. Her Galactic is obviously elementary compared to her family's. She shoots some rapid-fire Damei phrases at Wyrra. Then her long arm stretches down, extending a hand at Cory.

"Go-od even-in, Myr Corree."

Cory gives the hand a brief, delicate clasp.

Juiyn repeats the routine with Kip and adds firmly, "Also I thi-ink now go-odbye. Pleasantness."

Wyrra bows to all, and the two adults set off, walking, for their home. Juiyn paces the deck beside Wyrra on his coping path. Little Nyil lingers for a formal handshake with the Korsos and Baramji, despite her mother's abrupt calls. When she finally takes off to sail over her parents' heads, Kip and the others see Wyrra catch her foot and unceremoniously haul her down out of the air. He plonks her on the coping to walk before him.

"I'm afraid Nyil's in disgrace. Did you see her kidnap me?"

"She is a handful." Cory chuckles. "Let's see, I better leave the deck lights on awhile. I hope you folks don't mind."

A dozen voices assure her they didn't.

"I hope Hiner and Yule remember not to bang around," Kip says worriedly. "Maybe I'll just ramble down after them and check."

He sets off as he had before and again is stopped by the deep black shadows of the trees. Here he waits until he sees

470

Wyrra's light come on far ahead, cursing himself for forgetting his own. He'd left it recharging in the workshop, along with their three hand weapons, whose sights he'd checked. . . . He should recharge Wyrra's light, too. Better yet, teach him how.

All stays silent in the end room, aside from some mutters and the bump of a travel bag on vitrex. Finally Wyrra's yellow light turns the corner at the far end and disappears behind the hostel.

Kip walks back, enjoying the glorious green radiance of the sky and the luminous violet-blue auroral curtains which seem to ripple just above their images in the lake.

"All clear!" he calls as he approaches the group. "Douse the deck lights."

When the man-made glow goes out, the celestial splendor brightens tenfold; Kip is sure he will soon be able to see by it. He can hear Zannez' excited voice; the cameraman seems to be relieving pent-up feelings.

". . . absolutely marvelous, Myr Cory! Tremendous, unbelievable! This afternoon was so great I thought that was *it*, but then this Star-scene—whew!—and then actually having two of the wing-people here and one of them a little girl! Alien or Human, *the* most exquisite little girl ever in front of a lens. She makes Leila Carlea, the divine nymphette, look like a gods-forgotten lump. And the action she showed, the voice—oh, kids, wasn't that one glorious eyeful? What'll you bet the Feds are besieged by Gridworld idiots wanting to come out here and sign her up?"

Amid the laughter Stareem asks anxiously, "They wouldn't let them, would they, Myr Cory? I mean, they have so much money—"

"No way," says Cory firmly. Kip, arriving by the console, backs her up.

"Don't forget, they've had planetfuls of money waved under their noses for Damiem before. Plus some fairly wicked personal threats. That doesn't play, either. A few tragedies

471

happened, but they rolled up the biggest crime ring in the inner planets from Damiem leads. I trust your Gridworld friends will understand 'No.' "

"I guess we've been privileged," Zannez says soberly.

"Yes." Cory shakes her head in wonder. "I *never* expected them to come. Did you, Kip?"

"Nh-unh. It was Nyil's idea, Wyrra said. I guess she holds a lot of clout with her father. . . . Well! Can I bring anybody anything? More chow, a drink?"

"Just marvelous . . ." Linnix says dreamily, still dwelling on the Dameii. "That little Nyil . . . I keep thinking of your story, Kip. It was children like Nyil they tortured. . . . How could humans be so—be so bestial, so—" Her voice breaks.

Baramji leans over her, lifts her chin. "Linnie, don't— that's all in the far past. Think how marvelous they are now, enjoy it."

She looks up at him gratefully, manages a smile. "Yes. . . . But it mustn't *ever* happen again. Never, never."

"It won't," Kip assures her cheerfully. "That's what we're here for. . . . And now what can I bring who?"

X

NOVA MINUS 2 HOURS:
Doctor Ochter Reports

"Oh, my goodness!" Doctor Ochter struggles up from his chair. "It was all so marvelous I almost forgot! I brought along a little hostess gift, Myr Kip, in case the Guardians of Damiem turned out to be as gracious as reputed. You've been quite widely heard of, you know." Beaming, he makes a little bow to the Korsos and to Baram. "If Myr Cory agrees, I thought it might make a suitable toast to our good fortune while we await the Star."

"How perfectly lovely," exclaims Cory. "Whatever can it be? As to time, the probe is predicting at least ninety minim—"

"Shshsh!" Kip holds up a hand, pointing to the dark far end of the deck where the Dameii vanished. Everyone listens hard.

"Did you hear it, Cor?"

She nods slowly. "I thought it was Wyrra taking off around on the front side. But—twice?"

"I thought I heard a very faint voice," Stareem puts in shyly from the end of the screen where the four have been watching. "Like a call, or cry. Not words. Is it true they can't make loud sounds?"

"Oh, gods. D'you suppose Wyrra took a fall?"

"Go look," says Cory.

But Kip hesitates. "If he did fall and it wasn't too serious, the last thing they'd want is a Human poking in. If it's serious, Juiyn or Nyil will come for Bram."

Ochter speaks up. "Look, I'm going to my room anyway, and I have pretty fair night vision. Why don't I just take a good peek out, on the arcade side, before turning on any light? They'll never know I'm there. If I see anything that looks unusual, I'll report straight back here."

"Oh, thank you so much!"

"Good plan, if we're not overworking that leg," says Kip. "I'll come with you are as far as those shadows."

"No need, no need." Ochter bows his head at them and hobbles, with surprising speed, down the dark deck toward his room.

As his uneven footsteps die away, Prince Pao comes over to the console.

"You know that Patrol ship you said was in orbit? I saw it! Through the scope, just as it got really dark. That's what I was coming down to tell you."

"You—what?" asks Kip.

"I saw your ship!" Pao repeats impatiently. "The Patrol ship you said was in orbit. I wasn't looking for it, the scope just picked it up."

"But—" Cory broke off, looking at Kip; he recalls telling her that Dayan was taking *Rimshot* nearer to the new relay satellite. "What part of the sky did you see it in?" he asks the boy.

Pao gestures toward the southeast. "There was a strip of clear sky there, down low."

"What made you think it was a Patrol cruiser?" Cory asks him.

"Well, naturally—" Pao begins rather loftily. Then the Korsos' seriousness gets through to him, and his manner changes at once. "Inference only," he says carefully. "Knowing there was a Patrol ship, when I saw what appeared to be a ship I jumped to the conclusion—may I ask, why the concern?"

"That isn't the Patrol's normal orbit," Cory tells him. "And out here on the Rim things aren't like your Fed-Central traffic. Ships are very, very rare. Could what you have seen have been a stray rock or a satellite?"

Pao considers. "Unlikely. When I found I couldn't pick it up again, I fed my estimates of apparent brightness and velocity into your scope computer. I assumed it was moving normal to my line of sight, plus or minus fifteen degrees. Oh, I also assumed it was shining by reflected light. The parameters intersected at a ship-sized body at two hundred thousand km, plus or minus fifty. The, uh, albedo is awfully high for a rock, and the size is huge for a man-made satellite. And a closer distance puts you terribly slow. So I took it for a ship. Going toward the north, by the way; I estimated an angle of forty degrees from the horizon."

"Well done, Prince."

Kip and Cory look at each other for an instant while she unhooks the microphone and starts the old transmitter up. He sees her face taking on what he calls her "c-skip look." She's debating whether this information is hot enough to justify powering-up for the huge energy expense of transmitting it to Base via c-skip. The instantaneous transfer of information involves, among other things, supercooling the antenna, necessary to perturb the local gravity-field configuration. They've been around this before.

"Listen, Cor. The power-up will lose you half the time you gain, working through this rig." He waves at the old console. "And you don't want to do it upstairs—by the time that antenna is cooled down you'll be right into Star-rise time. You don't want to be sending then, do you? And that ship can't get itself lost out here, not for days. Unless it has 'skip, in which case it's an official vessel. Chances are a hundred to zip it's some joker who misjumped out here and is looking for a FedBase anyway. . . . Remember the *Golan*?"

Cory grunts; years back she *c*-skipped a warning of an unknown ship—which turned out to be an official visitor Base hadn't warned her about.

"Send a regular transmission with an override on it. It'll be there in a hundred minim—and let Base decide whether to pull Dayan in."

She nods, reluctantly convinced.

"Thank fortune I ran the voice relay down here."

Federation Base Number Ninety-six is in a huge, slow-orbit rock about a hundred light-minim away, made lavishly comfortable, by space standards, to compensate for the bleak Rim duty. The "override" signal will put her message in the Exec's hands as soon as received—if Commo isn't playing paddleball. She trips in the automatic recorder, which will loop the receiving wire, and jacks the transmission power to max, to punch through the Star's static. When the Ready light finally goes green she begins speaking quietly.

Only Bram and Officer Linnix are in earshot. Vovoka is clearly preoccupied, and the Lady Pardalianches's attention is divided between her sister and Zannez' screen.

Little Prince Pao watches the transmission with excited eyes. Once Cory breaks off to ask the time of his sighting, and when she resumes Kip catches the words "intelligent amateur." Pao nods to himself with a satisfied air.

Recalling his intention to get his hand light, Kip beckons the boy

"Would you do us a favor, Prince? Another favor, I should say."

"Pleasure."

"You know where my workshop is. My hand light is in

the recharger on the back bench, and I shouldn't leave here. Could you get it?"

"Two minim."

"Hey, wait. Our three Tocharis are on the bench, too. I meant to start one on the charger this afternoon. By any chance do you know how to put a standard Tochari hand weapon on to charge?"

"Oh, yes. But they aren't there, you know."

"They aren't . . . there?"

"No. I thought you'd taken them. I saw them this morning, but when I went to sharpen my pocketknife before supper— you have a really neat old stone, you know—I noticed the weapons were gone."

Kip's stomach is doing a slow cold slide toward his boots.

"You're sure?"

"Of course. Naturally I assumed you—"

"No, not me." Kip manages a grin. "Must be Doc or Cor, assuming they were charged. Things have been a shade uncoordinated around here. But I do need that light before I step on somebody, if you'd really be so kind."

Pao has been watching him sharply. Now he nods and heads for the lounge doors.

Cory signs off and turns to Kip. "Poor Dayan, he'll never forgive me if his men miss those games."

Kip takes a deep breath and leans across the console.

"Cory, listen. Due to my carelessness and stupidity, someone has taken all our three Tocharis. I left them in the open workshop to be charged. Pao saw them there earlier and this evening he went there again and they were gone. Any forlorn hope Bram has 'em—you can assess that. There's only one lucky point, if you can call anything about this lucky: I also forgot to put them in the charger and they're all dead dry. So whoever took 'em has only hunks of plastite. Unless he has some magic charger of his own."

Kip pulls back and drops his head in his hands.

"Oh, my gods, Cor, what can I say? Careless, criminally

careless. Stupid—lazy—*sloppy* . . . Guardian of the Dameii!!''
he says bitterly. "You have to report this, you know, Cor.
Or I will."

Cory is silent for a few breaths, taking it in.

"Oh, my dear," she says brokenly. "Oh, my poor dear
man." She straightens up. "We can discuss all that later.
Right now the question is, who—"

"Halloo, halloo!" Doctor Ochter's limping footsteps sound
behind them. "I return bearing large information and a small
gift."

Kip pulls himself together and sees that despite Ochter's
cheery tone, his face is drawn with fatigue and pain; he looks
ghastly in the emerald light. Clasped in his arms are a large,
thickly wrapped parcel and a travel pouch. Kip quickly pulls
a chair toward him. "Here, Doc, let me give you a hand."

Ochter all but collapses into the lounger. "Thank you,
thank you. . . . I also have . . . a confession to make, when
. . . I get my breath." He gasps a moment, gratefully accepts
Kip's water glass.

While he's recuperating, Prince Pao arrives with the
hand-flash.

"Is there anything else I can do for you and Myr Cory?"
the boy asks quietly.

"Just go on keeping your eyes open, as you've done damn
well so far, Prince. Oh, there is one thing. If Cory is talking
or listening on the transceiver, and you see someone apparently trying to overhear, we'd be eternally grateful if you
could break it up. You can do things I can't." Kip forces a
grin.

"I know." Pao grins back and goes along the hostel wall
to take a seat behind Zannez, where he can watch both sides
of the screen. Kip sees him lean forward and smile approvingly,
doubtless at Stareem.

Kip wants to tell Baramji of the strange ship and the theft
of the weapons, but Doctor Ochter has revived and is starting
to speak.

478

"Well—first things first," the small man says briskly. "On arrival in my room I left the lights off and was able to inspect much of the arcade and the area in front. No Dameii, no Humans, nothing. There's quite a breeze on the entry side of the hostel, you know; one doesn't feel it here. But apart from the wind all seemed still and silent. I trust my eyes more than my ears these years," he adds wryly.

"So I ventured to open my door and slip along the arcade toward Yule and Hiner's room, staying in the shadow, until I passed their side door and could see up into the treehouse area. The branches were tossing, but I caught glimpses of a greenish phosphor light. I also thought I saw some movement up there, and I watched for several minim, but it may well have been merely the effects of wind.

"From where I was one can see only the start of the parapet—you know how the rooms are offset. So I continued around the next corner until the whole curve of the parapet was visible, well past the point where Myr Kip lost the Damei family's light. Still nothing. I could also check that the deck was empty, except of course for the small angle directly beyond the hostel's end. There seemed to be nothing to suggest that your visitors had not reached their home in safety. But the sounds you heard; what could account for them?

"Listening hard, I had become aware of the muffled echoes of some activity in the two men's room behind me. Your walls are admirably thick; even in the lulls of the wind I could make out nothing. But just as I turned back toward their door, the most extraordinary uproar broke out. Loud imprecations, thumps, bangings, and what seemed to be one of them groaning or sobbing aloud.

"A minim later their door flew open in my face and Myr Yule rushed out, followed by Myr—ah, Doctor—Hiner, who was forcefully remonstrating with him.

"I could catch only 'You must!' or perhaps 'I must,' or 'We must,' and 'I can't,' or 'You can't'—all quite incoherent and emotional. Through the open door I could see their room in great disorder, open duffels and gear strewn about, a case jammed shut with garments protruding.

"Hiner saw me as he came out; I must say that I have never seen a man's eyes actually roll before. Next moment he'd left Yule and clutched hold of my shoulder quite painfully, pulling me about and in a loud whisper alternately demanding and pleading that I 'help Yule.'

"At first all I gathered was that they were *afraid*."

Ochter pauses to drink more water, sighing.

"Good glory—what *of?*" asks Cory. "Is it more of the insect-thing? I should go to them. Bram—"

Ochter shakes his head vigorously, swallowing water.

"No, wait please. . . . What they feared? Everything! Radiation of course, and the Star; but also those charming flights of tree leaves, and Myr Zannez' cameras, and Ser Vovoka here, and the poor paralyzed Lady. Virtually everything and everyone, even to the Dameii. Especially the Dameii! Yule kept muttering about 'eyes flying over' and dashing back inside to make certain their end door to the deck was locked. By this time I had observed two open liquor bottles, and their breaths were noticeable despite the wind.

"But the serious part of this idiocy was that Yule wanted to smoke. 'To keep them off,' he said. I surmise that he is also simply an habitual smoker craving his smokes.

"Hiner said he'd put a stop to that, although not, I think, in time. As soon as he mentioned it I recognized a faint smoky odor between the gusts of wind and alcohol. . . . It also occurred to me that this episode might have been the origin of the sounds you heard."

"I'll buy that," says Kip. Cory nods.

Ochter sighs again, sipping his water, and adds reflectively, "By the by, although Hiner was superficially more coherent, I did sense it as that type of pseudocontrol—you've doubtless met it—which can go quite far into unreality before overtly breaking down. . . .

"In the midst of it all, he muttered something about the power-cell shaft, which, if true, could be very serious. But that can wait till later." The little man paused for breath before resuming.

"A curious point which has baffled me all evening: From being slightly hostile strangers, these two have progressed to a degree of intimacy—if not exactly comradeship—with amazing speed. You'll see as I go on—it's as though they've discovered some overwhelmingly important need or bond in common that overrides their personal differences.

"Well. To make a messy matter brief, they'd seen me inject myself this afternoon and taken me for a medical doctor. First Hiner wanted me to give them something—he called it, oddly, a *special shot*—to calm Yule. Then he wanted it for himself, too. When I demurred, they became threatening. They were coming out here and, well, bother Myr Cory, and tear up the infirmary, if I didn't help them."

Baramji, who has come over to listen, grunts ominously.

Kip sees that. Ochter is really disturbed; he misunderstands Baram's grunt and hastens on apologetically. "Yes—of course I should have come for you, Doctor Baramji, and for Myr Kip. But I feared to leave those two alone in that state, and frankly, I wasn't sure I could. You see, at this point they were hanging on me at the door of my room.

"And here is where I must confess, Myr Cory. I recalled that our clinic had given me several syrettes for use in case of insomnia. So I offered Hiner two, quote, special shots, unquote, on condition they hand over Yule's smokes. D'you know, I was quite relieved when they accepted?"

He smiles shyly.

Kip gives an indignant snort, imagining the little old fellow in the clutches of those two young clots. He sees Cory's face has taken on her Administratrix frown: such things should not occur in her hostel.

"To, ah, add verisimilitude," Ochter goes on, "I managed to make an inconspicuous cryptic mark on certain syrettes as

I took them out." His twinkle has come back, with a tinge of mischief that tells Kip he had secretly enjoyed his little adventure.

"Which I duly showed to Hiner, as evidence that they were 'specials.' He seemed satisfied. . . . Of course I checked the true labels," Ochter concluded seriously. "Three milliliters of twenty percent ambezine hydrate solution each. Doctor Baramji can define it for you better than I. I've always understood it was harmless, apart from its soporific effect, but I worried about the interaction with alcohol.

"Did I do wrong, Doctor?"

Baram stirs. All nearby—except Vovoka—have been fascinated by Ochter's account, despite the growing marvel of the sky.

"No problem there, Ochter. Though personally I'd have been more inclined to give them a good strong emetic and a kick in the tail. But no, you did no harm."

"Your verdict is more than welcome." Ochter sighs again, relieved, and begins fishing in his pockets around his lapful of bundles. "Especially since the effects came unusually fast. Yule threw himself down on his bed as soon as they were back in their room, and had difficulty telling Hiner to lock the door after me. Which Hiner didn't bother to do. So—dear me, I nearly forgot to give you these."

He holds out two slim packets of cheroots to Kip. As Kip takes them he recognizes his old Federation brand and feels a momentary pang. For a moment he doesn't see that Ochter is holding up the travel pouch for him to take, too.

"In the confusion I seized the occasion to secure those," Ochter tells them in a lower tone. "Perhaps you will make out a receipt in the morning? The pouch, by the way, is mine. I glanced in an open bag and decided they belonged in your hands as soon as possible. It is, after all, a serious matter even to bring such things here. Though in their case it was inadvertent, I'm sure."

Puzzled, Kip peers into the bag. His eyes widen and he

reaches inside for an instant and then passes the pouch to Cory as fast as his shaking hands will work.

She doesn't look inside but only feels it appraisingly, watching Kip. He alone hears her faint gasp. He nods.

"Three Tocharis," he confirms quietly.

XI

30 MINIM TO CONTACT:
The Royal Eglantine

Cory hands the unopened pouch back to Kip. "Put these in a safe place, Kippo." To Ochter she says soberly, "I think we have much to thank you for, Doctor. . . . As for Yule and Hiner, while I'm normally opposed to doing things to people without their full consent, in this case they literally insisted on it, didn't they? It's not as if they'd demanded some substance by name. They wished to feel better, and I'm sure they do. . . . But will they be ill in the morning, Bram?"

"Only from the alcohol," Baram replies. "But by the way, Cor, does it strike you as odd to hear two presumably healthy young men asking for injections? The young Human male is usually my most needle-shy patient."

Ochter speaks up. "If I take your meaning, Doctor, a number of other small matters brought that thought to my mind, too. First, the peculiar sudden intimacy I mentioned. And then Hiner insisted on injecting himself and Yule, too, and he had quite a little ritual. He also turned so that I couldn't see their arms. But all that is strictly in the realm of invidious conjecture. I'd prefer to leave it there."

"Unless it translates to action," says Cory thoughtfully. She's thinking that Zannez' "hunch" may have been based on solid indicators—if these two turn out to be druggers, and stealers of guns to boot. What did they want the guns for? Invading Baram's infirmary supply seemed more likely than some Stars Tears plot. "Bram, dear, I think you'd best lay on some security. Remember that plan we worked up when Dayan put us through the drill?"

"Ah, seven devils take it," Baramji grumbles. "You're right, Cor, of course. . . . Oof . . . but there's no hurry, the doses those lads gave themselves should keep them out of trouble quite a while. I can do it in the morning. . . . And maybe they have some supplies of their own they couldn't find in the confusion, perhaps that's what Hiner was rooting for. Meanwhile I say let's forget it and enjoy the Star." He turns back to Linnix, who's been courteously ignoring the conversation. "Oh, my, look how it's changed while we talked!"

"So I'm forgiven?" Ochter asks Cory.

"Indeed you are, Doctor Ochter, and our thanks with it."

He beams. "But I shall never forgive myself if I fail to present you with this small gift before the Star is up." He hoists himself to his feet and formally presents Cory with the large wrapped parcel. "I do hope it proves enjoyable."

"Oh, thank you! But Doctor Ochter, you shouldn't—" She sits smiling like a girl, rather helplessly holding the cumbrous thing. "Kip dear! Could you . . . ? Is it all right if he unwraps it, Doctor?"

"Most certainly. How thoughtless of me!"

Kip starts from his private thoughts to find himself gripping the miraculous travel pouch so hard his hand aches. It takes him an instant to recapture what Cory is asking him to do.

"No problem. Here, let me lay this on the console where you can keep an eye on it, honey. Now, let's see. . . ."

At that moment the lights behind Zannez' screens go off, and the cameraman comes out, for once without a camera. He's sopping his shiny head, the monocle's dangling, his medic's whites are stained and rumpled: he looks dead beat.

"Whew! May we rejoin civilization, Myr Cory? I've got all we need in the cans and then some, and the automatics will take care of the sky. I told the kids to get decent and come on out. Green?"

"Green indeed, Myr Zannez. Do make yourselves comfortable. Would you or your actors care for some refreshments?" Her long smile twitches a trifle at the contrast between her formal words and the "acting" that must have tired them.

Zannez waves his hand exhaustedly and flops into the nearest lounger. "Ah, thank you, just tell Hanno where the food box is—no, on second thought, Bridey'd be safer. . . . I'd love some *laangua*, but what I *really* crave is a look at that sky without lenses in the way. . . . Oh! Hey kiddies," he calls, "for the gods' sake watch those artifacts! Don't try to move 'em; we leave the screens up to protect them. Hear?"

A chorus of assent comes from behind the barrier.

Kip sees Prince Pao unfolding two glittering, fragile robes, one silver, one gold, that he'd secreted somewhere. The boy gives them a last critical look and vanishes with them behind the screens.

Beside the parapet, the Lady Pardalianches is still looking through her peephole. Suddenly she gives a start and a faint squeak, and her eyes open wide. Zannez has spotted her and winks broadly at Kip. Now he abruptly shouts, "Snake!"

"Yes, boss," comes Snake's voice.

"Cool it—or I'll edit you out."

"Yes, *sir!*"

The Lady has turned away and begun energetically working on her unconscious twin's arms and hands. Her face is perceptibly flushed.

Aside to Baramji, Zannez says, "Tomorrow remind me to get Snake to show you how he got his name. It's one for the books." He chuckles, sopping his neck and head; then he glances absently at the mop—a scarlet lace garter belt—and stuffs it in his pouch.

Meanwhile Kip had undone the outer wrapping of Ochter's gift. It is now visibly a large, long-necked bottle, with a small package attached to its neck. Kip carefully detaches this and lays it aside before proceeding to slit open the costly constant-heat and blow-resistant inner layer. He's working with more and more caution, occasionally glancing quizzically at Ochter.

"Lords of the suns!"

The last layers fall apart, revealing a large, squared-off bottle elaborately scripted and sealed in gold. Its contents gleam deep purple in the mingled emerald and turquoise from the sky. Zannez, Baram, and Linnix stare hard at it; Cory and the four young actors, just coming out to join the group, look questioningly from the regal bottle to the others.

"If this is what I—" Kip begins, then breaks off to address the Lady. "Lady Pardalianches, you're from Rainbow's End—by any chance does this look familiar? I believe it's made there."

The Lady glances up. "Why, yes, it's just Eglantine, isn't it? Or perhaps an illegal copy, there're so many about. . . . Oh, Doctor Bram, her muscles *do* feel so, well, so different tonight."

Prince Pao has come up behind Kip to inspect the bottle. "It's no copy," he says. "We use a lot of it. See the numbering in that special FWA seal? Anyway, the smell will tell, as they say. You can't copy that."

"I smelled some once," Stareem says proudly. She looks almost luminous, an exquisite moon-child in Pao's silver lace gown and her own natural platinum hair. Bridey, sitting on

487

the parapet with one fine leg swinging, is a child of the sun in glorious golden lace. But Ser Vovoka, beyond them, is attending only to the sky.

"I've barely heard of Eglantine." Bridey grins affectionately at Stareem. "That shows you *my* class of friends."

"But Doctor Ochter—" Cory begins, and is drowned out by Zannez, who's been glaring at the Lady.

" 'Just Eglantine,' eh? Just Royal Eglantine—just its weight in zeranaveths, right? Cameramen's pay doesn't run to 'just Eglantine.' But I've tasted it a couple of times at the feed troughs of the rich—and my, oh my."

"Neither does Federation pay," says Kip. "But I can confirm. Just Eglantine—oh, my, my."

From the shadows, Linnix and Baramji murmur agreement.

"Nor do academic salaries." Ochter beams. "I've neither tasted nor smelled it; in fact, I'd never heard of it until my students gave me this as a retirement present. I didn't know what to do with it, till a friend volunteered to store it in his wine cellar. When I decided on this trip and heard of you, I inquired and was told that it was universally enjoyed. It seemed to be a suitable hostess gift for Myr Cory."

"Very good," says Pao.

"But Doctor Ochter!" Cory finally breaks in. "This seems a fearfully extravagant gift. A sip would be just lovely. But I am beginning to believe this passes the limits of what we may properly accept. Please don't think I'm being rude. I wouldn't for the worlds want to cast a shadow on your wonderful gift, but—"

"No problem, as the good doctor would say." Ochter holds up a lecturing finger: "You'll find that the regulations do not apply to—I quote—'potables and comestibles to be shared by all present, especially upon a special occasion; and/or the remainder thereof.' Note that 'remainder.' That's straight from a Federation legal body. Frankly, he objected to a trinket I'd first thought of, from my home planet. And that reminds me! Everyone I spoke with told me I must warn you of the salted peanuts effect.''

"You mean it's salty?" Cory asks.

"Oh, goodness, no, Myr Cory. That's merely an old phenomenological term from antiquity, for something you cannot easily stop eating or drinking if you take one. Today we'd say spice-berries, or those little biscuit-bites, I forget the name. It seems Eglantine has this property.''

"Of course!" says Cory. "Morpleases. But how amusing!''

"Not all that amusing if you want to keep any, Cor,'' Kip says. "Also, it's powerful stuff.''

"Everyone knows you don't drink Eglantine by yourself,'' Pao says severely. "I had a great-uncle who set the trophy room on fire that way.''

"Right,'' says Zannez. "You must not, repeat not, leave that bottle open near anybody you're not watching every minim. And that includes you and me and the most devout abstainer you know. The compulsion fades in five to ten minim, faster if you're talking. I'm not joking—I got briefed by the Gridworld wine board for a documentary. But we used—phew!—cold colored tea.''

"My goodness! Perhaps we shouldn't open it,'' says Cory. Zannez groans.

"Of course we will,'' Ochter reassures her. "I've been told exactly how, too. We all pour one drink apiece—I have the glasses in the little box. But before anyone drinks, two or three people escort the bottle to the next room, say, or any well-lighted place where no one could go unremarked for the next few minim. Then we all start at the same time, as one does a toast. And when it's properly time for another we just fetch it back and repeat. Isn't that what you do, Prince?''

The boy starts to speak—then shuts his mouth abruptly. It comes to Kip that the prince's style of home dining doubtless includes a wine steward and other liveried assistance. Next instant the lad finds the tactful words. "That is the proper principle. And you see, storage is no problem; it's like any other liquor unless you've just had some."

"Well, this *is* a new experience!" Cory laughs. "We have to thank you very much, Doctor Ochter— Oh! Look up, everybody, it's really starting at last!"

Kip looks up with the others, anticipating what they'll see.

The Green Fingers stage has passed during the Damei visit, giving place to an immense and ever-changing upper-atmosphere auroral display. The eastern sky, behind the black horizon trees, is a radiant green striped with a few horizontal black bands, which are out-of-season clouds; Kip has been privately fretting about these. But now, between the black treetops, a sparkle of scattered diamonds is erupting all along the east. As the watchers gaze, the diamonds float upward, joining, until the whole eastern horizon is one long blaze. The brilliance clears the treetops, passes behind a cloud or two, and emerges upward as a great arc of white light, in which facets of vivid spectral hues appear, change, and vanish, like flights of astral birds.

For an instant this fiery apparition could be a limb of the Star itself, and many watchers gasp; but Kip knows otherwise. Sure enough, just as the arc's edge approaches the zenith, down at the horizon its central area darkens. The darkness spreads fast, becoming an inner edge, and the vast curve of brilliance becomes an arc, a segment of a ring or halo whose center is below the horizon.

The arc spreads upward and outward, diffusing, changing, always with its internal play of color—and as it diffuses, the diamonds of a following arc break out among the eastern trees. It is as if the oncoming Star were shedding off great haloes.

On the hostel deck, people can be heard sighing out held breaths. As the second arc rises, pursuing its stately, ghostly course, only to give way to another—and another—Kip explains. "They're actually shells," he tells the watchers, "thin outer shells partly in the lower frequencies that we can

490

see. The apparently empty space between them has quite a hash of the shorter wave lengths, but nothing dangerous. Last time we had a dozen or two of these before we got to the maximum, the peak density of the nova that we call the Star. . . . I regret to say that some poetic soul christened 'em the Smoke Rings.''

A groan from somebody.

"Oh, look—it's all jiggling! Or is that me?'' It was Bridey's young voice.

"No, it's not you.'' Kip chuckles. "Actually, that shimmering, quivery effect has been going on since, oh, before dinner—but you don't notice it until the rings come up. They stay steady, see? . . . Later on, that perpetual flicker can get a little maddening; you feel as if you can't think straight. We don't know what causes it, either.''

In fact, he thinks, that skywide pulsing and strobing is already a little disturbing. It makes everything feel unreal. The eyes seek relief in the brilliant arcs, which seem to be immune.

"Perhaps we should make haste,'' little Ochter suggests, looking at the unopened bottle in Kip's hands.

"Righto.'' Kip returns to his struggle to clip the heavy wiring of the Eglantine's cork. Ochter picks up the little packet Kip has laid aside and opens it to reveal twenty elfin goblets, fragile as bubbles. . . .

"That's correct,'' Pao approves.

"They're so small,'' says Ochter, "I was amazed. But everyone assured me . . .''

"Not to worry. You'll see.''

"How many?'' Ochter counts heads. "Two and five and one and two, and you and I—I assume you'll take some, Prince?''

"Half a glass only at my weight . . . that's twelve so far.''

"And the Ladies will share one glass?''

Lady Pardalianches nods sadly. "I'll moisten her lips from mine.''

"So, thirteen, my young computer."

"I'll set them out on the ledge," Pao offers, "and stand guard while you stash the bottle, if you like."

"Excellent, excellent." Ochter counts out thirteen delicate glasses.

"You mean we all get some?" asks Snake Smith.

"Why, of course!" Cory is shocked.

"Oh ma'am, that's beautiful. Thank you very much." The others echo him. "It'll be a memory for always," adds Stareem.

"Ah-h-h!" Kip's labors are rewarded by a gentle pop. As he withdraws the cork, a vinous fragrance of a richness and delicacy beyond compare spreads across the deck. Prince Pao nods with satisfaction.

"Oh, my!" The little doctor sniffs appreciatively. "I do believe my advisers were correct. Myr Kip, would you pour it? These old paws are a trifle shaky for that freight."

"Righto." Kip carefully carries the Royal Eglantine back to where Pao is lining up the tiny glasses, with his own placed apart.

"I believe I'll take the bottle into your infirmary, if you don't mind, Doctor," Ochter says reflectively. "It's just a mite safer, if all this is fact."

"No problem," says Baram. "I'll go with you."

"No. With all due respect to you, Doctor, I have already chosen my guardians for the task." Ochter raises his voice. "Myr Stareem, Myr Eleganza, would you both be so kind as to accompany me into Doctor Baramji's domain, when our host finishes pouring? You see, there *is* a plan," the old man adds archly, to general chuckles.

The two beautiful girls rise and from long habit regally pace the few meters down the deck—Bridey the queen of golden fire, Stareem the queen of silver snow. Kip sees they can't resist the extra swirl of skirt and smoothing of waist that betrays their pleasure in the beautiful new robes. Ochter struggles up to meet them, bowing creakily.

Kip feels his throat choke up a trifle. They're such kids—
Stareem is what? Fifteen, maybe less? And Bridey-Eleganza
not much more. What a life for them. Don't think of it:
maybe their alternatives are worse. The Federation has a few
dark Human worlds, too. Maybe these two are fortunate. He
finishes with Pao's half glass and recorks the Eglantine. It
now displays a superb warm ruby glow beneath the whitening
light.

"Let me carry it, Doctor Ochter," Bridey says. "You lead
the way. If I trip you can have the Dameii fly me up and drop
me. Here. . . ." She scoops up the flowing skirt and tucks it
in her sash, so high that Kip sees where the scarlet item
Zannez pouched belong. Stareem hastily readjusts the skirt
while Ochter tactfully looks away.

Baramji rises to open the infirmary door and turn on a
light, Kip hands over the Eglantine, and the little procession
sets off. As Stareem closes the infirmary door behind them,
Prince Pao, grinning, takes up an extravagantly bellicose
sentinel station before the line of little ruby lights.

"This becomes more serious later," he says. "We'll have
to persuade the Lady Paralomena to take my place—sorry,
ma'am."

The Lady Pardalianches wheels on him, her face a mask of
fury. "You—you cruel boy! Oh—"

"I humbly beg your pardon, Lady. I meant no disrespect."
He bows to her, his plumed cap held across his breast. But
Kip, who can see his face, reads trouble brewing and hopes
to the heavens the Lady will shut up. Inspiration comes:

"Oh, look!" He points. "You sister, Lady Pardalianches—I
believe I saw your sister move!"

She's at the bed in a flash, Pao forgotten. And to Kip's
amazement he and the others can see real movement there.
The gleaming coverlet over the unconscious woman's legs
rises once, twice, as though Paralomena is trying to bend
both her knees. Her sister gasps out, "Doctor!"

Doctor Baramji is already at the other side of the rollbed,

493

his ear pressed to the invalid's chest. The bent-up legs subside as he listens. Kip's stomach lurches. Have they seen the poor creature's death throes? His mind begins to work on the grim practicalities of storage, transport—the Moom are notoriously averse to carrying the dead.

But Baramji raises his head, nodding reasurance to the marquise. Then he bends beneath the bed and adjusts something invisible to Kip. "A little more oxygen and blood sugar," Baram says, "if she's going to be so active."

"Oh, *Doctor*—oh, Doctor, my darling *lives*, she'll live again, I always knew—"

"We can only let time do what work it will, my dear." Baramji produces two more of the large blue capsules. "These will help you to be patient. Ah, thank you, Linnie." He takes the glass Linnix offers and presses it on the marquise. "I must insist you takes these quickly, my dear. Much might depend upon your steady nerves."

"Oh—"

Kip can see her hand shake as she seizes the capsules. Linnix is at her side, steadying the glass as she drinks.

"There. Now I suggest a light—very light—massage of those legs, if you have the strength." Baram pats the Lady's shoulder. "I'm right here, you know." He and Linnix retire to their loungers by the infirmary wall. The marquise is already at work on her sister, murmuring and cooing fondly to her.

Kip catches Baram's eye and looks a question. The doctor shrugs, letting both hands fall wide in total bafflement.

At that moment the main infirmary light goes out, and Ochter, with his attendant nymphs, emerges.

"We placed it by your night-light, Doctor," the little man says. He looks fatigued and limps straight to his chair.

"It took us hours to find it in these weird shadows." Bridey laughs, shaking her beautiful head. "We sure could tell a bachelor lives there, too. Do you always keep your soap in your shoes, Doctor Baram?"

"Ah, so that's where it went," Baramji says absently, watching the rollbed.

"Myr Kip," calls Stareem, "I thought you told us that you don't have any Damei servants."

"We don't," Kip tells her. "Why?"

"Well, when we were in there I heard somebody giving the arcade a good sweep-out. Are there any other Humans here?"

"No—at least, I hope not."

"I, too, noticed those sounds," Ochter puts in. "I concluded that one of those large featherlike trees must be brushing the outer wall. As I mentioned, there's a pronounced breeze on the entry side, though one doesn't feel it here."

"That's the *V'yrre,* the dry-season wind." Kip chuckles. "For sure we don't have any visible little helpers—wish we did, eh, Cor?"

"And I'll take a medical orderly while you're at it," says Baramji as he wrestles to let down the back of Linnix' lounger.

Kip quietly beckons him over to the console.

"Bram," he says low-voiced, looking at Cory. "I want you to put this in your infirmary safe, soonest." Cory nods agreement. "It's our three Tocharis. Ochter found them in Yule's and Hiner's bags. They're dry. They must have been taken from the open workshop, where I stupidly left them for recharging."

He can feel Bram's whole attention abruptly focus on him, but he continues to look away. After an instant Baram murmurs, "Yule *and* Hiner?"

"One or both, we don't know. In one of the open duffels, Ochter says."

"Hm'm. . . . Right." Baram tucks the bag under his arm and heads for the infirmary. At the door he checks and turns to the others. "I have to go to my quarters for a minim.

Anyone who fears I may be after the liquor bottle is welcome to observe."

"Oh, we trust you, Doc," Zannez says piously and adds, as Baram vanishes into the infirmary, " 'cause you haven't touched your drink yet."

Amid the general laugh Kip begins rechecking the console displays he'd been supposed to watch. On the eastern horizon, two arcs of white fire are now expanding quite close together; the invisible center of the rings—the Star itself—is now obviously very close to the horizon. They'd better get that Eglantine toast ready.

"I wonder if somebody would be good enough to pass out these drinks?" he says over his shoulder. "Then we can start as soon as Bram comes back and the Star actually shows."

"Hear, hear!" Zannez jumps up. "How about me and the kids deal it around? And seeing this is in your honor, Myr Cory, isn't there some way we can pry you off that computer for half a minim, so you can enjoy?"

Linnix pulls herself up from the comfortable recliner. "Myr Kip, you're monitoring overall inputs, aren't you? I believe I can do that for you, if you want to relieve Myr Cory."

"Sold to the first bidder," says Kip over Cory's protests, "with thanks from both. Cor's had quite a day. All right, Madame Administrator honey. Do you go quietly, or must I carry you? Frankly, I'm a little out of condition."

Cory rises and stretches, smiling gratefully at Linnix. By the lounge doors, Ek is handing Ochter a tiny ruby goblet. Cory says, "Doctor Ochter, why don't you go right ahead and have some? It's yours, you know, and—forgive me—you do look as if you could use it."

"No, no, I thank you, Myr Cory. That would not be right." The old man carefully accepts the tiny glass. "But I confess I'm very curious to learn whether all this is true, or is some great joke."

"You will, Doc, you will," says Zannez. He's presenting

a glass to the marquise. She leaves off massaging her sister's legs to clutch it with both jewel-lit hands.

"Oh, thank you! I'm *so* tired." She sighs sweetly.

The deck is steadily darkening, despite the blaze in the east. Kip can just see Bram come quietly out of the infirmary. The doctor peers about till he locates Linnix at the console and then sits down beside her empty lounger. Bridey sees him, too, and brings him his drink.

"All here and ready when the Star is," she announces.

Heads turn eastward, and Kip hears exclamations of dismay. He looks up to see that what had seemed to be the dark-forested horizon is in fact a solid black bank of low cloud, its edges glittering with silver light. The great halo of diamond light swelling above it shows where the Star will rise—and moving toward that spot, on the wings of the *V'yrre*, is a huge black-and-silver cloud promontory.

"You godlost cloud!" Kip explodes. "By the nine purple devils, with the whole sky to flap around in, why? . . . Well, we'll just have to wait till the Star rises past it. It does look to be moving pretty fast."

The current ring of light swells in majestic silence toward the zenith; beneath it is an unusually wide band of black, and from behind the cloud layer come rays of a somewhat different quality—the outermost fringes of the hidden Star itself. A feeling of something huge and alien and unnameable coming onto them grips the watchers on the deck.

Cory is lounging on the parapet behind her mate. He looks around and catches her smiling fondly at him. As usual, a warm, complex tenderness sparks. He smiles back, thinking, not quite experimentally, My Cory.

Permanent mateships are quite rare, and it's never occurred to Kip—or to his friends—that he might be capable of one. But he and Cor have been together far longer than either has been mated before, and it's getting harder and harder for Kip to imagine life without her, or with someone else. They've never discussed it. But he's pretty sure their mateships here on Damiem have been as happy for her as for him. . . . He grins, remembering Kenter's old joke: "All this and money, too?"

Right now, Cory's smile is untypically relaxed, almost dreamy. She's enjoying her unexpected freedom to watch the Star. In their life together she's so seldom without some background occupation or concern. Seeing her now so peaceful, he wishes for the thousandth time that he could give her some of his own easygoing nature. I'm good for her, he thinks.

Beyond her, along the parapet, Kip hears little Stareem urging a glass of Eglantine on Vovoka. Surprisingly, the sky-obsessed man takes it. Kip shifts to look past Cory and sees Vovoka lift and drain the glass in one draught, quite oblivious to the general plan.

"We-ell!" The Lady Pardalianches sounds scandalized.

Kip peers into the shadow beyond Vovoka and makes out the golden rollbed. That glimmering female blur beside it is the marquise. As he looks, a white elbow upraises itself from her veiling. Despite her disapproval, the Lady seems to be indulging herself in a generous sip. Kip grins.

Meanwhile, Vovoka hasn't turned back to the sky, as Kip expected. Instead he's lingering over his glass, eyeing it sharply, tipping it up to roll a last drop on his tongue, and rudely spitting into the treetops below. Then, as if satisfied, the tall man sets the glass bubble on the parapet and looks deliberately around the group until he finds Ochter.

"It will not work, you know," he says directly to Ochter, with a cold sound that might have been meant as a chuckle.

Everyone falls silent. Vovoka continues to examine Ochter for several long breaths, during which the small man gazes up at him like one helplessly hypnotized.

The odd scene holds long enough for Kip to puzzle over it. Vovoka's strange remark sounds as matter-of-fact as if he's referring to some well-known project of Ochter's. And Ochter's peculiar, almost cringing reaction seems to acknowledge it. Yet so far as Kip knows, the two men have barely exchanged a word. How could Vovoka be privy to anything Ochter plans?

Or—can Ochter and Vovoka be already acquainted, but for some reason not admitting it? And what "will not work" about the Eglantine? Could Vovoka have some strange notion that Ochter is trying to ingratiate himself with his handsome gift? Why? Or is this Vovoka's idea of a joke? If so, it doesn't look it. The tension between the two men looks real.

What the scene reminds Kip of, in fact, is one of the old grid-shows he'd seen as a back-planet youngster, where the villain reads people's thoughts against their will. That was kids' nonsense, of course; for centuries everybody's known that Human-Human telepathy doesn't exist.

Nonsense aside, Kip decides that this must have to do with some earlier conversation he's missed. Probably it's plain to everybody but himself.

But when he looks around he sees only expressions as mystified as his own. Cory's questioning gaze is moving from Ochter to Vovoka, from himself to Bram. And Bram is taking careful sniffs at his untasted Eglantine. Even in the strange light Kip's sure he can see Bram's eyebrows rising as he sniffs.

Kip raises his own glass to sniff, but at that instant Vovoka breaks the stasis.

"I haven't time. Pity," he says shortly, still in the same conversational tone, and turns his back on the group to resume his watch on the sky. Complete enigma, Kip thinks. He can hear Ochter exhaling as though he'd been holding his breath.

"Well! My goodness!" the little man says shakenly. He takes out his old-style cloth handkerchief and dabs at his face. "My!"

Kip's trying to frame a tactful question as to what Vovoka meant. But before he can speak, Ochter essays a smile and says in his normal genial tones:

"Well, if everyone is served, shall we ask Myr Cory to

499

lead us in a toast to the Star? And we shall drink to our hosts as well."

No explanation of the scene with Vovoka appears to be forthcoming. Ah, well, Kip tells himself, with the perfume of the Eglantine tantalizing his nose, probably the sculptor just frightened poor old Ochter into temporary paralysis with weird personal remarks of which only he knows the meaning, if any. Kip glances up at the artist's powerful figure. Anyone who'd seen Vovoka's tremendous strength and totally self-centered behavior might well be disconcerted if Vovoka suddenly singled him out.

"All set?" Ochter lifts his glass to the chaotic lights above. "Myr Cory, will you bring the Star out of hiding?"

Everyone raises their tiny drinks, looking at Cory. Kip swivels around to face her, glass high.

There is a tiny pause.

Cory lifts her wine to the dazzling sky: "To the passing of the Star!"

And just as she brings her glass back to her lips, a light, authoritative voice says clearly, "Hold a minim, all!"

It's little Prince Pao, who has his glass raised, not to drink but to examine. Everyone stares.

"You know," says Pao, still studying the glass, "he may have a point, that light-sculptor chap. The fragrance is there—in the Eglantine, I mean—but I've been here smelling it quite a while now. One becomes aware of a funny chemical undersmell that doesn't belong—"

He's interrupted by a sound from the vicinity of the golden rollbed beside which the marquise luxuriantly reclines. Her Eglantine glass is in the lounger's holder, and Kip can just make out that it appears to be nearly empty.

The sound comes again, now unmistakable. In the most refined, gentle manner, the Lady Pardalianches is snoring.

XII

CONTACT:
Kip Remembers

It takes Kip a minim to make the connection between the state of the Lady and the state of her glass.

Meanwhile Baram has gone to her and is attempting to rouse her. In vain; the light is now so bright that Kip can see Bram turn the Lady's eyelids and check the position of her tongue, while she sleeps on. She is not, in fact, asleep, but unconscious.

Something *is* off with the Eglantine, all right. Murmurs are rising around the deck.

"I suggest that no one should drink any more of this lovely wine till we find out what's wrong," says Cory pleasantly. "Don't you agree, Doctor Baram?"

"I do." Baram has produced his pocket kit and is listening to the Lady's heart.

Little Doctor Ochter has made his limping way to them, his face a picture of dismay. When Baram looks up, Ochter says anxiously, in tones loud enough for all to hear, "How is she, Doctor? Apart from my natural concern, a most disturbing thought has come to me. Is there any possibility that she has taken a fatal poison?"

"Fatal?" Baram eyes Ochter in puzzlement. "There's a strong odour of ambezine hydrate on her breath—that's the same drug you say you gave Yule and Hiner, a simple soporific. We didn't catch it in the wine because ambezine has the unique property of being virtually odorless until ingested. And all her signs are consistent with a moderate dose of it. But fatal? No. Why?"

"Oh, that *is* a relief!" The little man again mops his brow. "Of course I offer my inexpressibly abject apologies to Myr Cory and her guests for having presented such a questionable gift. But my first reaction, aside from wonderment at how some drug got into the sealed bottle—" He breaks off and looks around at Pao. "I suppose there is no question of Eglantine's going bad, or developing, say, a toxic mold, from improper storage?"

"Absolutely not," Pao replies. "It's easier to store than most wines, but if you do manage to spoil it, you just get some fancy vinegar."

"So it must be an introduced substance." Ochter sighs. "As I was saying, my first thought was simply to curse my own naïveté. Why had I not suspected that some of those so-surprisingly generous students might have thought to play a trick on their old professor? Such episodes aren't unknown. I should have been on my guard.

"But then I recalled that the bottle had spent five years in the custody of my friend, who is an active jurist in the Criminal Division. I know of two occasions on which his life has been threatened by vengeful convicts or their confederates, and only last year the Special Branch kept a protective watch on him for some months. Suppose some malefactor had got at his cellar and seen that bottle, believing it to be his?"

He shakes his head worriedly. "My students may have

found me boring, or even obnoxious. But certainly they would not carry a joke so far as actually to kill me. On the other hand, the death of my friend is exactly what an enraged, vengeful criminal—or his allies—would desire. Supposing *two* sets of persons, or two substances, were involved. Are you sure, Doctor, that the Lady's condition may not mask a far more serious agent, while giving it time to work?''

Baram is frowning. "I see your concern. . . . Well, I'm no toxicologist, but medical xenology pokes its nose into many places. . . . No," he says thoughtfully, "I'm not aware that there is any Human poison so tasteless that a lethal dose could be unwittingly drunk in wine. . . . Nor do I know of any which in lethal concentration would show no symptoms— pain, convulsion, gastric bleeding, nausea, heart arrhythmias, tremor, et cetera—over so long a time, with the patient apparently in normal stage D sleep. . . . There is a rare amanitoxin, an alkaloid which slowly dissolves the liver, but the process isn't symptomless and a very large amount is required.

"So I would say no. Even if we hypothesize that two separate operators had tampered with the wine, I conclude that the Lady has taken only a simple soporific, perhaps reinforced by this." He picks up the marquise's gold-chased flask and opens it to release the pleasant dry-wine odor.

"And as to how Soporin got into the Eglantine bottle," Baram goes on in his ordinary informal manner, "Kip here is the custodian of the cork." This is news to Kip, who looks about hastily and recalls that it's back in the bottle. It'll be wanted for examination; he'll dig up a replacement next time he goes in.

"And when we examine it," Bram finishes, "I'll wager we find puncture traces. There are sophisticated techniques for injecting through glass, but the cork is far more likely where the victim isn't suspicious."

Ochter chuckles bitterly. "That aptly describes me. . . . What a pity, though. If only I could bring it home to those

503

young rascals how many people's pleasure they've spoiled. . . .
If they thought at all, they probably envisioned me opening it
in my study with a couple of similar old fuddy-duds. . . ."

Two or three people laugh halfheartedly.

"Listen, all," says Cory's warm voice. "I've just remembered a most interesting bottle of Ice Flowers liqueur someone gave us. It's made by the hermits on Glacier. Of course
it isn't Eglantine, but if you've never tasted Ice Flowers, you
really should. When things quiet down here"—she gestures
at the console—"I'll go root it out and we'll at least have
something pleasant to celebrate with."

"Oh, ma'am, you shouldn't—" "No need to do that."
"Oh, how beautiful—" "Coloss!" The voices sound cherrier.
The deck darkens suddenly as the Star's light submerges
wholly in cloud, but there are glorious fringes escaping
toward the zenith which promise a grand spectacle to come.

Meanwhile, Cory's gesture has recalled Kip's attention to
the dials he's supposed to be monitoring. Linnix' hand is
pointing to three—no, four—readings, which are showing
very high averages of Star-radiation unstopped by the cloud.
Kip must run them over in detail to make sure the component
maxima are within safety limits. He sets to work just as
Ochter goes past on his painful way back to his chair. The
little man's face looks wretched, Kip thinks. Poor little chap,
to have his splendid gift turn out that way. Those students . . .

But as Kip's hands and eyes work almost automatically, an
odd thought comes to him: How strongly Ochter has injected
himself into the evening's events! In fact, their whole version
of what's gone on seems to have come from him. First there
are these students, mythical or otherwise, who doped Ochter's
gift-wine. And then—Kip thinks back—the whole story of
Yule and Hiner, and their sleep shots—and the Tocharis in
their bags—

—and even, gods! the safe departure of Wyrra and his
family. Only Ochter vouched for that.

Kip's fingers slow to a stop on the knobs as a voice replays

504

itself in his head. It's the voice of Pace Norbert, the Guardian from whom they took over. Kip had accused him of being a trifle paranoid. And Norbert had lectured him.

"All over this Galaxy," Norbert had said, "for as long as you live, there will be big crooks and little crooks and lonesome weirdos, Human and otherwise, dreaming up ways to get their hands on Stars Tears stuff. Too abhorrent? Don't you believe it. On the Black Worlds there are Human beasts who salivate over the prospect of torturing children. And passing in any crowd are secret people whose hidden response to beauty is the desire to tear it into bleeding meat."

Kip had flinched away. He'd fought a war, that was over now. This stuff he didn't want to know.

"And everywhere," Norbert had gone on inexorably, "there are beings who'd do anything for riches, for money, wealth, credits— Get it through your heads what the Tears you're guarding represent: pure treasure. Mountains of credits. Better than their weight in zeranaveths, those can be traced. Riches, worth taking any sort of pains for, worth scheming complex plans, worth killing off a dozen people for. One big haul can make a criminal rich for life. And the whole Galaxy knows it. Do you fancy nobody is dreaming about that?

"With the Federation guard, an ordinary armed raid wouldn't work. Entry must be achieved by cunning and stealth and the guard taken out from behind. And every quiet year that passes leaves us less alert. No, one of these years when you've forgotten all about him, the devil will show up. Say, maybe a lost Spacer girl—a genuinely nice girl. And some kind friends come looking for her. . . . Who's going to check them out before you're all dead, or poisoned, or your communications are cut?

"Don't go to sleep, Kip."

Dear gods of the universe, thinks Kip now, slowly resuming his task, have I been asleep? A harmless little old lame man, who's so helpful and sympathetic. . . . Of course he could do nothing alone, but by coincidence two odd young men have landed, uncleared, and so obviously angry at being here that it never occurs to me to wonder—and just in case it *does* occur to someone, the dear little old man can vouch for their being drugged asleep—and he even returns the guns they've stolen—after they proved dry, by the way. And he kindly gives us all some luxury wine that comes within a hair of laying us all out senseless!

As it should have, Kip sees. If it hadn't been for Pao—and who could expect a person really familiar with Eglantine among the handful of tourists to a minor astronomical event on a Rim planet? Not to mention a greedy, almost equally familiar marquise?

As he thinks this, Kip is distracted by the memory of the Vovoka and Ochter incident. Why isn't Vovoka flat too? He must have spat out more than they'd realized. . . . But—wait— there's a possible explanation for the strange dialogue—suppose *Vovoka* was Ochter's confederate and had decided to back out? "It will not work"—that would account for Ochter's dismayed reaction, too.

On the other hand, if Yule and Hiner are Ochter's confederates, there's no proof that they're out of commission in any way. They could be just waiting until everyone was unconscious from the wine. . . . And as for the coincidence of their being here—it's hard to think it, glancing at Linnix' starlit eyes, but she could easily have switched syrettes. A *genuinely nice girl* like that. Or they could have been switched on her; Kip's noticed that Ochter has very deft fingers. . . .

Kip's head is whirling; only a minim or two have passed since Cory spoke, but he feels as if his world has been turning over like a kaleidoscope, with each turn displaying a new, nastier set of possibilities. But—are they possibilities? They seem only barely so; what's truly impossible is for him to think that this is real, is the actual leading edge of a Stars Tears attack.

What he needs is proof. And the only available proof he sees is the status of Yule and Hiner. If Ochter lied about that, if they're in fact up and active, then any or all of the rest follows. But if—gods, may it be so!—they're deep in drugged sleep as the little man said, then all the rest recedes into fantasy.

Half rising, he spins the console seat to face Cory, his mouth opening to announce his plan to step down to the end of the deck and check out those two.

He finds her in low-voiced conversation with Baram. Before he can speak, Cory smiles and says firmly, "No.

"Kip, dear, I think I know what you were going to say." She straightens his scarlet neckerchief. "The answer is, you must not. If the improbable is true, you would be walking into a trap, and also leaving us in serious danger, together with these innocent, unwarned, unarmed people for whom we have responsibility. . . . Was I right?" She smiles mischievously for the benefit of the watchers, and Baram gives a surprisingly lifelike chuckle.

"Yes," Kip admits, "I guess I've been a little slow."

"Oh, no, darling. Three heads are better than two. But we can't talk long, if any of this is true—and we must act as if it is until we're sure. . . . Baram was just saying, this is the classic dilemma: if the danger is real, there *is* no safe way to confirm it. . . . My plan is simply to let the next Deadman's Alarm cycle go through. I explained to Baram that we don't have Mayday just now."

"I hope you explained that was my doing," Kip says morosely.

"My responsibility," she says shortly, grinning her good grin. "Do smile for our public, dear. . . . If Dayan's sore at having his boys miss that game, too bad. We aren't calling him on guesses alone; the three facts we know add up to Mayday by themselves." She holds up three slim, tanned fingers.

"First, two unlisted, uncleared landers—Coincidence A. And, parenthetically, when I think of what we could have missed in those duffels—and how much of that so-called

507

underwater gear could be used for climbing, I'm sick. . . . Coincidence B, a strange ship is accidentally sighted nearby. And finally, a drugged wine is offered to us under conditions that—by Coincidence C—would have rendered us all unconscious at once. What's the old saying? Once is coincidence, two is something or other, but *three times is enemy action*.

"And our question has to be, the wine trick having apparently failed, what do they do now? What's next? Is there a fallback plan?"

"By the gods, I'd missed that ship," Kip says. "Suppose it's full of bastards waiting for a signal to land and start work on the Dameii?" A pang strikes him; he has an instant of acute, almost physical longing to be sure that Wyrra and Nyil are safe.

"Or that ship could simply be their getaway," Baram says. "Yule and Hiner could work alone; more people means more splits, not to mention more risk."

He rises to stand with his hands on the console, apparently studying a readout. "I've got to get back to my seat before this looks too much like a council of war. But I want to impress this thought—we mustn't scare anybody into cutting our communications. That cable and those little webs up there are a very vulnerable lifeline, if any of this is true. Green?"

"Green as you go."

As Baram passes Linnix, who has been politely intent on the console, he pats her hand. To his surprise her other hand snaps around to cover his, holding him in place.

"Doctor Bram," Linnix breathes very softly, "and Myr Kip, too, if you can hear me. I couldn't help overhearing your general subject, and there's something you should know. . . . No, don't look at me, please, look at this readout here."

She removes her hand to point. They bend over it.

"That man Ochter," she whispers, "he's well acquainted with Hiner and Yule. On shipboard they were last to go down, they all three spent, oh, four hours, chatting in the view-room. They seemed very friendly, they laughed a lot. And then when they came in, Hiner was making a little fuss, and Ochter said something like, 'Don't make me sorry I chose you'—in a very sharp tone, that's why I heard. At the time I thought he meant he'd chosen Hiner to take the berth above him—we load from the top down, so he couldn't turn in until after Hiner. . . . And, wait, he added, 'Look at Mordy here.'

"I began to realize they never expected to see me again, you know. So I thought Myr Cory should know. I may have gotten it all wrong, probably it's nothing. And they said good-bye when they went down, not like they expected to all wake up together . . . or, wait, was there just a little something funny? . . . Oh, I could be imagining anything. But about the other, would you tell her, please?"

"Great Apherion, I should hope to say so," says Kip. "Look, we can't flank march this minim, Baram; I'll have to grab an inconspicuous chance."

"Good gods." Baram straightens up. "And good girl, Linnie."

"Wait. . . ." she says, remembering hard. "One other thing. After I left you, B-Bram . . . I looked at the lake. Hiner was swimming. The point is, I don't think he's a true Aquaman—he's, what do they call it, a spoiled Aqua? His gills must not work right. He came up and gasped and gasped and gasped. Poor man . . . I don't think he saw me. When people came out, he left the lake. There! That *is* all."

She starts running an analysis on the twenty-minim readout.

"Lords of space," mutters Kip as Baram departs. "What an earful." Now to find a likely minim to tell Cor that the probabilities have changed.

Thinking of Cor he smiles a little: his girl—and a real Spacer. It for sure hasn't escaped her that if any of this *is* true, it wouldn't be in the plan to leave any witnesses alive. But he won't get a word, a nuance, to admit *that*. No, it's "responsibility for other tourists." Well, let's hope that Deadman's Alarm works. Let's hope this is all one big false alarm. He'd give a lot to hear old Dayan cursing them out for a pack of spooky fools! . . . But Dayan would be first to admit that those three "coincidences" justify a Mayday, even without Linnix' news.

When he turns back to the console, he finds that Linnix has run out two of the worst-looking inputs for him.

"Hey, thanks. . . . That microwave is still plenty high, isn't it?"

"Yes. . . . Would it do damage?"

"Not unless it's intense enough to generate heat—we're a long way from that."

"Good. I don't want to be a smoked oyster."

Kip, chuckling, gets a look over her shoulder at Ochter, sitting by the main doors—and the contrast between his imagined enemy Ochter and the bewildered-looking, little lame old man there, with his anxious old-pixie face, shakes him. Is he insane?

As he starts to turn around again to Cory, every surface on the deck suddenly lights to glittering silver, and bizarrely colored shadows pool beneath their feet.

All eyes look up.

In the fringes of the cloud bank, a huge, sky-filling diamond is separating itself from the darkness and the green auroras, and welling upward, reflected in the lake. As it moves higher, it seems to loom closer and its facets shed flakes of ever-stranger and more violently colored light, which blend to spectral white. A last moment of tattered cloud edges—and then the great apparition comes totally free and floods the world with brilliance.

The Star has risen at last.

And with it, the whole Human situation changes.

XIII

NOVA ONSET:
Alien Eruption

Ser Xe Vovoka, who has ignored the others' doings, suddenly turns full east and flings both arms up toward the risen Star.

"O Beautiful!" he cries in a deep, rough voice. "Enslaver! Radiant enchanter! Killer of worlds from none knows where—at last you are avenged. *Avridar!*"

With that he puts a hand to his forehead and with the speed of long practice rips off what seems to be the skin of his whole ruddy face and head—eyelids, lips, ears, jowls, hair, and all. It's a stiff gauze mask. The revealed skin is a dusty-looking, pebbled, drab purple.

"He's—he's not a Human!" cries Stareem.

With two swift gestures, Vovoka peels his hands and forearms, crumples all together, and throws it down by the screens.

This all happens so swiftly that Kip, wheeling around from

the console, has time for only a bewildered impression of prune-dark skin and a long, vertical nose. Now he begins to take in the true Vovoka: The head is narrower than Human, but the features aren't too different, save for a prowlike forehead that runs with no break into the straight, nostrilless nose; long, thin-lipped mouth; downstretched eyes under heavy frontal bones that extend back, without temples, to circular ears; and pale stubbled crown that must have been recently shaved, showing an odd pattern. All trace of jocularity has vanished from Vovoka's expression, leaving a strong-jawed face of great gravity and sadness, and some menace. Without the Human head, it can be seen that his shoulders are disproportionately wide and powerful, even for his height.

The alien takes two quiet paces along the parapet to Cory's chair. She sits unmoving, gazing at him with an unreadable expression. As he nears her, a small object gleams in his right hand—a hand, Kip sees, that is abnormally large and five-fingered.

Vovoka has been moving deliberately. Now, so suddenly Kip's eye can't follow, he's holding the object against Cory's temple.

She still doesn't move or flinch away but only continues to look up at him watchfully.

Kip, beyond them at the console, has twisted out of his seat and started for Cory, too. Now he freezes in midstride, seeing the object at Cory's head.

"Get away from my mate, Vovoka."

Vovoka addresses him in level, curiously weary tones. "This is a weapon. It will do any degree of damage I choose, but she will never be the same. You will return to that console and set incoming communications on standby. If you do exactly as I say, your mate will not be harmed. But try no tricks. I know those boards well."

Unexpectedly, Cory speaks. "Do as he says, Kip. It's all right." To Vovoka she adds, "Most of those left-hand keys aren't functional, Ser Vovoka. I only laid in a channel to

512

Base frequency, and one broad-band sweep. The rest are data on the nova-front.''

"I know that," the alien replies, and tells Kip, "Deenergize the modular antenna, and that's all.''

Kip reluctantly goes back to the console, where he flicks two toggle switches and runs a slide switch to zero.

Watching him carefully, Vovoka says to the others, still in the same expressionless tone, "Please be calm and have no fear. I assure you that one person only, who is guilty of great crime, need be afraid. This weapon is intended solely for that person. The rest of you are entirely safe so long as you remain still and attempt no furtive action. If you insist on moving, I cannot guarantee your safety; and my reactions are very, very much faster than yours.''

To Kip he adds, "Reset that alarm, Myr Korso.''

The Deadman's Alarm has come on so recently that Kip himself hasn't seen it. Vovoka's claim about his reaction time appears to be true. Grimly, Kip resets it, thinking, A whole alarm cycle lost.

"May I go back to my chair, Ser Vovoka?" Linnix asks. "I should be near in case help is needed with the paralyzed girl.''

"Very well.''

Linnix carefully makes her way back to her place beside Doctor Baram. When she's seated again, Vovoka looks over at Stareem, while his weapon remains at Cory's head.

"Yes, small female," he says, his voice subtly more alien now and dark with sadness, "I am not Human. I am Vlyracochan, the last of my race. Others have given their lives, their vital essences, that I alone may live to complete our task. For—''

As he speaks Kip is wondering how in the name of the seven devils Vovoka brought that weapon on a Moom ship undetected and through the Federation check to Damiem. The first is virtually impossible, the second incredible. The weapon itself seems to be a relative of the X5 Daguerre, uncommon

513

but not unknown in military Spacer circles. Its merits are good accuracy for such a small piece and an easy adjustment from stun to kill. But is it really a Daguerre, or is it only a toy, a harmless piece of plastite for children playing Spacer? That would explain its presence here. . . . Possible.

And now Vovoka begins to talk. It's axiomatic that when a man with a weapon begins to explain himself, his attention is as distracted as it's ever going to be. Right now is Kip's best chance to act—if he can bethink himself of anything to do.

But he can't—knowing nothing of Vovoka's intentions—and in any event, the danger to Cory is too great. That Daguerre could be real.

At that moment he sees a twitch or jerk of Vovoka's weapon hand, and something happens by the lounge doors, where Ochter sat. Kip looks around and sees Ochter against the doors, bent over and gasping, nursing one hand in the other.

"I warned you," Vovoka says tonelessly.

"But my *finger*," Ochter protests. He holds the wounded hand up for an instant; Kip sees that the first finger is completely gone. The site is scarcely bleeding, it appears cauterized. "My error," the little man says gamely, "I was only going to my room to take some analgesic and lie down. Or to the infirmary, if you prefer. I didn't want to interrupt your talk."

Ochter must have figured along the same lines he himself had, Kip thinks. Thank the gods he didn't gamble with Cory's life.

He notices a tiny plume of steam or smoke rising from one of the door's lock handles, catching the multicolored radiance of the Star. Ochter must have placed his hand there when Vovoka picked off the finger. And Kip hadn't even seen the weapon swing away from Cory and back, so fast had been Vovoka's act! Whew.

"May I now go to my room? Obviously I am no possible threat to you, and I know I am not the one you seek."

514

"Go."

Ochter goes, this time hobbling down the Star-silvered deck toward his room.

This act of Vovoka's jolts Kip. "The one you seek"—subconsciously, he realizes, he'd been assuming it was Ochter. Now it's clearly not. Oh, gods, then—*who?* Zannez seems improbable. But Baram's a xenological doctor, he's treated all sorts of aliens. Could this be some crazed ex-patient? Or a relative? Oh, Lords of the Sky, please not Bram.

"Perhaps we may have an end to nonsense?" Vovoka sighs. "As I said, our investigations revealed that, contrary to the tale you heard tonight, there is one last crewman of the killer ship unaccounted for. A very young person. The regular gunnery crew seem to have refused to obey their mad captain's orders. Only this young one, little more than a child, would actually aim and fire the so-called planet-killer missile." He sighs again. "It has taken years and deaths, but our informants finally located the one who had been that child—here on Damiem."

All this while Cory has shown the strange peacefulness with which she submitted from the start. But the alien's next words galvanize her.

Vovoka looks at Kip. "And tonight I have heard it confirmed from your own boasting mouth. Kipruget Korso, perpetrator of abomination, prepare to die."

"No! No! No! No!" Cory screams. And to everyone's amazement she seizes Vovoka's gun hand with both her own and holds it tight to her own head.

"No!" Kip is shouting, too. "Don't harm her—she's crazy! Go ahead, shoot me if you have to shoot somebody."

"I do not intend to harm this female unless she forces me to it," Vovoka tells Kip. "I am giving you these minim to compose yourself, to die like a Vlyran."

Cory gets control of herself.

"Ser Vovoka, hear me! Doesn't the prospect of killing the

515

wrong, innocent person, and letting the guilty go free—doesn't this bother you at all?'' she demands. "Especially since I gather this is your last chance?''

"It would, very much,'' Vovoka replies slowly.

"Then forget Kip. He is the wrong person. I know, because—because—'' The words are halting and ragged and Cory's eyes stare up unseeing, as though ghosts are breaking through deep burial in her mind.

"Because—*I did it!*'' she cries. "Yes''—her voice is raw—"I was *Deneb*'s cabin girl. In those last days . . . Jeager only had me. I did it f-for him—'' The words are wrenched out savagely. "*I did it*. I aimed and fired. I am the right person, the one you seek. You must kill me.''

Kip's heart thuds, crashes. He simply will not accept or think of what Cory's saying, refuses also to recall what she'd let slip in their first days, when she mentioned that she'd been in Rehab after the Last War. So what? Many had. But he's bewildered. He needs a minim to counter this mad, dangerous notion of Cor's.

Suddenly Zannez speaks. "Ser Vovoka, may my girls get up and get their robes? They're cold in that metal lace. See, one's shivering.''

Stareem and Bridey, clad in their new finery, are sitting up in the loungers with their arms wrapped around themselves.

"Let them do that,'' Vovoka replies gravely. "I have no wish to commit unnecessary cruelty.''

The girls rise and go quickly behind the screens. Kip shoots a grateful glance at Zannez and tries furiously to plan. Bridey and Stareem return wearing the APC short robes.

Kip gives a bark of jeering laughter. "Unnecessary cruelty,'' he mimics, "Oh, dear, no!'' Can he infuriate Vovoka past reason? No good: the alien doesn't even look at him.

Cory is remaining calm, but still she clamps Vovoka's weapon to her forehead. Futile—he can break her hold any instant he chooses.

"Your spies were quite right, Ser Vovoka,'' she says

gravely. "The criminal is here. But you are in danger of wasting your whole great effort by mistaking Kip for me—as happened once before, didn't it? You see, I know about the two Dav Caltos. But in those days there were others of your race to correct it. Now you say you are the last one left. You *must* be right. And I can prove to you that I did it. That I am the criminal you seek, not Kip. It is I you must punish."

"Be silent, woman. Your effort to save your mate is, I suppose, admirable. But futile. Any doubts I might have had died when I heard the boastful tone and joking manner in which he told the story—while *preparing food*. Now let the brute compose himself and die with that dignity he can muster."

"Oh, no, no—that tone is his one stupid weakness—when those who know him hear it, we know he is telling false tales of what he has *not* done. Let me make him tell you of things he *has* done, you'll hear his true voice."

"Ah, she's only trying to confuse you, Vovoka. Believe your spies, shoot me and have done with it."

"Ser Vovoka! Did your informants ever specifically tell you the sex of the criminal? Or was it just taken for granted as male? Look—we need facts. I can give you facts and prove them! Allow me ten sentences—with all my heart I beg you. If you refuse to hear so very little, your life's great mission will end in shame and mockery."

Anger burns now in his alien eyes, but she's taken the right risk.

"Go on."

"First, Kip was never on or near *Deneb*. He knows nothing of the whole dreadful business beyond what I was fool enough to try to remember in our first years. Old—*Deneb* was *old*, she had major differences from other Class X cruisers. A question or two about her structural peculiarities would prove that Kip never was aboard her. But we don't have *Deneb* here, or even a diagram. By any chance did you go aboard before they took her out to her end?"

"No."

"Pity. What you'd have seen might resolve this in a moment. You might even have seen me—I was part of the last skeleton crew. Before that, of course, I was *Deneb*'s cabin girl. *I* was the young fool who still thought that Captain Jeager was the last great hero, a god. So when the gunnery crew refused to use our Class L planet-breaker missile on this world-sized 'weapon,' I called them cowards and mutineers. I convinced Jeager I'd memorized every manual—I had—and I could do it myself, for him. If we had time, you could ask me anything—mass-thrust ratios, gee-loadings, markings, missile-ready procedure, settings, point of impact—but we don't. Wait—here's a crucial one: Kip, when you say you fired, what was your last full view of the, the target, before the automatics cut in, and what did you see?"

"Well, the computers got the last good look"—Kip's a cool gambler—"and since their sun was behind the target I merely saw a huge unfinished-looking spherical body, with construction activity moving on one dazzling limb. And—"

"You hear, Ser Vovoka? Computers—*Deneb* had *no* computer capable of initiating an L-missile! *I* laid in the conversion factors and sighted that master launcher myself, eye-hand. We'd mounted an old AW-Four firing scope with primitive cross hairs. Jeager's hands shook too much and we were alone, so it was *I* who aimed visually, and fired. Unbelievable as it sounds. But the terrible thing—" She's losing control of her voice; it's as if the words are torn out of her throat. "Oh, Ser Vovoka, that head and face. *That face* . . . it slowly formed as I aimed—it wasn't there at first. . . . Beauty. Transcendence—no words. And I aimed and fired . . . right between the eyes. I had to watch it swell, and distort horribly, and break apart. . . . Child as I was, I knew then I had done something abominable. The appalling radiance—no one who ever—could ever—"

She draws a long shuddering breath. The watchers hang on the scene; Stareem is weeping silently.

"I still see it—very f-frequently. The days are worst, I see the cross hairs converge against the sky. I'll never be free. Ser Vovoka, will you believe I was not unhappy when I thought you had found me? Couldn't you *feel* it?

"But then, when you changed to Kip— Oh, I can only beg you, beg you, beg you—do not make an error and kill poor blameless Kip—and leave me alone with . . . that. . . ."

Quite disregarding the weapon, she covers her own face briefly with her hands, then looks at her mate.

"Beloved—beloved, let me go. It is just. And now I know. It's kinder."

Kip's face twists with love, but he's no fool and he is fighting for that love.

"This is a ploy!" he exclaims to Vovoka. "She should have been an actress; she's trying to rush you. I, too, have seen the face she speaks of—of course, I first described it to her. It haunted me, too, for a time. But our races are so different, Ser Vovoka. What was almost a god to you, was to me a piece of very fine sculpture wrapped around a sun-smasher bomb. And what you heard as 'boasting' is simply that for many males of our race it is considered improper to appear very deeply moved, and the more moving the subject, the more taboo to appear touched by it. Sorry? Of course I'm sorry—sorry beyond words. For a time I considered ending my life."

During this speech Cory sits in exhausted silence, her eyes pleading with Vovoka, both trembling hands still clasping his weapon to her forehead. The others watch mesmerized. Above them the enormous Star-diamond is growing, changing, convoluting, while all around, the auroral backlight pulses, strobes so that rational speech and thought are becoming difficult. The glory is passing beyond mere splendor into a realm of strangeness.

Vovoka studies them both in silence. Kip, returning his gaze, suddenly becomes conscious of a vague disorientation and remembers Vovoka's stare at Ochter. Oh, gods, no—is

519

the alien reading their minds? Quick, break it up—talk, say something!

Snatching at a memory of Spacer gossip years back, hoping against hope that it refers to Jeager, and that his voice conceals near panic, Kip says, "Moreover, although Cor claims she was a little cabin girl, she was still a *female*, right?

"It so happens—and your informants could confirm this by message—that Tom Jeager hated having women on his ship. He was truly crazy, you see—although he may have had a semirational aversion to the kind of emotional display you've just seen—forgive me, Cor. But the idea of a cabin *girl* allowed to fire their—our—biggest weapon by hand is pure fantasy. I can't recall a single woman on *Deneb*. He'd have found some excuse to get most of 'em off at the first stops."

"Nonsense," Cory says weakly. "N-nonsense!"

Vovoka makes an ambiguous sound. Gently, he releases one hand from Cory's clutch and takes from the inner pocket of his tunic a small sheaf of diagonally cut papers. Possibly an alien computer readout, Kip thinks. His heart begins to sink as Vovoka glances down the pages with lightning speed.

"Is Irien a male or female Human name?"

"Female," says Cory determinedly.

"Male," says Kip.

"And Glynnis?"

"No telling."

"Either," Cory says faintly. Her hands are shaking badly; she lets Vovoka carefully free his gun hand, too. He stands with the weapon pointing straight up as he reads on.

"Lee?"

"Male," says Kip.

"Not if it's s-spelled with, with an 'i,' Li," Cory manages to say.

Kip's own hands are trembling, his heart races. Has he really won? Was it really Jeager that Kenter had made that offhand remark about, twenty years ago? It seems so. For a moment he exults, quite oblivious to the fact that "winning" may mean his own death.

But then Vovoka speaks. "You do not recall any Human females aboard *Deneb*. And yet, without such ambiguous cases, the crew list shows thirty-two first names which I recognize as female."

Kip has lost, after all. His world collapsing around him, he forces his voice steady and belligerent.

"Such as?" he demands.

The alien sighs and consults his damned printout. Kip's gaze strays up to the glorious Star, then moves deliberately, meaningfully, from face to face of Zannez and his crew. Surprise, mass force, is the only hope left. ". . . four; Kara, two," Vovoka's saying; "Marye, three; Rhealune or Realune, five; Aytha, two."

"Oh, well," says Kip with the calm of desperation, "these are, if you'll forgive me, typical unskilled-worker names. Women from planets like Shoofly where they get no education. There could well have been some galley girls, or storekeepers, maintenance people who worked nights or in special areas one never saw. Forced on Jeager by the old equal-rights law."

From the corner of his eye Kip sees Snake untie his robe, while Zannez tightens his.

Vovoka consults his list again and says with finality, "Lieutenant-Commander Tali Temarovna, Chief Communications Officer."

Without visible warning, Kip leaps bodily onto the tall alien, both his arms locking around Vovoka's weapon arm, while his legs wrap Vovoka's free arm to his torso. The alien's body feels like stone.

"Take the gun, Cor! The gun, the gun!"

But she makes no move.

"Cory! *Get—the—gun!*"

His words are almost drowned in a stampede—Zannez and Snake are charging at them along the parapet, Ek and Bridey

521

rounding the rollbed to get at Vovoka from the other side; even little Stareem, naked, is sprinting at him. A pileup capable of throwing a robot is coming at the alien.

Doctor Baram catches Linnix by her belt as she takes off to help and yanks her back down into the seat beside him. He himself continues watchfully sitting by the rollbed. Little Prince Pao makes one leap toward Vovoka, then checks and, frowning thoughtfully, returns to stand by Baram.

Only milliseconds to go—but they're enough here. Kip finds his arms holding nothing—Vovoka has lifted his weapon arm free as easily as a man would lift his hand from water. Even as Kip grabs for a hold he hears the weapon's fast click—setting change—and Vovoka sweeps the oncomers with a whispering beam.

Four people become unguided missiles in midstride—slumping, falling, skidding, piling up around the console. Only Snake is untouched, still coming on the coping. The alien holds his fire and shifts place with a jolt—if he shot now the boy would certainly fall off onto the treetops below.

"They're merely stunned," Vovoka says at Cory. His words come out so fast they're high-pitched, barely comprehensible, like a speeded-up recorder. Kip, grappling the alien's stony neck, understands that Vovoka has some sort of ultra-high gear he can throw himself into.

Abandoning all standards, Kip goes like a madman for the alien's eyes. The eyes are protected by a hard, transparent shell. Vovoka merely blinks in annoyance. Kip whips out his pocketknife to stab or cut around the eyeball if the knife won't penetrate.

But the alien forestalls him before dealing with Snake. Kip feels one incredibly fast and powerful surge of muscles, feels himself seized by arm and leg—torn free—and flung whirling through the air.

He lands hard, a leg twisted under him across the edge of a heavy deck chair, his head ringing from blows. Consciousness gutters. He's scrambling to his feet by reflex, confusedly aware of bodies in motion around the console, as the leg gives way under him and sends him crashing again to ground.

He drags himself up by a chair, trying to force his good leg to push his body upright. The deck is a dark silver chaos of agonies into which he essays to step—only to go down once more, striking his forehead on the chair.

An instant of bewilderment, in which he calls, or tries to call out, "Cor, I love you!"—and then the world flickers away and does not return.

As Kip falls, Doctor Baramji comes quietly to his feet.

He looks from Kip to Cory—who during all this has moved only her head, to follow Kip—and from her to the alien. Vovoka is standing by the console, where he's just caught Snake's lightning karate double-kick, pulled him safely out of the air, and stunned him.

Behind his composed face, Baramji is in torment. His muscles ache from the effort to restrain himself from a suicidal attack on this alien who has injured Kip and threatens— incredibly—to doom Cory. Incredibly—yet all too convincingly to Baram, who has long sensed the shadow under Cory's cheer. Her first words of guilt instantly rang true to him; appalled, he understood that *this* was the trauma all Rehab couldn't erase from her young mind.

Yet that this should have happened to Cor! Cory, whom he loves so deeply, Cory who was a lifeline to him when his own mate went—only one implacable fact can prevent him trying to go to her aid.

His duty. Duty is there, chaining him: he is the sworn Guardian of the Dameii, in the name of Humankind; most probably the only one left. *And the Dameii may well be in danger right now.*

The events of the past hours have added up for Baramji— even faster than for Kip—to a growing conviction of menace from Ochter, Hiner, and Yule. Unproven but not rationally to

523

be dismissed. Until the Dameii are known to be safe, the lone Guardian may not waste himself for friendship or any personal concern. And now he is compelled to still other actions by his deepest duty as a doctor—an agonizing triple bind.

He addresses the alien, seeking frantically for some way, anything he can try.

"Ser Vovoka, may I, as a doctor, go to Kip? He has clearly broken a leg and seems to have other injuries. I will also need Myr Linnix to visit the surgery with me for splints and medical supplies."

"Do that." Vovoka's speeded-up voice slows and deepens as he goes on. "I regret . . . Was this why you did not join the others in attacking me?"

"No. I thought there would be needs, other than those you generate, I mean. And it seemed unlikely they would succeed."

"Wise."

"Tell me, are these unconscious people brain-injured or harmed in any way other than the obvious? Will they need my help?"

Vovoka has already turned away: he turns back impatiently.

"No. They will awaken in about an hour, just as they were before, apart from a few bruises. Now, doctor, go to your duty."

Suddenly a possibility comes to Baram.

"But *your* duty, Ser Vovoka—will you ignore the high duty so plainly before you?"

The alien eyes flash scorn at him—but Vovoka pauses.

"You have already disabled one Guardian of the Dameii. In the name of Star-justice, you must not disable the other until relief arrives. The innocent Dameii have suffered at least as gravely as Vlyracocha—yes," Baram says sternly as Vovoka's eyes blaze, "there are worse ways to die. I call on you to delay your revenge on Myr Cory. As you see, she will wait."

Vovoka glances around at Cory, who doesn't seem to hear them; her eyes never leave Kip.

Vovoka turns back to Baramji. He appears to be growing more alien, to have difficulty comprehending the Human appeal.

"Delay? . . ." he says effortfully. "I . . . I regret. Among other reasons. . . . I am soon dying."

Baram's hope dies, too. Has he waited too long to approach Vovoka?

"Then it is your duty at least to tell me one thing," he says desperately. "Do you know of any plot against the Dameii? You have read our minds—have you read dangers to the Dameii from any here? Have you?"

Vovoka's face has taken on a strange, dreamlike abstraction. *"Avra ki, avra koi,"* he says in no tongue known to Baram.

Then he turns definitively away.

Baram curses himself without seeing clearly how else he might have acted. He goes to Kip. Linnix has done what she could to make him comfortable.

A quick examination shows simple fractures of the right tibia and fibula, which Kip worsened by trying to stand, and an unknown degree of concussion. Normally Baram would take him at once to the infirmary for a full cephalic scan, but now he must stay here and watch for some possible opportunity to help Cory, however unlikely. It will be good to set the leg while Kip's unconscious, too.

With Linnix to help him carry, he goes quickly into the infirmary for his portable scanner and emergency kit. He's opening his safe by its lighted dial when Linnie's hand taps his arm. He looks up to a small shadow slipping through the infirmary door. There's a creak.

Pao! Wait—is there a possibility here?

"Prince, can you hear me?" Baram calls softly.

"No need to shout," says Pao's voice from beside them.

"I need to call on you for something that may be dangerous. You must feel perfectly free to refuse."

"What is it?" says Pao practically.

"Do you think you could slip unobserved down to Hiner

525

and Yule's room and check whether they're sleeping, as Ochter said, or gone, or up and active here? If they're asleep, fine—no danger. If they're gone or awake and up, we're all in bad trouble. That's the danger for you—they may have set a watch or a trap. I wouldn't call on you if there was any way I could do it, and it's not fair to ask a—" Baram stopped as he was about to say "boy," and finished, "a visitor to do our job."

His tact is useless.

"My younger brother is on active duty with our patrol service," Pao tells him coolly. "We consider most grown men ill suited to the best scout work. How do I signal you when I get back?"

"Um . . ." says Baram. From the corner of his eye he can see Linnix' intent stare.

"If everything's all right, I'll say so," Pao answers for him. "Same if they're gone and you're alone. If Ochter—I guess that's who worries you—if he's here, I'll give a chirr, like that lizard thing that was around." He pauses, and a moment later the metallic trill of a night-caller sounds behind them. "A single if they're gone and a double if they're here and active. Got it?"

"One means they're gone and two means they're active here," says Baram to the night.

"Right. . . . Oh, by the way, if those were your Tocharis you put in there, may I have one? I know they're dry."

The lad doesn't miss much; Baram fishes a Tochari out of the open safe and hands it down to the darkness.

"Thank you." The voice is moving away. "Did you notice the main lounge doors are fused locked? Vovoka's gun did that."

A shadow occults the surgery doorway for an instant and is gone.

"Amazing lad." Baram turns up the light to find Linnix grinning. But she sobers quickly. "Doctor Bram, do you really think that those two and *Doctor Ochter* could, could be . . ."

"I don't know, Linnie. . . . Here are the big splints. . . . There's a chance Ochter could be very dangerous. We'd certainly all be unconscious now if things had gone according to his scenario. . . . Or he could be as completely harmless as he seems. In any case I want you to stay well out of his reach until we find out." He shakes her arm gently. "Hear me?"

"Yes. Yes. . . . You mean they—the, the Stars Tears stuff . . . Oh, no—"

"What else? Reach down that RMSO, honey. Now let's get this load out, I'll take those blankets, too."

She reaches for the analgesics. He sees her brows furrow as she turns out the lamp.

"Yule and Hiner," she whispers. "You mean the cold-sleep . . ."

"Could have been a plant. Yes. Let's go."

But he pauses an instant. "I—I didn't mean to frighten you, my dear." What he'd been about to blurt out was, "I love you."

"You didn't, Dad." He can just catch the flash of an impish smile behind her load of bedding.

When they come back to the deck Cory is bending over Kip's head, kissing and caressing the unconscious man. Ser Vovoka stands behind her. As Baram approaches, the tall alien takes her gently by the shoulders and half lifts her away, turns her to face him. She resists only a little.

Bram and Linnix go around them to get to their work on Kip's leg.

"You shall have time for farewells . . . full and private," Vovoka is saying. He seems to regain Human speech again with Cory. "On my honor, I promise." He begins to lead her back to her chair.

But to Baram's dismay, Linnix suddenly is standing in their way.

"Please don't hurt Myr Cory," she pleads. "She's such a *good* person. Whatever she did when she was a child, it was out of loyalty. Please spare her, Ser Vovoka. Please."

Vovoka's weapon hand lifts ominously, but Linnix doesn't yield. Dear brave little fool! Baram moves to interpose himself. Still the alien finds patience to reply:

"Young female, did you not hear what she said to her mate when she asked him to let her go? 'It is both just and kinder'? She spoke truth, for reasons you can never know. Now will you be satisfied with that or must I stop you, too?"

Beside him, Cory nods speechlessly.

Linnix puts a hand over her streaming eyes and lets Baram pull her aside. Vovoka guides Cory to her chair.

When she's seated he says to her, "Look up."

Linnix and Baramji pause in their work with Kip to look up, too.

The great diamond is now filling half the sky. But it's a diamond no longer. Instead they see a great circular rainbow lined with lesser bows, sun dogs of hues and brilliancies no ordinary rainbow ever showed—quite beyond description. Its outer rim is radiant with eerie rivers of color and slow-moving fans of light that brush the horizons.

Any part of the great spectral wonder would have been a jewel, an emblem of fascination. The whole is ungraspable, unbelievable, yet there.

In the very center is an undefined swirl of pearly colors. As they watch, it begins to take on definition. But neither Baram nor Linnix can tell what it is. A head, perhaps a face? It flows and re-forms and flows again, tantalizingly.

A rasping sound comes from Cory: she is having trouble breathing. She lies with upturned face, eyes wide in apparent recognition. Beside her Vovoka leans against the parapet, staring upward, too, his alien face a mask of sadness.

"The last." Cory gasps for a moment and then goes on. "I was the very last to see it whole and unharmed, glorying in its beauty. The last. . . ." She falls silent, her eyes alternately wide and clenched shut, as if the sight is unbearable, yet resistless. Desolation ravages her once merry face.

Vovoka glances down at her, his strange face showing what they have not seen before, a trace of pity.

"Almost I would spare you if I could," he tells her.

"No." Cory still looks skyward. "Not now . . . now that I know. . . ."

Dreading what is to come, they watch helplessly as he checks his weapon and sets it to a new position, then places it against her head. She smiles faintly, like one who feels the touch of coolness amid burning heat.

Linnix clutches Baram's arm; Cory's strange acquiescence, almost eagerness, has made it hopeless to try to protest again.

"I do not know if this is kinder or more cruel," the alien says. "Know that I mean to be kind. I believe you deserve a few hours of peace and freedom that not I nor any of my race have ever known."

They hear a faint whisper from the gun. Then he withdraws it carefully from her glossy hair.

Cory shows no change but simply sits there, looking attentively from him to the preternatural splendor in the sky.

Baram is almost too dumbfounded to feel joy. *What happened?* Is she—can she be all right? A dozen speculations flash across his mind at once. Vovoka clearly hasn't missed—he appears satisfied, as if he expected no other effect. So it cannot be that some trick brain path allowed the ray—or whatever that thing fires—to cut only the corpus callosum, say. No, the aim had been diagonally down, toward the medulla, Bram recalls. Maximal damage.

Wait, could that "shot" have been a purely ritual "execution," like that business on Kaiters, where people died of symbolic punishments? . . . Maybe the effect comes later, he thinks. . . . A ray of hope touches him— When he can get to her, he can probably prevent *that*.

Now Cory's actually speaking, in a voice they can barely hear.

"Thank you, I think I . . . know a little. I wish I could share with you."

Vovoka smiles in great bitterness and despair, his gaze going back to the Star.

"Your mad captain was quite right, you realize, Myr Cory." He seems to wish to speak a little with the only Human who can understand. "It was a weapon. But self-generated. A seed from space, a germ of suns, who knows? It showed itself first in our clouds. And then one or two of our highest mountains began to . . . change. This was many, many lifetimes ago—ninety, a hundred. We had already a high civilization. This brought beauty such as no one had ever seen or imagined. And in many modes. Even to trees, weeds, rocks . . . like those here."

As he speaks he absently adjusts his weapon to another setting, and holds it loosely by his side. There seems to Bram no possible advantage to be taken here.

Vovoka's voice goes on. "But its wonder fed on the souls of the beholders. With too much exposure to that beauty one becomes strangely incapable of hope . . . and yet haunted by unquenchable, unnameable desire. You alone beyond our race knew something of this. The Federation doctors talked of cell fatigue, but we knew differently.

"And when it had fed full, and was almost through with us, it compelled us to build—what you have seen. Again, over lifetimes. So that it might go forth throughout the Galaxy, feeding . . . reproducing. . . ." He stares up at the Star and then down at the woman.

"Know this: *You have done no wrong.*"

Then his expression changes once more. He gives Cory a brief nod that says more plain than words, "Good-bye," and turns away for the last time. His gaze goes back up to the Star.

It has changed more while he spoke. The forms are breaking up, crystallizing differently, skywide. There is a raining or sifting of impalpable falls and drifts of color, down through the night. All blackness at the horizons has vanished under the silent, sky-filling light-storm. Is the Star upon and around them? Are they actually in it now?

Vovoka glances down briefly at the readouts on the console and nods. Baram hears him draw breath.

Then he throws up both arms as when he first addressed the Star. Now one hand holds a gun.

"We have done your bidding to the end, O Lustrous-Cruel. None remain save only I, who will soon be gone. And your revenge is ours, O Insatiable. Your ambition was too swift, your hatred for those who wounded you too absolute.

"So now you will be again as you were so long ago—a nothing, a spore on the winds of space, whence we drew you to our doom. *Averane!*"

He lets his arms fall slowly.

As the weapon passes his head it speaks again, a brief soft buzz. It is so quiet, and his demeanor so calm, that for an instant the three watchers do not realize that his head is simply gone. His neck ends in a thin gray-and-scarlet mist, dissipating in the air. There is no gush of blood; the whole neck seems to be cleanly cauterized.

For a moment the headless body stands leaning on the parapet, then crumples quietly to the tiles. With a metallic clink the weapon falls from the dead hand and slides out of sight.

XIV

THE NOVA GROWS:
Algotoxin

Stunned silence falls on the deck after the alien's apocalyptic death.

It is so still, under the uncanny radiance of the sky, that Baram, who is finishing Kip's emergency splint, can hear the soft brush of tree branches on the windward side of the hostel, and now and then a faint wind whine which inexplicably troubles him. Linnix, helping from Kip's other side, seems to hear it, too, and frowns.

The stillness brings it home hard to Baram that, of the dozen Humans here, only he and Linnix and Cory are conscious—and Cory may be gravely hurt. She's still sitting where she was when Vovoka fell, but she has turned to watch Baram with Kip. She seems alert, but once or twice Baram catches her looking into nowhere with an expression that reminds him too much of patients to whom he's given the worst of news.

And young Pao—where is his little scout? He should have been back long ago. Has he run into trouble from Yule and Hiner? Has he, Baram, done serious wrong in sending the boy?

Someone should go for him at once. And someone, most urgently, should go down to Yule and Hiner's quarters and settle the crucial issue: Are they locked in drugged slumber, from which it follows that Ochter is indeed the harmless, kindly old body he appears; or was that drugging story a lie and Ochter a dangerous enemy in league with them?

But Cory and Linnix must not be left alone while these three are unaccounted for. And someone should also check the too-long-neglected radiation counters, since this great new flux of radiation has come upon them. *And* Baram should examine Cory at once, not to mention taking a look at the others—

The conflicting urgencies racing through his mind dismay Baram. It's been a long time since the war, he thinks. A long time since a younger Baramji coped with a dozen life-or-death calls at once. Maybe too long since he's had to think of living Human enemies instead of microscopic pathogens. . . . He snaps the last lacing in and suddenly recalls a vital point.

"We're done here, Linnie. Will you go collect that weapon Vovoka dropped? I heard it fall on this side."

"Right, and I'll tend to the decencies." She snatches a blanket off Zannez' screens and goes toward the parapet near Cory, where Ser Xe Vovoka, last of all great Vlyracocha, lies headless in death.

Cory is rising, heading for Baram and Kip. Baram watches her come. She moves quite normally, but with great weariness—understandable enough—and he sees no signs of damage. Nevertheless, his doctor's prescience refuses to quiet; that weapon fired into her brain.

"Cory, my dear, what did he do to you? Let me look—"

"How badly is Kip hurt, Bram?"

"Not badly." He's trying to check her pulse, but she pulls her wrist away.

"I'm fine for now." Her voice strengthens. "Bram dear, stop looking at me as if I'm about to fall dead and tell me how Kip is." She sinks down by Kip's unconscious head. Linnix manages to slip a chair pad under her.

"Kip's fine, too, or will be in a few days." He tells her the details while he studies the glossy brown head, now in full Star-shine. He still can see no trace of injury, or even of disarray, unless it's that slim strand of silver over the left parietal. Surely that's been there some time? Women hide such things. Nothing else—save only that her glow seems dimmed in some way, as if he's seeing her through dust haze or a fine ashen veil. . . . Tiredness? A trick of the light?

"Kip may lunge about and need a restraining hand while he's coming to," Baram concludes. "And we have other urgent problems, Cory my dear—you haven't been exactly, ah, free to—"

"No." She gives a ghost of her old wry chuckle. "Oh, Bram—"

"Wait, Cor. First you should know that while you—a while ago—I seized a chance to send young Pao down to check on Yule and Hiner's room. He's overdue back. I hope I didn't do wrong to let him go; he claimed to be a proficient scout."

"Best you could do." Her gaze is straying back to Kip.

"Also, if Ochter had hoped to render us all unconscious with his wine, Vovoka has done most of his work for him. There's only you and I and Linnix left. And you may recall, Vovoka killed the last alarm cycle. If we still think as we did, I assume you intend to let the next cycle go through? Or do you want to alert Base now?"

Her eyes come back to him with some of their normal authority.

"Nothing . . . significant . . . has changed," she says thoughtfully, "except that we're in a far worse position to handle any violence. We still don't know if we're faced with two sleeping louts and a nice old man, or a deadly criminal and two accomplices who may be attacking, or preparing to attack the Dameii right now. And we can't determine which without placing ourselves and others in possibly fatal danger if the worse case is true. . . .

"Moreover, if the worst case *is* true, and we're heard telling this to Base, it's my feeling that Stars Tears criminals would exploit all here for their hostage value, and probably end with mass killing, before they let themselves be taken. Certainly they would leave no living witnesses. And there's no way of estimating the likelihoods—we have nothing but suspicious coincidences. Therefore it's the course of wisdom to act as if the worst case *is* true until we're certain it's not.

"So—I believe that the only safe course is to wait for the automatic alarm cycle to Base; it's silent. And meanwhile stay well away from Ochter or any vulnerable situation.

"But there is one call I think you can make." She bows her head and slips off the slender chain bearing the plastite-cased microchip that is her sigil of office; her hands are shaking so that it catches on her ear.

"Bram, I'm feeling kind of—spooked. I'd like you to take over officially. It would be normal enough to call and tell them that, and about Vovoka. . . . Will you?"

"Gladly." He sees how great an effort this has been; the weariness is returning on her so heavily that he's alarmed.

"Tell them, until further notice. Green?" She manages to smile.

"As you say, Cor, always." It was an old joke between them.

"Go. . . . Oh, and watch your output index, you'll have to holler to get through this mush."

"Right."

He goes to the console, trying to push his worry for her from the forefront of his mind and consider his Cory-imparted knowledge of the thing's operation. Adequate—he hopes.

He is stepping over and around the sleeping bodies of Zannez and his gallant troupe; Linnie has somehow found time to untangle and dispose them more comfortably. Zannez and the boys are on the near side of the console between him and Cory, and Bridey and Stareem are beyond it by the parapet. He can see no movements of returning life; well, Vovoka had said an hour or more.

When he succeeds in starting the transmitter power-up, several readouts change their spectral glimmering. Baram peers at them, ascertaining as well as he can that no components have passed the red lines Kip had marked. Through his shoe soles comes a faint hum of power, pervading the deck. Deep beneath him the power-cell is silently waking, activating the big transmitter.

The thrumming is so noticeable that he has a moment of panic, thinking that he has in error called up the monstrous energies required for a c-skip send. Among the factors necessary actually to perturb the gravitational field is a total chill-down of the sealed 'skip antenna; but when he locates its heat register on the board there is no sign of change. It must be that he's nervously sensitive to the normal transmission process he hasn't worked for so long. . . . And the Star-silence amplifies all.

To calm himself he looks up.

The Star is still in the midphase of comparative quiet. There is no longer a visible Star, but only this dense, dancing, pulsing rain of silver, shot with mesmeric reds, purples, green-blues, which means that the Star-shell, or its midmost layer, is all about them. They're passing through its denser zones. Other shells had showed this phase, only with less brilliant visual effect. Typically, this will be succeeded by a last burst of activity when whatever lies in the innermost zones comes by.

Baram says a silent farewell. The Star as such will never be seen again from Damiem. On the opposite side of the planet, where it's daylight now, the Star-blizzard is contending with the sun. When its twilight comes, there will be a glimpse of the setting lights of the Galaxy from behind the great, expanding wall of the explosion front. And when the turning planet carries the hostel around to night again, they will see only the last shreds of the inmost layer, gaseous wisps over the whole empty sky. The Star will be gone.

Baram suddenly recalls Cory's increasing gaiety over the past weeks. How she must have looked forward to skies forever free of that Star! That Star which, unbelievably, *she* had created, and to which, all unknown, she was so terribly linked. . . . The mysteries of destiny. . . .

Baram's thoughts have strayed only for an instant; now he is jerked back to the present by Linnix, rising from behind the rollbed, holding out empty hands.

"I just can't find it anywhere. Could it have fallen into the trees?"

Baram glances down into the treetops beyond the coping. "I really thought it fell here. If it's down there, we won't find it tonight. Well, neither will anyone else."

The needle is moving at last toward Transmit; only a minim or so more. The brief power-up time has seemed to Baram intolerably long. And he is quietly appalled that they have so far failed to be able to call for help. Is Cory right in her reasoning? She called it, with her usual accuracy, a "feeling" that it might be dangerous to be overheard calling for help. He agrees, in principle—but he has a strong urge to grab up that old-fashioned microphone and simply yell for *Rimshot*.

There's a number code he could use, but he hasn't learned it; maybe he would have done better to take some time from examining Damei uric acid function and learned that—but Cory would brief him if he asked. He's pretty sure that the reason she ignored it is that it's only a Star-Standard code and if these men *are* sophisticated criminals, they'd have made sure to have that, too. . . . His mind is circling unclearly; it's hard to feel sharp, surrounded as he is by flickering Star-light, and quiet sleeping bodies, hard to believe in the possible reality of small Human plottings under the cosmic beauty of this sky—and the light's unremitting pulse beat interferes with coherent thought.

"Linnie," he calls, "I left a pot of kaffy on to warm for us. Could you get it from the surgical stand? It'll do Cor good, too."

"Great thought." She vanishes into the infirmary.

The needle is almost at Transmit.

Just then, the flicker in the air intensifies, and the whole sky suddenly flashes black. Then flicker, white—and again black flash. Baram blinks, hearing himself say, "It'll do Cor good, too."

"Great thought," says a white-clad figure at the infirmary door, and a rush of shadow supervenes.

He frowns and slaps his head to clear the hallucination. There's a name for this, not *déjà vu*, something nasty having to do with synchronic foci in the brain; epileptiform. . . . Oh, no.

"Not *now*," he groans nonsensically, seeing with dismay how the quiet bodies around him seem to stir and change, becoming shadows rushing movelessly to and fro. Substance-less apparitions—people, chairs, blankets—are vibrating darkly in and out of empty space, like a breaking hologram. Everything flickers, overlaid by a centrifugal whirling that streams across his sight, and his ears fill with rustling sound, a rush of pounding footfalls, collisions, a dreamlike cry. Linnix has vanished.

With peculiar difficulty Baram twists in his seat, to find Kip's body indiscernible under dim transmutations of itself. And Cory—where is Cor?

He turns, seeking her but producing only more unreality— until chaos condenses into clear Star-light on the standing figure of Vovoka by the parapet—Vovoka with head intact, Vovoka alive! He's looking down at a brown-haired figure in the lounger beside him.

Baram stares miserably at the living, solid figures before

the flittering lake, which now reflects rainbow arcs, hearing Vovoka say, ". . . cell fatigue. But we knew differently."

And—gods!—understanding comes.

It isn't Baram's eyes or brain at all, it's a so-called time-flurry! He'd been under cover with the Dameii last time; he hasn't experienced one before. . . . Fascinating!

Rocked by relief and excitement, he watches the scene from the past unroll for a second or two. It occurs to him to try Pao's point—to make some mark, to change the past. Is it possible?

He raises his hand to shift Cor's stylus that's lying on the console. His muscles feel distant, tiny, weak; the very air seems to resist him. He recalls Cory saying that one felt "gluey." But he persists, and just as he succeeds in making the stylus roll, there's a weak flash, substance drains from the scene, and all blurs into rushing shadows again.

But it's time-forward now—Vovoka's figure crumples downward, the surging figures of people whirl through their courses and go to ground, and Baram, turning, sees the forms of Kip and Cory emerging into Star-light as he'd last seen them in reality. He sees, too, that Cor has dragged Kip into the protecting shadow of the overhanging eaves.

"Great thought." And the real Linnix disappears through his door.

Baram stares down at the bare console top; there's something he's trying to recall, but it eludes him.

The Transmit light flickers. And still the feared intrusions haven't materialized. Where is Ochter? Surely he can send any short SOS he pleases without being overheard. Should he? Cory has put him in charge.

As he hesitates, fingering the old microphone, a faint sound from the shadows distracts him. He turns to see Cory sitting bowed over, her hands to her face; he can see her shoulders quake. *Cory* weeping?

He can't go to her now even if she wished it, which she doubtless does not. He chokes back a pang of pity—pity and fear; she may know more of her injury than he guesses. The grayness of fatigue still veils her. Even that white streak in her hair, shining in the Star's light, seems broader than before.

A cup of steaming kaffy intrudes on his view—Linnix is standing over him, watching Cory, too. Her wonderful eyes, blue even by this light, turn on him, soft with compassion.

"Drink. I have hers here. Then I'm going to put on more lights to kill this rotten flicker. Green?"

A jewel of a girl, he thinks, thumbing the Send button. Pure zeranaveth. The hum and crackle of power are filling the air.

"Damiem to Base," he says, still thinking of an SOS. But as he identifies the station he remembers Cory's warning about the Star's static and checks the indicator. Sure enough, his words are being lost. He adjusts everything he can think of and repeats his call signal, finding he has almost to shout.

"FedBase Ninety-six, priority override," he repeats loud and clear, watching the led-back indicator. This is going to be work; talking at the top of his lungs does not come naturally to Baram. And partly because of this, partly from loyalty to Cor and concern for her, partly from a dozen wisps of causality, his intent changes.

"Administrator Corrisón Estreèl-Korso has suffered un-diagnosed head injuries," he howls, "in an encounter with an alien disguised as a Human tourist in today's landing party. Deputy Kipruget Korso-Estreèl has sustained a broken leg and some cerebral concussion in the same incident."

Linnix' hand flashes into his field of view, pointing. Catching his breath, he looks up to see her with her head cocked and one ear cupped by the other hand. What are those sensitive young ears hearing?

The hand she points with begins to beat time as she stares down the deck toward Ochter's room. Uneven beats—long-short, long-short. . . . No, it isn't the sound he'd dreaded,

540

the stride of two pairs of male feet. It is—of course!—the thud-tap, thud-tap of Ochter's lame footsteps.

Doctor Ochter is limping toward them, well within sound of his bellowed words. The gods had been with him, all right. Assuming Ochter is their enemy, he'd have heard every word of Baram's intended SOS. Whew!

Baram gulps an extra breath and shouts on. "The Deputy is unconscious, but the Administrator is conscious and she has delegated her responsibilities *pro tem* to me, Senior Medical Officer Balthasar Baramji ap Bye. On present evidence the Administrator's injuries must be considered potentially life-threatening, and I hereby direct—"

Thud-tap, thud-tap; very faintly he, too, can hear it now, above the humming of the deck. He listens as well as he can while specifying the equipment and the neurologist he wants *Rimshot* to bring soonest. The footsteps seem to be slowing as they approach.

"The alien responsible, calling himself Ser Xe Vovoka in your landers' list, is now dead by his own hand. Several tourists were stunned by his weapon, which has not yet been recovered; they are now unconscious but are believed to be otherwise unharmed."

Thud-tap, thud-tap. . . . Baram swivels to watch the place where Ochter will emerge into the deck light, suddenly conscious that he makes an ideal target if the man is armed. He searches his memory for ambiguous terms; why, oh, why hadn't he learned that code?

Thud–tap . . . silence. Just beyond the circle of light, Ochter has paused. Under Baram's white crest the scalp crawls slightly.

Suddenly, to his horror, Linnix deliberately walks between him and Ochter and drapes herself casually on the corner of the console. Gods curse this darling girl—if he could reach her, he'd knock her flat.

"Get away!" he hisses. She smiles serenely.

Well, he just must be twice as careful.

"In view of various events and circumstances, some of which have been reported earlier," he says haltingly, "and the condition of the Administrator, I now also direct—" Aha, one of the terms he needs has come back to him! "—that Captain Dayan treat this as a Class F priority. And I further request that he initiate voice contact with us in two standard hours."

Class F stands for Force in an old Rim War code, which Ochter is unlikely to know. Dayan will surely recall it, and it should mean to him that they are in some sort of danger. He puts the message on automatic repeat and signs off.

Thud-tap . . . Thud-tap . . . Ochter has resumed his painful march.

The instant the power drains down, Baram realizes he has botched it, several ways. How will Dayan know whether to come at once on the Class F, or delay to fetch equipment and neurologist on the medical priority? It could take a day or so to collect Dr. Schehl. And the two-hour reconfirmation might seem to mean that nothing was to start till then. . . . Well, at the least this should insure that somebody will be in shape to communicate in two hours—no, three, given the time lag. They are so ridiculously helpless. The man limping toward them could take them all if he's armed with a child's rocket starter.

Tap . . . thud-tap—

Into the pool of light hobbles a small, old, frail figure wearing a wrinkled sleep tunic and topped by wild tufts of gray hair; Doctor Aristrides Ochter.

His right hand is untidily bandaged.

Baram, like Kip before him, is rudely set back by the gulf between the malevolent, deadly Ochter of their thoughts and this harmless-looking little old man, who seems in constant pain from his leg.

Is the whole fabric of their reasoning insane?

Ochter halts and blinks about with an air of horrified astoundment at the recumbent bodies.

"Oh, my," he exclaims; "I thought I heard signs of trouble, you see, so I . . . But these poor people, are they . . ."

"So far as we know," says Baram, "they are only temporarily unconscious—except for Ser Vovoka there, who is dead."

"Dead!" Ochter stares at the ungainly shroud which does not quite conceal Vovoka's feet. "M-may I?"

Baram nods.

The little man limps around the console to the parapet by the alien's body. Only now does he seem to perceive Cory, back in the shadow of the eaves beside Kip. She has lifted her head to watch him. Ochter makes a respectful head bow to her, seeming to understand that she wishes no talk.

She acknowledges his presence silently and returns to her deep, private preoccupation, a statue of grief gazing down at Kip.

Ochter looks at her gravely for a minim or two more, than turns his attention to the corpse at his feet. Diffidently he lifts a corner of the blanket where Vovoka's head should be. His jaw drops open as he takes in the condition of the corpse.

"Oh, oh, my *goodness*—" he says, staring down. Then he drops the shroud and collapses feebly into the nearest chair.

Linnix comes over to him, standing close but not too close, Baram is glad to see.

"Would you care for some water, or something more reviving, Doctor?"

He peers up at her through his old-fashioned spectacles, bewildered and grateful. "Oh, thank you, Myr Linnix. Just some water, please. . . . I'm glad you appear well. Doctor Baramji, if you are not too occupied, could you tell me what has happened here?"

"Certainly. Well, let's see—you were at Vovoka's grand unveiling, weren't you?"

Ochter holds up the bandaged hand, smiling joylessly. "I was."

"Of course, sorry, my memory seems to be slipping tonight.

543

Would you like me to take a look, or make you a less bulky bandage? Doing up one's own hand is difficult.''

As Baram looks at the clumsy bandage it occurs to him that Ochter can have bound a small weapon, or who knows what, in there. But again, that amputation is probably too painful by now. "Are you getting much pain from it, Doctor? I could help there."

"Oh, no, no," Ochter says stoutly. "I have some topical pain relievers, and I've finally got things comfortable. Why don't we just leave it, unaesthetic as it is, till morning?"

"As you say." Apparently Baram is not to have a look in those wraps. "Now, let's see. Vovoka claimed that his purpose was revenge upon Myr Cory for an act in her long-ago wartime life. Kip attempted to defend her, tackled Vovoka, and got thrown there; he has some concussion. These five others charged Vovoka to try to help Kip, and he stunned them with that weapon. It's supposed to wear off"—enough caution remains in Baram to make him equivocate—"by morning. Vovoka also did something to Cory with his weapon, we don't know what yet. And then he blew his own head off.

"That leaves Lady P. I'm sorry to say she hasn't yet recovered from the deep stupor you saw, after drinking the Eglantine.''

"Oh, dear, Oh, dear. . . ." Ochter muses a moment, shaking his head. "As to the part of my wine in this terrible business, I still cannot think of any explanation other than what we discussed: a students' practical joke. I believe it had nothing to do with you at all. But oh!" he went on, quite fiercely. "If I could only teach them that when they sought to spoil my fun, they actually succeeded in spoiling a happy moment for some charming and innocent young people—to some of whom it seemed to mean much—on far-off Damiem. They'd hear something beside cerebration on informational asymmetry!''

The little man bobs his head vehemently, with surprising fire. Baram chuckles to himself, wholly convinced.

"And I may say," Ochter goes on, "that it was a wonderful stroke of luck we had our young nobleman to warn us. Such an uncontrolled and probably very excessive dose might have done actual harm—or am I wrong, Doctor?"

"No, under certain circumstances and for certain people you could be quite right," Baram admits.

Ochter harrumphs a time or two, a small volcano subsiding, and then asks, "By the way, where is that estimable lad? I'm happy that I don't see him among the fallen."

"No," says Baram. He's feeling entirely foolish in his suspicions, but a sudden resurgence of worry about Pao— really, something has got to be done about finding him! —combines with old habits of duty, and he says, "I believe Pao went up to his tower. I caught him yawning a couple of times despite his interest in the Star. These are long days, and the prince is still a kid."

An outright lie. Baram notices Linnie, who's checking Hanno's pulse with her face away from Ochter, glancing sideways at him or, rather, at his hands. An odd, almost mirthful expression crosses her face. Baram looks down at the loose switch plate he's absently fingering but can see nothing amiss.

Ochter suddenly starts and claps his hand to his head.

"My heavens, I *am* becoming forgetful. Here I've almost forgotten the very thing I was hurrying to pass on to you when I heard you transmitting. If I may ask, you were not sending by *c*-skip, were you?"

"No," says Baram shortly, wondering where this leads.

"Good. Although the vibration alarmed me. Did you not notice an extraordinary amount of throbbing and tension in the air, as though great quantities of power were being used? Or is that the normal performance of your machine?"

"Now that you mention it," Baram says cautiously, "I do recall thinking that there seemed to be an unusually powerful effect. But the transmission was quite normal, insofar as I grasp these things."

"Well then, this may not come amiss. I believe I mentioned that in the confusion in their room, before they became incoherent, Hiner was muttering about something he'd found underwater this afternoon? I really should have relayed this sooner, but so much— Well, as you know, Hiner went diving when we were all at your fairyland village, and he explored around the port leading to your power-cell shaft. The port, you may know, is over a hundred meters down— extraordinary to think a Human can ramble about down there as we would in a meadow, is it not?

"But the serious point is that he seems to have found that some water-dwelling creature has constructed an enormous hard-clay and debris blockage around the shaft vent—not the port, you understand, but the vent which is necessary to all operations. He said it was blocked completely, and that any heavy power usage like a c-skip transmission might blow the cell. He was getting a bit incoherent by then, but he was very clear about the vent being blocked and the explosive possibilities—he kept saying, 'Boom! boom!' with quite infantile enthusiasm. Of course, he may have been fantasizing. You realize I'm no expert at all, but it occurs to me that the blockage of the vent might be why normal use creates so much effect.

"At any event, I thought I'd better tell you at once, when I remembered. Do you know, I was really quite relieved, coming here, when I concluded you weren't powering up for c. . . . That 'boom, boom' quite gripped me." He chuckles. "The idea was that the hostel and everything in or near it would go skyward and come down as splinters. . . . Don't you think it might be a good idea to have a qualified Aquaman take a look at it fairly soon? Our friend Hiner does not quite fill the bill, but he may have given a useful warning. Although I'm sure," he adds politely, "that the unusual vibration and so on would have soon alerted you."

"Needless to say, I agree completely," Baram replies. "And my thanks to you for relaying it." He was thinking hard as he spoke, recalling Linnie's description of how Hiner "gasped and gasped and gasped." Surely a bit of exploration, a simple look-see, wouldn't be so exhausting? On the other hand, if Hiner *himself* had been sealing up that vent, it would be hard work. Some gasping would be in order.

But why should he seal the vent? Pure malevolence? Or part of a long-range plan for completing the job here—destroying the hostel, the other guests, the Guardians, and perhaps even their Damei victims—in such a way that only unidentifiable "splinters" remained?

Here, certainly, is the perfect mechanism for the "killing spree" Cory was afraid the criminals would resort to if driven to desperation. Hiner, Yule, or Ochter could simply turn on the c-skip power-up and have ample time to escape.

And such a blast might cover the fact that they'd survived; at the least it would destroy all who could identify them and knew of the crime. With luck, it might even be possible actually to conceal the fact that any crime had taken place.

Dameii are notably reluctant to talk to Humans; the survivors would just move away, which could be readily blamed on the blast. And the blast itself would be blamed on the presumably convincing-looking animal activities Hiner had simulated. Very neat indeed.

But again—totally hypothetical! Beyond Linnie's account of Hiner's fatigue, there isn't a reason in the worlds why Ochter's account isn't true, and a very helpful act. And Hiner's condition can be blamed on exactly what she'd thought, that he is one of those unfortunates whose gill structures haven't fully matured. The deficiency is sometimes so subtle biochemically that it defies easy test. Certainly Hiner himself would never voluntarily admit it—the "spoiled" Aquas are the most sensitive of all Human defectives.

Another devil-begotten ambiguity! Baram's mind feels torn in two.

To disguise his preoccupation, Baram has risen and is perfunctorily making the rounds of his patients. All are still unresponsive except Zannez; Baram catches a covert glance. Good—an ally. But in what cause? So far, Ochter has done nothing inconsistent with perfect innocence—and nothing inconsistent with secret criminal intent, either.

He concludes with a careful recheck of the Lady Pardialanches's heart action. Warm memories of the morning tickle him as he presses the stethoscope to her perfumed breasts.

"All her signs still suggest a simple soporific," he tells Ochter. "As you see, we're making no special attempt to wake her; such efforts sometimes do more harm than good. Nor have I done a gastric lavage; we've been a shade busy. But if she fails to show REM, and remains unresponsive to strong stimuli, after I've tended to things here I'll give her the full antitoxin treatment. Then we'll know the answer to your concern that some additional poison could have been present."

"Poor lady." The little man has risen too, and is leaning on the golden side of the rollbed. He glances down curiously at the silent sister, the lovely little Lady Paralomena locked in her endless sleep, and shakes his head in silence. Then he lowers himself into a nearby chair.

From the corner of his eye, Baram keeps close watch on Ochter's movements. Persons feigning a lame limb generally slip up. But Ochter's limp and favoring actions are letter-perfect. That bad leg looks miserably genuine, poor man.

Baram returns to the console feeling so emotionally remorseful toward Ochter that it serves to alarm him. Hold on a minim, he tells himself, this isn't rational, either. I'm swinging from hostility to gullibility, from fear to blind acceptance, like a child's toy. But nothing has changed except his own perception of Ochter. Looked at objectively, every response Ochter makes is as consistent with innocence as with deception and guilt. What Baram needs is a really clear-cut test. But he can see no way, nothing that Ochter would say or do only if he has tried to drug them and would not if he hasn't, or vice versa. And if Baram waits too long, and Ochter has evil intentions, too long may be too late.

But again, what can the little man do, alone here? If he has a weapon, he'd have used it by now—if he intended to. And if Yule and Hiner are in it, they're certainly giving no sign—unless Pao's absence *is* a sign? On the other hand, Pao *is* only a very young boy, distractable— Curse the Star's pulsing light! If only he could *think*—

"By the way," Ochter is saying, "whatever happened to that extraordinary weapon of Ser Vovoka's? It seems to have been astoundingly versatile." He looks ruefully at his bandaged hand. "Frankly I never heard of anything like it."

"Nor I," says Baramji, thinking that if the question had come a moment earlier, he would probably have blurted out that they've been looking for it right where Ochter sits.

"I presume you've examined it?" Ochter asks. "I admit I'm curious to look it over, knowing nothing of such things. Still, you might say I have paid a finger for a bare introduction." He smiles, eyes twinkling behind his lenses, a wryly jolly little gnome. "May I?"

"With pleasure, in the morning. The fact is that Vovoka—or rather, his headless body—dropped or flung it over the parapet as he fell. No use even looking down there in the woods till sunup."

Ochter sighs. "So much violence. . . . I confess, I . . ." His voice weakens, he seems to wilt abruptly as though he's been making an effort he can no longer sustain. Perhaps his analgesic has worn off.

He slumps back in the lounger, looking out at the light-shrouded lake and sky. Then his gaze shifts to the shadowed figure of Cory. Linnix is just urging more kaffy on her; Kip is still apparently out cold.

"You believe Myr Cory to have been gravely injured by that desperate being?" Ochter asks. "Yet I see no change beyond an understandable fatigue and grief."

Baram nods. "I know. But Vovoka discharged that thing

directly into her head, and then seemed satisfied. *Something must have happened."*

"Hmm. Let's see . . . our nearest Federation Base is, what, approximately a hundred light-minim away. How long will it take your expert to get here, assuming, say, that the Patrol helped him?"

An innocent query—and one of vital concern to the guilty, too. Baram closes off the answer he's been about to make and says that the neurologist will probably not start from Base, but from a med-center in the Hyades complex. "The fellow I want, best man in CNS work, is Mausbridge Schehl. He's notoriously hard to locate. Turns up visiting some patient on an asteroid nobody's heard of. He'll take time to find but there's nobody half so good."

Ochter seems to be about to ask more but sighs again and remains silently gazing out. The world is glorious, enveloped in the Star's iridescent, flickering mists of light. Yet Baram feels an oppressive, imperceptibly mounting tension. Some of Cory's ions, no doubt, he tells himself, checking over the readouts. High but still safe, as well as he can determine.

Ochter stirs. "I do believe I must go back to my bed," he says sadly. "I had hoped to see that the Lady—and all these poor souls—had recovered, and to enjoy more of the Star, but I find—I find . . ." He struggles up, making heavy going of it.

Linnix comes past on her way to the infirmary.

Suddenly the little man's limbs give way. He starts to collapse, catches himself on the chair, slips again, manages to grasp a straight chair, and falls across it, uttering a half-suppressed little cry of pain. His spectacles clatter on the floor.

Linnix is already beside him, helping him right himself in the chair. She retrieves the eyeglasses.

"If I could just sit here a moment before I make another attempt," he gasps, trying to push himself back.

"Of course." She goes behind him, and he gives another

550

cry as she takes him under the armpits and pulls him back and up. "There!"

Belatedly, Baram recalls his earlier warning to her. It doesn't seem to apply now, but nevertheless he calls softly, "Watch it, Linnie!"

They both glance at him. Baram realizes his warning could seem to follow Ochter's cry of pain.

"So embarrassing." Ochter tries to smile. "But . . . could I impose on you to . . . help me undo this? My medicines . . ." He's fumbling at his tunic sash, the hand bandage impeding all.

"Here." She comes around beside him, gently brushes the hands away, and loosens the knot. To do so she must go down on one knee; Baram feels a stab of uneasiness. But Ochter does nothing more than reach his good hand into his tunic pouch and bring out a small vial. Baram recognizes the golden color of Xyaton, a standard quick-acting—and addictive—analgesic. Linnix helps the old man click it open and convey two globes to his mouth.

In a moment he sits up straighter. "Myr Linnix, many thanks. . . . And now I believe you can get me on my way if you will allow me to do as they taught at the clinic, and loop my hands around your shoulder here? These loungers are so low—"

"Certainly."

He slides his good hand under her arm; she leans toward him and he bends his arms so that his hands meet on her shoulder, by her neck. "They tell me the elbow grip is too low, it requires too much strength," he explains to Baram. "Now you rise, my dear rescuer—if I'm not too much of an impediment?"

"Lords, no." She smiles, coming smoothly to her feet with the little man in tow. As he fumblingly releases his grip on the bandaged hand she suddenly starts and gives a tiny yelp.

"Oh, dear, that pin." Ochter quickly massages her deltoid

with his good hand. "And I've crushed your collar . . . I *am* sorry."

His tone is subtly different.

"It's nothing." Linnix grins and puts her own hand to her collar, looking a trifle puzzled.

"And now"—Ochter stands straight—"Doctor Baramji, there's—"

At that instant a night-caller chirrs loudly from the eaves right above them. Ochter jumps and peers up and about.

"Just one of our local night fauna," Baram reassures him as the creature jangles again. Two others answer from the trees around the lake. Why is Linnie staring at him so?

Ohhh—gods of death!

And Baram's world splits into horrifying fragments that whirl and reform around Pao's voice: ". . . a double if they're here and active." The call had sounded twice. But was that Pao? It was so real. But a real night-caller would answer the callers on the shore, and this one stays silent. And that means that—that—Yule, Hiner, Ochter—

It's only a microminim since Baram understood, but it seems an hour. Even his mouth moves with intolerable slowness to say the words, "Linnie! Get over to Cory, quick! She, she's having trouble with Kip."

Slowly, slowly, it seems to him, she slides free of Ochter's hand and heads for Cory. Ochter passively lets her go, looking intently at Baram.

At this instant the extraordinary point occurs to Baram that they have made no plans whatever for action if the worst case is true—all of them must subconsciously have regarded it as too remote, too unlikely. Only the no-alarm principle. Does it still hold? No matter, because his own course of action is plain—to lay hold on Ochter and force him to call off his henchmen.

It would seem that they have given Baram their own hostage, little Ochter—or rather he has put himself in that position. And he so vulnerable—why?

Even as Baram gets up and starts toward the little man, something in Ochter's apparently extreme weakness and defenselessness awakens suspicion. He simply *couldn't* have come among them so totally open to discovery and seizure. He must have some weapon. Or perhaps allies—could Yule and Hiner be on watch in Cory's room ready to pounce out and defend their chief? Surely Ochter is their chief? Yes—but the notion of the others guarding him doesn't make sense.

He must have some personal weapon. . . . Why has the little man come here, anyway?

Baram is almost within arm's length of Ochter now, but Ochter shows no sign of alarm. Nor has he produced any weapon. Indeed, he is standing so peacefully looking up at Baram that Baram finds it impossible to reach out and suddenly do him violence. Is it credible that Ochter actually intends to go on playacting?

"All right," Baram says brusquely. "No more games."

"Oh, I do agree," Ochter replies. "But Baramji, I implore you, before you do anything rash, think! There are three facts you must know if you care at all for Myr Linnix' life."

Baram scarcely hears this.

"I want your precious pair, Yule and Hiner, brought here at once, if you care for your safety."

"Myr Linnix' *life*," Ochter repeats louder. "If you attack me, she will be thrown into extreme agony and die, Baram. Die! I'm telling you that Myr Linnix' life is now bound by radio to an instrument in my right hand—if the connection is broken, or if I am hurt or killed, she dies."

Baram looks at him in silence, but halts.

"I told you there were facts you need to know. If you're ready to listen, here is fact one: *Algotoxin has been reconstituted.*"

As Baram looks blankly incredulous, Ochter repeats, as if to a child, "Algo-toxin. From *algos,* pain. The poison whose sole function is to cause pain and death. Don't tell me you haven't heard of the forbidden drug, *Doctor*?"

Baram frowns down at him, a sick fear stabbing his gut. "No," he says.

"Oh, yes! You doubt? Watch. Oh, Myr Linnix," Ochter calls over his shoulder to where Linnix stands by Cory and Kip in the dimness under the eaves. "I do apologize for what you are about to experience."

He holds up the bandaged hand.

"You see, Baram, the second fact you need to know is that this hand is maintaining a radio transmission which in turn is holding closed—closed—a very special remote-control, spring-loaded hypodermic needle. The instant my hand relaxes, the needle will open and discharge. Or if the transmission is blocked in any other way, the hypo opens and fires.

"And the third fact you must know is that this hypodermic needle, containing two LD—that is, twice the lethal dose—of Algotoxin, is now implanted in Myr Linnix' pretty neck."

XV

NOVA MAX:
Under Control

"Observe!"

Baram, struck numb in confused, half-unbelieving horror, stares at the uplifted wad of bandaging that is Ochter's wounded hand. He sees a slight shifting of the wrist tendons, and then—

"Aahh! Aaah!" An appalling yell from behind them, as quickly cut off. Baram has not heard that shocking, unmistakable outcry of agony since the dreadful war days.

He whirls, to see Linnix crouched with both hands clutching the side of her neck where Ochter's hands had locked. She's staring at them with eyes so adrenaline-wide that the whites show as rings, and her jaw is rigid with effort not to cry out again. In the instant that Baram can bear to watch her, the torture overrides her control and a pain-driven "Aah-ahh-h!" breaks from between her clenched teeth.

"Stop it! Stop it!" Baram roars, looming over Ochter.

555

He's maddeningly torn between his brute drive to grab and pound the little devil, and his fear of what Ochter can do to Linnie.

The little man steps back nimbly.

"I *have* stopped, Baramji. The Algotoxin lingers. That was the minimum, the absolutely least amount I could release, I promise you. And for heaven's sake, don't frighten me if you care for Myr Linnix!"

He shakes out his monogrammed kerchief and wipes his brow.

"You *must* control yourself, Baramji."

Ochter's voice is strong and clear, he holds himself like a much younger man. The old-pixie twinkle is long gone.

Baram gives a wordless growl and strides back to where Linnix stands, shaking, in the eave shadow. Cory has risen to put her arms around the girl. Baram can't see Linnix' neck clearly, only a gleam of metal under her torn white collar.

Linnix simply stares up at him in silence, her eyes sending love—and something else unreadable, thoughtful and dark.

"Let me look, Cor."

"Do not attempt to touch her, Baramji!" comes Ochter's menacing voice.

"He's right, Bram," Cory says. "I've seen enough to know it's a big spring-loaded hypo, with the spring held compressed by some radio signal, presumably from a transmitter under his bandage. You can't get at the main tube, it's fenced. Maybe with needle-nose wire-cutters and time. . . . But the point is that if the signal is interrupted in any way, the spring snaps open and the poison is ejected." She sighs with the effort to explain clearly.

"He's apparently holding it on transmit: if his hand relaxes, or tires, the hypo shoots. It would also be activated by anything which blocked off the transmission—say, one of those hats. . . ."

Her voice sinks to a whisper. "We could gain control if

we could duplicate his signal. But I don't need to tell you that would take time and luck, and probably his cooperation . . . and a slip would be . . . maybe fatal. . . ."

Her voice trembles off. She can't fight anymore against the unnatural, deadly weariness.

"Sit down, Cor," Baram says gently. "Linnie dearest, do you understand I have to leave you, to try to cope with Ochter?"

"Sure." She smiles strangely, takes a breath. "And Bram, dear, do *you* understand that you may have to kill me?"

The grotesque words, so coolly spoken amid the raining glitter of the sky, jolt him inexpressibly. *"What?"*

"Yes, unless there's a miracle. Or would you let me die of this stuff? You haven't had time to think; I have. It's a triage situation. When you think it out—"

"Baramji! Get back here!" Ochter calls.

"No time now," she says. "Just tell me one thing—you *can*, can't you? I can count on it?"

"If . . . if . . . if . . . but— Oh, my darling, my darling girl—"

"Baramji, when I call you, come. Do you need a lesson?"

"Tell me you can," she says implacably. "No if-buts. Cut my throat, or however's best. *Can you?*"

Baram is looking into her blue, blue eyes with their depths of real meaning. He suddenly realizes that he has been too long a man of ifs and buts, too far from any but medical action.

"Yes, I can. . . ." he says slowly. "And I have the means." He touches his pocket scalpel.

"Ah-h-h-h, good. I count—on— OH! AAH-eee—"

Apparently Ochter had found a more minimal dose; this agony is briefer—but to see pain's teeth shaking her as a predator shakes its prey—no. He couldn't let her die so.

"Baramji, that's only a taste. Get back here to the console."

Cory struggles to her feet to hold the girl again. Baram

557

pulls Linnie's hands away from the hypo, kisses them, and goes.

What he finds when he returns to the console makes him stare: Ochter is just freeing himself from a set of harnesses, or hobbles, that had been hidden under his night tunic. Baram had caught a glimpse of it by Ochter's jerkin edge that afternoon and taken it for a brace. Now he sees what it is—the source of Ochter's flawless limp. The little brute's a perfectionist, to endure that.

Ochter straightens up with a sigh of relief. Never taking his eyes off Baram, he kicks off one slipper and picks it up. A pebble clatters out. . . . Baram can only curse himself bitterly: gullible, gulled—a sucking fool.

And now he sees something more—a dulled, varnishlike gloss on the nail and ring finger of Ochter's good hand. The little beast is not as defenseless as he'd looked; that coating carries a so-called Death-Claw, a nearly invisible, surgically sharp point loaded with the poison of one's choice. . . . Sweet.

Meticulously, Ochter dusts off the knee he had fallen on, rewraps the dangling end of his bandage, and puts away his eyeglasses. He gives Baram one of his old impish smiles and says confidentially, "One does look so *helpless* with specs and a bungled bandage. Almost worth the finger, I thought."

Baram's icy blue eyes study him as they would study a purulent chancre.

"What is all this in aid of, Ochter? Why are you torturing Myr Linnix, who helped you when she thought you were in pain?"

Ochter looks Baramji up and down, and sighs. "Surely this is all quite clear to you, Doctor Baramji? Or will be with a little thought, considering which planet we are on? I do not wish to torture Myr Linnix. In fact, as a sensitive man, I deplore the necessity. My, ah, arrangements are simply to ensure that no one attacks *me*, or interferes with my task.

And particularly to enlist your help, since you are all so much larger and stronger than I.''

"*My* help? Are you insane?''

"No. And you will give it, when you find how little is required.''

"Which is what? Talk straight, if you can.''

"Nothing! That's the laughable part. I need all these people here to do absolutely nothing at all—oh, perhaps to sleep, peacefully sleep. Just as they—most of them''—he glances slyly at Baram—''are doing now. And you will be my bodyguard—yes, yes—because you are the one who is most deeply concerned for Myr Linnix. You will prevent any misguided souls who have not understood the position from attacking me and thus causing her that hideous agony you saw . . . and death. You see, she can recover from a number of small doses, but at some unknown point the effects cumulate and become irreversible.''

During this speech Baram has been very gradually maneuvering himself to within grabbing range of Ochter's hand wrap. But suddenly Ochter steps aside, holding up his good hand.

"Nah-ah! Do *you* want Myr Linnix to die? She really will die, you know, if I forget for an instant to hold tight on the spring switch inside this bandage. And''—he knocks the bandage against the console, producing a hard, hollow rap —''there's a very hard shell around my hand and the switch, so no one can seize it and hold the switch closed by pressing from outside. You're simply not going to outthink me on five-minim notice, Baramji.'' He smiles cheerily.

While Ochter speaks, Baram has been staring beyond him to where Linnix sits beneath the eaves with Cory and Kip. At Ochter's final words, describing precisely his own plan, a flood of helpless rage shakes him so that he almost bites his tongue in his effort to contain it. For an instant he's blind— and then, as his vision clears, he becomes aware of motion on the Star-lit eaves over Linnix' head.

It materializes into a small dark shape oozing toward the eave edge, near where Pao's night-caller trilled. Bram jerks his eyes away, saying desperately, "But why, Ochter? *Why?* Think what you're risking."

He cares nothing for Ochter's reasons, he wants only to keep his enemy's attention on himself and away from those eaves. From the corner of his eye he sees the boy-sized shadow withdraw uproof again—good.

Ochter is saying, "Baramji, take my advice and stop bothering your head with whys and wherefores. Instead, dwell on something more pertinent, like the characteristics of Algotoxin, for example. It really is a fascinating tale, you know."

"Tell me." Baram scarcely knows what he's saying. Pao has reappeared on the eaves, this time above a drainpipe that runs down behind Zannez' now dark screens.

Oh, no, no, stay up there, Baram implores silently, not daring to look. *Don't try it—oh, gods—* Pao is creeping forward, all too evidently about to try some acrobatic feat of swinging himself out and around and down to the drain. Even if he makes it, he'll be totally exposed till he passes the screens.

"Tell me, I mean it." Baram repeats, forcing his attention back to Ochter. "It's clear you do have some pain-producing material in that hypo—I can think of several that would duplicate such effects—but that it is Algotoxin, I take for a clever story. Algotoxin has been dead for decades. I don't underestimate your abilities, Ochter. Even to have learned of it by name and used the peculiar terror it induces is a considerable feat. But that you have it there, I doubt."

Baram's words end with a choke that he changes to a weak chuckle. Trying to focus only on Ochter, he nevertheless half sees a small cartwheel of flying limbs that dives headfirst around the eaves, ending as a kicking something dangling from the drain. An instant more and it shrinks to a mere blur, a thickening, darkly sliding downpipe to disappear behind the screens.

Ochter sighs. "I pray you don't force me to prove it, Baramji. You would be the saddest man in all the worlds. I daresay you would fairly soon take your own life to be rid of the memory of what you'd seen here. Perhaps if you know how it's come about, you may at least hesitate? There's some need for haste, but it will save time in the end if you believe me."

Baram stares at him in silence. Pao's made it safely down. Now Baram needs to think fast and hard. Let Ochter talk, it may let more people awaken. And if the little horror wants to reveal himself it might be useful.

"As you doubtless know, Baramji, Algotoxin was discovered by a woman looking for a cure for Krater's disease. Algotoxin is useless against Krater's or anything else, but she thought it worth a report. The first person who saw that report forwarded it to Special Branch. When the Federation found out what she had, they acted at once—destroyed all copies and all her notes, excised every conceivable reference to the process that produced it, and took everybody who even vaguely knew of it through Rehab to erase the memory. I may say everyone concerned cooperated zealously. You doubtless learned of it through one of the senior medical watchers the Feds briefed, to see it didn't show up again."

Baram nods slowly, interested despite his appallment. It was indeed a senior chief of pathology who had told him of Algotoxin, so long ago. He can still hear the change in old Doctor Ismay's normally genial voice: "Balthasar Baramji: You will forget what I am about to tell you. Bury it *absolutely* until such time, which I pray never comes, when it is necessary for you to remember my words. There is a compound called *Algotoxin* . . ."

Now his words come back: "Algotoxin has no beneficial properties whatever. Its sole known effect in Humans is to cause pain. *Algos* means pain. The pain is atrocious, unremitting, and continues unto death.''

"Unto death"; the strange formal phrase chilled Baram. And then came the shocker.

"The pain cannot be alleviated in the least by any known means. All have been tried. Even rendering the victim unconscious does not dull the terrible pain. Victims may tear out their own eyeballs, their veins and nerves, or bite the flesh from the bones of their limbs before finally expiring.

"The mechanism of death, and the lethal dose, will never be established. All data come from five accidental victims. Experimentation here would be morally detestable.''

But Ochter has said that the hypo on Linnix' neck contains "twice the LD.'' Has someone experimented?

He pulls himself back to the present, where Ochter is telling him that a solitary researcher, a crazy seeking revenge for his failure to pass med school entrance, had determined to reconstitute Algotoxin. "He set out to read everything recorded on Krater's disease. It took him a decade, Baramji, but he finally came on one overlooked half page; it carried the biochemical leads, and one mention of pain.

"It was enough, Baramji, just barely enough. He rented an infested room on one of the Dark Worlds. He didn't care who gave him the small monies to live and work—which is how certain people came onto it. He had to guess what lines the earlier researcher had followed. It took him another decade—I believe he actually came up with a cure for Krater's and threw it away—but he got it, Baramji. Algotoxin, or as near as makes no difference, lives again.''

Ochter's voice and manner are quite different as he tells this; something in this demented tragedy touches his wonder and admiration, almost his love. Baramji realizes they're up against a dangerous animal—the artist of crime. A mad, sadistic artist. Artistlike, he probably wants his cleverness known. Is it possible he'd rather talk about it than execute? Is it the Stars Tears riches that fundamentally attracts him—or pulling off the "impossible" coup? Could this weakness be useful? Certainly the man and his ego require very careful handling.

"Never mind how Algotoxin came to me. It was neither cheap nor easy; in fact, it involved me in some danger. But I deemed it suitable for this task." Ochter smiles proudly.

"A very beautiful composition, Doctor," Baram mimics Ochter's style. "Forgive me if I still have doubts. But a crazed researcher—"

Ochter interrupts him sharply. "It has been tested, Baramji. I insisted on that. Sometimes I actually regret it—as a sensitive man I am still shaken by what I had to witness. But yes, this is Algotoxin. Have no foolish hopes."

Baram's stomach turns at the realization that they *had* experimented. But he has no foolish hopes. Indeed, since he's had a minim to think, he has not much hope of any kind for the lives of either Linnix or himself . . . and little more for the others here.

In the first instant he'd seen clearly that the lives of ten innocent Humans are being held hostage to the pain Ochter can inflict on Linnie, and to his reaction to that pain. Baram, driven by Ochter's threats to Linnix, is to help Ochter inject the other ten with a soporific, after which Ochter can kill them off at his pleasure. And—have no foolish hopes—Baram himself will assuredly be injected the instant his usefulness is over and killed in his turn, while Linnix may well be made to perish horribly through the Algotoxin in her neck.

And Baram cannot, must not, cooperate in this course of action. First, because the attempt to save his own and Linnie's lives by killing ten others is unthinkably immoral. Second, it would be foolish; their own lives would not be spared. And third and worst, his allowing Ochter to protect Yule and Hiner through this blackmail is a breach of his sworn duty as Guardian of the Dameii—and the only Guardian now functional.

But how to prevent Ochter from drugging the others?

The moment Baram resists, Ochter will simply torture Linnie until Baram can no longer endure it—and he has no illusion that he could stand to watch her die so. Ochter will do the same if Baram tries to call Base.

So, either that thing must be gotten out of Linnie's neck, or Ochter must be killed. But how to do that without killing Linnie? Baram is pretty sure he could kill the little man fast, if he is willing to receive a mortal wound from that Death-Claw or some other lethal toy. The prospect of his own death does not, at this point, bother Baram—the point is that Ochter's dead or dying hand would release a doubly lethal dose of Algotoxin into Linnie's neck, and he would not be able to stop her agony. The Algotoxin death is too terrible to contemplate; and he has virtually promised to save her from that; his heart would force it. If only that vile hypo could be cut. . . . At the moment Baram would give his soul for a pair of wire-cutters and a minim's lead on Ochter.

And the other Humans now asleep must have time to awaken and be warned. They hadn't known of Ochter and the two others as their enemies. But if Baram can dispose of Ochter, he feels sure that Zannez and his boys will do their best to stop Hiner and Yule—who may even now be inflicting horror on some Damei prisoner.

Could they all simply ignore Ochter and go straight to capturing his henchmen? No—Ochter can't be left to work his sadistic will on Linnie, and any other helpless body as well. To go past Ochter would mean leaving all these to some horrible death. Ochter must be gotten out of the way first—but how, without killing Linnie?

All depends on getting that hypo out. If he can't, his duty is grim and plain. Linnix had seen it, when she called it "triage." The moment she dies, Ochter's power is all gone. But oh, gods, *is* she doomed? Perhaps, just perhaps, is there some way of releasing that devilish thing without killing his girl?

Baram is gazing absently at Ochter for the instants it takes to race down this mental track, and he becomes suddenly aware that the little man is gazing back somewhat as he had once gazed up at Vovoka. Why—the little butcher is *frightened!* Ochter's calculations tell him he is safe from Baram, but his glands are telling him otherwise—can he perhaps read his death in Baram's eyes? His reaction is to reemphasize his power, and his instincts take him straight to the point.

"By the way, Doctor Baramji," he says with an actor's coolness, "I trust you realize it's useless to think of an ordinary hypo, which can be cut? I will bring Myr Linnix closer so you can see. You will *not* of course attempt to touch her. . . . Myr Linnix!"

Baram goes rigid with suppressed fury at this maggot ordering his girl about.

She comes to them expressionless, only a little pale below her glorious hair. Her eyes pass over Ochter as if he does not exist and lock on Baram's own. Wordless communion— Baram's heart strives to leap to her through his gaze and hold her tight against harm. . . . And yet—his fingers touch the scalpel's steel—he cannot defend her, may instead have to do her dreadful harm. The best he can offer may be a clean death at loving hands. *To kill his girl* . . . How fast she understood this, how sternly she made him know that she accepts it. Even welcomes it, rather than endure Algotoxin or engage in Ochter's foulness. *Oh, my darling, my heart, my brave, brave girl. . . .*

"Observe," snaps Ochter.

Linnix turns so that Baram can see the right side of her neck. Her collar is torn and disordered, letting the tender throat show—will it be there that he must cut?—and Baram is startled by what appears to be a fat, loathsome, many-legged insect clamped to her milky skin.

It's about four centimeters long. Looking more closely, Baram sees a transparent central "belly" holding a bluish fluid; a milliliter, possibly more, he estimates. And dangerously near the carotid artery.

"On certain dark worlds this is known as a 'scorpion,' " Ochter says didactically. "Because it stings even in death. Those protective legs around the central tube are of ultrahard metal, in case you have notions. What Myr Linnix felt as a pinprick was a powerful, fast local anesthetic, to permit entry of the tube.

"But this is no ordinary hypotube, Baram. It is not meant to be pulled out. *Ever*. The shaft ends in long triple barbs which have unfolded themselves in her flesh. . . . And this scorpion has been tested, too, naturally." His grin is pure evil.

"Naturally," Baramji mimics him savagely, his heart sick with dismay. That venomous hypo looks impregnable . . . never to be pulled from living flesh. Baram shudders with rage and despair. But he must not, must not anger Ochter, lest he take it out on Linnie.

Ochter gives him a nasty glance and, resuming his insane urbanity, directs Linnie to return to Cory's area. "Or no, on second thought," he says, "you will sit here in this chaise where Doctor Baramji can see you clearly in case I have need to punish him."

Impassive, Linnix stretches out comfortably in the lounger— and as she does so, to Baram's amazed delight, she sends him a broad, unmistakable wink.

Gallant child, he thinks, trying to smile back with choked throat. She's teaching me courage. . . . *While we live, we live*.

Ochter eyes them sharply, as though they might be working some plot. To the coward, Baram thinks, simple courage is a deeply suspicious mystery.

At this moment a dark glimmering passes briefly through the light-filled air. Linnix' head snaps up, as if to see something looming on her. But nothing is there, only a momentary shadow. Baram himself feels an instant's disorientation and rubs his eyes. Ionization, perhaps. One of the Star's weird effects. He shakes it off. Ochter, too, shudders slightly, looking a trifle disturbed.

Then the little man extracts a small fat roll pack from his tunic pocket. "We will now get to our task," he announces, striding briskly over to 'Lomena's golden bed. The side-rails are down. Ochter lays his pack by the still feet and, working awkwardly with his left hand, unrolls it to reveal an array of tiny medical syrettes, gleaming multicolored in the Star's light. During this he has scarcely taken his eyes from Baram and Linnix. Now he begins humming the old space melody "Sleep," while selecting a pink syrette that Baram recognizes as more Soporin—if it has not been tampered with.

Meanwhile Linnix watches all this alertly, now and then exploring with delicate touch the horrid thing at her neck.

As Ochter rerolls his syrette pack, Linnix finds a chance to whisper to Baram, "Cory says the next Deadman's Alarm cycle should be soon."

Baram has an instant of slightly embarrassed confusion. The fact is, he had forgotten the automatic SOS—because it is irrelevant to Linnix and himself. The response—*Rimshot*—should arrive in time to save the Dameii and all the other Humans, especially anybody who'd gotten into trouble fighting Yule and Hiner. But by no possible chance can it bring help in time for himself and Linnix. Because they must refuse to drug the others: otherwise ten bodies will be lying here helpless at the mercy of these criminals when they discover they're about to be caught by the Patrol. No; his drama, and Linnix', will be over by the time *Rimshot* appears.

Nevertheless he feels the strange sensation of smiling and sees that Linnix looks different, too; at least *something* good is in prospect for most of those in danger, even if it won't help the two of them.

"Baramji! Are you deaf or dreaming? How many reminders does Myr Linnix need?"

"Oh, yes, yes—sorry," says Baram idiotically, and gets up. Just as he rises there's a flicker of light from the board. It's not the Deadman's Alarm, but two different readouts showing peaks above their proper maxima. This means he should switch them over to the large-scale track, to check whether these are true readings or summation effects. He's unpracticed at this.

Meanwhile Ochter is saying, "Ready, Baramji? As I told you, you will come and get down here by"—Ochter peers at the nearest blanketed form—"Myr Stareem. You will turn her blanket back and hold her leg down while I inject the, ah, hip. Your sole task is to make sure she doesn't jar my *right* hand." He holds up the bandaged fist. "Understand?"

Baram understands all right. Sadly, he realizes that he would fight the poor child to keep her from hurting Linnix. And he is aware, too, that by luck or design, Ochter has chosen as his first victim the one person who would be of least help in any physical struggle, the sensitive child whom it would be a kindness to let sleep through whatever lay ahead. A conveniently slippery moral slope down which Ochter proposes that he descend. . . .

"Oh, Bram, no—" says Linnix, just as Ochter snaps ominously:

"Baramji, I am *waiting*."

"Doctor Ochter," Baram says slowly, unsure of what he can contrive, "it's not that I doubt your word. You have quite convinced me that your meanings are to be believed. But I have spent my life as a doctor of medicine. Before I assist in the wholesale inoculation of unconscious persons, before I can function this way, I do need to know what it is that we're injecting. You have never told me, you know."

Has he chosen right? He watches Ochter's expression go from anger to impatience to self-satisfaction to a type of low-grade irritation resembling a man who has forgotten to complete some trivial task.

"Oh, very well, very well." Ochter sighs. "Put so, I owe it to the gods of medicine. The substance in these syrettes is ambezine hydrate, or Soporin, the same thing you diagnosed in the wine, and the thing I told you the clinic gave me for insomnia." His lip curls scornfully.

"And that you said you gave Yule and Hiner?" Baram is holding out his open hand.

"And that I told you I gave Yule and Hiner," Ochter says straight-faced. "Oh, here." He flips a pink syrette at Baram's hand.

Baram uses as much time as he dares examining the little thing. It does look untampered-with. Why not? Sleep is all that Ochter needs in his victims at this point. Baram has long since deduced that this dreadful crew intend to spend as long as they dare here and thus wish the corpses to be fresh in the scene of the final catastrophe they arrange.

His moment's inattention has lost him Ochter's tolerance.

"My patience ends here, Baramji. Give me that syrette and get down and do as I bid you or the consequences will be severe."

Linnie lets out a tiny gasp. Is she expecting him to cut her throat right now, or what? Baram gives her a pleading look and kneels down by Stareem. Resistance has no point here, and the other sleepers need time.

Gently he turns back the blanket from little Stareem's bare rump and lays a hand on the leg that she might hit Ochter's other hand with. Ochter is deft: the injection goes quicker than Baram had been prepared for and Stareem never stirs. In an instant Ochter is up again and summoning Baramji to the next sleeper's side. It is Bridey, poor little Myr Eleganza, still in her golden finery beneath the blanket.

Linnix is leaning forward, blue eyes alight with reproach.

As Baram rises, he manages to take a natural-seeming look at the console board and utters a grunt of surprise.

"What? Wait, Ochter, something goes on. This is no ploy."

He goes over and looks down at the peaking readouts as though he hasn't seen them before. The board looks somehow different; among other things, a third large blue readout is calling for attention.

"I'll be as quick as I can," Baram says without looking around, and sits down in the console seat to analyze the inputs.

Linnix suddenly speaks up. "I know these old things," she tells Ochter. "We had one on a Swain ship. What they do is to jump to sum, and if the data are dangerous or significant, you can't tell until you break it down whether it's a true reading. But three at once is rather a lot for a jump." She gazes up and around as if truly nervous—and by pure luck the sky cooperates.

A number of odd, beehive-shaped, fuzzy clumps of sparks, which have been hovering at an indeterminable distance over the lake, suddenly go into a slow spin and disperse—and those that come toward the deck reveal themselves to be gigantic. One passes over, or through, the deck, completely swallowing it, and as it does so, flares of cold Elmo's fire play through the empty chairs and up to the antennae above. The phenomenon apparently passes through to the front of the hostel, and the garage, and there is a startling hoot from the jitney's horn.

"Whew!" Linnix is doing a good job of acting like a person who is scared to death but trying not to show it, and thus rattles everyone; in fact, Baram is fooled for an instant before he recollects who this is.

She giggles very nervously. "The one on the Swain sh-ship kept summing so you'd get all the crew's meals for the week if you punched for a glass of w-water. And once, once— Oh, maybe I better not tell you about that now. . . ." She giggles again and falls silent, watching Baram work.

And then suddenly she makes another sound—but this is the real Linnix he hears. In a very odd tone of voice she says,

"Doctor Bram, don't you think it's really all right? Are you sure we need to do all that?"

The change is so abrupt that Baram looks around at her and catches a wildly warning look—which vanishes as Ochter turns her way. What—? It doesn't make sense, but he gathers that Linnie wants him to *leave that board.*

Well, he'd better; she knows more than he about such things. Preparatory to rising, he casts one last look around. A few more peaks, and one that had been there isn't now, a couple of lights, including a new-looking red one—rather conspicuous—that triggers a memory of a high little voice saying, "*the big red one,* what's it telling you?" And—

Oh, gods, gods, gods, gods!

He's been working right around the Deadman's Alarm while it came on. Drawing Ochter's attention just when it needs time, unmolested time to work—has his stupidity betrayed them all?

As casually as he can, he gets up, flipping a readout toggle at random, and steps over to Bridey's side. What does one more sleeper matter, if injecting her will distract Ochter long enough to get that SOS sent?

"Ready, Ochter?" But, oh, gods, he's overdone it again— Ochter gives him a puzzled look before opening his syrette case.

"You're . . . satisfied . . . with the readouts, Baramji?"

"Yes," Improvising wildly: "Basically a signal from the drone that the height of radiation is coming soon. It must be thinning out, ahead."

"Hm'm." Ochter takes out another pink Soporin, looking from Baram to Bridey. "You're ready to help me inject Myr Eleganza, Baramji?"

"As ready as I'll ever be."

And Bridey, on the floor, moves. She clutches the blanket clumsily and mutters "Hno . . . hn-n . . . No!"

Involuntarily, Ochter skips back a step. "Baramji!"

Baram kneels down by the girl, trying to soothe her, trying to release the blanket from her grasp, to expose a shoulder. "Get ready, Ochter."

"N-no!" from Bridey.

"I'll help you, Bridey! Can you hear me?" It's Linnix calling to her from the chaise. In a very clear, cold voice she says, "Ochter, if you try to inject that girl, I shall wrench this scorpion of yours through my veins and arteries and die! Right here and now. And then Baram will kill you. Do you hear me? Do you understand I mean it?"

Both her hands are gripped around the wicked thing on her neck.

"Bravely said, Myr Linnix," says Ochter in a scornful tone. "It's a great pity that there is some pain Human bravery cannot endure. When—"

"When I feel the pain it will be too late," Linnix says coldly. "No one will be able to revoke my act, unless someone may care to shorten my death." She gives a secret little smile—and Baram's back hair prickles in terror. He can do it, he can do what he must—but it will be hard, hard.

"Baramji, I believe we are going to have to tie Myr Linnix' hands down to the chair. I had hoped to spare her indignity—"

"And just how do you propose to get hold of my hands before they wrench your bug?" asks Linnix jeeringly. "The first person who moves toward me will end my life—even you, Doctor Bram."

"But why, Linnie, why now?"

"Simple arithmetic. My life—I have always intended to do this—my life can pay for putting Stareem in jeopardy. But one life can't pay for two."

"Oh, Linnix dear, no," Bridey says. "I don't understand—"

"They *will kill* you, if they can," replies Linnix. "Think. This man, and Yule and Hiner, are after Stars Tears. You will be a witness to the crimes this man intends to commit on

572

the Dameii. You can identify them. There is no chance they would voluntarily let you live—and that's true for everyone here."

"Oh-h-h. . . ."

Ochter rises and paces toward the rollbed.

"Stay in front of me where I can see you," orders Linnix. "And no nearer than three meters."

Obediently, Ochter turns and paces back along the parapet toward the console, taking thoughtful looks at Linnix and Baram. Baram does not at all like his expression. Meanwhile Bridey picks up her blanket and goes, somewhat unsteadily, to sit on Baram's old lounger. She looks as if she might be going to be ill. Linnix simply sits, watchfully gripping the hypo on her neck. Baram tries inconspicuously to interpose himself between Ochter's pacing path and the console. Every minim that passes is in their favor; soon, soon, that distress summons would be sent.

Ochter pauses; he has reached some conclusion.

"Something has changed," he says.

His head turns, methodically checking out everything in their previous field of action. When he comes to the console end of his arc, he lifts his bandaged hand meaningfully and steps past Baram to get a clear view of the board. Bandage held high, he studies the lights and dials. One or two flicker and change as he watches, but not the red light, at which Baram is resolutely not looking.

In the eaves' shadow there's a quite audible murmur from Cory. It sounds like—and is—a blistering self-curse. Unknown to Baram, she is not cursing herself now, but the lighthearted, light-headed Cory of so few hours ago, who without thought doubled the waiting-lapse time on her alarm . . . so she would not be inconvenienced by running to it. How many lives has she menaced by that carefree act? . . . And oh, instead of complaining of the bother, how happily she would set to work to lay in optional triggers, and the capability of canceling that cursed red light! . . . Too late now.

573

Ochter's beastly, methodical little mind has caught it.

"What's that red light, Baramji?"

A darkness comes over Baram's vision. Even his voice feels faint. "I don't know. Where?"

Ochter thinks a minim. "Switch it off."

"I don't know how," says Baram truthfully. How, how had he been such a fool? Ochter has the paranoiac's acuity; he can smell hope in his victims. Baram has betrayed them all.

The little devil turns to where Cory sits moveless by Kip.

"Myr Cory, the red light which you said you must switch off when the Damei child was here, and which Ser Vovoka called an alarm, is now on. I wish you to come here at once and switch it off."

"She's too ill," Baram protests. "Vovoka's shot—and it's not only that, she has a heart condition. Didn't your snoop tell you she came to the infirmary for another heart scan this afternoon? The mitral valve is under severe stress. Do you know what that means? What good will it be to you if she collapses now?"

"I know what you would have me believe, Baramji," Ochter says nastily. "And I also know that station personnel are required to pass a health clearance every planetary tour. And I know that Myr Cory is just commencing her fifth tour, Baramji. Now—"

"Then perhaps you also know—" Baram cuts in roughly. Time—time is their need: keep the little demon talking.

"Wait, Bram," says Cory's voice from the shadows. "I can do it, Ochter. But there's no use. I disconnected everything but the light while—while Vovoka was here. It was causing me too much trouble."

"Nevertheless, I wish it switched off right now."

"But it's complicated." Cory sighs. "That's why I left it, before. I'll have to get in behind the board. Leave it—it'll just kick on and off harmlessly all night." She understands the deadly game they are playing all right.

"Do *you* wish to hear Myr Linnix scream again?"

"No! Oh, no. Very well." She sighs again. "But I tell you, it's not connected to anything but a timer."

Ochter lifts his bandaged right hand threateningly.

Cory gives a little groan of protest and slowly rises and makes her way to the console. When she comes into the light Baram is shocked at her drawn and sagging face, the dark folds under her creased eyes, her strange stooped, stumping gait. She sits in the console seat he offers, bracing her movements with shaky hands. But when she speaks her voice is strong.

"Sit down there, Bram, and tell me if any of the dials go dead. . . . Oh, gods, what have you men been doing to my board?" She chuckles, in an eerie imitation of her old joking way.

"Myr Cory, I have warned you once."

She grunts and, to Bram's surprise, lays hold of the console with both hands. Click! The outer edge of the board swings away on hinges, revealing a complex of wiring—and a tool cubby, in which lies a fine new pair of needle-nosed wire-cutters. Two pair, in fact: a small one lies alongside.

The gods' blessing on you, Cor!

She has figured out the one tool that might help him, located it, and led him to it. Now it remains only for him to pocket it undetected and find a way to use it before Ochter releases his switch. In the sheer joy of seeing those cutters, of imagining them slicing through that lethal tube, he dismisses the devilish difficulty of the rest—it is so large a psychic leap from impossible to even barely possible at all.

Cory has picked up the small cutters and begun to probe beneath the board where the red light shows.

Ochter watches them intently.

Baram is bending all his attention on a slow movement to conceal his grab for the cutters, when he almost misses his chance: Cory's arm goes right above the cubby as she taps on a dial.

575

"Watch the reading there, Bram."

"It—it looks a trifle high to me." Bram snakes the cutters into his pocket. Now—now he has a chance to save Linnie!

Cor is saying some time-wasting nonsense about the rise in the readings.

Ochter starts to speak, but she cuts him off. "Ochter, you may not care if you get your brains fried, but those are theta microwaves." She raises her head and stares at him wanly. "These people should all have protective headgear. So should you, although I hate to say so."

For an instant Baram thinks the ruse has worked; Ochter hesitates, chewing his lip. But then, to Baram's dismay, the little man comes behind them and stares down at the board.

"It may surprise you to learn that I can read a simple flux detector," he says acidly. His lips tighten. "You chose ill. Moreover, I see no necessity for these maneuvers with the board."

"I told you I disconnected the alarm wires."

"Ah . . . now I recall. Yes!" He leans swiftly toward the board and his left hand darts down between them to flip an unmarked toggle before he backs away.

The red alarm light goes out.

Ochter's face is tight with fury.

"Return to your place, Myr Cory. I will teach you to try to deceive me!"

Cory rises slowly, painfully, and as she turns she catches Baram's eye and imperceptibly signals negation. Bad—bad; their hope is gone, they haven't managed to delay long enough. No alarm call has gone out.

And their loathsome enemy is meaningfully holding up his bandaged hand.

"No!" shouts Baram. "Ochter, in the name of— Take it out on me, damn you!"

"I am." Ochter wears a twisted, gloating smile. "You shall have something to think of the next time you are tempted to play games."

"Stop! No—here, jab me instead, you must have some more—" Ochter backs away farther, his right fist out.

"It's all ri—" Linnix starts to say, but the words turn to a scream of pain that rips Baram's heart. Both her hands go to her mouth, trying to stifle it—he can see her actually trying to close her own lips. But the pain is too terrible—her feet drum, her body arches, and the scream builds to a horrifying, ululating shriek.

Oblivous of Ochter, Baram springs to her side, is on his knees holding her convulsing body, trying to keep her from harming herself, trying to keep his ear to her twisting rib cage. In her agony she all but flings herself from the chair, rocking them both.

"Stop it, Ochter!" he yells above the screams. "You'll kill her, she'll stop breathing—respiration will quit! No, baby, baby, don't try to pull that out, you'll cut the artery."

He captures her hand that's tearing at the scorpion—a strong girl. But her screaming weakens as she runs short of air. "Breathe, baby, pull in." To Ochter he snarls, "If she dies, you're a dead man, Ochter. Dead! I'll stuff that death-claw down your gullet and tear your head off. You know that?"

Ochter looks a trifle thoughtful. "I have stopped long since," he says testily. "That's merely aftereffect. Come, Baramji, pacify your lady-love and get over here, you have work to do."

Baram growls. Linnix' shallow, airless panting falters, resumes, falters again: in some patients, extreme pain can leave all neural centers dangerously drained. No long-drawn-out death here. He has to get through somehow, restart the engine of her life. "Breathe, my brave girl—breathe! . . . Hold on just a little longer. . . . *Breathe,* baby, *pull in.*"

A resolve he hasn't consciously formed takes over his tongue. He speaks close to her ear.

"Listen, Linnie, you really are my girl. My d-daughter.

I'm the doctor you were looking for. I did it. I *was* on Beneborn, your home—I *was*. I've remembered now."

The breath hesitates again; he hopes it's an effort to listen.

"Linnie, it's true! I was there, on Beneborn. Remember the big gold building over the waterfall? It's come back. Honey, try to hear me—I did it, Linnie. You're mine."

The finality of it is choking him, good-bye, good-bye to dream—but he has to say it. For an instant he forgets the dream is doomed anyway and simply mourns.

"*I'm your father,* Linnie. You're my girl. My—my child."

It gets through. Pause . . . then two great ragged gulps of air. The screaming is only moaning now.

Slowly, carefully, Baram eases her back in the lounger, whispering, "Think that over, my love, my girl. Now breathe, hear me? Hold on, *breathe*. I'll get you out of this."

As he loosens her arms that have gone around him, Baram gets a clear look at the ghastly hypo in full Star-light. Yes, there's a space between the "legs" into which he could just get the wire-cutters' nose, to clip the central tube. The cutters burn in his pocket, but he daren't try now—her weight is on the pocket and Ochter's eyes are on him. That evil animal would hit her with another shot of poison before Baram could possibly get the cutters in place—and he'd risk losing them, too. He has to wait till Ochter's attention is fixed elsewhere. Thanks to Ochter's cruelty, Linnie's chair is close. . . . Dare he really hope at last?

"Baramji!" Ochter is standing over Bridey now.

"Oh, no," Linnix cries weakly.

Not knowing what to do, Baram goes over and picks up the empty syrette Ochter had dropped, as if to examine it more carefully.

"Give me that, Baramji. Oh, very well, as a doctor I allow you a moment more to satisfy your scruples. You'll find it's sleep pure and simple."

A shudder of darkness passes over Baram's vision as he smells it. Simple Soporin cannot do that.

"What else have you put in this syringe, Ochter?" he challenges, standing over Stareem. "Has it occurred to you, as a doctor—or a Human—I have no right to harm or kill a dozen people to save one?"

Ochter stares oddly, apparently truly taken aback. Baram's vision flashes black again, the Star-light darkens. Dear gods, what had he let happen to little Stareem?

"Ah, the arithmetic of morality," Ochter says vaguely. "Though I fancy another demonstration on Myr Linnix might change the odds. . . ." His voice trails off into peculiar echoes, as a rush of shadowy movement that is not movement sweeps across the deck.

Baram comes to his senses.

The flashing isn't the syrette contents at all, it's the start of another flurry.

And deep, deep— The flashing pastward flicker goes on, long enough for Baram to see strange multiple palimpsests of Ochter, his face in disarray—was this the first time-flurry he'd been caught in? Long enough for him to glance toward the frozen forms of Kip and Cory beneath the eaves and recall that for them this sequence does not exist. Long enough to turn to where Linnix lies in a blur of movement and hear her faint screaming in pain past. Is she frightened of the flurry? Is she again in agony? He must go to her.

"Linnie! Linnie, it's all right." He tries to shout, hearing his own voice fade into weird echoes, *"right-ight-ight-iii."* He exerts all his strength to lean, to lift a foot, to move. Like pushing through glue—and he is succeeding, only weirdly being helped forward and pressed back by the tugs of his own past motions. . . . Is that himself-past ahead there, crouching by Linnix-that-was? He doesn't want to know, wants only to move first this foot, then the other, the separate actions of moving to her. And he—or an aspect of him—does, as in a waking dream, while the scene slows and stabilizes.

At last he's close enough. "Linnie." *("Linnie-inni-in-n,"*

the echo wails.) She, or a past simulacrum of her, looks up at him. Is he a frightening figure, looming through the mad glitter? Or, perhaps, is he invisible? "Linnie! It's me, Bram." (*"Bram-ramm-amm-m-m."*)

"Bram! . . . Oh, Bram-m." She isn't frightened. Her arms open to him, regardless of the dreadful thing riding her neck.

He drops on one knee. Now! He can use the cutters, he can cut her free! *I'm like the Star,* he thinks. *I'm trying to go back and change things.*

His head clears enough to remember the difficulty and delicacy of this task, the frightful danger to her if he fails.

"Hold still, love-ve. . . ." His hand plunges to his pocket.

But—oh, gods, oh, evil gods!—

No wire-cutters are there!

Nothing—only a damned kerchief. He nearly upsets the chaise, ramming through every pocket, trying not to face the accursed fact: In real past time, at this point in the original sequence *he had not had them!*

The wire-cutters are probably "now" back in the cubby where he had found or will find them. Can he possibly get back for them quickly enough?

"Gods, Linnie, I've failed you. Wait, I'll try—" But as he makes to rise, the scene clouds, the Star-light flickers and speeds up to become a torrential substanceless rush and shuffle of shadows. Only now it is running time-forward again.

He has totally missed his chance.

He can only clasp her tight—yes, she is solid, flesh and warm—and enfold her with all his strength, so that he has to force his arms looser lest he hurt her. He trembles; she is hugging him, too, without heed to the menace at her neck. Wild notions of defying time and space rush through his mind, but they fade before a more rational fear: The pull of reality on this strange, anomalous realm may be dangerous.

Attempted defiance by force might cost a physical splitting—or worse, a damaged mind—

"Look out, Linnie. Oh, darling, we must let go."

Their arms drop away slowly; only their eyes hold one another through the eddying time-shadows. She is whispering—a lover's whisper. But the words are *"Father . . . Dad!"* It hurts Baram's heart. Chilled, he lets himself, or whatever aspect of him has violated time, be tugged, jostled by the rush of what is, and is no longer, there.

And just as the whirling flicker begins to slow, with Baram still kneeling by Linnix' low chair, he glances across her legs at the gold-hung rollbed and sees a flash of movement in the drapery below. Ochter had disarranged its drapes, leaving a gap—and through this gap there shows a small boy's figure crouching among the life-support tubes.

Pao!

The lad's head is down, he's scanning the floor; and something also seems to be distracting him. As Baram peers, Pao raises a hand to pluck at his neck and back.

Then the scene blurs—Baram finds himself somehow on his feet, tottering backward—but not before he's seen the thing they'd searched for, that Pao is apparently hunting for now.

In a fold of the bed's floor-length curtains lies Vovoka's weapon.

Any instant now Pao will see it, if he keeps on!

Baram gasps, his wind all but knocked out—the impact of real, unconditional hope after so long is like a blow.

He tries to stoop, to get sight of the boy and signal to him, but he can no longer command his body. Vague nonobjects brush him and vanish under the shimmering Star-light. The rushing time-tumult on the deck is clearing, slowing to solidity. He is now standing by the console, feeling oddly reunified. His head clears back to full present, the reality of his recent actions evaporating in his mind. Only the breathless, perilous sense of joy remains.

". . . might . . . change . . . the odds," Ochter is concluding, like a machine coming up to speed.

Baram is struck by a dizzying disorientation: the half-remembered events of, of—not the *past*, but a no-time; illusory moments that had been unlawfully inserted into the seamless flow of time—events, heartbeats, minim, which had not existed for Cor and Kip, shielded by the eaves. Are they true illusions? Or has Linnix really shared them? If only she and he could talk now!

His hand encounters the wire-cutters in his pocket! How could he imagine they had jumped out—and back in?

Illusion.

But wait—

His kerchief isn't there. The kerchief he'd flung down by Linnix' chaise in no-time! It should be in his pocket.

As he gropes again, his white hair is stirred by a breath of air; it must be backflow from the night wind over the roof. At the same time he notices something moving on the floor near Linnie. He peers . . .

It's his kerchief, now settling. It seems to have been blown about a meter toward him.

On Baram's back the skin crawls, and his ancestral hair follicles come erect. Had he been his own far-off, furred ancestor, that fur would now be standing straight out in horripilation, the threat response to fear. Surely he is seeing the very hand of Reality itself—or rather, Reality's impalpably fine finger—the tip of the force of What Is, and will not be otherwise.

In one or two more such soft gusts, all evidence of his acts during the regression will be gone—unreal, illusory, *gone*. He shivers.

But far more important than this fear: Are Pao and Vovoka's gun really there—*now?* If so, real help is possible. But Baram dares not tempt fate—or Ochter—again to look. It was such a brief glimpse, in shadow, it could so easily have merely been what he longed to see. Oh, gods of Star-justice, let not this be erased, too!

Meanwhile Ochter has been speaking, commanding Baram to hurry. But the little man seems somewhat subdued at the moment. He, too, has been through the time-flurry; what has he done, felt, attempted? If this was his first, he probably merely endured. Baram recalls his own bewilderment—and he had the benefit of Kip and Cory's talk.

Abruptly there comes a rattle and thud from the main lounge door—someone on the other side, not knowing the lock is fused. It must be Hiner, Yule, or both. On the deck, all who are conscious turn to look—including, Baram is glad to see, Kip. He's now lying propped up, rubbing at his eyes. Good.

But what new disaster is coming onto them now?

Desperately, Baram fingers the scalpel and the cutters in his pouch. Until and unless Pao produces another, these are their only weapons. Linnie should have the scalpel, he thinks, it's more use against an enemy and less temptation to try to cut a hypotube she can neither see nor feel.

As he moves toward her the infirmary door swings wide; whoever it is has given up and found the way. And out comes a figure so unsteady, so besmeared and bedraggled and fouled as to be barely recognizable as Yule.

He heads for Ochter, yammering incoherent complaints.

With him comes a sound.

Bridey and Linnix hear it first—a faint, very high-pitched keening that is almost beyond Baram's hearing. It is alive, it has a frightful heart-tearing quality; unforgettable. Baram has heard it twice before, once from a terribly burned young male, and again from parents whose child had drowned.

It is the sound of a Damei screaming in unbearable agony.

A Damei cannot scream or vocalize like a Human; only *in extremis* is there forced from one this soft, spine-freezing, whispering cry or stridulation that seems to come from everywhere and nowhere at once.

Almost as Baram recognizes it the sound cuts off raggedly as if the agonized one has been gagged. Horrified, Baram is realizing that Hiner and Yule are at their bloody crime, not in the village, but right here near or in the hostel itself.

And that means that the victims must be—he can't finish the thought, can only hear again Linnie crying, "It was children like Nyil they tortured."

And Kip's cheery reply, "That's what we're here for!" The Kip who now lies broken-legged, barely conscious, while the criminals have their way.

Oh, Pao, Baram implores in silence, if you exist—you *must* exist—get that gun to me. . . . Surely the boy has found it by now. But how can he approach Baram? Baram's gaze begins tracing out possible routes, deciding where he himself should stand.

"Mordecai! What's wrong?" demands Ochter as Yule staggers up to the rollbed. "Why aren't you at work?"

"Wrong? Everything's wrong!" Yule wipes his bloody sleeve across his smeared face. "Listen, you said your shot would fix me, it'd all be fun. Well, it isn't fun. Oh, Nat loves it, he thinks he's killing bugs. But it's—yehch, a mess! First we have to wait forever for the bugs to come to, and they're too big to hide; and you said to bring them here, everybody would be out, and then—hey, what goes on here? These types aren't out a-tall, look at him and her and—"

"That does not concern you," Ochter snaps him off. "They're under quite adequate control. But *are you getting the stuff?*"

"Some. But I hate it. You said fun—"

Ochter has looked his henchman over, visibly repelled by his state. But his voice becomes unctuous, soothing.

"Poor lad. Not to worry, Mordy, we really can make it fun. Of course you need a full shot. You see, I only gave you half before, you seemed so, ah, cool. Here, right away—" He selects a syrette. "Let me have your arm. Take that thing off."

Baram can scarcely listen. From his new position he can see the rollbed's floor drape—and a boy's quick hand emerging, feeling straight for the fold where Vovoka's weapon lies. It's real! And Pao is real, and he's about to get it!

Yule is stripping off his wet, stained sports tabard. Heartsick, Baram can recognize the purple of Damei blood and lighter, oily streaks that must be the back exudates, the Stars Tears stuff. Even from here he can catch the faint sweet scent.

"Remember, Mordy," Ochter is saying severely now, "you jumped the gun, with those smokes. I told you I didn't plan on starting with the aliens here, for security's sake. And then nearly smoking them to death! You have only yourself to blame for the wait and all the inconvenience."

"My good coat," Yule mutters. "And that big booger was sick on my shoes. Animals!"

"That's the spirit!" Ochter has captured Yule's muscular arm and smoothly injected him from a red syrette Baram doesn't recognize. "Now, Mordy, you'll feel marvelous in two minutes. Meanwhile, throw that thing away, you'll soon have the credits to buy a new outfit every day. Every hour, if you like. Get rid of that."

Mumbling, Yule flips the tabard onto the floor near Linnix, frowning down at his dirty boots. Under the rollbed, the hand still gropes, maddeningly blind to what's so near.

Hurry, Pao, Baram prays, uneasily trying to look anywhere but at the bed drapes. *Hurry—*

Oh, gods, a dire thought has come to him; should he try to rush Yule now, to give Pao time to find the gun? But it means torture for Linnie—Ochter will use the scorpion on her to stop him. And maybe it isn't necessary—

But it is.

Was.

Too late, he sees Yule suddenly stoop to the floor, saying irritably, "What gives with you anyway, Doc? I crotting well don't think that should be lying around."

Baram's breathing stops.

"What now?" Ochter asks.

"This." Yule straightens up.

Slowly revolving around his fat finger something gleams: Vovoka's gun.

Six, seven pairs of eyes stare in helpless realization at the thing dangling from Yule's hand: the weapon that would have saved them. And saved the Dameii, too.

After the hours of pain, threats, hideous prospects, painfully devised countermeasures that fail, fail—the Deadman's Alarm missed, the wire-cutters unused—and then this sudden unlooked-for miracle of reprieve all but in their hands—Baram is faintly surprised that he can still feel the anguish that invades him as he watches Yule's foul fingers close on the weapon; watches their last hope die.

XVI

STARSTORM:
Baramji Summons the Dead

The stillness of despair grips the watchers on that Star-bright deck. Even the pulsing, quivering beauty of the shoals of light around them feels cold; it will soon become their death-light. Against that weapon in their enemies' hands, there is no hope in superior numbers, surprise, courage—no help, no hope at all.

Yule, looking pleased with himself, plays with Vovoka's gun. Ochter looks up from rearranging his syrette pack.

"Give me that."

"I don't see why." Sullenly, Yule toys with the weapon a minim more, but he hands it over.

While Ochter examines it, Baram looks cautiously about. He meets Kip's squinting eyes; something still wrong there, probably Kip's having trouble focusing. But he's grasped the essentials of the situation. Beside him Cory sits with head bowed as if totally drained; she's drawn a Damei veil about

587

herself. Bridey, nearby, is protectively sharing her blanket with the unconscious Stareem. No more the queen of sunlight, her eyes are violet pools of dread.

Zannez, by his two boys, is also sizing up the situation whenever Ochter's gaze isn't on him. Baram sees a coldly alert speculative expression on the bald man's face, which grows more and more grim. Baram guesses he is realizing how that gun can be used to control them all, now that Ochter's control over Baram is attenuating in usefulness. That weapon will let him keep his victims alive but helpless— say, by blowing off hands or feet—without leaving traces to alert an investigator.

Hanny Ek and Snake are also stealing looks around, probably impatient for some leadership. Little Pao, invisible beneath the rollbed, must be on knife-edge. And Linnix, after one appalled stare at Yule, has turned to Baram with eyes blazing suicidal resolution.

But Baram is finally ready. He has settled his questions, or had them settled for him, and he has been taught a lesson—he wastes no more than an instant regretting he hadn't rushed Yule before Yule saw that gun.

The crux of the situation has in fact changed only slightly. Assuming only Ochter keeps that gun while Yule goes back to the lounge, Ochter now has another means of self-defense, and a very lethal one. But he must use his unbandaged left hand to fire it, and he will have to put it down to work a hypo.

And Ochter won't use the gun on them now; too many are awake and would make moving targets. He could easily kill someone by error, he might get into a struggle for the gun, and the small gun can have only a limited charge—it could run dry. Nor would Ochter allow Yule to use it.

No; he will continue with his drugging plan, using threats and indirection as before. Unless he could stun them all with one sweep as Vovoka had?

That question is answered.

"Don't play with this thing," Ochter tells Yule, looking up from his inspection of the weapon. "The settings are marked in an alien script I've never seen. It looks Human but it's definitely not. All we know is that its present point took off Vovoka's head. Now, back to work."

He lays it on the rollbed beside his open syrette pack. Baram's teeth clench; that gun is only centimeters above where Pao's head must be. It might as well be a light-year away.

Very well. As soon as Yule goes back to his devil's work in the bar, and Ochter comes back to his drugging scheme, Baram will take the first chance—maybe while they're bending over someone—to simply grab Ochter and cut his throat. Or break his neck; Baram glances with satisfaction at his own still powerful forearms and hands. That will cost Linnie some pain and undoubtedly get himself, Baram, mortally wounded by that death-claw.

But he's sure he can last long enough to get to Linnix and give her a better death; Ochter wouldn't have loaded that claw with anything instantaneous—it would be too easy to scratch himself.

After that it will be up to the others to take out Hiner and Yule. For that they'll have the gun, unless some impossibly bad luck strikes.

He can't get to Linnie first and—oh, my gods, he thinks, incredulous—and kill—*kill* her—kill *Linnie*—before Ochter can hurt her, because Ochter would get him first with the gun.

So be it—but for an instant Baram can only gasp, soul-stricken at the unbelievable acts and thoughts reality is forcing on him.

As his mind flashes over this grisly route, he sees Yule glance about nervously before saying to Ochter.

"And another thing. Nat wants to know where the crotty hell that ship is at. That *Comet*. So do I. Race is late, he should have showed by now. We want you to call him. Use that thing—" He gestures toward the console. "Their cruiser or whatever could come early; we want Race here."

"And bring the Federation down on our heads in an hour?" Ochter asks bitingly.

Meanwhile Baram is taking it in—they have their getaway ship all laid on, by the gods. Doubtless the ship Pao saw. Their worst hypotheses, all, all true.

Ochter sighs and says wearily, "Oh, Mordy, do use your head—no, on second thought, don't, that's my job. And tell Nat to stop worrying, that's my job, too. Now *Comet* isn't late. She'll be along when we need her. Because Race needs our credits or he'll lose *Comet*. I made sure of that early on."

"So why won't you call him? Just signal *Comet*, it could be any private ship."

Ochter sighs again. "Mordecai Yule, can't you get it into your brain that we're way out on the Rim? There *aren't* any private ships here, or any other kind. One call to *Comet* would tell that FedBase that an uncleared ship is heading to Damiem."

As they talk, Baram watches their distance from the weapon on the bed. Yule strays far enough to kick the blanket half off Stareem, but as Ochter lectures him he forgets her. "All right, all right, Doc," he says sulkily. "But I thought *Comet* was supposed to be an old Patrol boat. Why can't she go FTL?"

"Because all Patrol vessels have their *c*-skip drives spiked before they're sold into private hands." Ochter tells him. "And *Comet*—"

As Ochter talks to Yule, Baram's eye is caught by an oddity behind them. The brilliant gleam of the rollbed's satin coverlet *shifts* very slightly, unnaturally. . . . And not for the first time, either, his eyes recall. Significance suddenly strikes: Under that coverlet little Lady 'Lomena is moving her limbs!

Very minutely, but repeatedly. And—there it comes again, as Ochter is impatiently telling Yule why the *c*-skip can't be replaced in *Comet*. The paralyzed body stirs the Star-lit

590

silken folds. And it seems to come after the speaking of the word *Comet*.

What is he seeing, what—

Memory bursts like a golden bolt of lightning from that golden bed.

Only that morning he'd stood beside it in the marquises' room, his aching loins at last partially eased, listening to the marquise, in fetching seminudity, talk of her twin's terrible accident. How 'Lomena had been battered, jumping a beloved silver horse named—named—yes! Comet. *Comet!* . . . . And how, when Loma was dead to all else, she'd showed signs of protest when some fool had said in her presence that Comet would be killed. Yes!

Can that response be still vestigially there?

Can it be evoked? Strengthened?

Baram's breathing almost chokes; this million-to-one hope hits him bodily so that he has to struggle to remain impassive. The alteration between hope and despair has become physical pain. He dares not think, what if it works? Will young Pao be there, be alert? Will he fumble the chance? Will others interfere? Will—a hundred disastrous sequelae radiate— but Baram won't look at them. Certainly, if this fails, the suicide attack is his only course; neither he nor Linnix can hope to survive a fiasco. . . . Don't think of that now, concentrate on this one incredible chance.

The first essential is to capture Ochter's attention. A wild idea forms and grows as Ochter says:

"Now you feel better, Mordy. I can see it. Think about scooting back to work, think about getting rich-rich-rich!"

Yule squints his eyes.

"Hey, I do feel different." He licks his lips, grins. "Good ol' Doc!" With his bared torso he looks obscenely like an executioner out of history.

"Fine! Back to work you go!" Ochter claps him genially on his back, heads him to the infirmary door. "And good old

591

Doc has some work to finish before I join you." He turns away. "Baramji!"

As the youth shambles off, Baram addresses Ochter in a firm, carefully normal voice.

"Ochter, I'm really surprised you couldn't see the obvious solution to your simple problem. To depend on that lout! That pretty pair of louts, who doubtless intend to kill you as soon as they see their first money."

"Necessity makes strange demands," Ochter says absently, moving toward Bridey as he bites at the wrapper of a syrette.

"What necessity?" asks Baram. "None. None at all. Why didn't you at least check on the easiest and, I may say, the most profitable source?"

Ochter glances at him. "Baramji, I won't tolerate stalling. Does Myr Linnix need a reminder? Get over here."

Baram chuckles quite naturally, hoping that Linnix will stay still. "You don't grasp what I mean? Perhaps it will be plain to you if *you* recall which planet I'm a xenological medic on. Did it never occur to you that a man sitting on a mountain of potential credits might not wish to remain a little back-planet XMD all his life?"

A gasp from Linnix. Baram fixes her with a level stare, wills her not to speak.

"What do you mean, if anything?" Ochter asks crossly.

Smiling, Baram says slow and clear, as if to a child, "Simply that I have accumulated over a liter and a half of the highest quality Stars Tears material, in a *very* private place. And when you kill me, as you so blatantly intend, all knowledge of it will die with me. *And* you can't screw it out of me by torturing Myr Linnix—or myself—because she and I will die quite soon of our own choosing, not yours."

Linnix' eyes widen impossibly as she looks at him; across the deck no one seems to breathe.

"A liter?" Ochter asks tonelessly.

"A liter and a half, of superb quality. I managed to send one milliliter off-planet for test. Superb! And it was obtained,

592

I may add, without any of this messy torturing and illegality and confederates. The Dameii in question cooperated willingly." His tone turns reflective. "But there was, for me, a problem in disposing of it profitably without impairing my ability to obtain more. . . . I thought to wait until I had a dekaliter."

"A d-dekaliter. Baramji, you're bluffing."

"Also," Baram goes on obliviously, "I'm fond of my two co-Guardians here. I'd hoped to find a means of sharing the bounty with them, since it has no evil connotations. If you think I'm bluffing, Ochter, the more fool you. However, I may still have that report on my sample somewhere—though it's not the sort of thing one leaves about."

"You're a lying fool and I should punish you. Get over here at once."

"As you like." Baram makes no move to rise from the console seat. "When you kill me or Myr Linnix the question will become moot."

"Don't worry," Ochter says grimly. "I'll ransack that infirmary of yours, Baramji. If it exists, you probably have it on a top shelf—labeled."

This is so near the truth that Baram has trouble replying coolly. "Do. The place needs a good dust-out. But no, Ochter, I didn't consider the hostel safe enough; power-cells have been known to explode on their own." He has the little man's attention now, time to start. "But if you think I'm bluffing about this, you'll soon be convinced that I know where *Comet* is"—he stresses the name—"and why *Comet* won't get here. FedBase told me what they knew and I haven't had time to pass it on to anybody. Poor *Comet!* . . . Happy waiting."

The tension of the Star in the dazzling air seems to be growing; Baram almost jumps as movement shows on the golden rollbed. Does the syrette case slide just a little? Ochter is too preoccupied to notice.

"That's impossible, Baramji. I heard every word you said to that Base."

"Then you must have noticed my silence at the end," Baram says smoothly. "That was when Poma's all-station alert tape cut in, reciting her actions re *Comet*. I don't usually talk back to tapes."

It all sounds so palpably false; Baram, like many men of integrity, has no idea how fertile and convincing a liar he can be—save for one small trait.

Ochter frowns and asks reluctantly, "Are you telling me your Base was in contact with *Comet?*"

"Your *Comet* contacted Base. Race was lost, you see. It turned out he'd been trying to unspike *Comet*'s c-skip drive. That's not illegal because it's impossible. Base just laughed. The result was that he gained some speed and lost half his guidance. He was lucky—*Comet* could have bounced right out of the Galaxy. If you ever ship on *Comet*—which you won't, any time soon—I'd suggest you urge Race to stick to normal speeds. . . . Anyway, they got this call from *Comet* at extreme range. He wanted coordinates, that's his right. Poor *Comet!* For Race's sake, if not your own, you really should try to help save *Comet*. When *Rimshot* comes along with my CNS expert—you did hear that?—they'll pick *Comet* off like a netted goby. But I'll be long dead, of course. Pity."

Here Baram sees he's made a slip—Ochter steps toward the rollbed and his syrette pack just as Loma's legs move again. Will he see it and safeguard the gun? Baram holds his breath . . . and luckily, Ochter doesn't seem to notice; he begins pacing, taking hard looks at Baram, apparently in deep thought.

Baram switches tracks for a moment, to let him get away from the bed.

"It's all a pity. If you hadn't tied up with those two murderous clowns, Race would have made an ideal courier—

594

me working this end and you handling sales. However, I refuse to think about it with those two in the picture."

He can hear gasps and stirrings from around the deck. Linnix has her eyes fastened on him. She seems to be feeling the pain of the barbed hypo; her face is strained and her hands go often to her neck.

"Oh, I intend to get rid of *them* as soon as their work is done," Ochter says abstractedly. "But I don't get you, Baramji. Am I to understand that you have some proposition for me, assuming that any of this is true? Which I doubt."

Baram continues as if he hasn't heard. "*And* I refuse to remain alive if you hurt Linnie anymore. Oh, yes! I can be dead so fast you'll be astonished, Ochter." He rattles the scalpel and cutters in his pocket. "You never figured that, did you?"

Exasperated, the little man strides toward him, away from the rollbed. *All right,* Baram tells himself. *Now or never.*

"Baramji—"

"But that doesn't solve your immediate problem," Baram overrides him. "Where is *Comet*? Are you forgetting *Comet*? Every minim you waste, *Comet*'s going farther astray. Only I or Cory can save her now. Don't you want to save *Comet*, Ochter?"

"What *are* you babbling about, Baramji? Explain yourself this instant, or—"

"Easily!" He grins. "They gave *Comet* the wrong coordinates, you see. I doubt it was intentional—this sector was resurveyed last planetary year." Baram is improvising wildly, speaking past Ochter to the body on the bed. No response is visible now—and it won't be, he tells himself. He's a fool, a fool. Still he gabbles, unable to give up the forlorn hope.

"Poma wasn't in the office; some kid at Base gave *Comet* the old ones. *Comet*'ll be looking for Damiem till her oxy runs out—*Comet* was short there, too, you know. Poor old *Comet*!"

Suddenly, unmistakable motion on the bed. Loma's body heaves, her arms stir; he thinks that even her face changes a trifle. But it's the legs he needs.

Just as he opens his mouth for a last try, out of the infirmary door rushes Yule, a sight of horror with bloody arms and fists raised.

"I heard that! So you're going to 'get rid' of us, you rotten little scut. And *Comet*'s in trouble. Oh, lords—I should have known."

"Be quiet!" Ochter snarls with such authority that Yule actually shuts up, his face working. "Go on, Baram. Can you substantiate any of this? And if by chance it's true, what can you do about it?"

"Remember the strange ship our little prince sighted this evening? Or did you miss that, too? That was your *Comet!* Your silver *Comet*." Baram's voice rises at every repetition of the name: "*Comet*, going by on her course to nowhere. Your first priority is to rescue *Comet*. Save *Comet!* Don't let them shoot at *Comet*—what if *Rimshot* fires on *Comet*? *Comet* will be killed! Don't let them hurt *Comet*, *Comet* is your only chance. Help *Comet!* Send the right numbers. And don't let them take *Comet*, either."

As his words grow louder and madder, heads rise and turn toward him across the deck, and Yule and Ochter, staring, take an involuntary backward step, nearer the bed. Still no one notices the silken coverlet wrenched and moving. Linnix cries out, "Bram!" while Ochter and Yule try to shout him down at once. But he can't stop now.

"Save *Comet!*" He yells across twenty years at a girl's dead ears. Still nothing happens. He's a fool. "You can save *Comet!* Get on *Comet*, ride *Comet* away!"

And under the silks little Lady Loma's knees shoot up, while all that is on the coverlet slides and vanishes over the foot and side.

Ochter is closest; he whirls and stoops after his precious syrette case, brings it up in his good hand—and then suddenly leaps over the bed corner, shouting incoherently through the down rails at something or someone invisible on the floor. An instant later he pushes himself back and upright—and, before amazed eyes, abruptly *shortens* where he stands.

His body drops straight down, his chin jolts on the foot of the bed—he falls backward, arms flailing, syrettes flying, to the drape-strewn floor, and begins to scream.

At the same instant, across the deck there is a loud *crack!* and a crashing in the eaves as the main antenna snaps off and collapses into the cable. But Baram has no eyes for such incidental damage. He knows what must happen now.

Leaping from his seat to get to Linnix, he gets only glimpses of that which Ochter's fall reveals.

Standing on the floor where Ochter had been are two Human lower legs and shod feet, the remains of panters dropping down them. Where the knees should be is a mist of reddish smoke.

The grotesque apparitions hold for an instant, so like prosthetics that Baram, trying to get the cutters to Linnix neck, is slow to realize that they are the lower halves of Ochter's real legs. Then, amid rising screams, they topple one after the other onto Ochter's thrashing, almost legless body. His knees have simply disappeared.

When Baram next glances up, Ochter's free, Death-Clawed hand has vanished, leaving a waving wrist-stump; now the bandaged hand puffs out of existence, too—and with it the switch restraining the deadly hypo in Linnix' neck. There's no blood. Ochter's screams change to wilder cries as he shakes his handless wrists before his face.

Yule crouches paralyzed beside the bed, staring down stupidly at the wreckage of his employer. And behind him, Baram—his ears filled with Linnix' shrieks, his hands fighting hers—glimpses something like a rising wave of silk topped by a girl's blind head. Loma struggles up, reaching for the gods know what, and is falling over the edge, making a hoarse roaring noise.

As her long hair swings onto him, Yule looks up, gives a bellow of fright, and bolts for the infirmary door. Behind him Loma falls, to hang head-down over the bedside, her naked back unrecognizable under a welter of broken tubes, scars, wires, hoses spurting ichor and air—her life-in-death support, now ruptured forever.

As Baram struggles with Linnix he's marginally aware of young Pao darting from under the torn gold drapery to take steady aim at Yule, who's just reaching the infirmary door. With a last yell, Yule goes down, a smoking head-sized hole suddenly between his shoulders.

Then Linnix' heart-stopping shrieks and writhings of pain drive all else from Baram's mind. She's in full-body convulsions now, her knees jerking up to her chest, then straightening rigidly as she arches backward in the flimsy chaise. But she's breathing. Hyperventilating, in fact—possible Cheyne-Stokes coming on. Baram has to straddle her to hold her shoulders and neck, and tear away the top of her uniform to get at the ghastly scorpion hypo. Its belly is not quite empty, Baram sees. He strives to force the point of his wire-cutters underneath and keep her hands away. Perhaps the hypo mechanism failed, perhaps Ochter wasn't able fully to relax his grip. But he's said it contained "twice the lethal dose." Far more than half has gone into her.

Baram's mind wraps Linnix in the cold quiet that comes on him when a patient dies.

Still he fights to sever the scorpion's tube—until the tremendous paroxysm topples their chaise and sends Linnix screaming and sprawling away. Before he can crawl to her she gets both hands on the scorpion and wrenches it outward with all her might. Only a change in the timbre of her shrieks tells of the new agony that those barbs must have caused.

"Let go! Linnie, let go!" he shouts in her ear, working to open her fists. And then she lets go, but a bright red pulsing jet of blood bursts up between her fingers, sluicing everywhere. He knows what that means—she's cut into or severed her carotid artery. The filthy tabard is across her neck, and the scorpion lies half-out, revealing two of its sharp hooks.

He tries to get his fingers into the wound, but one hook catches the tabard cloth as she writhes and before he can free her, her shrieking dies down, her body goes limp. The sky around them gives a black flash. The blood gout is dying away.

As he finally gets a fingertip onto the torn arterial membranes, deep in blood, he's astounded to see her eyes come open. She looks up at him quite peacefully, almost as if she would smile—as though some secret sweet relief has eased her. He has seen death come thus. His fingers find the murdering barb, push it from the vessel. But there is almost no pulse—one weak beat more . . . another . . . none. The sky flickers.

Baram retains still enough sense of duty to lift his head and call strongly: "Zannez!"

"Yo?" comes the reply. People are on their feet.

"Take over, will you? Can you get Hiner?"

"Will do." It's Snake Smith's voice.

"And pull your people under cover, quick."

On that, Baram, sometime Guardian of the Dameii, lets his eyes and heart go back to his dying girl. She seems beyond pain; he gathers her to him under the darkening sky. And shortly she dies so, in his trembling, blood-soaked arms.

XVII

THE GRIDWORLD WAY

Zannez jumps up at Ochter's first screams, very glad of the chance to move. The deck is a bedlam of screams and shrieks. He edges around the console for a clear view, trying to grasp the fate that has befallen Ochter, and what it is that Baram has done.

When Pao emerges firing Vovoka's weapon, Zannez dodges back and bumps into Hanno and Snake coming the other way. Bridey is just beyond, wearing a blanket and hovering protectively over Stareem on the floor.

They all stare, breath held, as Yule dies.

"I think that thing is running dry." Snake whispers. "The hole didn't go all the way through."

Zannez shudders, but he thinks Snake's right. He's also very conscious of the rising tension in the air, the alien energies of the Star around them. It feels as if it's mounting to some peak. Like a sensi-effect special running wild, he thinks; but this is no Human made effect. For the first time he is really nervous about radiation. They should be back under the eaves, he thinks: get the girls.

At that moment Baram, struggling with Linnix under the strobing sky, calls to him, and he and Snake reply.

"I think Hiner's in the bar," Snake says then to Zannez. "With his—with the Dameii. We can take him."

"I want Bridey and Star under shelter first," Zannez tells them. "Doc says take cover. Things are going funny again. One of those was enough."

"One of what?" Hanno asks. Zannez remembers that they were both unconscious during the earlier time-eddies.

"Never mind—just move! Can you take Star?"

Bridey is sobbing when they reach her. "She's d-dead!" She clings to Zannez' chest. The screeching is dying down.

"Star?" Zannez drops to his knees, to feel Stareem's peacefully breathing flanks. She's curled in sleep like a silvery kitten.

"No. That girl-officer, that Linnix—I saw her die-ie—" Bridey's words are starting to echo in a way Zannez doesn't like. He looks toward Baram, bent over the white limpness of Linnix, but it's becoming hard to see.

Hanno stoops to get Stareem's arms and sling her over his back, as he's done a hundred times on camera. But now he staggers—everything is acting like high-gee. The air flashes darkly.

"Help him, Snako. Bridey, grab my arm. We don't—repeat, don't—become separated. Hear-ear-r?" Again the echo. "Hurry-y! Push hard."

He heads them for the closest point of sheltering eaves. All over the deck, shadows are beginning to glide and jitter, and a ghostly chorus of past screams murmurs in their ears. This one is coming on slower, Zannez thinks. Maybe it's big. They push, plow forward.

Just then he remembers Pao. Gods—the kid! Superboy. "I forgot the prince," he can only whisper.

601

Snake points effortfully ahead, and Zannez makes out the small shape of Pao; he seems to be going to their right, where Cory and Kip are. Longer that way.

"Nobody much alive back there-ere," Hanno pants. "How 'bout Doc?"

Zannez grunts again. If Doc wants to be with his dead girl, or die with her, that's his business. And Lady P.? Tough. She did it to herself. They can do no more than they're doing. Everything is becoming indistinct, each footstep forward is a fight.

The effort to traverse eight meters of level deck takes all their strength. Twice they circle shadow chairs, only to strike into something solid they can't quite see. The rushing, whirling effect is starting, but slowly, clumsily, thank the gods. Are they struggling upstream against time itself? Zannez doesn't want to think about it. It's warped time, anyway—one of the Star's crazy effects. . . . The ghost-sounds are getting louder. Push.

Just as the retrograde rush hits them hard, they reach the real darkness of the overhang and stumble, half-fall under it—

—and are suddenly in clear, silent air in a stable world.

Bewildered, gasping and panting, they stare back at the deck they fought their dark way across. It is brightly Star-lit, calm and empty. Baram and Linnix are gone. There's scant trace of all the violence, save for Loma's tragic little body hanging over her deathbed rail and, on the floor, a mutilated caricature of Ochter. Beyond the rollbed, a drift of sparkling violet veiling from a turned-away chaise marks where the Lady Pardalianches has slept safely through it all—or has not. Vovoka's body is only a still mound of blanket by the far parapet. Zannez remembers there's one more body— Yule's, out of sight somewhere along the wall by the infirmary door. But the whirling chaos of shadows, the echoes, all are gone. It's like striking a show set. The glittering Star-rain seems to have diminished a trifle, too.

"I feel funny," Hanno says, shifting Stareem around to carry her now easily over one shoulder: sleeping, she burrows her nose into his neck. "Like part of me is still out there."

"Hold my hand," says Snake, not joking.

"I know, I felt it," Zannez tells him. "Hold on, it goes away. Time to move, kids. Hiner's back there in the lounge doing terrible things to some poor wing-people. Doc laid it on us to stop him." It's like setting up a fast live show. He feels great, his team okay and a job to do. There'll be no suicide charges, either. All his people are coming out of this alive. I'll remember all my life, he thinks: for a few minutes I was in charge of defending a planet.

"This is the front of the Korsos' room," Snake says. "There's a door leading through to the lounge in there."

"Goodo. But we check in with the Korsos first. I think something bad happened to the boss lady while we were out, and Kippo's broke himself a leg. They have to know what goes down."

"I'll park Star with them," Hanny says.

"Do that."

They squeeze close to the wall to pass a place where the eave thatch is battered in. A big tangle of broken antennae is hanging over the edge.

"Hey, look, we may be out of contact," Snake says.

"Pao's gun did that," Zannez says. "Firing up at Ochter. See the big chunk missing?"

"Thank the gods he was pointing up."

They go along in the shadow in front of the lounge, toward where Kip and Cory sit beyond the big doors. As they pass they can hear faint sounds from within.

"I thought that was leaves," Bridey says brokenly. "It's— it's wings. Feathers."

"Hurry."

"Do we rush him?" Snake muses. "We have four ways in

603

from the sides: Korsos' room, infirmary, arcade doors. What if he goes out the front? Do we want him out or in? In."

"What weapons has he?" Hanny asks practically. Little Prince Pao, hurrying to meet them, overhears.

"A nasty harpoon thing," Pao answers. "Like a crossbow. It was disguised as underwater defense. It shoots a barbed bolt at almost bullet speed." His manner is sober, befitting one who has just killed. "One suspects they may be poisoned."

"Sweetheart," Zannez comments. "Hey Prince, well done! And thanks from us all." The others chorus appreciation.

"Thank you," the lad says gravely. "I was fortunate the weapon fell into my hands. After my unforgivable blunder that left you all unarmed."

"Blunder? What blunder? Oh, you mean the antennae?"

"No; that was unavoidable." Pao breaks off as they reach Cory and Kip. Cory has veiled herself in a Damei fabric; what they can see of her looks . . . different. But her voice is gracious and nearly the same.

"Myr Zannez—and your people. Is the little girl all right? Baram said she was merely drugged asleep."

"We believe so, Myr Cory, ma'am." Zannez bows, followed by the others. Hanny ends his bow by dumping Stareem into a nearby chaise, then straightens her out solicitously. "Pass me your blanket, Bride."

"Well . . . here." Bridey fetches another from the nearby line of screening.

"And Myr Kip?" Zannez is asking.

"Oh . . . I'll do," Kip forces a grin. "But I'm fairly useless. My eyes won't focus at all; Doc says it'll wear off. But how in the name—" He jerks his hand to point toward the lounge wall behind him. "Every minim he may be—of all times for me to—"

"The doctor asked me to attend to Hiner," Zannez says rather formally. "We think we can. With your permission we'll go right ahead. The, ah, Gridworld way." He grins ferociously. The Star's light reflecting from his bald head and red suit gives him the look of an antique demon.

"You can? . . ."

"I'll need someone to open doors. How about you, Prince? Can you open a door hushy-quiet?"

"I think so." The boy is definitely changed, Zannez sees. It's this unknown "blunder," more than the killings, at a guess. Proud little bastard. No time for that now.

"We need an idea exactly how he's set up. If he has the wing-people there, he's probably in the center space, between the stairs and the bar. But—"

"That's correct," says Pao. "I had a look in, from the roof. It's . . . quite abominable." Behind his formal words, the boy's upset. "He has the t-two adults tied to the bar, bent over so he can get their backs. He's in front of them by the stairs with Nyil, with the little girl. He's cutting her—cutting at her wings. And then he runs behind them and scrapes. It's . . . vile . . ."

"Easy, kid."

"You and your people face a terrible sight, Myr Zannez," Cory says. "I regret that the prince had to."

Kip grunts evilly but says only, "Weapons? Due to my—" and subsides as Cory grips his shoulder with a shawled hand.

"And Vovoka's gun is dry," the prince reports.

Snake nods.

Hanno and Bridey are exchanging murmurs.

"I saw a box," Bridey says. "Maybe there's more. I'll ask." She asks Kip and Cory her question.

"That's it," Kip replies. "No others."

"Means you two get across, what, at least ten paces bare-ass open," Zannez comments. "Hey, maybe Doc has some. Myr Cory, may we check the infirmary for more? We won't disturb—"

"Ask Baram, he's in there," Kip tells them. "He must have finished his clamps by now." They all looked puzzledly at him; Kip amplifies: "Linnix' neck. She needed stitches. Lords of death, that little devil."

"But, but she's—" Bridey starts to protest when a small hand comes up and clamps over her lips. It's Pao.

"I think one must be careful what one says," he explains as he takes his hand away. "While one is on this planet."

"Oh—" Bridey begins, and then just repeats, "oh."

"Forget it," Hanno tells Kip. "The box is enough."

"Okay, script session—one minim." Zannez beckons them around him. "You remember *Kiddy Cannibals,* three seasons back? And *The Corpse Fuckers?*"

They do.

"Keep remembering. Now: places. Pao starts with Snake and me at the Korsos' door and then scoots like a rocket around to the infirmary for Hanny and Bee. And—"

He speaks on fast, giving precise directions. He feels exhilarated, confident. He hasn't used all his abilities for so long! This is living as he'd never known it on Gridworld— yet they're working Gridworld skills.

"What I really need is some of those flashy gold drapes," Snake says as they brake up. "Only I'm goosey about trying to go back out there."

"No trouble," Pao tells him. "See?" He trots out of the shadow and back to them. "It's just the present, of course. The flurry's always in the past. You can only get in a time-flurry if you're there when it starts; I figured it all out." A trace of his old Superboy manner has revived.

"Goodo!" Snake hurries out to the rollbed and starts ripping drapes.

"I'm glad somebody has it all figured out," says Bridey. She and Hanno disappear into the infirmary.

"And what I need is *that.*" Zannez strides out to Ochter's body. "Myr Cory, maybe you better not look." Before he picks up Ochter he rearranges his own red suit, flips up the collar, and works his face.

Then, "Green, go! Pao!" he shouts, bounding with sudden energy toward the Korsos' room, Ochter held stiffly before him like a grotesque doll. He's done the actor's magic of face and body change, he looks frighteningly like an ancient picture of the Lord of Evil carrying the damned to Hell.

With Pao rushing ahead and Snake running behind, trailing golden stuff, they disappear through the Korsos' door.

Hanno and Bridey hurry into the infirmary, passing Baram by the operating table where Linnix lies.

"Excuse us, Doc, no time. We're going after Hiner." Hanno starts stripping off the robe and Bridey drops her blanket.

But her head snaps around as she sees Baram helping Linnix sit up and pin her torn white tunic together. Linnix smiles at her. Dumbfounded, remembering Pao's warning, Bridey only waves back.

Then, as Pao runs into the room, Baram picks up Zannez' hand camera and, to Bridey's and Hanno's astoundment, starts awkwardly taking a run of Linnix, with side takes at themselves.

But there's no time for more; they can hear Zannez yelling from the lounge and Pao is silently opening the door between infirmary and bar.

Naked, black leading white, they stoop low and move stealthily out into a scene of horror and peril.

Looking past them, Baram and Pao can see Nathaniel Hiner at bay above his victims, bare to the waist, his great red membranous gills standing out in desperate rage, from ears to chest in a blood-gorged ruff, while beyond him and taking all his attention, there sallies and gyrates and howls a demon of vengeance and terror. Blood and torn plumage are strewn about, and great fanning wings, crudely tied and pinioned, almost cover the bar, toward which the naked boy and girl swiftly and silently go.

*   *   *

Young Pao eases the door closed after them, leaving a crack to watch through. Behind him, Baram has laid aside the camera and is leading Linnix out to the deck to join Cory and Kip.

This gives Pao an idea. He turns briefly from the door.

When he comes back to peer, a screaming blood-red monster is dancing across the lounge, making skittering, howling dashes at Hiner. Zannez has burst into the bar leaping, whirling, zigzagging, and dangling Ochter's mutilated body with amazing strength, while from his throat pours such a barrage of whoops, snarls, roars, terrifying peals of devil laughter as Pao had never imagined an unamplified Human throat could make.

"Here's your boss, Nat Hiner! See your little bossy?" Zannez cackles with mad laughter, shaking Ochter's stump legs. "Say hello to your friend Nat, Ari Ochter! Hello, Natty-boy, hello!" He makes Ochter's handless arm wave cruelly.

Ochter isn't quite dead, Pao sees—he squirms in Zannez' grasp, crying weakly, adding to the horrible effect.

"You didn't know they have gods here, Hiner!" Zannez shrieks, amid inchoate yelpings. "See what they did to your pal? And Yule—Mordy Yule's in li-i-ttul pieces. Ha-ha-hah!" Zannez screeches, dances from side to side, forward and back, no part of him still an instant.

Hiner, momentarily paralyzed, crouches knife in hand above a tragic tangle of plumage, blood, small limbs, wires and rope, at which Pao cannot look. Then, with a peculiar neighing sound, Hiner flings the knife in the general direction of Zannez and grabs up his spring bow. He aims it one-handed at his tormenter while his other hand tries to stuff a bloodied flask inside his tunic, his wild ruff of gills in the way. Crack! Clang! A bolt shatters vitrex above Zannez' head and another hits the staircase beyond him.

At this moment something like a spinning golden comet

hurls itself into the lounge behind Zannez, giving out ear-splitting hoots and yowls.

Hiner fires another bolt that goes into Zannez' tunic, and breaks at a run for the main front doors.

But the gold-streaming thing reaches them first, circles to head him off from escape. Amid a riot of cartwheels, somersaults, leaps, and hand-walks, Pao finally makes out that it's Snake, his body almost invisible behind whirling gold drapes gripped in hands, teeth, and feet—a show that would tax a professional acrobat, which he is. But he and Zannez are performing for their lives now.

In another minim Hiner will realize they're harmless, but he's given no time. Zannez edges closer. As Hiner turns back, Zannez powerfully flings the wretched Ochter straight at him and dodges away, yelling falsetto, "They're coming for you, Natty-boy, gonna get you-oo-oo! Ha-ha-ha-ha-hee-hee-woo-oo-oo!" Snake joins in the uproar.

"Nat! Nat! Help me!" Ochter cries through the din, slipping down Hiner's body. clasping his stub-ended arms around one of Hiner's legs.

"Keep off me! G-get away, get away!" Hiner breaks free, kicking brutally, and suddenly sees Hanno and Bridey ducking behind the tied-down Dameii. He sends two more bolts at them; they clatter into the bar mirror.

Meanwhile Zannez has snatched up the skinning knife Hiner threw and is advancing in lunges, fencing fashion. Hiner fires another bolt which just misses Zannez' head, and then, to Pao's anguish, stoops and grabs up a tiny body from the tangle on the floor and holds it before him as a shield.

It's Nyil: one of her little gold wings droops brokenly, and there is only a terrible gash on her back where the other should be.

Clasping her across his chest, Hiner takes aim at Zannez with his free arm, snatching looks around the child's body.

For a second Pao's breath catches, while something pale whips up and down behind the center of the bar.

And suddenly a metal shaft is sprouting out of the socket of Hiner's aiming eye. He drops the child and, screaming, claps both hands to his face. Another knife flies into his open mouth, and another tears through his gills into his chest.

Bridey and Hanno have gained the open knife box by the stove.

Hiner staggers backward, turns, under a hail of knives. Knife handles march down his belly and sides, the impacts seeming to jolt him upright. Behind the bar, dark and light arms rise and fall together. Zannez and Snake fall silent. Then Hiner pitches forward and sprawls, away from Nyil.

And it is over.

Really over at last.

Hanno vaults the bar and begins the task of gently releasing Wyrra and Juiyn, while Zannez, roaring for Doctor Baram, converges with Snake above the heart-breaking form of Nyil.

But Bridey's in a killing rage. Her naked young body mounted on the bar, her white arms flashing like avenging lightning, she pours her steely missiles into Hiner and Ochter, making their bodies quiver and convulse.

"Turn her off! Turn her off!" Zannez shouts hoarsely.

"Okay, okay, sweetie." Hanny Ek cautiously reaches up to her. "Bee? Bridey! It's over now." He gets a hand on her throwing arm. "We have to leave enough of them to identify, honey. Sweets? It's over, you did it, Bridey-pie, you did it."

Slowly she comes out of it and lets him help her down from the bar, seeming fully to see the Dameii for the first time.

"But look what they've *done,*" she wails, her eyes flooding with tears of rage.

Hanno eases the rest of the knives away from her. "They're dead now, honey, we killed them dead-meat. You did just great, Bee, you never touched a feather."

"Oh, you Bridey-o!" Snake dances up to her. "If you were a man, I'd marry you!"

"Oh-h-h—" In reaction, she melts weeping onto Snake's chest; then pulls away to throw up into the bar sink.

Doctor Baram is bending over Nyil, his face haggard. "She's alive . . . barely." Cory, at the doorway, watches through her veil, impassive.

"How did you like the Gridworld way?" Zannez can't help asking the world in general. His arms and legs hurt, he has a bolt cut on his ribs, he's stiffening up all over, and his voice is almost gone, but he feels wonderful. He's done the job and his people are all okay.

"Fantastic. I'm shaking," Baram says. "But now I have to work fast with the Dameii." He has passed his wire-cutters to Hanno, and the two Dameii adults are slumping to the floor, so nearly unconscious that they seem only dimly aware that they are free. So far as can be seen, apart from their flayed backs, neither is physically hurt.

"Put this salve on them." Baram hands it over. "And tell your boys that most of those so-called feathers have nerves in them, go very easy. Let the Dameii move however they seem to want to." He says a few words in careful Damei, but Wyrra and Juiyn do not respond. "I'll take over Nyil. Oh, gods. . . ." as he feels more of the savaged little body. Then a desperate idea comes to him.

"Prince?"

The boy is beside them, emotions contending on his face.

"Can you take on one more small mission? Go out on the deck, and at the very first sign of a time-flurry—you know, that dark-flash effect—at the very first suspicion, dash into the surgery and call me. And better be wrong than miss one."

"Right." The prince salutes and hastens out.

"Oh, lords of pity . . . Myr Zannez, listen, if your people can stand it, would you get them to search through this mess for, for body parts? For fingers, Nyil's, the little girl's fingers especially. Toes. The adults', too." He clenches his jaw painfully. "Any bit of flesh. And any of the longer plumes

611

that look to have had a blood supply, bring them to me quick. We'll move all this into the surgery. . . . Dameii heal amazingly. I've sewn on a hand that'd been off half a day without refrigeration, and it's functional. . . ."

He gathers Nyil up in his arms, the severed wing in his hand, holding her facedown to spare her back. Zannez helps him through the infirmary door. To his surprise, when Baram lays her prone on the padded table, her neck lengthens and bends far back, and her small chin comes out naturally to point straight forward where a Human forehead would be. An adaptation to the wings, he thinks, choking down the sight; she looks so dreadfully like a brutally plucked, half-butchered little bird—who only hours ago had been all compact of life and fun.

"If you could help the other two in here," Baram says over his shoulder. "And bring Kip to translate for you—tell him I said to tow him on a blanket. Right?"

"Right." Zannez starts for the bar. He no longer feels exuberant. The helpless, sick rage that rose in him at the sight of Nyil, the aching pity for Wyrra and Juiyn, the shame that it is Humans who have done such irreparable vileness, will, he fears, live with him in nightmare to the end of his life.

XVIII

STARFIRE
PASSING

As Zannez leaves the infirmary, Prince Pao dashes in from the deck.

"It's starting! I'm certain it's a real one! Can I help?"

Baram brushes by the boy, carrying Nyil in his arms. He is a lifelong atheist, but at that moment he's praying with such silent fierceness that he barely hears Pao. *Oh, gods—God of Asclepious, god of Galen, of Pasteur, let this work! This one last time, oh, gods make it work—*

Aloud he says hurriedly, his eyes on the Star's light, on the flickering sky outside, "Yes. Get Wyrra and Juiyn out here. But—" he realizes he hasn't yet decided whether Nyil's parents should go through it: would they help? The memory of Linnie's screams decides him. Nyil would have to go back through torture, and terror; better they not see.

"But make them stay here, under the eaves," he concludes as he reaches the shadow edge, Pao running alongside.

"I think I'll be out very soon in real time." It crosses his mind that this extraordinary wave of time-flurries is what lay in the Star-shell's last and inmost zone; it must be a great concentration of the Star's special energies, its "yearning" to be back, back before *Deneb*. The other shells had shown nothing like it.

"Right." Pao starts off at a run, but the boy in him can't resist spinning around at the door to say, "Mind you don't meet yourself coming back!"

He disappears.

In fact it's good advice, Baram thinks, veering sharp left as he carries Nyil toward the brightest pool of Star-light. He must remember to take the other tack coming back . . . coming back, with what in his arms? The same heart-searing burden, or a miracle?

Don't hope, he warns himself. The peak of the Star's energies is passing. The air still feels charged, but not with quite the violent intensity with which it worked the miracle of Linnie.

Then the Star's retrograde time-pull was in flood. Swiftly it had borne Linnie back from death itself, through agony, to the near past, when the fatal artery was uncut, and blood filled her beating heart, and she lived again. She lived!

But he knew that if the time-eddy ran its course forward again with her, she would die again, and forever. He had to carry her alive from the time-flow's power, literally wrench her from the past to the present that existed so close at hand, in the shadow protected from the Star. So close—yet so agonizingly far in effort. It had taken all his strength only to move her, to lift and pull and tug her forward. He had ended crawling, just as the time-rush changed, dragging her beneath him with her wrists held around his neck, as he had once dragged the war-wounded under fire—and sick with terror that he had failed, that this was too gross a defiance of Time's power—until they fell across the shadow threshold and he could be sure she lived. Yes, she lived again—Linnie lived!

Yet even as he'd exulted, Ochter's damned triple barb had tangled itself in her hair, and he'd barely caught it starting to drag across her throat.

The memory of that kerchief blowing after the earlier eddy came back and scared him witless. Would this evil hook work its way from the ends of space, to reassert death's reality by killing her again?

He'd slammed it into his safe and frantically set about making this reality—the reality of Linnix alive—real. He made her speak to Kip and Cory, hand them objects, move chairs—anything to build the living Linnix into other's memories, to make her mark on *this* present.

It was then that he'd thought to make a camera record of her (shuddering with fear lest it turn out blank) and intermix her with scenes of *this* present. . . . It was then, too, that he'd understood the price this miracle had exacted; but he'd counted it as nothing, then.

And now he must hope that this last time-flurry will carry Nyil back a greater distance yet, to the moments before these unspeakable mutilations had begun—and that he has the strength to bring her out, to contest for her against Time itself once more, before the backflow spends its force and returns her to this grievous present again.

If he succeeds—will something be left behind? Don't think of it. You don't fight Reality unwounded. He'd been crazy enough to fight for Linnie's life. Now he's demanding another miracle.

So be it, he thinks, carefully spreading the barely living little body to Star-light. There's no other way. No Human skill can mend the dreadfulness that has been done to Nyil—that abomination, Hiner, not only slashed, but shredded, crushed the child's delicate wings, hands, arms. Baram can't stand thinking of what must have gone on: not clean cuts, but a progressive ruin, holding for a time the desperate hope of

615

repair. Oh, that they'd been able to act more swiftly—and he can't help adding, Oh, that he had the living Hiner in his hands! This time-flurry is his only desperate last recourse.

Courage, he tells himself; we have the aid of the Star.

Holding Nyil steadily to the dark-flashing sky, he sets his mind to believe. *Back—take us back!*

But the Star's influence is weakening. The active principle, whatever extra-Galactic entity gives it strange powers, is passing Damiem. He can see how slowly this time-flurry comes on; slow, so slow that only now is the familiar uncanniness beginning, the unmoving motion, the clutter of displaced objects, ghost-people.

Back, he wills. *Carry her back!* And then to his dismay the tiny body in his arms begins to writhe and struggle, and her all-but-ultrasonic wail pierces his ears. Oh, gods, she *is* back—in Hiner's grasp. Will it carry farther, take her back to wholeness? *Back, restore her,* he prays to the universe. Summoning all the Dameii tongue he has, he croons to her, "It's all over, Nyil my dear, you'll soon be better. You're free, Wyrra and Juiyn are free. The bad Humans are gone. Hold on, soon you'll be better—"

It seems to help a little; amid her pain she gives him one clear look.

But her legs and wing-remnants are making a curious drumming, vibrating movement; he recognizes it as the Damei response to great physical or mental pain. It crosses his mind that it must have been the great drumming wings of Wyrra or Juiyn that the little showgirls took for the sounds of sweeping. But now in Nyil he fears it may impede the miracle he hopes for.

There's a site between the wings where pressure sometimes quiets the reflex. On Nyil it is bloody meat, but he lays his fingers down hard, and the quivering eases. And as he holds her thus he feels something—*something*—brush his fingers where nothing was before.

Oh, gods of mercy—can it be her lost wing, coming back? Are they receding to a time when she is whole?

He peers down but can see nothing clearly through the dark-flickering air. Or is there what might be a transparent projection of *two* pale golden little wings, that spread and still, as he presses the reflex point? . . . Not solid substance yet, but *there?*

And now under his fingers there is a growing sensation of normal flesh, even downy skin. Other wounds he can see are healing, too; the pitiful stumps that were her hands have shadow fingers now.

Will it continue? Or will the Star's fading energies collapse too soon and let the flow rush forward again to anguish and ruin? *Go on, go on, go on,* he prays, as if one tiny Human will could aid the Star.

And wholeness *is* coming, solidifying—the wings fan once, and a perceptible flow of air touches his face. But is the healing real enough? Dare he take her out now?

He's half-mad with indecision: To stop too soon, or to wait too long—either may risk losing all. His eyes, ears, his very skin, are feeling for the first sign of the retrograde flow. He's oblivious to any weirdness around him, even to what might be his shadow self with Linnix, over there—he can spare no instant's attention from the ambient air.

Then he remembers: It will take time, getting out. Almost without willing it he begins to move. Or tries to move—the difficulty appalls him. They have gone deep, deep. All his being focuses on the extreme effort to carry her out. He is climbing beyond exhaustion, carrying a load too heavy to bear. For a time he despairs of making it. But a fierce joy gives him strength—the little form in his arms is whole, *two* gleaming wings shine up at him, and once she twists to send him, unbelievably, a smile.

Afterward he can recall little of the struggle to get out; the traverse of those few meters of deck drain him even of reserves he didn't know he had. The two things he remembers are that smile, and changing Nyil's position, as he nears the shadow, so he can pass her to her parents. He's learned how to do this—to stand her feet on one palm at breast height, with his other hand supporting her narrow front, her wings over his shoulder. The joy of her restored life thrills through her, it's like holding living lightening.

As she sights Wyrra and Juiyn through the flashing murk of the shadow's edge, her wings buffet his head, and just as they're reaching safety, she takes off with a violent beat and *flies* the last steps into her father's arms.

Baram, seeing her safe, lets himself fall to his knees. As he's done once before, he crawls feebly from the past into the sudden silence and clarity of the present beneath the eaves. He becomes vaguely aware of a cluster of Human legs around the three Dameii . . . and someone has gotten Kip into a rollchair.

But as he is trying to haul himself upright, he sees that all is not yet well. Nyil is leaning across her father's shoulder to embrace her mother's head. Suddenly her eyes close and she sags, limp.

Baram is so weak that he must cling to a chair back to get one hand to her breast, while Wyrra cradles her face upward, in his arms. The strong, running quiver of the central ganglion, the Damei equivalent of a heartbeat, is gone.

Baram has learned to restart it as he would a Human heart, but with a sharp, heavy double squeeze. At his first try the vibration resumes, and Nyil lives again.

Only there is a kind of darkness on her face, Baram thinks. It vanishes when she smiles, but between smiles and loving murmurs to her parents, there comes a look he's never seen before.

He steps back to greet Kip where he sits watching, with Cory standing, still veiled, behind.

"They're saying good-bye," Kip tells him quietly. "Bram, what is it? Didn't the time-thing work?"

"It worked," Baram says grimly. "But . . ." He doesn't

know how to phrase it without sounding crazy. Nyil has gotten back her wings, her body: what has she left behind? Her life?

"But there's a price," Cory finishes for him, in a grave voice.

"It took too much out of her—is that it?" Kip demands.

At that moment Baram sees her collapse again and steps forward to Wyrra. But when his hand reaches her chest, he gets a strong feeling of protest from both parents, He works the necessary compression as gently as he can. Too gently: he has to repeat the starting before her body takes over.

"No, no," says Wyrra in Galactic. Juiyn, looking wild, bursts out with a spate of Damei that Baram can't possibly follow.

"Don't they understand?" Baram asks Kip. "Don't they know I'm doing this to keep her alive?"

"They understand," Kip tells him. He ripples off a question to Wyrra in Damei, and both Nyil's parents reply at once, with Nyil herself joining in, until she sinks back exhausted.

Before Kip can begin translating, Nyil turns her face to Baram and crooks her fingers—her fingers!—at him, beckoning him near. He bends over her in Wyrra's arms.

And just as he does so, she takes two weak breaths, and he sees her quivering chest fall still. Baram brings one hand up to steady her back so he can seize the sternum area. She gives a plaintive little cry from almost airless lungs, and Wyrra's free hand plucks at Baram's. But the Damei's light touch can't break into the doctor's absorption; Baram's fingers squeeze in sharply, twice. Nyil breathes—and the life-throb is there.

When he's satisfied that function has been restored, Baram faces Wyrra. "Life," he says in his clumsy Damei. "Her life . . . not death, not dying." He mimics the hand squeeze. "Needed for life."

Wyrra gives the slow side tilt of his head that is the Damei

619

"No," and speaks in his own poor Galactic. "Pain," he says. "Too much pain. Have bad dream, say."

Baram's first thought, that Wyrra means that the restarting is too painful, changes when he hears that "dream." Is it that the child has simply been through too much and can endure no more? Helplessly confused, Baram can only repeat, "Life. Not dying," to Wyrra's unreadable negation.

Baram turns back to Kip. "What is it? What's wrong? Don't they believe she'll live?"

But Nyil beckons him to her again and speaks first.

"You save—you *have* saved me," she says carefully, faint but clear, and pauses to smile bewitchingly up at him. "You have saved me, terafore, no, *there*fore"—she brings out with unmistakable pride—"now I can die good; no right; well."

"But you don't have to die, my dear!" Baram explodes. "Now you can live!"

She tilts her head. No.

"No, I am to die. But well; it is all right now. I fly! Before you have saved me, it was no good." Her voice trembles. "Very, v-very bad."

"Yes." He understands that, at least. And evidently to these people not to die maimed, tortured, *wingless* is very important.

"But I *can't* let you die, my dear. We may have to do this"—he makes the squeezing motion—"a few times more, but you are ready to live now. Don't you want to live? Your parents—Wyrra, Juiyn, they want you to live."

The little head tilts, sways for emphasis. She sighs. "No, no. To understand diff-i-cult. I know you good, Doctor Baram." Again the heart-melting smile, this time with, incredibly, a tinge of mischievous mimicry. "Good-bye, my dear."

Her gaze goes from him to her parents, she says a word or two in Damei—and he sees the movement of her chest weaken and cease.

620

As his hands come up to restart the beat, a rough grasp fastens on his right wrist and jerks it away. It's Juiyn, towering over him with wings aloft. She makes the sharp sound that means emphatic "No" in Damei, holding his arm with almost Human strength.

Helplessly, he lets her pull him away.

Nyil's eyes have closed momentarily in a grimace of pain. Now they open wide. She looks at the faces that surround her, her gaze calm, clear, smiling, with only a scarcely perceptible shadow of what might be fear. Then her eyes go to Juiyn and Wyrra, and close.

She is whole, winged, untormented: she looks like a child in peaceful sleep. But a child who does not breathe again.

No one speaks. In silence the two tall Dameii, beautiful even in their ravaged state, turn away with their burden. They pace out of the circle of Human light, into the silvery mists on the deck beyond.

Just at the edge of visibility Baram sees Wyrra pass their daughter's body to Juiyn, and they turn to the parapet. Baram understands. Their horror of passing closer to those end rooms is so great that it has overcome Wyrra's reluctance to expose his defect of flight. A moment later comes the beat of his bad wing as they take off.

Baram, too, can't bear to think what must have gone on in and around those rooms. He'll have to, soon enough; tomorrow, the investigation doubtless will begin. . . . Afterward, those rooms—perhaps the whole hostel—will be simply destroyed. Erased, obliterated. . . . A pity, maybe, but there's no other thinkable way.

He's frowning absently at the spot where the Dameii vanished. Now he becomes aware of Linnie quietly holding his arm and pressing it against her warm side, as if to comfort them both. He looks down into her cerulean eyes. Some expression is coming back, he sees, a change from the vacant stare that so frightened him.

"I remember, I knew the little—the young one," she says softly.

He nods, smiles down at her. "Yes."

Then he looks up and deliberately meets the eyes that surround them. It's time. Linnie spoke quietly, but not so quietly that all did not hear.

Zannez is standing closest, his arms around the shoulders of Hanno and Bridey at his sides, his face carefully blank. Hanno looks frankly more and more curious, as the oddness of Linnix' remark sinks in; Bridey's violet eyes are open wide. Snake, quicker than Hanno, is examining the floor.

Even Kip, sitting in the medical rollchair, has paused in working at his eyes and is squinting at Baram. Behind him Cory leans against the wall; her face unreadable behind the veil; he can see that her hair beneath the cloth is now snow white. Baram's heart skips a beat as his gaze passes over her, but he has Linnix' problem to attend first. The boy Pao is sitting cross-legged nearby, beside Stareem. His head is up, studying Linnix. Only little Stareem, curled in sleep on Kip's vacated blanket pad, is peacefully oblivious to it all.

"Linnie, my dear," Baram says, "all these people are your friends, and we must tell them that you've had a loss—a lapse of memory."

She nods. Her response is childlike, docile, but light-years away from the drooling blankness he first saw. That was when he faced the terrible possibility that he'd brought her body out alive—without a mind.

"Call it traumatic amnesia," he tells the others. "We don't know yet if it's permanent or temporary, nor whether it's very extensive or localized and spotty. We simply don't know. Just don't be surprised if she doesn't recall your name." He smiles, then sobers. "There'll be plenty of time for introductions later if they're needed. Right now we have more urgent matters to attend to.

"Bridey, if I may I'll leave Linnie with you. And can you

622

also stand by Myr Cory and Kip in case they need anything? I should see about the marquise.''

"Oh, gods." Bridey moves to Linnix' side. "Poor Lady P.! I forgot all about her! And— Oh!'' She puts her hand to her mouth, glancing meaningfully toward the rollbed. "Well, yes sir, Doctor B. I'll stand by here, if Myr Linnix will stay with me. Oh, I'm Bridey. Hello.''

"Hello," Linnix responds interestedly. "I'm L-Linnix, I think.''

"And Myr Zannez," Baram goes on. "Do you suppose you and your boys could do one last dirty job? We seem to have a surplus of—'' He gestures toward the blanketed heaps that were once Yule and Vovoka, and the rollbed, where he'd pushed Loma's corpse back onto her pillows. 'Or have Snake and Hanny had enough?''

Zannez squeezes Hanny's shoulder. "You—and Bridey, too—remember what we said about props? Just keep telling yourself they're props—it's true. And you've seen a million worse ones, kiddies. Hold the thought—props.''

"Vovoka's can go in his room," Baram says, "and those three animals can go in Ochter's. Be careful not to disturb anything at that end; Base will need to see it all. And the rollbed with poor little Loma can go in my surgery. Perhaps you'll do that first.''

Zannez and his three get the rollbed moving, and Baram goes around them to confront whatever has happened to the Lady.

His first glance shows her not only alive but coming awake. She's tossing restlessly in the lounger, muttering, "Where's Loma? Loma!" with closed eyes—a charming sight even in disarray.

Now to tell her that Loma is dead, and her lifework gone. Baram gropes in his pocket for more of the blue tranquilizer pills and goes for some water.

Five minim later he's wishing he had one of Ochter's sedative syrettes. It has been decades since he coped with open, raving hysterics in a Human. At his first word, she rushes screaming after the rollbed into the lab and, amid vituperative denials and calls to Loma, attempts to climb into it. Despite her femininity, she's as strong as a wild animal.

Baram calls Zannez and his youngsters from their work, and among them all they manage to get the poor marquise into her room and into bed, and loaded up with calmants. But she will not relax until the rollbed with its still cargo is pushed into her room.

"That's the best we can do for now," Baram says. "I'll get the body into a coffin and work with her sister, as well as I can, when we've coped with the living. I think there's a Lord Protector of Rainbow's End I can contact to meet her at Central, if we ever get to that."

As he speaks he's conscious of a blended sound coming from somewhere and everywhere.

Partly it is a soft, high-pitched keening. That would be Dameii, singing or chanting in the trees around Nyil's home. He's encountered the death-song ceremony before.

But there's another sound underneath, a bass so low-pitched as to be more of a shudder than a sound. He knows it—but he's distracted by seeing Linnix abruptly straighten up and brush at her uniform, seeming for the first time to notice the rips and bloody smears on her breast. Of course.

The rumbling bass grows louder as he speaks till it drowns his words. A new light has sprung up in the Star-hazed sky, over the roof of the hostel. It's a ship's exhaust flare.

Somebody is coming in to land.

Baram's first thought is that it's *Rimshot*'s pinnace—but why would Dayan have come so soon, without their SOS or his requested callback? And he couldn't have picked up a neurological expert this fast. Besides, it doesn't sound like the pinnace, or like a Moom ship's lander. It sounds like a larger Patrol vessel capable of touchdown.

Which is exactly what *Comet* is supposed to be.

And *Comet*—wait!

Baram's story to Ochter, about *Comet*'s being lost and Race contacting FedBase, was made up of whole cheese. But he'd told it with so much effort and conviction that he's ended by half believing it himself. In fact he knows nothing whatever about *Comet*, and there is no mortal reason why this can't be Captain Race landing his ship to pick up his duly chartered passengers.

His lavishly chartered passengers.

How will he take the news that his passengers are dead, his promised payment gone glimmering—and he himself has landed on an Interdict planet and will be detained the moment FedBase learns of it?

All Baram knows about Race is that he's an adventurer who doesn't mind taking risks and is determined to get the credits to keep his ship.

These thoughts flash through Baram's mind as all activity stops to listen. They are followed by another.

An unarmed spaceship still has offensive capabilities: if its low-altitude guidance is good—as an ex-Patrol escort's would be—its exhaust and auxiliary thrust rockets can be used as flying torches to wreak havoc on the ground.

And Race has been told that his three passengers expected to get very rich here.

What are the chances that he's put one and one and one together and come up with Stars Tears? Or at least some gem find? Very good. And he has a threat by which to extract some or all of his payment from the station. He's already in violation; why should he care about further charges?

Oh, gods. Baram feels suddenly tired, tired and old. He's spent the night faced with an endless array of frightful threats and pains and dilemmas and assaults, and thought it at last over. But here's one more. For the first time, his internal feelings match his white hair.

He looks up at the strange ship; its trail seems to waver a bit, as though the pilot is looking the place over. And it is definitely not *Rimshot*'s pinnace.

When he looks down, Zannez' sharp eyes are on him. "More trouble?"

Baram beckons him over by Cory and Kip and explains the situation. Cory listens but says only, "That ship will have a transmitter . . . not *c*-skip, but better than—" She gestures at the wreck of the antennae.

Kip is reviving fast, though his eyes still squint. "If we can get at his caller. Race won't be eager to let us use it to report him in," he says gloomily, and then bursts out, "Amesha Spentas! Of all the accursed—I still haven't recharged the Tocharis. . . . Cor, you've got a stupid, blind, leg-broke Deputy, one overworked medico, and friend Zannez here—and two boys and a girl armed with kitchen knives!"

She lays a veil-covered hand on his shoulder.

Pao has been listening quietly from his seat on the floor. "Myr Kip, I have one of your Tocharis charging; it should be about full. I thought it might be useful. . . . You did tell me to, you know."

"Oh, my gods. Get it—no, we'll pick it up in the garage."

"Superboy," says Zannez.

"I'm the surprise factor." Pao grins at Zannez.

"Well, well, well!" Baram is purely astonished at good news.

Kip struggles to his feet in his excitement, frowning hard.

"And if we tape the LED indicators on the other two, they'll look functional." He grins. "So we give the charged gun to the best shot—that's between you and Zannez, Bram. Or one of the boys? The aim is to get Race and his crew under control, either in the ship or on-planet, in case he has ideas, while we use his caller. How does that sound, Cor?"

"Green. . . . But of course," Cory adds tiredly, "he may be quite peaceful."

"And we aim to see he stays that way. Let's see: How many crew would he be apt to carry for a charter of three? We can probably assume he isn't paying any more wages than he has to."

"Look," Zannez says, "numbers aren't everything. How about we bring along a girl? Bridey'd have the best chance of being invited in."

"With or without her cutlery?" Baram asks. He, too, feels a lot better.

Bridey touches her APC robe pockets and smiles.

"Best we put her in that gold thing of Pao's," Zannez says. "You can stick the knife up your sleeve; I taught you."

Snake gives a leer. "That outfit would get her into a Special Branch vault."

"Time to go!" Kip points upward. Insanely, everyone's grinning.

The unknown ship is coming in fast. Its thunder suddenly increases to a horizon-shaking scream as the ground retros cut in, then fade.

"Gods, doesn't it ever get light around here?" Zannez is trying to think. "Look, we need some tunics or something that looks like travel."

"I'll get ours," says Hanno.

"And I can get yours, Kippo." Cory moves toward their room, walking tall and fast.

"And we need—my gods, I almost missed—some dummy duffels. Snako—can you quick make up some from ours?"

"Done." Snake lopes off.

Baram has retrieved his own medical tunic at a trot and crosses through the lounge to help Cor.

In a couple of minim the group is reassembled, looking surprisingly different.

"Time to move it," says Kip. "My eyes are still no good, but I can't hurt anybody with a dry gun. Stick me in back, will you?"

Pao has been watching excitedly.

"You are the king of the castle now, Prince," Kip says. "We haven't left you much in the way of troops. You'll be green?"

"Go!" Pao tells him.

"We'll try to get word back," Baram says.

Bridey quietly kisses Cory as the others pick up their "bags."

"You really look like voyagers," Cory says, suppressing a cough.

"We are," Zannez says, grinning, as they exit. "That we for sure are!"

XIX

ON
THE RAMP

The jitney bearing Zannez, Snake, Hanno, Bridey, and
Kip, with Baram driving, arrives at the field just as the
strange ship flicks on its floodlights. In the glare on her side
Zannez sees a salad of scripts, topped by *COMET II*.

"Stop ahead," says Kip. "If we are where I think we are,
just turn the car a little crossways and we can block the road.
We don't want them roaring out past us."

Baram obeys. The ship has a Space-type drive, but her
landing rockets ignite the brush. She is also closer to the road
than the Moom ship's usual spot.

As the fires burn out, Zannez looks up and sees the huge
white wings of a Damei settling in the branches above them.
He nudges Baram to look up.

"Kip! One of the elders is here."

"No time." Kip calls out something in Damei. The wings
fold and seemingly vanish.

That Damei's staying really close to fire, Zannez thinks. Curious? Or maybe he has something important to say.

But what's in front of them is more important. The fire has sunk to embers now. He hears ship locks clank. Suddenly a landing ramp is angling down.

"I thought I heard the cargo latch let go, too," Kip says. "Let's stay right where we are, Bram."

A short, slight, erect figure appears at the port, with something in his hand. Captain Race? As the officer moves forward, a beefy-looking crewman comes out behind him and trots down the ramp.

"One," says Zannez. Kip is squinting hard.

There's a polite attention chime, and a nasal voice from a loud-hailer says, "This is the private spaceship *Comet Two*, landing to pick up a charter of three passengers for Federation Central. Ready now to board." After a pause, the voice adds, "Baggage will be hand-stowed, please. Pass your things to the crewman here."

"Now what? I—" Baram starts to say.

But to Zannez' amazement Kip has seemingly gone crazy. He's reached over and is hugging Hanno, Snake, and Bridey, and trying to hug him, too, and making weird whinnying noises.

"That voice," he chokes. "Oh, that accent—if only Cor was here!"

It's a minim before he calms enough to say, "Chums, I don't know how or why, but that isn't any Captain Race. It's Captain Saul Scooter Dayan of the Federation Patrol cruiser *Rimshot*—our friend! Bang on that hooter, Bram!"

"Friends?" Zannez explodes. He leans over Baram and starts tapping out the Federation anthem on the hooter.

"He must have taken over *Comet* somehow, and he's here to booby-trap Ochter and company. Oh, we have to tell Cor!"

"Oh-h-h, coloss!" Bridey sighs, once more resplendent in her Queen of Fire lace robe.

"Let's go!"

Everyone hangs on as they lurch out to the ship over the smoking sod. The familiar Horsehead accents from the port are repeating, sounding a trifle puzzled and peremptory.

"Hurry!" Kip urges from the back. "The tires'll hold; they have to."

Boom! Bffoom! Two tires blow as they near the ship. Baram careens to the ramp base on the rims.

"Saul! Saul! Scooter—it's us!" Kip bellows.

Cautiously, Captain Dayan comes halfway down the ramp, looking them over.

"Myr Kip, and Doctor Baramji, is it? I'm glad to see you seem well. But I must hold back until we establish certain facts and formalities, especially that you are what you appear to be. And who are your friends?"

"Oh, stow the formalities, Scooter! We've been fighting boogers all the long night—they've done awful things—and we've done a few—" But he falls silent. Even on far Damiem they've heard of Black World SC—techniques of simulation and control.

The hefty crewman has been joined by a sergeant carrying electronic gear.

"Retinal scanner there," says Baram aside. "I'll get him to check out your eyes, Kip."

"Green, Saul, Green," Kip concedes to the captain. "But listen, send a signal to Cory that you're here. She's not well and we've been fairly spooked. Oh, wait—the antenna's down; you'll have to send someone."

"Can't you get some of your flying friends to go?" Dayan's already testing Kip, Zannez thinks.

"No way, you know that, Scooter. And I tell you, terrible things have gone on."

"Very well," Dayan says grudgingly. "But it's against principle."

"If you'll step over here, Myr Korso," says the sergeant.

"I can't step, but I can hop if your pal there will help me."

As the crewman boosts Kip out, the cargo hatch flips down and three space marines in full battle dress emerge, tugging man-lifts. They mount and whistle off through the treetops toward the hostel.

The examinations are thorough but quick; soon Kip and Baram are up on the ramp, where the huggings and back thumpings recommence, and their story comes out in disconnected chunks.

"Gods, are we glad to see you!" Kip repeats. "But how in the name of All did you get here, in this?" He whacks *Comet*'s port. "Where's Captain Whatsisname, Race?"

"At Base."

Zannez, still at the ramp base, can see that Dayan is keeping one eye on the proceedings below as he goes on.

"Race took one look at your planet—you should see Damiem from space. He figured everybody was fried. So he went over to Base to find out what's what. Exec heard he was heading for Damiem, and I reckon Race is still explaining hisself. Meanwhile we decided to have *Comet* flown out to rendezvous with *Rimshot*, and some of the boys and I transshipped into her and came on here to look over these charter types."

"Beautiful."

At the ramp foot, Zannez is impressed by the sergeant's ingenious methods of countering any attempted audio surveillance, or control by hostage. Nice authentic touch for the documentary, he thinks—and thinks also to ask, "By any chance is this classified?"

"Yes sir," says the sergeant, not smiling. "And not by chance. We're getting to that."

And shortly Zannez finds himself being sworn, by his loyalty to the Federation, to keep it all to himself. Oh, well, he can see the point.

When it comes to the two boys' turn to be checked out,

Hanno is found to be incapable of speech above a hoarse whisper.

"What's the matter with him?" Zannez asks Snake.

"He's never seen a real live Space Patrolman up close before," Snake replies. "That's the problem I was going to tell you. It was bad enough when we were with Service people. But now the Patrol is here. He really *wants* it, you know? It hurts."

Zannez remembers: *"The Patrol doesn't take animals."* That was because of the porn. Damn. . . . But he's distracted by the increasingly unpleasant sensation in his left side, where Hiner's bolt hit.

"You, Myr-in-the-red suit," a woman's voice rings out from the ramp. Zannez looks up to see a big, rangy woman in medic's whites, standing by Doc Baram. "Do you always carry your left arm like that?"

"Uh. Well, ma'am, no, I don't—it doesn't feel—"

"I'm Siri Lipsius, *Rimshot*'s battle medic." She's striding down the ramp, giving Zannez a grin from a knobby, friendly-looking face. "I see your suit has taken a hit on that side. Were you in it?"

"Zannez is the name, ma'am. Oh, yes, I was."

She grabs his rubbery left arm and does something to the palm that he can't feel.

Snake speaks up. "Remember, Zannie, Pao said he thought those bolts could be poisoned."

"I'm getting my kit."

Doctor Siri lopes back up the ramp, passing Baram hastening down. He, too, takes up the arm, frowning.

"I've been very remiss, I fear," he says ruefully. "Good thing Siri saw you. You couldn't be in better hands; she's my idea of a top battle surgeon."

Doctor Siri returns and Zannez' rib cut is soon diagnosed, detoxified, and taped. The consensus is that he's had a narrow escape. The bolts apparently carried a neurotoxin of the Parat type, which could have stopped heart action if it'd hit head-on or near a major blood vessel.

"Don't forget he was shooting at Hanno and me, too," mutters Bridey as the examiner packs up. "Brrr!"

"A very beautiful young lady," observes Dayan from the ramp. "Do I understand that she killed one of your raiders by throwing knives?"

"That she did!" Kip chuckles. "Listen, time to head back to Cor. What time are you on?"

"Midmorning."

As he speaks a whistle sounds, and two large space marines issue from the port behind him, stretching and stamping their legs. Above them, the darkness is just graying toward dawn, behind the last drizzle of Star-shine. *Comet*'s floodlights suddenly look yellow.

"You've fed? How's about your men come over to the station for evening chow?"

"You may want to rethink that." Dayan grins, and steps back as several more marines emerge from the cramped six-passenger spaces of *Comet*. And more still, as everyone moves aside, until a full squad is unfolding tents and gear from the cargo hatch onto the field's cleared edge.

"Whew. You came prepared, Scooter. Let's see, with the crewmen . . . say, twenty-two? I think we—I—can make that, we have rations ahead for some characters who won't be eating. Ah—there's your car, let's go. But take it easy with that engine. We'll have to leave the jitney."

Rimshot's command car is rolling out of the cargo hatch, its hydride-fueled motor puffling out water vapor. They all start down the ramp.

Dayan waves the girl driver to the back and gets in to drive. "I fear you'll have to wait for the next trip, Myr Zannez."

"No problem, sir." Zannez finds his Gridworld kids have closed in around him, reluctant to be separated. So is he.

Dayan gives them a sharp look and a smile. An odd little

634

moment of empathy warms Zannez; the captain understands how it is when people have been through things together.

As they get Kip in, Zannez hears him ask, "Where exactly is *Rimshot*?"

"Looking for Doc's neurologist in the Hyades," Dayan tells him.

"Neurologist? Hey, Bram, listen, I'm green. My eyes just tracked in. I don't need anybody."

"Good," says Baram. "No, not you. I want Cory looked at by an expert. *And* by you, Siri."

"You can fix her up, Bram. Can't you? I figured you just needed a few minim without some godlost emergency cutting up."

"I can try."

Kip subsides, apparently satisfied. But Baram's tone chills Zannez. He listens closely as the two medics exchange a word before they get in.

"Don't forget, I'm only a battle hand," Siri tells Baram.

"Exactly what we need. The Administrator—that's Cory—had an alien energy hand weapon discharged point-blank into the parietal arch. There were no immediate signs of damage, but later—well, you'll see for yourself, Siri. You've forgotten more about alien artillery than I'll ever learn."

Then they're in. With Dayan driving, their car lurches sedately away and disappears into the dawn mists on the rocky station road.

Left alone on the ramp, Zannez leads his people over to the parked jitney, which is awaiting tires from *Rimshot*'s supplies. He feels naked without his cameras, but also easier for it in a way. Only, what shots he's missing . . . or is he? He looks around; the magic ship that bore friends—it would show up like any small space vessel sitting on a far-planet field before sunrise—he's seen a thousand such shots. And the Patrolmen who look like angels to him, not to mention to Hanno—could be any of a million routine shots. *Our Brave Space-Fighters* . . . He's losing his objectivity.

635

"Everything all right here, sir?" It's the squad leader with the interrogation sergeant, come alongside.

"Super. You'll never know how good you look to us."

"Glad to hear it."

Over their heads Zannez can see other large marines sauntering casually toward them and catches a good many covert glances in the direction of the golden flame that is Bridey. She is looking unusually demure.

Zannez has been in more situations like this than he wants to remember; he hopes the Code is as firm as it's said to be. From long habit, he starts a distraction.

"Am I allowed to tell you what happened?" he asks the squad leader.

"We'd admire to hear." That Horsehead twang, they must practice it.

"Well. The ringleader, see, was a little old fellow called Doctor Ochter, posing as a regular tourist. So kindly-acting, with a bad limp—faked—that nobody could believe he was a cold-blooded sadist. Oh, he was sweet.

"He had these two accomplices who did the actual dirty work on the Dameii—you all know about the Stars Tears thing, right?"

"Yes, sir," in a grave tone. "You mean they really . . ."

"Yes. They jumped one family before we could stop them. The wing-people who live by the hostel, they have—they *had* a little girl." The memory of little Nyil comes back sharply; Zannez pauses. This isn't just a Grid-show plot. Nyil was real, and she's gone.

"But, I should say, the butcher-boys got here uncleared by faking an error in the ship's sleep doses, so they had to be let off here—and their bags were full of bad stuff disguised as water-world gear."

"Grunions Rising." The sergeant nods.

"Right. And—" Zannez goes on tracing out the complicated events of the evening, the gift of poisoned Eglantine, Vovoka's devastating irruption, and Ochter's fallback plan of

control by hostage; the loss and final recapture of the gun—
though exactly what Baram did to make Loma move, Zannez
still doesn't know—and Pao's destruction of Ochter and Yule.

"Wait till you see Superboy." Zannez grins. "But the
last, best act was these kids—my kids here. They went in
after Hiner, unarmed, and Snake and I distracted him while
Hanno and Bridey got to the knife box, and whew!—you
should have seen those meat choppers fly!"

"It was Hanno, really," Bridey says. "He never misses.
And it was hard, the man held the little girl up to cover
him."

Hanno has again lost his voice, and his normal blue-black
face is turning a startling plum-purple shade. The Spacers
look at the youngster curiously. Several of them are part
Black.

"Knife throwing," the sergeant muses. "I tried it once. I
was no good."

Zannez swallows. "As a matter of fact, Ek here has been
trying to enlist in the Space Force. To be a Patrolman, like
you Myrrin. They won't take him because of his job. But
gods, people have to eat."

"Flat feet, eh?" the squad leader says sympathetically.

"No. He's fine physically. They turned him down because
he works for me. Some of my shows—well, I don't know
how to say it, they're somewhat low class."

"And they won't take him for *that*?"

"Right. It seems unfair." And what am I *doing* to myself?
thinks Zannez. "Sna—Smith, here, was too discouraged to
try."

"I've seen your Commune show," the squad leader said.
"Last time we went near the grid, Lee and I watched," he
told the sergeant. "It's not bad, it shows how the civvies
live."

"Well," Zannez says, "but we do other stuff, too. We
have to. Stuff you wouldn't see out here, thank the gods."

"Oh." The big squad leader stops himself staring.

The sergeant, more worldly-wise, grunts. "Still, if the boy's serious—"

"He is."

"Then he or you should speak to Captain Dayan. Out here on the Rim things are a little different. Any isolated Patrol unit can accept field enlistments, subject to evaluation. And that could be done at FedBase. Would you like me to have a word with the captain?"

"Oh, my-oh-my. That'd be tremendous. Hey, thanks!" Now he's done it. Godlost fool. Glory.

Hanno has his face under effortful control, but his eyes give him away. He ducks his head at the two Spacers. The sergeant nods back, a slight smile on his jaws. Those eyes, Zannez thinks. You wouldn't think black eyes could do all that, he should remember to use it. . . . When, fool? If this doesn't work out, he'll have one heartbroken boy on his hands. And what about Snake? Oh, gods. . . .

"Here comes your ride. Need help with that baggage?"

Bridey has jumped out and is hauling out stuffed duffels.

"Oh, no, thanks." She smiles at last; the sergeant backs into his friend. "They're just props." She tosses one up. "Fakes!"

"Nice meeting you." Zannez stops himself from reminding the sergeant not to forget; this isn't Gridworld. The sergeant doesn't look as if he forgot much.

The command car is driven by a hearty young Patrolwoman, Ralli. She and Bridey look at each other with obvious eagerness; Zannez can see about a tonne of temporarily suppressed questions each side.

Hanno gets in, radiating obliviously.

Snake sits quietly beside him, refraining from certain slyness with Hanno that the presence of a strange woman normally provokes him to.

"Snako, did I do right to hint about you? Do you want to decide this on your own? Or shall I . . ."

Snake smiles, a lopsided version of his sinister look. " 'Whither thou goeth . . .' "

"Huh?"

"Maybe it's 'goest' . . . old saying. Anyway, I will go, too . . . I've nothing for or against the Patrol. Even if I had . . ." He sighs, then breaks out a real grin. "Somebody's got to see our boy gets fed."

XX

TO
THE SUNRISE

Baram, who has gone ahead with Dayan, Kip, and Siri, is very anxious to get back to the hostel.

They've left Cory alone with a young lad, two unconscious women, and an amnesic girl. More than that, Baram is sure that Kip has no idea how severely stricken Cory may be. Kip wasn't able to see her clearly, beyond the whitening of her hair. Baram himself doesn't know precisely what's wrong, but he's seen enough of Cor to be very fearful. That gun in Vovoka's hand had not misfired, whatever she's told Kip.

Behind his fear for Cory lies a deeper, visceral fear for Linnix, that Baram can't shake. Superstitious idiot, he calls himself. Yet, after the early time-flurry, when he'd displaced that piece of cloth, that kerchief, it had come blowing back to its original position on gusts contrary to the steady *V'yrre* breeze.

No. Wonderful as it is to have Saul Dayan and his men

here instead of an angry, unpredictable Captain Race, Baram cannot be easy about Linnie's life—not until that beastly triple-barbed hypo now in his safe is somehow destroyed, made incapable of getting back to Linnie and killing her again. He has an idea about that.

They arrive at the hostel just as the first rays of *Yrrei* come towering up from the east. The sky is still quietly spectacular. Cut by the western horizon, the passing Star-front shows as a great contracting lens of multicolored light, fading up to the pale green zenith, that is embroidered with pearly filaments and tendrils of light. And there is a sense of change, of leaving, passing away, as the Star-light almost perceptibly withdraws.

As Baram looks, a disquiet touches him. *Is* something leaving? Something quite other than Nyil's life or Linnix' memory. Has something Star-borne been here that will soon be forever gone away?

His attention comes swiftly back to Damiem Hostel.

There's a quick view of Wyrra and Juiyn's treehouse as they enter the drive. It looks crowded. Several pairs of big wings are fanning from the porch, and Damei faces turn to the car. There seems to be a meeting going on.

As they pass the garage he glimpses two of Dayan's battle-clad marines checking it out. The third stands guard by the main doors.

As soon as the car comes to a halt, the driver's side snaps open apparently of its own volition, revealing little Pao holding a handsome salute.

"Meet our Commanding Officer, Liaison, Logistics, and Intelligence," Kip announces, laughing. "Prince Pao, meet Captain Saul Dayan."

Baram, watching, has seen the boy's face tighten at Kip's ebullience and gives thanks to the gods that Kip is too far to hug him or tousle his hair. A prince is a prince. But Dayan has spotted it, too, and gravely returns the salute as he gets out.

"Nicely judged, young man. The door, of course, I mean."
Pao's face melts into a smile. Baram's mystified.

"What?" ask Kip and Siri together.

"Tell them," says Dayan as they're helping Kip out.

Baram, taking medical license to push ahead, hears Pao say, "You exit a closed vehicle in inverse order of rank, as a usual thing. But I felt this was an operational situation where the commanding officer would wish to be first on the ground."

"Inverse *what*?"

"Don't sneer at protocol, Kipper. Our young friend's royal life will be full of it. All right, Ralli, back you go for the grid-show people. . . . Oh, great gods, what an unholy mess!"

Behind him, Dayan has seen the lounge.

The infirmary door cuts them off. Baram is just going through his quarters to the deck, when he sees Linnix in the shadows smiling at him.

She's too damn close to that safe where Ochter's scorpion is.

"Hello! Look—I know how this works!" And her hand goes to the knob, turning. There's a click. Gods! By pure chance she's hit the first mag point. With the sureness of sleepwalker she starts to spin it back. It all happens so fast that Baram, panicky, can do nothing but grab her arm and yank her away.

"Get out! Gods damn it! Get away from that, my dear—my dear Linnie, forgive me. I'll explain later—just for now, never, never go near that thing. Hear?" He shakes the arm, shakes her in his fright.

"Come." He's scared her. "It's all right, it's all right, dear, Come out with me." Oh, gods, if he'd been a minim later . . .

He pulls her with him out to the deck.

For an instant he thinks it's deserted, then sees Stareem on Kip's pad, holding her head over a basin. Beside her in the shadow is the shawled figure he knows is Cory.

"Hello, Bram—is Kip all right? Dayan sent word." The voice is Cor's and not Cor's. . . . He's heard such changes before.

"Hello, my dear—yes, everyone's fine. Kip's vision seems to be all cleared up."

She makes a strange little sound. "Then my small . . . stolen time . . . is over."

"What, Cor?"

"You'll see in a minim. Bram, can you do something for this poor girl's headache?"

Stareem peers up at him pleadingly. Of course, that Soporin leaves unpleasant effects.

"A minim. Linnie dear, stay out here."

He goes in for his kit. As he's getting it he hears Kip's voice from the deck outside.

"Hallo—hallo! Where's Cor?"

"This is Cor," the hollow voice replies. "Kip . . . my dear love . . . you might as well see it now."

Baram comes back out with a capsule and a drink for Stareem just as Cory is clumsily loosing the shawl. (Cory with fumbling hands?) It drops and she leans forward into the dawn light.

She is an old, white-haired woman, with lined and sagging face; her legs are veined and wrinkled, the knobby knees cruelly exposed by Cory's shorts.

"You—you're not Cor! Cory!" Kip tries to shout but his voice breaks.

"I *am* Cory, my dear. I . . . was. Vovoka didn't misfire—I let you believe that for a while. . . ." She draws a panting breath. "What it is, I'm . . . aging very fast . . . as well as I can estimate . . . a year or two per hour now. . . . He said I'd have time to say good-bye. . . . That means, Kip, that . . . some time tomorrow . . . I'll be dead of old age."

"Bram!"

It's a cry from Kip's heart, but Baram isn't hopeful. He goes to her, just as Siri comes out to join them.

But Cory waves them off, feeble but firm.

"Please," she gasps. "I know what's happening to me . . . quite well enough, Bram dear. Or do you . . . think you can reverse old age?"

Siri speaks up.

"I've heard two reports of effects like this, Myr Cory. Basically it's destruction of glandular function by selective resonance, at the atomic level. In one case mainly the pituitary was affected, and yes, we could reverse the effects by replacement therapy."

"That's it," Kip cries. "Do it! Get the stuff! Scooter, can we use your caller?"

"And the other case?" Cory's asking quietly.

"In the other, whole glandular systems were knocked out, and we couldn't help much. Now we need a blood sample from you, then we won't bother you anymore for a while. I can get the medication by emergency 'skip."

"Get it," Kip orders.

"All right." Cory makes the croak, or cackle, again. "But I don't think that alien. . . V-Vovoka"—she struggles for the name —"would have failed."

"Don't be gloomy, Cor. We'll have you out of this," Kip says heartily, not looking at her.

"Thank fortune you're here, Siri," says Baram. "I can take the sample, while you go signal Base."

Dayan has been standing to one side, quietly watching. Now as they hear the car come back, he nods to Siri. She follows him. Baram can hear Zannez admonishing his troupe as they enter the lounge.

"Wait, kids." The cameraman shows himself and bows briefly to Cory. "We'll be in our quarters if needed." He disappears, a tactful man.

"I'd like to go to my room, too, now, Bram," Cory says. "You can take the blood there. Kip . . . my dear, if you don't want to . . . look at me . . . or be with me . . . I truly understand."

"It's only for a while," Kip says. "I know my girl is there waiting."

"She . . . is," and Cory's old-woman chin quivers, the easy tears of age brim her sagged eyes. She veils herself, and Kip helps her rise. His touch is halting, as if he were forcing himself to touch something icy.

As Cory reveils herself Baram catches a glimpse of a familiar beauty-spot mole on her nape, and for one flash the young, vital Cory of yesterday is there. Next instant she's lost in the white-haired scarecrow figure of Cory-now. He finds himself close to tears.

"Oh wait." Baram remembers the sigil. "Cory, you should have this back."

"Give it to my . . . Deputy." She's trying hard to hold herself tall and walk well. "Tell . . . Dayan to notify Base, with Siri's opinion . . . *both* her opinions."

When the medical doings are over, Baram corners Pao and asks him a question. Then he goes to Dayan, who has made his first inspection of the dead.

"Sir, I am about to destroy some evidence. Or I should say, I intend to attempt to. The automatic hypo, that demonic so-called scorpion that Ochter put in Myr Linnix' neck. I think you should look at it first."

"Oh? And why are you going to destroy it, Baram?" Dayan's walking with him toward the lab. They pass Prince Pao.

"That's what I feel I can't explain to you fully until much more time has passed and we're safely off this planet. I think it's only safe now to say that the thing nearly ended her life once before, and there seems to be an affinity—an unnatural affinity between it and Linnie, that suggests to me that more than simple physical effects exist here. Such things are possible. You may call me farfetched, or impose any penalty you please, but the point is that I intend to disperse that thing down to its constituent atoms, right now, if possible."

Dayan considers. He respects Baram, but he's never seen him in this light. "Linnie?" Evidently more is at stake here than normal concern for Human life.

Baram pushes the lab door closed—it sticks, where he's been meaning to plane it—and goes to the safe.

"This is the thing." He puts it on the lab sink. "I'm going to call in young Pao. He thinks there's just enough charge left in that weapon of Vovoka's to destroy a small object at close range."

The scorpion, fully revealed, is even more hideous with its vicious triple barbs besmeared with blood and ichor.

"Nasty piece of work. . . . No, I don't believe the investigators will miss it."

"Oh, I didn't tell you, I photographed it. Do you agree there's no point in looking for fingerprints or other body traces?"

"Agreed."

Baram opens up and calls the prince in: they position the thing on an expendable box, before the dense metal splashboard.

"All set. I'll turn it so the barbs at least will go— Oh, damn!"

The door is pushing open.

"Excuse me," says Linnix. "I know you don't want me to come in here, but Myr Cory sent me—"

"Get out!" Baram yells, rushing at her. "I don't care if the gods themselves sent you—get away!" There's a tiny clink.

In his haste to get her out, Baram doesn't notice that the scorpion has caught in his sleeve. When it appears on the ground by the door he almost screams.

Linnix, frightened, is pulling the door to. Baram bangs it shut and sighs relief—and then sees that the scorpion is gone. Somehow his foot or the door must have knocked it away. He looks around the floor.

Nothing.

It takes him a horrified minim to realize that he must have knocked it *outside* with Linnix when he banged the door.

Oh, no—no—*no*.

"Linnie! Linnie!" he yells, wrestling with the sticky door.

She's about two meters away, stooping curiously over the wicked thing. Her hand going down—

"No! No, darling! No!" Baram can only throw himself bodily on the hook. Linnix stumbles backward in alarm as his arms and body knock her away.

And the worst pain he's ever felt tears through him from the barbs in his chest. "Aaiiee! Ah—" He rolls and kicks in agony; dimly through the pain he is startled to find he can't draw breath.

A moment—or a year—later he has a temporary, precarious control. Someone is bending over him. The pain is unrelenting.

"Go," he gasps, "go into my—lab cooler—bottle, top shelf—labeled—aah-aah! Oh, forgive me—label—"

"Yes, bottle in cooler top shelf. Don't you want morphine?" It's Siri.

"No! No morphine. Al-alg—" He can't say it. "Bottle, label WYRRA. W-Y-R-R-A. Try, fast. *Please*— Aaii-oh—"

An eternity later the bottle is swimming before his eyes. He's afraid he's been yelling and groaning shamelessly. How did Linnie stand it? . . . Bottle, WYRRA, a blur of dates.

"Yes! Pour on pad—apply—don't waste," he gets out between screams.

Another eternity . . .

. . . And then the most blessed ease he's ever felt, the truest, purest no-pain, spreads through him. A sweet familiar smell fills his nose.

He closes his jaw, blinks, finds Siri has bared his chest and is holding gauze to it. He can't help smiling, beaming. Beautiful Siri. Beautiful world.

He looks around at quite a lot of people, all beautiful. Dayan is somewhere.

"I'm going to surprise you," he tells Siri and Dayan. "Two surprises. The stuff—on the barb—is Algotoxin. Algo-toxin," he repeats as Ochter had. "It's been remade on a Black World."

"Algot—" Siri breaks off, obviously remembering. "Oh, *no*."

"Yes. And you know the pain can't be stopped. But it *was* stopped." He still feels wonderful but awfully weak.

"I saw it happen once before. Linnie—" He finds her sitting on the floor on his other side, holding his hand. "Linnie had a bad dose of that pain. Twice the lethal dose, almost. But she—you, darling, you rolled on that tabard Yule had been wearing when he scraped the Dameii's backs. It had that sweet smell. It was their nectar, the secretions of their back glands. And it stopped your pain, Linnie. . . . *It stopped the pain of Algotoxin*. Do you understand what that means? Siri?"

"Yes," she says, very gravely.

"Dayan, maybe you can't. She'll tell you. . . .

"I collected the nectar during medical procedures . . . where there was pain. Wyrra and others let me sop their backs. We hoped, if we could get enough to analyze and synthesize, it would stop the Stars Tears horror forever. . . .

"As to the Algotoxin . . . I was going to experiment . . . I guess I *did* experiment. Very messily. Sorry, all." He's about to go to sleep but remembers he can't and struggles against Siri to sit up.

"I've got to destroy that thing! What did you do with it?" He stares wildly around, holding Linnix by the arm.

"Rest easy, Baramji." It's Dayan's voice. "The thing is destroyed. The lad and I carried out your plan; the whole thing is in vapor, gone. It can't do any more damage."

As Barem lets himself slip off, his next to last thought is that many decades from now, a frozen hunk of painfully regathered molecules might come blasting down from space through some planet's atmosphere, to intersect with Linnix. No help for that . . . best they could do.

His last thought is that Linnie's eyes look different. Better. Vaguely, as he drifts off, he hears her say, "Doctor Bram, I think—I think I've . . ."

An hour later, he is awake and in Cory's room, with Kip and Dayan, at her request. The morning light is clear gold green. Prince Pao comes as far as the door; when Cory hears his voice she asks him to come in, too. She's on the bed, fully dressed and shawled. Only the silver of her hair can be seen clearly through the gauzy stuff.

"This is intended as business, not an emotional orgy," she says clearly, and chuckles in nearly her old way. "Bram, thanks for the stim-shot. It helps. . . . I think I got the weepy stage over last night. One comes through, you know. Now I need to dispose of a couple of decisions . . . that you'll have to make otherwise."

Kip stirs, says vigorously, "Cut it out, Cor. Rest now, for the gods' sake."

"Let me speak, Kip dearest. Please . . . I know you believe this is reversible—but if it's not, I don't want to leave loose ends."

Kip grunts, folds his arms, and looks away.

"The matter of Vovoka. We spoke, you know," she tells Kip's stony face, "after you were knocked out. I believe he was a fine, honorable being, and the very last of a great race. In his tragic end, he tried to be kind. His body mustn't be— Saul, Captain Dayan, I leave it to you to see that his body is laid away with honor. Unless we find other instructions in his effects, I suggest Damiem's moon, where he will be nearest the place his world was. And please—this is a strong wish— don't use a short coffin because of his, his condition. I believe that Myr Zannez must have images of him as he truly was. Put it to him to provide good ones for the burial place. Will you undertake this, too, Saul?"

"I will. And we'll put his effects with him. . . . Last of his race—it's a terrible thought. You've met a being from history."

"Yes," she says. "People who hear of the Star may visit his tomb.

"Now, me. . . . Yes, Kip, please. Even if you think it's all nonsense. I'd like my body to be—do we have the resources to stick me up there on this moon, too? I'd love to think I was in sight of the world of the happiest years I've ever had. Oh, Kip, please. My dear, what will you do with me, if I'm right—or if I die of the treatment? Or if I stub my toe dancing for joy and bash my head in? I guess they'll put that chore up to you, too, Saul. What do you say?"

"I say yes, will do. If necessary. . . . Near or far from Vovoka? After all, he may be your murderer, Cory."

"Near. Funny, I don't feel murdered. I feel it was just the end of what I started at fourteen. It *is* odd," she says reflectively. "I've had such a busy life; if you asked me—yesterday—I'd been Administrator here, and Deputy on Herrick's, and had an expedition to Hundanaro Vortex and all the rest. Years and years of exciting work. But to anybody on the worlds who ever thinks of me, I'll always be only the cabin girl on *Deneb* who pulled the trigger that killed the Star. It's possible . . . to do something in your childhood that changes and dominates your whole life. Prince?" Her head turns restlessly, then she sees Pao.

He's obviously sleepy, but he straightens and nods gravely. "Yes, Myr Cory."

"If you wish any words of aged wisdom, I'd say, everything you do in your youth, everything that happens, *counts*.

"One last thing." She's tiring, Bram sees. The shot he's given her is wearing out. He hopes he hasn't put too much of a strain on the damaged adrenergic system. But a person is a mind, too, and Cory had demanded it.

"Zannez. . . . There's a reward for warnings, information

650

about Stars Tears raids. No one but me knows that it should go to Zannez. Yes. He warned me clearly. I was too busy to do more than listen, but he was right. His data were purely subjective, he simply perceived them as criminal types who came here deliberately, and knew the Tears were here . . . but he has a history of such perceptions and I . . . should have listened. Will you, Kip or Saul, raise the question of the reward and see it goes to Zannez? I think he can use it. . . . And my failure to heed him could have cost their lives."

"Right," Kip says briskly. "Old Zannez will appreciate that. His team is breaking up."

"Now . . . if I *am* irrevocably aging, I want everybody to carry out their normal lives around me just as you would . . . if I were aging slower. No . . . long faces and tiptoeing and whispering . . . right? And I want you to serve the Ice Flowers tonight. I'd like some. . . .

"And finally—Kip, it's about you. If you ever wonder what . . . Cory would have wanted—" She makes an effort, her voice clears. "Remember Cory would want you to be happy. Really happy. That's not just sentimental. Kip, you're one of those people who should be happy in order to be you. . . . You function best, you're most valuable then. Bram, Saul, never let him make himself miserable because of me. Hear, Kip?"

As Kip squirms uneasily she manages a little laugh. "Darling, you're a booby trap for any woman with eyes—the temptation to make you happy is irresistible." She tries to laugh again but ends in a fit of feeble coughing.

"We've got it, Cor," Baram says. "Time to rest now."

"Overtime!" says Kip. "If you want me happier, stop this and rest till the drugs come."

"Right. I'm finished. . . . Thank you, all." She lets herself sink back. Baram, touching her hand to say good-bye, hears her whisper, "I wonder . . . is it possible? . . . No."

She means there's no hope. Despite himself, Baram agrees.

He and Dayan and Pao go out; Siri passes them going in.

She's taking charge until Baram can get some rest. Nobody on Damiem has had any true sleep that night—except Stareem, who can be heard, leaning on the parapet in the morning sunlight, singing and strumming her little zither. *"We have made it, we have made it to the sunrise."*

Pao goes to her.

It's a beautiful Damiem morning, framed in the unreal rim of Star-light. Kip comes out after them, unspeaking, until he lifts his head sharply and makes a faint sound in his throat. Baram looks, and sees a young, brown-haired trooper, arms loaded, looking for an instant like Cor . . . Cory-that-was. What's left of Cory now is in there behind them, on her bed. . . . Hard to believe. Kip doesn't believe it yet, Baram fears. The gods send he's right.

Half an hour later, Baram has dragged a lounger into Linnix' small room. He's so exhausted he doesn't feel sleepy. Nor, seemingly, does Linnix; her eyes have a wide, unseeing abstraction he doesn't like, as if she looked upon private dread.

And that's just what must be happening, he thinks. She's told him she was remembering. At first it seemed to be a good experience, coming to herself, but now the darker side of the past could be coming through.

Her silence, her air of aloneness, bothers him. This must be what her life was like—solitary, stoic endurance of whatever hurt. That can't go on. But how to break through? Is she withdrawing from him now as a stranger—she, who'd been so childlike and confiding when her memory was gone?

Or is it deeper, more chilling—the difficulty of pulling her whole self from a reality that killed her, to this reality of life? Despite himself, he shudders a little. He has actually fought Death bare-handed, has reshaped reality itself to bring her here. And he'd accepted the scorpion's pain to keep her; that counts as nothing, but it gives him an idea.

"Linnie, it strikes me we have something in common that

652

no one else has. Not that it's very nice. Excepting whatever poor devils Ochter and company experimented on, you and I are the first Humans in generations to know what Algotoxin feels like. Of course, you got it worse than I, but I got the idea. My dear, I knew it was terrible—but believe it or not, I'm glad now I've shared it.''

"Oh, *no,* Bram—''

"Yes. You know my one thought was, How did Linnie stand this?''

"I didn't,'' she says. "I was awful.''

"You saw *me.* Remember how I yelled? That's another reason I'm glad. You're a proud girl, you might get some insane idea you were cowardly. I don't normally holler, either.''

She's looking at him, really at him now.

"And to be at the mercy of that monster . . .'' he reflects. "Gods!''

She gulps. "I—I kept telling myself he wasn't Human—it was like being attacked by a crazy alien, or a w-wild animal—'' Her voice breaks, her hands cover her face.

"Ohh, I wanted to die—the *shame*—''

"Linnie, Linnie darling, look at me.'' He's out of the lounger on his knees beside her, gently pulling down her hands. "You did it—now it's all over, it's all right—''

"No!'' And the flood breaks; for the second time she's weeping in his arms. But this is a different weeping; raw, uncontainable. "But I pulled it out, I did, didn't I? I pulled it out?'' The sobs stop as she looks at him anxiously for confirmation.

"You certainly did, my dear. You frightened me out of my skin.'' He smiles tentatively. "I knew you didn't have that red hair for nothing.''

Answering small smile. He's so pleased he fails to see the danger.

"F-funny,'' she says. "You really can't remember pain. I

653

can remember what I *did*—yelling and k-kicking around—but I can't remember the *feeling*. Can you?''

"No. And that's good. Let it lie.''

"I . . . I just fainted, didn't I?''

Too late, he sees where this is leading.

"Yes. You fainted. A momentary syncope due to hypertension and general trauma. Anybody would have. And now I suggest we let this topic go, my dear.''

"Yes . . . I just remembered how great it felt when the pain stopped, and the sweet smell.'' She sniffs. "And trying to fight you or something when you said, 'Move.' And bumping—being bumped along. My tail's sore.'' She laughs, and he thinks it's all right, but then she frowns.

"Bram, we were in—there was a time-flurry going on, wasn't there?''

"I don't recall,'' he gets out, sick with dread. "Linnie, I want you to think of something else, right now. Think—think of being an officer again. I'm serious, darling.''

But she mutters, "I think there was, a time-flurry, I mean. Something . . . queer. I wonder—''

"Stop it, Linnie!'' he shouts. Gods, is she going to talk herself dead, the damned redheaded little fool darling? "Linnix! Stop it, do what I tell you, right now this instant. What—'' He forces his voice down. "What was the name of the last world you stopped at? Tell me.''

"We didn't stop.'' She's stubborn: her gaze is inward again, he can't get through.

"Linnie, I know it's hard to stop yourself thinking, but if you're an officer, you have to have the self-discipline to do it. Can you? I tell you, it's necessary, and I can't tell you why. Later you'll understand. Right now, *if you value our lives*, you'll turn your mind away from—from what you were saying. And keep it turned away until I tell you it's safe. Hear me? Hear me, Linnie darling?''

She looks at him opaquely.

The terror of the threat—it's as if some personal enemy

keeps trying to return and kill her, using now her very mind. This isn't Linnie alone, he thinks. The force of that other reality is pressing on her, pressing her to know herself dead. And die again, for good, in his arms. He trembles, fighting away from the thought of how she had lain thus before. Maybe the very act of holding her is too much like, is dangerous. He makes himself let her go and sits back. Yes. Better.

"I'll help you. What was the name of the Moom captain on your last ship?"

"There wasn't any."

"No captain? Honey, how can that be?"

Very reluctantly, she amplifies. "The loser, I think has to be captain."

"Loser? What loser? *Tell* me, Linnie." He would have listened to her recite timetables if it would keep her mind off that terrible quarter hour.

He takes her through what she knows of the Moom Life-Game: it comes out in stiff sentences that only gradually relax. When the topic seems exhausted he realizes that he and she are, too—in fact, they're both stunned silly with fatigue. He hitches the lounger over and rests an arm on the pillow beside her flaming head, tentatively smiles down. Suddenly she grins up at him, the old Linnix again. He's inexpressibly warmed.

"Oh, Doctor Bram, I'm such a—I *know* you've done so much, and I . . . I . . . I think I love you."

Is this gratitude? Or Daddy? He's too tired for tact. "What about your father, all that searching?"

"Strange . . ." She smiles pensively. Somehow they've moved so he's more or less beside her on the bed.

"What's strange, darling girl?"

"I remember all that, I really do—Beneborn, the Sperm-ovarium, Lintz-Holstead . . . Were you really on Beneborn, or did I dream that?"

655

He takes a breath. How much hangs on this? But he's too tired to think; the truth wins.

"No."

She squints at him, then reaches for both his hands. "Say again?"

"What? Oh. No, I never was, I'm sure."

She nods, letting his hands go. "Oh, Bram, when you said all those things, and I thought you meant them—and then I saw your fingers!"

"My fingers . . . what about them?"

"Crossed."

"Oh . . . oh, gods, if Ochter—"

"But he didn't." Her eyelids are drooping.

"You were saying . . . about Lintz-Holstein . . ."

"Like a story," she says sleepily. "As if it . . . happened to somebody else."

The force with which he exclaims, "Oh, darling, darling!" wakes her briefly. "Then you'll come . . . with me . . . r'search," he concludes, and just catches himself falling asleep on her neck.

As he struggles up, her breathing changes; she's asleep, too. He collapses into the lounger and knows nothing more.

An unknown time later a nightmare of paraplegia wakes him. Linnix is sleeping peacefully. But one of his legs is numb and his old shoulder wounds hurt. The lounger has developed strange lumps and horrid angles; he's cramped all over.

Kaffy, he thinks. A nice cup of hot kaffy. He'll go make it.

But when he gets up he stands gazing down at the girl in bed. His girl now. His Linnie, sleeping hard. She sleeps attractively, rosy and warm amid that wonderful hair. The bandage on her neck is untouched.

He's pretty sure, now, that he'll have many nights and days to look at her so. And to shepherd her through: she mustn't be left alone for a while. His long leave is overdue,

656

he can go tomorrow. But where? There's his research to do, the Damei nectar and its miraculous neutralizing effect on Algotoxin pain. Maybe one of the Hyades schools will give him lab space. But it's sensitive; he'll have to take a lot of security precautions. The Hyades rumor mill works overtime. Not ideal. He rubs his stiff shoulder, pondering effortfully.

Kaffy.

He stoops and touches his lips to her sweet, sleep-scented mouth and stumbles out into Damiem's noon light. Thankful that no one is about, he makes it to his red-cross door.

The infirmary smells alive—that's right, Siri was working here. He dreads what she's found. But that's for later.

As he's brewing up the kaffy, he imagines Linnix in the musty but splendid bridal robes of his House, becoming the Aphra Bye. When he takes her back to Broken Moon, on one of his rare, brief visits. He has told her a little of his home world.

On Broken Moon, he is no longer Doctor Baramji, XMD, but *the* ap of Bye, fifth Balthasar, ninth Baramji, and nominal owner of the vast estates of the Clan Bye.

Like all of Broken Moon, Bye is rich only in tradition and gorgeously rugged scenery, relieved by occasional glens in which half-civilized clansmen raise Terran-hybrid sheep. Its chief exports, aside from a special wool, are rugged young people who want to do something other than sit in unheated castles adjudicating the squabbles of the yeomanry and planning the endless tourneys, jousts, and games that have more or less replaced the clan wars. Luckily he has a blood cousin who is content to occupy the Seat of Bye while Baram works in the Galaxy. But his few visits home are occasion for endless ceremonies of fealty. Linnie can take it—and she'll make a resplendent Aphra. . . . He smiles, thinking of red hair.

The kaffy is ready—but a vague sense of trouble from the marquise's room is making itself felt. Oh, no. . . . But he'd better check. Groggily he sets the kaffy down after one sip and goes through the connecting door.

The bed is empty, open and cold to the touch. A trail of lacy bedding shows where the Lady has staggered away. It leads toward the golden crib in the corner, with its cold freight . . . gods.

He goes to it.

What he feared is there. Lying beside Loma's body, her finger in her mouth, is the Lady Pardalianches.

"Marquise! Lady, Lady—Pardie!"

Despite the massive load of tranquilizers in her system, she blinks at his call.

" 'Oma," she mumbles around her finger, essaying to smile. " 'Oma . . ." and something that sounds like "at last." There's a rictus smile on dead Loma's face, too—the sight is grisly.

Baram looks closer: the Lady's pupils are unevenly dilated. Real trouble here. On impulse he bends to inspect the controls on those golden caps.

What he sees makes him curse himself for negligence again. He should have torn that cap off the corpse, and off the Lady as well.

Somehow she has managed to turn the power way up. And has lain there "receiving" from a dead, disintegrating brain, for who knows how long.

Receiving death through that cap.

Clumsy with fatigue, he slams the controls off, and as gently as he can, over the Lady's agitated flailing, he finds the cap deep in her hair and pulls it from her scalp. She lolls back on his hands during the process, still sucking her finger, and is asleep before he gets it free.

What to do? He can't leave them thus, living and dead, and no one seems to be stirring. Is there no end to this? He goes out the arcade door and into the lounge.

Two of Dayan's men are cleaning up, and Dayan himself is working on his report at a side table.

Baram explains his problem.

"There's a fridge compartment in *Comet*," Dayan tells him, "and we have body bags here. Jordan can transport the dead woman to the ship right now. You can leave the other poor creature where she is; I'll ask Siri to get clean bedding on her. And you go back to sleep, Baram."

"My fault, my fault," Baram mutters.

"Shut up and go to sleep and forget it," Saul Dayan says. "You're clean pizzled out of your mind."

The comfortable drawl has its effect on Baram. Maybe he is a little irrational. As he's told so many students, nobody can do everything for everybody, everywhere, all the time.

He picks up his kaffy and takes himself back to the lounger in Linnie's room. Pity that bed isn't wider.

He thinks of his own bed, and of the fact that the scorpion is destroyed. Be rational, he tells himself. She's sleeping like a rock. He lets his mouth brush Linnie's cheek and turns to go back and sleep in his own place.

But as he goes out he glances toward Ochter's room, only one door away. Unspeakable little devil, Ochter; his hellish fate doesn't melt Baram's loathing. That scorpion hostage act must have been his fallback plan, in case the drugged wine didn't work. . . . But one hostage wouldn't have been enough to control them all, if Vovoka hadn't stunned them. Ochter must have planned on capturing the group. How? No telling how. But perhaps, just perhaps—are there *more* scorpions in his luggage? . . . It's so near, so close . . . and people will be opening those bags.

Without noticing it, Baram has turned and is gathering up a pad, a blanket, pillows, with numb hands.

Be rational: too much is at stake.

Back in Linnix' room he lets down the back of the lounger and lays the padding. Really quite a decent cot. He kisses Linnie's brow again, collapses onto the lounger, and gratefully lets go of consciousness.

* * *

Two hours later, while the Damiem people are sleeping, the parcel of hormones shrieks into upper-atmosphere orbit and is remote-landed from *Comet*.

And an hour after that, Siri, completing the analysis of Cory's blood samples in Baram's little lab, realizes that any attempt at therapy is useless. Vovoka's weapon was sophisticated, lethal; whole glandular complexes are missing from his victim's system, and there's other damage she can't define.

Cory's little speech was necessary after all. She may see Damiem's sun rise tomorrow, but she will never see it set.

XXI

STAR'S
SONG

When Damiem's long afternoon sends up blue-and-gold reflections from the lake, Saul Dayan, in the hostel's cool, newly cleaned lounge, finishes his report. It's in written form; he doesn't trust what the vocoder printout makes of his accent. And he likes the stable feel of a document in hand.

He's been conscious of a gentle presence in the room. Now he looks up and sees that the little silver-haired girl he's come to know as Stareem is leaning on the bar, watching him. Ah, yes, she's the one who was unconscious through it all. Even prettier than her knife-throwing friend, too.

He smiles. "Hello."

"Please, sir . . ." She has a gentle, clear voice. "If I'm not bothering you . . . I wonder if you could tell me—I mean, I slept through the whole thing. Only I had bad dreams." She shivers a little. "First that alien stunned us and then Doctor B. had to drug me. They explained that—but I still don't really understand. What were those men trying to do to us? I mean, why didn't that Ochter person kill us all right then while he had the chance, if he was going to? I mean, I'm not sorry he didn't, but I don't *understand*.''

"Well . . ." Dayan respects the appeal for clarity. Somewhere under the extravagant looks is a Human mind. "The answer is a mite gruesome, Myr Stareem."

"That's all right." The chilling Gridworld maturity behind the child's face.

"H'mm. Well, he planned to blow the place up, you see. Going to overload the power-cell down below. Seems Hiner had done demolition study, too—we ran onto manuals on power-cells in among those music tapes. That way Ochter hoped to get away clean; he hoped the blast would make such a mess-up that a few bodies wouldn't be missed. Probably would've worked, because there'd only be one absent. Ochter said he figured to cool off his little helpers after they finished the job for him."

"I see—but I still don't see—"

"Why he didn't do you in right then? Well, he knew there'd be an investigation. And it would look pee-culiar if folk's flesh was found to be full of poison, and dead for a day or so too long."

"He was keeping us fresh." She nods, satisfied, and then shudders despite herself. "Oh, my—and Doctor Baram and the others saved us all while I just slept."

"Best thing you could have done," says Dayan gruffly.

While they're talking, the small figure of Prince Pao comes down the stairs, rubbing his eyes. He bows to Dayan and advances to Stareem, takes her hand, and kisses it lightly, to Dayan's amusement. Kip has told him of the boy's devotion to Stareem. Fine smile the lad has, he thinks, catching the scent of what's doubtless very expensive cologne. Pao's three-plumed gold cap is tucked under his arm. Quite the little dandy.

"My dear, I'm sorry I left you alone so long."

"No problem. Want some juice?" She goes to the bar cooler.

"It's good practice for her," Pao says confidentially to Dayan. "She doesn't get much solitude. On Pavo I shan't be with her as much as I'd like."

This sounds serious, on the part of the future monarch of Pavo. "You plan to take her away from, ah, Gridworld?"

"Yes. I believe it's time now—thanks, Myr Star." He drains the glass at a gulp.

"I'll get more. And how about saniches? I see some that look like cheese."

"Goody-o!" Pao plunks himself down at the table beside Dayan, suddenly a boy eager for food. "Yes," he tells Dayan. "She's had adequate experience now. On Pavo it's customary for young ladies to have full sex training before the happiness of love and marriage. Young men, too, of course. And Star needs to go to school for a proper education. Including music— Oh, that looks fine," he breaks off, opening the huge sanich Star has put before him. Between bites he explains to Dayan, "Myr Star's untutored things are quite lovely, but one really can't stay untutored on Pavo long—we discussed all that, Myr Star."

"Yes," she says gravely. "I'd love it." She bows her head, thinking, then suddenly bursts out at Pao, "Do you *really* mean it? I mean, joking's fine, but I— And Zanny says—" Her huge eyes are like a wild thing's, wondering whom to trust.

The boy gives Dayan a man's look—or a mother's—as if to say, "Isn't she a gem?" He takes her hand.

"Did you think I was joking, my Star? I assure you I'm not. And with all respect to Myr Zannez, as regards Pavo or me he doesn't understand much. I suggest you listen to *me,* from here on. I am really, really serious."

"Ohhh." The eyes melt, brim. Then she ducks her head and says very low, "You won't be when you know my real name. It's awful. It's—Sharon. Or Sharone."

"Oh, I know all that," Pao says airily, Superboy again. "It's Sharon Roebuck, to be precise. When our Special Information Branch saw I was interested in this APC person, they looked into you. Very thoroughly. They were able to trace Star's mother," he tells Dayan. "On Pavo we feel it's essential to observe how a young lady's mother ages. More often than not, it gives advance notice of what the young lady will become. Of course, it's not infallible"— he digs into his sanich—"but Star should age very acceptably, given better care."

Star's hands are at her throat.

"But my mother's dead. They always told me she'd died."

Pao swallows hurriedly. "I forgot, my dear. Of course, this is a shock." With surprising gentleness he says, "Myr Roebuck is indeed dead now. I'm sorry, my Star. She was in very difficult circumstances, which I was able to improve without her knowledge. We think she was unaware that she was breeding babies for a flesh mart. Your father we don't know for sure: it's been narrowed to three possibilities, all—"

"Babies?" Star interrupts. "You mean I have brothers and sisters? Oh—"

"None living, my dear. Oh, I am sorry—I didn't mean to drop it on you this way." He looks in appeal at Dayan, who's engrossed by the little drama. "She'd have to know sometime, and she has friends here."

Dayan nods agreement. "Right."

The lad's fluency and seriousness have so diverted him that he can't believe he's not dealing with a much older person. But Pao looks in all respects like a normal, healthy lad of ten or twelve, who will be shooting up taller soon. And the voice in which he speaks his grown-up words hasn't changed yet.

"Myr Roebuck lived, ah, near the spaceport," Pao continues after another bite.

Dayan nods. That's by custom defined as the worst area on most planets.

"And two of the children perished from the effects of the fuel dump. Then, there was a tragic crash—not on the regular lines," he clarifies to Dayan.

But Star gets it. "Oh. A *Black World*!" she cries.

"I'm afraid so." Pao puts his sanich down carefully to reach up and pat Star's shoulder. "Be brave, my dear. I know you will. This doesn't affect anything." He smiles winningly and waits for her answering smile before taking up the sanich. "Look at it this way, my Star . . . as the SI Branch said, those tragedies preserved them from miserable lives." A pause for bites. "Your own life was only saved by your promise of beauty and a series of incredibly lucky accidents."

Zannez has come quietly in from the arcade stretching and rubbing his arms; he overhears the last. He nods at Dayan, then nods again because what Pao said is so true: he recalls that Gridworld night, and the thing on a rope.

"Morning, all—or is it evening? Gods, I'm stiff. Getting old. Where does that juice come from, Star?"

"I'll get," she says. "More saniches, Prince Pao?"

"Yes, please. And you don't have to use my title, Myr Star, except on formal occasions, of course."

Dayan and Zannez find themselves looking at each other blankly. Zannez rolls up his eyes.

"Just what is your status with respect to these young people, Myr Zannez?" Dayan asks thoughtfully.

"Contractual. Contractual employer." Zannez puts a foot up on a chair to rub his leg. " 'Scuse me."

"Contracts with their parents or guardians, I reckon?"

"No. With them."

"And he's great to us," calls Star from the cooler. "He's not like the others. We love Zannie."

"They seem a mite young to be self-employed," Dayan persists. "How old is that little girl?"

"Thirteen, going on fourteen." Zannez pauses in his rub-

665

bing and looks at the floor as he says, "On Gridworld kids of five can sign valid contracts."

"Valid? You mean to say, a court would enforce it?"

"All the courts. . . . A few are starting to require the employer to show the kid continues in good health, or is getting treatment for whatever."

Dayan digests this a minim and then says mildly, "Seems like the Federation might blacklist your Gridworld one day."

Zannez laughs, not merrily. "Oh, they can't. That's been tried. Their people demand our product."

Prince Pao is consuming his second lot of saniches. Now he licks his fingers judiciously, saying, "Naturally, I intend to purchase Myr Star's contract from you, Myr Z., if you will."

"Why not? Oh, lords, I'm a softy. The team is bust. I'm letting Snake and Hanno go to the Patrol."

"I reckon you don't have a choice there," says Dayan dryly. "Enlistments if accepted take precedence over civil contracts. But I'm real glad the parting's friendly."

"Oh, sure it is . . . but I'll never see another team like that again."

Dayan remembers Cory's requests. "I'm not sure you'll need to, Myr Cameraman. Anybody tell you yet about the reward?"

"The reward? What reward for what? Nobody's even seen the doc—the documentary."

Dayan laughs. "This isn't for any picture show. It's for something you said to Myr Cory. You best talk with her." He bethinks himself. "When you go to, ah, say your farewells."

There was a short silence.

"Yeah," says Zannez. "Thanks, Captain. . . . So! You young ones are all set. Wait a minim. I'm as close as Star has to a father, so I better ask you what you plan to do with her on Pavo, Prince? She'd best stay with me rather than be abandoned on a strange planet."

"Oh, no danger of that. I respect your interest, Myr Zannez"—Pao selects a sausage sanich—"and you will receive formal documents, plus a periodic report, if you wish. I plan to appoint Myr Star Royal Concubine A. That's a constitutionally protected position—all the royal concubines and consorts are. I have a copy of our Constitution, if you'd like—"

"Great—but not now," Zannez rubs his neck.

"You'll receive one, of course. Later on, she will move to the position of Senior Hostess, Hostess A, that is, on the informal side. She'd think up things and find talented people . . . we do an awful lot of royal entertaining," he groans, suddenly boyish. "Part of the diplomacy." He pounces on a ripe *lopin* fruit.

Zannez frowns. "Informal, eh? . . . I get it." He takes a *lopin*. "What's 'consorts'?"

"Well, if Myr Star proves to have other talents and passes the exams, I'd love to have her as Royal Consort One. Otherwise I have to choose betwen Alwyn and Jo's Paradise—two of our client worlds—they both have, uh, marriageable daughters." He sighs. "I have to see a lot of whoever's Consort Number One, you see. And she gets a try at bearing the heir. Later on, she becomes Senior Hostess Number One on the *formal* side." He sighs again. "The statuses—A, B, or One, Two, Three, whatever—are for life. It's all planned and programmed, it's part of our diplomatic work. . . . It isn't as though we were having fun," he says wistfully. To console himself, he selects another *lopin* fruit.

"Hm'm," says Zannez. "Hm'm! . . . Well, how does that sound to you, Star? I'm not selling you off against your will, Star baby."

"He's told me a little about it before," she says, wide-eyed. "I thought he was joking. It sounds coloss."

"Never, my Star," says Pao. "And by the way, that's a word we want out."

"What? 'Coloss'?"

667

"Yes. Horrible."

"I've a lot to learn," she says humbly.

"Yes. But you'll make it. I've observed you learning acts."

"You were *watching* me," she says wonderingly.

"I wonder what else is in that cooler," says Zannez. "Will you join me, Prince?"

Pao needs no urging. But as they're uncovering dishes of spiced *bicklets* he sighs heavily again.

"Anything wrong?"

"As soon as Doctor Baram awakes I must apologize."

"What for? Oh—the 'blunder.' Want to tell us?"

"Why not?" The boy seems genuinely depressed. "Dreadful. . . . Captain Dayan, it was my fault Myr Linnix was trapped by that despicable man. If only I'd been on time. . . ."

"What'd you do," Zannez asks, "stop to pee?"

"Much worse. When I went down to Yule and Hiner's room, on the roof, I stupidly blundered right into one of the nets they must have used on the Dameii. Unforgivable. I've been trained on them and Myr Kip actually mentioned nets. And I trod right in." He makes a disgusted noise and fiercely bites a *bicklet*. "I still have pieces of it on me."

"Nets. You mean those sticky, stick-tights? They're illegal."

"That's right. You're acquainted with them?"

"We used one in a show one time; we had to cut three people loose. Almost choked to death. . . . They cost, too."

"They must have jerked. That tightens them."

"It cursed well does. . . . How'd you ever get loose?"

"I have been trained, you know. This thing was on the eaves; Yule or Hiner must've fired it and missed. I could have spotted it if I'd sighted along at foot level, as is correct. But I was *sloppy*." He's really angry at himself, Dayan sees. It occurs to him that the lad could become quite a little tyrant if Star doesn't take whatever lessons she'll be given seriously.

"*Overconfidence*," Pao is saying grimly. "There I was in midstep, with one leg up—it took me nearly ten minim to get

668

that foot down—and another half hour to get at my knife. You have to move slowly—slowly—slowly—slowly—and all the time I knew I must hurry. It was horrible. The only thing I can say is," he tells Dayan, "I didn't tighten it once."

Dayan nods. "Good."

"Even when you get your knife you have to know how to cut," he explains to Zannez. "Whew! I've certainly learned a lesson, but at what terrible price to Myr Linnix and Doctor Baram—and the little Damei child."

"It could happen to anybody," says Zannez. But Pao ignores him. Pao doesn't identify with "anybody," Dayan sees.

"Unforgivable," Pao says again, and chews for a minim in silence. "I must make my confession to Doctor Baram and Myr Linnix. But how can I make it up to them?" He's suddenly an appealing boy again.

Dayan is listening interestedly to the future royalty of Pavo reproaching itself while consuming a monstrous meal. The appetite is certainly that of a boy. Could it be that General Federation educational standards are a trifle low?

"I know!" says Pao, swallowing briskly. "It won't be adequate, but it's something." He pursues a last *bicklet* methodically. "The doctor should really get some leave after this. And I believe Myr Linnix will go with him, don't you?"

"Looks that way," says Zannez. "I don't see her taking up as a Log Officer again right now."

"Yes, that's what I thought. So I could invite them both to Pavo. I have to return, you know." He grimaces. "They can just relax and rest—or maybe he has some research to do." He takes his plate neatly to the bar, then opens the cooler for another look. "He could use our facilities. I'm told they're quite good." He brings a dish of sweet dessert to the table.

"I bet they are." Zannez stretches, extends his legs, and

rubs his lower back. "Never again. Hey, Prince, how did you like our act?"

"I was most impressed." Suddenly he chucks his maturity. "Beautiful! As Star would say, coloss! Oh, how I wish I could do that. Especially—" He sketches a no-hands spin in the air with his spoon. "Can you do that?"

"No more. I could once, that's what you learn when you're too broke to afford a double. I taught Snake."

"You did?" Pao thinks a minim. "Could you teach me?"

"Yes, I'm pretty sure. But Prince, it's not too safe. You can take some spills."

"No matter. A modicum of real danger is thought essential to royal education. And skis and horses bore me. I'm entitled to choose." He draws himself up, grinning. "Myr Zannez, I hereby invite you to Pavo for a tour as Royal Tutor in Advanced Gymnastics—all expenses paid. How about it?"

Zannez, eyebrows high, mumbles something about his contract and then about Bridey. Pao waves his spoon airily.

"Can all be arranged. I'll signal from Central. And Myr Bridey can come with you, of course. She'll be company for Myr Stareem—after classes. And Pavo can have the first showing of your Damiem documentary— Why, wait, you can also act as consultant to our holodocumentary staff! They're good, but just a bit *dull*."

Stareem is beaming. "I love Bride; I hated to think I was leaving her forever."

Dayan, highly amused by the fairy-tale turn of events, says reflectively, "I'd really admire to have seen that act you finished Hiner with."

"Oh, but you shall!" the little prince exclaims. "I almost forgot. It's on your hand camera, Myr Zannez. At least, I hope it is," he amends worriedly. "I've only had one lesson. I don't know how good a job I did. I just started shooting as soon as my two charges went in."

"*What?*" Zannez is purely astounded.

Pao repeats.

"Listen, am I still asleep and dreaming?" Quite seriously, Zannez pinches himself twice and shakes his head. "Reward, job offer—and now this. Wait—Prince, did you take the lens cover off?"

"Naturally." It's Superboy again.

"Whew! Then you got it. . . . Gods—the greatest act we ever did in my life, and I thought it was all gone bye-bye. And you say—oh, man—" He jumps up, visibly checking himself from mauling Pao. "This I've got to see! Camera, camera, where are you? Bye, all."

He bolts for the infirmary, Pao puts down his bowl and follows at a run.

Dayan reckons the boy has forgotten all about Royal Concubine A, but at the red-crossed door Pao checks to say, "Oh, good-bye, sir. Till later, Myr Star!"

He kisses his hand to her and then tears after Zannez, a boy again.

There's a silence in the lounge; Dayan turns his gaze on the charming girl-child beside him.

"Well, little lady, and how will you like it on Pavo, with your life all mapped out?"

"Oh, col—no, uh, very much, sir." She nods seriously. "Well, you see, sir, I think my life on Gridworld was all mapped out, too. Only it was all *down* . . . and maybe not very long, either. . . . And on Pavo I think they like you to learn a lot. Like, keep on learning. Oh, I'd love that. I love to understand. I was in a—a *library* once. There's so much to learn, you'd never run out. I guess you know all that, sir."

"By no means," he says guiltily. "Tell me, Myr Stareem— or should I call you Sharon now?"

"Oh, no, please! Sharon is—is gone. Never was."

"I reckon that's so. Well, then, Myr Star, tell me honestly: Is your prince really a young boy? The age he looks? Do you know how old he really is?"

"Yes, sir." She smiles dazzlingly. "He's just turned eleven.

He told me his birthday the day we met. He's two years younger than me. But I don't think that matters so much. Do you, sir? Especially since he says I'll age all right?''

"No," agrees Dayan gravely. "I reckon two years won't matter. But it's hard to believe that boy isn't a lot older than he looks."

"You mean, because he's so grown-up? People say 'mature,' but it sounds so dismal." She cocks her head, studying him. "You mean you really, really, don't believe it?"

Dayan grunts. "Should I?"

"I think so, yes." She nods. "I saw some papers—from Pavo—something's s'posed to happen when he's twelve. 'Man's estate.' That's why he has to go home. Zannie asked him about it, too; that's when he showed the papers. Why he's so mature—ugh—is because of what they do to children on Pavo. 'Specially to children—wait . . .'' She looks up, remembering hard, a darling sight. "Destined for great responsibilities. Yes. That's what he is, right? So some ancient philosopher, Miles or Mills, I forget the name—I have to start learning and remembering now, don't I?"

"You do, little lady. What about this ancient man?"

"He said, Keep the child away from other children. Don't waste his best early years learning how to be a child. Because he'll just have to unlearn it, see? So they put him with grown-ups right from the start. Bright grown-ups, the best. Even his mother wasn't allowed to talk baby-talk to him."

"You mean Pao never had any playmates? Pretty rough on the kid."

"Oh, no. Adults play with him. Zannie's playing with him right now, isn't he? Partly because he's a prince, but mostly because he's—what's the word I need, sir?"

"H'm. Word for Pao? Well, 'mannerly' is a word we used around the Horsehead."

" 'Mannerly'—that's nice. He is." She sighs. "And I have to learn to be mannerly, too. I wouldn't ever want him to be *ashamed* of me. Do you think I can, sir?"

"I do."

"I hope so. . . ." She sighs again, pensively. "In a way, they did that to us, to me, too. We're always with grownups. But they don't teach us anything but a little acting and mostly sex—but not really that."

"How do you mean?" Dayan asks incautiously. He's mesmerized by this delicate, fresh-looking little Human, raised in a life he conceives of as inhabited only by loathsome subhumanity.

"Well, you know, I've never— Oh!" She puts a hand to her lips. "Zannie told us not ever to talk to space people, we'd offend them. I don't want to offend you, sir, Captain Dayan."

"You can't offend me, Myr Star. Since I asked the question I have only myself to blame. What were you going to say you 'never'?"

"Well, let's see . . . I don't know your word for it, but is it all right if I say I've never done—oh, you know—never with anybody I *liked*? Except Hanno and Bridey and Snake, but they don't count."

Dayan is transfixed. There's some shouting outside he should check on; it will have to wait a minim. But out of a hundred questions he can't phrase, all that comes to his lips is, "Why don't they count?"

"Because it's just their job, you know. Like me. And Hanno and Snake are really *for* each other. I've never been for anybody," she says wistfully. "But Pao says that's all right, it's training. He has to get his training, too," she says. "It's even more important for boys. And then he'll be for me. He says that being *for* somebody grows, it doesn't come all at once like the stories. I'm really looking forward to being with him. Captain Dayan, do you think really possibly, we could be *for* each other? At least for a while?"

It's a serious question. The shouting outside is louder, too. He must go. He rises to leave and takes her small hand.

"I think there's a real good chance, Myr Star, and I most certainly hope so, for you."

She has heard the shouting, too, and understands. Oh, lords, Dayan thinks, heading out, something's happened to Valkyr, the crewman who's making up cheap utility coffins.

He shows his teeth in a brief grin. One thing there's no doubt about is those dead-boxes: they're *for* Yule, Hiner, and Ochter.

Patrolman-Tech First-Class Valkyr, out behind the station workshop, curses the portable plastic-formant rig. The ratsass thing is made for midgets, which Valkyr is not. It's late afternoon and he's finishing the last of the five coffins the captain says they need. All vacuum-seal. That station must be full of corpses. If he only had his proper shop on *Rimshot*, they'd all be long done.

Still, this is a pretty little planet; everything safe for Humans and the locals are supposed to be worth seeing, but shy. Most of the dead are said to be Black Worlders who came all this way to kidnap some for a nasty job. That's why the bodies have to be preserved, for the Crime Section.

Whatever, as soon as he's finished this last dead-box, he's going to take a swim in that fine lake down there. And then go see what's to be seen before chow time. Chow's to be at the station, too. Nice change . . .Valkyr appreciates fresh food.

He steals a glance at the glittering lake behind him—and the inadequate holder on the hot plastic tilts. Some plastic goes on the ground, setting up fast.

Valkyr snaps out of his reverie and takes one step for his tongs. His foot goes onto the plastic puddle and skids, smoking.

Off-balance, he slides into the rig.

Next second a scream tears out of his throat as the hot plastic hits his pants, sticks, and burns through. No help for it; he goes down in a yelling frenzy of spilled plastic and the stink of burning flesh.

"Doc! Doctor Siri!" Another Patrolman runs up shouting and gets the rig off him, but he can do little with the stuff sticking to Valkyr's body, face, and arms.

Siri gets there fast, as usual. She grabs up the can of solvent and gets his vital parts clear before the can runs dry. Her impartial curses at the solvent, the rig, and Valkyr blue the air comfortingly.

"Ice! Tally, you scoot back with the first double handful of ice you can get your paws on. Bing, you search out every godlost piece of ice they've got. Including frozen food. Run!"

Even more comforting is her needleload of painkiller. Presently Valkyr feels green and go. But he is not; he's lost a lot of skin, and he needs *Rimshot*'s tissue bank. Help will come, but during the hours ahead his life will depend on skilled nursing.

Dayan is watching.

"I'll have to take him up myself, Saul. How soon can *Rimshot* get here?"

"Under an hour after I signal." He's already in the command car.

"Meanwhile I'll get some fluids into him and get a wetbunk made up on that trailer of theirs. Can your car tow it to the field?"

"It can."

"Right, then. And I'll have to stay with him at least until we know the first grafts have taken. This'll change some plans. . . . All right, Rango and Maur, see he doesn't move. Hold his hands quiet. Rip, Jorge, come and help me carry." She heads for Baram's infirmary.

This will indeed change plans, Dayan thinks as he bumps along the spaceport road. Siri had been going to stay behind with Kip and Cory, until Cor either improved or died. That would permit Baram to take off with his redhead he's so nervy about; the gods know the Doc has enough leave coming.

But now Kip would be left alone with—whatever. Cannot do. . . . Too bad; looks like Baram stays on. . . . "Move it,

Ralli,'' Dayan says, ''a few bumps won't break me.'' Ralli grins happily and corners on two. Dayan hangs on, thinking, It's a pity there's no one to take Baram's place.

In the rearview mirror he notices a surprising number of the winged folk taking off from the station grove, in the evening light.

A great, faintly quivering rim of Star-light is brightening eerily all around the horizon, as the sky light fades above.

XXII

GREEN,
GO

Dawn is brightening to daylight over the landing field of
the small planet called Damiem. Two fiery sparks move in
the pale sky, one receding, the other descending. Above the
horizon there glimmers a fading ring of opalescent light that
no sun ever cast; it has a just perceptible pulse or flicker in it.

At the edge of the field stands a ground-jitney, attached to
a freight trailer. Six Human civilians and a Space Patrol
officer wait in the jitney. On the trailer is strapped a modest
pile of luggage and a long, plain official Patrol coffin.

In the car's front seat sits a very old, frail woman. The
driver beside her is a handsome man in early midlife who
might be her grandson. Behind them is a man with white hair
and startling blue eyes, holding the hand of the red-haired
girl beside him, whose eyes are the same turquoise blue. Her
other hand rests protectively on the shoulder of the old lady
in front. Behind these sits the Patrol captain; beside him sit

two youths, one ebony black, the other tan with oddly slanted eyes. Their hands lie close but not touching.

"See, the . . . new moon," says Cory Korso, gazing east through clouded eyes. "Tomorrow . . ."

Kip, in the seat beside her, presses her hand briefly and clenches his jaw. Then his face resumes its look of dismayed bewilderment, as of one who has returned home to find his house gone and his friends strangers.

Captain Dayan clears his throat and addresses his young seat mates. "I assume you two don't need passenger accommodations? I'm bedding you down with the crew."

"Oh, yes, right, sir," they say together. Then Hanno bethinks himself. "Sir, are the eats the same?"

Dayan chuckles. "Better."

"We'll be up to see you, Myr Linnix," Snake says, "if they let us."

"That can be arranged," says Dayan. "Just don't either of you mistake this for duty."

"Oh, no, sir. No."

All fall silent again in their separate preoccupations.

They are awaiting *Rimshot*'s descending pinnace, which will take off with Captain Dayan, and Hanny, Snake, and Linnix, all bound for FedBase. But without Baram.

Wearily, Cory speaks. "Bram . . . it isn't fair, making you stay. . . . If it's for me, please go . . . Siri will be . . . back so soon, Kip dear."

"I know," Kip says. "Bram—you know how I feel. Go. Your girl needs you worse than we do."

Baram smiles and shakes his head no. His face is drawn and worried.

It had been a nasty blow to him when they found that Siri was held up on *Rimshot* by a badly burned crewman and couldn't be expected down for several days. If Baram went with Linnix now, it would mean leaving Cory and Kip alone to face what lay ahead—with Kip as sole Guardian. That couldn't be.

So Linnix is headed for Base hospital alone, to await Baram. Siri of course will be what help she can without full knowledge. Baram has warned Linnix and warned Siri to keep Linnix from talking of the scorpion episode. But Linnix must then wait alone in Base, until someone comes to relieve Baram. And she is so vulnerable, so exposed to the first well-meaning idiot who wants the story. Baram can hope that being off this planet will lessen the menace, but his heart rebels. He terribly fears her danger—not only of physical harm or death, but that some essential part of herself could be pulled away to that not-quite-extinguished *other* reality. Suppose, when he finally gets to her, he finds her as she'd first been, a mindless body?

Brooding, he's vaguely conscious that Kip and Dayan are remarking on the presence of several Dameii in the high streamer-trees overhead. Presently old Quiyst floats down to them, sending up a cloud of the mobile tree leaves. Kip greets him, and the old Damei speaks volubly, pointing at Dayan.

"He wants to talk to you, Saul," Kip reports. "He's not too clear, but he knows you're chief honcho over us." Dayan is in fact on the Damiem Reparations Council.

"Talk away, if you interpret."

"It seems they're waiting for two more of their people before they begin."

"Not to wait too long."

"Right. . . . He says it's *franivye*—superimportant. Gods, I can't see what it could be; we've apologized till we're hoarse, we've offered reparations, plus keeping all tourists off, plus destroying the hostel. The gods know we've lost all kinds of face."

But Dayan's gaze has turned up to the other, receding light, now almost lost in daylight. It's the exhaust flare of *Comet,* leaving for Federation Central under a Patrol scratch crew. It will pause at a staging asteroid near Base to exchange Dayan's men for Race and his crew. Race is being released on his own recognizance, to deliver himself and his ship to Central's Far Planets Branch, which supervises Damiem; they will impose his penalties if any.

But Race is less unhappy now. Since Moom ships will not board Human passengers without a Logistics Officer to supervise cold-sleep, FedBase is paying Race a reasonable fee to carry the five live Humans and four coffins bound for Central. Up there behind those fires go Zannez, Bridey, Stareem, Pao, and the poor marquise, still mute and smiling in her twin's rollbed. Prince Pao and his Star will change at Central for Pavo, along with Zannez and Bridey—it's felt that Zannez' contract and documentary copyright negotiations will go better if he's not in Gridworld's grip. And the two marquises, living and dead, will be put into the waiting hands of the Lord Protector of Rainbow's End, while the three criminals' remains go to Special Branch.

The parting has been emotional: as always, in this great Galaxy, friends, once parted, too rarely meet again. Beyond *Comet*'s flare are doubtless a few moist eyes. Down here, Snake and Hanno look up from time to time unsmiling. "You don't get many like old Zannie," Snake says. Hanno nods. "And if we ever see Superboy again, I guess it'll be Your Royal Majesty." They sigh.

Dayan watches until *Comet* is seemingly beyond sight, then continues to gaze. Shortly he's rewarded by a brief flash as *Comet*, under Dayan's pilot, changes to space drive. Dayan nods and transfers his gaze to the descending pinnace.

At this moment the jitney's transceiver bursts into life. Amid whistles and squawks, a coded message is coming through from *Rimshot*, in orbit high above. Dayan bends to hold an ear to the speaker.

"Say again?"

The screeches repeat.

When Dayan answers, his normally soft twang changes to a bellow so penetrating that his companions wince. To their surprise, Kip and Baram make out "sixteen-sixty"—return to ship—and another code group too.

"What's up, Saul?"

There's a sky-lightening flare of flame from the pinnace.

Dayan grins a broad 'I-have-a-secret' grin. "New passenger."

"Not Siri?" asks Baram.

"Nope." The grin broadens. "How'd you folks like a little surprise? Want to guess who's come dropping by to stay awhile?"

Blank looks.

"What would you say to your old pal Pace Norbert, first Guardian of Damiem?"

"*What?* But he's—"

"Yes. But it seems the good soul heard there was trouble and bundled himself into a one-seater freight pod and came all the way here to help you out. He's just docking with my ship."

"No!" Kip is beaming; even Cory is trying to smile.

"Do you think Norbert could stand in for the Doc here, till we get Siri back?" Dayan asks. "I understand he's qualified as an MD since you've seen him last."

"Yes, he was into medicine," Kip remembers. "Pace Norbert! I can't believe!"

"Wonderful," whispers Cory. She means, wonderful for Baram; she alone understands why he needs to stay close to Linnix: to keep her alive. Cory, too, had clearly seen her die.

Baram and Linnix are looking from Dayan to Kip to Cory. Baram has never met the former Guardian, was unaware of their friendship. Does this mean . . . ?

It does. Kip and Cory are delighted with Pace Norbert's company as a substitute for Baram's. Indeed, the prospect of a new face, an old friend, in place of the poor worried doctor cheers Kip mightily.

"You see those man-lifts over there the crew left for us to bring up?" Dayan asks Baram. "Can you navigate one?"

"I have done. Why?" Baram is so happy and relieved he's forgotten all else.

"Green. I'll help you get started. Then back you go to the station and pack everything you can in ten minim. Go!"

After a couple of hair-raising tries with the man-lift, Baram finds the knack again and sails away at a very conservative altitude above the road. Linnix turns to look after him with eyes like blue stars.

Overhead, the light of the pinnace has visibly reversed direction and is dwindling upward and northward toward *Rimshot*'s orbit.

Dayan walks back to the jitney to find a cloud of Damei wings fanning out overhead. The missing must have arrived, and the Dameii are ready to parley.

"Hallo, there's Black Golya, from Far Village," says Kip. His face clouds; Golya has been a troublemaker. "And there's Juiyn! Weird." He switches to Damei and greets the group.

Old Quiyst speaks briefly, making a sweeping gesture at Dayan.

"They have something they want you to record and act on, Saul."

"I can only lay it before the Council. But naturally, any reasonable requests will be honored."

Quiyst ducks back, and another Damei from the Far Village group, whom Kip knows only as Yrion Red, comes forward along the branches. With wings formally leveled, Yrion delivers himself of quite a long address in Damei, punctuated by the Galactic words, "He-ar me!"

Kip tries a running translation.

"They no longer wish—wish *us*? I could understand that— No, wait, he means they no longer wish Guardianship as it is today. But they still want protection on call—that's you, Saul—and they want more instruction in Galactic, and medical help, and—wait, something— Great Apherion—wait—"

He asks two questions in Damei.

When the answers come, Dayan thinks he hears the words, "Sta-ree Te-Yas."

"Well! Well! Well! Well! In the name of Holy All! The thing they want, Saul, beside protection, teachers, et cetera, is a kind of commercial consul! It seems—it seems they plan to manufacture and export Stars Tears themselves! Yes! And they want a chemist to show them ways of distilling it from the raw nectar. . . . Great Apherion in flames! *They want to make money!* I've been explaining the financial facts of life to Wyrra, and it seems he told it to Juiyn, who got her Far Village family all hotted up, and— Oh, whew! They even think people should pay to *see* them!"

"What use do they have for Galactic credits?" asks Dayan practically.

Kip asks the question. He receives a voluble reply from Yrion Red; and others join in. Kip starts to say something in reply or objection, but the dialogue is cut off by old Quiyst:

"Talk finish."

"Well!" says Kip. "Primarily they want a water system. Seems they're tired of lugging water. Gods—we were going to make them one, when we found a silent pump—but I guess we've been a little slow. They never *looked* unhappy. . . . And they want other things. They want to live like us. Yrion says we have a book of things—that'd be the *Federation Supply Catalog,* I think. Anyway, they want one. Oh, my, my, my!"

Cory coughs, trying to say something. Finally she gets it out, in a hoarse wheeze: "How . . . how do they plan to . . . to get the nectar?"

"Right. Good point." He questions Yrion. Again there's a voluble response, cut short by Quiyst.

"Well? Are they setting up to torture each other?" Dayan asks.

Kip frowns. "I don't think so. Yrion was saying something to the effect that they know good ways, although I don't know whether he means good-and-efficient, or good-as-opposed-to-bad. But old Quiyst just said it was none of my business. . . . Great purple gods!''

"Looks like your pets are growing up," says Dayan dryly.

"But what about it, Saul? Can they do this? Oh, I forgot—they want to *use* the hostel; we're not to destroy it. So much for sensitivity. . . . So what do you say?"

"Speaking unofficially, my flash reaction is that their plan is within the Terms of Human Restitution—provided their methods of, ah, extractions are humane. We don't want them massacring each other. . . . Do they know about this pain-killer business of Baram's?"

"I don't see how. But here comes Doc."

They watch as Baram parks the man-lift with a mild flourish, leaving his duffel on it, and walks over to them. He bears a quilt-wrapped package.

The light of the pinnace has reappeared again, descending as before—but now bearing Pace Norbert to the rescue. It's coming fast, already they can hear it.

"This doesn't leave me." Baram laces the package carefully into the shoulder-hung travel medkit under his cloak. "It's the Damei nectar I intend to work with."

Kip and Dayan fill him in on the new developments. Above them the Dameii are leaving as the pinnace's sound grows louder.

When they ask Baram what the Dameii know of the nectar's analgesic properties, he hesitates.

"Of course I haven't had occasion to tell them," he says. "But you'll note that the nectar changes character when the donor is in pain. It may be that it's part of their natural pain-control system, and they could well know that. In any event, after this new revelation I just wouldn't be too sure what they don't know. We—you—may be in for some surprises."

Last of the Dameii to leave is old Quiyst. He holds his ground long enough to ask a question.

"He wants to know whether you have heard and will act," Kip tells Dayan.

"Tell him I hear, and I will carry their desires to the Council. And the Council will, I'm sure, take action—but probably not as rapidly as they wish."

Quiyst, who knows some Galactic, disappears before Kip finishes translating: the sky roar from the pinnace has grown shattering.

As the big g-blockers cut in, the decibels rise still more. Only Cory can hear Kip's exclamations to the world in general—broken phrases of wonderment and amaze, half-uttered plaints about their own projected hydraulic system, astonishment at the Dameii's knowledge of the *Federation Supply Catalog*, astoundment that they should wish to change their immemorial way of life, dire predictions of their disappointment, bewildered curses of dismay. And amid it all, Cory hears distinctly, "D'you know, they even *looked* different to me! Oh, they're beautiful. But I never really believed they were evolved from, from *insects* before. Maybe that's how that devil Hiner saw them, that's why he could . . . Oh, my goodness, it'll all change—"

She understands too well what all this means—beneath his excitement is heart-hurt, the pain of rejection. And beneath that again lies something only she knows, waiting to come . . . the thing Vovoka spoke of.

And she won't be . . . here to help him through that, to share it.

She longs to comfort him, to open her arms to him as she used—was it only yesterday? But she's locked in this shattered scarecrow body that he fears and hates. Perhaps she could stroke his hand or his knee? But she has no strength, she'd topple sideways. It's not hour by hour she's going now, she thinks: it's minim by minim.

And she *must* have strength, to help Kip, to greet Pace; and there are instructions to give.

"Bram . . . Bram . . ." she whispers hoarsely.

By chance Bram has leaned forward between them, thinking Kip wanted to be heard. His ear is near her cheek; to turn those few centimeters takes all her power.

"Bram—Bram . . . listen!" she mumbles hoarsely. "Oh, please!"

Ah, he hears! "Yes, Cor?"

"Stim-shot. Now. Quick. You . . . have?"

He's dismayed. "Yes, but Cory dear, remember! *Try* to remember what I warned you of—the risk—"

She closes her eyes, tries perilously to shake her head no. *"Stim-shot now* . . . urgen' . . . Order, Bram." She gets that out clearly. "After . . . no matter."

He gives her a deep look from those unearthly azure eyes. "Very . . . well."

To her impatience his hands in the medkit seem so slow. Slow enough that she remembers something. After he plunges the needle in her unfeeling triceps she says: "Bram . . . try to hear me."

"I'm listening, Cor."

"Bram—'nother order. . . . Do not . . . no matter what . . . you'n Linnix . . . must not . . ."

"Must not what?"

Oh, lords, didn't she say it? "Not turn back," she gasps. "If I . . . trouble . . . not turn back, not look. . . . She . . . mustn't see." Her voice is suddenly clear—but an instant later she feels a front tooth give and puts up a hand. Please, fate, for Kip's sake, don't let me go toothless.

"You, Linnie, do not . . . turn back. . . ." she says muffledly. "Order. . . . No matter what. . . . Repeat please . . . Bram dear."

He sighs. "Yes. You order Linnix and me not to turn back—from boarding I presume."

Cory nods. "N-not . . . come back."

"Or if we are boarded, we must not come back out . . . all this regardless of—of whatever may be happening behind us,

686

with you— Oh, Cory, my dear—my dear, do you know? Do you?'' he asks incoherently, meaning simply, love.

He captures her shaking, gnarled old hands and kisses them tenderly, pushing heedless against Kip, who is absorbed in the pinnace landing. Neither Baram nor Cory notices when the uproar from the pinnace dies. As it grounds a brief flare of burning brush crackles out around it, then subsides.

Baram sinks back to his seat and meets Linnie's understanding smile. After a pause she says, ''That man-lift ride must have been exciting. I've always wanted to try.''

''I'm glad you didn't see some of the gyrations I cut. Look, the ramp is down. I've never met this Norbert, but I bless his name.'' He squeezes her hand. Never to be separated again, if he can help it.

Cory, waiting for the stim-shot to take effect, peers toward the pinnace. A slender man's figure appears on the ramp. Kip is waving joyfully, starting the jitney.

''Green we run up there now?'' he remembers to ask Dayan.

''Go.'' The new set of tires from *Rimshot* are flameproof.

But the short run to the ramp jolts Cory almost to blackout. Her strong legs that used to brace her are no longer there. Just as she crumples down she feels steady hands slide beneath her armpits, pulling her back to safety. That nice red-haired girl behind her, Linnix. Cory manages to pat her hand.

But how fast everyone moves! Baram and Linnix are already out and going up the ramp; she has a confused memory of good-byes. And here's Pace at the car, in a barrage of rapid-fire talk with Kip. Has she greeted him? ''Hello . . . Pace dear,'' she says painfully—and just then her heart changes rhythm and the stim-shot comes to her aid. Her voice clears and strengthens. ''You came all that way in a freight pod? Lords!''

''It wasn't too bad.'' He's trying not to look at her—and the odd thing is, how old he's grown himself!

687

She retrieves her shawl from where it fell, covers herself. "It's pretty bad, Pace, isn't it? And it's going to get worse before the end. The one thing is, it's natural. It's what you'd see at the end of our lives. Just think of it as a kind of time-warp, a preview. . . . Now Pace dear, I have to tell you something in confidence . . . but I can't hobble far—" She casts a pleading look around.

"I'll get the bags," says Kip, sliding out.

Dayan says abruptly, "We've got to get Vovoka's coffin aboard," and heads for the pinnace, followed by the boys.

Pace climbs into Kip's vacated seat.

Cory thinks a minim. "Pace, were you told that an alien did this to me?"

"Yes, but why, Cory, why?"

"Because he was the last Vlyracochan—the last member of the race of the Murdered Star—and his mission was to kill the last surviving crewman from *Deneb,* the ship that did it. . . . Pace, I was that person . . . I was young, and war-crazy. When the regular gunners refused to do it, I was the criminal fool who fired the fatal missile at Vlyracocha. . . . They sent me to Rehab for memory erasure, but it came back as soon as Vovoka, the Vlyracochan, spoke."

"Oh, dear lords of space, Cory, to take revenge on a child—"

"Pace, it wasn't quite like that, but we can't waste time. I've had a stim-shot specially to tell you something. Please listen, Pace."

"Right."

"Before he died . . . the alien told me something that changed the whole picture. He said that in their antiquity, when they already had a high culture, an invisible entity, a space-borne *something,* quite likely from outside the Galaxy, somehow impinged on Vlyracocha. There was no doubt of its presence; its effect took the form of a great and growing beauty in all things; in Vovoka's words, 'Beauty such as no one had ever seen or imagined . . . even the trees, weeds, rocks . . . like those here.'

"And after generations of exposure to this beauty, the people of Vlyracocha began to weaken and die. They had no doubt as to the cause."

For an instant she gasps for air, her hand on her withered breast.

"Cory dear, you shouldn't be exhausting yourself like this," Pace says. "Rest, lie back a minim."

"I'm aging—correction, I'm dying—every minim, Pace. Don't you understand? No rests. It's now or never. Please, listen, there's a point.

"The form of the disease seems to have been a terrible loss of the ability to hope, a boundless despair—coupled with what Vovoka called 'an unquenchable, unnameable desire,' a yearning, I think. As if the entity had fed on the souls of the beholders. And then . . . he said . . . 'When it had fed full, it compelled us to build'—the thing *Deneb* destroyed. It was a gigantic work of art, with all the culture and history of their race, and powered so that it might, I quote, 'go forth through the Galaxy, feeding and reproducing.' It housed the entity, you see. Vovoka seemed both to reverence it and to hate it bitterly. . . .

"At the end he told me I had done no wrong in blowing it to atoms. . . . And he addressed it, saying, 'Now you will be again what you were—a nothing on the winds of space, whence we drew you to our doom.' His tone, his words are graven on my mind."

Pace is silent an instant, shaking his head. "An evil marvel beyond easy grasp. . . . I've heard of nothing like it in the Galaxy. . . . Was that what you wished to tell me, Cory?"

"The—the prelude only. . . ." She's tiring. "Understand, Pace, it *was* blown to atoms. Its particles were mingled with those of the Star. If it was still alive . . . or latent, it rode in the great . . . explosion-fronts that passed us here.'' She breathes for a minim, speaks more strongly.

"But did they all pass? Did some remain, or adhere? Or were we judged unsuitable, if such a dispersed entity can be said to judge? I don't know.

"All I know is that the one being, the Vlyracochan who had experienced it, who knew it, said two things very pointedly. The first I've told you, that the entity gave beauty to 'trees, weeds, rocks *like those here.*' The second— He was a very silent being, but he took occasion to tell me that Damiem has *'a peculiarly flattering light,'* . . . and Kip says he added something like, *'Don't feel too secure.'*

"You know for yourself how lovely all things are here. The Dameii—if one isn't careful, one can feel an almost sickly infatuation with them, Pace. . . . Incidentally . . . do the Dameii feel it, too? Remember, find out that. . . .

"What's convincing is that no . . . no mention of the beauty of the planet or the people is found in the very old writings. . . . Of course I haven't examined them all, and they were the work of unimaginative men—soldiers, criminals, engineers. But still . . . See, that would be before the first Star-fronts came . . . before Damiem . . . began to live in the explosion's ambience.''

She pants again, jerking up a hand to stop Pace's protests.

"The Star has passed now, Pace. I don't know whether something of it . . . some traces of glamour or magic . . . still remain, or will . . . and I don't know if that's good or bad. I fear . . . fear; it's headed into the Galaxy. Will it infect other planets in . . . its path? Terrible. . . . But point is, Kip immersed himself in Damiem's Star-beauty . . . I, too. I, too. We lived in an enchanted garden, Pace . . . all aglow. So—'' She is shaken by rattling coughs, she looks deathly, but somehow energy is still there.

"When the Star has all passed . . . everything may seem cold, dry. Shabby—a bleaker . . . ordinary landscape . . . perhaps . . . Even the Dameii will be . . . more like big

690

insects. But the point"—again the dreadful coughing—"point is, *Kip* . . . may be a very sick man . . . on your hands." She takes a ragged breath, struggles to sit straighter.

"Pace, maybe psychologically a dying man. . . . *Get him off this planet*. . . . Can't order, only beg. Get him away."

Pace says slowly, "The loss of illusion, eh? But that's reality, Cor. We all—"

"Reality—" She tries to laugh, jeeringly, coughing, shakily holding up one feeble, crabbed, vein-encrusted hand that's like a little clutch of deformed twigs.

"*That's* reality, Pace. . . . Yesterday that . . . was a h-hand. . . . People . . . say, 'Be realistic.' As though reality needs encouragement. . . . Tell you, Pace . . . *reality doesn't need friends*."

The almost-laugh catches, turns into frightening coughs.

Pace gives a bark of laughter, marvelling.

"Ah, you're Cory—you're Cor to the bit—" He stops himself.

"Bit . . . bitter end?" she gasps, or maybe she's trying to laugh. "Strange thing . . . it isn't bitter, Pace. . . . If . . . I could only—tell you—"

But it's all gone now, all really gone, forever. Her eyes hold his for a desperate minim, and then she collapses back in the seat, a shrunken, feebly choking, dying old woman. It's an instant before he realizes the coughs are rasping: "Don't call . . . Baram. . . . Order, Pace. . . . Do not . . . call Bram."

Her eyes close, her breathing is noisy.

Pace puts his ear to her chest and hears the dreadful price of that stim-shot. Kip and Saul Dayan are nearby; he calls them over.

"She doesn't want Doctor Baram called," he tells them. "Get him and his girl into the ship. Saul, can you spare the time to drive us back to the station? That way Kip and I can hold her from each side."

"No problem." Dayan strides up the ramp and slams the

port closed behind Baram and Linnix. "Put that last man-lift on the trailer," he calls to the crewmen who are loading them. "I'll use it coming back."

Kip and Pace are crowding in on either side of Cory now, to leave driving room for Dayan. The front seat will just hold four, and the tight fit will help. As they settle, Cory, with enormous effort, turns her head enough to see up.

She sees the flowering tree branches arching overhead, against an opalescent sky. The flowers show as lapis-blue plumes, downy lilac puffs—and between them is her last view of the crescent moon, fading into sunrise.

It's all still beautiful, as well as she can judge. But the horizon is still ringed in Star-light; the Star-front has not completely passed from Damiem.

Her movement has caused a small commotion. Such looks, such long faces! She'd asked them not to do that, before she was even sure. If only I could tell them how I feel inside, she thinks. So light and free, all duties done. . . . *And at last I know it all; my whole life is my own.* . . . All known. Like a child on a high hill, like a first plane ride—I can see it all from horizon to horizon, and think it all over. There are patterns, where I didn't know patterns were. . . .

Like overfondness. Overfond of Kip, overfond of Captain Jeager. I suspected his gunners were right, but Jeager's lonely mad heroics wrung my heart. . . . Same about Yule and Hiner: I knew I should get them off the planet, but Kip's smile—that dear smile—melted my wits. . . . And little Ochter, I couldn't see past that mask of pathos. . . . Unfit for command I was, really. . . . But it doesn't matter now. . . .

The eyes watching her are amazed at the smile that spreads the deep wrinkles of her face. Next instant her hands are up, fumbling at her mouth. Curse the teeth, she tries to say, pushing at the shrunken roots. Talking's over. . . . But that doesn't matter, either.

She's gotten everything said. . . . Baram will be all right with his girl, and she's warned Pace. Kip . . . He'll be unhappy, but Pace will get him away, and he'll wait in some new station with his wonderful looks and his sweet nature and his red neckerchief, and another woman will come.

Even that funny brave cameraman and his young ones will be all right, and the little prince. The only one who isn't is that poor marquise—but who knows what the very mad, very rich, really want?

A happy ending to the tale of the great Star, really—except for tragic little Nyil. But even she said it wasn't so bad, because she flew . . . flew to her death. I can understand that, somehow. . . .

And me . . . funny, I'd forgotten myself. I suppose they count this as tragic. Oh, if I only could tell them—all they see is this rotting body; they don't see I'm perched in it like a bird in an old tree. When the tree goes I'll only float away. Maybe, when it crumbles, could I just fly away, free? Flying to death, like Nyil?

No. That's nonsense.

I must have made more sounds; they're all saying things. ". . . her own bed."

Do as you wish, my dears.

Starting the car, now. Starting—oh, good lords, the jolting! Hands everywhere—they're trying to hold me together, with their fine young strength. No use, I fear. But it's not so bad . . . not too bad. . . . Oh, pain. Not much . . . only I can't breathe . . . *pain* . . . can't—GODS, GIVE ME AIR—

What happened? What're they doing? Car's stopped. Pace—I think it's Pace—is squeezing, pounding on me.

Oh, please, it hurts—

"I think we have a problem." She hears that. No, dears. *You* have a problem. I don't. Oh, if I could only tell them. . . .

Problem is, I'm alive. Technically, I guess.

But they don't dare start the car.

And life goes on. . . . How strenuous the living are. I think it's Saul Dayan, driving . . . and the ship waits.

But such a beautiful sunrise—so comfortable, so radiant

and limitless! I wish they had time to enjoy. . . . When you're dying you have time. And you don't need help to die. No arrangements. You can just do it, all alone. Right the first time. . . .

Won't be long—but I was given back my life just right, just in time. In time to be whole. . . . I wonder if that Rehab's really so good? I lived all my life *muffled*. Until now. . . . I guess something has to be done . . . for people where unbearably bad things happened. But . . . it's amputation. Until now I was an amputee.

They're still debating their "problem." Hello! One of my little friends.

Perched on the windscreen beside some leaves is a furry, bird-sized, brightly colored arachnoid, a sort of flying spider. They're usually nocturnal. Its color is peach and green, with bright vermilion knee joints, and it has a comically surprised expression in its large, stalked eyes. Cory's vision is dimming, but she can just make out that one of its eyes is bent toward her. . . . She wishes now she'd ignored the regs and tried to tame one . . . but that was never her style.

"Thank you, Saul," she whispers to herself. His delay has gained her this last sight.

But delays must come to an end; she knows that.

She feels a new jostling. What? Oh, it's Pace, putting his ear to her heart again. She tries to hold her breath so he can hear, is suddenly conscious of the hoarse racket she's been making. Wheeze-in, wheeze-out; wheeze-in, wheeze-crackle-out; wheeze—

Pace looks closely into her face; she tries to look back, hoping he will see some trace of a spark deep in the ruined eyes. Maybe he does. He pulls back to let Kip come closer. But Kip doesn't know what to do, finally brushes his lips against her wattled cheek.

You didn't have to do that, darling, she wants to say, but can only cough feebly . . . in, out; in, out; in, out . . .

"If you shake her up, that heart will stop," Pace says. Her ears still work, after a fashion.

She must speak, must. No matter about teeth now. Must. Mouth, *move*. . . .

But not enough breath. Must try again.

Try. Try, for the gods' sake. . . . Tremendous effort—

"She's trying to say something," Pace says. "Yes, Cor, dear. What?

Again the groaning whisper is achieved; she's panting in total exhaustion.

Kip utters a wholly incomprehensible sound. He understood, she thinks, but he can't make himself say it.

Studying her face, Pace says carefully, "I thought it . . . sounded like 'Green, go.' "

Yes, the spark in the old eyes tries to say.

Kip chokes. He's not overly imaginative, but the memory-picture of a brown-haired girl putting a bunch of bright yellow flowers on their breakfast table suddenly devastates him.

There's a silence. Air rasping laboriously through an aged throat; out . . . in , . . out . . . in . . . out . . . in . . . out . . . in . . .

Green, go?

Dayan breaks the silence. "Right."

Carefully, he starts the motor, engages the drive. The car moves off, not smoothly despite his care, on the rock-strewn road under Damiem's empty sky.

695

THE STAR PASSES

DAMIEM

SUN

to center of Galaxy

Nova front
expanding and dissipating

mkJ/abs

APPENDIX:

Cast of Characters and Glossary of Terms, Titles, Places, and Things

Damiem—The planet.
Dameii—The people of Damiem, plural.
Damei—One of the people; or adjective, as in "Damei music."

1. The three Human residents of Damiem, all co-Guardians of the Dameii:

> *Corrisón Estreèl-Korso* (Cory or Cor): Chief Federation Administrator of Damiem and mate of Kip.
> *Kipruget Korso-Estreèl* (Kip): Deputy Administrator of Damiem and Liaison to the Dameii; mate of Cory. (Mated couples take each other's surnames as hyphenated last names for the duration of the Mateship. This facilitates computerized records. Although Kip and Cory are overdue to redeclare, they keep the forms as evidence of intent.)

Balthasar Baramji ap Bye   (Baram or Bram): Xenological MD, doctor to the Dameii. Bye is Baramji's vast feudal estate on Broken Moon; "ap" is a hereditary landowning title. At home he is the ap of Bye, but abroad he is simply a senior doctor with a xenological specialty.

2. The tourists, Human and otherwise, listed in order of appearance from the ship:

Zannez (Beorne—last name never used; Zannie): Subdirector and cameraman for four of the 35 stars of the popular interstellar soft-porn grid-show, *The Absolutely Perfect Commune*.

Stareem Fada   (Star): Her stage name. One of the four *APC* actors here.

Hannibal Ek   (Hanny or Hanno): His real name. Another of the four actors.

Snake Smith   (occasionally Snako): His permanent but not real name. The third of the four actors, and a professional acrobat.

Bridey McBannion   (Bee): Her real name—she refuses to use the stage name, *Eleganza*. The fourth of the four actors. A knife-thrower.

Prince-Prince Pao   (Pao, Prince, or Superboy): The heir to the royal throne of the planet Pavo. His actual first name is "Prince."

Ser Xe Vovoka   (Vovoka, but not to his face; "Ser" is an honorary title): A light-sculptor.

Doctor Aristrides Ochter   (Ari, occasionally): A retired professor of neocybernetics-E.

Lady Marquise Pardalianches   (Pardie or Lady P.): Of the nobility of Rainbow's End.

Lady Marquise Paralomena   ('Lomena or Loma): Lady P.'s twin sister, paralyzed.

Mordecai Yule   (Mordy): A student of water-worlds, bound for the next planet, Grunions Rising, and at Damiem by error.

Doctor Nathaniel Hiner (Nat): An Aquaman, also bound for Grunions Rising and wakened at Damiem by error; a representative of the Aquapeople's Association doing a survey of water-worlds to update the old *Aquatica Galactica*. Aquapeople are the successful products of a long-ago genetic effort to achieve a true-breeding gilled human, able to live underwater or in air.

Linnix (Linnie—no other name): Logistics Officer tending to Humans on the Moom ship.

3. Other Humans (Humans are but one of many races in—and out of—the Federation, like Dameii or Moom; hence Human is a proper noun and is always capitalized):

Captain Saul Dayan (Scooter): Captain of the battle cruiser *Rimshot*.

Doctor Siri Lipsius (Siri): Battle surgeon of *Rimshot*.

Valkyr: Technician First Class of *Rimshot*

Jordan Tally, Bing, Rango, Maur, Rip Jorge: Patrolmen from *Rimshot*.

Ralli: Captain Dayan's command car driver.

Poma (never seen): Chief of Communications at nearby FedBase.

Captain Race (never seen): Captain/owner of a charter ship, *Comet II*.

Pace Norbert (Pace): Former Guardian of the Dameii prior to the Korsos. Now an MD.

Kenter, Janny, Pete, Saro (mentioned only): Wartime colleagues of Kip.

Captain Tom Jeager (mentioned only): Mad wartime commander of battleship *Deneb*.

4. Dameii:

Quiyst: A Damei elder, spokesman for Near Village.

Wyrra: (m)
Juiyn: (f) The Damei couple who live adjacent to the station.

Nyil: Their young female child.

Feanya: Second Damei elder, friend of Quiyst.

Zhymel: Damei elder from Near Village, part of group inspecting Humans.

Black Golya: Dynamic-type Damei from Far Village.

Yrion Red: Ditto.

5. The Moom (barely glimpsed and heard): A large, pachydermatous, slow-living, virtually immortal race of aliens who run most Federation interstellar shipping.

6. The Swain (mentioned only): Another race of ship-faring aliens.

7. Ships:

The Moom ship (no name given): A more-or-less regular Federation passenger and freight ship on the Rim-and-back run.

Rimshot: A Federation space Patrol warship assigned to guard Damiem.

pinnace (no name): A small craft berthed in *Rimshot*, for landing capability. (*Rimshot* cannot land.)

shuttle (no name): A small landing craft berthed in the Moom ship, which likewise has no landing capability.

Comet II: A passenger/freight charter ship precariously owned and operated by Captain Race.

Golan: A former official ship, mentioned only.

8. Places:

The Rim: That part of the rim of the Milky Way Galaxy that terminates one arc of the perimeter of Federation space.

FedBase: Short term for Federation Base, the nearest to Damiem being about 100 light-minim away.

Grunions Rising: The nearest planet to Damiem. It lies in the direction of the Rim and is the end of the Rim shipline. A water-world.

Rainbow's End: A wealthy planet, home of the Marguises.

Vlyracocha: The name of the Murdered Star. The planet, along with its sun and an artificial satellite, was destroyed at the end of the Last War, and formed the nova-front now passing Damiem.

Gridworld: The interstellar Hollywood planet, originator of all shows for transmission over the Grid, a *c*-skip (FTL) communications network linking star systems and other Human and alien habitations. Technically under Federation law, but in dubious compliance, internally.

Broken Moon: A romantic, backward, feudal world; Doctor Baram's birthplace.

Beneborn: A biologically high-tech world, mad about eugenics, where Linnix was born.

Pavo: A small but important world, a royal principality, where Prince Pao will rule.

Alwyn and *Jo's Paradise:* Two planetary neighbors of Pavo, dependent on it as the financial, economic, diplomatic center (mentioned only).

Rehab: A quasimedical center for compassionate and other rehabilitation of Humans and others deeply traumatized as victims—sometimes perpetrators—of violence and crime. Mem/E is the Memory-Erasure section.

9. Glossary of some Damei and other unfamiliar terms:

Yrrei: Damiem's sun, a GO-type star.

V'yrre: A wind that blows WNW during the Damiem season of the Star events.

Avray: A large (50 cm diameter) plum-colored arachnoid or tarantuloid animal of Damiem. Like all Damei fauna, including the Dameii, it has an extra pair of limbs as compared with its Terran homolog, making ten in all. Though harmless, shy, and rare, it is hated and feared by the Dameii as an ill omen.

Tochari, Daguerre: Two Last War hand weapons, nonballistic.

c-skip: Faster-than-light-speed (*c*) transmission, by inducing temporary perturbations in reciprocal gravity-field configurations. Requires super-cooling of transmitting nuclei.

Myr, Myrrin: Myr serves for Mr., Mrs., Ms., or Miss and is often prefixed affectionately or jokingly to a person's first name or nickname. Myrrin is the plural, corresponding to "Ladies and Gentlemen."

"gods," "lords,": As ejaculations, these are always in the plural and lowercase; this convention, now automatic, was a part of the treaty which, it is hoped, ended forever all religious factional strife. Only when a god is named, which is only done jocularly, using a mythical entity, is the exclamation singular. All this has of course no effect on private personal prayer.

"The All": The only singular entity that may be secularly referred to, all religions having given their assent to it.

Saniches, Morpleases (and native-tongue edibles): Food items.

Algotoxin: Is, so far, by the mercy of Fate, a fiction.

Zeranaveth: A carbonaceous gemstone similar to colored diamonds, but more beautiful. Found only on a few planets such as Rainbow's End and the Hallelujah system.

ABOUT GOLLANCZ

Gollancz is the oldest SF publishing imprint in the world. Since being founded in 1927 Gollancz has continued to publish a focused selection of bestselling and award-winning authors. The front-list includes **Ben Aaronovitch**, **Joe Abercrombie**, **Charlaine Harris**, **Joanne Harris**, **Joe Hill**, **Alastair Reynolds**, **Patrick Rothfuss**, **Nalini Singh** and **Brandon Sanderson**.

As one of the largest Science Fiction and Fantasy imprints in the UK it is no surprise we have one of the most extensive backlists in the world. Find high quality SF on Gateway written by such authors as **Philip K. Dick**, **Ursula Le Guin**, **Connie Willis**, **Sir Arthur C. Clarke**, **Pat Cadigan**, **Michael Moorcock** and **George R.R. Martin**.

We also have a strand of publishing in translation, which includes French, Polish and Russian authors. Gollancz is home to more award-winning authors than any other imprint, with names including **Aliette de Bodard**, **M. John Harrison**, **Paul McAuley**, **Sarah Pinborough**, **Pierre Pevel**, **Justina Robson** and many more.

The SF Gateway
More than 3,000 classic, rare and previously out-of-print SF novels at your fingertips.
www.sfgateway.com

The Gollancz Blog
Bringing you news from our worlds to yours. Stories, interviews, articles and exclusive extracts just for you!
www.gollancz.co.uk

GOLLANCZ
LONDON